Career School

A Novel By

Mike Colahan

TELEMACHUS PRESS

This book is a work of fiction. Names, characters, places and incidents are either the product of the author's imagination or are used fictitiously. Any resemblance to actual persons, living or dead, or to actual events or locales is entirely coincidental.

CAREER SCHOOL

Cover designed by Elliot Colahan

Cover art:
Copyright © iStock_000016981806 druvo
Copyright © iStock_000026453645 VvoeVale
Copyright © iStock_000038083490 Ventura69

Published by Telemachus Press, LLC
http://www.telemachuspress.com

Visit the author website:
http://www.mikecolahannovels.com

ISBN: 978-1-942899-42-6 (eBook)
ISBN: 978-1-942899-43-3 (Paperback)

Version 2026.04.29

My gratitude to Bonnie Lee Behm, Adrienne Glerum Dichter, John Dysart, Chris Entwisle, Mick O'Toole, Jennifer Shropshire, Sondra Stevens, Tory Stozek, and Kristina Wilhelm-Nelson for offering their time, expertise, guidance, and support during the writing of this story.

To Meg, Michaela, and Elliot—always.
And to Katharyn Howd Machan, my best teacher.

Contents

Author's Note:

This story is set in the mid-1990s, when secretarial schools like Burr were more prevalent than they are today. The descriptions of Philadelphia are offered as accurate for the time. The ruinous Southwark Towers are no more, and the Richard Allen Homes, the Martin Luther King Plaza, and the housing project that served as the model for Caulfeld Homes, have long been razed and renewed.

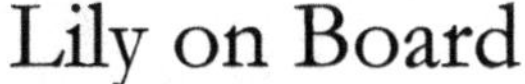

Lily on Board

1

DORIS ROBINSON PEERED through her kitchen door at the angry flash of cars on the expressway twenty feet from her back stoop. Separating her from this ceaseless hurricane force was a patch of grass considered her back yard, and a metal fence ten feet high topped with sloppy curls of barbed wire.

Javaughn asked, "We got coffee?" He was hunched over a bowl of Cheerios.

"No, we ain't got coffee. I'll get some next week."

"Naw, I'll pick up some tonight."

She whirled on him so unexpectedly that he flinched. "No you *ain't!* You don't buy nothin' for this house. You hear me?"

Her son's shoulders tightened. Anger filled him quicker than lightning, but in this house Doris, Lord knew how, was still master. She stood by the screen door, her fat body filling its frame, and placed her hands on her hips. Between them sat two-year-old Corey, strapped in a high chair, gurgling happily. After a moment Javaughn scooped more cereal onto his spoon. Pride dictated that he leave the room, but he wanted to finish his breakfast.

"Whereat's Keone?" Doris asked.

He didn't answer.

Doris walked heavily to the living room and stood at the foot of the stairs. "Keone!" Her big hand rested on the stairway banister, and the entire wooden railing rocked loosely.

A thin voice. "What?"

"Git down here. You ain't sleepin' your life away, girl."

"I be right down."

Javaughn called out from the kitchen, "Axt what she done yesterday."

"Yesterday?"

"Wasn't home all day."

Doris returned to the kitchen and looked at Javaughn to see if he was making trouble. Her son continued to eat. She watched him, helpless to say more. She didn't want to be like her husband, she wanted to stay in touch with her children. She felt she was fighting something lost decades ago. Her gaze drifted to the empty coffee maker.

Javaughn muttered, "It's stupid you not lettin' me get some."

"I ain't stoppin' you from doin' your business," she snapped. "I ain't takin' your money. Just leave it." But in fact she thought it stupid too.

Keone walked in, quiet as a mouse. Her face had an adolescent starved look: pitted eye sockets and pronounced cheekbones and jaws. Bone-thin legs extended from puffy blue shorts and a pink cotton tank top. Without a word she grasped the Cheerios box and poured a bowlful. She sat and spooned it dry. Corey laughed at his sister and flapped for a handout.

"I hate that you don't put nothin' on 'em," said Javaughn, who was three years younger than his sister.

"Then hate it," she said. She took a Cheerio and placed it in Corey's eager fist. Corey crunched it and chortled.

"Aw, you gettin' crumbs all over!"

"I ain't doing it, Corey is."

"You're givin' 'em to him!"

"Yeah, but I ain't tellin' him what to do with 'em." She handed another to Corey who happily crushed it.

Javaughn slammed down his spoon and left, storming out of the house without a word. No one watched him go. Keone gave Corey another Cheerio and he squashed it, then studied with a round serious face the crumbs in his wrinkled palm. "Boke," he said, and let the crumbs rain to the floor.

"I should get to work now," Doris said without moving. She was staring out the screen door at the traffic again.

"Mama?"

Keone's voice, so quiet. Strangely high and insecure. Doris had a sudden weird flash that if she turned around she would find her daughter a ten-year-old, about to ask for candy or maybe money to go to the movies with friends, all her early sweetness still intact. She could hardly bear to turn around, so strong was the feeling plus her desire not to disturb it. But of course she did turn around. Her daughter sat at the table, the spoon resting in her hand, the cereal uneaten. At eighteen Keone was no longer a virgin but, thank you dear Lord, not yet a mother. At eighteen she was one year older than Doris was when Doris birthed her. Keone's face disconcerted her. Something different this morning, and Doris couldn't figure it out. For the first time she tried to be attentive.

"What is it, honey?"

Keone hesitated, a sure sign of dreadful news. With quick reflex Doris' brain transmitted an old message to Heaven: *Lord, give me strength.*

"Mama, I wanna go to school."

"School?"

"Yeah. I wanna get into business."

Doris couldn't follow this. "School?"

"Yeah." Keone looked angry and nervous.

"Why, when'd you decide this?"

"Last weekend. I—I already looked into it some. There's a school in Center City what teaches you to be secretaries. That's what I want."

"A secretary?"

The girl nodded silently, braced for her mother's wrath.

Doris sank onto Javaughn's chair at the table. Corey stopped laughing, startled to see his mother so close. She took Keone's hand, and realized that her daughter was perspiring.

"Jesus, baby. I don't know what to say. I'm speechless."

"I wanna go even if you say I can't."

"No, honey, no—I think it's wonderful. But I don't see how we can do it. What school is it?"

"It's the Burr College. On Sixth Street acrost from a park. They teaches secretary classes and computers and things. Mrs. Hooper says they teach you computers the best way, and computers is everything."

Mrs. Hooper was their case worker, a white woman in her mid-twenties who routinely interviewed them to justify a dwindling welfare continuance. She conducted these meetings in the manager's office by the gated entrance of the project instead of interviewing them in their home as she was supposed to. A lot of case workers did that. Few outsiders deliberately transgressed Caulfeld Homes. Even the cops disavowed any responsibility for what might happen to someone reckless enough to enter what they collectively called "no man's land."

"Oh baby, I know that school. That's a fine school. But I gotta tell you, a school like that's gonna want you to have a diploma. And Keone, baby, you ain't got yours."

Keone's tough façade melted. They looked at each other in mutual agony. Oh that bad time! Doris had cried to no avail when Keone dropped out of Southwest High School at sixteen, shedding education like a thick coat she'd been forced to wear for eleven years against her will. Doris knew what would happen next: pregnancy, abandonment, and a growing impenetrability on her daughter's hard-bitten face, her eyes gray, her mouth a rude slit to protect it from a world bitterly indifferent to a failed life. It happened to everyone's children here. You couldn't help it. That's what Caulfeld did—taught you to accept defeat because that's how life worked, and learn nothing from it.

"Mama, I'd have to go back to high school two more years to get a diploma!" Keone's voice rose in panic. "I can't wait no two years!"

"Baby, you should of thought about that before. Remember how I begged you? But you was too smart for me. You knew all the answers. That school was nothin' but bullshit, you said, and nothin' you was learnin' was important and wouldn't do you no good. Remember all that?"

An angry wail escaped Keone's lips. She leapt up from the table and ran out of the room.

Doris jumped up too. "Keone, I'm sorry!"

The girl dropped on the couch in the living room. She folded her arms across her chest and stared furiously at the TV where two Muppets sang in a bathtub. Javaughn had turned the TV on earlier, and once on no one ever shut it off.

"Honey, I shouldn't of brought that up. But that's the single worst moment of my life, when you dropped out of Southwest. You was my hope, honey. Javaughn's always hated it, I've known for years he'll drop out soon's he can. And Corey was just born then."

"You don't think I can do it!"

"No, baby. It's just I don't see how they'll take you. Places like that wanna see high school records and such. What they gonna think when they see you dropped out?"

Keone's answer was a sullen frown.

"Baby, let me axt you," Doris tried gently. "Don't get mad. You ain't done nothin' with yourself all this long time, why suddenly you want to be a secretary?"

Keone looked anxious. Though they both knew her brother had left the house, they spoke in whispers. "Mama, Javaughn deals."

"I know it."

"He's gonna die in this place. He ain't takin' hisself, not yet, but he will. He thinks he's too smart, but everybody does it sooner or later, and he will too. He ain't around here for days sometimes and—and remember that night last year when he come in with his face all bust up?"

Doris saw again the bloodied face of her son, the animal glare in his eyes, the rank panic in his movements, the unsteadiness in his voice as he barked orders at them all. Javaughn never told what happened, but for two weeks he wouldn't leave the house, not even at night, and shut off all the lights before venturing to a window.

"Darcy lost her baby 'cause a crack." Keone grimaced saying this. Darcy was her age, her closest friend. "Mama, I promise I won't hang out with no boys, and I'll study every night. I won't buy no clothes or jewelry or treats. Just say I can go."

"Why, of course you can go. How could I axt you not to? I wish other people felt like you." Without looking up at the bedroom over their heads, Doris managed to convey her meaning. "What else Mrs. Hooper tell you?"

"Well, I got me a brochure. Wanna see it?"

"You got a brochure? Where? From the school?"

A careful nod.

"You already been there?"

"Just to get the brochure. I didn't talk to nobody. I wasn't sure I should."

Doris studied her with slight amusement. As if she were proud of Keone. "Yeah, get it. Let's see what they got."

Keone started for the stairs. She paused on the first step, and her tough scowl returned. "Mama?"

"Yeah?"

"Do I gotta tell Daddy?"

"No," Doris said flatly. "You don't lie to him, but there ain't no reason he gotta know straight out. Get your brochure. Show me all about it."

2

"She was eating a banana *in the library!*"

Daphne D'Abrosso's reddish-blond hair spilled down the back of her head from a gold butterfly barrette. Her face was narrow with luminous brown eyes and small rosebud mouth. Her slim legs displayed a well-tended summer tan. She perched in the chair across from the director's desk, her back, shoulders, and chin stiff with indignation.

"Daphne, that's wrong, I grant you—"

"You're darn right it is!"

"Daphne, just chill a moment, okay?" Oliver Dunbar assumed a counselor's smooth patience. "Let me ask you, did you talk to Safina about it? Did you tell her that eating in the library was against the rules?"

"No I didn't! That's not my job! That's *your* job! I don't ever want to talk to her! That banana stank up the whole room! She left the peel in the trash can! All afternoon everybody could smell it!"

The library was modest but adequate, like so much of the Burr College: a single large room on the second floor, with metal shelves on three sides and several circular tables in the middle. With the afternoon sun baking through the south windows, an abandoned banana peel could turn rank pretty quickly.

"Daphne, I'll certainly talk to her about it. But you know some people need a little tolerance when they're learning new ways."

"Oh *come on*, Dr. Dunbar! What new ways are you talking about? Is acting decent a new way?"

"Daphne—"

"If my parents knew someone like her was in the same class with me, they'd be outraged. They'd be down here chewing you out something fierce!"

"Daphne, Safina comes from a different background. She hasn't had the advantage of a well-off family—"

"Oh right! My parents say you don't have to be rich to know the difference between right and wrong. They say it every night when we watch murders and robberies on the news. And besides—" the student's voice turned nasal, "my parents are *not* well off! I have two brothers in college too, you know. Dad's very squeezed right now."

Word from David Hurley, Oliver's financial aid director, was that Mr. D'Abrosso earned $268,000 a year as an executive at NFL Films.

"Look how she dresses, Dr. Dunbar! That ugly brown horror she had on today, that wool thing with the fuzz coming off it—you call that professional?"

"Daphne, give her a break. Maybe she can't afford better clothes than that. That's why many less-fortunate students come here, you know. To get a decent job and upgrade their lives and come away with a little dignity." Oliver's voice was a smooth tenor designed not to irritate. All angry students hurt a school, but Daphne D'Abrosso was a special asset. Halfway through the two-year Executive Secretarial Arts Associate Degree Program, she was by far the best in her class. Her shorthand was over 130. She typed in the dizzy upper nineties. Her business letters were superb, her office manner and organizational abilities a joy. Dean's List consistently captured. Valedictorian in the bag. Every executive in Philadelphia would want her greeting powerful clients at the front desk. Placement would get a whopping high salary for her, maybe even something in the thirty thousands, a salary plateau yet to be achieved by the Philadelphia Burr College for a starting graduate.

"Daphne, we could talk in circles like this all day. What is it about Safina that really bothers you?"

The student hesitated. She knew an honest answer could be taken the wrong way. When she did respond, it was with enough contempt to protect herself from ridicule. "She's a goddamn nigger, *that's* what's wrong!"

Oliver sighed and sank back in his chair.

"I'm sorry," the girl said with prim dignity, "but that's the way I feel. I know my parents would agree with me. I don't see why they should pay good money for a school whose Admissions Department allows that kind of person to attend. I don't care if it's not polite—it's still the truth."

So at last Oliver allowed a hint of his own anger. He was easygoing about most things, but not this. "Well, thank Heaven your feelings don't rule the rest of the world. In this country everyone is entitled to a good education. For all your worldly judgment, Safina Howard *did* pass the admissions test, and has just as much right as you to be in class."

"But Dr. Dunbar, you can't honestly think—"

"Yes, I can. She's here to learn, she's doing her best, and this school is proud to have her. You have no right to judge her, and I won't hear any more about it. I'll speak to her about eating in the library. She won't do it again. Anything else?"

Daphne stared at him, wide-eyed.

"Let's be clear," he said firmly. "If equality of education is too much for you to accept, then maybe you're the one who doesn't belong here." Oh, but her parents were wealthy. This could really hurt.

Daphne stood. Her pretty face was granite. "I'm sorry, Dr. Dunbar, to have taken your time. Please excuse me, I have to go back to class."

He tried to ease things. "Always a pleasure, Daphne. I mean that."

A harsh bell beyond his office blatted the start of Fifth Period. Daphne strode briskly out the door.

Oliver Dunbar took a moment to clear his head, then stood and stretched. He was in his upper forties, six-foot-two with a narrow carriage, and long limbs. His forehead was high and faintly furrowed, his hair black with clear patches of gray coalescing at the temples. Black-framed glasses made him look like what he was, a born professor. Slipping on his suit jacket, he stepped outside.

The school director's office opened on a large room gridded by partitions to create a series of work cubicles generously dubbed "offices," one each for the admissions secretary, the evening school coordinator, the placement secretary, the dean's secretary, and finally the business manager, whose "office" was a cramped corner by the window. Besides Oliver's, there were four actual offices with doors for privacy, and these opened along one wall of this larger room. Three belonged to Admissions, the fourth to Financial Aid. The entrance to the business manager's cubicle was beside the school director's office, and Oliver leaned around to peer in.

Louise Mallory sat at her desk, scanning book lists and locker numbers for the new class registering today. In her mid-sixties, with scant white hair and a face devoid of cheekbones, Louise was considered a mean old hag by the students and only slightly less so by staff and faculty. She lived by herself outside Philadelphia, commuted on a growling SEPTA train both ways, and held no fear of the city after dark. She appreciated paperwork and numbers, and begrudged any breathing person who needed her attention. Despite this, she was a seventeen-year fixture at Burr. She handled all vendor accounts, student accounts, the physical plant, personnel benefits, payroll, and the list went on. She glared at everybody from between a two-drawer file cabinet on her right and a computer table on her left which, with her desk before her, socketed her in. She lusted for an office of her own, but understood the ins and outs of small school politics and resigned herself to the primacy of Admissions. The only time Oliver ever saw Louise smile with genuine pleasure was years back when he permitted her to include office walls for herself on the annual capital expenditure request. The President's Office in New York squelched it as unnecessary, preferring to order new cassette decks for the shorthand classrooms. Every year thereafter Oliver continued to include the wall request, but never saw the business manager look hopeful again. Louise was not someone you could fool twice.

She said, "Ms. D'Abrosso stomped out of your office with quite a pout on her puss. What'd she want?"

"The repeal of the Emancipation Proclamation. I think I was hard on her. You get so frustrated when you don't reach them."

"Well, what were you trying to reach?"

"A little dormant compassion, maybe." Oliver pushed up his glasses and rubbed his forehead. "She's griping about Safina Howard. Safina is a black student from the Logan section of North Philly. She's a victim of poverty and a weak high school. Daphne hails from affluent Cherry Hill in New Jersey. I wanted her to appreciate that."

"Oliver, you can't teach against Mom and Dad. They got to her a lot sooner than you did."

"I know. Still, I do wonder what a girl like Daphne thinks education is about."

"Who, her?" Louise's face rumpled with cheerful disdain. "That chicky-babe doesn't think about it at all. We're just part of a long-range plan to snare a sugar daddy."

Oliver grimaced.

"You know it too. She's in a two-year program at a prestigious school with a guaranteed job as soon as she graduates. She'll join some high-power outfit, meet an insufferable yuppie, and get herself engaged within two years. Why else does a smart girl come to a junior college like Burr instead of attending a four-year college where she could get a bachelors?"

"You know I hate to think like that."

"Just the same, it's true. Dean Harris was telling me about her niece. The kid had her eleventh birthday two months ago, and Ethel asked her what she wanted to be when she grew up. And the kid said, with these wide serious eyes, that she was going to study hard and get accepted to Princeton. At Princeton she would find a successful law student and marry him. He would make lots of money, and they would buy a big house where he would then leave her alone to do whatever she wanted."

"Good gosh." Oliver was impressed.

"Damn right. Kid's all of eleven and got it figured out. Wish I had a plan like that when I was her age." Louise squinted at a half-finished letter scrolled through her Selectric typewriter. By her elbow was a computer bought new two years ago when New York finally bent with the times and splurged for computers for all personnel. For months the secretaries, staff, and even the teachers struggled to learn how to type and save documents, how to click with a mouse, and store everything on slim square floppy disks. Even Oliver was still getting the hang of it. Louise couldn't be bothered.

"So what's happening?" Oliver asked, changing the subject.

"I'm assigning lockers and checking inventory. We're missing books from New York."

"Missing books?"

Louise held up a hand to stop him from drawing closer. "I'm working on it. Don't bug me until I need you."

Thus chastised, he left her, and crossed through the maze of partitioned cubicles to the lobby.

The Burr College lobby tried to combine all the elements of corporate success with the charm of being housed in a legitimate Philadelphia historical landmark—a three-story red brick mansion once owned by a powerful English Tory. The walls were plain white-washed colonial plaster, the fireplace mantle painted patriotic blue to match the carpet and wall trim. The window glass was primitively blurred with imperfections consistent with windows of two hundred years ago. The furniture was old-fashioned, overstuffed, and supported on brown cabriole legs. Two portraits hung over the couch depicting the 1907 founders of the famous Burr empire: Reginald Burr and his mother Evelyn. Beside a giant fern stood a TV set on a high metal stand, and the furniture was arranged to allow visitors to relax while they viewed a ten-minute video tape that explained why the Burr College was one of the best two-year liberal and secretarial arts colleges in the nation. Standing by the receptionist's desk was Elaine Margolis, Oliver's senior admissions rep. Currently there was no director of admissions, and while the search continued Elaine was holding down the fort. Tall, with long chestnut hair, Elaine carried herself with a polished Main Line elegance that was the common signature of a Burr graduate.

"Oliver," she said immediately, "the final count will be ready soon. Deirdre is doing one last tally."

"Okay." He registered the unhappiness in her voice. Everyone knew that the poor enrollment for the new class was not Elaine's fault, and Oliver was prepared to reassure her if she needed it. "Where do you think we'll land?"

"Last count came to one hundred and sixty-nine."

"Okay. Come see me when Dee's done."

Elaine nodded and walked off. Oliver stared morosely at a print of Thomas Birch's *Philadelphia Harbor* hanging over the receptionist's desk. To the receptionist herself he said, "How's your day been?"

Julie Fitzgerald smiled sympathetically. At thirty-three she was older than the average Burr secretary, with round gold-frame glasses and blond hair usually pulled back in a simple bun. Mature and bewitchingly efficient, she kept the front area organized with the unpretentious skill of a friendly hostess, while also serving as Oliver's secretary. "Good enough," she answered. "I saw Daphne D'Abrosso sail out looking ruffled. What did you say to her?"

"Nothing she wanted to hear." Oliver rubbed his eyes, then stared at her, perplexed. "Now what did I come out here for? I guess I'm losing it."

"Mr. Nostrand?"

"Oh hell, yes. Did he call?"

"Twice. Wants you to call back right away." She held up two pink *While You Were Out* slips.

"Of course he does." Oliver studied the messages. The URGENT box on both was checked. "How'd he sound?"

"Not so thrilled when I put him off the second time. Are you going to call him?"

"Well, I guess I'd better. He's not gracious about waiting. I'll—no, wait. What time is it?"

Without looking, Julie said, "Quarter to three."

"Shoot, I'm on now, aren't I?" For no reason Oliver patted his pockets.

"According to the itinerary, you're to speak to the new class at two-thirty."

"Damn! Think the dean is still on?"

"No way I could know, boss."

"Okay." He scanned the lobby hastily, as if searching for something. "Right, I'm on my way to the lounge. If Nostrand calls back, just ..." He tried to think of something and failed. He shrugged feebly.

"I'll handle it," Julie said amiably.

"Thanks. Here, take these messages back. I already know what he wants. I just don't know what to tell him. Okay, I'm going. Wait—what about that three o'clock appointment? Is that confirmed?"

"Yes. Mr. Jameson for the admissions director position. And then a Ms. Martin at four for the same."

"Two in one afternoon, eh? Maybe things are looking up. You wouldn't have copies of the resumes, would you? I'm not sure where I put mine. They might even be on my desk at home—"

"I have copies right here."

He grinned. A little embarrassed, she grinned back. He said, "You know I've heard that you keep copies of everything you give me."

Julie fluttered her lashes. "Why Dr. Dunbar, why would I need to do that?"

"Damned if I know. Listen, if you're so smart, answer me this. How come we've only had you for six months? How did I survive the past two decades without you?"

"Good help takes a while to find, I guess. Go wow the new class, Oliver."

"Thanks. Listen, put the copies of the resumes on—or wait. If Nostrand calls then ... oh, to hell with it! I've got to get down there." He hunched up his shoulders in the loose jacket and looked at his watch. "Catch you later!" He darted out of the lobby.

3

Oliver trotted down the carpeted hallway at a brisk pace, passing the large Willard grandfather clock, some charming cherry wood antique side tables and chairs, and a row of black-framed historical photographs documenting the rise of the Burr institutions since the first college was founded in Boston in 1907. That founding, by Reginald Burr and his mother Evelyn, reverberated with social significance as well, for it was a clear feminist thrust into the hallowed masculine halls of turn-of-the-century Boston commerce. The satellite campuses that followed: New Haven, Hartford, New York, and others, also opened resistant professional doors for its female graduates. Though the Philadelphia college was only twenty-two years old, Oliver liked to think that it contributed as well to this progressive history. He squeezed past a few milling girls by the water fountain and bounded down the stairs to the basement, a room dramatically renovated nine years ago from a leaky cinderblock shell to a large student lounge with vending machines, chairs and tables, and watercolor etchings of Independence Hall, Franklin Court, the Betsy Ross House, and Elfreth's Alley. A luminous photograph of the Museum of Art at night dominated the wall over the hot-and-cold food bar, run by little Betty Driscoll every day from eleven a.m. to four p.m. The new class sat at the tables, listening to the introductory remarks of the dean. The door to the lounge had a small glass window, and Oliver paused a moment to peek in.

Dr. Ethel Harris stood at a podium before an avid group of women. The dean's stance, hands on hips, legs apart, feet clamped to the floor, looked formidable even from behind. She was tall, broad-shouldered, with the commanding voice of a single woman who has raised four boys on her own.

"… will not be easy," she declared. "The work here is accelerated and challenging, and before you know it you'll think you are drowning. You cannot afford at any point to slack off and take a breather. If you do, you'll never catch up.

"This is deliberate, of course. This school trains the finest executive secretaries in the country. This is our faculty's commitment to you. The hard work you do these next two years will be worse than anything you will encounter when you go into the business world. When you've earned your degree from us, you will be ready to do anything, face any amount of pressure, meet any deadline. You will be able to live up to the reputation of the school, and the prestige of having the Burr name on your resume."

Oliver stepped into the room and she glanced at him. He didn't like this drill instructor approach but never argued. Ethel earned her doctorate from Temple University and had been dean here for fifteen years, controlling a passionate faculty of twenty-five with both authority and physical presence. These new students already sensed that nothing got by her. They would fear and hate her—and yet two years from now they would cry at parting from her. Ethel, who gave no slack, received more flowers and gifts at graduation than any other school employee. Students admired this husky, African-American woman even as they knocked timidly on her office door.

"A boss can be sloppy. His secretary cannot. A boss can mislay papers, but his secretary has to know where they are. A boss can misspell every third word in a memo, but his secretary has to catch the errors and correct them. Smart employers recognize the vital role secretaries play in the work force. The program you are taking will turn you into an executive supersecretary. This can lead to great opportunities. *Don't* expect it to be easy. *Don't* expect a social life while you're here. But *do* expect an exciting challenge, and do expect to reap great rewards when you leave."

It was the same speech every time. There were four starts a year for the major Burr secretarial arts programs, and Ethel never saw reason to change her introductory remarks. It did amuse those staff members who got stuck listening to it every time: David Hurley in Financial Aid; Deirdre Smith, the admissions secretary; Clara Peterson, the placement director. They all made little speeches of welcome to the new classes, taking turns standing before a long table with the red and silver Burr College banner draped over it, topped with liter jugs of soda and cookies arranged on trays.

Suddenly Ethel raised her arms, her one dramatic gesture. "Consider yourselves pregnant," she declared movingly, her eyes on Heaven. "Pregnant with hunger and ambition. The education you'll receive is the fetus inside you, constantly growing and evolving. And when you graduate you will proudly give birth to a diploma. Good luck to you all!"

As always, Oliver winced. Ethel got this inane metaphor from a poem printed in an education periodical years ago, but though it never failed to make the school director cringe there was not one amused face among the new students. They applauded with faces glowing.

Ethel moved away from the podium, and Oliver stepped forward. He clasped his hands behind his back and surveyed the group of women with a broad smile. "Good afternoon."

A genial chorus echoed him. "Good afternoon."

"My name is Dr. Oliver Dunbar, and I'm the Director of the Burr College. I know Dean Harris has given you the hard line. Let me add something I'm sure the dean—if I know her well—neglected to mention. Please remember that although the work *is* hard, it will also be a lot of fun."

The women smiled gratefully. Most were students just out of high school, and he found their mix of eagerness and anxiety endearing. But a sick panic palpitated within him, *for there were only one hundred and sixty-nine students in this class!* That was half of the September goal set by Bill Nostrand, vice-president of operations in the President's Office in New York. It was the biggest failure ever suffered by the Philadelphia school. Nevertheless these women, dressed in their best, electrically attentive, were counting on him to make them feel good about coming here, so he kept his face cheerful and his sentences coherent.

"Two years from now you will be graduating as the Class of 1997. A new millennium will be upon us, with all the opportunities of the world at your fingertips. Burr will help you get there. You'll meet classmates who will become the closest and most dependable friends in your life. You'll feel a thrill like no other as your skills increase. I've stood in this room introducing new students to the Burr curriculum for twenty-two years now, and I've been doing it that long because to me the greatest satisfaction is just watching women like yourselves blossom. Enjoy this day. There is no feeling like what you are feeling right now. Be proud of the choice you have made, and feel good for having the courage to work hard and pursue an education. I admire you for it. And in a special way, I envy you. Good luck to you all. Have a wonderful, successful two years!"

The women clapped joyously. No mean feat getting them to do so, Oliver thought with grim pride, after having to sit through Placement's gushy pep talk, Financial Aid's pleas for stragglers to get the complex forms in, and the dean's hard academic line. He always wanted the new students to leave Orientation Day filled with anticipation. It was why he spoke last and kept his remarks short and positive. After two decades in this business you did learn something.

Orientation Day finished with Oliver's leaving the podium. The new students stretched and milled about. Their hands clutched course descriptions and the red policy handbook that dictated where they could smoke, how they must dress, and other mundane matters. Their actual first day of class wouldn't start until Monday, and this was only Wednesday. No pressure yet.

Oliver cut out fast, trotted up the stairs, and nearly galloped down the long corridor to the front lobby. "Hi, did Nostrand call back?"

Julie waved a pink slip. "I told him you were greeting the new class, and that you had an appointment at three o'clock with Mr. Jameson."

Oliver stared, uncomprehending.

"Alex Jameson," Julie said gently.

It still took a second. "Oh jeez, yeah." He looked at his watch, which read 3:10. "Is he here yet?"

Julie's eyes slid sideways to the couch.

A large man pushed himself to his feet. He looked about fifty. Formidable acne scars pocked a flabby face, and loose jowls crushed his shirt collar. His waist bulged beyond his unbuttoned jacket. "How are you, Mr. Dunbar?"

"Dr. Dunbar," Julie corrected.

"And I'm Alex. Pleased to meet you!" Heedless of his error, Jameson grinned and whipped out a hand the size of a tennis racket. His teeth were small and green, the gums blood red.

"Uh-huh," was all Oliver managed, so bombastically confronted. He tried to remember if his office was clean enough for a guest. Usually he tucked extraneous papers and folders in a drawer, but with Jameson catching him in the lobby he didn't have the chance. "How do you do? Sorry to keep you waiting. Why don't we go to my office? Oh—would you like some coffee?"

"Hey, that sounds marvelous!" Jameson's voice rattled the loud words, as if gargling grit.

Having offered, Oliver now saw a problem. "Uh, Julie, I hate to ask …"

"Sure," she said cheerfully. "Would you like some too?"

"Uh … yes. Why not? Thanks."

Julie stood and stepped past them. She was taller than Jameson, with an attractive hourglass figure, and the job applicant grinned a bit too wolfishly as she disappeared out the doorway. Oliver led him back through the cubicles, grateful for his secretary's good nature. After all, if there was one place where you *never* asked a secretary to get you coffee, it was a secretarial school.

They entered his office, and Jameson sank with audible relief on a large vinyl chair. His smile was not the ingratiating smile of a job applicant, but coarse and cryptic, suggesting a menacing appetite that made Oliver nervous.

"Mr. Jameson, you wouldn't have a copy of your resume on you, would you?" The school director despaired at the high stack of paper on his desk.

"Naw, sorry. Guess I should of thought to do that. My mistake."

"No, don't worry about it. It should be here somewhere. My secretary will know." Poking at the bottom of the stack, Oliver felt the files on top start to slide. He whipped down his hand, catching them before they cascaded to the floor, and pushed them precariously back in place. "Well, let's wait for her. How was the drive in?"

"Oh, I live right here in town."

"You do?"

"Sure. Sixth and Fitzwater. Just moseyed up here."

"Well, that's good."

"Yeah. One of the pluses for my working here, I guess. I'll get all the exercise Doc keeps saying I need. I can also hop over any time you got like an emergency too. Whaddya say to that, hey?"

"Great."

Julie appeared with two steaming cups of coffee on a silver tray, plus little containers of cream and Sweet'N'Low. "Mr. Jameson, do you take anything with it?"

"Just a little love, hon. Meanin' sugar. Everything goes better with a little sugar, don't ya think?"

"Dr. Dunbar?"

"Thanks, Jule. I really appreciate this. Say, you haven't got Mr. Jameson's resume, have you?"

She produced it from a folder held under the silver tray.

"Fantastic. Give yourself a raise."

"Why sure, Dr. Dunbar. Right away." This "Dr. Dunbar" stuff was for Jameson's sake. With an affectionate wink, she sauntered out and closed the door.

Jameson sipped his coffee with an admiring shake of his head. "Christ, that's some girl you got. She go to school here?"

"Just graduated last March."

"We got a girl at our office too. We should send her here. She won't do none of this stuff."

Oliver gave the resume a hasty scan. Jameson's single appropriate job was as admissions director of a trucking school located somewhere in South Philadelphia. Oliver knew it from TV commercials only, where an excited male voice barked that classes were fast filling up while the camera offered shots of shadowy figures (grads presumably) pulling tractor-trailers out a gated lot. He didn't know what to ask. At the beginning of the summer, when the admissions director position first became vacant, hardly any resumes came from admissions directors of good four-year private colleges—and that didn't surprise him. He never expected a junior college to attract professionals from that ideal sector. But he *had* expected a lot of interest from local community colleges and other junior colleges. Yet this interest never materialized. All summer the resumes that trickled in were from places like this, small niche trade schools offering quick programs that didn't require serious academic quality or polish. In many ways it was a professional slap in the face, one he hoped was just bad luck and not a developing academic trend toward two-year junior colleges.

"Tell me about the Truck Driver Academy," he said, his eyes still on the resume searching for inspiration.

"That was okay, wasn't bad," Jameson said with a cough. "Kind of took that on as a favor for a pal. He owned the school, and enrollment was starting to drop off. It's not a bad place, but you can't believe the hours."

"Long?"

"Real long. Shouldn't be legal, how long the hours are. Sometimes Saturdays too. Maybe if I was younger, know what I mean?"

"Of course." All admissions directors worked long hours, it came with the turf. For Jameson to complain about it was ridiculous. Oliver decided to avoid any further truck school questions. "I see you're currently working for an employment agency."

Jameson waved contemptuously. "That's Al Primoni. Al's my brother-in-law. It's a legit business, you know, don't get me wrong. But between you 'n' me there's too much racket crap going on in employment. A lot of stuff he's got me doing is non-union work, see? And lots of times that's finding scabs for trucking and waterfront outfits. Though at least that ain't boring."

"Scabs?"

"Sure thing." Jameson took the school director's grimace as a need to explain. "You know, you find guys to fill positions left open by employees on strike. It's harder than you think. Those union guys play rough, and sometimes the scabs get attacked."

"Yes, I've heard about that." Oliver imagined the hoots and cackles of his staff when he told them this one.

"It ain't dull. But I'm getting kind of tired of the fighting and threats. I can take care of myself, but I'm starting to get up in years, you know. Just don't want the hassle."

"Certainly."

Jameson leaned forward, tugging his collar with one hooked finger, and Oliver saw how the acne scars on his cheeks and neck continued down under his shirt. "That's why I'd be good here, see? I mean, girls learning to be secretaries is one of those naturals. Shouldn't be nothing to persuade 'em."

Oliver hesitated. He spoke as if trying to coax a response from an animal. "Well you … you do see that the girls could *go on* from being secretaries, don't you? That it might be a stepping stone for them, and they could work their way up in business and be something more?"

Jameson frowned. "Well, I guess. Why—do you?"

The rest of the interview, like the celebrated tree falling in an empty forest, made noises no one heard.

As soon as he could, Oliver walked Jameson to the double glass doors of the lobby. He did not offer him a business card, and only relaxed after the big man exited through the heavy oak door that was the main entrance to the school.

Julie also felt free to laugh out loud. "Who was he? Vito the Chopper?"

"He was a little scary."

"He'd have eaten the girls alive."

"He recruits scabs to cross union picket lines."

"Are you kidding?"

Oliver shook his head. "I'll tell you the whole thing later. Isn't there another one today?"

"Yes. She's due any time. I put her resume in the folder. She hasn't shown yet."

"You mean she's late?"

Julie nodded.

Oliver sighed and rubbed his chin, feeling the beginnings of a five o'clock shadow. "You may not believe it, Jule, but there was a time when responsible people applied for these jobs."

"Well, I'm here."

"You are the equivalent of a Biblical miracle. And thanks for the coffee. I won't ask you for that again."

"It's all right, Oliver. I didn't mind. It's not as if you expect it."

He re-entered his office. Draining cold coffee, he read the next resume in the folder. Cindee Martin. A fresh college degree from Rosemont College, which probably made her twenty-two. Her major work experience was as admissions rep for a family-run computer school in Norristown, with a side business at an ear-piercing booth in the King of Prussia Mall. Some business with the silly name *We Lobe You*. Oliver read further. Last year under Martin's leadership, ear-piercing increased twenty-six percent. Oliver removed his glasses and pressed his forehead to the desktop. He groped blindly for the intercom button.

Julie's voice cracked in the speaker. "Front desk."

"Julie, is she here yet?"

"Not yet."

"Isn't—" He firmed his voice to avoid sounding so defeated. "Isn't there another appointment tomorrow?"

"Yes. At four. That resume's in the folder too."

"Thanks. Did Nostrand call back?"

"Not yet."

He checked his watch. Quarter past four. If Nostrand didn't call in forty-five minutes Oliver could cut out on time for a change and not have to talk to him. He might still be able to end the day in one piece.

He picked up the second resume. The woman's name was Lilia Espirito. She lived in a very toney part of Radnor Township and was a graduate of Temple University. And she had some experience as an admissions director in a small school setting. Unfortunately—and Oliver recognized this immediately—the two schools she previously worked for were now closed. And currently the woman wasn't in education at all but working as a hairdresser. Self-employed, which probably meant out of her own home.

So who was better qualified to interview candidates for the prestigious Burr College of Business—the twenty-two year old ear-piercer, or the wealthy woman of unlisted age who styled hair? Oliver shut his eyes and returned his forehead to the desk. The cold coffee weighted his stomach like heavy petroleum. Somehow he had weathered every crisis at the Burr College. Somehow after twenty-two years he was still kicking. But he couldn't remember a time when he felt so exhausted. Before his closed lids he saw again the cheerful September class in the student lounge. Smiles, rapt faces. That ... that *small* class. One hundred and sixty-nine students. One hundred and sixty-nine eager, happy students ...

The goal had been three hundred and forty.

Buzz. "Oliver?"

He hit the intercom. "Yes, Julie?"

"Mr. Nostrand, Line One."

He looked at the white flashing light, so tiny and threatening. "Did the Martin woman ever show?"

"No."

On his desk was a gold-plated clock given him in 1988 by ABCAA, the college accreditation agency when he had been its Member of the Year. It read 4:45. Obviously the ear-piercer wasn't going to show. Yet he wondered if he could have Julie tell Nostrand that he was interviewing someone anyway. After a moment he quashed that plan. He might lie himself, but never through his secretary.

"Okay. Thanks." He hit the button.

"Oliver? This is Bill." Nostrand's voice, a hard tenor to begin with, had acquired with the summer's dismal recruitment numbers a deeper grimness that could fossilize the bones of any still-living creature. Oliver felt it happening to him now. "Oliver?"

"Yes. Hello."

"I spoke to your admissions secretary this morning and got a projection for the September class."

"Yes."

"You haven't returned my calls all day."

"Well, Bill, it's Orientation Day. It's been pretty hectic."

"Yes, I can imagine. Okay, Oliver … let me tell you where we stand."

4

He left the school at six-thirty, having capped the long overwrought day with a brutal analysis of the low class numbers with Elaine Margolis, and felt slightly punch-drunk as he stood a moment in the cool September twilight. It was six concrete steps from the door to the sidewalk, and as he descended two girls trotted past him sporting red Burr bookbags.

"Hi, Dr. Dunbar."

"Hi there, Lauren. Hi, Marcia. Stayed late too, eh?" They nodded with weary pleased smiles. He should let them go, but couldn't resist asking, "Lot of homework, hey?"

Mock groans. "Oh, way too much! I think you should tell Mrs. Cavanaugh to let up on us."

"Why don't you tell her yourself?"

"No way! She's too scary!"

Oliver grinned. "I know what you mean. She scares me too."

The girls laughed and moved on. He loved the look of the red canvas bookbags. Wasn't it Alexander Pope who said if you bent a twig you'd incline the tree? Oliver decided to walk tonight, rather than take the bus up Walnut Street.

The Burr College was housed in a large three-story building, a colonial mansion with a cornerstone of 1756. The original owner's wealth was reflected in its size, the inordinately high number of rooms for a colonial dwelling, and the black and red Flemish bond brickwork that stippled all walls of its exterior. The school faced west on Sixth Street across from Washington Square Park, one of five block-sized parks from William Penn's original Greene Countrie Towne. Oliver loved that his school faced so many trees, small statues, a flowing central fountain, and the Tomb of the Unknown Revolutionary War Soldier with its flickering eternal flame. In fact the Burr College, one block south of Independence Hall and in the heart of the Historic District, was surrounded by old churches, cemeteries, huge gardens, and cobblestone streets. It was a rich and varied setting, better than any four-year private college campus he ever visited.

The Philadelphia Burr College was one of seventeen such institutions from Massachusetts to Louisiana. The first school was founded in 1907 by a young man named Reginald Burr in anger over the social mistreatment of his mother. The family business was a string of Boston grocery markets that had thrived since Cotton Mather days, but when it was Reginald's father's turn to inherit the business his happy taste for extravagance and a sad tendency to drink nearly forfeited the family income. His wife Evelyn, in the shadow of her husband's office each night, used her own natural business acumen to pay the bills, track the profits, hold overhead at bay, and keep the business solvent. But when Joseph Burr died of tuberculosis in 1888 (Reginald was six), the family will transferred the stores to his younger brother Benjamin, who bore little affection for Evelyn's forthright spirit. The new widow was ostracized by the Burr family, and eventually supported her son and two daughters by scrubbing floors and washing linen for two families on Beacon Hill.

The family ostracism extended only to the widow; Benjamin Burr felt a need to nurture his brother's sole male offspring, and he footed the bill for Reginald to attend Yale. Reginald accepted the money and education, and with vengeful energy studied marketing, finance, and commerce. Upon graduation Benjamin transferred to Reginald a withheld portion of the family inheritance to start him in business. To his uncle's subsequent shame Reginald used the capital to open the first Burr school just off Charles Street with the socially defiant name Burr Business Academy for Women. He was twenty-five years old. His mother and two sisters, Linda and Suellen, taught the first classes. Its opening caused nary a ripple in the Boston conscience. Women's roles in business were insignificant, and the thought of a school devoting itself to this foolish minority was a joke, a brief subject of lampoons at high society cocktail parties.

And yet, applications for the school did come in.

Evidently there *was* a female population hidden in the silent recesses of red-brick Boston yearning to step into business. Whether jobs would be offered afterward might be a question, but female students trickled to the academy with growing steadiness, and the school made it through its first year without folding.

Riding the crest of the cause that his school embraced, Reginald became a prominent advocate for women's rights. A year after opening his Burr Academy, he hit raw nerves with a notorious interview in *The Boston Herald* while the financial community buzzed over a big strike among twenty-five thousand women garment workers in New York City fighting for higher wages. "Women belong in business," thundered Reginald in the perfectly-timed interview. "I'm talking about an equal footing with men. The girls who study at our academy have intelligence, ambition, grace, skill, as well as that so-called masculine trait, the desire to succeed. Someday women will be managers, department heads, and finally they will sit on the boards of major corporations, working in equality with their male colleagues!"

The backlash from this filled the Boston print media. *The Globe* ran a cartoon of Reginald in a dress, petticoat, and bonnet, looking dismayed over the caption, "I wonder why no one will hire me?" (A copy now hung in every Burr College.) Businesses, men's clubs, and government officials castigated the Burr Academy, railed at Reginald—and secretly hired his students. For the truth was these Burr secretaries were exceptionally skilled, and could be had at much cheaper wages than their male counterparts. And although Reginald and Evelyn bridled at the wage discrimination, they realized it was the only way to get their graduates in the door.

In 1915 Reginald opened a second school in New Haven. That school suffered an initial setback when vandals, convinced the school was a headquarters for female immorality, smashed windows and painted anti-suffrage slogans on the walls. The vandalism only brought sympathy to the school; when the damage was repaired its enrollment soared.

The World War sent America's men off to Europe and business personnel pools had to fend for themselves. The feminine secretarial market flourished. Reginald quickly opened schools in Newport and Hartford. The Hartford school was built from a renovated farmhouse, and the first graduating class had its picture taken before an unused cow barn.

The schools filled steadily throughout the 1920s. The 1929 Crash and subsequent Depression slowed expansion, but none of the schools closed. In late 1942 factory production for munitions in America hit stride, and positions opened up that hitherto had been unheard of for women. All along the upper East Coast it was Burr women who first acquired the managerial positions Reginald had envisioned thirty years before. It prompted him to take the schools' biggest gamble to date, and he opened the giant New York and Washington schools simultaneously. Each were three floors in major office buildings, with twenty classrooms, a staff of fifteen and a faculty of forty. Both schools succeeded beyond Reginald's dreams. The Manhattan corporations and the Washington war machine hired the women as quickly as they graduated. The "legend" of the Burr secretary was growing. The stories of businesses sending recruiters with fistfuls of cards to graduation ceremonies, where they tried to hire grads as they unpinned their mortarboards, were true.

Opening the two big schools was Reginald's last major decision. He was sixty-one years old and extremely wealthy. He retired, and his son Henry became the head of the growing Burr secretarial empire. Henry, in turn, passed the baton to his own son Charles in 1959. There were now thirteen schools operating from Boston to Chicago and from New York to New Orleans. Burr schools thrived in Atlanta, Miami, Cincinnati, and Memphis. Charles realized a need to officially charter the schools and develop a staff to govern the campuses. He established a board of trustees and a President's Office in New York City, with himself elected the first Burr College president. In an effort to elevate the prestige of the schools even further, he got the board to change the name to the Burr Colleges of Business. When he retired in 1972, seven of the schools honored the occasion by naming their libraries after him.

The board elected John Coyne to be the new president. Coyne was not a member of the Burr family, but he and Charles were good friends, and they had worked together to expand the schools throughout the 1960s. Coyne was forty-seven, a self-made businessman self-conscious of his own lack of formal schooling. He loved serving on the Burr board, and it was he who first saw a burgeoning of small trade schools in the Seventies and worried that Burr would, as a mere secretarial school, become part of this pedestrian mix. He persuaded the board to revise the charter, and changed the schools' mission to include a combination of liberal arts courses he wished he had taken himself in his youth: English, Drama, political science, the fine arts, and some serious math. All of this allowed the Burr Colleges to achieve greatness. They were the premier finishing schools on the East Coast. Movie stars, congressmen, and even two presidents sent their daughters there. So did a prime minister of Ireland. The core of the programs remained secretarial in nature, and thus the schools retained everything they had already achieved: it was educational quality and job pragmatism rolled into one. Businesses responded with healthy enthusiasm to the rounded curriculum, and when they needed secretaries they asked specifically for Burr grads. Alumni rose to positions of prominence in banks, publishing houses, and fashion centers. Six and a half decades of tradition and success backed these grads. Schools displayed framed letters from Presidents Eisenhower, Kennedy, and Johnson praising Burr graduates as "models of integrity in the American work force." When he assumed the presidency at the peak of this good feeling, John Coyne reexamined the East Coast and decided to plug the gaps. Over the next four years colleges opened in Trenton, Baltimore, Philadelphia and Richmond. At the same time a young Oliver Dunbar, clutching a freshly minted doctorate in education from the University of Pennsylvania, contacted Burr for a job. Eager and exuberant, and possessing a liberal feminist spirit, he was exactly what John Coyne needed. He was enthusiastically hired, making Oliver Dunbar the first Burr College director in sixty-six years who was not a woman.

*

It was a twenty-minute walk to Rittenhouse Square where the apartment houses towered over the treetops as impressively as they did across Central Park in New York, a similarity not lost on Oliver's wife. She had a lot of money now, and they lived in a huge apartment for the astonishing rent of $4,400 per month.

The doorman greeted him with a smile and brisk, "How are you this evening, Dr. Dunbar?" Oliver looked for mail, found none, and realized that Tina might be home. If so, it would be the first time in three weeks. His heart tripped impatiently as he rode up the elevator.

"Tina?" he called as soon as he opened the door.

"Hi honey," she responded brightly from her study. The apartment boasted eight rooms and a balcony, all furnished in accordance with Tina's marginally-researched spiritual tastes: framed Japanese watercolors, lots of odd—and oddly placed—buddas, and wicker bookcases supporting sinuously twisted candleholders. The walls were robin's egg blue, the furniture light tan, the latter including a plush L-shaped sectional sofa, a glass coffee table, and a brown meditation bench positioned before a forty-two inch TV. The fireplace mantle was cluttered with disparate family portraits.

Oliver dropped on the sofa with his coat still on and yanked off his shoes. "Was I supposed to know you were coming back?"

"Not at all. I knew your Orientation was today, and I thought it'd be nice if I were home to greet you."

"That's so great, sweetheart. Thank you."

She emerged from the study. In khaki shorts and a red pullover jersey, she looked at forty-five as if she were still in her twenties. Her arms were slim and round, her legs long and firm from years of dance lessons. Strange thick creams applied nightly kept crow's feet from her eyes. Her bright eyes, emerald-green with the contacts in, sparked life in a sweet, high-cheeked face that was somehow even prettier when captured by a camera. It was Tina's earliest asset, her face. She asked, "Was it bad?"

"It was tough. Though at least I still have a job."

"Do you? I know you weren't sure."

Oliver smiled weakly. "I think the only thing that saved me is John Coyne likes me."

"Then let's hear it for John Coyne." She sat beside him on the puffy arm of the sofa, and let her hand caress the back of his neck. "Tell me about it."

"Well you know what the summer's been like. We finished way below goal. Bill Nostrand's furious."

"But he can't be mad at just you. Didn't you tell me all the schools are hurting?"

"They are. Everybody's applicant pools have been shrinking for years. Anyway, he said we'll need to recruit one hundred and sixty students in January and April each to even things out."

"Is that possible?"

"No." He laughed too loudly.

Tina crossed to a pristine tan wood bar in a corner of the room and began mixing drinks. Her head was down, her wide mouth puckered. It was a sign she wanted to talk. He accepted the martini she handed him, and let her sit across from him on another part of the sectional.

"Hon, I might have some news."

Oliver smiled. "You look like you do."

"Fred called. It seems that Sidney really does want me for his film. This after not hearing anything from anybody for weeks."

Oliver felt embarrassed. "Sidney?"

"Wallace."

"Oh of course."

"The director."

"Yes, I know who he is. This is that police script, right?"

"It's a courtroom film. It centers around a powerful career prosecutor who has to break down the psychological armor of this street punk, a Latino kid, real dangerous. They don't have him cast yet. And in doing so she actually falls in love with him. It'll raise all sorts of moral and ethical issues regarding our legal system."

"Sounds terrific, hon."

She grabbed her pack of cigarettes from the glass coffee table. "God, Oliver, can you imagine me in a Sidney Wallace film? So many of his actors have won Oscars, I can't even begin to tell you! He's worked with Hepburn, Bogart, Steiger, Fonda—both Henry and Jane—Brando, Pacino, and … well, a lot more, but that's an incredible gallery of talent already."

"He must be a million years old."

"He's brilliant, is what he is. With a long career to show for it. His films are significant. You know how important that is to me."

"Yes, I know. Honey, this is great. We really should celebrate, don't you think? We can—"

"Oh *no no no!*" she said in sudden panic. "It's not confirmed! Fred was just telling me what he heard. Sidney's been all over the place casting this. Fact, last I heard he was seriously considering Gwyneth Paltrow. That one spooks me, Oliver. She's half my age."

"You'll get it, hon. You know you will."

"They're projecting a seven week shoot, most of it in Brooklyn. I want you to join me for it."

"For the whole shoot? Tina, I can't get away."

"Except I think you can." She looked at him sternly, enough to break the little buzz his martini was giving him. "I'm not asking you to stop working. Just asking you to come to New York and see what your options are. You'll like the place in West Village—I've done a lot with it since you saw it last."

"Tina, we've been over this too many times. I'm not giving up my school."

"Then take a vacation." She struck a match hard, and lit up. "God, I've watched that school rip you apart all spring and summer. It's not good for you."

"Tina—"

"I'm asking as nice as I know how. I really want you to be there for me. For this."

It was such a worn out conversation. "I can't," he said, and hated it.

She sighed and began to move about the room. Eventually this put her in front of the foyer mirror, and she stopped to look at herself. "Can't you even try to be reasonable? There are tons of schools in New York that are better than Burr. Places that would welcome a real talent and commitment such as yours."

"Burr will turn around. These things are cyclical."

"Cyclical? Christ, Oliver, it's a *secretarial* school." Tina twisted her lips a little, it made her look angry. "This is 1995, not 1907. Why would any intelligent woman study at the Burr College when she can get a degree from Columbia, or Villanova, or Stanford? Some place with a real career path."

"Businesses are starving for good secretaries."

"So what? Nobody wants to *be* one." Tina widened her eyes and angled her head a little. "Suppose we had a daughter? Suppose she was of college age, intelligent, outgoing, assertive, the whole nine yards. Would you say to her, 'Darling, I love you, I want you to be the best you can be. So go to this school and become a secretary'? Would you tell her that, Oliver?"

He was silent.

"You'd never want her to settle beneath her abilities, and neither would I. We couldn't stand it if she did. You know I'm right."

He was so quiet she finally turned to look at him. "What are you thinking?"

"I'm thinking that our marriage is twenty-one years old. We should have a daughter in college."

Now Tina was quiet. She carried her empty glass back to the bar. *"Touché,"* she said softly.

Oliver stood up to put his coat in the hall closet. By the front door in a brown wood frame hung the one ornament in this eclectic home that still affected him: their marriage certificate, the parchment signed by their families and friends at the Quaker wedding in Abington, his boyhood town. He read over the signatures—Tina's parents, his brother Earl, Dale Thurston who was Oliver's closest friend when they were high school students and then grad students together at the University of Pennsylvania, and some of their classmates. He felt the little shock he always did at seeing his dad's signature, for his father had passed away two years before. Tina was not a Quaker. Her family was from Connecticut where her father owned a prosperous plastic bag manufacturing company, and although Tina was technically Jewish she held no religious beliefs. In fact, when he asked her to marry him—he had just finished his first year working at Burr—she agreed to the Quaker service because its lack of trappings, the fact that no minister presided, seemed a good compromise.

"Oliver." She was behind him, balancing a fresh martini. "I don't want to argue with you tonight. That's not why I came home. I knew your day was going to be bad and I wanted to be with you." She clicked her glass against the one he still held.

"Thank you, Tina, for coming home."

"Oliver, please. For God's sake, never thank me for coming home."

She put a hand to his cheek, tilted her head, and gave him a slight knowing smile. It was her most beguiling look, natural and unpracticed. He kissed her.

Tina kissed back more erotically than he expected. With a throaty laugh she plucked the drink out of his hand, set both glasses on the coffee table, and said, "You quiet intellectuals can be so much trouble."

"Can we?"

"Yes. Especially tall handsome ones like you. You cling to these old ideals as if it's the rest of the world that's gone mad, and yet it's impossible to stay angry with you." She unbuttoned the neck of her blouse. "That's an ambiguity some of the best actors in the world can't manage."

"Are you saying I'm talented?"

"I'm saying that you are still the dearest man I've ever known."

Oliver embraced her, affected as always by the earthy sexuality of his tall limber wife, panted over by a sea of faceless fans and yet still his, only his. His hands fumbled with her blouse and Tina laughed, leaning back in his arms. "Let me." She whipped the shirt over her head with feminine magic and threw it aside. Her naked shoulders and long neck glowed. "Now, Professor, I do you." She deftly unknotted his necktie and flicked free the buttons of his dress shirt. Oliver stood in wonder, feeling a blood-rush that hadn't lost its edge since their courtship days at college. Tina trimmed him down to socks and a wristwatch, then stood back, admiring the statue she had made by removing the unnecessary marble. She looked great—beautifully bare-breasted, wearing only the khaki shorts, grinning so deeply that even her smallest dimples emerged. She turned toward the bedroom but Oliver grabbed her hand. She responded with a deep voodoo chuckle as he pulled her down on the carpet …

Sometime later they lay looking up at the ceiling, taking medicinal breaths and basking in an afterglow of pleasure and gratitude.

"Part of the sectional has moved," Tina remarked.

"Don't know how that happened."

"And the drinks on the coffee table have slopped."

"That I kind of remember."

A clock over the fireplace chimed. Tina raised herself on an elbow and grasped Oliver's arm to read his watch. With a businesslike grunt she sat up and took the TV remote from the coffee table.

"I guess that replaces cigarettes," Oliver observed.

"You don't mind, do you, hon? *Pulp Fiction* is on HBO. I have to watch anything with Harvey Keitel, you know that."

"I do," he said with a smile.

The TV's giant forty-two inch screen shimmered to life. They remained naked on the carpet, and Oliver admired Tina while she avidly admired the film. His breathing was back to normal.

5

Elaine Margolis checked her face in a hand mirror for sake of a ten o'clock appointment, a possible last minute entry into the failed September sit. In an anything-goes era of short skirts and dangling earrings, the Burr senior admissions rep consistently wore long, slim dresses that expressed an elegance reflective of her wealthy Main Line family breeding, and sported the pearl earrings that were a birthday present from her husband Steve. She had graduated from the Advanced Secretarial Arts Program four years before, and credited Burr for her professional manner, her personal confidence, and business smarts. Steve, a rising financial advisor for Merrill Lynch, hated the long hours his wife put in, the stupid policies from New York that made her goals all but impossible to achieve, and the endless criticism from self-righteous teachers who felt (wrongly) that she used no discretion in accepting prospects for a class. But Steve couldn't talk Elaine out of loving a school that had done so much for her.

She passed inspection, put away the mirror, and walked out to the lobby. "Keone Robinson?"

A skinny black girl sitting on the couch glanced up. She wore a black T-shirt, black jeans, and gray buck shoes. Gold earrings the size of maple leaves swung from either side of her head. Her humorless eyes stared distrustfully as the rep approached, the way many economically poor girls did when confronted by Elaine's grace and expensive clothes. The rep knew in a glance that this prospect was a disaster. Probably she would end up talking her into going someplace else, a trade school perhaps, or a less demanding secretarial school, since students like this invariably failed out. On the other hand, another recruit for the September class would raise the sad percentage of forty-nine on the monthly report to a still sad but at least even fifty percent.

"Are you Keone?" she asked with a smile that showed no trace of her low evaluation.

"Yeah'm."

"I'm Elaine Margolis. Why don't you come with me, please?"

They shook hands, and Elaine felt tiny bones in the girl's grip. She led the way through the cubicles to her office and closed the door.

"Have a seat, Keone. Is that your application form? Why don't you let me take a moment to review it?"

Keone handed her the blue form. A large majority of the questions were left unanswered. The lines provided for the essay question, WHAT I WANT MOST IN A CAREER, were blank. But the girl's address was filled in, and Elaine's suspicions from the lobby were confirmed. One eight-three Virginia Street was in Caulfeld Homes, a morbid housing project in South Philadelphia. Elaine sometimes passed it on the Schuylkill Expressway where a chain fence and her car's own speed provided a safe buffer. She read further. Southwest was a bleak, notoriously crime-ridden South Philly high school. Students either dropped out or graduated from Southwest, no one was allowed to linger simply because of failing grades. The two field reps, Joyce Miller and Marcia Matteo, finally refused to visit the school, which was the loggerhead for getting out of visiting any other high school on the infamous "C" list. Elaine flipped the app over. No job experience, no special interests. Single, but Elaine wondered if Keone was a mother. Like most well-off white people, Elaine assumed all poor black girls had babies.

"Well, Keone, I see you're a graduate of Southwest High."

"Yeah'm."

"You'll have to get us a copy of your transcript from there."

"'Scuse me?"

"Your transcript," Elaine said gently, and smiled. She talked this way to her three-year-old niece. "Or a copy of your diploma will do. It's your proof that you're a high school graduate."

"But it says right here I graduated." The girl pointed at the application where one question, ARE YOU A HIGH SCHOOL GRADUATE? was checked "yes."

"Well, but I'm afraid that's not proof. We require an official transcript from everybody who comes here. The Burr College cannot accept a student who doesn't have a high school diploma or G.E.D."

"Or what?"

"G.E.D."

Keone sat rigidly. Outside the window a dog barked in Washington Square, and unseen children squealed happily.

"Awright, I get it."

"Sure. It won't be a problem. Just ask your high school. They'll mail it to you, then you bring it to us, okay?"

"Yeah."

"Now, let's take a look at what you want. You're interested in the Two-Year Executive Secretarial Arts Program, right?"

"Yeah'm."

"Well, you're very lucky, Keone, because we're starting that class on Monday. Even though it's such short notice, I'm sure I can squeeze you in. I believe there are one or two seats left." Such harmless lies tripped unthinkingly off Elaine's tongue. She flipped through the September class list, took a moment to study it, then smiled. "Yes, Keone, we can fit you right in."

Keone nodded, and the sullenness faded a little. Elaine talked easily. She had recited the course descriptions a thousand times now, but could still keep it conversational, and the black girl dropped her guard more and more as the classes were described: business writing, shorthand, office procedures, endless computer classes, accounting and advanced math, economics, literature, current events, a very rounded curriculum for the two-year program, all leading to an associate's degree and a rewarding career.

"Keone, how does it all sound to you?"

"Good."

"Would you like to start on Monday?"

"Uh-huh."

"Terrific." Elaine flipped shut the catalog. "Keone, it's a twenty-five dollar app fee, and a one hundred dollar tuition deposit to secure your seat in class. Did you bring any money with you today?"

"No."

Of course not. Par for the course. "Well, I really ought to have the twenty-five. I can't even have your name entered in the computer without that. That's the rule."

"I don't got no money on me."

"Can you get it for me when you come on Monday?"

"Uh-huh."

Elaine let it go. She needed this kid. "Tuition is $9,125. You're taking a two-year program, and assuming tuition doesn't go up next year—which it might, you have to be prepared for that—then your total tuition expense could top eighteen thousand. Plus your books and any additional expenses. Do you know yet how you plan to pay?"

Keone's eyes flickered nervously. "I want some financial aid."

"Okay. That's fine, Keone. Maybe we can talk to the financial aid director right away."

On the "Office Use Only" part of Keone's application Elaine neatly checked the spaces marked "H.S. Trans/Dip" and "App fee." Beside this she wrote, *Follow up and collect.* At the end of the interview the app would go to Deirdre Smith, the admission secretary, who would have to chase Keone and about forty other students in the class to get these items to complete the files.

Elaine smiled and rose. "Keone, just keep your seat a moment. I'm going to see if David Hurley is free. It'll just take a sec."

"Can I look at this?" The girl pointed at the catalog, which showed happy Burr girls descending from a chartered bus in front of Independence Hall.

"Certainly. That's yours to take with you."

David Hurley's office looked like a massive dumping ground. Manila folders stuffed with papers lay in stacks on the floor with no visible room for anyone's feet. David sat before a computer terminal punching up state grant awards and comparing them to the funding notices he gave his students. In what looked like a separate project, David's student worker, Becky Wright, was refiling folders of graduates into the scarred old fireproof file cabinet that ABCAA accreditors required for storage. The financial aid director looked in a good mood and Elaine considered this lucky, for David hated surprise appointments.

"Hey, David, how busy are you?"

He sighed dramatically, but did so with a smile. "You can see. Look at this mess. Plus a ton of loans to certify. What's up?"

"Can you talk to an applicant?"

"God, Elaine. I don't know. I've got to get this stuff done or we'll never get the money. And Becky's pulling all the files from last year to count family incomes for the federal FISAP report. New York's screaming for that info."

Elaine nodded sympathetically, then pressed. "Well, I've got a new applicant. She's for the two-year program. I don't think she'll take you long. She doesn't have any papers or anything, it's just to get her started. She wants in, and if you'll talk to her we can squeeze her into the September class."

"September? Oh hell! Absolutely not!" David bristled and shook his head. "Elaine, you've got to stop taking these last minute cases. They're too disorganized, they never have any up-front money, and none of their financial aid paperwork is in order. They're always the first to drop out too."

The senior rep pressed her lips in annoyance. "Look, the accreditors will let us accept kids five days into the program, which means I could accept her *next week* if I wanted and still be in compliance. I'm giving her the admissions test in twenty minutes. If she passes, she's a legitimate entrant to Monday's program."

"I'll bet she has no money," he grumbled.

"That's why we have you," Elaine's manner turned cheery, "to spring one of your miracles."

"Yeah, right. Crap. Let me clear some room. I'll talk to her in a minute."

"Thanks, David. I owe you."

"Doesn't everybody?"

Elaine left. David sulked at the papers before him. Admissions wasn't supposed to spring surprise interviews on him; they promised never to do it, then did it anyway. And of course he didn't want Oliver to hear he had turned an applicant away, so there it was. A rock and hard place. He faced his student worker.

"Beck, why don't you move that box to the corner? And go see if Julie has something for you to do for the next half hour."

"Sure, David."

Alone now, he sighed out loud. David Hurley was twenty-six, a college grad with a B.F.A. He had studied and painted in happy bliss for four years at the University of the Arts, then graduation came and with it a world that didn't jump up eagerly and embrace him as his faculty had. Recognizing (or perhaps pitying) his lack of practical skills, the University's placement office found him a position on its own financial aid staff. Though he never imagined himself holding a desk job, David took to financial aid, studied the handbooks, read the letters from the Department of Education, and went to training workshops. He found it to be ideal work for a would-be artist who needed a job: it offered him challenges and autonomy, and he could also see how his efforts went directly toward helping the students, who were generally likable and pleasant. He was conscientious and courteous by nature, and when he left the University of the Arts one year later to become Burr's financial aid director (for twenty-five hundred more a year), the new school saw right away that they had someone good. He had worked here now for three years and was comfortable with everything about the place, even though he was a single African-American male in a staff of mostly Caucasian women, even though his salary was only $21,000 a year, even though he still lived at home in Roxborough with his parents (who were not pressuring him at all to move out), and even though he currently didn't have a girlfriend and was beginning to see, by listening to the secretaries in their cubicles talk to each other about their own significant others, that staying at home with mom and dad was probably a romantic impediment. On the other hand, his situation could be worse: some of his former painting classmates were still minimum-wage stock boys in super markets, or tearing tickets at the local cinemas.

Elaine led a tall bony black girl into the office. "Just have a seat, Keone. David is our financial aid expert. He'll answer all your questions about forms, grants, loans, every bit of it, okay? Then he'll buzz me and I'll come get you."

The girl nodded without a word, her hard shell back in place.

Elaine left. David smiled pleasantly. "I'm David Hurley. Sorry about the mess. It doesn't normally look like this. Very happy to meet you."

She said nothing and barely nodded.

"Keone, isn't it? Keone, have you ever applied for financial aid?"

"No."

David produced a booklet entitled *Free Application for Federal Student Aid*. "Have you seen this form?"

"No. I remember seein' it in the high school, kinda."

"A lot of high school guidance counselors have it, yes. What high school did you go to?"

"Southwest."

Oh God.

David folded out the application. "You have to complete this. That's what starts the whole process. After you've done that you'll schedule an appointment with me, and I'll calculate your expected family contribution."

The girl stared at him.

"It's the amount your family is expected to pay," David gently explained. "We have to know that before we can figure out how much financial aid you can get."

"My family can't contribute nothin'," Keone said quickly.

"Well, *if* that's the case, the formula will show it. Depending on your parents' earnings—"

"My parents don't make nothin'."

A counselor at PAATP, the Pennsylvania Aid Administrators Training Program, once advised David never to use the word "poor" when counseling the disadvantaged. Pitching his voice so as not to offend, he said, "Excuse me, Keone, but in all fairness your parents must have some kind of income. Nobody can live on nothing."

"Welfare's all we get. My dad ain't workin', and Mama just does little stuff at a grocery."

"Well, then she *is* employed."

"I don't think she call it that. It's all under the table." Keone started to look annoyed. A lot of the disadvantaged black students got this way when talking to David. They expected leniencies from him, and resented when he treated them by the book like everyone else.

"Does she file a tax return?"

"I never seen her fill out somethin' like that."

"Okay." David hid his irritation well. He was less aggravated by the girl's lame answers than he was the fact that Admissions was recruiting her. At times like this he felt there should be a special purgatory in the afterlife just for Admissions reps. "Let's go over the form so you won't be confused when you fill it out at home."

Keone stared at the tiny print. "I can't fill this out."

"Well, it looks scary, but if you take it one question at a time you'll eventually finish. The easiest way is to start with your name."

"Where's it go?"

David didn't bat an eye. "Right here, on the first line. Where it says, 'Name.' Then your address goes right below it, where it says 'address.'"

Fifteen minutes later Elaine returned and led Keone to an empty classroom. She handed the girl a test booklet and an answer sheet, then sat at the teacher's desk at the front of the room while Keone struggled in silence for the next ninety minutes. Elaine perused a small stack of correspondence and kept a cool front, but inwardly she waited anxiously for Keone to finish. At last the test time ended and she took the answer sheet. She walked Keone back to the lobby, then returned to her office to check the girl's answers. Elaine's hopes plummeted fast. The test was one hundred math and English questions, and to be accepted a prospect had to pass a minimum of seventy. Keone had only forty-two correct answers. Elaine put down her red Burr pen, sat quietly for a while, then finally walked out to the lobby to break the bad news.

So much for raising the September class to fifty percent.

6

Oliver's four o'clock appointment turned out to be a strikingly beautiful Hispanic woman in her early forties, smartly dressed in a Liz Claiborne navy blue business outfit, silk blouse, and gold droplet earrings. Her first words were, "Dr. Dunbar, well, well. At last we meet!"

"Really? I'm afraid I don't understand."

Lilia Espirito's smile was dazzling, framed by large lips and a strong square chin. Her eyes were glinting black onyx under arched brows, her hair an astonishing whirl of bronze and gold swept atop her head in a modern chic beehive. Her business suit's miniskirt and five-inch stiletto heels were unquestionably brassy by Burr standards, but otherwise her appearance was impeccable. Her voice was high and a little breathy. "*Surely* you know that your name has gotten around, sir?"

Oliver returned the smile. He didn't know this, but sensed a compliment.

"Oh absolutely, sir! Your reputation for integrity is as high as that of the Burr College *itself!*"

It was a snow job, but still nice. And maybe it was true. Hadn't he worked in education for over twenty years? Wasn't he a past Member of the Year for ABCAA, which he earned chiefly by lobbying ceaselessly against education cuts during the twelve bleak years of Reagan and Bush? He probably did have a reputation "out there," if he ever bothered to notice.

"Well, that's very kind of you to say. Won't you step into my office? Uh, Julie …?"

"It's on your desk."

"Thanks."

With outstretched arm he pointed the way. Espirito walked before him with a finishing school mix of professional poise and feminine allure, putting one foot before the other so that her hips swung gently, like a model on a runway. As they passed through the cubicles the secretaries stopped their work, startled by the job applicant's conspicuous beauty, and even Oliver, despite twenty years' experience working with professional women, felt a flush of male pleasure to be escorting her. He opened his office door. "Please have a seat, Mrs. Espirito."

"Thank you. And please, Dr. Dunbar, call me Lily."

"Lily. Thank you. Please sit."

She did so with that same finishing school grace and crossed her bare legs. Her smile, the well-tailored clothes, the immediate ease instead of the normal tension of a job applicant, made Oliver suddenly feel good about himself. As if working in this office day after day and year after year was something special. He said, "Thank you for coming in. Did you have a good commute?"

"Oh, I drove. I hate public transportation, don't you?"

"Well, I live in town."

The black eyes glistened. "Do you *really?* Oh wow! I think that's grand. That's what I'd love. I've asked Luis about it, but he prefers the suburbs, so I don't anticipate being a city girl again for quite some time."

"Luis is your husband, of course."

"Yes. He's chief of reconstructive surgery at Walter Welles Hospital."

"Really? Well, I take my hat off to him. That's got to be an enormous responsibility." And he wondered what a plastic surgeon at a major hospital brought home a year. It had to be substantial. Why would a wealthy woman apply for a position in a business school that held so much stress and grief?

"Luis is very good at what he does. Terribly dedicated. Half the time I don't even see him. They're very exposure-conscious at that hospital. He's always flying off to conferences, seminars, whatever. He's their highest ranking minority and he's published so much they're anxious to get his picture on everything."

"May I ask what his national origin is? Do you mind?"

"Brazil," she responded brightly. "Not me. I was born and bred in the USA. Been a Philly girl all my life."

"Really?" He smiled. "Whereabouts?"

She blinked. For a moment her smile lost its energy, it became a stiff facial tic. Then she laughed and wrinkled her nose. "Packer Park in South Philly."

"That's a really nice neighborhood."

"Simply beautiful. Thank you."

"Do you have any children, do you mind my asking?"

"No."

The answer confused him, since he asked a double question. "No, you don't mind?"

Her laugh had a startling melody to it. "No—no we don't have any children."

She took that moment to recross her legs, and Oliver's concentration floated out the window. A cavernous silence followed, during which he realized that his questions regarding her husband and non-existent children were frightfully inappropriate. So he picked up her resume and, like a bad actor, cleared his throat.

"Well, I've reviewed your job history, of course. You last worked for the Stanley Business School in the Northeast."

"Yes."

"It closed last year."

"That's right."

"And you've done hairdressing since then?"

"Well yes, but that's more of a lark. I have my own salon in back of the carriage house, and serve only a few select customers. That was my passion when I was a teenager, and it was fun to fall back on it again. I'm very good with hair and cosmetics. It was almost my life's vocation."

"But you'd rather stay in admissions?"

"Oh yes! The hairdressing only passed the time. Basically my husband convinced me after Stanley closed to take the year off and relax, have some fun. And so I did."

"Well, I'm sure it was excellent therapy after losing your school. Can you tell me a little about the circumstances that closed Stanley? I don't think I ever knew anyone who worked at that school."

"Oh, but you wouldn't have," she laughed, flipping her hands. "It was a dinky operation. The kids didn't know how to *spell* 'secretary,' much less learn the skills to be one. It was nervy to call the grads 'executive assistants.'"

"Really?" Though he already suspected this. The Stanley School was an infamously bad business school, perhaps even a scam operation. What surprised him was the woman's merry candor about it. "Then you don't know why the school closed?"

"Not really. I'm not too clear about it." She shrugged with such nonchalance that Oliver incongruously smiled. "I know the feds came in and did an audit, and that's what shut it down. But I never knew the particulars."

"Of course. Well … uh, why not tell me about yourself then?"

"Goodness! Well, I've been working in admissions for four years now, not including last year's time off for good behavior. I was two years with the Stanley School, and two years before that with the Institute of Beauty and Fashion, that used to be over on Spring Garden Street. Before that I worked with Kelly Girl as a recruiter."

"Uh … the Institute of Beauty and Fashion closed too, didn't it?"

"Well, yes it did."

"Can you tell me the circumstances?"

"No, I'm sorry. Wow, I wish I could." She smiled impishly. "Actually, now that I think about it, the feds visited the Institute too."

Oliver nodded solemnly. This wasn't good at all. Lily Espirito's entire admissions experience belonged to institutions that had been closed by the Department of Education.

She caught his silence. She leaned forward, and the foot of her upper crossed leg extended, and from it a tiny ankle bracelet glinted, a little string of diamonds. "Dr. Dunbar," she said earnestly, "I know I don't have what looks like a good track record. It's embarrassing, as I'm sure you can imagine, to work for two schools that eventually went under. But I *am* a good admissions director. It was *not* on account of the admissions department that those schools closed."

"Yes, I'm sure." Oliver's attention was drawn to the ankle bracelet. Were those really diamonds? Didn't things like that break and get lost?

"They were closed by the feds for technical reasons involving educational and financial aid infractions, areas that were completely outside my province. I was never questioned by the feds. I want you to believe that."

"I do."

"I ran a spotless department. And I can say that the productivity of the admissions departments at both schools during my tenure was unsurpassed. I increased the Stanley enrollments by thirty percent. At the Fashion Institute it was over sixty percent. I also increased enrollment in the evening school programs by over seventy percent. These figures are all on my resume."

"Yes … I see that. Oh yes, right there. Um … how do you account for that? I mean, what did you do at those schools that was so different from how they'd been handling their recruitment before?"

Lily laughed, her hands flipped again. "It's just sales knack, Oliver. The ability to size up a prospect and recognize what she wants. The beauty school was easy. Cosmetics is my forte, and besides, we all know beauty sells itself, right? *Everyone* wants to be beautiful. I coached my reps on beauty tips so they looked like models. And I gave tips to the applicants during the interviews that just fascinated them. We turned it into a very glamorous school."

"I'll bet you did. What about—"

"Now the Stanley School was harder, of course, because that was a business school, and your students needed to know proper English and possess some rudimentary skills before they even came through the door." The black eyes crinkled and she tilted her head. Her wide smile was both coy and dazzling. "It doesn't pain me to tell you that both schools were crappy operations. I wouldn't try to fool a real professional like you by pretending otherwise. Frankly, I believe it a small miracle that you even considered my resume. But Oliver, I need this chance. I don't want to work forever with the dogs. I believe—and I hope this doesn't come out too corny—that the most thrilling prospect of being your admissions director is that I would finally be working with the winners. The college that does it right."

"Oh, I wouldn't dare think that's corny. That's exactly how I feel about this place. Sometimes I—"

"And I can't help thinking that the Burr College must give a good admissions director an edge. All seventeen schools have a reputation that can't be beat. Almost ninety years of quality service. Your secretaries work in Washington in all seats of government, and at least two have worked for the President himself. They hold executive positions at Eastman Kodak, Shearson Lehman, the Rouse Company, all the big shore hotels and casinos, the TV industry, and that's just from *this* school. Everywhere you go, if you mention the Burr College there's *some*body who knows it or went to one, or their mother or grandmother did. That's wonderful material for a salesperson."

"Well, you've read our catalog, I see."

"Oh dear." She put a hand to her mouth. "Well yes, you caught me. Ha! Ha! Though I knew all that information anyway. After all, when I worked for Stanley we were competitors."

"Were we?"

"We weren't in your *league*, of course, but we were fishing in the same student pool. We were always fighting the Burr image. We couldn't compete except by copying you. So we sent spies here. Our admissions reps posed as applicants to learn your methods and find out exactly what you were offering."

"Really?" This revelation both startled and disconcerted Oliver. No matter how charming, this woman was obviously outspoken and not at all ashamed by anything she did. Spying was hardly ethical, and to have a job applicant confess so breezily that her previous school did it was … well, unusual if nothing else. Yet it was flattering too. To be spied on by the competition and have them actually admit it was an awkward but genuine compliment.

Lily said, "I hated being a copycat. You know, you're either a leader or a follower in this business, and Stanley was a follower. Their intentions were good, but they had no savvy. That's why I want to work for you, Oliver."

A warmth spread through his nerves, pleasant prickles like goose bumps. He realized he was experiencing something he hadn't felt in ages: actual joy at talking to someone he truly wanted to hire.

"Good, good. Well, I guess I should tell you a little about the school, our different programs and such. We have an enrollment of about six hundred students a year, not including the evening school. For day classes we have basically three types. There's the one-year Advanced Secretarial Program, a one-year Information Processing Program, and a Two Year Executive Secretarial Arts Program that leads to an associate's degree. The Advanced Program starts in July and April, the IP Program in January. The two-year program always starts in September. Students earn certificates in the one-year programs. The college mandates a rounded educational experience, and many liberal arts classes are built into the core. Our evening school runs the same programs, but on a part-time basis. That means some of the students, going at half or a quarter the rate, can take a very long time to finish. We're supposed to have an evening school coordinator, but the position's currently unoccupied, so as admissions director you'd be expected to cover evening as well—at least until the position is rehired."

"I have no problem with that."

"And I should tell you that the previous director, a woman named Rose Bradshaw, quit last June and took a rep with her. As a result, we fell far below the September class goal."

"Really?" Her eyes widened.

"Yes. It's only fair to tell you. It means you'd be starting a job already in catch-up mode."

"Oh my. Well." Lily pursed her lips in thought, then crinkled her dimples and shrugged. "Well, we've all been *there*, haven't we, Oliver? Ha! Ha! Ha! Just makes the challenge more exciting, is all."

"That it does." Oliver suppressed a heavy sigh of relief. "Now, you do have two reps. Elaine Margolis is senior rep and she's terrific. Been here four years now. The other rep is Trudy Weiser who just graduated in June. She's been here two months, but I think she'll be solid too, once she gets a little experience."

"Sounds excellent."

"And that's our basic structure. I could break down the curriculum for you, the academic standards, credit counts, progression and so forth, if you wish." He smiled and decided to tease her, and felt daring for doing so. "Or were your spies very thorough?"

"Oh dear!" She laughed so hard her body rocked the chair. "Ha! Ha! Ha! I see now that you'll never let me live that down! *Please* tell me about your school, Oliver. It's obvious that you truly love it."

Oliver was overwhelmed. "Well, uh, maybe we could just tour the school, and I'll talk as we go."

"That would be lovely."

It was a memorable tour. Lily praised the atmosphere of the historic mansion, the quaint small classrooms, admired the banks of glowing computers, and the giant dictation consoles where girls practiced using cassettes of different word speeds. Yet her praise was not blind; she was lucid and shrewd as she noted these things. She insisted that the computer equipment was much more up-to-date than the Stanley School, and jokingly expressed her jealousy for the chalkless blackboards. "Stanley couldn't afford them, so of course they paid for computer repairs instead," she said with a derisive laugh.

At the end of the second floor corridor Oliver opened the library. "It's not much," he said, "but I can't help feeling proud. I remember when it was just an empty storage room."

"No, it's just right." Lily strolled in and gave a brisk pleased inventory. She lifted a copy of *Smart Women, Foolish Choices.* "It's not big, but it has the essentials."

"It keeps getting better. Two teachers, Sobolewski and Harding, take care of it. On their own time they scout out trade bookstores and library sales. They petitioned with the dean for the computers you see here. Upper administration wasn't keen on it at first, since there were already computers in the classrooms."

"It is a changing world, isn't it? And your teachers must be terribly dedicated to go to such trouble."

"They're the best."

Through the wall they suddenly heard the loud noise of many typewriters pounding at once. Lily raised her brows. "Typewriters, Oliver?"

He grinned. "It's funny, I know, especially after what you just said. You're hearing the last IBM Selectrics in the school. Each year we get fewer kids who don't know basic typing, but when we do this is where they learn it. All the teachers believe they can teach typing better on a typewriter. There's a discipline that develops when you have to manually set your tabs, align your paper, and type knowing that any corrections you make have to be fixed with white out or an ink eraser."

"That is fascinating. Tell me, Oliver, do your students learn Gregg?"

"Actually, no. Our dean still thinks it's the best shorthand system, but it takes so long for the girls to learn, and it's so much harder. We find that students do just as well with phonetic systems so we've implemented them instead. And employers couldn't care less what system a secretary uses. All they want is speed and accuracy."

Lily nodded briskly. "I agree with everything you're saying. Stanley wasn't bothering to teach dictation at all by the time it closed."

"It's surprising how many employers still want a secretary who knows how to do it, even with all this new technology."

"Almost comforting, eh?" She grinned.

Oliver looked toward the sound coming from the other room. "Guess it's my turn to be corny. I spent so many years hearing the thunder of typewriters in the typing rooms, and now that we've replaced them with computers it isn't the same. The little clicking keyboards just don't have that force."

"The price you pay for progress, hey?" Lily laughed.

"Yes. Well—oh hey, I didn't realize it was getting this late. Shall we go back to my office and discuss the details?"

"Oh please. Let's!"

Twenty minutes later she was signed on. Oliver felt no need to wait, and Lily saw no reason to think about it. She would start immediately and receive $70,000 a year, full medical and dental, four vacation weeks and ten sick days. It was a package offered only to the most experienced and high-powered of sales backgrounds, a starting package not much less than what the employees in the President's Office received, and in a way Oliver was dazzled that he offered so much. He knew there'd be a squawk with Nostrand about it. But he didn't care, and felt up to the battle. For the first time in months he felt his problems coming to an end.

7

Of the one hundred and sixty-nine newly recruited students for the September Two-Year Executive Secretarial Arts Program, all but twelve showed at eight-thirty a.m. on Monday for the first day of class. Despite the previous week's Orientation they still stumbled the halls in confusion, and approached any of the staff, especially the secretaries unprotected in their cubicles, to ask where lockers, bathrooms, the lounge, the bookstore, and vending machines were located. At Oliver's insistence Deirdre Smith, the harried admissions secretary, stationed herself by the front door to catch those who hadn't finished their enrollment paperwork. Deirdre needed to complete the files so that a final class count could be made, and also so they could then be delivered into the iron hands of Dean Harris. At that point they became Education files. And when the students graduated, two years hence, their files would become Placement files stored in a large room be-hind the faculty lounge in the basement, a cobwebbed enclosure lit by bare light bulbs and known to all as "The Dungeon."

Louise Mallory was at her most embittered on the first day of a new class. Instead of working on payroll or invoices, jobs requiring no human contact other than getting Oliver's docile signature, she was trapped in a room on the third floor, something that might once have been a giant walk-in linen closet during the rich Tory's happy days, but now was the Burr College bookstore. For a linen closet it was enormous, for a bookstore it was a cramped joke. There she and Jessica Harrelson, the amiable freckle-faced placement secretary, a grad from the July '93 Advanced Secretarial Program, knocked elbows trying to open cartons in search of the English I books promised by Andy Abrams in New York.

"Goddammit!" said Louise, finding herself frowning into a box of steno pads instead. "I knew it. They're not here."

"He never gets anything to us on time," said Jessica, who learned this from the business manager. "Did he say we'd have them today, or only that they're coming?"

"Oh, they're probably winging their way down the Jersey Turnpike right now. Fat lot of good it does us. Was it put on the student checklist?"

"Natalie would have been the one to do that." Natalie Spicoli was Dean Harris' secretary. "But I'm sure it was."

"Shit," Louise said, since Jessica was no longer a student.

The missing book was indeed typed on the student checklist, and as soon as the new class missed it in their lockers they crowded the bookstore's half-door, believing it an oversight. Jessica said, "No, it's not here. You'll probably get it tomorrow," over and over until Louise was ready to scream.

"Well, do you know exactly when they'll be here?" persisted one obtuse student.

"When they ARRIVE!" bellowed Louise, exercising the omnipotent power all mean spinsters possess to intimidate the young. It was the first day for these kids, and they needed to learn right away the necessity of not riling her. It worked too. The students shied away before her beetle-eyed hostility, at the violent way she grabbed a box between her sapling thin legs and tore open the flaps so that large copper staples ricocheted off walls and metal shelves. The students watched this scary white-haired bird of a woman, the business manager of what was, in fact, a business school, and prudently decided to go to class. For the rest of the year they would do their complaining to teachers or Dr. Dunbar. The few who chanced approaching Louise Mallory with a problem—a locked locker, a missing coat, a freezing classroom—would only be queried about their outstanding tuition balance, and quickly learned to steer clear. It was how Louise liked it.

Oliver stood by the front door with Deirdre, and gently checked the exasperation of the young secretary as so many students admitted they forgot their enrollment agreements, their high school transcripts, college placement scores, and swore they'd bring them tomorrow. Oliver watched the new students traverse the long hall. Most of these kids didn't know what an associate degree in applied sciences meant. What they did know was their need for self-improvement, and they were determined to do something about it. Most would work hard, and on this first day in particular the ambition to do well was high. They wore their best clothes, and they chattered exuberantly as they squeezed past the antique furnishings that lined the corridor, and pounded up and down the stairs. Friendships were being made, and some would last a lifetime. Unlike Louise, the first day to Oliver was the biggest thrill of the whole educational process. He loved the palpable optimism on this day even more than at graduation. Inclining that tree.

The September class ran from September to June for two years, a total of four semesters with summer off in the middle. This first semester, starting September 3 and finishing December 20, right before Christmas, was a particularly easy one. New York had debated the wisdom of this for years. Should students in a two-year program be brought along gradually or start on their skills right away? But skills didn't need two years to develop, not in typing and shorthand anyway, and now that dropout rates were starting to climb New York opted for a soft, gradual beginning to the curriculum.

This calculated approach worked like a charm on the new class, which was divided into six sections to accommodate classroom space. Section One left its first period class, Professional Development, charged with happy adrenaline. Calculated to interest, like the first chapter in a book, the initial lecture was on cosmetics. Given by Mrs. Carol Sobolewski, an older but dynamic teacher of engaging personality who was once a cosmetics media consultant, the entire fifty-minute period was spent discussing wardrobe and make up approaches appropriate for the conservative business office. Short skirts were okay up to a point, but absolutely no minis. Never more than one string of pearls. Never more than two rings on one hand, or more than three on both hands. Shoes should be mid-heel and the toes closed. Hair should be cut short, but if you wished your hair long then this was what you did with it—and with harmless quips about dazzling the good-looking males in the office, Mrs. Sobolewski demonstrated four or five different pinning styles that were not only acceptable for office decorum but foxy as hell. The girls left the classroom tittering.

Office Procedures came next, another deliberately easy lecture class. Mrs. Donna Harding ran this class with elegant charm. Previously a seller of computer software, she brought to her students a slick professionalism worth emulating. Fresh from a talk on business appearance, the class scrutinized her with hungry expertise and found themselves entirely satisfied. Mrs. Harding was tall, with bright aqua eyes and long brown hair that was *not* pinned up because she could obviously get away with it. At thirty-seven she was the stunning image of the self-assured business woman, confident and in control. She started the class by asking, "Who's had an office job before?" and most of the older students raised their hands. "So what was it like?" she asked next, and there was enough humor and insight in her voice that the stories came. Anecdotes about stupid bosses, arrogant bosses, and arrogant bosses' wives. They quickly hit the topic without bottom: male chauvinism. There were plenty of juicy tales to tell. The boss who kept his female office manager in an open work space rather than the private office she deserved, just so he could look at her. The supervisor who led one girl Friday into the storeroom and showed her a magazine filled with ads for various dildos. "I hope you asked why he was showing you his family photo album," Mrs. Harding said, and the girls laughed as if at a slumber party.

English I, at 11:00, was the first period to actually feel like a class. Robert Lawrence, blond-haired and pale-eyed, and somewhat rumpled in his business suit and scuffed shoes, punctuated the rules of grammar with a humor that bordered on the morose. He was the first person they met at Burr who wasn't professionally perfect or as sweet as candy. He actually seemed a little miscast as an instructor, and his rueful comments about the missing textbook were strangely self-effacing and cracked everybody up. The melancholy in his manner was affecting, and some of the girls would actually, for his sake, learn some grammar.

Lunch at twelve. Two out of five days each week lunch was at one, as the students participated in elective classes from English, drama, art history or world history, to harder academics like calculus and statistics. After lunch, the remaining five days, there followed a free period or a second elective if the students wished. And then Section One had Jean Cavanaugh.

The soft approach ended with Cavanaugh for Economics. She was thirty-eight years old, with a chubby face, large thick glasses, and a thrusting jaw. Married to a policeman for eleven years but with no children in sight, Jean Cavanaugh ran her class with a tyranny worthy of a third world dictator. A self-proclaimed crusader against the laxness of American education, she refused to let her students succumb to an undemanding environment. She brooked no misbehavior, and graded papers without curves. She did not hesitate to blacken a favored honor student with a justified F, and perpetually marched students into Oliver's office for chewing gum, slouching, whispering, and the persistent passing of notes. And yet it was this woman, alongside the imperious dean, who received the most letters of gratitude and flowers from the students at graduation, and whose arm at the receptions which followed was eagerly tugged by girls wishing her to meet their parents. Her name was known in all seventeen Burr schools. Jean was her own institution.

She rose from her desk as the first face peeped timidly through the door. "Back of the classroom!" she barked. Her plump arm snapped like hard rubber, pointing so there would be mistake where the "back" of the classroom was. "Line up! No sound! No talking! I can hear every word! Just do as you're told! *That* way!"

The new class formed a single line along the wall. Mrs. Cavanaugh took a sheet of paper and held it scroll-style, one hand over the other, as if to read the charges before these students were summarily executed. "Alphabetical order as I call your name. *No talking!* Just move to your seat! Front right-hand desk first, then backward until the row is finished! Then start at the front of the second row, and so forth!

"Abel, Kelly!"

"Yes?" a little red-headed girl piped, shaken at being singled out. She was from Upper Darby, west of the city.

"*No!* No talking! Abel, Kelly!"

The girl barely nodded.

"Well?" said the teacher.

"Ma'am?"

"I said *no talking!* Move!"

The girl was frozen to the wall.

"Front right-hand desk! You sit *there!* MOVE!"

There was no comedy in this. The girl scampered between the desks like a frightened fawn. She sat, and Mrs. Cavanaugh immediately pointed to the desk behind her.

"Albretti, Amelia. *There!*"

The girl ran.

In her own random place in line stood Heather Feeney. Tall with long black hair dyed green at the ends, fudge-brown eyes, a tiny slip of nose, and a hard jaw that widened the whole lower half of her face, she was unfamiliar with the city and not too thrilled to be at Burr. She hailed from a dingy blue-collar neighborhood in Norristown where her father worked in a warehouse and her mother on an assembly-line with the shared dream that their daughter do well at this school and make them proud. Heather herself didn't know what she wanted, but factory work didn't look so hot, and her parents were really sacrificing the bucks for her to come, so here she was. She stood against the windowsill cooperatively, but a voice in her head told her that this teacher was wrong, that Mrs. Cavanaugh had no right to yell and bully, and under Heather's resistant skin lay the temptation to do something about it, to appear defiant, to slouch or look bored. She already didn't feel right among these richer bitches who all looked alike with their big styled perms, prosperous clothes and—well shit, even the black girls looked stylish, sort of. All that gold jewelry. Mrs. Sobolewski said too much jewelry was wrong for the office, and Mrs. Cavanaugh reiterated this in no uncertain terms as the overly-bedecked girls hastily took their seats. Heather wore four cheap rings on each hand, like a double set of brass knuckles. When the heavyset, bellowing woman turned her way, defiance gave way to self-preservation, and Heather tucked her hands behind her back where they wouldn't be seen.

"Feeney, Heather!"

Heather swiftly took her seat. She did try to look bored, but Mrs. Cavanaugh called forth the next name with nary a glance at her.

When all were seated, the teacher opened the fat green economics book. Morale slumped lower. Even the English teacher, Lawrence, hadn't made them work on this, the first day of class. Mrs. Cavanaugh was a monster, they all saw, but it was too late to jump ship. They opened their books and stared foggily at a red and blue graph while new phrases like "Gross

National Product" and "Supply and Demand" were tossed at them with the portentousness of Mt. Sinai tablets. Fear of being called upon made the clock crawl.

Accounting I followed. Another male teacher, Mr. Cassidy, paternal and gentle as a middle-aged priest, which some girls in the know said he once was, coaxed them into believing that a simple understanding of the four basics, addition, subtraction, multiplication, and division, was all it took to master basic bookkeeping and accounting. Credits and debits were simply positive and negative numbers put to practical use. He joked about the exacting Burr image but in a very positive way, and let them out of class early without once asking them to open their stiff new book.

Four o'clock and the day was done.

A short day, but that was the arrangement of the first semester. When the skills classes began, chiefly shorthand and the ever-progressive computer classes, the days would stretch to five o'clock and beyond. But that hard work was still far ahead of them. Right now this all looked terrifically easy, and none of the new class believed they would drop out or fail. Pleased and confident, they dashed back to their lockers and stored all the books but the economics book (for Cavanaugh alone had assigned two chapters to be read by the Friday class), and the eager chatter and warming of friendships began anew. They felt grand as they left the large red-brick mansion. They had plunged headfirst into the swirling waters of intellect and personal growth. They had climbed, if not Everest, then at least the Matterhorn, and were flushed and exhilarated to find themselves unscathed.

8

At nine a.m. that same day, Lily Espirito showed for work in a lilac business minidress, cream blazer, and five-inch stiletto heels. She installed a coffee machine in her new office and set a full pot brewing, then sat at her desk, testing the chair while the sun from the window behind her glinted off her bronze and gold beehive hairdo and caught the light of her diamond ankle bracelet. When the coffee maker finished she filled a large mug and walked out to the cubicles where her new secretary was stationed.

"You must be Deirdre, right? I'm Lily. Nice to be on board. Can I see the appointment book?"

"Sure. Right here." The girl was quick in front of the new boss. Deirdre Smith was a petite girl, delicate-boned and almost doll-like, with a round cherubic face, large eyes evenly spaced, and lips appealingly full. Just cute all over, Lily thought.

"Only five appointments for the week?" Lily stared in dismay at seven nearly naked columns on the two-page spread.

"That's all for now." Deirdre evidently did not find the low booking unusual. "Maybe more later. Trudy's got a coupla new leads."

"Yes. Now what's this fifth one? I can't read the writing."

"Oh. Oliver put that in. His scrawl's kinda funny but you get used to it. That's Mona Otterbach and her dad. They want the one-year program, but don't know whether to start in January or wait till next July."

"She'll come in January." Lily handed back the appointment book. "Say Dee, we're pretty much a chick operation, aren't we?"

"I'm sorry?"

"We're all girls. Except for Oliver."

"Oliver and David."

"David? Oh yes." Lily sipped deeply from her mug. "What's his position here again?"

"He's the financial aid officer."

"Ah! Financial aid." Lily nodded importantly. "Any idea what his background is?"

"Got his degree from the University of the Arts. He's a real nice guy."

"Oh, he studied art." Lily smiled as if that made perfect sense. "Well, I'll have to get to know him. Do you find that his being black puts the poorer applicants at ease?"

"What?"

"Never mind. What's this?" She pointed to a letter on the desk which began *"We regret to inform you ..."*

Deirdre said, "It's a reject letter. The girl wanted to start in September, but she blew the Admissions test."

"By how much?"

"She scored forty-two. You gotta get at least seventy to pass."

"Oh for Pete's sake." Lily picked up the letter. It was for a girl named Keone Robinson and bore Elaine Margolis' signature. "Doesn't Elaine realize that every kid who comes in September helps relieve the deficit for January?"

"But she failed the test. Missed it by a mile."

"Yeah. Hmmm." Lily's brows knitted. Her foot tapped the carpet briskly. "One eight-three Virginia Street. Hell, she's a project kid. Probably went to some crap high school like Buchanan or Southwest. That's a mitigating circumstance if ever I heard one." Lily crumpled the letter. "Send her an acceptance. For God's sake, let's not be so hard-hearted around here."

Deirdre looked more confused than ever. "We can do that?"

"It's why God put 'mitigating' in the dictionary." Lily's eyes rested on a snapshot pinned to the lower left corner of Deirdre's bulletin board: some sinewy T-shirted male straddling his Harley, blue eyes glowering at the camera. So little Deirdre like 'em rough, hey?

The secretary said, "I think Elaine already told her she can't come."

"Then call her back. Tell her she's been re-evaluated. If she starts tomorrow she'll only miss one day of class. Sound good?"

"Sure."

Lily returned to her office and drew a second mug of coffee. For the next hour she perused a stack of monthly reports submitted by her predecessors. The first report shocked her. Then she read the others with bleak resignation, recognizing the same diminishing enrollment figures that had plagued her previous employers. The import of this was deep. The glamorous Burr College, with graduates working for Warren Buffett, Donald Trump, Rupert Murdoch, the White House, plus various government offices and the CIA, and on the international scene, Buckingham Palace and the Vatican, was not supposed to have enrollment problems. Coming in this morning Lily had wondered at the many drab working class girls mixed with the polished Main Line wealth, including quite a few more blacks than a white-bred school like this needed to show a good liberal face. Now it made sense.

She sat for a while with these pages before her and cartwheeled a pen through her fingers. Finally she pressed the intercom button on her phone. "Elaine, stop by my office when you get a chance."

"Yes, Mrs. Espirito."

"And bring Trudy too, if she's free."

A moment later the two reps appeared in the doorway and watched in respectful silence. Lily smiled to put them at ease. "Sit down, girls. I hope I'm not taking you away from anything."

"No ma'am," they said, and Trudy added, "My nine o'clock didn't show."

"Please sit."

Elaine sat gracefully on one of the client chairs. A remarkably pretty woman, Lily thought. Tall, slim, a regal powerhouse at age twenty-six, tastefully dressed in a light pink business jacket and skirt, with classic pearl earrings and a diamond wedding ring on her left hand. Elaine was the postcard Burr rep.

Trudy Weiser was similar, but without Elaine's calm maturity. Also a product of Main Line wealth, Trudy was smartly tailored in the standard blue blazer, skirt, and low-heel pumps, her short black hair curled into sausages above a round, plump face. At twenty, she still looked like somebody's sweet kid sister, although Lily had heard that she was engaged to some Drexel engineering geek named Ira. She sat on a small loveseat near Elaine's chair, and unconsciously sucked her lower lip.

"Well well, girls. Let me say right off that I'm terribly excited to be on board with you. Oliver has told me wonderful things about you, and I can tell already that his opinion was right on the *money!* I'm sure we'll be a great team, hey?"

Elaine said, "Yes, ma'am," and poor Trudy just nodded.

"Eww! *Don't* call me ma'am. Gracious, call me Lily. You're making me feel like an old biddy! Ha! Ha! Would anybody like coffee?"

Elaine declined. Trudy said, "No, ma'am. I don't drink coffee. I'm—"

"Lily, dear."

"What?"

"Call me Lily, please."

"Lily. I don't drink coffee. I'm a tea drinker."

"A tea drinker? Really? *Tea?* Goodness, I can never drink it myself. Doesn't give me enough zip! Now Trudy, you've been here what? Two months?"

"Yes. I started right after I grad—"

"And Elaine, you've been here four years?"

"Yes."

"Well, the school looks wonderful, and I'm sure it's a reflection on your efforts for this office. Now Trudy, I know Elaine is a graduate of Lower Merion High School. But you—now where did you go to school?"

"Radnor, ma'am. I graduated—"

"Are you sure I can't interest either of you in a cup of coffee? It's right here, already made."

"No thanks, Lily."

"How about a bagel? Or a croissant?"

Again the two reps declined.

"Well," Lily's voice tightened slightly, the lilt faded. She set her coffee mug on the desk and clasped her hands around it. "Much as we all hate to, I guess we'd better hunker down to business. Trudy, did you tell me your nine o'clock didn't show?"

"Yes." Trudy's skin whitened around her eyes.

"Does that happen a lot? Applicants not showing for appointments?"

"It does happen some—sometimes." Trudy looked anxiously at Elaine, who remained silently watching their new boss. "We try to, uh, overbook when we can, just in case."

"I see. Are we overbooked today?"

"No. There's hardly anything scheduled for today."

"And you, Elaine?"

The senior rep said, "Not at the moment. But it's usually a slack time right after a new class sits." Her eyes met Lily's steadily.

"Elaine, Trudy, I'm brand new here. I don't want to push you around. You're both a pair of sharpies, and I'm sure that together we can achieve great things. Still, I have to speak frankly." Lily's brows lifted, her eyes black and glittering. "It looks like we're in trouble. More so than I expected when I accepted this position. Wouldn't you agree?"

The reps said nothing, though Elaine cautiously nodded.

"You know, I'm finding this a real eye-opener. The Stanley School, where I worked previously, was in a lot of trouble too. In fact, during their last two years they simply accepted every kid who came through the door, smart or stupid, black, white, green or purple. You know the old joke about the mirror test? The admissions officer holds a mirror to the applicant's face and if the mirror fogs, she passes. Well, that was the Stanley School. It wasn't how I wanted to recruit, but they were so desperate they gave me no choice. It was do it, or close the place down. You know how it is, don't you?"

Trudy looked pale. Elaine simply nodded again. Her gaze at Lily was non-committal and offered no sympathy. A real Burr snob.

"Of course, this school isn't that bad. But you're talking to someone who's been around a while, and I'm telling you the writing's on the wall. And the *black* girls, ladies! I've been reading these reports." Lily patted the thick stack on the desk. "At least seventeen percent of the annual student body is made up of minority students. Predominantly black, with a few Hispanics and Vietnamese around the edges."

Elaine grew attentive. "Do you have a problem with that?"

Lily saw the subtle danger. New employees had to be careful. "Dear, I'm not a bigot. Over the years I've met some truly charming African-American men and women. But I'm being realistic. Statistically most blacks who attend inner-city schools come from impoverished backgrounds, and that means inadequate high school education. It's a reflection on the high schools, not anyone's skin color, are we clear about that? These disadvantaged girls proliferated the hallways of Stanley. Like ninety percent of the student body by the end. And where's the Stanley School now?" She lifted her hands and smiled placidly.

"Well! The failure of the September sit means we have to recruit nearly triple the number of students originally planned for January." Lily checked a few notes scribbled on a yellow legal pad. "We were supposed to sit sixty in January. Split the missing half of the September sit with April, plus seventeen more to compensate for cash flow loss, and we now have to sit one hundred and sixty-two students in January, and probably a similar number in April. I think it's an impossible goal. What do you think? Honest answer, Elaine?"

"Well, it *sounds* impossible, Mrs. Espirito—"

"Good! Good for you! Now observe!" Lily straightened and suddenly clapped her hands—SMACK! "As of this moment you may no longer think that way! From now on we will all believe the January sit IS possible!" She clapped her hands on each stressed word. "We will sit ALL one hundred and sixty-two students! DESPITE the fact that it's the second week of September and we have maybe three months to recruit. DESPITE the fact that no prospective applicants loom on the horizon. Do you hear me? We WILL make the January sit!"

"Yes, ma'am," said the reps. Elaine's face twitched.

"All righty then! I see that we get most of our leads from newspaper advertising and high school presentations. Obviously that's not cutting it for us, ladies, not if we're going to make January. We're going to have to hustle."

"Hustle?"

"Telephone, telephone, telephone. Greatest recruiting tool ever invented. At Stanley I designed a twenty-two-call-per-applicant plan that really paid off."

"You called each applicant twenty-two times?"

"It got them to come," Lily grinned proudly. "Just wait. You'll see for yourself."

Trudy asked, "Don't you piss people off calling them twenty-two times?"

"That's not the point," Lily said cheerfully. "It gets them to come. *That's* the point. It means putting in more than a seven-hour work day, since telemarketing works best in the evenings, but since we're all dedicated to Burr that shouldn't be a problem. I'll show you how to do it. I have a whole script. I see also that when a prospect calls we only send out a catalog. Why don't we send them an application?"

Elaine said, "Because we don't want them to think we're pushing them. Choosing a college is an important decision, and applicants need to think about it. If they really want to come they'll—"

"*Wrong!*" Lily laughed. She stood, crossed to the coffee maker, and topped off her cup. "This is what we're going to do. We'll get all the info we can on each kid and put it in the database. Then we'll send out catalogs, applications, addenda, brochures, congratulatory cards for when the applicants finish high school, birthday cards, parent wedding anniversary cards— I've got a whole array of correspondence cooked up that'll keep the Burr name prominent in any prospect's mind."

Trudy said, "What if they tell us to stop sending this stuff?"

"Well, you *never* stop sending the stuff. That's Cardinal Rule Number One."

"Even if they ask us to? What happens when they call up angry?"

"You apologize, then wait one business day and send the next letter. And if they call *again* to complain about you, then Elaine or

Deirdre takes the call and we just start the cycle over again. It really works."

Elaine said bluntly, "Mrs. Espirito, that's not how we recruit."

The room went silent. Lily rested her eyes on the senior rep and sipped coffee. Elaine's expression softened; she realized she had stepped out of line.

"Mrs. Espirito," she said gently, "what I mean is, it's never been our way to high-pressure applicants. Burr isn't that type of college. When a student decides that we're not the right fit, we have to respect their decision."

"Well, of *course* you respect their decision," Lily said brightly. "And then it's your responsibility to make them understand that you know better. You're a professional college recruiter. You're *supposed* to know more than they do."

"Lily, no. With all due respect, this isn't the Stanley School or the Beauty Institute. The applicants' desires come first here, and they're made to feel it. They know we're an honest school."

"Honest, dear. I'm not sure how practical we are."

"Well, our reputation has always been our biggest asset."

"That's nice, of course," Lily snapped with sudden scorn, "except we failed to sit fifty percent of our most important class despite our marvelous reputation!"

Elaine stiffened. Lily permitted herself the barest of smiles. The senior rep obviously considered her new boss' career background shabby, and didn't anticipate Lily finding the Burr College wanting. Well too bad, Miss Stuck-Up Burr Princess. Just learned a little lesson, didn't you?

Again Elaine backed down. "Mrs. Espirito, please understand what I'm saying. I don't think you realize that a lot of students who apply to this college are not qualified to be here. They don't have the academic background, for one thing. You should see the college placement exam scores on the 'C' list."

"Excuse me, dear, what is that? The 'C' list?"

"Yes. It's in the computer. Deirdre can run you a fresh copy. Every two years we do a survey of all high schools within commuting range and divide them into three lists. All area high schools are rated by educational standards, make up of surrounding neighborhoods, things like that. The 'A' list has the most desirable schools. Central High, ever since they had to admit women, Girls High, Great Valley, Cherry Hill, these are schools where we recruit our very best students, naturally. The 'B' list has high schools in more marginal areas—Norristown, Upper Moreland, Paulsboro. They're more blue-collar. Not as good as the 'A' list, but definitely recruitable. The 'C' list is the bottom of the barrel, economically depressed areas like North Philly, Chester, or Camden in New Jersey. We never use the 'C' list."

"Never say never, Elaine."

"No, ma'am. We *never.*"

Lily set her coffee cup down with a brittle clack, clasped her hands together, and waited.

With a quiet dignity that belied her young age, Elaine said, "Mrs. Espirito, I'm not saying our system is the most effective. It certainly isn't, if all you want is to sell students. I have friends at other colleges and they're very aggressive. Maybe as a result they sit more students, I can't say. But I think our way is right. You can't hard-sell education. I know the ridiculous pressure New York puts on Oliver and … and you, but still—these are kids. And it's a commitment of two years for the ones who come here, and thousands of dollars for their parents. I've seen moms and dads, some of them the sweetest people you could ever meet, hand over their life savings, every dime from the bank, so their daughter could get her education here. I've seen tears of pride in their eyes when we tell them their daughter passed the admittance test. Moments like that only emphasize the importance of what's at stake here. These kids are too young, most of them, to really know what they want. They need guidance and advice, not shoving and being sold to. Do you see that, ma'am?"

"Call me Lily, Elaine."

"Yes. Thank you. Do you see that, Lily?"

"Elaine, do you consider us a good college? Within our niche, I mean."

"Yes. No question about it. Other schools can't compare."

"Thank you, Elaine. This was very helpful."

It took the senior rep a moment to realize she was dismissed. The new admissions director stared at her with wry amusement. Disconcerted, Elaine rose and left the room.

Lily puckered her lips and shrugged at Trudy, as if to say, *What are you gonna do?* She stood up and casually removed her suit blazer, and Trudy was taken aback by the audacious display of her boss' large bosom. The lilac dress fit the admissions director like a corset, pushing up her breasts and allowing a square-cut decolletage to display four inches of naked cleavage. "Would you like some coffee?" Lily asked as she hung the blazer on the back of her chair.

"No, ma'am. Lily. I—" Trudy was genuinely flustered. No woman at Burr ever dressed like this. "I, uh, I'm not a coffee drinker, ma.am."

"Oh, that's right. Tea, wasn't it?"

"Yes, ma'am."

Lily sat behind her desk again. Her black eyes glittered eagerly. "Okay then, now that it's just you and me, let's get down to business. That one-year Information Processing Program starting January 4 is a bread-and-butter program. You, me, and Elaine are going to have to concentrate very hard on it together."

"Yes, ma'am. Lily. I'm sorry."

"But I also have another *special* area I'm interested in grooming you for."

"Yes, Lily?"

"Evening school. Right now the Burr College's evening programs are small and their potential only half-heartedly explored. But I can assure you they are an untapped *gold mine*. Our sixteen sister schools have been running various low-cost programs at night and doing well by them for years. These include graphic design, accounting, restaurant management, travel agent training, cosmetics—my particular specialty—real estate training, paralegal, oh the list just goes on and on, a wide range of programs Oliver has been resisting. Would you like a Granola bar?"

"Pardon me? Oh, no thanks. Lily, why is Oliver resisting these programs?"

Lily's hands danced playfully across her desktop. "The wonderful thing about these programs, most of them anyway, is that they have no sexual stigma attached. Accounting, restaurant management, and travel can be done by both men and women. It's the avenue to get some men to attend this school. Do you realize that there are one hundred and twenty-three million men in the United States today? That's forty-seven percent of the population. What an incredible, *unrealized* applicant pool! And do you know why we haven't tapped that pool? Because the Burr College, for all its posturing as a *business college,* is still seen by the world at large as a secretarial school. That's the foundation of our reputation, it's what we're known for. And let's be candid between our own four walls, honey. Men *don't* want to be secretaries."

"But I've seen men take classes here." Trudy's loyalty was challenged. "I've seen them in the hallways."

"We average maybe five or six male graduates a year. All of them hold degrees in History or English or Sociology and couldn't find jobs. Big whoopee. No, I'm talking about aggressively selling to the male population. *Masculinize* the Burr image. Get this school genuinely respected by the business community. Anyway, that's what I want you to head up."

"Of course, Lily." Trudy was a little mystified, but tried to hide it. Her boss was experienced, she was not. She had to learn.

"Frankly I'd much rather sell to men than women. You, with that cute face and figure, should have no trouble."

Trudy blinked. She wasn't sure she heard correctly. "Lily, I'm sorry. But ... *what?*"

"You know what I'm talking about. We'll have to work a little on your wardrobe. What you've got on is perfect for impressing proud moms and dads, but it's not quite right for evening school."

"Ma'am?"

Their eyes met. The smile on Lily's face dried a bit, and her voice lowered, losing its melody and developing a harder edge. "Trudy, love, what you're wearing is fine, please get that bewildered look off your face. The classic business attire has its purposes, of course, but what we need right now is ... well, call it professionalism with *zing*. We've got to loosen up on the old conservative Burr look. These are not conservative times."

"Like how?"

Lily grinned. "Sell for a cosmetics school sometime, you'll catch on. Remember this and never forget it. *Everybody wants to be alluring.* That's the all-time guiding influence on human behavior. If you put a little sex into your professional appearance, I guarantee the men will fall over themselves giving you their $125 tuition deposits. And the women you interview will sign up thinking they'll learn how to look as good as you."

Trudy didn't know what to say. She stared at her boss.

"Start with boots. Do you have some leather boots that come up to the knee?"

"I—yes."

"Good. Bring them. Keep them in your office and use them when you need to. Also wear miniskirts. You might even consider bringing a selection and keeping it here, although we don't really have the closet space. I'll have to talk to Oliver about that."

"Lily—you really want me to wear miniskirts? Dean Harris used to send girls home if they came to school in minis."

"Times have changed, dear. Besides, you've got nice legs. You shouldn't hide them. Are you athletic?"

"Well, tennis and jogging. With my fiancé."

"Ah yes, I saw the ring. Lovely. Earrings, Trudy. Get yourself some that dangle a little. Something with more sparkle than those you have on. It'll add such light to your face. What are those, anyway? Silver?"

"Yes."

"Lovely, of course, but they don't sparkle. You should wear gold."

"Lily ..." Trudy faltered. She was afraid to speak.

"Go ahead. Are you all right?"

"Yes."

"Would you like something to drink? I have coffee, you know."

"No, I'm fine. I'm just ... I just—" She took a deep breath. "Lily, I didn't expect any of this. This is not how we were taught to dress when I came here."

"You're in the real world now, Trudy. You're not living inside a stodgy Burr catalog any more. But don't look so scandalized. You happen to be a very pretty woman. Are you ashamed of that?"

"No."

"Movie stars use their beauty all the time."

"I guess. Well, yes, but—"

"And models too. They use their beauty and find nothing wrong with it."

"I know." The rep wet her lips uncomfortably. "But in an office it just seems, well, unprofessional, and—"

"GOOD GOD, Trudy!" Lily's laughter was a bellow from the gut. "What planet are you on? There's nothing *professional* about women's business attire! Do you think high heels are worn because they're practical? Women wear them because men like the way they emphasize the shape of a woman's leg. And lipstick, making your mouth bright and shiny, what professional purpose does *that* serve? Fuck, honey! Our whole appearance—pardon my French—our whole appearance is a man's wet dream: eye shadow, mascara, hairstyle, lipstick, earrings, shaved legs, skirts instead of pants, *pantyhose* for Christ's sake!—none of us wear this rigmarole because it's *professional!* We wear it because men have dominated the fashion world since time immemorial, and they like seeing us dolled up nice and sexy. Am I right?"

Trudy didn't know how to answer.

"You don't see *them* going through this daily crap, do you? Holy Mother of Saint Andrew, wouldn't that be a sight? A board room of male executives fluttering Bambi lashes and crossing naked shaved legs. *Ha!* Trust me, Tru, if the bastards had to do it themselves they wouldn't expect us to! Really, I'm not asking you to do anything outrageous. I want you to be your absolute professional self. I'm *not* asking you to flirt. Heavens, that would be disastrous! On the contrary, you're a cool professional sales-woman who just happens to be a knockout. You'll impress the hell out of everybody: Mom, Dad, male and female applicants—everybody!"

"I don't know, Lily. It just makes me uncomfortable. I'm not trying to be difficult, you know."

"Of course."

"It's just not what I expected. I—I do have some short skirts."

"How short?"

"Like this?" Trudy made a cutting motion just above the knee.

"Shorter, Trudy. Has to be shorter. Buy what you need and charge it back to the school. I'll make sure it goes through."

"And the boots?"

"Yes. You'd be surprised how many men have a fetish about boots."

"Fetish?"

"Exactly. A man who finds a woman alluring has a hard time saying no to her. Never forget that. Men will judge you superficially whether you like it or not, so as long as they expect you to be sexy, you might as well use it to your advantage. Fair is fair. This is great strategy, dear. You're going to make one hell of a commission."

"I thought commissions for reps was against the law?"

"Fringe benefits. I meant fringe benefits, of course." Lily studied her new rep closely. "Trudy, are you having a problem with this? You still look troubled."

Trudy slowly shook her head. "No, I'm just surprised."

"I'd rather you were more excited than surprised, dear."

"Ma'am, I'll try. Uh … are you going to have Elaine dress like that too?"

Lily's mouth tightened. "Elaine's been here a while. She's more settled, but I'll work on her."

"Oh."

"Say, would you like some coffee, Trudy? It's a fresh pot."

Trudy sighed. "Sure. Thank you, ma'am."

"Lily."

9

Bob Lawrence's schedule finished at four, but instead of heading for home he drifted downstairs to the faculty lounge for a last cup of coffee. Two teachers were in the lounge when he got there.

"… nowhere near the quality of the Julys!" Carol Sobolewski declared. She was a chronic complainer, like most teachers Bob knew. Faculty didn't need more than a day to determine that Admissions had recruited a mediocre class, and she and Arthur Cassidy were already at it. Bob poured a cup of sludgy coffee, then sat by himself on the couch near the compact refrigerator. He wasn't interested in criticizing the new class. He had a date tonight with a Two-Year Executive Secretarial Arts student who had started school the year before. Her schedule wouldn't let her out until 5:15, so he had some time to kill.

Arthur Cassidy responded to his fellow teacher's tirade without looking up from *The Chronicle of Higher Education*. He was a large man in his upper fifties, with a portly stomach and a face made kind by salt and pepper brows and bulbous red nose. "Carol, the September class is never as good as July. The Julys are more ambitious. But the September class is never a *bad* group."

"Well, I think that's a pretty sorry crowd we got handed." Carol nibbled an Oreo cookie. "That Elaine did some pretty desperate recruiting. Did you see the grades some of those girls got on the admissions test?"

"Well, no I didn't."

"I didn't either, but Jean Cavanaugh did. She checks every class, even though Admissions kicks about her looking through the files. She saw the scores on their tests and, my God, she was fuming! Fuming something awful!"

Bob spoke up. "You mean they didn't pass? Oliver wouldn't accept students who didn't pass."

"Oh, certainly they passed. The state would fine us if we took 'em when they didn't pass. But I'll bet that's the *only* reason keeping them from accepting the ones who don't. No, they all passed—but only by the skin of their teeth, a lot of them."

"And what color would that skin be, Carol?" Arthur dug ever so gently. These former priests, man, you had to watch them. They stayed priests, no matter what they told you. All that time in the seminary, learning the chants, practicing guilt, sitting all day in confessionals hearing God knew what—it had to stick deep. Arthur's easy cadences always had a Hail Mary tucked in one cheek.

"Don't pin that on me, Arthur," said Carol. "I'm not prejudiced, and neither is Jean. What I'm talking about includes the white girls too. They're not recruiting the cream any more. They're settling for second best. And this school was not founded on its graduates being second best."

"Well, I know Oliver rejected a lot of applicants. I think he's being as selective as he can. As it is, he didn't get the class he wanted."

"Well, I shouldn't be saying this," started Carol. She caught herself, went to the door, surveyed the empty hall, then shut it. "I think Oliver's going to be fired."

Bob said, "I don't."

"Neither do I," said Arthur.

"Well, it stands to reason. And for exactly the reason you said, Arthur. He only brought in half the number of students he was supposed to. How can New York let that go, hey?"

"Still," said Arthur, "Oliver's been here since they started this place. They'd be fools to let him go."

"Well, I shouldn't be saying this," Carol said, "but I hear that New York thinks he's inept."

"Oh, New York never knows what it's talking about. Who said it?"

"Someone Jean knows. She's got a few connections in the President's Office. Ever since she was on the committee to re-evaluate the Advanced Program a few years back."

Bob drained his coffee and felt lumpy particles brush his tongue. The gritty sensation turned his mind away from the gossip. With practiced reflex, he ran his own mental inventory on the batch of new students. Instead of desks, his classroom had plastic chairs with tan writing tables attached to the front by a single chrome tube, and this minimalist design obligated him to view every slim waist and supple leg placed before him.

And those students …

They were pretty, they were young, and with few exceptions they were very, very trusting. So eager to grow up that it didn't take much for even an English teacher to put that look of worship in their eyes. This school, unlike the high school in Baltimore where he taught five years earlier, was almost one hundred percent female. A secretarial school, for God's sake—of *course* it was mostly female! That added up to a lot of worshipful looks. The pressure on someone like himself was practically a given. Human nature, after all. Bob's prime interest in life, oddly enough, was *not* teaching language arts to an ever-revolving group of disinterested bimbos. No, he wanted to write. A novel boiled in him. A serious work. Literature. So he had a healthy respect for human nature, and could understand almost clinically each time he succumbed to it.

Arthur turned a page of the newspaper. "I can't imagine the Burr College without Oliver. He's kept the curriculum up, you have to give him credit for that."

"That's Dean Harris," Carol said stubbornly. "I feel sorry for Oliver. It's too big for him."

Children, Bob thought. He pulled from his briefcase the seating chart of his third period class, Section One of the new September students. Reviewing it, he thought as always how the students' names never changed. Nor did their faces and bodies, except of course each year they grew younger.

Janene Boothe, Caryn Carrolson, Lisa DiCicco, Phaedra Eccles, April Gercke, Fran Hodge. A pretty nice batch, actually. There was one girl in the front row near his desk, a tall brunette with nice legs and a summer tan. His eyes rested on her name: *Heather Feeney.* This sultry girl stuck in his mind, already picked out in a way, for as the new kids trooped in he recognized immediately that she most intrigued his taste. She wore dark eye makeup, and the tips of her long black hair were dyed green. That was an interesting touch. A good chance she was Catholic, and Catholic girls had sexual buttons that were easy to press, praise God. What his chances were didn't really matter, for he wasn't giving any of this serious consideration, not with Mary Grace Whitman ready to rendezvous at a Society Hill pub in half an hour. And besides, he didn't do this sort of thing rampantly. It was just fun to think about. He was thirty-six now, and wasn't yet sure if that made him old. He didn't feel old, but that "-six" had some sting. He was certainly *on the way.*

With a warm smile, Carol Sobolewski changed to a healthier topic. "One of my girls in transcription, Arthur, a January girl this is, just hit eighty words. She's been trying so hard. That'll give her a B, if she can keep it up for four more letters. She was so excited she almost cried. The entire class cheered her. You know, Arthur, I sincerely think that for some of these kids a moment like that becomes one of the lasting memories of their lives."

Arthur beamed. "It *is* wonderful to see such selfless team spirit, that's certainly true. You can't help loving these girls. Right, Bob?"

"Absolutely."

Bob checked his watch, then put away the papers. He bid his colleagues a quick good-bye and departed the cigarette-cloudy room, leaving Arthur and Carol to outdo each other with examples of the exceptional students they had taught over the years.

He headed east on Pine Street, and within minutes was in Society Hill. Two Street was a wide avenue gentrified to suggest colonial America: commercial fronts were housed in brick, and simulated gas lamps lit the corners. Horses pulled tourists in carriages. Patches of the street lay open to exposed cobblestones. Bars were pubs here, restaurants were taverns. Bob passed under the wooden sign for *"Mad" Anthony's* and peered through the bar smoke. Mary Grace stood near the back, dynamic in a purple leather dress. He approached, smiling, and in the inner giddiness of her youthful beauty kissed her several times before taking her to a corner booth.

"You wore the tie, Bob," Mary Grace said, as happy as one mortal girl could be. She said the single syllable of his name with petty joy; all of her classmates had to call him Mr. Lawrence.

"It's my favorite tie." She had given it to him last Valentine's Day, and he made sure he wore it often.

They ordered drinks, and she said, "What do you want to do tonight?"

"Do you still want to take in a movie?"

"We could. I guess." Her large eyes studied him with a lurid burn. The seven-and-seven in front of her couldn't be her first.

"You want to do something else?"

"I think I'd really like to go back to your place. Maybe order take out."

"Really?" Though he couldn't be displeased. Mary Grace in this purple leather was a quasar he could enter without ever finding a limit. The one good thing about dating young girls was *not* that they were young; in fact, their youth tended to be problematic. But young girls were willing to dress like knock-outs. They still possessed the desire to want to blow you away. Mary Grace was stimulating every inch of him, so acutely it felt like happiness.

"Do you mind?" she asked. "Or were you really looking forward to a movie?"

"Of course not. What can Hollywood produce to compare with you?"

She giggled and blushed. Sipping her drink, she said, "We could rent a movie, maybe."

"Oh, I think that would be a waste of money. Our time is limited, isn't it? Frankly, there's no way you're entering my apartment looking this good without me immediately taking you to bed."

"That sounds great." Her smile broadened. "Dad said I could stay out to midnight."

"Did he? You're kidding. He always wants you home by ten."

"Well he still does, usually. But, um ..." She hunched down a little, looked at him coyly with the tip of her tongue between her teeth.

"What did you tell him?" Bob asked cautiously.

"I told him I had a date with a boy from Jefferson Medical College. I said he was twenty-four and very sweet. Mom and Dad both got excited. I knew Dad would like it if he was a doctor."

"He doesn't want to meet this ... boy, does he?"

"Sure he does. But I said it's too early yet. Dad understands."

"Honey, you don't play games like this." Bob looked at her severely. "Burr has a no-frat policy regarding students. Anybody finds out about us, you'll get me in trouble."

"No, it's okay. It's just something I told Dad so I could stay out late. Next week I'll tell him we broke up. Well, maybe in *two* weeks."

That got them both laughing. They leaned across the table and kissed. "Let me pay this and we'll go," he said, surprised at the huskiness in his voice.

He took the tab to the bar. Waiting for his change, he studied Mary Grace a little solemnly. She lived in a South Philly row home with a protective middle class family, but she had her own car and a fair amount of independence. Seeing her these past nine months (including summer when she had no classes) had been fun. Still, that was a long time to date one kid, and the start of school with its crop of fresh faces was making him antsier than he cared to admit. He pictured Heather Feeney with her dark hair tinted green at the ends. What was *she* doing tonight?

Bob got his change and they left. Walking across Two Street, Mary Grace clung to his arm, light-headed and clumsy as she navigated her high heels across the cobblestones. They headed toward his apartment, his arm around the girl's waist and her head resting on his shoulder. With each step his fingers rode the muscles of her thigh, and he didn't think thirty-six was so old after all.

10

Ethel Harris sat in her cluttered office reviewing grade reports. Students were measured at the end of every semester, and with four program starts staggered every three months this caused sudden gluts of overwhelming paperwork. Stacks of more grade reports lined the front of her desk like a metropolitan skyline. Shoved about by these files was her phone, a gilt-framed picture of her boys, a small figure of the Virgin Mary, and a desk plaque quoting First Corinthians: *God Hath Chosen the Foolish Things of the World to Confound the Wise.*

"Why Jean, these aren't so bad. The way you were sounding off, I expected everybody to have zero GPAs."

Jean Cavanaugh sat in the chair normally reserved for students who came to the dean with complaints or a need to plea-bargain. The teacher looked both angry and ashamed at the cards in Ethel's hands, for they represented the first semester efforts of the April class, easily the smallest and worst class currently running at the school. At least this was Jean's opinion, and she felt no qualms in expressing it to anyone who would listen. "Some of them are certainly trying," she said. "Valerie Deems, there. Look at that. A 1.23 GPA. And Charmaine Hoyt, 1.09. It's not like they're skipping class either. They're attending and *still* getting these grades. I don't know what to do."

The dean nodded without comment.

"They *can't* stay in school. It's embarrassing to talk to them in front of the rest of the class. They can't learn anything!"

"Well, yes," Ethel murmured softly, "we'd all like to think they could learn *some*thing." She stared at the incredible numbers. Only three of the eleven students had the requisite 2.0 GPA mandated by federal regulations and the school's own policy manual for maintaining satisfactory progress and therefore staying in school.

"Please, Ethel, drop them. Put them out of their misery. Keeping them is a scandal." Jean, though terrifying to her students, was quite kind-hearted and generous outside the classroom. Her voice, offering this edict, broke a little.

"Just these two?"

"Yes, at least. Deems and Hoyt are unteachable. I'm telling you that, and when have you ever heard me cry uncle?"

"Never before, that's true." Ethel considered, still registering the dismal grades. "But *eight* of the eleven students are below satisfactory progress. You can't just single out Deems and Hoyt. By rights we should cancel the whole class."

"Then that's what we should do," Jean said with the unwavering righteousness of all good teachers.

"I don't know," the dean said dubiously. "I've seen classes canceled for low attendance, but in all my years I've never seen a class canceled for low GPAs. I know we think of ourselves as trendsetters, but that's not the kind of trend I'm interested in."

"I don't see how we have a choice."

"Jean, you know Oliver isn't going to close a class or even expel two students and leave a class of less than ten as a result. He was supposed to sit thirty-five for April to begin with, and only got twenty. Nine have dropped out already."

"Well, they're beyond my help. I throw in the towel. Those kids can graduate if we're too wimpy to expel them, but they'll never get jobs. You could drill them for five years and they'd never learn to compose a coherent letter or write a report. Doesn't Oliver know this?"

Ethel shrugged.

Jean started to get up. "Maybe I'd better talk to him myself."

"You will NOT!" Ethel barked. "Jean, you are not to bother the administration about these students, is that clear?"

Jean froze in mid-rise, then dropped back in her seat. A guttural noise issued from her throat.

"Jean ..." coaxed Ethel.

"All right."

"Good. Bother *me* all you want. That's okay. In fact, I want the feedback. But I just learned recently that you and Carol Sobolewski went into Elaine Margolis' office and yelled at her for accepting these students. Oliver was livid."

"Oh, Oliver." Jean shook her head in disgust.

"Well, he's right, Jean. You can't do that, and I don't ever want to hear about it again. We've run an April class for three years now. It's *always* the worst class. It starts in late spring and that's too unusual a time. The only students who come are the ones not organized enough to attend school during the normal starting months, September and January. People that disorganized are naturally the scholastic dregs."

"Then why the hell do we run an April class?"

"You know why. Because the President's Office looked at a calendar once and saw a big gap of time between January and July and said, 'Gee, we could put a class right in the middle there and grab some extra revenue.' But Admissions has never successfully filled such an unusual start, and the girls who do come are bottom-of-the-barrel. Oliver knows it, but if New York can't be convinced the class is a bad idea he has no power to stop it. According to Louise we don't get enough kids in April to cover the cost of running the class, much less turn a profit. There's nothing anybody can do. So as long as we're stuck with these kids, let's keep cool heads and figure out how to help them the best way we can."

"But Ethel," Jean pleaded, "isn't it illegal to keep a kid on if she isn't making satisfactory progress?"

Ethel's sly smile betrayed fifteen years of higher education experience. "Well, we *are* allowed to expand academic probation periods for our students when special circumstances are involved."

"Ethel, I don't think obtuseness is a special circumstance."

"I'll think of something."

Jean sighed. She stood and stretched, and somewhere within her jacket a bone joint cracked. "I ought to head home. It's so dark now, and the time is only what? A quarter past six? Can you believe the days are already getting shorter? And I hate taking the train out to Narberth. It used to be nice, but they're letting more and more hoods get on."

A hood to Jean was probably any young black male in a sweatshirt. "Good night, Jean. See you tomorrow, bright and early. Thanks for the grades."

"'Night, Ethel. Well," and Jean smiled pleasantly, "at least *last* year's September class is strong, and the graduating Januarys don't look so bad."

"One thing I've learned, Jean, is the good and bad eventually balances out in this business."

The phone suddenly jangled by Ethel's elbow. Jean took the cue and went out, leaving the door open. Ethel picked up the receiver, and with her free hand continued to flip through the grade reports.

"Eth? It's Harry."

The rumbling bass voice wiped the evaluations from her eyes. She said coldly, "What do you want?"

"C'mon, you don't gotta start with that tone, do you?"

"I'll give you whatever tone suits me. What do you want?"

"The check bounced."

"It did not."

"I swear it did, Eth. I need a new one."

"You stupid ignoramus, don't you know that I get bank statements? I already know for a fact that check went through. Where the hell do you get off saying things like that? I'm hanging up."

"Wait, Eth, Please—"

Ethel wanted to hang up, but could not quite do it. The voice on the line was deep and broken, familiar and yet not. After a moment she resumed scanning the grades again, comforted by the knowledge that this voice no longer had any power over her.

"Eth, can't you spare me just a little?"

"What's a little?"

"Five hunnerd."

"Five *hundred?* Are you nuts? Don't call here anymore."

"But you changed the home number—"

"Yeah, imagine why!"

"Eth, I can't make—"

"Listen, I told you not to call any more. You promised you wouldn't. You also promised to stop asking for money. Now hang up."

"I'm going to the meetings again."

Ethel was silent. His telling her this meant nothing to her, but … well, in case it was true, she'd better not say anything negative.

"Good. Proud of you. What do you need the money for?"

The voice hesitated. "Rent."

"*Rent!* Aren't you still living with your mother?" That old hag, black-skinned and white-wrinkled, huddled on her Germantown Avenue porch in a shawl, arguing incessantly with Ethel about the babies. Must be ninety now, the indestructible bitch.

"Well yeah, but her pension ain't much."

"Shame she's gotta count on you."

"Don't be mean. I was thinking. Maybe the boys …"

"What?"

"Stevie. Couldn't he maybe … help out a little? Get a job after school, maybe. He could do something."

"NO!" All at once she was shouting, arched back in the creaky swivel chair. "Don't even think it! You don't go near the boys, any of 'em! You do, Harry, and I'll have you behind bars! Is that clear?"

Silence.

"You think I'm fooling?"

"I know you ain't," he said softly, his voice as gray as driftwood. "Eth?"

"What?"

"How 'bout three hunnerd?"

She hung up.

Ethel looked at the open door and wondered if anyone heard. She could change the home number again and again, but she couldn't change this one. She tried once more to look at the grades but couldn't. It was too late, too close to evening class time, and her blood pulsing too fast. Ethel made sure her purse was locked in the desk, then shut her door and went downstairs. Her office was on the second floor, due to an unfortunate shortage space among the offices on the first.

All of the secretaries' cubicles were empty, the windows black with speckles of light from the office buildings framing Washington Square. Ethel looked in Oliver's office and found it vacant, the radio broadcasting a Sibelius symphony to empty air. She leaned around the partition of Louise's station, and there they were.

"Hi."

Oliver and Louise looked up. A sprawl of colored invoices covered the business manager's desk. Oliver's smile was cheerful, but his eyes looked puffy. "Hey, Eth."

Louise looked just as weary, her gray head down, tiny eyes burning angrily under pursed brows. "We've had another robbery."

"Oh no, not again! You must be kidding!" But, of course, Louise never kidded. "What was taken?"

"Four Dells."

"Jesus, Mary and Ralph. How'd it happen?"

"The same way it always happens," Louise growled. "Somebody— probably that night school teacher, whatever her name is—didn't put the alarm on before closing up, and the thief jimmied the lock to the kitchen window." She looked accusingly at Oliver. "They've come in that way before."

Oliver stirred to feeble life. "Well, we got bars for that window, but someone tore them off. Other than bricking it up I don't know what else to do." To Ethel he said, "We asked around among the teachers and students today. Some girls in the July class thought they saw a strange man age thirty to sixty standing in the alley beside the kitchen, but it's not enough to go on."

"Thirty to sixty?" asked Ethel.

"The best they could do. The police took a report, of course. All we know is that four computers from Lab II were lifted sometime between when we closed, and today at eight when we opened. Evening school went to nine last night. Who can say? This is an old three-story building with lots of large windows, and front, back, and side doors. It was built at a time when the only enemy was the British, an entire ocean away. We're just asking for it."

"Who opened this morning?" Ethel leaned her shoulder on Louise's partition.

"Deirdre," said Louise. "She's always here by eight."

"And who reported the theft?"

"Arthur Cassidy. Right at nine o'clock. Four of his students stood at their empty stations and asked him how they were supposed to do their assignment."

For a long moment no one had anything to say. All three sighed simultaneously, though none noticed. Ethel shrugged. *"C'est la vie."*

Louise bristled immediately. "What do you mean? This comes out of our budget, I hope you know! Jodi Myers in Accounting will love to hear it. That makes six computer thefts since the beginning of the summer. Not to mention last May when someone blithely walked off with the VCR from the lobby. This school's a sieve, but New York won't pay for better security. Jodi keeps saying we have no respect for the equipment, and puts those comments in her monthly reports. You can imagine how that makes me look!"

The bell in the hall sounded its ugly blat, and Ethel looked at her watch. "I've got to teach the steno class tonight. Oliver, do me a favor?"

"You do? What about Ellen Pfeiffer?"

"Called in sick again."

Oliver contemplated that. "How many times has she done this now?"

"A lot. I think she's scared to be in the city at night. Perfect attitude for an evening school teacher, right? I can really pick 'em sometimes. Anyway, can you call my son and make sure he's got dinner going for his brothers? And remind him to leave a little hamburger for his old lady. Will you do that? I won't get home 'til after ten."

"Of course. Is this Kurt?"

"Yeah."

"You got it."

"Thanks. Good night." Ethel left.

Oliver watched silently as Louise checked through each invoice and carefully shuffled them into alpha order by vendor. Before leaving tonight she would tick them off in her ledger and ship the invoices to New York, where the actual payments would be made. New York didn't care what order they received the invoices, but Louise had her methods and the alphabet was, for her, the backbone of all business organization. She asked, "How's Tina?"

"Going through a rough spell," Oliver said. "Thanks for asking. She wants this Sidney Wallace film badly."

"I'll bet she does." Louise halted her work for a moment and gave him a friendly grin. "Did you ever imagine, back when you two hit it off, that one day your wife might be working with a director like Sidney Wallace?"

"It's pretty crazy," Oliver admitted. "But then most of Hollywood blows my mind. I hope she gets it. Fred Sheldon, her agent, keeps saying Wallace wants her, but no one will commit. Tina just mopes around the apartment with nothing to do."

"Then for God's sake, stop staying late at the office and take her someplace."

"I want to. I was thinking maybe this weekend. Dinner and dancing."

"There you go." Louise shoved the invoices in an overnight envelope and licked the flaps.

"How late are you staying?"

"Guess about twenty more minutes. I still have to make the rounds and check the doors and windows. Hang the 'THIS WAY TO THE OFFICE EQUIPMENT' sign outside the kitchen window so the thieves can save time. Oh—I wanted to remind you about the capital expenditures request. New York wants it by Thursday."

"I know. Julie's still typing it up. I put in the request for your office walls again. Just wanted you to know."

"Sure," said Louise. "What the hell."

Oliver rose with unbearable stiffness and returned to his office. He dropped in the swivel chair and blinked at the red 6:25 on the gold clock on his desk. He felt he had been at the school for three straight days. After a moment he reached for the phone to call Ethel's son. But when the receiver was in his hand he decided to call Tina first.

After four rings the answering machine clicked on, some goofy pre-recorded nonsense that Tina got Kevin Costner to recite during one of her L.A. jaunts. He didn't bother to hear the greeting through, and hung up. Obviously she wasn't home.

He punched his home number again, plus a four-digit code to prompt the machine into playing any messages back to him. Through thin surface hiss he heard a male voice say, "Tina? ... Tina? ... Hey, hon, if you're there, pick up." A long stretch of low breathing as the caller waited, and then a click as he disconnected. Oliver knew the voice. It belonged to Dennis Skye, one of Tina's New York actor friends. Oliver disliked Skye more than any of his wife's colleagues. The man was arrogant and unfunny, his wit basically dependent on sarcastic barbs aimed at fellow professionals and innocent bystanders. All of Tina's movie friends called her "hon" or "sweetie," and those were standard addresses in the business. But Skye made the endearments ring with a shady propriety that offended Oliver's personal space. He wished Fate would stop allowing Skye and his wife to be involved in so many projects together.

A second beep went off in his ear. "Tina? Hello baby, it's me." Skye again. This was becoming intolerable. Oliver unconsciously held his breath for the entire length of the message. "Tina? … Okay, hon, listen up. Big things going on here. Call me just as soon as you're in. I mean pronto, get me? Love ya." Another click as the phone hung up. Oliver exhaled.

A third beep. Oliver felt a shock, for this time it was Tina. "Oliver! Listen, hon, I waited until five-thirty, but I guess you're staying late again. No surprise, right? I should have called you anyway, sorry, but I've been busy getting things together. I'm calling from Thirtieth Street Station. Fred called and I've got to rush up to New York. Oh, I'm really excited, hon! I can't say I've got the part—God, I don't want to jinx it! But it's looking *goodish!* Might be back tomorrow, but more likely nearer the end of next week. It's that topsy-turvy right now! Love ya!" The phone clattered to silence, and after a moment three beeps went off in Oliver's ear, telling him there were no more messages.

Oliver punched another number from memory.

"Joey's."

"Let me have a small with peppers and anchovies. And a Coke."

"Address and phone number?"

Oliver gave the Burr College address.

"Okay. That comes to $9.65. It'll be there in thirty minutes."

"Good enough. Thanks."

Oliver called Ethel's son, then pulled out a sheaf of papers and began to jot notes in the margins. It was the rudiments of his budget proposal for next year, due in the President's Office by mid-November. In a few minutes Louise shuffled by, clad in a shapeless brown overcoat and yellow stockings hiked high on her spindly legs. A bandanna over her white hair hid all but the large owlish glasses. She waved wordlessly at him. Oliver waved back. He stopped writing, and sat motionless at his desk until the outer front door clicked shut behind her.

11

"Information Processing is one of our best-paying programs," Trudy Weiser said with a big smile. "It gives you all the proper business skills you need to get your foot in the door."

Annie Duncan nodded, staring at the open catalog in her hands. The applicant was a big woman, twenty years old, with a large, almost comically expressive face. "Yeah, it looks pretty good," she said, but then shut the catalog and frowned.

Trudy grew nervous. The rep had done everything she was supposed to: described the program, given the tour, and finished the morning with the test. Annie had nothing but good things to say about the school. And as a Burr representative, Trudy believed that she herself looked good. Despite Lily's instructions, Trudy was still wearing conservative business suits with proper length skirts, medium heels, modestly applied make up and minimal jewelry. Her anxiousness at this defiance of her boss lifted immediately after talking to Elaine Margolis. Elaine had coached her on this model attire, and the senior rep was so impressive herself in dress and sophistication that Trudy happily followed her directions. She now believed, since two weeks had gone by without a comment from the boss, that Lily's earlier instructions were, in fact, not orders but suggestions, and not particularly good ones at that.

"Great!" she said a little too quickly. "There are still seats open for the January class. What I need is a twenty-five dollar application fee and a one hundred dollar tuition deposit. The hundred dollars is important because it holds your seat in class."

"Yeah, I know. See, I'm really just feeling my options. How about this? Lemme give you a check for twenty-five, and after I've looked over the stuff you gave me I'll mail you the hundred. Do I have time to do that?"

"Well, sure …" But Trudy's mind inwardly raced. Annie Duncan was her fourth interview since Lily's hiring, and the first three had gone over with wonderful ease. All three applicants paid both the app fee and deposit right up front. Now Trudy was faced with having to convince an applicant to pay more than she wanted, and it went against the rep's grain. In fact, it struck her as faintly dishonest. But she had to try. Lily would expect the full one hundred and twenty-five. "Well, of course there's no *official* cutoff, but obviously the sooner we get the deposit, the quicker we can secure your place in class."

"Do classes really fill up so fast?"

"Well, you just never know." Trudy felt she was slipping badly.

Annie wrinkled her face. "See, I'm simply not sure a secretarial career is what I want. It's so far from anything that interests me. God, what I really love is raising Great Danes. We have two at home now, Harley and Ebony."

"Gosh, that's great." Trudy laughed to hide the fact that most big dogs scared her.

Annie picked up her purse. "Will a check be okay?"

"Sure … for what amount?"

"Twenty-five."

"Oh. You know, it really would be better to pay the hundred too. Seats *are* going kind of fast."

"Well, like I said, I want to think about it first."

"You know the hundred's refundable, right up to the first day of class?"

"Yes." Annie filled out a check in quick easy strokes and handed it to Trudy.

"There's no risk or anything," Trudy said.

"It's okay. I'm really pretty sold. Call it insecurity." Annie wrinkled her face again, this time at herself. "I just don't like putting out so much so fast. Even though I'm sure I'll come in January."

"You do? That's sure?"

"Pretty much. The facilities look great. I still don't know if it's what I want, but I'm sure it's what I need. I can't keep floating forever. Thank you, Trudy. It's been terrific talking to you."

"Same here." Trudy stood. "Let me walk you out."

Walking an applicant to the front door was something Elaine told her always to do. A lot of selling was simply playing hostess, according to Elaine. Trudy actually felt best on her feet, walking side by side with the applicant, and felt more Annie's equal as she took Elaine's metaphor at its word and composed herself the way her mom behaved when Rabbi Pasternak and the rest of Temple Council came to their house for meetings.

"Very glad to have met you." She smiled while Annie wriggled into a floppy windbreaker. They walked through the double glass doors of the lobby to the heavy oak door that opened onto Washington Square. Trudy watched Annie go, and held the twenty-five dollar check tightly to keep it from flapping in the late September breeze.

She returned to the lobby and looked at the receptionist. "I only got twenty-five dollars from her."

"Well, that's good," Julie said.

"But it's the first time. You know, since Lily started."

The secretary stopped typing. She sensed the young rep's apprehension and beckoned her closer. With an encouraging smile she said, "Listen, you can't expect to get the hundred dollar deposit every time. Nobody can do that. Life would be too easy."

Trudy smiled shyly. In some ways Julie was a mystery to her. The secretary was somewhere in her thirties, which made her an adult, and her organized desk and effortless handling of customers made her seem knowledgeable and worldly. Her heart-shaped face, wire-frame glasses, and long blond hair neatly pulled back, gave her a fresh-scrubbed prettiness that also seemed mature—a grown up commonsense approach to beauty. Julie didn't chit-chat like the other reps and secretaries, and this added to her stature. It also meant that no one knew much about her. Sometimes on Fridays the girls would go out after work for dinner and drinks, and though Julie was always invited she consistently declined. She did it in such a friendly way that no one took offense, but it still set her apart.

"Oliver thinks the best students usually *don't* pay the hundred up front," Julie said. "He thinks it's a good sign when they want some time to think about it. Shows they're serious about the decision. You think the girl wants to come?"

"Well she said so, just before she left."

"Then you have nothing to worry about. She'll mail the hundred in, and you'll get it by the end of the week. That's how most of them do it."

This sounded so right that Trudy was finally heartened. "Thanks, Julie."

She cut down the hallway to the bathroom and checked her appearance, then returned to the lobby and passed through the cubicles to Lily's office. The door was open. Lily stood by her coffee maker, pouring a fresh cup. She glanced over her shoulder at the rep and smiled pleasurably. "Yes, Tru?"

Trudy hesitated. The admissions director stood tall and glamorous in a red-and-white striped minidress and signature stiletto heels. Her ears, throat, and one ankle shimmered with gold, while the dress's low-cut neckline flashed far more cleavage than was permitted by *The Burr Guide of Professional Standards*. The junior rep's confidence melted on the spot.

"What have you got, hon?" Lily carried her fresh cup back to her desk and pushed aside the library's latest copy of *ELLE*.

Trudy hung in the doorway. "I uh—just finished with Annie Duncan. She's definitely interested in the January program. Looks good, too. Did real well on the test."

"Excellent. Did you get the app fee and tuition deposit?"

Trudy lowered her voice and held up the check. "Just the twenty-five for now. But she doesn't think there'll be a problem getting the rest."

"Just the twenty-five?"

"She's coming back on Tuesday to talk with David, and she said she'd bring the rest then. She really wants to come."

Lily stared at the young rep. Trudy's stomach tightened.

"Okay. Shut the door and take a seat."

Trudy tried to do both. She closed the door, but when she turned to sit Lily was already up and advancing. "Goddammit, Trudy! What do you think this is, some fucking GAME?"

"What? Well, but Li—"

"What the fuck is wrong with you? You're a SALESMAN! You're supposed to SELL! Selling means getting what you SET OUT for!"

The terrified rep stuttered, "N-no, see—but Lily—"

"And twenty-five lousy bucks IS NOT GETTING!"

Trudy's flapping mouth couldn't utter a word to save her soul. Lily's beehive hair filled her vision like a bronze and gold nimbus, red stripes rippled harsh kaleidoscopic lines before her eyes, and the admissions director's piercing voice reached down the rep's open mouth, coiled about the girl's spine, and shook it as if it were a sapling.

"What the BLOODY CHRIST am I supposed to tell Oliver? That my dumb rep hasn't the GUTS to dig in and pitch? You're in the REAL world now, honey-buns! There's no happy Main Line insulation HERE! Those cuddly good looks won't make the world love you, not anymore! I'll bet that's what you're USED TO, huh?" Lily thrust her face into the rep's, a terrifying distortion of purple fury and dazzling white teeth. "A baby-faced cutie-pie like you? ANSWER ME!"

"I—I don't—"

"What? WHAT?"

Trudy couldn't breathe. Surely the whole staff was hearing this, even with the door shut, and this realization defeated her. She dropped on a chair, covered her face, and broke into wracking sobs.

"Oh right! *Cry!*" Lily threw up her hands. "You BABY! Jesus H. Christ, how am I going to make goal with tenderfoot twats like you? I could just SCREAM!"

Trudy shook her head, unable to stop. Lily backed off, pushed up her hair, and smoothed her skirt with both hands. She returned to her desk and sipped coffee, taking a moment to muse on the junior rep's black sausage curls and pretty legs. Trudy was the type of girl who mistook her voluptuousness for fat. This made her both emotionally insecure and physically sexy—an irresistible combination to the male mediocrities who tended to show for evening school certificate programs. Trudy's sobs slowly digressed to chokes and hiccups. When finally she sat up, her eyes were swollen pits of smeared mascara.

"All right," Lily said. "Let's not overact here. It's only a hundred dollars, after all. But you failed to get that applicant to commit, and that's a serious breach of salesmanship. She wanted time to think and you obviously felt she was entitled to it. Isn't that correct?"

Trudy reluctantly nodded.

"Well, let me postulate a fact of human nature, dear. People with time to think never do *anything!* They don't sign up, they don't pay out, and they damn well don't go to school. Certainly not to places like this. The people who come to small career schools are not gifted with foresight; they're not great planners. When they do something like this it's always on impulse. They're fed up with their jobs, or they're having a particularly bad day or a blue night, and they happen to come across our ad in the phone book or newspaper and *that's* how they decide to come. And that's why you can't afford to let them think about it. Do you understand?"

Trudy nodded.

"What, can't you speak now?"

It took a moment, but she managed to whisper, "I c-can speak."

"So can a trained toucan. Are you getting anything out of what I'm saying?"

"Yes."

"Okay." Lily smiled. Her hands began to flip. "Oh Tru, you think I don't know what you're going through? You're at a point in your professional career where you need to learn aggressiveness and yet, at the same time, *real* aggressiveness isn't a part of your good nature. You're a very sweet, kind-hearted girl."

Trudy snuffled.

"I guess you haven't been yelled at like that before?"

"No, ma'am."

"Well, forget it. Consider it a morale boost. We understand each other now, and I know you'll try extra hard next time. This is a critical juncture for you, Tru. Now is when you must recognize the needs of your job and harness your energy in the direction that will make your work produce. After all, you *did* get the tuition deposits from the last three applicants you interviewed. Remember how proud you were each time? Remember how pleased Oliver and I were with you? How about some coffee?"

"Um ... no, Lily. Thank you."

"Oh, you look pretty frazzled. I think you'd better have some." Lily moved to the coffee maker and poured. "Cream, dear?"

"Sure ... thanks."

Lily meditated as she shook a container of Half-N-Half in the rep's cup. "Incidentally, didn't we have a little talk a while ago regarding your attire?"

Trudy, whose lungs had calmed enough to permit the articulation of complete sentences, felt them constrict again. "Yes, Lily."

"We *did* have such a talk?"

"Yes, we did."

"Hm-hmmm. So then why aren't you wearing what we discussed?"

"Well, I … well, I—"

"Go ahead, hon. Make this good."

"No, ma'am. I just … well, I thought when we talked that I was supposed to wear, you know, the boots and skirts and stuff only for the Accounting Program. But I haven't had any interviews for Accounting yet."

"I see. And what were you planning to do? Change clothes depending on the type of interview you had?"

"Well, I … you see—"

But Lily was grinning. "No, don't be embarrassed. I think it's a wonderful idea. Still, I haven't *once* seen you in the attire we discussed. Now I know for a fact that you have an interview this afternoon with a young man interested in the Evening Accounting Program. Were you planning to dress appropriately for that?"

Trudy said helplessly, "Yes."

"Oh? You mean you brought the clothes with you today?" Lily's smile grew icy. "I don't think so. Do you want to quit, Trudy?"

She did, she really did! But how could she when that face with the penetrating black eyes and mocking smile was set to write her off as a spoiled fool the minute she said so? Trudy didn't have the courage to quit.

"I think it would be a shame. Any job you get, Tru, is going to be as tough as this. Don't kid yourself. Hell, the whole world is cutthroat. Do you want to do well here?"

"Yes."

"Look at me when you say that. No fucking around now."

Finally in a position to utter a whole-hearted truth, Trudy lifted her head. "Yes, Lily, I *do* want to do well here."

"Fine." Lily reached into her purse and withdrew an enormous leather wallet. She tossed a card onto the girl's lap. "That's my AmEx. On your lunch today you go straight to Lord & Taylor and get what you need. I don't care about the price, just get something *right*. Sign my name and bring the receipts back, and I'll charge them to the department. Got it?"

"Lily, I—"

"Got it?"

Trudy picked up the credit card. "Yes, Lily."

"Okay. Now one last thing. *Why* didn't you follow my orders? About this wardrobe business?"

"Well," Trudy sat up straight. Here at last was a chance to deflect her boss' wrath on someone else. "I, uh … well, I asked Elaine about it."

Lily's eyes widened. "Is that so?"

"Yes. And, well … she said that it wasn't right to wear leather boots and miniskirts, even if some women do wear that stuff in business. She said it would just make us look … well, she didn't think it was right."

"What did she say it would make us look like?"

"No, Lily. I don't remember."

"Yes, you do. What did she say? Tell me."

"No, please, I really don't remember." Elaine said it would make the school look tacky and unprofessional, and to even suggest such a wardrobe for a rep made Lily the biggest dodo bird in admissions history.

"So you listened to Elaine and not to me."

"I'm sorry! I am, really! I shouldn't have, I know! It's just—"

"Oh shut up. Stay here. *I'm* going to have a little talk with Ms. Margolis." Lily strode to the door.

Trudy said, miserable that everything she told her boss was bad news, "She's not here. She's doing that high school presentation in Wayne since Joyce got the flu."

"Then I'll talk to her this afternoon."

"I don't think she's coming back today."

Poisonous silence. Trudy resisted curling up in the chair again. Lily stared murderously at the grainy tan of her closed office door. Her piled hair trembled.

"Stay here!" she barked. "I'm going to set some things straight once and for GODDAMMIT all!" She swung open the door with a velocity that blasted Trudy's black bangs, and made the steam from her unsipped coffee cup vanish.

One wall over, Oliver Dunbar had John Morris of ABCAA on the phone. The acronym stood for American Business College Accreditation Association, one of several nationally recognized agencies that monitored many educational institutions as well as all seventeen Burr colleges for quality control and regulatory compliance. John Morris was not only the finest walking library of academic regulations, he was an old friend, and he and Oliver had pooled each other's expertise for over ten years. Oliver held the latest ABCAA questionnaire and said, "I know what you're getting at, John, but we don't have any crimes enacted against students on this campus."

"Oh come on, dude. Not even a little petty theft? How about some pocketbooks stolen, or somebody's jacket."

"Surely that's not what they're asking for on this survey?"

"Oh, anything will do. It's just for your file. Your school doesn't get its accreditation renewed for another two years, and by then this'll all be forgotten. Meanwhile, somebody at Department of Ed is demanding that accreditors gather this data from every school they represent. So be a good boy and comply."

"Happy to," said Oliver. "We report crime stats for this school every year anyway. But I've never seen the survey ask for such a detailed breakdown. This is pretty extreme, even for you guys, don't you think—"

"Oliver, *hang up!*"

A flurry of red stripes, cleavage, and gleaming bronze hair filled his doorway.

Oliver put his hand over the phone. "Lily, one sec. I'm talking to the accreditors. Yes, John, what was that? No, something happened here—"

Lily lunged forward, grabbed the receiver with Oliver's hand still on it, and shoved it down on the cradle. "Tell me right now!" she shouted. "*Right now!* Whose department is Admissions?"

"Lily—what?"

"Whose department *is* it? It's an easy question!" She jerked a thumb at her chest. "I thought *I* was admissions director! That's what I interviewed for!" She raised an arm to the wall that separated their offices. "That's what it says on my goddamn *door!* So you tell me, *am* I the admissions director?" She crouched like a boxer, fists ready. "Well? *Tell me!*"

"What?" Oliver was dizzied by all the violent gestures. He couldn't comprehend that John Morris' voice was no longer in his ear.

"Because if I *am* admissions director then I assume I should be allowed to direct *Admissions!*" Lily stormed back and forth before his desk. "Make the decisions! Set some goddamn policies! Tell me if I'm stupid to think it works that way!"

"Of course you're in charge. Why would it be otherwise?"

"Then how come Elaine Margolis can undermine my authority?"

"What are you talking about? Of course Elaine can't—"

"She is! She is! *Grrr!*" Still pacing, Lily's hands throttled an invisible neck. Her lethal heels scored the carpet. "I gave some simple instructions to

Trudy, and Elaine *flat out* told her to disregard them! What is that, if not undermining?"

"Oh, that can't be right. Elaine's a professional."

"*Don't* give me that 'professional' crap! Elaine's a career woman! She's smart and she's got ambition! I know *all about* people like that! And she's been here longer than me, and believes she's better qualified for my job! She's trying to sabotage me!"

"Come now, Lily, you know that's not true."

She stopped pacing. Everything in the room seemed to drift. "Oliver, I don't make idle accusations."

"Lily, please," he said calmly but a little desperately. "I've worked with her for over four years. I can assure you with all confidence, Elaine is *not* trying to undermine your authority. It's unthinkable. Forget it."

Lily stared at him. Her anger dimmed, but her eyes grew cold and remote. She said flatly, "Okay, I see where the sympathies lie."

"Please, Lily, it's not that way—"

"Want me to pack up right now, Oliver? Is that it? I'll do it, you know. I don't need this shit."

No! *No!* Not after only two weeks! He couldn't face Bill Nostrand and tell him. He couldn't face another employment search. And the January sit would *die!*

"Lily, sit, please. Just tell me what happened. If something's wrong, we'll fix it. I'll support you, I promise. Please sit." He sweated until Lily, after much deliberation, finally took a chair. She didn't smile. Her hands laced together on her lap like a corset, and the balls of her feet pressed the carpet as if pushing a strong coil into the floorboards, a coil that might rocket her out of the chair again at any second.

"Two weeks ago I gave some selling advice to Trudy. Today when I asked her why she wasn't following my advice she said, to my profound astonishment, that Elaine told her to ignore me."

"Ignore what? I don't understand."

"Just some special advice on how to sell the new programs."

"New programs? What new programs?"

"Accounting, for one. We're going to start Accounting in January, for the evening school."

Oliver was completely baffled. "Wait a sec, Lily. I'm not following you. I never authorized that program."

She looked genuinely surprised. "Why, of course you did." She laughed a little. "You *must* have."

"No. Absolutely not." He shook his head, and his glasses slipped. "I don't like the Accounting Program. It's far from adequate to teach the material. I've said so to New York on several occasions."

"Huh." Lily looked perplexed. "Well, New York seems to think differently. Didn't you get the memo?"

"No. Did you?"

"Of course. Want me to show it to you?"

A queasiness pushed upward in Oliver's stomach. "Who sent it?"

"Bill, certainly."

"Bill Nostrand?"

She raised her hands. "Who else would?"

"Wha—wait a minute! Lily, what are you talking about? Does Dean Harris know about this? She hasn't discussed hiring a teacher for it."

"Really?" Lily laughed, more than a little surprised. "Well, if you don't mind my saying so, she should get cracking. New York's expecting an Accounting class in January. I already have three students signed for it."

"You *do?* For the—for the *Accounting Program?*" Blood rushed to Oliver's brain as if he were plunging in an elevator.

"It's not a difficult sell. A tuition cost of two thousand easily covered by a federal student loan. Meets three nights a week for six months, and students receive a certificate at the end."

"Yes, I know how it works. I wrote a six-page report years ago castigating the whole idea." The very memory stirred his panic. "Good gosh, Lily! Do they really think we're running that awful program?"

"Best of my knowledge, Oliver. I sure hope I haven't been recruiting for nothing." The admissions director chuckled, her dimples teasing.

"But ... but ... have you looked at the curriculum?" He swung sideways in his chair and pulled open a credenza drawer. His fingers walked over deteriorating files jammed in the overstuffed drawer. "It's a horrible syllabus. The Miami school originated it three years ago. It's not accounting, it's just glamorized bookkeeping. The text they use is kindergarten level. Our own two-year Executive Secretarial Arts Program uses a harder book. The lesson plan is simplistic and the assignments a joke. The whole thing is patently designed so the students can't fail."

"Really?" Lily was intrigued.

"Yes. Miami picked it up big time because the kids don't get discouraged, and the student loans cover the whole cost. Ever since then New York's wanted everybody to run it." He gave up looking for the file and shut the drawer.

"Oliver, maybe I'm a fool, but it all sounds rather shrewd to me."

"No!" He pushed up his glasses. The lines in his high forehead flexed harshly, and his jaw thrust forward with resolute authority. When it came to the education, he was still king. "The program is dishonest. The students learn how to add, subtract, multiply, and divide in neat columns on green ledger paper and nothing more. They can't get jobs afterward, certainly not as accountants."

"I see." Lily backed off a little, watching him closely. She was a little surprised, having written Oliver off during her first week as a quiet, well-intentioned mouse. Now she was actually seeing a little fire in the school director's veins, a flash of moral rectitude. She waited a moment to give it time to go away. "Oliver, let's be real. What do I know about academics? I run the Admissions Office. It's my job to sell the school's programs to interested applicants. I *know* I can sell this program. That's what I told Bill, and he was elated."

"Bill? You were talking to Bill Nostrand?"

"Of course. We got chatting one day, and he mentioned the Accounting Program and how he's been trying to get the schools to take it on, and I said I thought it would help break the sex barrier and get some male students into the school. I spoke very enthusiastically about it, Oliver, but of course at the time I didn't know you were so set against it. And really, I'm sure Bill's right when he says it won't be hard to place the grads, because they'll be able to say they're Burr College accountants. On a resume it'll look great!"

Oliver's face was white. "When did you talk to Bill?"

"Oh, I guess shortly after I came on board." Lily's answer was dismissively sweet. "He always calls the admissions directors. He *is* the executive in charge of recruitment. Really, Oliver, I'd suggest Dean Harris shake a stick and hire a teacher. And get Louise to order the books. Bill's expecting at least twenty in that class, and I've got three already. And little Trudy's interviewing another one this afternoon."

No! He couldn't let Nostrand get away with this. He had to nip this in the bud now, or who knew what else Bill would make them do? Oliver planted both hands firmly on the desk and said, "Lily, I'm *not* going to run that program. It's a travesty. It's a piece of crap."

"Miami runs it."

"The Miami Burr College has a difficult student demographic. They get a lot of immigrants who hardly understand English. They have to sell *any*thing to make their enrollment. I shouldn't be saying that, but it's true. We're not like that here."

Lily said dryly, "That's a brave stand in such tough times."

"Sorry, Lily. Some of us still care about the kids getting a good education."

She sighed. "Yes, I suppose. But surely, Oliver, the program can't be *that* horrible or New York would never approve it."

"You'd be surprised." Oliver glanced gloomily at his scattered correspondence. A cloud passed overhead outside, and the top of his desk turned a dull gray before his eyes.

A hand rested on his shoulder. Looking up, he was startled to find Lily standing very close. Her black eyes were soft and friendly. "Oliver, you've run no cheap programs all these years. For a little school in this day and age that's quite anachronistic. It's one of the reasons why you have such trouble making your yearly revenue goal. Why, you should know that it's the little programs that fill in the cracks. The big one- and two-year programs will always be our bread and butter, but these little programs, where the federal aid covers the whole cost so students bear no burden at all, are what keeps the profit line possible. This school is going under."

Her hand began to massage his shoulder, the very medicine he needed. Under its gentle caress he miserably conceded, "I know ..."

Lily stood behind him now, and worked his shoulders with both hands. "I can help you, Oliver. I can make your goals, and I'll fill your classrooms. I'll make your job so easy you'll begin to enjoy it again. All you'll have to do is make the teachers teach, Financial Aid finance, and Placement place. The rest I can handle."

He shut his eyes. Lily's fingers brought forth a delicious drowsiness. A light exotic scent surrounded them both, an aura of moist ferns and rich dark earth. What a strange perfume.

"Oliver, because of that failed September sit, the goal New York has set for January is virtually impossible. Yet I'm *telling* you I can make it. And I will."

"But ... but we can't just do it ... do it any old way ..."

Lily chuckled lightly. She leaned forward, her face close to his. The sugar-scented puff of her words brushed his cheek. "Oliver, I know it's integrity that makes the Burr College special. Your teachers are excellent and committed, and so is your staff. I can make your goals and still not lose sight of what we are. Don't I deserve a chance to show how well I can work for you?"

"All right. Okay. Thanks. Thanks for that." With heavy regret he straightened up. "I guess I'd better, uh … give Ethel a buzz. And I'd better thank you, Lily, for calling this to my attention. I appreciate it. Or wait—I'd better call Bill before I talk to Ethel. I want to know why I was never informed of this. And let me see a copy of the memo you got."

"I'll dig it out." Lily strolled around his desk and went to the door. "It's going to be good, Oliver. You know it is. We're going to be a remarkable team. Goodness, what a day this has been! And still so much to do, don't you know?"

*

That afternoon Trudy Weiser returned from lunch wearing a Versace leather miniskirt, gold cascade earrings, and knee-high calf boots with five-inch heels.

12

A company has 1,000,000 shares of stock at par value of .25/share to sell. A capital investment of $500,000 is made. How would you record this?

a. Debit stockholders' equity for $250,000, credit cash $250,000.
b. Debit stockholders' equity for $250,000, debit A.P for $250,000, credit cash for $500,000.
c. Debit cash $500,000, credit stockholders' equity $500,000.
d. None of the above.

Keone was in over her head. She stared at the test page, ten multiple-choice questions in the neat fussy scrawl of Mrs. Greenwald, her accounting teacher. She had no idea how to answer any of them. It was as if she hadn't studied, and she *had*, every night! Her scratch sheet was a jumble of equations merging into each other. This was a forty-minute quiz and the clock galloped; she could see the minute hand move. She glanced surreptitiously at her classmates. They were hunched over their quizzes and busily circling answers or pensively studying questions. Their faces were untroubled. It made her furious.

"Two minutes left," said Mrs. Greenwald, smiling from the front of the room. Keone circled anything.

"Okay. Pass 'em forward and have a nice weekend."

Everyone passed their sheets to the front row. Keone surrendered hers, grabbed her bookbag, and was one of the first out of the room. Scalded, she stomped down the stairs to the cafeteria in the basement.

She was getting killed in this place and knew it. Almost immediately after the first easy week the school work began to grow harder and more exacting, and she couldn't keep up. The English was confusing and humiliating. The other subjects, especially Cavanaugh's economics class, were hopeless. She hadn't taken a test yet where she scored better than a D. At Southwest she pulled A's and B's all the time. What the fuck was going on?

In the lunchroom she bought a candy bar from the vending machine and sat at a corner table to munch it. It was all the lunch she could afford. The rest of her class quickly trickled in. The girls chattered as they ordered from the lunch buffet, or opened the bag lunches they took from their lockers. No one sat at Keone's table until all the other tables were filled. Then two girls, Courtney and Rita, sat across from her. They spoke to each other without the slightest inclination of engaging the sullen black girl in the plain cotton dress.

Keone was scared. Her student loan check had come in, $1,250, more money than she had ever seen in her life, and Mr. Hurley made her sign the back of it, and then that mean Ms. Mallory put it directly in Keone's account to reduce the bill. It was money Keone would never get to use, yet when she graduated she'd have to pay it back. A similar check would come in the spring. Mr. Hurley sent her a notice recently awarding her a $2,340 Pell Grant and a $2,360 Pennsylvania State Grant, but all this money went—again!—right into the account, not a penny for Keone herself. At least she didn't have to pay the grants back. But the student loan was serious shit, because the bank would collect even if she dropped out, and while Keone didn't give a fuck about banks or bad credit, Mr. Hurley explained that not paying the loan would keep her from ever getting another, which meant no other school would accept her if she didn't do well here. Burr was her only shot, *and she was failing out of every motherfucking class! And nobody cared!* The teachers didn't, and her classmates—well, fuck *them*, they hardly spoke to her, and their clothes, all neatly pressed, good fabric, unscuffed shoes, how she hated them. Keone hadn't cried since she was a kid, but sitting at the lunchroom table, thinking about that quiz, ignored by the two girls across from her, she felt like crying now. She wouldn't, not in front of them, but … someplace. She wanted to scream and howl and claw something, but there was nothing to get her hands on. At home sometimes she hurled her books across the bedroom, but stopped doing that after realizing her father in the room next door might hear. Friends like Darcy rarely came to see her anymore. Dashiell she hadn't seen since he disappeared, months before she even thought about going to school. Coming to Burr was supposed to change her life, get her into something better. Instead, it had made her the loneliest person in the world.

Courtney broke off talking to Rita and said, "Excuse me, have you got a pen? I just need it for a sec, d'you mind?"

"Uh-uh." Keone dug a red pen with *Burr College of Business* inscribed on it from her bag, and gave it to the white girl.

"Thanks." Courtney jotted down a phone number as Rita dictated. She handed the pen back and Keone, with a feeling that she was somehow groveling, took a plunge.

"That's a beautiful dress."

Courtney immediately glanced at herself and smiled. "Thanks."

"You make it yourself?"

"Shit, no." Courtney laughed, flattered. "I don't know how to sew. No, I bought this at Nordstrom's. It was on sale for like a hundred and ten dollars. You can't pass up a steal like that."

The dress was a handsome yellow and blue print, all shiny silk, and Keone envied both its style and the girl's assured way of carrying it off. "Sure is pretty," she said slowly.

Courtney assessed Keone in return. Her look was friendly enough. "I'm really sorry, but what's your name again?"

"Keone."

"Where you from?"

"South Philly."

"Oh. Well, God, thanks for the compliment. And the use of the pen. Rita, do you think he'll be home tonight? Do you think he'll mind if I call?"

They resumed their talk, and Keone sat with them, alone, holding the pen. Keone watched them, then her gaze traveled the room to watch all her busy, happy classmates. Her eyes were dull and veiled. She hated them all.

13

Driving back from a high school presentation in Ardmore, her catalogs, applications, and T-shirts in three cardboard boxes on the rear seat of the VW Jetta she bought a year ago, Elaine made her way from City Line Avenue to the treacherous two-lane curves of the Schuylkill Expressway and eventually toward the skyscrapers and sunlit haze of noontime Center City. Boathouse Row and the Museum of Art reflected across the river like a serene foreign country of parks, culture, and healthy activity, a taunt to anyone trapped in a business suit, for Elaine's side of the river was congested traffic, cluttered Amtrak wires, and approaching office buildings. Elaine felt a hollow dread as she came in sight of the city skyline. It was sheer emotional physics. The closer she got to the school, the closer she was to Lily. Amazing how the addition of one new employee could erode four years enjoyment over coming to work.

Elaine didn't see herself as a rebel; she just believed Lily was dishonest with applicants, that what the woman called her "sales technique" was no more than petty trickery. Elaine didn't play that way. A successful admissions rep for Burr four years running, she was not about to change her style, and she had Oliver's assurance that he would never fire her. So Lily could stick her angry admonishments up her wazoo. The woman was dangerous because she could seriously wreck the school's image if not checked soon, but she was not a personal threat to Elaine.

The alley beside the school was just wide enough for a single car. Elaine lodged the Jetta there, and walked through the front door lugging the box of pamphlets. Julie, on the phone, merely waved. Elaine waddled the heavy box back to Deirdre's cubicle and dropped it on the desk.

"Hi, Elaine." Deirdre was sticking student names on file folders. "How was Ardmore?"

"Okay, once we got started. Dee, it's beautiful outside. You have lunch yet?"

"No, I like taking it late. Breaks up the afternoon."

"Well, would you consider having it early? Like with me right now?"

"Can't. I gotta get these labels done. And I'm supposed to send out notices to the students whose files still aren't complete. I'm just behind on everything. Besides, you've got a twelve o'clock."

Elaine stared at her. "Who says?"

"It's in the book. I saw it this morning."

"Wait a minute. It's twelve *now.* I've got appointments at one, two, and two-thirty. When the hell am I supposed to eat lunch?"

Deirdre said quickly, "Don't look at me. I didn't put it in."

"No, I'm sure." Elaine took a deep breath. "Christ. Okay."

She made a beeline to the lobby. The appointment book was maintained by the admissions secretary, but the day's page was always photocopied and kept up front for the receptionist to reference. "There it is," she muttered grimly, noting the entry on the page. She recognized Lily's handwriting.

Julie said, "Didn't you know about this?"

"Just learned of it now. When was this put in, this morning?"

"Yes. She took all the messages left last night by the answering service, and anybody who wanted an interview she parceled out. She had Deirdre and me confirm them all too."

Elaine couldn't help noticing that Lily's day was empty. "Is this Hannah Siegel here yet?"

"Not yet, but she's coming. She called from a Bristol gas station and said she was stuck in road construction. Guessed she'd be about a half hour late."

Elaine looked at the clock, which read 12:15. "It's nice of her to call."

"Yes, that's always a good sign."

Elaine permitted herself a sigh. Since no applicants were in the lobby, she sat on the corner of Julie's desk.

"Lily's been looking for you," Julie began.

"Don't mention her right now, okay? I'm attempting a little sanity preservation here."

"Okay." But since they were friends, Julie asked gently, "How bad is it between you two?"

The senior rep looked at her and said nothing.

"Elaine, you can't hide tension in this place. We all know by now what Lily is like."

But Elaine didn't think so. She believed she was the only one who really knew. She witnessed Lily outright lying to applicants, inflating the starting salaries of Burr grads, downplaying the difficulty of the curriculum, and poo-pooing the cost. She saw her on the phone daily, chatting with that Nostrand guy in New York, or taking two-hour lunches to get her hair or nails done, or to do some quick shopping at Lord & Taylor. Elaine, who in the beginning was cordially invited to join her on these excursions, got to watch Lily quaff a lot of martinis too, sometimes to the point where by the afternoon the woman's hands trembled as they gripped her perpetual cups of coffee. Elaine saw these things, but didn't think anyone else did. Lily had the instincts of a cat, and was adept at hiding evidence whenever facing applicants or Oliver. Elaine could even admire the skill involved, but she had to report to this woman, and her own upbringing and Burr training made her writhe at such unprofessional behavior. Elaine ached to tell someone—especially someone down to earth and sensible like Julie—but couldn't. She kept her mouth shut, and prayed quietly for the day when Lily would slip.

"What's she want me for now?"

"I think about an envelope of lead cards. Like fifteen leads you brought in yesterday from Great Valley High School. You remember?"

"Of course. What about them?"

"Well, Lily had to get her lead numbers together first thing, and she said you told her you would give her the Great Valley cards. When she didn't find them in her in-basket this morning she got all pissed."

"Oh for God's sake. I never told her that. The cards don't go to her. They go to Deirdre so she can input them in the computer. That's how we do it, that's how we've always done it. Lily knows that."

"Well, you may have to explain it to her again. She was charging around like an angry rhino all morning."

"The woman's crazy. Give Deirdre a buzz. I'll bet you a paycheck she's already entered them in the computer. Go ahead."

Julie punched Deirdre's intercom button. "I don't take the bet."

The intercom beeped. "Deirdre."

"Dee, this is Julie. Do you have an envelope of lead cards from Great Valley High School that Elaine dropped off yesterday afternoon?"

"Wait a sec. Sure do. They're already in the system. Why? What's up?"

"Nothing. Lily just didn't know where they were."

"Oh. Well, they're right here. Want me to buzz her?"

"No, don't bother. Elaine'll let her know." Julie punched off the intercom. "So you think Lily's a crazy woman, eh?"

Elaine hesitated. "She and I just have different views on how to sell a school, I guess."

"I can tell you firsthand that Oliver admires you enormously. You don't have to worry about anything on that front."

"I know. He told me too, which was sweet of him. But I wish he'd bring *her* into line."

"He does what he can." Julie, saying this, seemed to know.

Elaine frowned thoughtfully. "Actually, in some ways I can sympathize with Lily. She's running scared. There's no way in hell we're going to make the January sit, and it's all going to fall on her head."

"Well, maybe that'll solve your problem. If she fails in January, New York might replace her."

"No. They don't give them much rope, but they give them more than that. Usually about a year's worth of bad sits. I've been here four years now, and I've watched three admissions directors come and go. I outlasted them, I'll outlast Lily."

Julie chuckled. "Now I know why you didn't apply for the position yourself, last summer when it was open. I know Oliver hoped you would."

"It's a hot seat, Jule. I'm not that stupid."

At that moment the carpet vibrated, and both women looked up. Lily strode in from the cubicles. "Oh, you're here now. Good. I had to plug a twelve o'clock on you today. I hope you don't mind. There wasn't any other time the girl could come."

"Fine, Lily." Elaine decided not to get off Julie's desk.

"I do feel bad about it. I know this means you'll miss lunch."

Julie picked up the calendar page. Uninvited, she said, "Lily, actually you're clear all day."

Lily stared at the secretary. Her vivid black eyes hardened, then the faint lines in their corners slowly crinkled. "Yes, but I'm afraid I have several reports to put together. Now—" she faced the rep, "I must take you to task regarding a different matter. Yester—"

"The Great Valley lead cards are in the system."

"Pardon me?"

"Deirdre has the cards." Elaine glanced at Julie. "Didn't she say they were already in the computer?"

"Yes," said the secretary.

Lily looked from one to the other. Her square chin pushed forward like a shield. "How do you know?"

"We asked her."

"Oh. Well, why didn't you give them to me?"

"Because that's not how it's done, Lily. Deirdre has to load them first into the computer. That's how we produce the mailing labels for each applicant, and how she draws the figures for your weekly reports. Then she gives them to you."

"I see. And how long has this policy been in effect?"

"For about twelve years. Ever since we got the computer."

Lily took a slow step back, keeping her eyes on the senior rep. "Well, good then. That's good to know. Is your twelve o'clock here?"

"No. But she called to say she's still coming."

"You have a one and two o'clock as well."

"And a two-thirty. I know, Lily."

Lily turned to leave, then suddenly stopped. "Oh, one more thing. Trudy has a student taking the admissions test in your office. She just started, and it'll take ninety minutes. So you won't be able to interview in there."

Caught off guard, Elaine blurted, "But Lily, I can't interview without an office! What am I supposed to do? Why is she taking a test in my office in the first place?" She slid off Julie's desk as if pushed.

Dimples wreathed Lily's dark, beautiful face. "Obviously this sort of thing is going to happen from time to time. One thing we do not have at this school is surplus space. There were no empty classrooms available at this hour, and she has to take the test in a private area with a closed door so she won't be distracted. You wouldn't want her to take the test out among the secretaries with all their bustle and phone calls, would you?"

"So what do you think I should do?" Elaine's face was taut with anger.

"Maybe nobody's in the library," Lily shrugged. "If so, you can interview there. Now, I've got to get back to work." The admissions director strode briskly through the cubicles, causing various fliers thumbtacked to the partitions to flutter in her wake.

A graveyard silence encompassed the lobby. The phone rang, and Julie took a message. She dropped the pink note in the dean's slot on the message rack.

Elaine puckered ruefully. "Notice how she doesn't say my name anymore?"

"What are you going to do?"

"I don't know. But the library at this time of day gets the sun baking through the south windows. And those windows don't open. It'll be an inferno in there. You can't expect an applicant to come away with a good impression."

"You think Lily knows that?"

"I have no doubt." Elaine looked past the cubicles to the admissions director's half-closed door. "Right this minute she's sitting in there, swilling coffee and having the best time thinking about me interviewing in the library at this time of day. *Wait a minute!*" She turned on Julie with wide eyes. "This is noon!"

"So?"

"So most of the classes are at lunch! There are *plenty* of free classrooms for someone to take a test!"

Another long silence. Elaine puckered her lips again. "I guess that's two for her, one for me."

Julie said delicately, "You think Lily knows about the classrooms?"

Elaine shrugged. "Is Oliver in?"

"Going to complain?"

"No. Is he?"

"Sure. Go on through."

Elaine walked past the cubicles and stood in Oliver's doorway. He sat at his desk writing on a yellow pad, or trying to—his hand with the pen kept soaring up to conduct the rising crescendos of a Tchaikovsky symphony playing on the radio. Elaine knocked on the doorframe. When he saw her he smiled, and reached to lower the volume. "Elaine, hi. How was Ardmore?"

"Fine. Can I ask a big favor?"

"Sure."

"I hate to ask, but it's a real problem. I've got a twelve o'clock and a one, and Lily's allowed Trudy to give the admissions test to an applicant in my office, which ties it up effectively for the next hour and a half. And I can't use the library because at this time of day it'll be a kiln."

Oliver frowned. "Why are they using your office for a test?"

Poker-faced, Elaine said, "According to Lily there was no other room for her to take it."

"No, that's not correct. At this time of day there are plenty of empty classrooms."

"Maybe you should tell her that."

Oliver looked puzzled. He quickly assessed the work on his writing pad. "Okay. I'm just jotting up some memos, anyway. I can do it in the faculty lounge."

"Thanks, Oliver. This is greatly appreciated."

Elaine returned to the lobby where a small woman in a tan blouse and blue jeans sat stiffly in one of the overstuffed chairs. Her face was narrow and serious, her long brown hair tied back by a red hair band.

Julie said, "Elaine, your twelve is here."

Elaine smiled and held out her hand. "Hannah? I'm Elaine Margolis. Very pleased to meet you."

The woman stood anxiously. "Hi. I'm so sorry to be late."

"That's okay. These things happen. It was wonderful of you to call us. Not many do."

"If I'm way too late, I'll reschedule another time."

"No. I do have someone coming at one, but she's interested in the same program you are, so maybe we can combine your tour with hers. We'll work it out, don't worry. It'd be silly for you to go home and come back again. Julie, we'll be interviewing in Oliver's office."

The secretary's brows raised appreciatively. "Oh? Where will he be?"

"In the faculty lounge. He said it was okay."

"Does Lily know?"

"No. But she will. Maybe it'll signal something to her."

Julie grinned. "It will if she's smart."

Elaine said to her applicant, "Why don't you take a moment and fill out the application form? Then I'll take you back and we'll talk. Okay?"

Elaine returned to Oliver's office just as he came out, clutching his pad and a can of club soda. "Hi. I'm out of your way as of now."

"Just wanted to say thanks again, Oliver."

"No trouble. If we're good at anything, it's self-sacrifice. Say, listen to me a second, Elaine."

She looked at him.

"I know there are some personality conflicts between you and Lily. I'm not asking you to rat on her, but still—in general is everything okay with you?"

"Yes."

"It is? Will you ever tell me if it's not?"

"I will."

"Okay. You're not a complainer, Elaine. That's very noble, and I admire you for it. But it also means you can get walked on. Don't let that happen."

"I won't."

"You're too important to us. Good luck with the interview."

He smiled and walked away. Elaine watched him go, then went into his office feeling good about herself for the first time in weeks.

14

On Halloween the college was invaded by witches, goblins, hobos, firemen, belly dancers, black cats, Playboy bunnies, doctors, nurses, convicts, football players, soldiers, human-sized toothpaste tubes, candy, and walking abstract art. Disguise was not limited to students. Julie Fitzgerald at the reception desk answered phones in a tawny lioness outfit, and Jessica Harrelson answered placement calls in the rags and shawl of a gypsy. Natalie Spicoli, the dean's secretary, was dressed as a bride, Deirdre Smith a white-sheeted ghost, and David Hurley modestly masked as a burglar. The teachers too: Donna Harding's chic professional image shattered by a dazzling red and blue clown suit with big pompom buttons, frilly wig, white grease paint, and rubber nose. Until she spoke no one knew who she was. Jean Cavanaugh, as if to mock her own reputation, dressed as a witch with a green face, long warted nose, black hat and cape. She astonished her class by cackling maniacally, and flourished a broomstick instead of her usual blackboard pointer.

Dean Harris patrolled the halls as an austere Marine drill sergeant, complete with hat, baton, holster, and pin with her name on it. This blatant symbol of her authority traumatized the students, who already understood Ethel as the grim, imposing dean, a tall black woman who chewed out offending pupils with the sharp-tongued voice of God, and who rated their hard-earned progress in clipped, withering reports every three months. Ethel intended the costume to amuse the students, but in reality it only increased their awe of her.

She peeked into the faculty lounge, crowded with lunch trays and cookies and sodas for the party at three. Arthur Cassidy, clad once more in a turned-around collar and black cassock, sat with Bob Lawrence at a table in heated discussion. Bob looked bizarre and ethereal in white suit and vest, foaming white wig, and white bushy eyebrows and mustache that gave him just the right fanatical look.

"Well, well, Father Cassidy and Mark Twain, I do believe. Gentlemen, I am impressed."

Both men laughed openly at the sight of her. Bob said, "Ethel, I thought you were coming in costume today."

"Well," Ethel grinned and straightened the stiff brim of her hat, "I thought I might have to put some of the girls on KP after the party, and this was probably the best way to make them agree."

Arthur said, "This is why your sons do everything you tell them."

"Oh don't I wish. If I thought wearing this would get them to mind me, you'd never see me out of it."

"Where did you get that uniform anyway?"

"My boyfriend. He's a minister in Mount Airy."

"Colorful guy," Arthur murmured.

Ethel's good humor suddenly disappeared. Her face assumed its more familiar hardness. "Well, this is nothing compared to Lily Espirito. Have either of you seen her?"

"No. What's she got on?"

"Not much. Frankly, I'm embarrassed. She shouldn't have been allowed in the school."

"Well, it's Halloween," said Bob, leaning back and stretching. "A lot of questionable things are okay today. Have you seen Carol Sobolewski yet? She's in a nun's habit with a pillow stuffed under her waist so she looks pregnant. Don't get me wrong, all the girls are laughing. But when you think how highly Catholic our student population is, you might wonder if that's good taste too."

"Lily's just … oh, never mind." Ethel shook her head. "We all know what Lily's like, don't we? Anyway—" She turned cheerful again. "Bob, I want to confirm with you—we're replacing your eleven o'clock with Jean's economics class. She still wants them to take their test, and if the party's at three she'll have to cancel. Natalie got that info to you, didn't she?"

"Sure. I don't mind. It means I get a free period. But that's particularly heartless, don't you think? A test on Halloween? Jean has no mercy." Bob's face twitched, as if about to sneeze from the hairy mustache.

"Oh, and before I forget, would one of you elegant gentlemen help judge costumes this afternoon?"

Arthur said, "I'd be happy to, but a lot of these young ladies' costumes are fairly revealing. I think Carol has given Catholicism enough of a pasting today without the resident ex-priest ogling the contestants."

"Mr. Clemmons?"

"Sure."

"Great. Three o'clock then. Bob, that's a terrific costume. When you glare and thrust your chin like that, you look just like him."

"Good. Tell my students, will you? They all think I'm Colonel Sanders."

Ethel continued down the hall, feeling the fresh holiday laxness in the air. Her businesswoman's stride, with its practiced bravado, fit the imposing uniform perfectly. Each time a student passed she saluted, and sometimes they laughed and sometimes they just stared with open mouths. Ethel loved it.

She strolled deep into the lobby before spotting a young man seated on the couch with a blue admissions application across his lap. This unexpected encounter with an applicant halted Ethel, for on principle she preferred new people to see the college at its professional best. There was nothing to do now except brazen it through. She marched swiftly to the receptionist's desk.

"Is Louise in?" She felt the young man staring, and fought to suppress a smile.

Julie snapped erect in her chair. "Ma'am, yes, *ma'am!* She's in her office, *ma'am!*"

"At ease, Fitzgerald. Thanks."

The phone rang, and Julie reached for it. She had to bend aside her left whiskers to hold the receiver close. "Burr College of Business. How may I help you?" Ethel left her.

The secretaries went through distracted motions of work in their cubicles, quite a surreal sight. Deirdre was dwarfed in her ghost sheet. Trudy stood beside her in a billowing blue Cinderella gown. Natalie, in white dress and veil, was a round-faced bride frowning over academic transcript cards. In her corner cubicle sat Louise Mallory dressed as, of all things, a gunslinger. Her narrow frame was clad in a fringed brown leather vest and skirt, with a yellow kerchief around her wattled throat. A holster supported a pistol on either hip. Ethel burst into laughter, unable to help it, and from under the brim of a black Stetson Louise's square spectacles glared.

"Why Louise, you've donned your new collections outfit, I see."

"I thought about that. Unfortunately the guns are fake."

"Jesus, Mary, and Ralph. Somebody should do a psychological study on the costumes people choose for this crazy holiday. I hear Oliver's Julius Caesar, I've *seen* Lily Espirito, and here you are brandishing six-shooters."

"I'm sure it's been done," grunted Louise. She lifted an inch-thick stack of invoices and jammed them viciously on a large spindle. "But if you're coming to work dressed like that, Ethel, you'll be the first for analysis."

"What do you think of Lily's costume?"

Louise laughed scornfully. "I think it's the funniest thing to hit this school in years."

"I don't find it amusing at all. I think it's atrocious."

"Well, we all know the school's going downhill." Louise reached for her cup of black smelly tea. "Nobody said we had to do it with dignity."

Ethel let that sink in. "Oh well," she said at last.

"Oh well."

"Listen, I wanted to ask if you'd be the other judge this afternoon. I've got Bob Lawrence already. That would make one faculty member and one staff member. There should be a third, I suppose, but I can't think of another faction to pick from."

"The secretaries?"

"No. They're all too chummy with the kids. You and Bob won't cause any hard feelings."

"What's the prize?"

"I'm embarrassed to say. A one hundred dollar gift certificate to Victoria's Secret."

"My, we *are* a patron of the female mind." Louise curled her lips, less than thrilled. "Okay. As long as I've got to be there anyway."

"Great. That finishes my one duty for today."

In the lobby, the young male applicant on the couch recrossed his legs and watched the costumed women flitting past the glass doors that led to the hall. He looked at the receptionist in her lioness outfit and suspected that she was probably pretty sexy under that tan fuzz. She caught him looking at her, and he laughed. "I didn't expect you all to look like this."

Julie smiled. "It's for Halloween, of course. Normally we're quite a staid old-fashioned business school. You're just applying on the wildest day of the year."

"Oh, I like it. It gives the place personality."

"It's a great school, Mr. Davis. May I ask where you're from?"

"Havertown. Melrose Street. I want to get in the Evening Accounting Program. I was shooting for a degree in the social and behavioral sciences, but I think I'd better take some business classes. I have to become more marketable."

"Certainly."

"My fiancé wants … well, frankly I'm not sure she'll *stay* my fiancé if I don't get a good job soon."

"I see. Well, good luck to you."

"Thanks." He laughed, thinking what a pretty lion she made.

And then a soft voice said, "Pardon me?"

"Yes?" He looked around, and all thoughts of the lioness went away for good. Before him stood an exotic jungle queen in a leopard-print dress so small and clinging it nearly stopped his heart. The skirt's hem barely covered the woman's crotch, and was cut at a diagonal so that the skirt covered the upper half of her right thigh while leaving her entire left hip naked. Her bare legs were pedestalled on spiked high heels patterned with leopard spots. The flimsy upper portion of the dress barely contained the woman's bulging breasts, and was held up by a single thin strap over her right shoulder. To complete the jungle effect, a necklace of shark's teeth ringed her throat, and a bracelet of plastic green grass stems encircled one ankle. Her gold and bronze hair was sprinkled with glitter dust.

"You must be Harry Davis. I'm Lily Espirito, admissions director."

"That's right, yes. That's me." He stood so fast his head dizzied. She squeezed his hand shaking it, and he took in large oval eyes and mischievous dimples. Her nose was a little wide and her lips very full, and he suspected some Spanish in her, or Mexican maybe. She flashed him a stunning smile.

"Now you're interested in what?"

"The Evening Accounting Program, ma'am."

"Oh yes, of course." The black eyes gleamed affectionately. "Goodness me! Will you step into my office?"

"You bet."

She turned to lead him back. As she strode briskly before him the raised side of the short skirt exposed her entire left buttock, a clear view of smooth naked skin that shocked and flustered him. He wondered if she realized it. He couldn't think of a way to tell her that wouldn't embarrass her. His own walk was guarded; he felt his carriage melting. She held her office door open and he stepped through ahead of her. The door banged loudly when she shut it.

"Dee said you're taking classes at Temple." Ms. Espirito laughed with wonderful high-pitched melody. "I approve right off! That's my alma mater!"

"Yeheheh," Davis said, to his horror.

She motioned him to a chair, then with a girlish hop seated herself on the front edge of her desk, so that she sat a little above him and quite close. "I know this is kind of ridiculous," she said in a singsong voice tempered with embarrassment, "but it's Halloween. We're throwing a big party for the staff, faculty, and students this afternoon. Obviously this isn't my normal work dress."

"You look fantastic."

"It's all in fun, you know. The girls really get into dressing up. I've seen the most darling costumes today. You're certainly observing first hand that the Burr College isn't all stuffy pomposity. You *have* to have fun with your work, don't you think, Mr. Davis?"

"Sure." He gave her his most winning smile.

"I know I always need a little fun. Fun keeps the pipes clean! Ha! Ha!"

Harry Davis nodded, and his smile gathered strength. Off balance he may have been at first, but now he recognized that this was as great a moment as he might ever know, close and alone with this beautiful creature. Jesus *Christ*, what a body! Perched on the desk, her hands holding its edge on either side, the Burr College head of admissions hit him in great frontal globes; she was all breasts, knees, and calves. She crossed her legs, and her raised foot with the little bracelet of grass stems absently tapped the air.

"Mr. Davis, the value of a Burr education cannot be measured by mere tuition. The Burr name will automatically open doors for you. You'll have access to the highest strata of corporate business. You'll have a guaranteed secure future. Burr graduates are valued for their depth of knowledge, superlative skills and boundless integrity." She picked up his application. "You live in Havertown, I see."

"Yes."

"And you're what? Twenty-six?"

He had to think. "Yes."

"You're a graduate of Archbishop Prendergast High School, and currently you're enrolled at Temple."

"That's right."

"Mr. Davis, our best students come from Archbishop Prendergast. I don't know why, nobody's ever done a survey, but it seems to be the case."

"Really? I wonder why."

"Who knows? Some things just *are!*" She laughed and shrugged, teetering a little on the desk edge. Her crossed legs lifted slightly, less than three feet from his face. "Now you've already taken some algebra and geometry. And I don't want to dismiss those Latin credits. My goodness! I can't believe the background you've put together for yourself!"

He laughed nervously. "Do you think so? 'Cause I always felt it was kind of unfocused. My fi—a friend of mine said I'm lacking in direction."

"Oh, your friend must not be in academia, Harry. I've seen a lot of applicants in my day. You have to trust me to spot the Cadillacs."

"A Cadillac, huh?" He grinned. He was beginning to notice that although Ms. Espirito kept her lovely legs crossed, she seemed unable to settle comfortably on the desk. She talked with unbroken ease about the program, yet every time their eyes met she would shift slightly, as if something disturbed her in there where her bare thighs were squeezed together. He didn't think she realized she was doing it. She smiled innocently and continued to talk only business, but he wondered if he was right in reading something more in this. A plea for action from him. Something she eagerly awaited. The oldest challenge in the world. He wished he could be sure.

"You just need that little bit of gloss the Burr College can provide. It *is* gloss, but it's vital to you. You're going to be more marketable than you ever dreamed! Ha! Ha!"

"You think so?"

"Oh yes! Oh *yes!*" She rocked happily on the desk. "The people who graduate from the January IP program get all the best salaries. We have one student who—"

"Whoa, wait! What did you say?"

"The January IP Program." Her smile gleamed with Amazonian red lipstick. "It's our information processing class. Frankly, it's the best program we have, Harry. You'll—"

"No, no," he said quickly. "I'm not here for the—what you just said. I'm here for the Accounting Program."

She looked confused. "Accounting?"

"Yes."

"Oh." Ms. Espirito seemed taken aback. "I'm sorry, I didn't realize." She looked down at her lap.

"Are you all right?" he asked anxiously.

"Yes. I just—well, I have to tell you, Harry, I think you're making a mistake. You shouldn't be in the Accounting Program."

"No?"

"No. With your qualifications you belong in the January IP Program. That's where I want to see you."

"That's the full-time day program, right?"

"Yes. It only costs $9,125, but what you get—"

The amount was just big enough to pierce his reverie. "Huh? Oh no, I can't afford that, Lily." There! He had braved her first name. If he was right about her body language, then she wouldn't be offended. The room felt oppressively hot, and forced his lungs to push harder for their quota, but the rush that filled his head was also … what was her word? *Fun!*

"But Harry," she looked up at him eagerly, "it's an investment you're making. You—"

"I'm sure," he said gently, even ruefully, "but I don't have that kind of money. I just haven't got it."

She looked down at her lap again. "I see."

"Lily, I'm serious. I really don't have it. I'm sorry."

"It's all right."

He began to panic. "Well look, I shouldn't talk out of hand. You know your job better than me."

"No, Harry." Her voice was a whisper. "I certainly can't tell you what to do."

"Look, I jumped the gun there. If you don't think accounting's for me, I should listen to you."

She didn't look up.

"Please, Lily, tell me about it."

"Well, but you're right," she conceded miserably. "It *is* a little more expensive than the Accounting Program. Oh, but *Harry!*" She faced him with glistening eyes. "You come away with so much more! More training, a better known program that so many of our employing companies are familiar with, and a much better salary! I truly believe that your full potential won't be reached in that puttery little Accounting Program. Your qualifications for the other are just *too good!*"

"You think so?"

"Oh, I know it! Ha! Ha! Ha!" Ms. Espirito threw back her head and laughed. Her lips gleamed. Her left breast nearly jiggled out of its sling. Her crossed knees lifted, affording him another astonishing view of her bare left buttock. Harry stared helplessly.

"You are definitely over-qualified," she declared, awestruck.

"Well, but I'm not sure I can afford that tuition—"

"Oh, anything good *sounds* expensive until you look into it. We have a financial aid officer who's a crackerjack at getting aid to students who need it. I'm sure you'd qualify."

"But isn't that mostly loans? See, I can't—"

"It's not all loans. You'll get some grants too, you'll see. Listen, why don't we take a tour of the school? Just you and me."

"A tour?"

"Sure! Let me show you what we have to offer. You'll see the equipment, you'll see the dedication of the faculty, you'll see this is precisely the career track you need for a satisfying and lucrative future. When you study at Burr, you know, you're not just a secretary, you're one of the elite!" She laughed again, then teasingly winked at him. "And you'll also get an idea of all the cute girls you'll be sitting with. Ha! Ha! Ha!"

"I'll bet they can't hold a candle to a beautiful lady like yourself."

It was a bold thrust and it worked. Ms. Espirito blushed and looked down. "Oh Harry! Oh *my!* Isn't that sweet!" She turned away to hide her face. Harry Davis' soul sang; he reached in his jacket pocket for his checkbook. He didn't dare say no to this.

"What do you need for now?" he asked.

"A hundred and twenty-five," said the admissions director. "For starters."

Elaine Margolis walked through the front door to the lobby, dressed in her regular business suit because she was returning from another high school presentation. Julie quickly waved her over with the knife she used to open the mail.

"What's up?"

"Hold on. Let me buzz Natalie." Julie did so. "Nat, can you take the front desk for fifteen minutes? I promised the dean I'd help lay out the food. Thanks."

Elaine stepped closer. "Something's happening, I can tell. What's up?"

Julie glanced tactfully toward yet another male applicant seated on the couch, a heavily built teenage boy with thick round glasses and a barely realized pencil mustache. He idly flipped through last year's yearbook. Natalie trundled clumsily to the desk in her long wedding gown, tugging a floppy train behind her.

"Holy moly," said Elaine. "Congratulations! Why didn't you let us know?"

"You like it?" Natalie's big smile glowed through her veil. "It's Mom's."

"Nice to see it getting some use."

"Oh, she's given it use."

Natalie settled gingerly at the front desk, and Julie practically pulled the senior rep back among the cubicles. "I couldn't talk in front of the applicant," she said, keeping her voice low. "Elaine honey, you're gonna love Lily today."

"Oh God, what now?"

"No, I won't tell you. You'll have to see for yourself."

"Jesus Christ." Elaine turned to the little admissions secretary. "Dee, that *is* you under that sheet, isn't it?"

"Sure is. Boo."

"Any interview activity today?"

"Sure. All excellent."

"Excellent? Watch it, Dee, you don't drop that word casually around here."

But Deirdre held up the appointment book. "No, look at this. Nine interviews for Lily today. All male applicants. She's had seven in so far, and she's gotten the app fee and full tuition deposit from every one of them."

"Oh that can't be!" Elaine grabbed the book. "Nobody has a record that good."

"She had the whole thing planned," Deirdre explained eagerly. "Some of these guys expressed an interest in the school as far back as a month ago. But instead of scheduling appointments right away, she made me save them up and stick them on the calendar for today. Told me it was a little trick she learned at the cosmetics school."

"Trick?" Elaine looked at Julie. "What the hell is she doing?"

Julie said, "I'm not telling. It'll be more fun watching you discover for yourself. History's being made here today. See you at the party." She turned away, grabbed her lion's tail, twitched it back and forth at them, and sauntered off.

"This whole place is nuts," Elaine said.

In his office, Oliver tried to primp his bed sheet toga into proper senatorial shape using his limited reflection in the glass covering a print of Renoir's *Two Sisters*. A silly crown of green plastic leaves, bought at a theatrical store, rested on both gray temples. A harsh knock jarred his concentration. "Yes?"

Ethel Harris stormed in. She slammed the door behind her so hard it swung back open, and Oliver braced for the worst. "We have to talk!"

"Of course, Ethel. What about?"

"What everyone is talking about! What the whole damn school is talking about! Your admissions director!"

He closed his eyes. "Don't."

"Have you seen her? Have you seen what she's wearing?"

"Yes, I've seen it."

"And you let her get away with it?"

"Sit down."

"No, I'm too fired up!"

So Oliver sat, dropping on his desk chair with a sigh and glancing out the window. A lot of strollers were being pushed through Washington Square, mostly by black women although the babies were white. The leaves were rich with autumn color.

"Ethel, she's just doing her job," he began.

"Her *job,* Oliver! Go to hell! She's crass! She's shameless! Worse, she's destroying everything sacred we try to teach these girls! We teach them they can be successful with their brains, not their bodies, and we tell them to insist on the same professional respect that men receive. And then that … that woman in plain view of everybody prostitutes herself—"

"Ethel, hold it right there—"

"I will not—"

"Yes you WILL!" he barked. They were both startled when she shut up. "It's just Halloween," he said lamely. "It's the costume she chose, nothing more."

"Don't act stupid with me. You don't believe that. I don't care how you defend her, I know in your heart you don't like what she's doing."

He pushed up his glasses and rubbed his eyes. "All right." He yanked a thick manila folder from the stack on his desk. "Come over here. Let me show you something."

"What am I looking at?"

"It's the President's Office report telling me what the goal for January is. Originally it was sixty students. Because of September they've almost tripled the stakes. We now have to seat one hundred and sixty-two students."

"Jesus, Mary, and Ralph!" Ethel exploded. "We've never sat more than sixty students for January in all the years we've run the program!"

He eyed her coolly. "How about that?"

"New York's crazy!"

"New York *is* crazy. That goal is impossible. I know it, and you know it. Whether Lily knows it, I can't be sure. She probably does, she's extremely intelligent even if her colleagues don't want to admit it. But she's telling me she can do it. She's the only person left with any faith, Ethel. The only one."

Oliver flipped a page, which showed budget figures in three clean columns. "The way revenue is distributed, we lost half of our year-end income when we failed that September sit. Bill Nostrand has informed me that if we fail to sit one hundred and sixty-two students in January he'll make us cut staff. That's something we've never done. Don't you see? We have to get over this hump. One way or another, we *have* to."

Ethel chewed her lip. "So what happens to our reputation, Oliver?"

"I truly believe, Ethel, that at this point the only way the college can keep its reputation is for New York to close us. It's the only *respectable* option left."

"So now we trick students into coming to school, and we get them to sign up for all the wrong reasons? Oliver, what's going to happen to them? I mean, hooray we get to stay open, but what about them? They're paying thousands of dollars, and they're trusting us to do well by them."

"The students ..." Oliver began morosely. He tried to think of a way to finish the sentence. He looked up and saw Julie standing in the doorway.

"Hi. Sorry to interrupt. The party's started, and the dean and director are conspicuously missing."

"See you down there." Ethel strolled out. Julie stepped into the office.

"How much of that did you hear?" Oliver asked.

"Most of it. I'm sorry. I guess if staff got cut I'd be first to go, wouldn't I? I've got the least seniority."

He stared at her. The possibility shocked him. He hadn't thought it through that far. Trudy Weiser was the most recently employed, but she was an admissions rep. Bill Nostrand would expect him to cut a secretarial position first.

"It's not worth getting into now," he said quickly. He couldn't imagine running the school without Julie.

"Oliver, you look so tired."

"That's because I'm not a school director anymore. I'm a businessman. I used to think only about helping students get the best education they wanted. I can't afford to do that anymore." He rubbed his eyes again, digging deeply. "Education is so important, Julie. It should be above money, don't you think? It shouldn't be subservient to making a profit."

She took his arm. "Come and eat."

"You're a hell of a lioness, Julie."

"Well, I'll treasure that. A compliment from the Emperor himself."

Director and secretary, Roman emperor and lioness, walked down the corridor to the Halloween party in the student lounge. Happy clamor rose from the staircase as they descended. The lioness kept a hand on the arm of the emperor, and the emperor, in a cloud of numbers, students, and dire presidential edicts, seemed more than content to let it stay there.

15

Oliver walked out of Penn Station via Madison Square Garden and strolled north along the Avenue of the Americas. It was mid-November and the street blazed with Christmas glory. The intricate works of commercial art in the shop windows of the big department stores: animated elves and Santas amidst diamond necklaces and fur coats, was all of holiday New York at a glance. The city to Oliver meant, as it did to any city dweller whose city was *not* New York, crowds, immeasurable wealth, commerce, unseen crime, and celebrity. And to one outside city dweller at least, it meant Tina. Only here was an irony, for this was his first trip to Manhattan in months and she was off in Brooklyn somewhere for a two-day shoot. When she told him this, a week ago, she cursed and apologized, and Oliver still couldn't believe it himself.

The President's Office of the Burr Colleges of Business was housed on the forty-third floor of a massive office building on 54th and Sixth Avenue. Oliver was a bug walking through the lobby. The security guard gave him a bored look. The elevator rocketed past the first twenty floors before it began to count.

In the reception room he was greeted by Eloise Mahwat, Nostrand's secretary. "Hello, Dr. Dunbar," she said in a soft Pakistani accent. "Mr. Nostrand is expecting you."

"How are things with you, Eloise?"

"Very fine. Would you like some coffee?"

"Is Bill having any?"

"Not at the moment."

"Well, maybe later then. Thank you."

Walking through the cluster of offices, he got the feeling he always did when he came here: that the President's Office was just a Burr College without students. With the exception of an accounting and promotional department—both behind glass partitions—and a computer team located on a different floor, each office represented corresponding departments found at each of the schools. Andy Abrams was executive business coordinator (Louise's corporate boss), Abby DeSalvo the executive dean (Ethel's), Lisa O'Toole the executive of placement (Clara's), and Lana Kaufmann the executive director of financial aid (David Hurley's), who also monitored all regulatory matters. There was, however, no executive director of admissions. That position had merged with the office of the vice-president of operations two years ago when Bill Nostrand signed on. The CEO, crafty old John Coyne, wanted everybody to know that school operations and admissions went hand in hand.

None of the offices were elegant. Only a few even had pictures on the walls, but if you were Bill Nostrand you at least got a view of the East River, though you had to catch it in sections between other buildings. Bill's rank did allow him twice as much office space as anyone else, with a big desk before the window on one side, and an expansive floor-to-ceiling bookshelf on the other, filled with business and computer literature where in Oliver's office tomes and journals on education were displayed. Bill's one touch of elegance was the glass covering his desktop, and it worked to his demagogue's advantage. You never saw Bill's face when he sat at this desk, for the bright window behind him silhouetted his entire upper body, and the glass plate simply reflected an upside-down duplicate of the silhouette. When he moved his arms he looked like an octopus.

"Hey Philly! Have a good ride in?" Bill stood, smiling, and shook Oliver's hand.

"Fine." Oliver returned the smile. He saw for the first time how gray the vice-president's hair was getting. Two years ago it had been jet black. Nostrand motioned him to a chair, then returned to his desk. His head and body lost all features to the bright window.

"Ready to give your budget?"

"Yes. Right here." Oliver bent sideways and lifted his briefcase. Before he could snap it open the silhouette raised a hand.

"Wait a bit. We'll go in to John together."

"I'm seeing President Coyne?"

"Don't look so worried." Nostrand laughed. "I'm sure you know all the school directors are flying here to present their budgets for next year. They were just seeing me, but the first three, Joan Barkley from Atlanta, Rhonda Harrison from Orlando, and Teri Lee from Boston, presented budgets so ridiculously padded that … well, let's just say I made sure they were all completely embarrassed with themselves before they left. Their operational needs were so exaggerated I had to show John, and of course he blew his stack. He decided to go over the budgets of the remaining directors personally. You get to be first, lucky boy." He laughed again. "So I hope your figures aren't *too* padded."

"No. Uh—no, I don't think they are."

The phone buzzed. Nostrand picked up his receiver. "Okay." He hung up. "That's it. The big man beckons."

John Coyne, president of all seventeen Burr Colleges, possessed the one luxurious office on the forty-third floor. The long office was surrounded by rosewood paneling, with one end furnished with couches, a fake fireplace, and a fully stocked bar. Coyne had worked with Charles Burr, Reginald's grandson, since 1960, and was voted president upon Charles' retirement in 1972. Coyne's personal wealth was self-made, and he himself possessed no more than a high school diploma. But the man loved education, believed his work for Burr was his contribution to Mankind, and intended, when his own time came, to leave behind an array of institutions that would thrive and benefit generations of future students. In person he resembled Harry Truman, small and compact, silver-haired, puffy-faced, with round-framed glasses. Others had mentioned this similarity to the president, and he enjoyed living up to it. His manner was buoyant and youthful, his eyes restless with energy. His language was coarse in an old-fashioned way. He rose and stepped around his desk as Oliver and Nostrand came in.

"Oliver, good to see you again. Attending meeting faithfully?" Coyne asked this every time they met. Oliver's religion always tickled him, as if being a Quaker from Philadelphia was something quaint, like an actor dressed as Ben Franklin strolling through Independence Hall.

"When I can, John."

"Got all your Christmas shopping done?"

"Almost."

"Let's have the budget." Coyne returned to his desk. Oliver removed the report, which he had given to Julie only yesterday to type. Coyne ignored the introductory cover letter and turned to the first page. Both Oliver and Nostrand remained standing. The president sucked his lower lip on some items, and on others he fairly chuckled. Oliver's gaze dropped to a framed photograph on the desk of John Coyne and Charles Burr shaking hands in this very room, the one coming in and the other going out. Both looked pleased.

Coyne scanned the fifteen-page report in four minutes, put it down, and smiled. "Ah, budgets, budgets, budgets. It's always interesting to get the school's point of view on what they think they need. Shall we go to work?" He smiled with unnerving exuberance.

"Yes, sir," said Nostrand.

"Okay, first things first. The property tax in Philly went up. We'll be paying something like seventy thou for the building. Well, they got us by the balls on that one. Christ, where do they think we're located? The school's on Rittenhouse Square, not Park Avenue."

"Washington Square," corrected Oliver.

"Right. We gotta pay it, though."

Nostrand said, "We don't have a choice."

"No, we sure as people piss in pools don't. All right, so let's see what we *do* have a choice with."

In a blitzkrieg Oliver saw slashes go through his prized requests for updated computer programs for the classes, paper stock increases for classes, equipment repair, the chalkless blackboards desperately needed for two of the personal computer labs, and of course, Louise's walls. What stayed was maintenance of physical plant, the security system, and the twenty-four hour answering service. ("You never know when an applicant might call," said Nostrand.) Raises, always awarded annually, would henceforth occur every eighteen months, and the merit increase of five percent would drop to three. When it was over Coyne nodded and grinned pleasantly with tight lips and little pebble teeth. *Dewey Defeats Truman,* Oliver thought.

"Good, good, boys. Looks do-able! Away we go now!"

Oliver found his way out of the room only by following Nostrand's back. He sank onto a chair in the vice-president's office. Nostrand sat behind his desk, converting himself to a silhouette. "Oliver, you look drained."

"I feel it."

"You couldn't have been too surprised."

"No. I did pray for a miracle the whole train ride up."

"That's no good. You should only pray for the things you know will happen. That's how prayers get answered." Nostrand lit a cigarette and waved out the match. He said with vague sympathy, "You know most of this is because of that lousy September sit."

"Damn it, Bill, I couldn't do a thing about the September sit!" Oliver heard his own exasperation and tried to calm down. "Rose Bradshaw walked out last May, just when the recruitment season hit its peak."

"I know. We've been through that. At any rate, the past lives with us. Everything now pretty much hangs on your January sit. How are you with that?"

His nerves still raw from the hatchet job Coyne did to his budget, Oliver said tactlessly, "Don't you know? I thought you were on the phone with my admissions director every day."

"Of course. But I always assume the sales people are glossing when they talk to me."

"The Philadelphia school does not gloss its numbers," Oliver said indignantly. "When they're below goal we take our lumps. You know that."

Nostrand did not admit if he did. He stubbed out his cigarette and studied Oliver without a word.

Hoping to change the subject, Oliver said, "If it means anything, Bill, the September class is doing very well."

For the first time the vice-president showed his anger. "Christ! What do you mean, doing well? You failed that sit by fifty percent! Your school lost a projected revenue of one and a half million dollars, the worst loss in your whole goddamn history!"

"I realize that, Bill, I do. But I'm talking academically. The Septembers are about to go into first semester testing, and we anticipate pretty good grades. It's a very motivated class."

Nostrand stared as if Oliver had weeds coming out of his scalp. "Hooray. Maybe one will graduate smart enough to haul you into the black. Goddammit, Oliver, it makes no difference if they all graduate four-point-fucking-oh and take jobs dictating for the Pope! If you fail this January sit you're going to have to cut. It happened in Miami, it happened in New Orleans, it happened in both New Haven and Boston. Philly has no special protection."

"But Bill, we're a skeleton crew already. We can't function properly if you take someone away. The secretaries are burnt out as it is."

"By definition your school already isn't functioning properly. Your January goal was sixty students, but because of September you now need an additional one hundred and two just to catch up. Espirito tells me she has a hundred and eighteen commits already. You tell me now—what's the *real* figure?" Nostrand's hands, flat on the desk, showed white angry knuckles.

Oliver felt he should protect Lily, but it continued to rankle that she did all this talking to Nostrand without going through him. He said, "I think it's seventy-eight."

"Seventy-eight." Nostrand nodded with satisfaction; he must have known it was seventy-eight. "I guess the Philly school has learned to gloss after all. And what's seventy-eight? About forty-eight percent of goal? And you have, say, five weeks to go, but of course Christmas is right in the middle there, so it's really like four weeks. Not much time. At least you've reached the core sixty, provided they show, but how the hell are you going to make the extra? It's impossible. So then what do you think happens?"

"I guess we cut staff."

"I guess you do."

A long silence followed. Nostrand coughed and seemed to take pity. "Look I realize you had a tough setback during the summer. And I want you to know that I think you're on the right track now. Too late to help you in January, but still better late than never."

"How am I on the right track? I don't understand."

"That new admissions director. I like her. Haven't met her face to face, but I'm looking forward to it. First time we talked she gave me the most incisive analysis of the marketing problems for liberal arts that I've come across in years."

Oliver said quietly, "You should have been in Philly on Halloween."

"You know, I heard about that. Must have been outrageous. I mentioned it at the board meeting and John near busted a gut laughing. And of course your October monthly report has the best numbers for your school to date."

"Thank you."

"Some of her tactics sure took me by surprise. What she's doing with the Accounting Program, for example. Totally unique. Most schools recruit for their big programs, and when an applicant can't afford the nine thou tuition they talk them into attending a short program that's less expensive, so at least the school gets maybe a couple thou. The better-than-nothing approach. But Espirito recruits for Accounting, which costs two thousand dollars, and when they come to interview she sells them into taking the bigger expensive class instead. That's fucking gutsy, Oliver. She must be persuasive as hell."

"She is."

Another long pause. The silhouette crossed its arms. "God, Oliver, what's bugging you?"

Oliver stared hard at Nostrand, trying without success to find a face in the silhouette. "Bill, I was just wondering. You and John took my budget and cut out everything needed to increase the educational quality of the classes. The upgraded computer equipment, for example. We need that, or in a year's time we'll be teaching students on equipment businesses aren't using any more."

"Didn't cancel it, Oliver. Just put it on hold. We had to."

"But it makes me wonder. I mean, it seems like we never talk about the education anymore. It's all goals and numbers and projected revenue, isn't it?"

Nostrand's response was unexpectedly angry. "Don't patronize me, Oliver. Don't get sanctimonious. Your school isn't even earning its upkeep, and right now that's your primary concern. Maybe that's not Ivy League pedagogy, but it's the way things are. Even a school as prestigious as Burr has to show a profit. Son of a bitch, Oliver—the other schools are *carrying* you. Yes, it'd be nice to get state-of-the-art equipment for the girls, *but first you have to get the girls!* Now you sit your classes like you're supposed to, and *then* we'll talk educational improvements. It all starts with that. Cause and effect."

"Okay."

Nostrand turned amiable again. "Start with that new Paralegal Program. I'd like to see at least twenty enrollments for a March 17 start."

Oliver straightened, horrified. "Bill, the Paralegal Program? Come on, don't push that one, please!" Good heavens, he was *begging!* "We talked about this. The prerequisites are too weak, and it just won't play in Philadelphia."

Nostrand's sigh was like a soft growl. "I really hate defeatist attitudes."

"Bill, wait! When that program was proposed last year my placement director did a study. Did it at your request, in fact."

"That's Clare Peterson?"

"Yes. She—no, it's Clara. Clara Peterson. Anyway, she polled law offices. She polled Pennsylvania University's Law School and several other schools that run paralegal programs, and she worked up some figures." Oliver leaned forward, almost off his chair. He spoke rapidly, spurred by panic. "There's currently a lawyer glut in Philadelphia. Graduates from *regular* law schools can't get jobs. Lawyers are begging to be paralegals just to get their feet in the door. *Lawyers* as paralegals, Bill! Do you understand? There's no room for someone who's trained just to be a paralegal! Clara got this info from a top Philadelphia legal placement service. Hell, Clara's husband is a lawyer—he confirmed all this stuff firsthand." Oliver could hear the stridency in his voice, knew it was hurting his case. "And even when times are good, Bill, even in the *best* of times, no firm will accept a student in a paralegal position who isn't at least a college graduate with a GPA of 3.0. That's the *minimum* requirement. But our paralegal program accepts applicants straight from high school. Bill, *nobody's* going to hire them! The program costs three thousand dollars, they'll study three nights a week for twelve months, and they won't get jobs when they finish! They'll still be so under-qualified they won't get past a personnel screener!"

"Oliver, please."

Nostrand's quiet voice shut him up. Oliver froze in his chair, humiliated by his outburst.

"Oliver, you're going to run the class. Why are you telling me this?"

16

The fall semester ended on December 20.

In a sudden strange madness Oliver pulled out all stops for the office Christmas party. He secured a third of the tables at the new Kiki Lounge on the Franklin Parkway, and told everybody to invite spouses, boyfriends, relatives, street people, whomever. On the company account he covered full dinners for everyone, plus the first round of drinks. Louise was flabbergasted, but Oliver grunted and insisted she send the catering bill north. Louise later told Ethel about it, commenting with uncharacteristic concern that their school director had finally gone off the deep end. "Maybe he has," said Ethel. "But at least we're getting a party out of it."

Faculty and staff took him at his word. Elaine brought her husband Steve, Natalie brought a younger sister, and Deirdre came with some dangerous bearded lug who looked more like her kidnapper than a boyfriend. David Hurley's date was a young woman on the local singer-songwriter circuit, and since David had never mentioned a girlfriend everyone gravitated immediately toward the couple. That is, until Jessica Harrelson arrived with a hunk straight out of *GQ*, with blond hair and an English accent that left all the reps and secretaries buzzing. Louise Mallory and Julie Fitzgerald arrived alone, and Bob Lawrence was the only one not to show at all. Best of all, Tina agreed to come. Oliver was delighted and proud to lead her on his arm into the noisy club.

Lily saw them first, and rushed to embrace them both. "Oliver! It's all FABULOUS! And you must be Christina! So glad you could come! Heavens, I'm in AWE! I've never met a genuine movie star before!"

Tina smiled demurely. "I'm only Christina on a marquee. Call me Tina." Both women scanned each other with mute female ruthlessness. Tina, in a clinging black dress with one string of pearls around her throat, black nylons, her black hair cut razor-short, was all New York sophistication. Lily wore a sequin-shiny red dress high to the neckline, with green emerald beads and clever earrings made of Christmas balls. Oliver thought Lily even more extroverted than usual, almost manic in her greeting. She chattered without pause, and her eyes flashed from face to face without focusing. She looked feverish, and her hands jerked in broad gestures.

"I know I saw one of your movies at least, Christina. A jungle movie, I think. Have I got it right?"

"You certainly do. *Lost Treasure of the Amazon.* It was crazy camp, but it gave me my start."

"Oh ... well, I thought you were absolutely wonderful in it." Lily's sudden hesitance betrayed the fact that if Tina asked one question about the movie she would not be able to answer. So Tina merely said, "How sweet, thank you," and side-glared at her husband.

Oliver asked, "Where's Dr. Espirito?"

"Sitting at the bar. He's not much of a socializer. You'd think a man who gives lectures at symposiums here and in Europe would—oh hey!—it's the DEAN!"

Ethel approached, shimmering in a silver dress. She held the arm of a tall, handsome black man in a sharp blue pin-stripe suit. "Hello, everybody. Merry merry Christmas."

Lily burst into teeth and melody. "Ethel Harris, you foxy dish you! Oh my Heavens! Who is this charming gentleman?"

"Hello, Lily. Oliver, Tina—gads, Tina! It's been a while, hasn't it?"

"Yes it has, Eth."

Ethel took her tall date's arm. The man actually towered an inch over Oliver, and was broad-shouldered under the expensive jacket. "Everybody, this is Alex Garber, who is minister of the Methodist Church of the Holy Lamb in Mt. Airy."

"Oh dear, oh dear!" said Lily. "Well, we'll have to be on our best behavior, won't we all, with a minister on the premises? Ha! Ha! Ha! How do you do? Actually, my husband and I are Catholic."

"How do you do?"

"Yes! Oh goodness, Ethel! I *can't* get over how ravishing you look! Don't tempt this good man astray! Well, well! Let me make my rounds! I still haven't said hello to everybody! Looks like the whole school is here, practically, doesn't it? We never had this type of social turnout at Stanley, I can tell you! Is that Arthur Cassidy over there? Why don't you introduce the good reverend to Arthur, Eth? Reverend Garber, Arthur's an ex-priest. You'll have lots to talk about." Lily ran off in a flurry of red sequins.

"Jesus." Tina pulled Oliver's arm and they started walking. "Why don't you put solar panels on her and light up the city?"

Oliver turned and watched Lily laughing with Arthur Cassidy by the buffet. "She's putting on a show. We got the latest weekly figures today, and January looks bad. She's been depressed most of the afternoon."

"Well, she's only had the job a few months. New York can't blame her for a sit that was in trouble long before she was hired."

"Oh, but they can. They're not interested in fair play. Tina, thanks for coming."

She smiled dryly. "It wasn't easy, you know."

"I know. I want you to know that I know."

They reached the edge of the dance floor, which vibrated under pounding heels. The dance floor was in the center of the Kiki Lounge, with tables at different levels surrounding it like a theater-in-the-round. The lounge was spectacularly adorned for the Yuletide, with Santas, reindeer, snowmen, and wrapped boxes under glittering trees. Cocktail waitresses sported mini red jackets and floppy Santa hats, their bare legs thrust into black boots. A live band imitated established holiday hits.

"A lot of teachers showed," Oliver said, scanning the mob of dancers. "There's Elaine and David and their significant others, out there dancing away their woes. And good old Louise."

"Where?" Tina searched the dance floor in disbelief.

"By the bar."

"Oh. Her I always liked."

"You just like any of the personnel who don't fit the wholesome Burr image."

"Let's say hello."

Oliver pulled her hand suddenly. "No, darling. Let's dance." And they went out on the floor.

Trudy Weiser and her fiancé, Ira Gold, stepped into the lounge. Clara Peterson spotted them first and waved. She lurched noticeably, having spent the early part of the evening at the bar arguing with her husband.

"Trudy! You made it! Elaine was wondering where you were. Is this Ira? Ira, you're fiancé is one of the *finest* employees in our school! One of the finest grads we ever *had* too, right?" She kissed the rep's cheek before Trudy knew to pull away.

Ira's arm slid possessively around Trudy's shoulders. "Well, I always knew she was special."

"Please come in. Get a drink. There's tons of food. Merry Christmas and Trudy—watch out! They've got mistletoe hanging just *everywhere!*" Clara giggled and weaved away. Fascinated at seeing the director of placement in such shape, Trudy allowed Ira's arm around her for almost a minute. Then she shrugged it off angrily.

"What did I tell you?"

"What, babe?"

"I told you, no affectionate gestures while we're here. I have to work with these people."

"Yeah, but it's Christmas. I'm sure they don't care. Everybody's putting their arms around their spouses."

Trudy reddened. She loved that he already thought of her as his wife. "Well, we've got to be more grown up here, okay?"

"Sure." And to prove his sincerity, he courteously offered his arm. They walked down to the dance floor.

Jean Cavanaugh stood at one end of the lounge's horseshoe-shaped mahogany bar, leaning an elbow on it and sipping her token glass of Chablis. To Carol Sobolewski she said, "This must be the most extravagant Christmas bash we've ever had."

"You need something like this after a semester with those kids, you really do."

"I had my usual share of last-minute miracles. Kids who kept dragging their tails all semester still pulled through for final testing."

Carol nodded. "Happens every time. Oh look, there's Oliver dancing with Tina. I haven't seen Tina in ages."

"Is that her? It's funny, but I wasn't quite sure. Last time I saw Tina her hair was much longer."

"Got it cut for that new movie she's making."

"Yeah, well, I guess as long as her career's doing well he's got nothing to worry about."

Donna Harding joined them, towing her short thin-haired husband. Though hardly impressive in appearance, Robert Harding was a successful CPA for a major insurance firm, and they were quite well off. Donna said, "I see old Lily out there, kicking up her heels with some lawyer-type. See her?"

"No," said Jean, "but then she's hard to recognize with her clothes on."

Everyone except Robert, who didn't know Lily, pealed with laughter.

Donna said, "Yes, her red dress does seem a tad conservative, doesn't it? Actually, though I hate to admit it, she looks very nice. The beads and earrings are cute. I mean, if the truth be told."

Jean shook her head obstinately. "Anybody with big boobs can make an impression."

"That's for sure," Carol nodded.

"What can you say," said Jean, saying it, "about a woman who brings her husband to a party, then dances with someone else?"

"Her husband's here?"

"He's that white-haired gentleman sitting by himself at the other end of the bar." She nodded toward the other leg of the bar's horseshoe, where an older man sat alone with a drink.

"That's her husband?" gasped Donna. "He could be her grandfather."

"Why am I not surprised?" said Carol.

"He speaks in this low, cultured accent," Jean continued. "I found him rather charming. All I did was say hello, and he seemed grateful for the attention. I guess Lily doesn't show him much at home."

"I'm sure," said Carol. "I'm sure it's that way."

Donna squinted through twirling cigarette smoke. "He's well dressed, isn't he? Isn't that an Armani?"

"He's head of reconstructive surgery at Walter Welles Hospital, if that gives you a clue. He lit my cigarette for me, and you should have seen his lighter. It's gold with eight diamond studs on it. He said there's a stud for each year he's been married to Little Miss Devotion. And he's got a diamond ring worth six figures if it's worth a dime." Jean suddenly looked annoyed. "Things have sure come to a pretty pass. Hear about our budget, guys? The new personal computer equipment Oliver was supposed to push New York for went right down the tubes. Everything got cut."

"I hadn't heard," said Donna. "Where did you get this?"

"Abby DeSalvo in the Executive Dean's office told me. We talk all the time. It's a numbers racket now, we all know that. Let me tell you, I've been checking the test scores of the upcoming January class." She nodded portentously. "They're pret-*tee* poor indeed!"

Carol said, "I wonder whatever happened to Oliver. Remember the Olivettis he got, years ago, when they were all the rage? And how we were the first secretarial school back in '83 to get IBM Displaywriters for our students, when they were the latest thing? And Wangs—everybody remember them? We were on the cutting edge then. And I remember how he stood up to New York when John Coyne said no to budgeting that stuff. He *made* them shell out for the equipment. God, he was good then."

"Glory days," Donna said. "All gone."

"Everybody enjoying the party?"

Louise's sharp voice made all three teachers jump. They faced her uneasily, not sure how long the business manager had been standing behind them.

"Sure," said Jean. "Much nicer place than last year's."

"Good." Louise's acid smile was clear in the bar's overhead track lighting. "Maybe before you come down on the boss you'll remember to thank him for this bash. You know, we were specifically told not to have a party."

"What!" exclaimed Carol. "They did? How could they?"

"New York told Oliver to cut any unnecessary expenses. But he was so furious over the way they butchered his budget he said he didn't care, and arranged this anyway."

"Wow," said Donna.

"He's already sweating it," said Louise, whose loyalty stretched only so far. "We posted the bill to New York this afternoon and he knows Nostrand will excoriate him for it."

After a long silence Jean grudgingly said, "Well ... yes, that was brave of him, I guess. But it's so typical of him to fight for all the wrong things. I mean, if he has to take a stand, it should be over something important, like the personal computer equipment for the students, not a Christmas party for the staff."

"Go stick it in your ear," said Louise. "You people would have rioted if Oliver hadn't gotten you a Christmas party. You'd have raised more bloody hell than you did when you learned the computers were axed."

All three teachers bridled. Jean said stiffly, "I hope you don't seriously believe that, Louise."

"Well, you can always hope." Fresh drink in hand, Louise walked away.

Out on the dance floor a well-dressed member of the lawyers' party cut in for Tina's hand. Oliver stepped back without protest and Tina whirled away. He came off the dance floor and stood at the bar, further down from where the little knot of teachers was going at it. He smiled, watching his beautiful wife. Even in the dense crowd, Tina shone. She had come to his party, and he couldn't feel happier. He watched as yet another man cut in for Tina. He was glad she was having such a good time.

Julie Fitzgerald was making a survey of the buffet with Elaine and Steve, when she saw Oliver standing alone and wormed through the crowd toward him. She balanced a small plate and a glass of wine. Because of the loud music she had to shout. "Hi, Oliver. This is all wonderful."

"Julie, hi. Yes, it turned out pretty well."

"Tina's here, isn't she?"

He nodded toward the dance floor. "In the black dress."

Julie picked her out immediately. "She really looks—" She stopped herself.

Oliver laughed. "Looks like herself, doesn't she?"

Julie smiled, embarrassed. "She dances well."

"She's a terrific dancer."

The bartenders hustled behind them, and shoulders crowded them on all sides. Julie stood close, her back to the bar, not sure what to say next. The school director stood tall and dark in his navy blue pinstripe, one of his most frequently worn suits and, in her opinion, one of his best. Usually his necktie was a conservative earth tone, and it was funny tonight to see a bright red tie dotted with reindeer. She sipped the last of her wine, and Oliver leaned to shout in her ear. "You look ready for another. What are you having?"

She shouted back, "Just Chardonnay."

He signaled a bartender, then faced the dance floor again. Julie watched Oliver as he watched his wife dancing with another man, and some base instinct told her something was wrong. She couldn't define it, it was pure feeling. Oliver's face was still rooted with the fatigue and worry that had plagued him since the summer. She wished there was something she could do about that. The bartender returned with a fresh glass of Chardonnay, and Oliver held it out to her. "Thanks," Julie said, taking it from his hand. She stood beside him watching the dancers, wishing it was his hand and not the drink that she was holding.

Overhead lights began to strobe the dance floor, raising a cheer from the crowd. In the pixilated confusion, Tina Dunbar stood out as a gyrating dynamo. She kicked and whirled from one partner to the next. The black dress slithered like a snake, her pearls flew. Julie tiptoed to shout in Oliver's ear, "She's amazing! Does it ever feel strange to be married to a movie star?"

"Not really. She keeps out of the gossip, so at least I don't have to see her on a tabloid. Taking her to one of her own films can be weird. You're sitting next to her in the theater and yet, you know, there she is, the size of a garage, talking to Robert De Niro who's just as big."

"I can't imagine. It must be fascinating."

"Actually, it's probably done more to deglamorize movies for me than anything else." He leaned closer to her. "Would you like to kiss?"

"I'm sorry—what?"

"Would you like to dance? I'm feeling remiss here, standing next to you."

She hesitated, looking out at the swirling crowd. *Dance,* he had said. *Dance.* "Oh, I don't think I should. I hate to say it, but they're going way too fast for me."

"Okay."

"I'm sorry, Oliver. Thank you for asking. I will if you want to."

He smiled and shook his head. "No, it's okay. Actually I'm relieved. They're going too fast for me too." He looked out at the dancers again. Julie gulped her wine.

Louise approached, took advantage of six inches of counter space next to Oliver, and set down her empty glass. She immediately tapped it for another. "Quite the soiree, boss."

Oliver smiled. "You enjoying yourself?"

"Some. I just chatted with the teachers and that was fun. That man on the other side of the bar is trying to catch your eye."

"What man?" Oliver squinted in the shadows.

"Lily's husband," Julie said.

"Oh? I guess I should say hello. If you ladies will excuse me."

Oliver came around the long curved bar to its other side. The man smiled to see him approach. He was squat and squarish of head and shoulders, and much older than Oliver expected. His face was dark and seamed, his hand holding his drink covered with liver spots. But there was certainly nothing aged in the strength of his grip.

"Dr. Dunbar, yes?"

"Yes. You must be Dr. Espirito?"

"Luis, please."

There was no empty chair, so Oliver remained standing. Espirito caught a bartender's attention and signaled for him to give Oliver what he himself was having. Oliver noted the man's beautifully tailored suit, the sheen of a fresh expensive dress shirt, two gold rings on his right hand, and the large diamond on his left.

"I won't keep you," Espirito said cheerfully. "You've got a lot of guests and I know you have to make your rounds. I just wanted to tell you how happy you made Lily when you gave her that job at Burr. She was so thrilled when she broke the news to me."

"That's nice to hear." Oliver accepted a drink from the bartender, and found himself holding a vodka and tonic.

"Those other schools were dog operations, totally beneath her. She'd come home every day burned out and depressed. I'd tell her to quit but she wouldn't. I don't think Lily knows *how* to quit, she has too much drive."

"It's a marvelous quality."

"Yes. I never stand in her way. Cigar?"

"No, thank you."

"It's Havana."

"Thanks, I don't smoke."

"Med school started me." Espirito pulled a long thick cigar from his jacket pocket. "Must be a joke there somewhere. Anyway, I know you're busy. I just wanted to tell you how grateful I am that you gave her this opportunity."

"We were lucky to get her."

"You and me both." Espirito grunted happily. "She's my salvation, Oliver, she's my saint." He laughed at Oliver's surprised look. "I'm not ashamed to admit it. I bless God Almighty every day for letting me marry such a vivacious and caring wife. I'm thirty years older than she is, you know, and hardly the virile man I used to be. I'll never understand the good Providence that let her say 'yes' when I proposed." He pulled a solid gold lighter from his pocket and lit the cigar.

At that moment the saint slipped off the dance floor, crossed to the bar, and ordered bourbon and water. It was her fourth this night, but she was not drunk. Lily was good at keeping off drunkenness when eyes were glued to her, and every goddamn eye in this place was glued and glued tight. She downed the drink and rapped the bar with her glass. "Again, please."

Earlier this afternoon she had received the latest weekly figures, and she was in a lot of trouble. The green-barred computer sheet, even with the padded figures she slipped in behind Oliver's back—or that she tried to, since that monstrous bitch Margolis caught her and told Oliver and he made her take them out—even with the padding, the figures told a ghastly truth. January was going to *die*. At first it hadn't looked so bad. All twenty Evening Accounting students had at least paid their twenty-five dollar deposits. That was her doing, and little Trudy's. Trudy was a good rep, possessing two attributes essential for an underling: malleability, and a fear of fucking up before the boss. And also on the positive side, the base sixty for

January was also committed, though some were only promises without even their app fees paid. And some, like the handful of boys whom she more or less buffaloed into the big expensive IP class when they wanted the smaller accounting one, were in a state of bewilderment and kept having second thoughts, and even some of the girls kept calling to say they weren't sure and wanted to back out or maybe attend a later class. Lily took every one of these maddening calls herself, and sometimes they lasted over an hour as she cajoled, promised, commiserated, and tenaciously steered them into staying. She believed she would keep this crucial core of sixty, but the class was hanging together by wire and chewing gum; new students were not considered part of the admissions count unless they sat a full month in class—a harsh rule the Stanley School never dared impose—and so the cajoling might go on even after they were in class. Once the month was up the kids could drop out if they wished and be someone else's worry, the dean's probably.

No, what hurt on the report was the extra students needed to fill the fiscal gap. Of the one hundred and two needed to compensate for the loss in September, Lily's staff so far had coughed up a whopping forty-nine. Where were the other fifty-three going to spring from? She only had half a week before Christmas, followed by Christmas week itself which was rarely good for interviews (kids went looking at regular four-year colleges with their parents during Christmas break, if they thought about school at all), and then January 4, the first day of class for the new IP program. *There was no time left!* Two weeks *tops* to get fifty-three students to come, interview, and sign contracts agreeing to pay $9,125 to learn secretarial arts. It was absolutely impossible!

Lily gulped the last of her drink while her eyes traveled the crowded, happy room. Elaine Margolis and her husband were standing near a giant twinkling Christmas tree, talking to Julie Fitzgerald and Jessica Harrelson. Watching the tall senior rep, Lily began to chew the ice cubes in her glass. She chewed one cube, then another, and felt the vibrations channel like a massage through her skull. By the time she put the empty glass on the bar, she was starting to feel good again.

Elaine had one hand on Jessica's arm, the other around her husband's waist. Over their heads a speaker blatted out the live band's rendition of "Blue Christmas." "Elvis they ain't," she laughed. Loosened by a few drinks, her laughter was loud, her face pink, and she looked happier than either Jessica or Julie had seen her in weeks. Elaine said to Steve, "You want to hear the latest?"

"Sure."

"Lily won't let anybody look in her office closet. She actually put a lock on it. Deirdre's the only one who knows what's in there and she isn't supposed to tell—only Deirdre can't keep a secret to save China. Want to know what Lily's got in there?"

Steve's smile was polite. Married to Elaine, he had been hearing about the Evil Dragon Lady every night since September.

"Outfits," Elaine said distinctly. "All kinds. Every type imaginable. Business suits, casual suits, party dresses, tennis skirts, plus the good stuff: fishnets and hooker heels—at least forty different pairs of shoes. Dee swears she saw a woman's military uniform hanging in there, and even a funeral dress. Lily has Dee go out and case the applicants in the lobby. Then Lily decides what to wear and changes, right there in her office."

Julie said, "I didn't know that."

Jessica did, and nodded. "Isn't it outrageous?"

Elaine snorted. "Well, it's sleaze-city like you never believed, but at least it's original. I don't know why I'm laughing. I've got to work with this bitch."

Julie said, "And Oliver doesn't do anything about it?"

Elaine said dismally, "Oliver doesn't do anything anymore."

Looking past her shoulder, Steve said, "Ease up, hon. I think she's coming."

"Oh, who gives a shit? It's Christmas."

"Well, well!" Lily glided up to them, her wide full-lipped smile tainted slightly with the suspicions of a mother hen. "Everybody's so jolly. Can a fifth enter into all this mirth?" She turned to Steve. "You're Elaine's husband, right?"

"Yes."

"I'm Lily Espirito."

"Yes. We met earlier at the door."

"Would you mind terribly if I talked to Elaine alone for a moment? I won't keep her long."

Steve looked at Elaine, who was sober and submissive. "Hon, I'll stay right here by the tree, okay?"

"Sure. See you in a few."

Lily took Elaine delicately by the shoulder and they moved past the band. They stopped at a corner settee near the kitchen and restroom doors. "Have a seat, dear. We need to talk."

Elaine sat willingly, but said, "Lily, do we really need a lecture tonight of all nights?"

"Dear, I'm not going to lecture. I want to patch things up. Please, Elaine, it's Christmas. Indulge me."

Lily sat across from her and, to Elaine's extreme discomfort, gently took both the rep's hands in hers. "I feel bad that there's so much undue tension between us. It's so counter-productive and psychologically bad. Don't you feel that way?"

Elaine nodded slowly, warily.

"I thought—this being Christmas—that we might try to put past hostilities aside and clear the air."

Elaine said in her best business manner, "Lily, I'd be happy to try. We might be able to 'clear the air' as you put it, if you would answer one question for me."

"Yes, dear?"

"What do you get out of this? Admissions, I mean. What's your personal satisfaction in doing the work you do?"

"Elaine, sweetie. If you don't know what the satisfaction is, then you don't belong in sales."

"Lily, I'm in this because of the school. I'm a Burr graduate. I received an excellent education from this establishment and that's why I'm selling it. That's why I'm here."

"Well, honey, I believe in Burr too. But I think we're operating from two different viewpoints, you and I." Lily's voice kept its sugar, but developed an edge. "You see Burr as an excellent college that students should want of their own choosing to go to. I see Burr as an excellent college that *very few* are interested in going to. These days we kill to get students, don't you see?"

"I appreciate that, Lily. I'm not blind to our problems. But I remember what you said about the Stanley School and the mirror test, how they were recruiting anybody whose breath could fog a mirror. I don't think you're that bad, Lily, please don't get me wrong. But there's still a lot of trickery and manipulation in how you're selling the Burr programs."

"You're very candid," Lily said coolly.

"And I know you're my boss," Elaine continued, shaking a little and hoping it didn't show, "and you could fire me for this. I don't want that either, because I love the Burr College. But I can't sell based on tactics or tricks. I can't high-pressure applicants into enrolling. It's not my way, and I can't change. I'm sorry if that upsets you, but I can't."

Over the speaker the band did a flat imitation of Elmo and Patsy mourning their grandmother. Lily was quiet for a while. "All right, dear," she said at last, sweet and maternal, "I know where you're coming from, and I do see your point. I'm not fond of conducting business this way myself. If times were different I'd be more than happy to … well." She sighed and daydreamed a moment. Then she brightened. "Elaine, how about a compromise?"

"A compromise?"

"Yes. A little bit of your sales philosophy with a little bit of my technique. What do you say?"

Elaine looked interested, but remained wary. "What did you have in mind?"

"I won't insist on high-pressure sales tactics, and I'll leave you to sell the way you see fit. You just do one tiny thing for me."

"What?"

Lily's eyes twinkled as she pointed to Elaine's hand. "Take off your wedding ring when you interview."

"Take off—what? My wedding ring?"

"Exactly. You don't know how people notice, dear."

Elaine whipped back on the settee. "I don't care! Are you serious? Of course I'm going to wear my wedding ring!"

"But Elaine, it's not like you'd be lying. You just wouldn't be advertising it. That diamond sticks off your hand like a stalagmite, and it's rather intimidating to the less well-off girls and boys who come to us."

"Not in a million years, Lily! This ring means more to me than anything!"

"Well, that's a fine attitude, isn't it? *There's* team spirit."

"I don't care what you say! It's the most insensitive thing you could ask me! The very worst!"

Lily's voice hardened. "It comes *off,* Elaine. This isn't open to discussion. It's an order from your *boss.*" She hissed the double "s."

Elaine jumped to her feet. She could hardly see in the shadows and pounding music. She shouted, "Well, maybe you're right, and I have no business being in sales! Goddamn you, Lily!" She stormed off. Lily stood and craned her neck, trying to see through the crowd. With the lightness of a gazelle she hopped up on the settee and strained to see above the bustling heads.

Oliver and Tina, Louise, Julie and Steve stood by the big Christmas tree. Louise, telling one woeful office anecdote after another, had Tina in stitches. Elaine strode up and grabbed Oliver's arm, spinning him around.

"That's it! I'm done, Oliver! Finished! Two weeks and I'm *outta* here!" She grabbed Steve, and pulled him toward the door.

Oliver and Louise looked at each other. Then he darted frantically after her. "Elaine, wait! What happened? Wait—"

Sweet blood circulated in Lily. She felt it race down her arms to her fingertips and tingle within her toes. It thumped throughout all her veins, a sub-dermal massage that made her dress, belt, shoes, Santa earrings, watchband all feel pleasantly tight against her skin. Her very clothes tickled, and she started to laugh. Immediately she sat down, for she couldn't afford to be seen laughing, but the blood thumped harder and the tickling grew more piercing against her sensitive skin. She ducked toward the restrooms, and in a narrow passage bumped into a couple already hidden there. They parted guiltily, and in the murky light of a red exit sign she recognized Trudy and Ira.

"Hey," said Lily. "Well, well! Good for you!"

"Excuse us," Trudy said, horribly embarrassed. Ira hastily tucked in his shirt.

"No, honey, no! *Don't* be embarrassed! Let's have a little more of this Yuletide joy, hey? Do you mind?" Lily reached over and kissed Ira fully on the mouth. Before Trudy could even register it, Lily leaned over and kissed her mouth too. Her face inches from the rep's, she whispered, "You're my best, sweetest little daughter, Trudy. Do you know that?"

Trudy said shyly, "Merry Christmas, Lily."

"It is now, dear. It really is now!"

Louise and Tina caught up with Oliver outside the entrance of the club. High apartment buildings rose along the length of the Parkway, and the Art Museum glowed like a fortress at the end of the avenue. The night air was cold. Oliver stood on the sidewalk, stunned and alone.

"Did you talk to her?" Louise asked. "What happened?"

"She wouldn't tell me."

"Do you think she means it?"

"Yes. That's the one thing she said. Two weeks, that's it. She's furious."

At that moment the cars parked along the curb flared and flickered, and lights danced off a multitude of plate glass windows. A staccato thumping reverberated through the air. Of the three of them, only Tina looked up.

"Fireworks," she said. "Exploding over the Art Museum. Somebody's happy tonight."

17

Those same fireworks rumbled through the walls of a small apartment on Waverly Street, where the remains of a quiet candlelit dinner lay spread on a modest kitchen table tucked under a plank staircase leading up to a giant loft. Two wads of crumpled Christmas wrap lay discarded on the floor, and the gifts—after-shave for him, a gold tennis bracelet for her—were forgotten on a chair. The meal was over but the wine glasses refilled, and Bob Lawrence smiled and lifted his. Heather Feeney giggled and quickly raised her own.

"Merry Christmas."

"Yeah." She couldn't stop smiling. In the scented candlelight her straight black hair with the green tips appeared as rich as chocolate. The clink of their glasses triggered a gentle chirrup from the floor. Heather leaned down and smiled at Bob's tabby. "Sorry, baby, there's no more." But the cat mewed louder. His wide-eyed hopefulness for a handout made her laugh.

"He's so fat," she said.

"Yeah, he's a porker all right." Mr. Wemmick weighed in at twenty-seven pounds. His bulging stomach flopped like a cow's udder when he walked. "You'd never know that eight years ago he was a starving stray on my doorstep."

Heather giggled and rubbed Mr. Wemmick's ears. They always loved his cat.

The windows rattled gently. He said, "Listen to those fireworks. Sure are a lot of them."

"Can we see them from here?"

"I don't know. I doubt it."

She stood and went to the window. She looked painfully young in her Christmas-red knit blouse and jeans. He found her cowboy boots sexy, but hated that she was duck-footed. "Can you see anything?"

"No. there's some big building in the way. I think your apartment's so cool, Bob."

He rose too, holding both wine glasses, and stood behind her. "I do love it," he agreed.

The apartment was both the third floor and attic section of an old brick building purported to have once been a convent. The attic floor had been cut back by a third, supported by exposed beams, and this made the attic a giant loft. Bob's salary was thirty-three thou a year (less than his age), and although $850 a month was steep without a roommate, he thought the place hip for an aspiring writer.

He touched the girl's shoulder and turned her toward him. Heather blinked solemnly, expectantly. He kissed her, then led her toward the loft steps. She pulled back and asked, "Your bathroom's down here, isn't it?"

"Yeah. You need it?"

"Just for something. You go up. I'll be right there." She picked up a tote bag she had brought with her, and walked off.

He ascended the creaking steps and snapped on the loft light. Half of the loft was taken by a full-size bed, the other half by a chair and table that supported his computer and his novel, a stack of pages three reams thick. The computer was new for twelve hundred bucks, a steep price but necessary to get the Internet, for it was clearer every day that a modern writer needed to know how to do research on the 'net. Only since getting this access several months ago, he hadn't done much with it except scan porn sites and read a few movie reviews.

It wasn't long before the steps creaked again. Heather rose above the loft floor, and Bob's heart gave a primal thump. The girl stood grinning in red silk panties and a pink see-through negligee. Her breasts were small and cloudy through the gauzy silk. "Hi."

"God, hello."

"Do you like it?"

"Of course."

She moved to the bed and stretched out on it, raising one knee and lifting her arms above her head, a *Playboy* pose. "I got it with the gift certificate."

"With the what?"

"You know. For winning first prize in the Halloween contest. I've been waiting for this time. So I could wear it for you."

"Well," he said.

He undressed quickly and joined her on the bed. Heather's body was shorter than Mary Grace Whitman's, and in the tangle of sheets seemed mostly arms and legs. She had no sizable breasts to speak of, just bruise-colored patches with a modest pucker of nipple. Initially she lay on bottom, and he buried his face in her neck to hide his own, and wished he had thought to snap off the light. Heather's little tongue flickered like a moth in his mouth. The negligee melted off easily, and her hot young body gripped him like a vise. "I can't believe this is really happening," she breathed, pressing her cheek against his.

They all said that. Every one of them. "Oh yeah, I know what you mean."

She seemed tiny with her clothes off. He tried to hug her, and embraced both her body and the two pillows she lay on. His hands felt large and brutal on her girlish ass. It shamed him, and he felt all his semen recede to a sleepy backwater. He raised his head to look at her. Heather's mascaraed eyes were shut, her mouth open and half-smiling. Her body wriggled nonsensically under him. "Come on, will ya?" she whispered. She raised her head and kissed him hungrily. "Don't hold back, Bob," she whispered. "I want to feel you inside me, feel you loving me—loving me—"

When was he going to learn that fucking a student was never as great as the titillation promised? He'd seduced maybe seven of his pupils in the last ten years, big deal, that wasn't so many, but at thirty-six he could no longer pretend they were contemporaries. Their youth was becoming more alien, and their bodies lacked the seasoned grainy definitions older women's bodies offered, a certain organic wear-and-tear he was beginning to find attractive. The green tips of Heather's hair were stiff and spiky from whatever godforsaken goo she used, and stabbed his face like toothbrush bristles.

She finally realized that he was having trouble, and suggested they trade places.

On top Heather almost had breasts. At least they hung with a hint of feminine roundness. Her stiff hair swung gently. Bob still couldn't come, try as he might. He felt irrevocably soft, and knew she felt it too.

"What time is it?" he asked.

She looked at his glowing digital clock. "'Bout ten or so."

"Really? Guess you'd better get home."

"Why? Don't you like this?"

He was not in a position to be honest. "Sure. But I don't want to get you in trouble."

"They know I'm here."

"Who does?"

"Mom and Dad."

"*What?*"

Heather laughed. "Sure. Well, they don't know it's *you*, but they know I'm staying overnight with a guy."

"Over night?"

"Didn't you want me to?"

"Uh, sure. I just didn't think you could."

"Well, I am." She kissed him. Her hair tickled his ears.

He pushed her up and studied her face. "Heather, can I ask you something?"

"Sure."

"Don't—don't your parents worry about you? Don't they have anything to say about you staying overnight with some guy they've never met?"

The girl's eyes sparkled. "Are you worried about me, Bob? That's so sweet. No, of course not. My parents trust me. I'm a big girl now. I'm eighteen."

Half his age. "I need a drink. Is there any more wine left in that glass?"

"Yeah. Hold on." The bed was close to the writing table. Heather stretched to reach it, her body long and slim and smooth. Bob gulped the last two swallows.

"What's distracting you, baby?"

"I ... I don't know. Just a lot of things, I guess."

"Want me to get you hard?" She bent down to take him in her mouth.

"Hey, stop that! Get up here." When she didn't listen he pulled her by the shoulder. Heather looked at him, a little hurt.

"Your parents," he said miserably. "They really don't care?"

She snorted, and rested her cheek on his chest. "I think you're the sweetest guy in the world, Bob. No, they don't care. They know I'm responsible. They know I wouldn't get involved with just anybody."

"Jesus God," he whispered.

"Hey, you get back on top. I think you're better when you're not submissive." And she swiftly pushed them both around, and wiggled under him.

Bob's loft dissipated in a murky cloud. He felt a black mortal doom, felt the corruption of the whole planet leaden the air around them. Everything was for nothing. Parents didn't care, young girls jumped into bed with anybody, nobody read any more. Maybe Revelation was right. Bob was hardly a Bible guy, but still—maybe the Second Coming had come, and now here was all that was left: a little wine, some sputtering lust, and a big dead end.

"Look, stop thinking, okay? What can I do for you?"

"Huh?"

Her head was a narrow stone in the sack of the pillow. "Want me to whisper to you?"

"No, please don't."

Grabbing the back of his neck with one hand, she raised her mouth to his ear. "Fuck me, Mr. Teacher," she panted. "Shove your big cock in me. Make me your bitch—"

He jerked away from her in horror. "Stop that!"

"Aw, baby, come on." She looked up in real confusion. "Then tell me what you want."

He stared at her expectant face and didn't know what to say. She was eighteen. He would have just started college when she was born. They would have both been virgins.

Heather stretched against him, her eyes still bright but beginning to worry. She thought she was failing him, and he couldn't stand her thinking that. His hand drifted along the curve of her ass, felt the incredible silk of her thighs. She really was a beautiful girl.

Shove your big cock in me, she had said.

"Hey," Heather grinned and cupped him lightly with both hands. "I think something's happening."

He felt it too, a pleasant firming below, nurtured by her fingertips. His hand played up and down her leg while he focused on the echo of her words, the chime of her young voice.

Make me your bitch …

"Good, good," Heather breathed beneath him. She began to push his pelvis up and over her, centering him above her spread legs with the precision of an air traffic controller.

Make me your bitch …

She gasped as he penetrated her, then held him tight and pressed her cheek to his. "Oh baby," she smiled. "I told you you weren't old."

Essential Self

18

THE TALLY WAS in. On January 4 twenty-two students registered for the Evening Accounting Program. It was a satisfactory sit, for twenty had been the goal. And the nine-month January IP Program had ninety-six students, easily covering the core sixty required by New York. But as Lily read the report her eye kept dropping to the last column, marked PREV SHORTFALL, where a black 171 cast an evil taint over the whole report. Her staff had fallen tragically short of the extra students necessary to re-coup from September. Trembling with anger at the injustice, she signed the report, then walked it over to Oliver's office. He signed it without a word, then gave it to Julie who shot it overnight to New York.

On January 7 Bill Nostrand called to say he would visit the Philadelphia school in two days. It was only the vice-president's second visit to the college since he was hired by John Coyne two years ago, and there was not one staff member who did not wake early that morning and dress in his or her best.

A department head meeting was scheduled at ten. Nostrand was offi-cially a guest, but in fact he presided. Julie took a seat in a corner and scribbled notes, but Nostrand didn't have a lot to say. The sit was a failure, he declared, and it was the fault of every person in the room. Without ex-planation he faulted the dean, Admissions, Placement, the Business Office, Financial Aid, and met the fuming stares of Ethel, David, Clara, and Louise without weakening. He went on to say that Burr couldn't open its doors and simply expect the world to rush in, that maybe the College could do that once but those days were gone and he wouldn't tolerate minds living in the past. Students needed to be hand-held, coddled, nursed along. They didn't understand forms, they didn't understand deadlines, and it was up to the staff to take up the slack. He didn't give a damn about titles or depart-ments. Anybody who dared think admissions wasn't in their job description had better find new jobs fast.

He sat down to a poisonous silence, crossed his legs, and sipped the coffee he'd asked Julie to fetch for him. He looked to Oliver for comment (as did everyone), but the school director had nothing to add. Nostrand adjourned the meeting.

"Shut the door please," he told Julie, who was the last to leave. The secretary gave Oliver a worried look as she closed the door. Suddenly the hardness went out of Nostrand's face. In an almost genial tone he said, "Well, Oliver, now let's talk. The sit wasn't really as bad as we expected. Nobody, including John, figured you'd actually get one hundred and sixty-two students. But after the way things have been going here, we didn't expect you to keep the sixty."

Oliver fairly exploded, "Dammit, Bill! Why didn't you tell them that? They all walked out of here with their tails between their legs."

"That's okay. We've got the April, July, and September sits ahead of us now, and this meeting will light a fire under them."

"Sure. If they don't quit first."

Nostrand laughed. "Statistically speaking, people at this level of management don't quit. They get pissed, but they stick around. And anyone who *does* quit because they don't want to work hard isn't someone we want on the Burr team anyway." He opened his briefcase and pulled out a memorandum. "Tony Gallagher worked this up. With the revenue generated by the thirty-eight extra January students, you won't have to do as harsh a staff cutback as we originally envisaged."

The school director stared nervously at the report.

"Tony and I went over your personnel list. You don't have a lot of fat, but we can still make an adjustment. For one thing, you've got four secretaries."

"Bill, please. Is this really necessary? Why don't—"

"Oliver, you can't lose money and not lose personnel."

"Even if we're already a skeleton crew as it stands? Even if by losing a person it'll be that much harder to make the April, July, and September goals?"

"We decided you can lose one administrator, though I don't recommend you do so, or two secretaries. I'd probably cut that secretary of yours. What's her name?"

"Julie Fitzgerald."

"Her and maybe the placement secretary. Incidentally, your placement revenues are some of the best in the whole system. I forgot to mention that."

"Bill, if you were here on a daily basis you'd realize how invaluable Jessica and Julie are."

"Well, that's true. I might think differently about a lot of things if I worked at one school. But I work in the President's Office. My job is to oversee the whole picture. We trust school personnel to do what's right at this level. Everybody has a perspective."

"I can't cut Julie. She's the best secretary we've got."

"Then cut someone else. I really don't care." Bill checked his watch. "I need to catch the two-forty for Miami. I've got to ream Carol Nixon's ass. They didn't make January either, as I guess you know."

"I didn't."

Bill stood. "We'll be in touch. I'm gonna talk to your admissions director and then get out of here. Have Julie call me a cab for, say, half an hour. Don't bother seeing me to the door. I'm sure you've got work to do."

Oliver thought how David, Ethel, Clara, and Louise were somewhere in this building, snarling and gnashing their teeth. He did, indeed, have work to do.

Bill Nostrand found Lily in her office scooping black grounds into a coffee filter. "Lily, may I have a word with you?"

"Certainly, Bill. Would you like some coffee—it'll be fresh."

"No, thanks. Well, on second thought, maybe I will. When it's ready."

Lily prepared the coffee maker, then sat at her desk. She clasped her hands primly, but her eyes were tense and alert. Nostrand sat in the love seat across from her.

"What's your plan now?" he asked.

"Well, Bill, I think I need you to be more specific."

"Okay. There's another nine-month Basic Secretarial class to start in April. And you have a huge July one-year and a September two-year class to sit that'll be the bulk of your revenue for this year. You've been here for one sit, and I'm curious to know what your strategy is."

"Well, let me tell you right off, Bill, we *will* make July and September. They'll be no problem at all. They're far enough away that we can really get rolling—"

"What about April?"

"Well, it's a small sit. We'll make that too."

"I don't believe you."

Lily felt a chill. Nostrand smiled with the cold superiority of a self-made man. Her husband's friends often looked at her like this, smug in their education, their successful careers, and feeling justified that she was nothing without them. Lily relaxed in the face of it, and let herself grow sharp from her own controlled anger.

"Bill, we'll make April but it'll be hard. Not because it's only three months away, but because the students who traditionally attend April stink."

"They *stink?*" He was thrown by the word.

"Yes. Any student so disorganized as to attend school at that weird time of year just hurts everybody."

"Oh, don't give me that," Nostrand said with quick irritation. "All the schools fail the April sit year after year, and the directors feed me that excuse all the time."

"Well, maybe you should fucking listen to them."

Nostrand's eyes widened.

"Pardon my French," the admissions director said, "but what a little common sense from you could do for me."

"Really?" His tone was frosty.

"Goddamn right."

Nostrand said nothing for a bit, and studied her with the beginnings of respect. "What do you want me to do?"

"First off, scrap the April start."

"Scrap it? Are you out of your mind? Where do you get off—"

"I mean it! April is a start we had at Stanley too. It's the crappiest time to run a class. Nobody wants to come. We might get twenty-five kids total and they'll all be losers. Listen to me, Bill. It won't cost us. Any bozo willing to come in April I can talk into waiting ten weeks to attend in July, which is a much more important sit. The recruiting you get in April only takes away from July anyway—everybody at the school level knows that."

"I see."

The coffee maker gurgled. She got up and lifted the carafe. "How do you like it?"

"Black's fine."

"It's how I like it too, Bill."

She handed him a brimming cup and returned to her desk. "Another thing. You need to know why we failed January. You need to understand the uphill battle I'm fighting. There's very little cooperation here. Oliver is good-hearted, but he doesn't know a thing about business."

"I'm aware of that."

"Now two major problems hindered me for January. Oliver wasn't as supportive of me as he should have been regarding these issues. I'm talking about the lack of cooperation on the part of David Hurley and, of course, Elaine Margolis who defected."

"You're saying the financial aid director isn't cooperating?"

"Christ, Bill, you know how financial aid people are! They're bigger prima donnas than the faculty! They get their rules and regulations from the feds, and they'll be damned before they bend a single one. Like they're the fucking consciences of the school, pardon my French. Try to do something clever in this office and they jump right on you saying, 'You can't do that, it's not in the regs!' As if somebody in Washington is going to say, 'Oh heavens, let's shut down the Burr College, they gave a few extra bucks to the wrong student.'"

Nostrand laughed. Lily hesitated. "No," he apologized. "Go on, I like this."

Lily sipped coffee deeply. "I've had a couple of skirmishes with David, just minor matters. Cases where he should be giving more financial aid than he is, simply because he thinks it isn't *right* to give more. And you know how that kind of thinking impairs enrollment. Still, that's not the main issue. You need to appreciate the impact on this office when Elaine quit."

"Yes, what caused that? I never felt like I got the right story from Oliver."

"Oh, it was just pettiness. She resented that I was made her boss. She'd been here a long time, and didn't want to take orders from a brand new person. She never treated me with any respect for my authority."

"Okay."

"But even that I could deal with." Lily's hands unclasped and started to flip. "For goodness sake, I don't have to be friends with my colleagues to work with them. But she wouldn't follow my orders. She believed that she alone could sell the school. I couldn't get her to do anything. Well, then right before Christmas I tried to reconcile with her. I told her how much we needed and appreciated her, and how critical these last two weeks would be—and as soon as I said that she smiled at me. And she said, 'If that's the case then I'd better quit now.' That's what she said to me, can you believe it?"

Nostrand frowned. "Wait, I don't understand what you're getting at."

"Hell, Bill, it's plain as *day!* Elaine deliberately waited until she knew we needed her most, and then she quit! She told me so *right to my face!* Completely premeditated! My God, could she have acted cruder? How's your coffee?"

"Pardon me? Oh—fine."

"So now it's just me and one rep. It's not enough. Christ, Bill, what's it going to take for you to see what you have to do? I can *guarantee* your goals for July and September, and can even promise to surpass them. I can guarantee you so much additional revenue you'll never worry about the Philly school again. But you have to do a few things for me or it'll never happen."

"Okay." Nostrand sat back and viewed her soberly. "Which brings me back to my first question. What do you want me to do?"

"Scrap April, for starters."

"Let's pretend that's done. What else?"

"I need to hire a rep to replace Elaine. But more than that I want to take Deirdre Smith and make her a rep as well. I'd rather have her in that capacity than as a secretary. We won't have a secretary—I'll just distribute those duties to everybody and we'll get by. But I want her *selling,* not collecting papers for a file."

"You don't have the budget to make her a rep."

"*Goddammit,* Bill! It takes money to make money! Pump some dough into this place. Let me make it pay off. We won't make July and September if you don't agree to this, but we will if you do. And making July and September will bring in more than enough revenue to cover it!"

He hesitated, then smiled again. "I'll consider it. What else?"

"Publicity. All we do is put ads in newspapers and the Yellow Pages. I want big, colorful ads on billboards, in the subway system, all over. Maybe even a commercial. We're talking bucks, I know, but again—it'll pay gold dividends."

"Shit," said Nostrand, but he still smiled.

"To help offset this, I want to start an Evening Paralegal class in May. I know we're scheduled to start a class in March, but I want to run *two* classes. I know I can sit them."

"You want to *add* an extra start to the schedule? My office will never argue with that."

"Good."

He put his cup down and looked at his watch. He fairly leaped to his feet. "My time's up. Lily, it's been an interesting talk."

Lily stood too. "Listen, I know you think I failed January. Well, that's bullshit and now you know why. There were problems down here, and there were problems at your end too. I can handle the problems here, but I need you to start taking care of yours. I want my new rep, and I want that publicity. I want you supporting this office and not sitting in New York yelling 'Move it, move it!' at me every day while you don't lift a finger yourself."

"Is that so? Say, aren't you afraid you're committing professional suicide, telling me this?"

Lily snorted. "There's no suicide, Bill. This school's in a lot of trouble and we both know it. I can turn it around, and frankly I relish the opportunity. But it won't break my heart to just walk away either. I'm financially set for life."

They measured each other, then suddenly both laughed. All tension melted out of the air. "God," Nostrand said. "I don't know if this school can turn around or not. I don't know if I believe you or not. But I'm gonna take every one of your proposals to John Coyne." He reached out and they shook hands. "I'll do it, Lily, because if anybody can save this school it's you. If *you* can't do it, we'd all better give up."

"Why Bill, that's sweet. Let me walk you out."

Oliver tracked down most of his department heads in Ethel's office, where the grumbling contest was in great heat. Louise and Clara were there, and Ethel presided behind her desk. "Oliver," she said as soon as he entered, "I want to kill him! To *kill* him!"

"I know. My apologies to everybody."

"It's not your fault," said Louise. "The goddamn bastard."

Clara trembled like a pudding. "How could *I* be responsible for the poor sit? I only place the grads. I don't even sit in on admissions meetings. I don't even know what the goals are."

"It's all right, Clara, don't worry about it. Ladies, we're all upset and I can't blame anyone. I'm not going to talk you out of feeling this way, but we have a more immediate concern." He shut the door, then leaned his back against it and put his hands in his pockets.

Ethel asked, "What's up?"

"After the rest of you filed out, Bill dropped the other shoe. We have to cut two secretaries."

"Shit," said Louise.

"Jesus, Mary, and Ralph," exclaimed the dean.

Clara put a hand to her mouth. A silence settled over the room.

Louise asked, "Who goes?"

"Well, I need to talk to you about that. Seniority would make it Julie and Jessica."

"Julie!" said the business manager. "No way! No way, Oliver!"

"I don't want to lose her. We can't *afford* to lose her. But I don't know how else to choose who stays and goes."

"Well, Natalie's no mean shakes," said the dean, who rarely kept a secretary past two years.

Clara's wide mouth opened twice before she timidly said, "Oliver, I can help you in one regard. Jessica gave notice yesterday afternoon."

"She did? I didn't know that."

"Well, I guess I'm telling you now. You were so worried about the Nostrand visit, I hated to burden you. She'll be here another two weeks, and then that's it. She got a job at a travel agency in Upper Darby, very close to where she lives."

"That saves one spot," said Louise.

Clara looked pained. "But I really can't afford to lose my secretary. Oliver, does this mean I can't even advertise for one—"

Ethel said stiffly, "Clara, if we lose two secretaries then none of us will have one. The hands that remain will be spread too thin."

"All right," said Oliver. He spoke slowly and painfully, as if a dozen critical thoughts passed through his mind before every word. "That's opportune, bad as it is. Jessica and who else? There's still one more who has to go."

Ethel said, "It can't be Julie."

"Amen," said the business manager.

"I don't know what to do," said Oliver. "Natalie has been here longer. And letting Deirdre go is out of the question."

Ethel leaned back in her chair. "Oliver, Natalie isn't that good. She's a poetic speller and terrible proofreader, which is the worst possible combination. She's also quite absent-minded, to my eternal irritation. A sweet kid, but nowhere near as critical a loss as Julie. Julie is just too damn good."

"You can't let Natalie go based on that," Oliver said. "You gave her a glowing review just last summer."

"Hell, Oliver, I always give them glowing reviews. I don't expect that much from them, not anymore. As long as they're conscientious and don't lie or steal, I give them good reviews. They'd never get their raises otherwise, and they're paid crap to begin with."

"Fine. But it still doesn't change the fact that Natalie has a good record on file."

"Oliver," said Louise, "we all understand the rules. Now understand this—we can't lose Julie."

Oliver stared at his shoes. No one said anything, or if they did he didn't hear. As a student Julie had been just another face in the hall until she applied for the director's secretary position. She sat in his office, dressed in the standard blue business suit, and answered his basic job interview questions, then somehow their discussion evolved to the most recent books they had read, the films they liked, and discovered from hearing his radio playing that they both enjoyed classical music. Since that day Julie had proved to be a secretary of rare quality. He couldn't remember the last time he had an assistant whose cheerful, down-to-earth manner at the front desk made the school look so good—or made *him* look good, for that matter. The thought of losing her struck a nerve deeper than mere professionalism. The school would be an empty shell without her.

"Oliver," said Ethel. "People are trying to talk to you."

He blinked. "What? Oh gosh, I'm sorry."

"Let me work out something," said the dean. "I'll have a motherly chat with Natalie, and tell her she's been here two years now and that it's high time she moved on. And Clara will find the best job possible for her."

"I certainly will," the placement director nodded bravely.

"And we'll keep Julie. We'll only lose Jessica and Natalie." Ethel shook her head angrily. "They're really decimating us, aren't they?"

"Okay."

"Good."

"But it's not fair. It's not fair to Natalie at all."

Ethel blew out her cheeks. "All right, Oliver, then make a choice. All of us here will do whatever you want. Who do you want to keep?"

"Julie."

"Then we'll take care of it. Just let us be."

"All right." He turned and opened the door. His hand played with the knob, made it rattle slightly. With his back to them all he said, "It's just I've never done anything like this before. Natalie's getting screwed, no matter how nicely we do it."

"Oliver," said Ethel, "at that meeting just now we all got screwed. Getting screwed *happens*."

Louise nodded. "That's the way of business everywhere."

Oliver stepped out of the dean's office and shut the door.

19

Lily was not bluffing with Bill Nostrand. She was determined to make the July and September sits, despite the astronomical numbers. Adding the shortage from January, plus cash flow compensation, plus compensation for the requested publicity and cancellation of the April sit, her department was now expected to bring in two hundred and forty students in July, and four hundred and sixty-five in September. (Normally the combined goal of these two sits was only five hundred.) She had a high opinion of herself and her abilities as a saleswoman. The only obstacles she ever faced were the limitations of the people around her.

That—and the money factor. Still compensating for losses, the Burr board of trustees agreed to raise tuition by nine percent, setting the July and September costs to $9,950. For the two-year program this meant a projected price tag of at least twenty thousand dollars. Even Lily couldn't imagine anyone paying that much for a secretarial liberal arts degree. To applicants' concerns about the high cost, she fell back on standard answers. Don't think of the expense now, but consider instead the long-term rewards garnered by holding a Burr College degree. Don't call it student debt;

consider it an investment in *Education,* that great limitless intangible which would benefit you for the rest of your life. Who could put a price on that?

Lily was doing all she could, but saw quickly that unless conditions changed her task of achieving the massive goals was next to impossible. In the revolving cycle of multiple starts (where a school offered the same program several times throughout a year) the profits of one sit fed into the next. The Burr College had fallen drastically behind. Lily needed the freedom to try new ideas, to do some truly aggressive salesmanship and not just sit ladylike behind a desk and pretend Burr was still an elite finishing school. She tried, almost immediately after her chat with Bill Nostrand, to put some obvious ideas into effect, but a barrier rose before her. It was a most unexpected obstacle, and one over which she should have had the most control. The obstacle was Oliver Dunbar.

Something had changed in the school director since the vice-president's visit. Lily sensed a new toughness. Oliver refused to grant even her most critical requests, such as sending Joyce Miller and Marcia Matteo, the field presenters, to the high schools on the notorious "C" list, or getting New York to budget ads for the Philadelphia subway system. Oliver hated subway ads, and told her such marketing only brought in riffraff, not the type of student Burr specialized in. Alone in her office, Lily threw pens and a tape dispenser and cursed him. Okay, so it brought in riffraff, what the hell—it brought in *somebody!* This school was dying! Why didn't he see that?

Lily considered resigning. She even called a few headhunting friends of hers, drinking buddies from the Beauty Institute and even some from good old sorority days. But then fate took mercy on her, and brought about a circumstance that put some aces back in her hand.

*

Tina called at a quarter to five to say she was at the Rittenhouse apartment and would stay the weekend. Oliver was delighted. He told her he would pack up and head home immediately.

"No hurry," she said quickly. "I just got in myself. I'll be here whenever you come."

"Are you done filming?"

"Officially yes, though we're supposed to stay available for reshoots, if Sidney decides he needs them."

"I'll come right now."

"Oliver, wait. There is some news."

"Good or bad?"

She hesitated. "Well, just news. Maybe a little bad, I don't know. But we've got the weekend. Come home when you can."

Oliver was out the door by five o'clock. Julie was surprised to see him tug his coat from the closet, but she was busy with a phone call and merely waved good night. It was the second Wednesday in January, and Oliver faced a cutting wind as he passed through barren Washington Square. An enormous blizzard had hit the city a few days earlier, and snow in record-shattering amounts still piled in drifts against buildings and blocked whole streets. Any commute by foot was treacherous from large patches of un-breakable ice.

The doorman gave him his habitual greeting. When Oliver opened the apartment door it struck a suitcase. "Tina?"

"In the living room."

She sat on the couch watching the local evening news. She wore jeans and a gray Aryan sweater. Her shoes were on, which was a little odd, for she liked to go barefoot when in the apartment.

Oliver stamped the snow off his shoes and shucked aside his wet coat. "This is a great surprise. You look wonderful." He was beside her in two strides and kissed her warmly. Tina's kiss was a little stiff. He asked, "Are you okay?"

"Sure," she said, and smiled.

But a moment later she sharpshot the remote, muting the TV. "Well, maybe not. I guess I'm not sure."

He sat beside her on the sofa. "What's up? Is this what you were talking about on the phone?"

"It is. I'm not sure how to bring this up." She took his hands. "I kept thinking I didn't have to rush this, that I'd come home and we'd have the weekend together, and then I'd break it to you Sunday night. But then riding on the train it really started to feel bad, and I knew I wouldn't manage a whole weekend."

"You're not staying?"

"I think it would be a mistake." There was white insecurity in the beaten-back lines of her eyes. Not since the cuter moments of their court-ship had he seen her look so much like a child. She put a hand to his cheek.

"Now I look at you and I feel like I owe you the weekend after all. I'll hang around if you want. But I won't be able to bear it."

"You haven't unpacked." He looked at the suitcase by the door.

"No. That's how up in the air I am. Oliver, look at me. I'm going to say this now. I want a divorce."

He stared hard at her green contact lenses. "Oh no."

"I don't know what to say next," she admitted. "But I do know I want one."

"Oh, Tina. You mustn't. No."

"This can't be a complete surprise to you."

But it was. He didn't know what he expected; he hadn't expected this.

"I kept wondering how I should tell you, because I knew it would hurt. Living in New York, you know, I was free and doing my thing, and whenever I pictured telling you it all seemed natural and honest. You can imagine how much I rehearsed this."

"Sure. Gosh." He tried to say more and couldn't. "Gosh. I can't believe it. Talk to me."

She did. She described the film project, gave him the whole plot, talked of a terrible night shoot in Bedford-Stuyvesant in the pouring rain. She spoke of her co-star, Dennis Skye, and the late-night discussions they had over what she should do, for it was plain that she needed the opportunities of a big international city like New York, and couldn't bear to return to the provincial city caught in New York's southwest shadow. The window light faded, the room darkened. The national news came on, the TV bisected by Peter Jennings' long face.

"Dennis was thinking that maybe you were bothered by my income, since it's higher than yours." Tina looked at Oliver closely. "I told him that was never the case, that it's always been the Burr College that keeps you here."

"That's right."

"He didn't mean anything by it. He was just helping me come to grips."

Oliver's stomach took a nauseous dip. "This isn't only about your career, is it?"

"No, it's not." And she looked so miserable that he instantly forgave her.

"Skye?"

"He's been a good friend for a long time."

Oliver couldn't speak.

A blue-lit stage whirled into view on the large TV. *Jeopardy*. It must be seven o'clock. The evening was leaking away from them. Tina stood up. "I've got to take dinner out of the oven."

"Honey, I can't eat anything."

"Neither can I. But I made a pot of macaroni and cheese. It was all I could find. It's been baking on low for an hour. I have to take it out."

After she was gone he stood up. Save for a little vertigo he experienced no sensations, not the carpet under his shoes or the heat hushing from the central air. He was incapable of thinking. He stood by the double glass doors of the balcony and stared down at Rittenhouse Park, eleven floors below, a smoky muddle of frozen treetops framed on all sides by bottled up traffic. He felt bad for everyone down there.

The second round of *Jeopardy* started on the TV, and with Tina still in the kitchen there was nothing to do but take the remote and raise the volume.

"At more than four and a half billion years old, it's the closest star to Earth."

The Sun, he thought, and watched as the three contestants got it wrong.

"Oliver?"

Tina stood in the doorway. Her arms were at her sides, her face worried. The gray Aryan sweater made her look infinitely huggable. "Are you okay?"

He shrugged.

"There must be something you want to say to me. Obviously, I feel terrible about this."

"Thank you."

"Okay, maybe you should tell me how you feel. Help me a little, Oliver, and then I'll take whatever lumps you want to give."

"What I feel?"

"Yes."

His mind turned inward. He didn't feel anything. Or maybe he felt so much it didn't seem like anything. He thought of all their firsts: their first meeting in a French Lit class at the University of Penn, their first drink at a pub, their first expensive dinner at Bookbinders which he couldn't afford but took her to anyway, and their first home in Powelton Village with whatever furniture their parents could spare. He thought of the Quaker wedding in Abington, exchanging vows and a ring, the erotic way she kissed him after the marriage certificate was read aloud, to the mirth of their friends on the benches.

"Waste," he said.

"Oliver?"

"All I feel is an incredible waste. I don't believe in reincarnation. We can't take back twenty-one years of marriage. We've wasted each other."

"God, I feel bad about this." Tina approached him and put her arms around his neck. "Honey, talk to me. I need to know what you're thinking."

"But I really don't have anything to say. I've said what I can. You really want a divorce?"

"Yes." She looked terrific this close, shiny black hair, large oval eyes. He loved her lashes. "This is all my fault. I won't contest a thing with you within reason. I know you're a fair man, I don't expect to be taken advantage of. Would Ken Allenbach be your lawyer?"

"I suppose."

"I know this is a blow. I swear I couldn't think of any way to make it easier. We'll get the whole thing settled as quickly as possible. We're not enemies, it shouldn't drag long. Oliver—are you all right?"

"Yes."

"Why do you keep looking away?"

"I don't know. No reason." The *Jeopardy* category was literature. Oliver tried not to listen, but it was one of his favorites.

"This is all a big mess. I'll go now and stay in a hotel. We'll keep in touch. There are things I'll need to take back with me, but actually the place in West Village is pretty well stocked. I've done a lot with it since you last saw it. Would you keep this apartment, or do you think you'd move somewhere else?"

"I have no idea."

Alex Trebeck said, "He's the villain trapped in a cave with Tom and Becky."

"I know you weren't expecting to think about this, but I'm not going to stay in Philadelphia after tonight, and anything you can decide now would be a big help."

"Injun Joe."

"What?"

"Who was Injun Joe?" Their eyes met, and he hung his head. "I'm sorry, what were you saying?"

Tina's contriteness vanished. She removed her arms. "I'll call you." She took her coat and suitcase and walked out the door.

20

Jean Cavanaugh, at thirty-eight, remembered nuclear air raid drills. If you were outside at recess when the bell rang, they made you kneel with your head against the brick wall. If in the classroom, you were to squeeze under your desk. It affected kids in different ways. Most thought it fun, an adventurous break from arithmetic or vocabulary. Jean was terrified by it. It was clear that putting your head under your desk during a nuclear onslaught was the smart thing to do, but she sensed the undercurrent in her teachers' instructions that implied your chances were still a little slim. She was nine years old and her teachers, even as they yelled "Duck and hide! Duck and hide!" were admitting that she was vulnerable to a horrible bombing. Death was a big worry for a kid whose legs were too chubby, who had fat cheeks, and who hadn't been kissed by a boy although Tommy Gallagher spun the bottle once and it pointed at her, but then he ran out of the room without doing it, leaving her to face the stares of everyone. A nuclear bomb would set all of Pennsylvania to rubble, and turn her friends and family into air pockets. Completely dispirited after one such drill, Jean put her head on her desk and gazed sidewise out the window at the grass she might never see again, and pictured the baseball diamond's metal fence blasted to fragments like a swatted spider's web.

Miss Bartholomew spotted her moping and put a swift end to it. Miss Bartholomew was sixty going on two hundred, and had been teaching fourth grade for so long the standard joke was that the elementary school had been built around her. You didn't lay your head down in Miss Bartholomew's class and live to tell of it. Jean slowly grew aware of a fearful silence in the classroom. A hulking shadow passed over her desk and she knew she was in trouble. The back of Miss Bartholomew's hand, hard as a Ping-Pong paddle, struck the girl's spine with a terrific WHOMP! The sheer force snapped Jean into rigid, perfect posture.

"We do not sleep in Social Studies!" the teacher barked. She started sluggishly toward the front of the room. She was squat and spectacled, and tended to mutter to herself when she walked, whether in the classroom or passing down a corridor.

"Ma'am," Jean said through the lingering sting, "I wasn't sleeping."

Miss Bartholomew's broad back stiffened. She turned to face this new effrontery. She had a grandmother's face gone to rot, jowls dripping, eyes sunk in folded wrinkles, and white eyebrows hanging loose from her forehead like pinches of lichen. "Are you lying to me, Jean?"

"No, ma'am."

"Were you asleep?"

"No, ma'am."

WHOMP!

Jean yelped this time, but the teacher's face remained a stone gargoyle's. Teachers by the mid-Sixties were no longer allowed to strike students. Paddles were forbidden. So were old reliables like making the pupil face a corner with his or her pants yanked down. Psychologists were deploring such corporal measures, declaring they caused mental scars instead of positive reinforcement. But in the Sixties the common folk were not yet conditioned to scream lawsuit at the slightest offense, and the old breed, gray and beyond change like Miss Bartholomew, successfully resisted any enlightened attitudes toward classroom discipline.

"Well," she declared, "you certainly weren't watching the board."

"No, I wasn't. Sorry."

Honesty was the only way to soften Miss Bartholomew. "Then what were you doing?"

"I was worried about dying."

"Dying?"

"From the drill. I'm scared about it." Jean dropped her voice, hating that her classmates were getting to hear this embarrassing confession.

For a moment Miss Bartholomew was at a loss. "But Jean, the drill is for your safety."

"Yes, ma'am. I know that."

"Jean, we're all scared of dying. These are very scary times. But we can't just lay our heads down and surrender. It's up to your generation to make the future a better place to live in. Don't you see?"

"Yes, ma'am."

"So don't neglect your studies. Learning is important for all of us."

"Okay." But Jean said it wistfully, and her eyes strayed to the window again.

Hot air exhaled from the teacher's nostrils. Miss Bartholomew's attempts at teacher-student counseling did not hold patience as a virtue. The broad rough hand whipped out again.

WHOMP!

"Face that blackboard this instant, and let me hear no more of this! If you don't know what's good for you, miss, then trust your elders. Now everyone turn in their arithmetic books to Page 23. Jean, you can go to the board and do the first three problems."

Jean Cavanaugh grew up remembering that. She would never openly admit that three whacks on the back from a scary fourth grade teacher were enough to influence a teaching style that, within the small network of the Burr Colleges of Business, would become notorious. But she told the story often to friends and colleagues, for the truth was that Miss Bartholomew left the firmest and most lasting mark. Jean never again used the insecurities of daily life to lower her aspirations. She took great pride in this. She was smart enough to recognize a sad truth: that when the boss was a bastard people did their jobs well. Hence the tyranny in the classroom. She loved her students, and they were going to learn. She wouldn't hit them like her old teacher, but she did twist the screws hard. And her students hated her for this bullying manner, for the heavy workload she imposed on them, and for refusing to apply curves to mediocre test scores. At the same time, Jean made herself entirely available to them, and ultimately they recognized her deep devotion to them. Before any class graduated, the hatred invariably changed to respect and gratitude.

On this particular day, shortly after the new semester began, she stood before the September class and finished up the first lesson of Finance II. Just as the bell blasted its ugly squawk, her eyes focused on a student she had decided would be the next recipient of the Bartholomew Technique. "Chapters Twenty-five, Twenty-six, and Twenty-seven by Friday," she said. (This was Wednesday.) "Pay particular attention to Twenty-six, which deals with intangible assets. Twenty-five goes into greater detail about depreciation."

The class knew better than to groan.

"Okay. See you Friday. Ms. Robinson, please stay after class."

The black girl looked up, startled. Her classmates shuffled out the door, and the room felt empty and cold. Keone could hear her own heart. Jean advanced only after the last student had exited.

"Ms. Robinson, don't worry. You haven't done anything wrong." Yet the teacher didn't smile, and Keone sat rigid. "You do have a problem. I saw it all last semester, and when I reviewed the final fall grades I knew I'd better act. You obviously want to succeed. You're working hard. In fact, I'll tell you to your face you're the hardest worker in the class. You are also getting the worst grades. The only students doing worse than you are the ones who are exactly your opposite—that is, the ones who aren't applying themselves at all. How do you account for this?"

Keone, convinced this was a scolding, blanked her face the way she did when her father was on a rampage.

"Do you have an answer for me?" asked Jean.

"No'm."

"Well, *I* can account for it. Let me tell you why you're doing so poorly." And Jean thought again about that WHOMP!

"Yeah'm."

"You're failing because you came to us under-qualified for this curriculum. Your high school, Southwest, pushes students in one door and out the other. They don't teach a damn thing. You received no educational development, no discipline, and no character. That school readied you for nothing."

Keone's eyes flashed with indignation. Jean didn't flinch.

"You want to deny that? You mad enough to prove me wrong? Well, I'm mad too, Ms. Robinson. I don't say things like this to a student for the fun of it. Let's look at your test scores, just to pick one thing. Three primary tests in this class alone during the fall semester. Two F's and a D-minus. That averages to a grade of F-plus, Ms. Robinson, and I hate to break the news to you but there is *no such thing* as an F-plus. You're just flat-out failing."

Keone said angrily, "Why you ridin' me?"

"It's rid*ing*," snapped Jean. "And I'm not riding you. What I'm doing is making you an offer. Listen to me now, and don't sulk. I'm here five days a week this semester, and I finish every day by four. However, I'm going to stay until six every night and do some special tutoring in accounting, and maybe some other subjects as well. Whatever I see fit. I'm not offering this to everybody, but I am offering it to you."

"'Cause you think I'm stupid."

"No. Because you're working hard, and your lousy high school let you down. The system wasn't fair to you, Ms. Robinson. If you didn't give a damn, it'd be different. As it is, you deserve fair play, so here I am."

Jean turned and walked to the front of the room. She picked her pocketbook off the desk and irritably snapped it open. "You should know that you're not the only one who will attend these extra sessions. I've asked three other girls in your class and I've got two others in mind that I haven't approached yet. We'll start on Monday. Are you interested?"

Keone's heart thumped hard. She hated herself for floundering in and out of these classes all these months, fucking up the tests and not understanding what she was reading. She had expected to be kicked out at Christmas but by some miracle the dean kept her on.

"I be there."

"It's 'I'll be there,' Ms. Robinson."

"Yeh'm."

"Say it!"

"I'll be there."

Jean allowed herself the thinnest of smiles. "That's a taste, Ms. Robinson. After school sessions are open season to me. We won't limit ourselves to accounting. You'll want to be a top Burr administrative assistant when you leave here. *That's* what you're going to learn. You're not going to be unmarketable when you graduate. You've put too much of yourself into this to let that happen."

"Thanks, Ms. Cavanaugh."

"You're welcome. Go to your next class."

As she said it, the one minute warning bell blatted. Keone scooped her books in both arms and darted out of the room. Jean took a pale lipstick from her pocketbook, ran it quickly over her lips, put the lipstick back and dropped the pocketbook in her desk drawer, where she locked it in. She stood with her back to the chalkboard, her feet spaced apart, and watched, frowning, as the new group, the January kids, trooped meekly into the classroom. Only two weeks in, they hadn't yet reached the *respectful-but-getting-comfortable-with-it* attitude. They were still scared of her.

This group was a real mixed bag. Easier than ever to tell apart the girls who really wanted to learn and those chosen by Admissions simply to fill the class. Jean's practiced eye singled out fifteen already who would probably get WHOMPED before the spring semester finished.

"Spot quiz," she announced.

The class looked stunned, and two or three groaned.

"No noise!" she barked. "Books on the floor! Pens ready! Ms. Otterbach, take these sheets and pass one out to everybody! You have twenty minutes! *Do it!*"

21

A student knocked timidly on the half-open door of the dean's office. "Dean Harris, can I talk to you a moment?"

Ethel's office was a holocaustal mess of stacked files, books, papers, grade sheets, newspapers, boxes, and several pairs of high heels lined against one wall. Most of the stacks were current student files transferred from the now empty cubicle that had been Natalie's, and Ethel had no idea where to store them. The dean was rummaging through a large file box with the silk sleeves of her blouse rolled up. She saw the student and knew with a veteran educator's instinct what was about to transpire.

"Ms. Whitman, are you all right? Do you need to sit down?"

"No, I'll be okay." Mary Grace stepped into the room. Her eyes were bruised, her cheeks pale. She kept looking everywhere but at the dean. "Ma'am, I have to drop out."

"Drop out? No, you can't. You've already put in a year and a half. You're in your final semester. You can't afford to lose all that."

"I don't have a choice."

Ethel shook her head. "There has to be a choice. Dropping out is not an option. Tell me what's happening to you."

Mary Grace looked at the floor. Her hands tightly gripped each other. "Nothing's happening to me. I found a job."

"Did you? What kind of job?"

"Secretarial. It's a real good paying job, and it's just what we need."

"You mean your family?"

"Yes."

"What's the company's name?"

Mary Grace looked up, meeting the dean's eye for a moment. "Ma'am, I *do* have to drop out."

"Ms. Whitman," Ethel said gently, "you've got a home situation, don't you?"

The student looked wretched.

"I want you to tell me what's happening to you. But close that door first. No reason for the rest of the world to hear your story." Ethel said this because her office was located on the second floor, and opened directly onto a classroom corridor.

Mary Grace shut the door, but said firmly, "I don't have a home situation. I just have to leave."

"Even though you're in your final semester?"

"Yes."

Ethel thought a moment. "What if, instead of dropping out, you took a leave of absence?"

"What's that?"

"It allows you to come back and resume your studies after this interruption is over. We'll say that you're leaving as of today and we'll—well, we'll just keep your return date open. Maybe you can join the nine-month January class that just started. Their second semester starts in May. You could join them, and graduate in September."

"I don't know if I'll be back by May."

"Then we'll keep the return date open. You're a good student, Ms. Whitman. You deserve a few breaks. Have a seat." Ethel offered this before realizing that her client chair was buried under paper. "No, I guess you can't. Hang loose a moment, Ms. Whitman." While the dean rummaged through her desk for a form, Mary Grace stood silently. She didn't ask what happened to Natalie. The dean's stock answer was "She's gone on to bigger and better things," and since Nat was a grad of Burr, the answer seemed credible. But in truth Clara Peterson was still sending Nat out on interviews. Her layoff was three weeks old.

The form she wanted was in an overstuffed drawer, and Ethel betrayed her middle age by grunting as she tugged it out. "Here it is. You fill out the top section."

"Do I have to get all these signatures?" The form required the signature of the financial aid director, the business manager, and the school director.

"Don't worry about that. I'll take care of it."

Ethel went back to her clutter, and tried not to watch the unhappy student fill out the form. A moment later Mary Grace said, "I'm done."

"Okay, I'll take it."

Ethel reached for it and their eyes met. She knew this kid was never coming back. Family situations were too volatile, and the resulting messes never went away. Whatever blow had been dealt poor Mary Grace, it was bigger than her education at Burr. "We'll see you in the spring."

"I'm very sorry," said the girl.

"Take care."

"Thanks for everything, Dean Harris." Mary Grace smiled shyly, and then she was gone.

Ethel stood among her piles, angry and helpless. She quickly completed her portion of the form, then strode down the stairs and through the long corridor to the front of the school. Stray students backed against the antique furniture to let her pass.

Ethel stopped short of assaulting Oliver's closed door. She forced herself to knock gently. David Hurley's face popped around the edge of Louise's partition. "Oliver's not in."

"Where is he?"

"Beats me. Louise says so."

Ethel walked into the cubicle. Louise was at her desk, mulling over unpaid accounts. David sat across from her. These two always got together before bills went out, so Louise would know exactly what financial aid was outstanding before she tracked down delinquent students to confront them with what they owed. The stack of outstanding accounts looked higher than usual.

Ethel asked, "Does anybody know where he is?"

Louise said, "He told me he was going to lunch, but then he never came back."

The dean looked at her watch. "It's three-thirty. That doesn't make sense."

"It does if something's wrong."

"*Is* something wrong?"

Louise chuckled. "You want to tell me something recent that's gone right?"

"Okay. As a matter of fact, I'm here to add to the hard luck list." Ethel slapped the LOA form on the desk and Louise's tea mug rattled. "As long as you're both here, deal with this."

"Oh my God," said David. "It's Mary Grace."

Louise grimaced. "What's her problem?"

"I wish I knew. She showed at my door just now and said she was quitting. Looked terribly distraught, and tried to tell me she found a job, but I know there's something more."

"Family?"

"Probably. I couldn't get her to tell me anything."

"You think she'll come back?"

"Who can say? I know I'm not supposed to, but I'm leaving the return date empty. She's an excellent student, and she can come back five years from now as far as I'm concerned."

"You know she's three weeks into this semester. She'll get charged ninety percent of her tuition."

Ethel winced. "Isn't there anything you can do about that?"

"I would, but New York won't. It's in the kid's enrollment agreement, which I'm assuming she signed. All the kids who drop out get burned like this, you know that." Louise looked at David. "Make sure all her financial aid came in."

As soon as the financial aid director left, Louise punched Mary Grace Whitman's name on her computer screen. She grinned with cold satisfaction at the fully paid account. Hardship or not, Mary Grace was one of the reliable ones.

Louise finished her own part of the LOA form, then walked it out to the lobby. "Where's Oliver?"

Julie looked up guiltily from a magazine she was reading. The lobby was empty, the phone silent. The page from the appointment book was blank. "If he isn't in his office then I don't know."

"Did he come back from lunch?"

"I thought he did. I took lunch at one and Deirdre covered for me. I just assumed he was back in his office. Did he say he was taking the afternoon off?"

"I've never known Oliver to take time off without memoing everybody two weeks in advance. Julie, is there something wrong with him?"

The secretary was silent.

"Is there? If something's going down I need to know."

Julie looked very unhappy. "I'm not sure. He seems sad, though that could be from anything. I know it was hard for him to let Nat and Jessica go."

"True," said Louise and no more. No one had told Julie the real story about that.

"It's like … like suddenly he doesn't have a sense of humor. He's buried by his problems, whereas before he used to take even the worst of them in stride. You've known him a long time. What do you think it could be?"

"With Oliver?" Louise raised her brows. "It could be anything. Global warming or a traffic ticket."

"This seems different."

"Not if you know him. Did you know this college has a ninety-seven percent placement rate? That's a terrific number. Any other school director would kill for a stat like that. You know what Oliver does? Each year when Clara reports that figure he anguishes over the three percent. Wants to know who they were, what were their grades, wants to figure where the school could have done better."

Julie frowned. "Isn't that admirable?"

"It can be," Louise acknowledged. "Most of the time it's a pain in the butt. Has Oliver ever told you about the perfect good act?"

"The what?"

"Listen to this, this is good. According to Oliver, the perfect good act is when you deliberately sacrifice for someone else but they never learn that you did so. They don't find out, and you don't tell them. But more than that, you don't tell anyone else, so no one ever knows. But even more than *that,* you yourself don't know, even though you made the sacrifice deliberately."

"But that's impossible!"

"Of course it is!" Louise cackled loudly. "It's certifiable! Who would set a standard like that? Who even *thinks* like that? Don't get me wrong, I love Oliver, I really do. But he's also a fruitcake." She handed over Mary Grace's LOA form. "Anyway, get him to sign this, if you see him."

Louise returned to her office. Worried now, Julie picked up her phone and started calling around, trying to find Oliver. She buzzed the faculty lounge, the library, and any other room in the school that had a phone extension. No one had seen him. She even asked several students who passed through the lobby, but they merely stared at her. Julie finally tried his home phone, but when Kevin Costner's voice came on she hung up.

It was Lily who found Oliver. Bill Nostrand had just gotten off the phone with her. A recalculation of the loss for January and the carryover from last fall put both the July and September goals up another seven students each. Well, fourteen more on top of a combined seven hundred and five didn't make much difference. But she needed Oliver to know. He had to see what a bind she was in.

He was in the library. Lily didn't know Julie had buzzed this room without getting an answer, and so finding him there didn't strike the admissions director as strange. There were no students in the room. The school director sat at a table, one hand resting on it. His suit jacket and overcoat were folded on a chair. He had no papers spread out before him. He was just sitting there.

"Hello!" she sang in her best teasing tone. "Hiding from us, eh? What a great idea."

Oliver looked up dully, which disconcerted her.

"May I join you?"

"Sure."

She sat across from him and clasped her hands earnestly. Lily's black dress was interwoven with gold threads, enough to give her whole body an animated luster. Her gold and bronze hair was swept atop her head, as glamorous as the day he first met her. "Oliver, Bill Nostrand just got off the phone with me."

He grunted, "More good news."

"He's adding another fourteen to the July-September sits."

"Why?"

"Recalculating our losses. Oliver, we're in trouble."

"We've always been in trouble, Lily. Saying it again doesn't change anything."

The flatness of his manner truly surprised her. "Oliver, is everything okay?"

With an embarrassed smile he said, "I was feeling sorry for myself. I came back here until it passed."

"Office or home? Don't answer if you don't want to."

"It's mostly office stuff. The problem at home," he pushed up his glasses and rubbed his eyes, "is already gone."

"Well … whatever I can do to help, Oliver."

"What's up, Lily?"

"Right." She hunkered down to business. "Oliver, our lead cards are as low as they've ever been. The presentations are filling high school auditoriums, but for some reason we aren't getting the lead cards back. Dee now comes in at eleven and works till seven, four days a week, so she can do evening telemarketing, but there aren't even that many leads to call. Dee's pulled a list of inquiries dating back a year and we're contacting anybody who asked about us but never enrolled. The response has been abysmal."

"Well, someone who called a year ago isn't going to—"

"But the recent inquiries aren't any better." Lily's face darkened with anger. "People who phoned as recently as Christmas are pugging out on us. We're going whole days without a single interview. Julie sits up front twiddling her thumbs with nothing to do. The lobby is empty."

"So how can I help you?"

"You need to review our options in realistic terms and keep an open mind. Then you can make the right decisions. Going as we are, this school will fail and possibly close in July."

"They won't close the school."

"Bill told me otherwise just a few minutes ago. He sounded kindly about it too, the way a veterinarian explains euthanasia."

"Yes, I know that tone. But Burr has never closed a school. He'll fire you and me before shutting the doors and declaring publicly that a Burr College failed."

"Then let's worry about you and me, okay?"

He heard the urgency in her voice. It was a rallying cry, a call for action. Against his will he felt a little energy come back. He looked into her worried eyes and felt ashamed. Other admissions directors faced with a low lead pool generated through a predecessor's poor management would embrace it as a predetermined cause for a sit's failure, and therefore keep their own track record clean. In his experience, most admissions directors sought excuses for their low numbers as hungrily as they sought their applicants. "Lily, what do you have in mind?"

She smiled eagerly. "First off, I want to start using the 'C' list. Listen," she said quickly as he predictably stiffened, "we've exhausted the 'B' and 'A' lists. Our girls are going back and presenting before the same students. A third of the lead cards Dee's processing are repeats from girls who've already applied. The 'C' schools haven't been touched by us in over three years."

"Yes, with good reason."

"Because they're lower class schools, I know. I don't think Burr can afford to be snobbish right now—"

"It's not snobbery," he said. "Well, not much, at least. The last time a presenter went to a 'C'-list school she got a brick through her windshield. You can't ask reps to go back to places like that."

"Sure you can. That was one incident. Listen to me, Oliver. The business schools that recruit from ghetto high schools like Buchanan, Southwest, and Western High are the bargain basement schlocky ones. Crap operations interested in getting tuition out of the students but not in giving them an education. Places that offer computer training without a computer on campus for the kids to learn on, or where kids pay for books they never get. The high school counselors would go wild if the Burr College of Business with its sound reputation went to where these other schools are recruiting. We'd clean up."

"I'm sure," Oliver spoke hastily. "But if you bring a lot of ghetto girls here, what's going to happen to our standard population, the upper-middle class white woman from Bryn Mawr or Haddon Heights?" And an inner voice mocked him with shame for asking this.

"We're losing that demographic anyway. We're losing it to real colleges, the Villanovas and the Bucknells. You know I'm right."

He was silent.

"Well?"

"Okay."

"Okay what?"

"You can start using the 'C' list."

"Thank you." She laughed, crinkled her nose, and patted his hand. "Don't look so demoralized. We're actually doing the type of good deed you admire most. As long as those kids are going to get talked into the crappy business schools anyway, wouldn't you rather they learned at Burr where the curriculum is good?"

"Well, that's true."

Lily sat back, beaming. The gold threads in the black dress quivered. She reclasped her hands and waited.

"What else?" he asked.

"ATB."

"Oh no!"

"Ability to benefit." Lily leaned forward, flushed with enthusiasm. "It's high time, Oliver. We can't afford not to."

"Lily, ability to benefit students aren't even high school graduates. That's lowering the admissions standard to the point of nothing."

"We can't afford to be snobbish. Just because some poor girl couldn't make it through high school because her parents weren't supportive, or because she made a bad decision and dropped out when she was too young to know better, doesn't mean she should pay for it by remaining ignorant the rest of her life."

"Lily," he said, thinking less about the students than of facing his dean, "I don't know how I can even consider this."

"You'd *better* consider it. We're not getting the kind of applicant you want, so we either get the ones we don't want or take no one at all. Besides, Oliver, I'm sure you don't believe these kids should be left out in the cold."

"Well no, but—"

"And I'm sure the Burr faculty can handle them."

Oliver put a hand to his head. "The faculty."

"All right, they won't be happy about it, but they'll do it. And they'll do a better job teaching those kids than the schlock outfits can do."

"But don't you understand? There's a stigma to schools that accept ATB, Lily. We're just not that kind of institution."

"Bill's thinking of closing us down. Do you want to be *that* kind of institution?"

He put his head in his hands. "Ethel will go through the roof."

"Well, Ethel could use a little modern day reasoning as well." Lily stood up, primed and shimmering. "Oh, I do have some very good news. Paralegal for March looks solid, and May is promising. Have to give Bill credit for that. He thought Paralegal would sell in Philly, and he's right."

"No one doubted it would sell," said Oliver. "The problem is finding them jobs when they get out."

"Clara is a whiz. Do you want the door shut?"

"Please."

Lily strolled out.

Silence again. A fluorescent light fluttered over his table, casting a sickly blue wave across the tan Formica. Oliver leaned on the back legs of his chair, removed his glasses, and shut his eyes.

Friday's staff meeting would be hellish. When he announced Lily's policy changes Ethel would kill him. Oliver couldn't believe the changes himself, and he'd conceded to them just minutes ago. They were the scariest choices regarding the future of his school that he had ever made, and after stalling Lily for so long he had now, almost at the drop of a hat, given in. He wasn't sure why. No, that wasn't true. Actually he *was* sure, but wasn't prepared yet to be so honest with himself.

He no longer cared.

22

"You are out of your goddamn skull!" the dean declared in a voice so thunderous the department heads around her cringed. He had never seen Ethel angrier. No one had. Even Louise tucked her head down and preferred to study the doodles on her notepad. David looked horrified, and Clara seemed near swooning.

Oliver found himself defending the ATB decision by echoing Lily's argument to him. "It's just something we have to do for now, Ethel. We can't afford to be snobbish. In concept ATB is just—"

"Snobbish!" shouted Ethel. "Bullshit! You can't be trying to justify ability to benefit, Oliver! Not to *my* face! Not in front of everybody in this room! I can listen to anybody talk about it but you."

Lily sat on the couch in a purple lame minidress, her bare legs raised off the floor and curled under her. She held only coffee. With a wide smile she said, "It's actually a very exciting concept—"

"You just shut up!" Ethel whirled on her. "You think I'll believe this is Oliver's idea? You think we don't know who's pushing this?"

"Ethel!"

"We are *not* doing ATB, Oliver! Do you hear me?"

Oliver said with quiet firmness, "I hear you, Ethel. Except we are."

For a long time the only sound in the room was the harsh breathing of the dean.

"When last I heard," said Oliver, "nobody gave you any special veto powers on admissions practices. Something's got to be done to get students in the door. Wouldn't you say that's right, Louise?"

The business manager stared at him. Lily chimed in, "You betcha we do!" and Louise closed her eyes.

Ethel said, "Then I quit."

Oliver's answer was to simply look at her.

To the others in the room, David, Louise, Clara, and Julie taking the minutes at furious speed from the corner, the import struck them like a dream. This was incredible. People came and went at Burr all the time, that was the nature of small college administration everywhere, but not Ethel Harris. Not the dean. Save for Oliver, no one had worked here longer. The corridors and classrooms radiated with her authority. This standoff was a frightening thing for the staff to witness. It spelled a profound and terrible wrenching of the very foundation of the Philadelphia school.

Ethel waited him out, but he continued only to look at her. Finally her breathing calmed and the muscles in her face relaxed. Her large fists unclenched, and she nodded slowly.

"That's it then." She walked out of the office.

"Oh my!" said Clara.

Lily frowned. Half-sitting on her calves, she rubbed one ankle thoughtfully but knew not to say anything.

"All right." Oliver picked a sheet off his desk. "This is how it is. The federal government has specific regulations regarding ability to benefit. We have to—"

"Oliver!"

"Yes, Louise?"

"Ethel isn't really quitting, is she?"

"I have no idea."

"Oliver, are you crazy?"

Out of his goddamn skull. "Louise, people do what they have to." He felt his words squirming through a wall of fatigue. "We are going to become an ability to benefit school. I'm sorry for anybody who doesn't like it, but I can't be swayed by mere discontent. Nobody's staying here because I'm holding a gun to their head. They're here because they want this school to turn around."

"I want it to turn around too, but you said yourself ability to benefit is—"

"I don't care what I've said in the past. I'm not going to argue this. Not at this late date." He put the paper down and leaned back in his chair. "Lily, why don't you explain it?"

Lily uncurled and sat forward. Dimples flitted at everyone. "Well, this is really a terrific opportunity. It means we no longer have to collect high school diplomas or G.E.D.s from students in order to accept them. As long as a student can prove she will learn from our program, which she does by taking a test—"

"And which is not the same as the admissions test," Oliver cut in.

"Right. It's designed to show that the applicant, despite not being a high school graduate, will benefit from the program of study. If the student passes the test, she can be a legitimate candidate for the Burr College. It's going to be a major answer to our enrollment problem!" Lily beamed and nodded and touched her bright hair.

"There's nothing sleazy about it," said Oliver.

"Oh heavens, no!" chimed Lily.

"And it's completely sanctioned by the federal government. It's all spelled out in the regs. The test cannot be designed by the school, nor can it be proctored by someone who works for the school. The government has authorized several tests that students may take, and I will leave it to Ethel to choose the test and determine who will be the authoritative outside agent to proctor it."

"You mean the new dean," muttered Louise.

He was brought up short. "Right. The new dean will decide these things."

Lily twitched but remained silent.

"Oliver," Louise said, "even though the federal government sanctions it, it's still a lessening of our admissions criteria. You're not going to deny that, are you?"

He said with hard determination, "No. Done with discretion this will not lessen our admissions standards. I want the … the dean to monitor the results of the tests, and I want her input on every individual case that utilizes ATB."

"Can I say something?" Lily raised a hand.

"No!" barked Louise.

"I don't think we should think of this as a negative thing." The admissions director smiled and nodded and flipped her hands. "It's actually a very positive move for us. We're broadening our field of admittance. We're saying that anyone, regardless of past mistakes and personal errors of judgment, is entitled to a good education. ATB is a screening device, ladies. A screening device can hardly be a scam."

No one appeared convinced. A pall hung over the office. Dust was felt as it dropped on skin and hair.

Oliver said, "Anybody else got news?"

There was either nothing new, or people just didn't feel like talking. The staff meeting broke up.

The word passed swiftly through the faculty that Ethel Harris had resigned. Clara told Donna Harding in the faculty lounge, and Donna actually interrupted Jean Cavanaugh's Econ II class to whisper it in her ear. Ethel had gone straight from the staff meeting to her office on the second floor and locked the door. Several teachers tried to buzz her, but she did not pick up her intercom. No one could get to her.

Bob Lawrence heard about it at lunch when he stopped in the lounge to get his mail. Along one wall of the lounge were little square cubbyholes where every morning Julie Fitzgerald put each teacher's mail after sorting it.

"It's the end of the world," Carol Sobolewski told him. She was sipping tea at one of the tables and eating a pastel-colored salad in a plastic tray.

"It is?" he said. "Again?"

"Ethel's quit."

"Get out." He sat down across from her. "Where'd you hear this? I don't believe it."

"She got fed up with whatever they're doing up front there. I can't say I blame her. Just look what they let in the door for January."

"Well, January is always a weaker class."

"What about Suellen Colby?"

Bob fought and failed to keep a smile off his face. "Well frankly, Carol, I think the Suellen case is a little funny."

"Funny," said Carol, aghast. "The girl's *blind!*"

"Well … yes. Yes, she is." Bob was still smiling.

It was true. One of Lily's last minute entries into the January IP Program was a Hatboro girl who was eighty percent blind. She walked with a cane, took the train by herself every day, and wanted with all her might to be an executive assistant with computer experience.

"I've got nothing against the handicapped," said Carol. "In fact, I don't even like the word 'handicapped.' I don't like 'challenged' either. They're just people with individual problems like we all have. But Bob, we're not set up to teach blind students. How is she going to learn personal computing if she can't read the keyboard or screen?"

"Well, they're coming out with systems like that now—"

"Sure, but we don't have them here. Donna Harding is beside herself. She's going to get that girl next semester to teach personal computer training. I don't know what she's going to do."

"Maybe Donna can teach her seeing-eye dog. Teach it to bark when she makes a typo."

"That's not funny, Bob," Carol said so seriously that he finally got the smirk off his face.

"I'll see you later," he said, going to the door. "That's hell about Ethel, huh?"

"I don't expect many of us will stay long after she's gone," Carol predicted ominously, and seemed to enjoy saying it. Bob was happy to quit the lounge.

He hadn't brought his lunch today, so he entered the student lounge and got in line at the food stand. He pulled a plastic tray off a rack and ordered a roast beef on rye with Swiss and mayo, potato chips, and a Coke. He paid, then held the tray while he scanned for a seat.

Heather flagged him. She was seated at a table with two classmates, Kristin Rutherford and Jennifer DeAngelis. He weighed the risks briefly, then thought the hell with it and approached. He gave the table his best smile. "Got room for a fourth, ladies?"

"Sure, Mr. Lawrence, come on in." Kristin shifted to make room. She was thin with freckles and non-descript brown hair, and her smile revealed crooked lower teeth. But she wrote good B papers in class.

"I'm not breaking up any boyfriend talk, am I?"

"Naw," said Jennifer. "Kristin's talking about her ski trip over Christmas break."

"Really? Kristin, do you ski?"

"Sure. My family rents a place up in New Hampshire. Been doing it since I was four."

"I've never skied," said Heather. "Someone should take me sometime."

"I've gone on Camelback in the Poconos," Jennifer said. "Scared me shitless first time I skied down that. Oh I'm sorry, Mr. Lawrence."

"That's okay. You're allowed to say 'scared.'"

Jennifer laughed, and proved she liked him by punching him on the arm.

"So guys," he said, "any of the plays we're reading this semester look good to you?" For this was what they had him for now, Drama I, part of their liberal arts credits on the way to the associate's degree.

"I can't even remember the name of the one you just assigned," said Jennifer, laughing and putting a small fist in her mouth.

"*You Can't Take It With You,*" said Kristin. "God, you don't ever read your assignments, Jennifer!"

"That's not true," Jennifer yapped, but seemed flattered. "I'll read anything fun."

"Well, it's supposed to be a comedy," Bob said.

"That's my problem with it," said Kristin. "I'm not laughing at anything. It's just dull."

"Well, it was written during the Great Depression. The idea of a family saying 'To hell with you,' to the government at a time when everybody hated the government had a lot of strong appeal. That's where the comedy is rooted."

"But I don't see how they could get away with it. I know my dad couldn't. He'd get himself arrested if he didn't pay taxes and stuff."

"It's wish fulfillment," said Bob. "It's what everybody would *like* to do. That's what makes it funny."

"That's what makes it dumb," insisted Kristin.

Heather spoke up. "Do we really have to read a Shakespeare play? I can't stand that stuff."

"Well, *Romeo and Juliet*. The dean chose that one. That's not what I'd have picked."

"What would you have picked?"

"*Hamlet*. There's a good play. There are a million interpretations of *Hamlet*. You guys could write anything about it you wanted and I'd have to give you all A's. You can't go wrong, it seems, interpreting *Hamlet*."

"What's that about?" asked Jennifer.

Kristin rolled her eyes. "You know that one. The ghost tells him to kill his mom."

Both Bob and Heather ate slowly, and as the hour progressed the other two finished lunch first. Jennifer in particular seemed reluctant to leave, and because of that he was reluctant to let her, but both she and Kristin wanted to catch a smoke before Period Five, and finally they said good-bye and left.

Heather shifted around the table. "You mind if I sit next to you?"

"No."

"I like this. Eating lunch with you."

He merely smiled. Most of the cafeteria was empty now, just a few lingerers, students probably debating whether to go to Period Five or cut it. It was Arthur Cassidy's Accounting class, and Arthur rarely took the attendance he was supposed to. "Well, this is sort of a one-time thing. Once is just an anomaly. Twice becomes a pattern."

"You look real good, Bob."

"You're quite the charmer yourself, Ms. Feeney."

"I think it stinks. I really want to kiss you good-bye before going to class."

"Well, I wouldn't recommend it."

"Are you sure, Bob? Nobody's watching. I'd love to."

"No," he said firmly. His good humor vanished. "I'm not kidding, hon. You'll get me in a lot of trouble if you do that."

She put on her "boo" face, pouting her lower lip in a way intended to be cute. Bob overrode this ploy easily.

"I'll take you some place this weekend," he said. "Some place nice. Let me give it thought."

"I'll have to bring my books."

"Sure."

"Can we maybe go back to New York again?"

"Well," he hesitated, "that's a little hard on my budget. We'll go back again soon though, don't worry." He pushed his tray aside and stood up. Heather looked so dejected he felt compelled to give her something. "Hey, can you keep a secret?"

"Sure."

"Some news happened, but you can't tell anybody."

"What?"

"The dean quit."

Heather's eyes went big. "Really?"

"Just gave her notice. Walked out on a staff meeting. Now don't tell anybody."

"I won't. Boy, what's gonna happen now?"

"No one knows. Don't breathe a word of it."

"I won't, Bob. God!"

By afternoon's end the entire student body knew of the dean's resignation.

In her cubicle, Louise sat at her desk and flipped paperclips. Finally she got up and strolled out to the lobby where she saw Clara Peterson by Julie's desk. "Hello, happy people."

"Louise," said Clara, "what do you think of something? I asked Julie and she says no. But you'd probably know better than anybody."

"What's on your mind?"

"Well, we were—"

"Don't include me in this," said Julie, looking very angry.

"Okay, I was—" Clara scanned the empty lobby, then dropped her voice low. "Do you think Oliver and Lily are having an affair?"

"An affair?"

"Yes. You know …" She couldn't finish.

Louise burst into a cackle so loud the placement director hunched her shoulders in alarm. "Jesus Christ," exclaimed the business manager. "You guys are the best! You really are!"

"I guess that means no, huh?" said Clara, miffed.

"Lordy, lordy. I love this place. It's more entertaining than a season of soaps. No, Clara, not those two. Not in a million years. She's too rich and he's too married. Trust me."

"Well, then why does he keep giving her what she wants?"

"Why do you think?" Louise dried her eyes with a sleeve. "Remember Bill Nostrand's visit? And how Natalie and Jessica got axed? I'll bet you any sum of money he scared Oliver to death when they were alone in his office. I'll bet Oliver is running so scared now, he'll do anything to get his goal, even use ability to benefit."

"Louise," said Julie, "is ability to benefit really so bad?"

"Well, not on paper." The business manager puckered her gray lips. "In concept it's honorable. It's just too damn easy to abuse. And you know Lily won't—"

Julie's intercom buzzed. She picked up her phone. "Front desk."

"Jule," said Oliver, "when you have a sec can you come in here?"

"Sure." She stood up and faced them both. "That man," she declared, "is dealing with more problems than any of us know. I have no idea what's happening to him, but speculating like you're doing—" she pointed angrily at Clara, "is the worst thing anybody can do. He needs our support, not our gossip." She strode past them and went through the cubicles.

She halted in his doorway. Oliver sat at his desk, his eyes black sockets in a white face, his shirt creased and baggy. "Hi, Jule. Have a seat. Some day, huh?"

"Oliver, can I get you anything?" She had never seen him look so bad.

"No. Actually, I've got something for you. Please sit."

She did so, but then he didn't speak. He stared past her at the wall, almost too tired to move.

"Oliver, please—isn't there anything I can do for you?"

Someone knocked on the doorframe, and they both looked. Julie was startled to see Ethel's brooding dark face.

"Oliver," the dean said flatly, "can we talk?"

"Absolutely." He waved her in as well.

Julie started to rise but Ethel said, "It's all right, Julie, stay where you are. I don't care if you hear this. Oliver, I'm not going to sit down. I just want to ask you, face to face and free of a certain party that will go unmentioned, why in God's holy name are we doing ATB?"

"We need to," he said simply. "Ethel, the idea's been bounced around the President's Office for years now. Nobody wants to do it because it admits a lower class of student. That worries me too, as I'm sure you realize."

"Yes."

"But I believe ATB will help Lily bring more students into this school. Scowl all you want, but that's critical. I also believe ATB will not take advantage of applicants if the right supervisor is in charge of it. You're the person for that job. You won't let any bad apples through. Your integrity will keep us in line."

"Dammit, Oliver," she said, unappeased. "This is all Lily's doing—"

"No. Actually Lily's not too pleased with me. She doesn't want you monitoring ATB. She thinks you'll be too tough, but that's exactly what I want you to be. That's the way it has to be."

"Oliver, my teachers are going to have a holy fit when they learn about this. Jean Cavanaugh even now is saying—"

"If Jean doesn't like it, she can quit."

"Jesus, Mary, and Ralph—!"

"And you may quote me." He stared her down.

"All right, you win." Ethel went to the door, then turned around. She planted her hands on both hips and scowled. "You've got some kind of bug up your ass. I don't know what the hell you're doing, but I hope you're having trouble sleeping nights. You deserve to." She walked out.

Oliver took off his glasses and rubbed his eyes. His forehead came down on the desk with a mild, weary thump. He tried to exhale from this cramped position and found he couldn't. Before he could summon the strength to straighten up, fingers brushed the back of his neck and slowly worked into the flesh. He lifted his head.

"Wow," he murmured, eyes still closed.

The fingers dug in, massaging harder. He put his forehead down again, but this time comfortably on his hands. "I hope this is you, Julie."

"Why?"

"Because anyone else would do this as a prelude to strangling me."

She laughed. Her fingers worked harder, the massage started to really hurt. "You know," she remarked, "it's like I can feel a steel pole inside your neck. Don't you ever lose this tension?"

"I've been tense most of my life."

"Even as a kid?"

He chuckled. "Especially as a kid."

"You're going to give yourself an ulcer. I can tell you're one of those burning-up-inside types. They can be the most aggravating bosses, you know."

"Well, you said yes when we offered you the job."

It was such a moment, standing behind him, rubbing his shoulders and neck, no one else around, that she could say what she wanted to say. "It was the best decision I ever made."

He sat up and turned his head back and forth. "Jeez, you're what the doctor ordered. Give yourself a raise."

"Well, thank you."

"Sure. Don't run off. I've got something for you."

Julie returned to the client chair. Oliver opened his top drawer, pulled out a slim white envelope, and held it out to her. "I hope you're interested in this. It's tickets to *Les Miserables*. It's coming back to Philly and everyone says it's spectacular."

"Oliver, are you serious?" She reached for the tickets, amazed. "This show sold out months ago."

"Well, I bought them when they first went on sale. I thought I'd take Tina when she was in town. It's her favorite. But she's got something else going."

"She doesn't want to see it with you?"

"It's okay. It's my fault. I should have checked with her first. They're no good to me without her. And you've been terrific, putting up with my idiosyncrasies, if I can politely call them that. I just thought you might enjoy it."

"Oliver, this is incredibly generous. I haven't been to a show in—God knows when." She looked at him carefully. "But I guess I have the same problem. I don't have anyone to go with either."

"Well, the show isn't until February 26. That's almost a month away. Plenty of time to ask a friend."

Julie looked at the envelope. It wasn't sealed, and she could see the tickets within. She tapped its edge on the desktop, felt a deep rush in her chest. "Oliver, would you go with me?"

He was visibly jolted. "Oh, I think that would be a little awkward."

"I don't. I think it would be nice."

He laughed appreciably, but shook his head. "I do too. Gosh, what a surprise. But I don't think I should. Thank you."

"Why? For professional reasons?"

"Well, that and …"

"And what?" She was still smiling, but behind the smile Oliver sensed a steely resolve.

"I don't know," he admitted.

Julie held the envelope out to him. "You'd better give the tickets to someone else. I appreciate the gift, I really do. But I can't use it unless you come with me."

"Why?"

She swallowed but still met his eye. "Bad question, Oliver. Don't embarrass me."

"I apologize."

"Here."

But he didn't take the envelope. A weird spark flickered in his brain, a realization that if he didn't go to the show with Tina then who would he take? His close friends were all married, and anybody really interested in seeing *Les Miz* no doubt already had tickets. If he had to choose the one person whom he would probably most enjoy the show with, it would be, well …

Julie.

He would not have thought of it on his own, but now that the prospect lay before him, he realized it was true.

"I'll pay for dinner," she said. "Does that make it more fair?"

"You don't have to."

"Well, it makes it fair for me, then. I think it could be a lot of fun, don't you?"

"Sure. Okay, let's." And in an obscure recess of his heart he felt his integrity drop yet another notch.

23

"We're talking about poise," said Trudy, leaning into the microphone. "Poise, taste, and intelligence, all of which makes a professional *appear* professional. It's image, of course. The unfair but very real truth is, ladies, that an intelligent woman who doesn't dress to advantage is worse off than a dumb woman who does. The first thing about yourself that strikes *anybody,* a prospective employer, a colleague, a boyfriend, is how you look. And it is how you look which ultimately helps you maintain your respected standing in a company and paves your way up the corporate ladder. Hard work and diligence will only get you thanks and a pat on the back. You have to dress to match your ambition. Dress short of your dream, and you will fall short of it yourself. Now let's see how a modern professional business woman dresses."

The heavy blue curtain pulled open with a loud swoosh, showing three girls in tight leather slacks and loose shirts with silver studs. One girl's pants were ripped at the knees. Another's bare midriff showed. Deirdre Smith had her hair tied up in a kerchief. The other two, Karen Louden and Bonnie Beecher, were students granted leave from class to model in this fashion show today. They all stood on the stage in the auditorium of St. Luke's Catholic High School for Girls in Northeast Philadelphia, and slouched and pretended to puff invisible cigarettes. Bonnie, an acknowledged classroom clown, even lurched a little. Trudy, in her best office suit, stood behind a podium off to one side of the stage and read the copy she had put together with these girls, for the clothes they would display today were all their own.

"My goodness!" said Trudy, feigning embarrassment. "These girls aren't doing much to project professionalism, are they?" The audience laughed loudly. Lily had supervised this whole production, and this was her touch, to start off with a chuckle, to get all these eighteen-year-old juniors and seniors warmed up. "Well, in that get-up they might prove successful on a corner on South Street, but I guess I'd better not say at what." The girls in the audience cheered and applauded. It was, after all, exactly how they dressed themselves on Saturday nights when they hung out looking for guys or a place to party, or to browse in the punk clothing stores lining that most eclectic of Philadelphia streets. Only the blue-clad nuns standing in the back of the auditorium, who had laughed at the initial sight gag, remained silent at this second comment of Trudy's.

"All right," the senior rep said, waving thanks to the three, "perhaps we should try again to see how a professional career woman dresses." With her foot she tapped on a cassette player, and a pulsing disco thrummed through the auditorium speakers. Deirdre and the two students stepped into the wings and the curtain pulled tighter until there was just an opening in the center of the stage. Amelia Albretti stepped through. The current class president wore a trim double-breasted suit with knee-length skirt and mid-heel pumps. A briefcase bumped her knee, and her long hair was pinned up tight, putting ten years on her. She crossed to stage left, then right, spinning stiffly on her heel. Lily had rehearsed them all.

"Amelia is wearing a Brooks Brothers navy blue suit," Trudy described with a delicate cadence, trying to imitate the soft-spoken voices of the fashion commentators she watched on TV. "Pure wool, this is the classic business suit. Timeless and peerless, you cannot go wrong wearing an outfit like this on a job interview, and for that reason alone it is still in vogue. But ladies, as good as it is, we must also admit that it is a predictable outfit. After all, what about *after* the interview, when you already have the job? Do you want to look like every other blue-suited business woman tromping around Center City? *Men* in business are obliged to wear uniforms, certainly if they want to be taken seriously by their superiors, and their fashions rarely change. Women are more fortunate, for they are granted professional leeway. After all, the business industry is still governed primarily by male minds, and let's be frank here: men still desire professional white- and pink-collar working women to remain visually attractive and varied in their appearance. Well, rather than be indignant about this, the enlightened woman knows how to take advantage. Let us show you, by adding a little more pizzazz."

Karen emerged from behind the curtain. She wore a pleated pink skirt of midi-length and white blouse with a small round pendant. Her bright blue blazer looked large, even though she was five-eleven.

"Karen," Trudy intoned, "is wearing a swing-back jacket, which helps if you haven't got much in the way of shoulders and don't wish to appear mousy. It makes a serious statement, yet doesn't look baggy or cumbersome. A tall woman, Karen lessens this potentially intimidating trait by wearing flats. Her pearl earrings express to the immediate onlooker that she has class and taste. Incidentally, this is an excellent outfit if you have to do a standing presentation before an audience. This particular ensemble is by Lawrence Ruce."

Deirdre came next, stumbling a little from nervousness. She paraded left, then right, same as the others. "Deirdre is a short woman, let's see how she compensates for this. She is wearing a long mahogany blazer, pinstriped, with one button fastened. She wears this over a gray cotton turtleneck. Her tan skirt, also cotton, just reaches over the knee, coordinated with flesh hose and dark brown shoes with four-inch heels. This is a moderately conservative suit, both serious and laid back, and the pinstripe lines of both blazer and skirt give an optical impression of height. Even in this day and age, ladies, people still associate height with personal power. Short women need to dress accordingly, to compensate. This is obviously casual work attire—it has a certain sporty look that your colleagues can appreciate. The skirt and blazer are Ralph Lauren, the turtleneck by Eddie Bauer."

Amelia emerged again. "Here we have real individualism with dash," said Trudy. "A black and yellow large check jacket, then smaller checks for the skirt, which stops just above the knee. Checks are wonderful: they give you immediate energy; you look alive and vital just wearing a checkered suit, and when you vary the size of the checks from skirt to jacket as you see here, you break the regimentation. Amelia is certainly anything but boring no matter how long you look at her."

As Amelia pirouetted off, Trudy smiled. Behind the podium her foot tapped unconsciously to the mindless disco. "These are variables, of course, presented today so you can get a taste of the many directions you can explore—directions, incidentally, that men in their blue and gray uniforms cannot. Now, let's see how far we can go in terms of personal power. Bonnie?"

Bonnie Beecher emerged from behind the curtain, and a palpable gasp rippled through the auditorium. A short white blazer opened at the front to reveal a tight-fitting black blouse with a low V-neck cutting straight down the front to a single gold button near her sternum. A matching black miniskirt emphasized Bonnie's thin waist, then stretched snugly over her hips with the hem cutting high up her thighs. Bonnie's blond hair was short and chic; her bare legs, shining brilliantly in the floor lamps of the stage, were long and athletic, for outside the classroom she was an assistant aerobics instructor. As she strutted confidently on black pumps with skyscraper heels to the left of the stage, every face, framed in a wimple or not, followed her every move. Lily had picked both Bonnie and this suit, and designated which point in the program she should appear.

"Bonnie," Trudy continued her calm cadence over the hushed room, "is wearing a black blouse and skirt. Barely visible silver threads give the blouse its marvelous sheen. The skirt is a tight bold rayon wrap. Black heels give her a strong sensual power that knocks you out immediately. The large gold button daringly placed down the front of the dress is for show only." Bonnie reached stage right and let the white blazer slip off her shoulders. She tossed her head at the audience with a big smile, and began a pre-arranged second sweep of the stage. Trudy said, "Ladies, this brings us to an important point. Although she looks like she's dressed to kill, Bonnie's dress still meets the standards of contemporary business fashion. Women in offices dress like this quite often. At the same time, Bonnie looks terrific in this outfit for her own sake. She has, and I'm sure you'll all agree, dressed to maximum personal strength. You can tell that she will graduate from the Burr College with an excellent high-paying job, and you know she would achieve this even if her grades weren't particularly good—which, incidentally, they are. Bonnie is one of our most academically accomplished students, currently holding down a 4.0 GPA. Thank you, Bonnie."

The St. Luke's girls cheered and clapped. Bonnie grinned good-naturedly and bowed before leaving.

Now Karen emerged, and although there were not as many gasps this time the rigid attention was the same. Her red dress had gold buttons down the front and the skirt hem, like Bonnie's, cut high up the thigh, exposing a dynamite pair of legs. Red stiletto heels elevated her to the stratosphere. She posed on stage left, smiled over her shoulder at the audience, then pirouetted stiffly.

"A red nylon dress with gold buttons and trim," praised Trudy. "Ladies, red is just one of *those* colors. Who *doesn't* notice a woman in red? Even a woman with a limited wardrobe budget can still go to a mall and find a solid, striking red dress—it's a business essential. Karen, who dressed to scale down her height when last we saw her, has now dressed to upscale another aspect of herself. The square cut shoulders give instant presence and confidence, and the red shoes extend this strength throughout her whole person. Karen knows she could wear this outfit in the office by day, and zoom off to a nightclub for drinks and dancing the same evening. You will find that women's business attire crosses that very thin line quite easily these days."

Trudy leaned into the mike and sweetly lectured. "You see, ladies, women's dress in business has finally caught up with modern thinking. Businesses over the past—" She stopped at a sudden banging from the back of the auditorium. She tried squinting past the stage lights. Several blue nuns were storming out the back, letting the heavy auditorium doors clang shut behind them. "—over the past, uh, ten years has grown more fast-paced and unforgiving than ever. In a hardball climate like contemporary business, the professional abilities of women have never been fully appreciated. Like it or not, historically our sex has kept our male colleagues from taking us seriously. How many out there think that's a stupid attitude?"

The auditorium happily booed.

"Well, the Burr College teaches that we don't have to defend our sex any longer; we don't have to apologize for being women. Our gender is not a handicap; rather it is a vital asset, and fashion is allowing us to take full advantage. The ability to be both professional and sexy in an office is a power few men can manage, which makes it an essential power for us. And the secretarial field in particular can truly utilize that power to its fullest potential. The Burr College philosophy will," and here Trudy's smile was so big it could be seen in the last rows, "make you feel strong and glamorous about yourself. In our classes we teach everyone how to find their Essential Self. Essential Self, ladies! Everybody has it, but not everyone knows how to bring it forth and use it!

"Now, how about another example? Let's try something gentler this time."

Deirdre strode out and posed clumsily.

"Ah, dear old gray," said Trudy. "Nothing is more traditional than a good gray suit. But here we go for a subliminal soft effect. Deirdre is short which gives her an immediate appeal, and her silk gabardine double-breasted blazer falls gently from her shoulders, and her matching skirt carries the same soft warm accent. The buttons are jeweled and give a dash of glamour. Deirdre looks sweet and almost cuddly in an outfit like this, which a lot of men would find appealing. If she doesn't have the best confidence in herself as a skilled businesswoman, she can still learn how to take advantage of this, her Essential Self. It's best, perhaps, to approach this with—"

Sister Margaret had heard enough. She left the auditorium and charged red-faced down the hall, her blue habit flapping. Sister Margaret was St. Luke's student advisor, and a long-time advocate of the Burr College as a venue for the well-groomed if somewhat sheltered Catholic girls of St. Luke's. Her office was just off the Principal's near the front entrance. She opened her door with a bang and grabbed her phone, not even bothering to sit. She knew the number by heart.

"Burr College of Business, Julie speaking. How may I help you?"

"I need to speak to Dr. Oliver Dunbar right away!"

"I'm sorry, but Dr. Dunbar isn't in today. I'm his secretary, perhaps I can help you?"

"Well, I need to speak to *some*body!" Sister Margaret felt with amazement the sharp hammering of her heart.

"May I ask what this is in reference to?"

"I'm Sister Margaret at St. Luke's. I'm calling to talk to somebody about the fashion show that's going on here! I need to talk to someone now!"

"Well, Mrs. Espirito is the admissions director. Her department runs the fashion shows for the high schools. Would you like me to switch you to her?"

"I certainly would!" declared Sister Margaret.

A moment later her ear was greeted by a pleasant melodious voice. "Hello? This is Lily Espirito."

"Mrs. Espirito, this is Sister Margaret of St. Luke's."

"Yes?"

"Your employee, Miss Weiser, is conducting a fashion show for our students right now."

"Yes, that's right."

"Mrs. Espirito, I have never been more shocked and outraged in my life! What your Miss Weiser is saying to our girls is appalling! Elaine never spoke like this when she ran the fashion shows—"

"Ms. Margolis no longer works here—"

"Your Miss Weiser is showing off the worst attire, incredibly revealing … And how she's telling them to behave in an office is … is … I don't even know how to tell you, or how to describe it!" For a scary moment Sister Margaret felt herself starting to choke. She tried to calm herself with deep breaths.

"Well, I can't really comment, Sister, if you're unable to put your objection into words."

"Well, I … well, then let me say this! This is hardly what we expected from the Burr College, and you can be sure you will never run a fashion show or anything else at this high school again!"

"Oh."

"I am so angry, I can't believe what I just witnessed!"

"I see."

The indifference in the other's voice disturbed Sister Margaret. She began to feel the weight of her lunch, a hard lump pulsing in the folds of her habit. "Mrs. Espirito, have I made myself clear?"

"Oh, you certainly have," the other's voice trilled. "And I do thank you for calling, Sister. Input is always helpful, and we're always here to listen to good advice. Thanks for calling. Do take care." The phone clicked dead.

Sister Margaret leaned over her desk, clutching the phone and puffing for air. She had dealt with the Burr College for three years now, and had been on wonderful terms with Elaine Margolis. She had even visited the college, loved its colonial atmosphere, and believed it a charming healthy environment for the girls of St. Luke's to mature in. She enjoyed watching the yearly fashion shows as much as the girls in the auditorium.

With sudden violence she slammed down the phone, then looked up to see a young male teacher staring at her through her office doorway.

"Sister," he said anxiously, "are you okay?"

"What?" said Sister Margaret.

"Is something wrong?"

Sister Margaret stared at the young man until his question registered. She looked down at her phone. "I'm hoping I just had a wrong number."

"You're *hoping* you had a wrong number?" He raised his eyebrows.

"Yes," she snarled. "What's it to you?"

The young teacher scurried off.

Back in the auditorium, Trudy said in summation, "Burr recognizes that today's working woman can now have her cake and eat it too. For the woman who wants to get into business and use her brains, we'll train her how to succeed best that way. For the woman who wants to do well in business but isn't quite sure she has what it takes, we can train her as well. At the Burr College everyone comes out a success! You are women preparing for the work force at the best time in American history! Let us show you how to make the most of it! Our wonderful models will be passing out cards. Please fill them out and send them postage-paid to me at the Burr College!"

All four models walked out on stage applauding. Everyone in the auditorium cheered and applauded back.

"Remember," Trudy raised her voice over the jubilant noise, "to always strive for your dreams! Don't be afraid to reach for the glamour a business career has to offer! *You* are all women of power! *You* are all secretaries!"

24

"I graduated from Buchanan High School," said Dorothee Jackson, and Marty Nolan wrote it down, for the applicant had oversighted this bit of information when she filled out her academic history.

"And when was that?"

"June. No, July. Wait—it *was* June." She giggled and flashed large white teeth and rose gums.

"And you're eighteen, right?"

"Yeah."

Marty smiled a moment, as if he found her age personally appealing. He jotted notes in the *Comment* section of Dorothee's app form, and the girl watched the pen, fascinated that facts about herself were important enough for this good-looking guy to write them down. Watching unobtrusively from a corner, Lily was delighted.

"And you're interested in the Secretarial Arts Program?" he asked.

"Yeah. My guidance counselor thought I might be good at that."

"Excellent." Marty leaned back expansively in his chair. "You should realize, Dorothee, that Burr doesn't just teach you to be a secretary.

Burr teaches women how to become *executive* secretaries. That's a big difference."

"Yeah?"

"You bet. You're going to be multi-skilled. You're going to graduate an extremely marketable career woman, with a sizable salary to match." He laughed appreciatively. "You look like someone who deserves a lot of money, Dorothee."

The girl smiled hesitantly, not sure if it was a compliment. Marty smiled as if it was, and she did like that smile.

Marty Nolan was twenty-seven, a graduate of Montclair State who had briefly done admissions work for his alma mater before moving to Philadelphia five years ago and landing a rep position at, of all places, the Beauty Institute. Although his tenure occurred just before Lily's time, they were able to throw out names of former colleagues and enjoy mutual gossip. Marty was tall and clean cut, with skin more brown than black. He himself joked that more than one massa's blood circulated through his chromosomes, and explained this historical circumstance by confessing that all the Nolan women were beautiful. Wallet pictures of his mother and sisters bore him out. Although he brought a framed shot of his family to work his first day (two little girls and his wife, a lovely creature hugging a bouquet of flowers), he did not object when Lily suggested he tuck the photograph out of sight whenever he interviewed.

It was easy for Lily to see that Dorothee Jackson was enchanted by this older man. Marty's square-shouldered sports jacket communicated a fine muscular build, his bowtie a hint of dash. His cool brown eyes studied Dorothee with a pleasant glint, and she kept breaking into little smiles. Every time she did, he smiled back.

Marty described the Advanced Secretarial Arts Program with jaunty charm, then asked, "What do you think?"

"It looks good," said Dorothee, whose pinnacle of work experience was a Duncan Donuts cashier job. "But I don't think I done good on that test."

"What? Our admissions test? Shoot, miss, I'm sure you did just fine." He took the answer sheet from her file and counted the answers. Dorothee had gotten sixty-four correct out of a hundred.

"It felt like I was blowin' every other question," the girl confessed.

"No, this is good. You're well within our acceptance range." And he looked so pleased that she laughed.

"Well, I only had an hour and a half to do it in."

"I know. It's a tough test, no getting around that."

"And now I can't wait for July, Marty. Feels a million years away."

"Dorothee," his smile paled a little. "We're going to have to talk a little business. I'm afraid I'm going to need a twenty-five dollar app fee and a one hundred dollar tuition deposit."

The girl's face fell. "Are you serious? Today?"

"Well, today would be best. You can imagine how popular the Advanced Secretarial Arts Program is. Seats are filling up rapidly. You know we were supposed to run an April class, but it was taken off the schedule, which means all those students planning to come in April are now taking up many July seats. You shouldn't wait."

"Lemme see, okay?" Dorothee dug through her purse. A lot of used tissue and change came up in her hand. "I got forty dollars, Marty. I was gonna buy a blouse while I was in town."

He nodded gravely. "Well, and I know how important new clothes are. But you might want to think what's most important in the long run—the blouse you buy today, or the education you'll have for the rest of your life."

"Forty dollars is all I got."

He looked past her while she rummaged through her pocketbook again. Lily nodded.

"Forty's fine," he said. "But you'll have to get the rest to me just as soon as you can. I'll maybe be able to hold your seat forty-eight hours with this. How's that?"

"That'd be super, thanks so much. I do appreciate it, Marty."

Lily watched as he showed the girl out. Marty walked with stiff solemnity, holding her arm as if he were leading her to a ballroom dance. Dorothee couldn't take her eyes off his clean hatchet profile. Lily noted the girl's wardrobe—black stretch stockings, jogging sneakers, and a K-mart blue sweater. The clothes were cheap but the jewelry wasn't: large gold hoop earrings, a gold star punched through her left nostril, and hands and wrists rattling with bracelets and rings. The whole package probably cost, to Lily's knowledgeable eye, over three hundred dollars. These inner-city kids lived so poorly, yet still had money to burn. It was an important fact for a college recruiter to keep in mind.

A moment later Marty strolled back to his office and the admissions director gleefully clapped her hands. "Bravo, Marty! You were terrific!"

"Thank you." He dropped behind his desk and stretched his long legs. "My apologies, Lily, for only getting forty bucks from her."

Lily waved that aside. "You get what you can. My guess is she'll bring the rest tomorrow. Cash is always tougher. It's better when they bring a checkbook."

"I know."

"Marty, you've got the looks, the manner, and the ability to be tactless without appearing rude. I'm very pleased. And that thing you said about the April class—" She pointed a finger at him, trying to recall. "What was that? How because we canceled April we've got fewer seats in July?"

"Something like that." His grin was enormous.

"Genius! And you're speedy too. You sold her in about twenty minutes. When our interviews pick up that'll be critical."

"Well, to be truthful, she wasn't a difficult sell. She already wanted to come."

"But she's more and more what comes through the door. Sometimes I think I'm the only one who understands that. She's poor, and her high school education sucks. Now it's my experience that when a poor city girl who's not too bright meets a friendly, well-dressed school rep such as yourself—"

"Who is also black."

Lily registered that he was smiling before allowing herself to smile back. "You're gonna go far here. With your brains and that gentlemanly manner, you should be swimming in bucks come commission time."

"We both will." He laughed deeply, and playfully tugged his bow tie.

Lily reached for Marty's desk phone and buzzed the intercom. "As long as you've finished early, let's get the staff meeting rolling right away."

Five minutes later Deirdre and Trudy joined them in Lily's office, clutching yellow legal pads. Dee, in her new role as a sales rep, now boasted a tight spongy permanent, her business suit was pressed and free of pet hair, her shoes polished—a far cry from the casual attire she wore in her days as a secretary hidden behind a cubicle partition. Lily offered coffee, which Trudy and Marty accepted. Lily then hopped onto the front edge of her desk, sitting over them all. She hooked her ankles together and let them swing freely, a sign the two female reps knew meant she was feeling good.

"Ladies, Marty—this is what's going down. We're getting a lot more publicity out of New York. The newspapers are getting larger flashier ads. Does everybody know that shot we took of Bonnie Beecher in that dress of hers?"

"The black one?" asked Trudy.

"Yes. That's the one Bill decided on. We've got a shot of her sitting at a desk talking on a phone. Taken from the side, of course, so you can see all of her. It's a hell of a shot, and it's on all the ads.

"We are also advertising in the subway and city streetcar systems. And possibly a TV commercial, although Bill isn't convinced the cost will warrant the apps we'd be likely to get from it. We are also advertising in movie theaters. That—" she extended a proud hand, "was Trudy's inspiration. There are theaters in and around town that show advertisement slides on their screens before the feature begins. The competition's been doing it for years. We never did, of course, because the Burr schools were above that sort of thing. Well, we're not above it *now!* Ha! Ha!

"And, of course, we've expanded the number of high schools we present in."

She twisted on the desk and picked up a page cut from a newspaper. "Anybody see the wanted ads in yesterday's *Philadelphia Inquirer?* Two secretarial jobs both asking specifically for Burr secretaries. Did you see them?"

"Hey!" said Deirdre, and she took the page excitedly and scanned it.

"This is great!" Trudy exclaimed, reading over her shoulder.

"They're both administrative assistant positions too," squeaked Deirdre. "That always sounds better than just a secretary position."

"Read one for Marty," said Lily.

"*Wanted: Administrative assistant for large Center City firm. Must be hardworking, independently motivated, capable of handling multiple tasks simultaneously. Heavy client contact. Burr grad or Burr-type assistant preferred. Good salary, excellent benefits. Send resume and three references to P.O. Box—*'"

"Jesus, how about that?" said Marty.

"The other one's just as good," said Deirdre.

"Okay, okay," said Lily. "We have a national reputation. Don't be afraid to say that employers ask for us by name. Those ads are worth more than all the TV commercials in the world."

"They're terrific," said Deirdre.

"Glad you think so," grinned the admissions director. "I wrote them."

"*You* wrote these?"

"Both."

The two female reps could not hide their disappointment.

"I used to see legitimate ads asking for Burr secretaries," Lily said breezily. "I hated the sight of them when I worked at Stanley. But I haven't seen a real ad like that—" she tapped the page in Deirdre's hand with the pointed toe of her shoe, "in two or three years.

"All right, gang, now let's talk strategy. As you know, we've restructured. Dee is no longer an admissions secretary, she's a bona fide rep. We do not have an official admissions secretary any longer. The services Dee provided in that capacity are being split among ourselves. We'll arrange our own appointments, do our own follow up, be responsible for cultivating our leads. It won't be that much more work because the applicant pool will be divided among four of us, when previously it was just two reps and myself."

"But Lily," said Deirdre gently, for she alone knew what was involved in this major change, "what about making sure the proper documentation is in the students' files? That was one of the most time-consuming duties I had when—"

"Frankly, dear, I'm more interested in getting cheeks in the seats than papers in a file."

"But we're *required* to keep certain things in the files—"

"Of course. I know that. We're all responsible for our own files now, that's all."

"It's still a lot of work," the new rep warned. "It's going after high schools for diplomas, getting citizenship proof—"

"*If* they need diplomas," muttered Trudy, less than thrilled. She was referring to the new ATB policy. Like most grads, she didn't like the idea of other students coming to her alma mater with less qualifications than herself.

"Everybody is responsible for their own prospects' files," Lily repeated with a flash of impatience. "Is that clear? I don't want to spend time discussing it now, we have more important matters to go over. I have perfect confidence that you, Deirdre, can show us all how to do it.

"Ladies, Marty—you should know that we have to bring in seven hundred and nineteen students in July and September. We also have an

April Evening Accounting class, a March and May Paralegal start, and both an Evening Accounting Program and a Travel and Conference Planning Program starting in June. That last is a new program, the brochure's still at the printer. These evening classes are small, but they're going to take the heat off some of the July and September numbers. We *don't* have an April—that's the good news. Oh yes! When I was observing Marty just before this meeting, he said something really brilliant to the applicant regarding the fact that we don't have an April class this year. Marty, please tell them what you said."

In the student lounge, where the TV on its high stand played *All My Children,* most of the girls sat eating lunch with eyes on the screen. Some studied textbooks, and looked up only when the music swelled. Donna Harding watched them through the glass window in the lounge door, and Bob Lawrence trotted down the stairs and saw her.

"Spying, Donna?"

"Oh! No, actually I was debating whether or not to snitch a Milky Way from the vending machine."

"Why don't you?"

"Mm-mm." She shook her head and patted her tummy. "Summer's coming. I have to work on my bikini belly."

No you don't, Bob thought, but kept his mouth shut. Donna Harding was easily the best-looking teacher in the school: tall, smart, and cunningly sexy in her corporate career business suits, her brown hair always done up in the latest Fortune 500 style, her aqua eyes twinkling behind olive frames. Her husband was a wealthy somebody-or-other, a CPA Bob seemed to recall.

He followed her into the staff lounge. Louise Mallory sat at a table reading a newspaper, and didn't look up when they both said hi to her. Donna took a paper bag lunch from the refrigerator, then sat at a second table. Bob grabbed a can of soda and impulsively joined her.

"You live in the city, don't you Bob?" Donna asked, popping open the plastic container holding her lunch.

"Yes. Nineteenth and Waverly."

"That must be nice. I always fancied a place in the city. The idea of coming out your front door and simply *walking* to the Academy of Music makes my heart ache."

"Is that a passion of yours, classical music?"

"Of course. And shame on you, Bobby, if it isn't for you too." She stabbed at a salad that looked like a pile of green leaves.

"Oh it is," he said truthfully. "That's the music I grew up on. Mozart, Beethoven, Stravinsky, Copland. Those were the rock stars in my parents' house."

She smiled pleasurably. "At the end of the day, it really is the best music of all."

Bob nodded, warming to this. Donna was a colleague he didn't know much about. Although they had both worked here for several years, they had never really talked. Now, suddenly, they were comparing their experiences as teachers, discussing politics (she was a Democrat, which surprised him), social concerns, even the environment, and finally they both confessed to feeling weird at having careers that promoted business even though neither particularly admired the business world. Donna talked about growing up in West Chester in the days when farms surrounded the city, and expressed her unhappiness at seeing the land plowed under for housing developments that were then named after the farms they destroyed. Bob talked about growing up in Baltimore where his father still lived, and mentioned some of his wilder exploits as an undergraduate at American University, just to gauge her reaction. Donna laughed in all the right places. It was almost magical, talking to someone his own age. He couldn't believe how much fun he was having.

Quite suddenly the one o'clock bell blatted.

"That," he said to cover his disappointment, "is the ugliest sound in the world. Why didn't they just put in a proper ringing bell?"

"My theory," said Donna, "is this one wakes up the girls in study hall."

"Say, Donna, I really enjoyed talking to you."

"So did I." She stood up, holding her texts and vinyl calendar binder.

"Do you ever stay in town after work?"

"Sometimes. Why?"

"Well, this is going to sound silly, I guess. But I think I'd like to buy you a drink."

She studied him, and she was definitely flattered. But he could see her mind go through a process, and that saddened him. "I don't think so, Bob. Thanks, anyway."

"I didn't mean anything improper. I hope you know that. I just—I haven't had so much fun talking to someone in ages, that's all. I didn't want it to stop."

She was friendly about it. "Sure. But it's probably not a good idea. It shouldn't be like that, I know. But it is."

"I guess that's true." There was a very large diamond ring on her hand. He thought of his little loft apartment with its one bedroom, cat, and a manuscript going nowhere. Donna waved and walked out.

He felt bad about it. Just talk it would have been. He didn't think he could have tried for more. Still, it was an enlightening moment. Donna Harding might not be available, but she was clearly what he needed. She was his age, educated, and understood his cultural references. Which was all fine, except where would he find someone like that who also wouldn't care that he made thirty-three thou a year? He didn't believe such a woman existed.

Ruminating on this, he slowly realized that Louise Mallory was grinning at him. Her newspaper was neatly folded with each section back in alphabetical order.

"What?" he asked.

"Nothing. I just thought that was interesting."

"Think I'm hitting on married women?"

"Why no, Bob. Actually I thought you quite sincere. But you know, I like music too. Why don't you ask me out for a drink? I'd be thrilled out of my gourd."

He stared at her, at Louise's big glasses and white wattled neck, at her scrawny angular body. She had to be twice his age at least. At *least*. "That's okay," he said, not sure he was being polite. He stood and was at the door when a horrible creaking noise stopped him. Turning in wonder, he saw Louise doubled over the table, laughing.

"Gotcha!" she shouted, and pointed an index finger between his eyes.

Bob tried to laugh too, then went out.

Louise went to the sink and rinsed out her tea mug. She left the lounge and took her time going up the stairs, frowning at scuffle marks in the paint where thoughtless students bumped the walls. At the first floor landing she almost collided with Clara Peterson, whose chubby hands fluttered with excitement.

"Louise," she exclaimed. "Check this out! Check it *out!*" She held up a sheet of paper.

"What's that?"

"It's a job position from Fred Strom, of Sutherland and Associates! They've just put in new offices at Liberty Place and want us to screen five secretaries for them! *Five!* Can you believe it?"

"That's an excellent company," Louise said.

"I've been after them for *years!*" Clara moaned dramatically. "They were always put off by our placement fee. But quality secretaries are so hard to come by, Fred told me himself, that now they're willing to pay for someone good."

"Clara, that's great news. Congratulations. Hope you find him some good placements. That's a large firm, you can probably do a lot of repeat business."

"Don't I know it! And I'm not worried about giving him quality, because our July class finishes in March, and the Julys are always the best."

"Sounds like you know what you're doing. Good luck." Louise walked past, heading for her office.

Clara hummed to herself as she trotted up the stairs to the second floor where the Placement bulletin board was hung. Looking at the board, she couldn't help thinking what a gold mine the day had become. She tacked the Strom sheet beside the two beautiful ads she had cut out of yesterday's *Inquirer,* ads for administrative assistants that asked specifically for Burr grads. Clara was still humming as she trotted back down the stairs to her office.

25

Julie Fitzgerald was not the first woman to fall in love with a married man, although up to now she believed she had done a good job keeping her feelings mute. Her attraction to Oliver Dunbar traced back to when she was a student at Burr catching glimpses of him working tall among his staff in the front offices, or watching him pass through the halls with his buoyant long-legged stride. She felt it again when she applied for the director's secretary position and had a chance to talk with him one-on-one in his office.

She was struck by his easy manner, his respect for people, and his unwavering enthusiasm for the students. She liked his calm clear voice, his lean good looks, even the gray in his temples. Clara Peterson had fluttered with dismay when she accepted the position, for the placement director knew Julie was good enough to work in a big corporation for an important executive, and thereby earn more money and status than Burr could ever afford to give her. But Julie didn't care. She needed to respect the person she worked for, and after interviewing with Oliver she couldn't imagine working for anyone else. Time had proved her right. She liked working at Burr, enjoyed managing the front lobby and interacting with her co-workers, and she basked in a passionate but very private love for her boss. That she felt this way was her own problem. He was a decent man, and she would never do anything that might complicate his life or cause him trouble. Even their upcoming dinner date was just a chance to spend time with him, a pleasant one-time opportunity. At least that's what she told herself.

Still, as February 26 approached Julie began to feel a low-grade anxiety that proved justified when she awoke that morning and still couldn't decide what to wear. Her instinct was to dress up, to make a real night of it. After all, it was a show they were going to see, and it would be fun to go all out. But she still had to put in a day at Burr, and it wouldn't do to be overdressed for the front desk. With the clock ticking, she stared at the limited choices in her closet, and finally selected a silk blue dress that was simple and elegant although still too nice for the office, then spent far too long in front of the bathroom mirror pinning her hair in a perfect French twist. Finally she surrendered all pretense by putting on the pearl necklace and earrings that her grandmother had given her on her sixteenth birthday. She drove her car into the city instead of taking the bus, and kept breathing deeply to calm herself while her hands tightly gripped the wheel.

All day she sat in the Burr lobby, grinning self-consciously as her colleagues continually complimented her. More than one asked who she was dolled up for. At five o'clock she puttered aimlessly at her desk while the rest of the staff pulled their coats from the lobby closet and waved good night. A few minutes later Oliver emerged from his office, tall and handsome in a gray wool pinstripe, and took his own black overcoat from the closet.

"All set?" he asked with a very sweet smile.

"All set."

Julie had reserved a table at Garibaldi's on Locust Street, one of Philadelphia's premiere restaurants for celebrity spotting, although they saw no one special this night. The waiter asked up front if they were attending the show, and when they answered yes he assured them they would be out on time.

"Now what was I talking about?" Oliver asked after dinner was ordered.

"You were chatting about education and low salaries."

"Right. I knew it was something cheerful. The truth is, Jule, unless you do consulting work there's not a lot of big bucks to be made in education. It's a job with a moral duty attached, and the people who take it up are following a genuine calling. So since it's idealism that motivates you, it's a matter of course that you don't get paid well."

"Even for a school director?"

"Well," he acknowledged gently, "I'm not doing badly, but I've also been at it twenty-two years. My salary is based in large part on longevity. Want to hear a funny but true story?"

"Sure."

"It happened to me right after we started the IP Program back in '85. New programs always have to be cleared with all the agencies—Federal Department of Ed, Pennsylvania Department of Ed, ABCAA, everybody sticks their nose in. One of the agencies was Veteran Affairs, located in the Commonwealth Building on Spring Garden Street. To help speed things up, I decided to walk the documentation over rather than put it in the mail.

"So I'm walking up Broad Street with everything in my briefcase: four copies of the catalog, letters of eligibility and such, and I'm just north of City Hall when a bum spots me. He's maybe fifty or sixty years old and very disheveled. And he says, 'Can you spare a dollar, mister?'

"Now I'm actually a pretty soft mark. We don't pass a hat in Quaker meeting, so maybe giving money to the homeless is my answer to tithing. Anyway, I dig in my pocket for a dollar. While I'm doing this, the guy eyes my business suit and briefcase and says, 'I'm sure you can spare the dollar, mister, because you're a lawyer or something.'"

Julie laughed. Oliver went on happily. "'No,' I tell him. 'I'm not a lawyer.' He says, 'Well, then you're a consultant or big executive or something, right?' And again I say, 'No, still wrong.' And now I've got the dollar in my hand, and I give it to him. He looks at it, and the most hurt expression comes over his face. He's disappointed that it's only a dollar. He says, 'So what the hell *do* you do?' And I say, 'I'm a teacher.' He laughs and says 'Okay!' and walks away."

"Oh no! Really?"

"That's when I realized this would never be a lucrative profession."

Salads arrived. Julie started hers, thinking that Oliver Dunbar might be special, but he shared something in common with most men—the desire to talk about himself. It was a great relief, for as much as she admired him, Julie realized there wasn't a lot for her to say. They had never socialized before, and unless she wanted to talk shop there wasn't much to discuss. And she was afraid to talk shop because this night was supposed to take his mind off it.

During one lull she asked, "Is Tina doing well?"

He took a sip of wine before answering. "Haven't heard from her in a while. Probably doing very well."

Shit. Instinct radared that this was a sensitive subject. Was anything about this evening going to be easy? "You don't really see each other much, do you?"

"Not much."

"I'm sorry. I shouldn't be asking this. Please don't take offense."

"Offense?" He looked surprised. "Gosh, it didn't occur to me."

She smiled. "Gosh indeed. Oliver, you don't curse, do you?"

"Not really, no." He grinned self-consciously.

"Don't get me wrong. It's nice, actually."

"And I'm not apologizing. In my parents' house you never used the Lord's name in vain. Raised that way, 'gosh' and 'jeez' were all I had."

"You're fairly religious, aren't you?"

"No more than the next fellow." Oliver sat back and patted his mouth with his napkin. "I do attend meeting, and I believe in God. And I believe in principles. All good school officials are creatures of principle. We've got to have our values in place, and we'd better practice what we preach. And do it without judging others or becoming supercilious. *That's* the challenge."

"Well, you do that last very well," Julie said. "You don't judge or criticize anybody. I always thought that was a Quaker thing."

Oliver laughed. "Actually Quakers can be quite judgmental. Ah, here we are."

The food arrived, roast duck with fruit stuffing for her, New York strip for him.

"This looks wonderful," Oliver said. "Thanks for dinner."

"You're very welcome." She raised her wine glass. Oliver smiled and raised his. It was a moment; she *knew* it was a moment. But all she could think to say was, "To a night out."

"Yes," he agreed. "To a night out." They clinked.

Les Miserables was magnificent. The theatrical special effects were dazzling and state of the art on a revolving stage that continually transformed into stark dungeons, smoky sewers, and moonlit Paris streets and bridges. Oliver was mesmerized. And yet the best moment of the evening came for him at intermission. Julie, holding his arm as they navigated the crowded lobby, looked up at him bug-eyed and said, "Oliver, thank you so much! This is the greatest time I've ever had in my life!" Her saying this changed his whole perspective. Oliver had been watching the show the way he was habituated—that is, through his wife's professional eyes. He kept imagining Tina's comments all during the first act. But seeing Julie's happiness at intermission helped break through that a bit, as if he suddenly recognized his own right to enjoy the show on his own terms—and with the person he was with, not the person he was without. He enjoyed standing in the lobby and watching Julie fight her way to the ladies' room, and smiled when she returned, laughing as she jostled her way through shoulders and handbags to get back to him.

After the final curtain, she held his arm again as they pushed through the jam outside the theater. "Oliver, thank you so much!"

"You're welcome. I'm glad you talked me into this."

"Oh please! I'm embarrassed about that. It was shameful. I really put you on the spot that day in your office."

"Don't worry about it. You've done me a world of good."

Her car was parked in a garage on Sixteenth Street. An attendant took her stub, and they stood among other theatergoers waiting for their transportation to be brought down. Julie stood rigid by the curb, watching each car roll out from the ramps above. She only had a few minutes left.

"Oliver, can I tell you something?"

"Sure."

"I'm a mother."

"You're a what?"

"A mother. I have a seven-year-old daughter named Kelly."

He waited, as if for a punch line. A particularly loud car pulled up close, its brakes squealing so shrilly that everyone winced. Oliver touched Julie's shoulder and she looked up at him, her eyes hard and steady behind the round wire-frame glasses. He started to laugh.

"I don't believe it. How old are you?"

"I'm thirty-three."

"Are you married?" He recoiled immediately. "I'm sorry, that's not my business."

"I was married straight out of high school."

"But you're not anymore?"

"No. Sam and I were wed the summer after graduation, then we took an apartment in Pittsburgh so he could study Music Ed at Carnegie Mellon. He got a job teaching in Downingtown so we moved back here. Then Kelly came. Babies are a big responsibility, you know. They just change everything. And so ..." She looked away, watched the cars coming down the ramp. "So one day Sam left."

"I'm sorry."

"Yeah." She took a deep breath. Without looking at him she held out a hand. Oliver took it. "I don't know how you do that to your daughter. He's back in Pittsburgh again, teaching band at an elementary school. He's supposed to pay child support, but I never get anything. My parents are sweet but they don't have much, we couldn't move in with them. And because of Kelly I couldn't hold a job. After a few years on food stamps I wised up, borrowed some money from an uncle, and came to Burr."

"You shouldn't have bought that dinner tonight."

"No—please!" She turned to him with tears forming in her eyes, even as she tried to laugh. "I loved buying your dinner tonight."

She released his hand and fished through her pocketbook for a tissue. Oliver immediately offered his handkerchief. She smiled at the courtliness of this.

"Oliver, I need to blow my nose."

"Do what you have to do."

She did, loudly, which made them both laugh. "I'm keeping this," she said.

"I'm not sure I want it back. Where's Kelly right now?"

"At my parents. She stayed the night there."

He thought a moment. "Louise must know."

"Yes, but she's the only one. Kelly's the beneficiary on my life insurance plan. I don't know why I've never told anybody. Some stupid vanity, I suspect. None of the other secretaries are mothers, and I already feel so old among them as it is. Kelly goes to a special school by day. The bus drops her at Mom's house at four each afternoon, and she watches her until I can come pick her up. We have an apartment in Manayunk. It's small, but there's a nice view of the river."

"Well, you could just knock me over with a feather," Oliver said. "Why are you telling me all this?"

"Because you're you." Julie gave him a marvelous smile. "Because I don't want to hide anything from you. I don't think you realize how special this night is to me, Oliver. It's one night more than I expected. One night more than I ever could have hoped."

The lenses of her glasses were thin enough to cause no distortion; he saw in her bright hazel eyes a humor and intelligence and an unmistakable affection for him that caught his breath. He was struck, suddenly and a bit foolishly, by how attractive she was.

Julie said, "This one's mine."

A cream-colored Oldsmobile with a bad engine rattle and more than a few dents pulled to the curb. Oliver tipped the attendant and held the door for her. As soon as he shut it she rolled down her window. "Oliver, thank you for everything."

"Thanks back at you. It was fun. I'll see you Monday."

He watched as she pulled out carefully and steered left onto Sixteenth. He stood for a moment in the mouth of the garage, detached from the sidewalk and floating, unaware of the exhaust fumes behind him or the cold in his face. Although west was the way home, he turned and walked east.

The stores on Locust Street were shut tight. Traffic was minimal, the streets quiet. Beggars slept in stairwells and bus stop pavilions. Oliver walked without thinking, and soon reached Society Hill. Washington Square Park spread before him like an odd chunk of displaced forest. The park's lights were shut off, the only glow coming from the Tomb of the Unknown Revolutionary War Soldier, where the eternal flame flickered like a lonely campfire. He walked through the park, despite the darkness. The walkways were lost to shadows, forcing him to step slowly. The central fountain was a cold empty basin, shut off for the winter. He reached the east edge of Washington Square and there the Burr College greeted him, facing him from the opposite side of Sixth Street.

It never lost its appeal to him. Though the colonial mansion's three floors were dwarfed by the office buildings that bookended it, it still won on sheer Philadelphia charm. The windows all had little white Dutch shutters, and the big oak door had a brass knocker shaped like a lion's head. Two tiny chimneys rose on either end of the roof apex (neither chimney worked), and a lit window on the third floor glowed over the park like a lighthouse beacon. He realized suddenly that few of his classmates from Penn still kept in touch with him. Most now worked in lofty universities where their names would occasionally appear in book announcements or college publications. He knew that they looked down on junior colleges, and would certainly think that their one-time colleague Oliver Dunbar had squandered himself. But Oliver knew better. The core of education was purest in that building across the street. Those same colleagues would laugh at that, but he knew it was true. Education was about improving your fellow beings, cultivating ideas and preserving and enhancing culture. Surely there was no field of employment more worthy of the human race! Even doctors were nothing without education, or lawyers, or entertainers, or politicians. But his aging classmates, with their titles and multiple doctorates and degrees, were embroiled in office politics, grant underwriting, and preserving their standing in the Great Ivory Tower. The careerist in education eventually reached a plateau of academic management where contact with students became negligible. Burr had kept that from happening to him. His eye traveled up to the light on the third floor. He stared at it, first puzzled, then in wonder.

Why was a light shining on the third floor?

Before he had a chance to convince himself that it was nothing, that Maintenance simply left a light on; before he could think of any reason not to worry, a shadow passed before the window. Hairs prickled on the back of his scalp. It was the middle of the night, *and someone was in his school!*

No cars passed, and the sidewalks were empty. Oliver felt monumentally stupid standing across Sixth Street watching his school being robbed. Louise would kill him.

"Oliver!"

He jumped a meter. His first thought, that the robbers had spotted him, quelled when he realized they probably wouldn't call him by name. Julie's car was parked by the curb at the south corner of the park. She got out and ran toward him, hugging her unbuttoned coat. The sound of her heels striking the quiet street scared him, and he said angrily, "What the hell are you doing here?"

"Well, what are you? I saw you walk off in the wrong direction, so I circled around. I guessed you were heading here."

"So what?"

"So nothing," she said, mad enough herself not to be put off by his sharp tone. "Except it's almost midnight. What were you going to do, Oliver? Go inside and work?"

"Is it any of your concern?"

"Right now? Right this minute? Absolutely it's my concern. Try to tell me it isn't!"

Her anger cooled his own. He pointed up, and her gaze followed.

"Someone left a light on," she said.

"No."

She gasped. "You think someone's up there?"

"I'm sure of it. I saw movement."

"Oliver, get in the car! We'll call the police!" She tugged his arm, but he didn't move. "Oliver!"

"What?"

"Let's get out of here! Let's call the police!"

He gently pried her fingers from his coat sleeve. She saw his face then, and stepped between him and the building. "Don't you dare go in there! You can't! You don't even know how many there are!"

"That's true."

"Oliver, this is scaring me. Get in the car."

"Jule, we get robbed all the time. I'm sick of it. They shouldn't be in there. I have every right to confront them."

"And what will you do?"

"Tell them to leave." He touched her shoulder lightly and stepped around her. He was across the street in three bounds.

"Oliver, if you go in there I'm coming too." She ran up to him, still hugging her coat.

"No, Jule. That doesn't make sense."

"Oliver, telling thieves to leave doesn't make sense. Only calling the cops does. If you're going in there, I'm coming too. I'm not waiting out here and I'm not going home. We'll check it out together. Maybe it's nothing."

He didn't look happy.

"Besides," she said, "I've never liked thinking thieves can scare me."

"Me either. Okay."

Together they climbed the steps to the school. Oliver pulled out his key, unlocked the heavy oak door, and pushed it open. The corridor beyond was a borderless void. He and Julie looked at each other, then cautiously stepped inside.

26

The lobby light switch was just inside the double glass doors, but Oliver was afraid to turn it on. He had thirty seconds to cross the lobby and switch off the security system behind Julie's desk before the alarm sounded, and he lost the first fifteen tripping over a curling corner of the oriental rug under the coffee table and falling flat on his face. His knee cracked hard on the oak floor beneath the carpet.

"Oww!"

Julie fought the urge to bolt. She stood by the glass doors, straining to see him in the dark. Oliver crawled on hands and knees to the desk, found the red light on the wall behind it, and groped for the square code box. He blindly pushed the buttons and the red light winked to green. He blew out his cheeks in relief.

Julie whispered, "Are you all right?"

"Yeah," he whispered back. "Can you see yet?"

"Starting to."

"Where are you?"

"Still at the door."

The windows let in a little yellow street light, enough to navigate. The two large portraits were black squares over the couch. Oliver stood and limped to her. "Take my hand. We'll head for the stairs."

The first floor corridor was eerie and opaque. There were no windows, for classrooms lined either side. Oliver and Julie groped past the grandfather clock, the antique furnishings, the old-fashioned grilled radiators. For all his years of working late, Oliver had never once traversed this passage with the lights off, and the hall stretched twice its normal length, filled with inexplicable black shapes and hints of peril. They passed the closed door of the Placement Office and reached the staircase.

"We have to go up," Julie whispered.

"I know."

"Can you hear anything? I hear something."

He tried to listen, but his heart was too loud, and his knee ached more than it should. "Nothing."

"Careful now."

Holding hands, they started up the steps. His eyesight improved to the point where he could see Julie's pale arm and bracelet, her feet arched in their pumps, and her pearl earrings. The black stripe of his necktie bisected his white shirt. They were dressed far too nicely for crime-fighting.

"Oliver, we don't even have a weapon."

"I'm not planning to fight them. I'm just going to tell them to go home."

"Okay. I was afraid you didn't have a plan."

The ancient stairs creaked, forcing them to halt repeatedly. "Rotten old building," Oliver muttered.

Julie asked, "What if they're in the lounge too?"

That was a scary thought. The lounge was in the basement; if the thieves were down there as well as on the third floor, then they could be rushed both ways.

"Well, it doesn't look like the lights are on downstairs. I don't think anybody's there."

"Burglars don't always turn on lights," Julie pointed out. "They're not reliable that way."

"Let's go up."

They reached the second floor landing. The corridor extended like a morbid black tunnel, with the classroom doors on either side shut and locked. A tile of moonlight shone through the smoked glass window of the library's door at the far end, lit from the alley outside. Julie whispered nervously, "We're not going down there, are we?"

"No, we want the third floor. What's that noise?"

A soft clicking sounded over their heads.

"That's what I heard downstairs," said Julie. "Oh my God, it's a keyboard!"

"So it is." Oliver felt along the wall for the light switch. The second floor corridor flared with florescent light.

"Oliver—"

"Don't worry. I doubt they're testing the equipment before stealing it. That's not a thief on the third floor."

"Still, I don't think—"

"No, it's okay. I know what it is." He bounded up the steps, three at a time. Julie raced to catch up with him.

The light was on in Computer Lab III. The lone keyboard clicked a bit, paused, then clicked some more. Oliver halted by the half-open door. Julie pressed up beside him. They both leaned around the doorframe and peered in. A black girl, a student, sat at one of the twenty-five terminals, squinting at an assignment propped on a vertical stand. She typed with stiff fingers. A yellow slicker was flung over the teacher's chair at the front of the room, a Burr bookbag propped beside it.

"Ms. Robinson?" Julie asked softly.

"JESUS MOTHERFUCK!" the girl screamed and jumped to her feet. Oliver and Julie jumped as well. They could see the girl's white eyes all the way across the room.

"It's okay," Oliver said, and held up a hand. "It's just Dr. Dunbar and Ms. Fitzgerald."

The student clutched her throat. Realizing who they were did not give her any comfort. Oliver and Julie stepped into the room.

Julie said, "Hello, Keone."

"Am I in trouble?" the student barely whispered.

"That depends," said Oliver. "What are you doing here?"

"Just workin'."

"It's past midnight."

"Is it?"

"How come Maintenance didn't kick you out?"

"I hid from 'em."

Julie felt Oliver shaking beside her, felt he might—for all his surface control—explode with fury at any moment. He asked, "And how did you manage that?"

Keone was also waiting for an uproar. "They … they always does the girls' room first, then the men's room, then the lounge. I hid in the lounge while they done the girls' room, then I hid in there when they done the others."

Oliver asked, "Aren't you exhausted?"

"Well, I slept some on that couch in the lounge. After them clean up people left."

"Keone," said Julie, "how often have you done this?"

Startled, Oliver looked at her. But Julie's intuition was on target, for Keone said reluctantly, "Not often, ma'am. Just a few times."

"What?" said Oliver. "You've really done this before? Why?"

The girl stood silently.

"Why?" demanded Oliver.

Julie said gently, "Go ahead, Keone. Tell us everything."

It took some time for her to get it out. She was receiving extra tutoring from Jean Cavanaugh, but the work was hard, and concentrated not just on finance but English and writing skills as well. Consequently, she had no time after school to practice her typing and shorthand, two skills her class had just started learning this spring semester. She had no computer at home, and so had to get the work done here.

"Keone," Oliver said severely, "you can rent a computer."

"I can't, Dr. Dunbar. It coss a hundred forty dollars to rent a computer through this school. I don't got that much."

"But …" Oliver was at a loss. "Well, but even so, you can't go on like this. It's not good for your health, for one thing. And for another, it simply isn't allowed. We can't have students in the building by themselves late at night. Our security isn't the greatest. Do you understand?"

"Yeah."

"Am I clear about this?"

"Yeah. I guess I won't do it no more."

"Where do you live?"

"South Philly. Caulfeld Homes."

"Okay. Pack up. We'll give you a ride to the subway."

The girl winced and looked down at her open composition book.

"Keone," Oliver said firmly, "don't get mad at me. You know I'm right."

"I ain't mad, sir," said the student. "But I don't got no subway fare."

Oliver felt ashamed. He pulled out his wallet. "That's okay. Here, take a five. I know it's extra, but don't worry about it."

Keone took the money without hesitation. "I'll pay you back," she said quickly.

"I know you will. Now pack up."

Julie tugged his sleeve. "Oliver, let's wait out in the hall. I want to talk to you."

He followed her out, and she said, pitching her voice low, "Oliver, you can't make that girl take a subway at this time of night."

"I know that," he said just as softly, "but the kid lives in Caulfeld Homes. There's no taxi stupid enough to drive her there or I'd gladly pay for one."

"Then let's take her home."

"In your car?"

"Of course."

"Julie, do you know what Caulfeld is?"

"Sort of."

"It's a notorious crack nest. It's in the news all the time for shootings and what-not. I don't think you want to drive in there."

"Well, truth be told, I don't. But there isn't much choice, is there?"

Oliver smiled.

"What?" she asked self-consciously.

"Where did you come from? How did the Burr College get someone like you?"

She reddened a little, then turned toward the lab door. "Keone, let's go. Dr. Dunbar and I are driving you home."

The most direct way to go was down Broad Street. Stores, Laundromats, bars, ice cream shops were all dark. Southern High School passed as an imposing granite edifice to their left. Keone said nothing from the back seat. She didn't know what to make of Dr. Dunbar and Ms. Fitzgerald; she was grateful for the ride though she really didn't see the point. Ms. Fitzgerald knew enough to turn right after passing Vet Stadium, but then she slowed and finally braked. "Keone, I've only seen Caulfeld from the Expressway. I don't know how to get to it."

"There's a coupla ways. Best is through here. Watch it, though. It ain't wide."

Julie nosed the car down Haggard Street, a residential lane thin enough for only one vehicle, with porch stoops and phone poles nearly brushing the Olds on either side. At the end rose a metal fence that marked the boundary of the project, and to the left was the open-gated entrance. The manager's shack was a silhouetted box with a dim blue light glowing inside. No lights shone on the empty expanse of playground. It was so flat and open that Julie felt she was driving across a razed field.

Keone said suddenly, "Is you two married?"

Oliver and Julie both laughed. Julie said, "No."

"You datin' then?"

It was Oliver's turn. He smiled. "No."

"You look it. 'Cause you're dressed up so nice."

Julie said, "Well, thank you."

"We're not dating." Oliver looked at their driver. "I'm not sure what you'd call this."

"Keone," Julie said carefully, "where do I go from here?"

"Oh miss, you don't wanna go in here. Leave me off. I be all right."

"I'm not leaving you here. It's pitch black."

"I walk through here all the time. It's nothin', Ms. Fitzgerald."

"Where's your home, Keone?" said Julie. "We're here now. Let's do this right."

"Take that way. Go along Carolina Street."

Julie drove down a street that took her between white-washed two-story buildings she had seen and yet never seen from the Schuylkill Expressway side of the Caulfeld fence. There were no working street lights, and invisible potholes made the car jiggle and bang.

"Straight ahead?"

"No, turn here."

"Where?"

"Right here."

Julie slowed to a crawl. "Keone, I can't see anything." She rolled down her window, and cold air flooded the inside of the car. A black gap about the width of two cars appeared between a pair of white buildings. She had to presume it was a street opening, and turned toward it.

"Nobody's out," remarked Oliver.

"You don't wanna go out at night here," said Keone.

"How long have you lived here?"

"M'whole life."

"How many in your family?"

"Four. Me, Javaughn, Corey, Mama, and Dad. Five."

The car rocked from the cratered street. The wobbling headlights picked out tall grass stems and weeds thrusting through the asphalt. Parked cars looked crippled by the curbs, none of them new, many of them incomplete, patched with different colored parts or up on blocks. TVs glowed in a few windows, and some lights shone very low to the ground, coming from horizontal basement windows. Julie concentrated on avoiding the largest potholes while Oliver scanned the blackness between the white buildings, expecting some great evil to leap out. From one apartment hip hop thudded through the walls like an angry heart.

"That house up ahead," said Keone, pointing.

"With the lights on?"

"No, crost from that one. That one's Mister and Ms. Tarrant."

"They're up late," said Oliver.

"Naw, they's old folks. They sleep with lights on all the time."

"Okay."

Julie pulled up before Keone's building, and dogs barked ferociously across the street, rattling metal mesh. A light in the basement at the other end of Keone's building winked out. Keone got out of the car, dragging her bookbag across the seat.

"Thanks. You circle around the block making left turns, it'll bring you back to the gate."

"Better get inside," Oliver said.

His nervousness made the girl smile. "Ms. Fitzgerald, Dr. Dunbar, I do appreciate this."

"You come see me Monday morning," said Oliver. "We'll see about a computer for you. You're not coming back here at night any more, okay?"

Keone nodded. She walked up the sidewalk. Julie and Oliver waited until she unlocked the door and went inside.

"God, I hope she's right about going around the block," said Julie. "I can't tell the road from people's lawns in this dark."

"Been a full evening, hasn't it?"

"Tell me about it. Nobody can say you don't show a girl a good time, Oliver Dunbar."

Keone's instructions proved correct. Julie turned at each corner she saw, and quickly spotted the far off (and much better lit) lane of Haggard Street through the fence in the distance. She worked the car over ruts and bumps, and grimaced every time her tires crunched glass and cans. The dwellings on this street were entirely boarded up.

"These don't even look like houses," remarked Oliver. "They look like flat warehouses. How do people live in these?"

"I can't imagine. Yet she said she's been here all her life. You getting her a computer, Oliver?"

"Yeah, I'll work out something."

They drove out of Caulfeld without incident, made it onto Patterson Avenue, and drove east to the sports complex and Broad Street, where Julie turned north.

"Tired?" Oliver asked. "It's one o'clock."

"No. It's funny, but I don't feel tired at all. I don't think I'm going to get that kid's home out of my mind for a while."

"Same here."

"How about you?" she asked. "Are you tired?"

"Not at all."

"Then I have an idea. Come out to Manayunk tomorrow and spend the day. I'd love for you to meet Kelly. We'll do something fun."

He smiled, touched. "I don't think so, Jule."

"Tina's not home this weekend, is she?"

"No."

"Then why not? Get the goddamn school off your mind. That place is bad for you, Oliver. You need a break from it. We'll go for a long drive. Out to Lancaster, maybe, and see the Amish. Kelly's never done that."

Oliver said nothing for a moment. He hated returning to the empty Rittenhouse apartment each day. But he also realized that there was more to Julie's offer than just meeting her daughter. For one brief moment the potential sweetness of it filled him, he felt her company with the ache of his entire being, a grasp at happiness as real as a grasp at Heaven. He tamped it back. He would not use Julie as an antidote to his misfortunes. She was smart and young with a life of her own. Besides, she worked for him.

"Jule, thanks but—well, no thanks. I admit, I'd feel awkward doing that."

"You shouldn't."

"Just the same. It is what it is."

Julie said no more. The humor left her eyes, and her hands gripped the wheel a little too tightly.

"When you mentioned Kelly before, you said she went to a special school."

"Yes."

"Why?"

"She's deaf."

"She is?"

"Yes. Born that way."

"You didn't mention it."

Julie frowned. "Well, I'm used to it. And I hate having her thought immediately by people as a deaf person. She's only seven, for God's sake. I guess I kind of dodge mentioning it on the first go-round. Kind of a courtesy to her, except I'm not sure it is."

"Is she profoundly deaf?"

"Yes." Julie turned onto Walnut Street, and headed west toward Rittenhouse Square. "She's pretty good. She signs fluently, and even lip-reads well."

"Can she talk?"

"A little. She's not as good at it as her teachers say she should be."

"Well." Oliver studied the young woman's profile as the lamplights of Walnut Street flashed past her window. "I don't think I'll be able to look at you the same way again."

"If you're smart, Dr. Dunbar, you'll find the right way to look at me."

"Okay."

"I mean it. I know I'm being forward. I know I shouldn't be saying any of this. But I'm watching you every day, Oliver, and I can tell something bad is happening to you. I don't think the job is helping you and—forgive me, *please* forgive me, I know this is none of my business—but I don't think your wife is helping you either. I think I can. Dear Lord, I don't want to complicate your life, that's not what this is about. I just want to see you happy."

Rittenhouse Square broke into skyscraper jewels before them. She pulled up by the canopy entrance of his apartment building.

"Julie," he said with difficulty, "I think going to your house would be the most fun I've had in ages. But let's be honest. I don't think it would stop at fun. I think more than that would happen."

"All right," she said, more than ready for this.

"My wife left me."

"I know you feel awk—what?"

"Tina now lives in New York with another actor. We're going through a divorce, but I haven't spoken to my lawyer in … I can't even remember. I don't know where the hell we're at."

"Oliver, my God! When did this happen?"

"About five weeks ago. The sixteenth of January."

"You never told anybody?"

"Well, what would be the point?"

"My word! Oh Oliver, I'm sorry!" Her hands went to her face. "I had no idea. I feel horrible."

"Don't."

"It's like I'm trying to take an emotional advantage of you. Please forgive me."

"Julie, it's okay. It really is." He climbed out of the car, then bent down to look at her. "You might just be the best friend I've got."

Julie's eyes were wet. "It was a wonderful show tonight, wasn't it?"

"Gosh, I forgot we even went to a show. Yes, it was terrific. Good night, Julie."

"Good night. Oliver!"

"Yes?"

She bit her lower lip. "I'm in the book."

He straightened and watched as her white battered car worked its way around the perimeter of Rittenhouse Square to reach Walnut Street again. He watched long after it was lost from view.

The building he lived in was a skyscraper, designed to thrust at God, like Babel, and make small those who could not afford to live within its portals. Tina had loved it. Oliver felt no connection to it at all, and this made him feel helpless, like a bit of flotsam.

He tucked his hands in his overcoat pockets and started walking. He headed east.

The July/September Sits

27

THE THREE REPS and Lily were busy now. The guidance counselors of the "C" schools were delighted to let the Burr College come in. As senior rep, Trudy had to visit these high schools, and the first time she went she was terrified to see students trudging through metal scanners as they entered the building, video cameras mounted everywhere, and uniformed security guards patrolling the halls with their holstered automatics in plain view. Looking her professional best in a pink business jacket and skirt, powdered and well-groomed, Trudy just knew she wouldn't take six steps inside the entrance before being grabbed, dragged into a closet, and raped. She was so scared it took her half an hour to find the guidance counselor office. But her fears proved over-reactive. The students were rowdy and her assembly presentations disjointed, but the audiences were never *that* unruly, and in truth she was never molested or even rudely spoken to. The counselors and teachers were open and friendly, and this bridged the gap to the girls themselves, who were an ill-educated but interested and lively group, and Trudy was excited along with everyone else when the lead cards started rolling in.

Added to this, the publicity campaign promised by Bill Nostrand took root in late February and the results were available by the middle of March. Large colorful Burr ads now adorned the Philadelphia subway system where no Burr ad would have ever appeared before. Billboards depicting black women dressed in superb executive regalia smiled down on the ghetto neighborhoods in South Philadelphia, West Philadelphia, and North Philadelphia east and west of Temple University, the cheapest locations in the city to buy billboard space.

The effect of all this newfound publicity was to bring the illustrious Burr College a different type of student than what smiled from the glossy cover of the school catalog. Students the caliber of Keone Robinson applied to the school in droves. From the slums of Chester to the south and from Camden to the east, from the weary blue-collar towns of Eddystone,

Norristown, Essington, and from the darker repressed shadows of the city itself: Logan, Brewerytown, Yorktown, Strawberry Mansion, Kingsessing, these rough-hewn girls arrived and applied.

The Admissions Department meeting on Monday, March 18, started with a wonderful show of initiative. A small bargain-basement school, the Harper Cosmetics Institute, had closed one week earlier in part, according to the grapevine, because a federal audit found its fiscal practices wanting in legality. With a self-indulgent flourish, Marty Nolan produced a computer list of all students eligible for federal Pell Grants from the dead school.

"My lord!" Lily fell hungrily on the list. "Bless you, Marty! What did you do?"

The rep grinned tartly. "It doesn't take much to get something from a school that's closing. The good people who worked there, if there ever were any to begin with, are long gone. The handful left don't care. I also figured the feds must be going in and out of the place, so I walked in, flashed my old Montclair student I.D., and asked for the list."

"You flashed a student I.D.?"

Marty just laughed.

"That's a riot," Lily said. "Let's take a look at this." She flipped through the blurry pages. "No phone numbers?"

"No. What I wanted were class lists, but it doesn't look like Harper bothered to keep serious enrollment records. I had to think fast then, and this was the best I could come up with. Kids eligible for Pell Grants come from low income families; I figured Harper must have a lot of them. The list only gives names and social security numbers, but we can do a local name search off the Internet and probably get most of these. A friend of mine is a Web idiot; he can find anything."

"Love, this is terrific. All right." Everyone could see the boss' brain clicking. "Now I happen to know that the Harper School failed its fidelity bond, so the feds—"

"Fidelity bond?" asked Trudy. "What's that mean?"

"It means," Lily chortled, "the school didn't have enough money to cover its ass once the feds started fining them right and left. The school couldn't even pay back the students who didn't get to finish the program because of the closing. Dee, this may be a project for you."

"Yes, Lily?"

"Punch up letters for these kids. Tell them how much we commiserate with them over their interrupted educations, and that maybe they should try something more secure like the secretarial field. Tell them if they want to come to Burr in July, we'll reimburse them for whatever they've already spent up to fifteen hundred dollars."

"Can we do that?"

"Well, Bill has to okay it, but why wouldn't he? We shell out fifteen hundred for tuition and they pay the rest. That's an eighty-six percent profit. I wouldn't sneeze at that, would you? We'll call it a … an incentive scholarship, maybe. We'll work it out. This is wonderful stuff, Marty. I hope the rest of you see what a little oomph and imagination can do.

"All right." Lily popped open the pencil drawer of her desk and extracted three chocolate almond Godiva bars. "Ladies, Marty—our hard work is finally paying off. The numbers are going up. We still have a long way to go, but we have three months before July, and five months before September." She passed out the candy. "Everybody gets a 'Making Good Progress' bar. If we keep up this momentum we will definitely have enough students to make the July goal." She was interrupted by cheers and loud clapping. Her voice sailed high above it. "Ladies, Marty—I have never missed a goal in my life. I don't count January, that was botched before I got here. The person responsible is no longer in our employ, so that's ancient history. But we are well on the way to making July, and even though the September numbers are even tougher, we will make that goal too. Because failure in this department is un*think*able! Right?"

"Right!" they all shouted.

Lily leaned forward. Her earrings clicked. The ankle bracelet winked. "Let me pass onto you what Bill told me this morning. Any of the seventeen Burr schools that make both July and September will go on a five-day Caribbean cruise! That's no joke. So between that and our regular commissions we've got some pretty damn good incentives, don't you think?"

"A cruise?" gasped Trudy. "Really?"

"For all of us! Just be careful, okay? It's actually a staff improvement seminar if anyone asks." Lily grinned wickedly. "One where you come back with a helluva nice tan. Ha! Ha! Ha! Sound good?"

"Oh yes!"

"Eat up." She leaned back in her chair, sipped coffee, and watched with deep satisfaction as they munched the candy. Deirdre and Trudy gobbled their chocolate quickly. Marty unwrapped his bar halfway, and held it out to the admissions director.

"You can't sit this out," he said. "We know this is all your doing, Lily."

Lily laughed and broke off half his bar. They all chomped contentedly.

"Well, let's get to work here," Lily said at last, wiping her fingers on a handkerchief. "Dee has pulled a massive mailing list which I've broken into thirds by alphabet. It's telemarket time once again, ladies and Marty. Anybody who ever expressed the slightest interest in this college in the past twelve years is going to get a call."

"The past twelve years?" said Marty. "The names go back twelve years?"

"Couldn't be helped," said Lily. "We bought the computer twelve years ago, and the lists won't go back further than that."

Deirdre asked, "Why would anybody still be interested after all that time?"

Before Lily could reply Trudy whirled on the youngest rep. "Because every straw is worth examining. Because if these people were unhappy with their lives once, they might still be now. Maybe all they need is a reminder that we're here to help them."

"A-plus!" trilled Lily. "Any questions? Any old business? Any new business? Okay, *scoot!* Get the lists and good hunting. Trudy, stay a moment."

The others left. Lily beckoned, and Trudy stood close to the desk. Lily produced tweezers and plucked at the young woman's left eyebrow. "Excuse the liberty. You don't mind, do you?"

"No. Is something wrong?"

"Just a mascara clump. There, you're picture perfect. By the way, how did the church raffle pan out?"

"Not well at all, Lily. I'm sorry. They offered it, but nobody bid for it."

"*Nobody?* What's the matter with those Coatesville rubes, don't they know a good thing when they see one? Do they think colleges auction seats to an accounting program all the time?"

"I guess it just wasn't the type of thing people plan on paying for when they go to a church raffle."

"Hmmm." Lily's face creased irritably. "Well, maybe not. Hell, it was worth a shot. Okay, dear, go get your list."

"Lily?"

"Yes, Tru?"

Trudy's rosebud mouth twitched. Her hands fidgeted. "I got the bonus check yesterday. It was higher than I imagined."

Lily laughed. "Well, good!"

"I can't tell you how great it made me feel. Thanks."

"Listen sweetie, those fashion shows brought in *tons* of lead cards. No way was I going to let New York ignore that."

"Well, I really appreciate it. Thank you."

"No dear. Thank *you*." The admissions director's black eyes danced affectionately. She watched the rep skip out of the office. She lifted the phone to call New York when suddenly Marty stuck his head in the door.

"Lily, a second?"

"Sure, hon. Come on in."

The rep's face was grim. "I got a problem. David won't process a federal loan for one of my kids. Says she's reached her aggregate limit."

"Her *what?*"

"Evidently you can only borrow so much over time in the federal loan program. This kid's gone to other colleges before us, and now she's used up her eligibility. David's being a real prick about it."

"Christ." Lily shook her head. "Look, have the kid mail her loan note to you, then *you* certify it."

"I can do that?"

The admissions director's tone grew sharp. "You can if you don't tell David. Fill it out and put it in the mail. If you have questions, come to me."

"Sure. Great. But won't David know when the funds come?"

"One problem at a time. The main thing is to keep that kid wanting to come here. We'll deal with Mister By-The-Book when we have to."

Lily grinned mischievously, and Marty grinned back. He admired his boss' gleaming black eyes, her high cheekbones and full lips.

"Listen hon," she continued, "your telemarket list is somewhat larger than the others. I hope you don't mind."

"Not at all."

"We're doing well here, Marty. You and me. Don't think I don't know it. Don't think I won't reciprocate either."

"That's great, Lily. Cool."

Marty returned to his office and punched the first phone number with his pen. "Yes, may I speak to Bernadette McCue?"

A rough male voice said, "Who wants her?"

"Is this Bernadette's father?"

"Yeah. Who wants her?"

"Sir, I'm Martin Nolan from the Burr College of Business. Your daughter—"

"Heh? Christ. We're not interested." And the phone clicked dead.

Marty punched the redial button on his phone.

"Hello?"

"Mr. McCue, Martin Nolan again. The thing is, sir, Bernadette responded to a postcard expressing interest in our Secretarial Liberal Arts Program. I think it b—"

"My daughter is seventeen years old. She signs every damn thing that comes to her in the mailbox. We're not interested." And again the phone clicked dead.

Marty hit redial again.

"Hello?"

"Mr. McCue, I fully apologize. I know I must seem rude to you. But stop and think, sir—Bernadette expressed an interest in this college, which is an institution of higher learning. She is obviously motivated to pursue a good future for herself. I think it would be terribly remiss, sir—forgive me for saying so, I do apologize—I think it would be a shame if you summarily dismissed her good initiative. So few young people even give a thought to their future. You should feel proud that Bernadette has the foresight to be so responsible about herself."

An irritated sigh on the other end of the line.

"If she's looking at education, sir, then she's looking for what will fulfill her and make her happy for the rest of her life. A good father wouldn't want to be a roadblock to that, don't you think, sir?"

"All right," the voice said, very tired. "What's the name of this school again?"

Marty smiled and leaned back in his chair.

28

The bell blatted, ending Third Period, and students filled the corridor and tromped up and down the staircase. Taller than most but not all, Bob Lawrence wormed through. It was his lunch hour, but instead of going downstairs to the teachers' lounge he climbed to the second floor and stood outside Carol Sobolewski's Practical Business 205 classroom, acting casual until Heather Feeney emerged. She was chewing gum and chatting with two other girls, but she saw him and smiled. With the barest tilt of his head, Bob indicated for her to follow, then descended the stairs without waiting. The Burr College was not large enough to have a health center, nor could it afford to employ a full-time nurse. Still, there was a room marked INFIRMARY at the foot of the stairs on the first floor. Bob checked to make sure Heather saw him, then ducked inside. A moment later she opened the door and slipped in too. Only after she closed the door did he snap on the light.

"Bob, what's up?" She giggled, delighted at this impromptu adventure.

He didn't answer. He flipped the door bolt, then faced her. He looked pale, and his eyes bulged with nervous liquid.

Heather walked toward him with a gentle sway of her hips. "Am I cutting this class?"

"No," he whispered. "I just have to talk to you for a moment."

"Sure, Bob."

"It's important, and it concerns the two of us."

"So I gathered."

She was too close not to embrace. A failure to do so, he knew, would not be politic. With one arm he gave her a quick strong squeeze. "Baby, I've got to ask you something critical."

Heather put both arms around his neck. "You locked the door."

"Yeah. Just to be safe. Nobody ever uses this room anyway."

"Oh, I don't know. *Some*body might find a use for it."

"What I mean is … I need to know—" He was startled by her upturned face. Heather's eyes were lustrous, her lips parted, he could feel her breath. "Honey, what—"

"Kiss me."

"Heather—"

Her hands pressed the back of his neck, pulled his face close. "Kiss me, please."

He did, and got a hell of a kiss in return. There was a tongue on this girl. Thrusting it into his mouth, she fired shock waves down his throat and out through every limb. Automatically his hand slipped up her skirt. Heather felt it, and smiled against his lips. He tried to pull his head back, but the girl's hands on his neck were unexpectedly strong. "Mmm," he grunted. "Mmm, mmm." Finally she broke off.

"What's all this?" he gasped.

She looked surprised. "What do you mean?"

"Well, I haven't seen you like this in—in a while."

"Sure you have."

"No," he said firmly.

"Sure you have. You must be crazy. I love you." And she kissed him again.

No, he hadn't. Things had been hot that first night before Christmas and for a few weeks afterward, but recently when they got together the desultory themes emanating from her were *I'm bored* and *What have you done for me lately?* This ardent arousal was totally unexpected. Even the way Heather's hands gripped his back felt different.

"Oh baby," she whispered. "This is great. Isn't this so great, baby?"

And in an intuitive flash he knew! It was this closed room! The two of them hidden in the heart of the school while her classmates walked past in the hallway just inches beyond that door. The danger of immediate exposure was turning this girl on like the safety of his apartment or a hotel room never could. Christ, and he thought *he* had strange fetishes!

"Baby, I can't," he said around her mouth.

"Honey, come on—"

"I can't. Really, no. I can't."

"I'm already missing class."

The makeshift infirmary boasted a tiny hospital cot with two sheets and a prune of a pillow. It probably had the noisiest springs in the world. Heather, kissing like a leech, was trying to pull him there. But these walls were only sheet rock. He didn't dare, he didn't dare—

"Heath, listen to—listen to me, baby—please. I think there might be something wrong."

"Like what?"

"Well, I don't know if there's anything *really* wrong, it's just a possibility. It's probably not even that. Something's bothering me very much, and I need to—to ask you something."

"What?" She looked up at him with her chin against his chest.

"Have you been talking to anybody? About us, I mean."

She looked very surprised. "No, of course not, honey."

"Are you sure?"

"Sure I'm sure. You told me not too. I know how it worries you."

She sounded sincere but … but wasn't that what she *would* say? "Okay. Because you'll get me in a hell of a lot of trouble if you do, you realize that, don't you?"

"Bob, I'm not an imbecile."

"I know that. Believe me, I don't think you are. That's not what I'm saying."

Heather's grip on him loosened. She looked appropriately insulted, but was it because he was questioning her word or because he'd backed off from her amorous advance? Either possibility could be sticky.

"Don't you trust me?"

"I trust you completely, honey. But I know how it is with secrets. You have every intention of keeping them, but there's always one close soul mate who swears that she'll keep the secret just as well, and so you confide in her—"

"I haven't told anybody!"

He quickly kissed her forehead. "Please, baby, keep your voice down. I know you haven't."

"Bullshit! You think I have!" She stepped away.

"No, I don't. Not at all. Baby, please, try to understand. I got a little shook up about something, that's all. Some of the girls in my classes are grinning at me, and I don't know why."

"Who is?"

"Nobody. I'm sure it's nothing. But when it happened, you know, it got my imagination fired up."

"Who's grinning at you?"

"It doesn't matter." He smiled affectionately and reached for her. "I realize now it was nothing, okay?"

"Fuck you," she snapped. "You're a big jerk, Bob."

"Yes, I am. I'm a big jerk. I'm sorry for that too. Sweetheart, the last thing I want to be is a jerk around you."

The contrition worked. Heather let herself be mollified, but still pouted. "Who's grinning at you?"

"Nobody, now that I think of it." He shrugged and laughed. "I guess I'm suffering an irrational attack of nerves. I'm only human too, right? I mean, this *is* a little risky, what you and I have going, you know?"

"Well, nobody better be grinning at you, honey. Not if they know what's good for them."

He kissed her again. "No one is, I swear. Sorry to trouble you, Heath. Go on to class, okay?"

"Okay." But it wasn't that easy. She glanced at the infirmary cot, and he knew she was remembering this whole scene, all he had said, and most of all what he hadn't done. "Can I talk to you tonight?"

"Okay."

"You call me, or I call you?"

God, it was like he was a teenager too, having to answer questions like this. "You call me."

"Eight o'clock?"

"Fine."

Bob switched off the light and Heather stepped out of the room. He shut the door after her but was too afraid to immediately step outside himself. He turned the light back on and sat on the little hospital cot, close to despair. He hated their phone conversations, how incredibly long they were, the *hours* they ate up. Conversations filled with insufferable lapses when neither had a word to say, but if he tried to suggest they hang up too soon she got upset. He sat on the cot for ten minutes before remembering his lunch. He went out and ran downstairs to the faculty lounge.

Donna Harding, Arthur Cassidy, and Jean Cavanaugh were there, sitting at tables eating their bagged lunches. Jean marked papers, and Donna was skimming headlines in the *Philadelphia Inquirer.* As soon as he entered Jean pointed a plastic spoon at him. "You ought to be ashamed of yourself!"

"What?" said Bob.

"You know exactly what I mean!"

Time suspended. All eyes were upon him.

"It was you who put that topic in the suggestion box, wasn't it?"

"Which suggestion was that? I put in a couple."

"'The Advantages of Sleeping With the Boss.' We all know it was yours, Bob. No one else would dare suggest that as an essay contest topic."

He looked at their faces, but they were all grinning. Donna was outright laughing. "It made my day to read it," she said.

Bob laughed too, loudly. "Well, it's not like I expected you guys to accept it."

Jean shook her head. "You are such a wiseass. Lord knows where we got you from, Bob."

"I don't think the Lord had anything to do with it," said Arthur.

Bob opened the refrigerator for his lunch, a tuna fish sandwich he made for himself three out of five days a week. "I think it's a great topic. And you gotta admit the essays would be much more fun to read."

Donna said good-naturedly, "Let's not come down too hard on our hedonistic little Bobby. It's an inbred male condition to want to see women barefoot and pregnant."

"Actually, Donna, I must repudiate that. I don't care for children, and I'm partial to high heels." He sat down beside her. "So where are we with the essay contest?"

She folded up the paper, bored with it. "The suggestion box is full. We'll go through it and have a topic picked by the end of the week."

The essay contest was an annual event, one of the few things students from the January, July, and September classes could compete in as a group. A theme was chosen and the students wrote a five hundred word essay based on it. The winning entry was read at graduation, and its author received both a plaque and a one hundred dollar gift certificate to whatever was the current hottest clothing store in town. The faculty or staff member who thought up the chosen topic got a gift certificate as well.

"Oliver has a good one this year," Arthur said. "'Setting Goals is the Key to Success.' I like that one better than my own."

Jean asked, "What's yours, Arthur?"

"Real simple. 'Attitude is Everything.'"

She nodded. "That's good, Arthur. Except I think we used it about three years ago."

"Did we? I thought I knew it from somewhere."

"I'm embarrassed to confess," said Donna, "that I'm drawing a blank this year."

"Mine," said Jean eagerly, "is 'Equip Yourself for Opportunities.' Do you think they'll understand what I mean by that?"

"I understand it," said Bob. "In fact, it sounds like my old fraternity motto."

Jean made a face at him.

"Dean Harris has a great one," said Arthur. "'Fortune Favors the Prepared Mind.' How about that?"

"That *is* good," said Donna.

"Didn't Ethel win last year?" asked Jean with a small frown.

"Yes, she did," said Arthur.

Bob sat on the couch and watched his fellow teachers as they talked about the essay contest, about their students, about their work. He felt removed from them and, sadly, wished it wasn't so. They were a good crew, the teachers at this college. Decent, dedicated, passionate. He liked them a lot. But wouldn't it be nice, wouldn't it make things a little bit easier, if one of them just had a surreptitious meeting in the infirmary with a student? He looked at them each in turn, the intelligent, attractive business teacher, the affable former priest, and the tough but passionate economics teacher. He hated to admit how much he wished it.

29

If Julie Fitzgerald ever believed that just working for Oliver Dunbar would be good enough, the dinner date put an end to it. She was hit hard by the man, by his kindness, his respect for her, and his caring nature. At the same time she no longer had the protection of keeping her feelings secret. She had let herself get too close to him, had even propositioned him (sort of), and thus put her entire relationship with him at risk. Coming to work the Monday following their date she didn't know how to speak to him, and what hurt most was Oliver's own reticence; they both said little more than hello to each other all day.

The next morning was better, and by afternoon the necessary routines of the job forced all remaining discomfort to ebb. Oliver resumed asking if she would write up his reports, screen his calls, take dictation, and he treated her with the same breezy, self-effacing good humor that had originally and innocently captured her heart.

One day Julie arrived for work with a picture of Kelly in a silver frame, and positioned it on her desk. All morning the child smiled back with gapped teeth and whiffs of feathery blond hair. It didn't take long for the picture to cause a sensation, and Julie was bombarded repeatedly by the same two questions: "That isn't your *daughter,* is it?" and "Why didn't you tell us you had a child?" Julie answered the first with a pride that increased her embarrassment at having to answer the second. She felt stupid for not mentioning Kelly to these people, her colleagues and co-workers, and thoroughly enjoyed their attention.

Late in the day Oliver buzzed her intercom. "Jule, would you be able to take a letter for me?"

"Of course. Let me get somebody to cover the lobby." Julie buzzed around, found Deirdre, and asked her.

A harpsichord piece tatted on the radio in Oliver's office. He was leaning back in his chair, staring at the ceiling. His glasses were upside down on the desk blotter. His jacket was off, which was normal, but his tie was yanked loose at the knot and his collar unbuttoned. This sloppiness shocked Julie.

"Hi. Take a seat. I need you to jot something down for me. I tried doing it myself and I'm getting nowhere with it."

Julie sat and flipped open her steno pad. He didn't speak. His fingers idly pushed his glasses back and forth on the blotter.

"How's your day going?" he asked after a bit.

"Fine." His manner was making her nervous. "How about you?"

"Up and down. The President's Office issued our new catalog for next year. It's on the credenza if you're curious. Not as glitzy as in the past. They're cutting corners there too."

"Oliver, are you okay?"

He looked at her curiously. "I've got a lot on my mind."

"Does that include me?"

He smiled. "No. I'm fine with you."

"Are you sure? I mean … well, it would be perfectly natural for you to find it awkward having me here."

Still smiling, he leaned forward. With his glasses off she could see how weary he looked, how deep-set were his gray eyes. His nose had red marks from his glasses that looked freshly sore. "Do you think I'm acting awkward around you?"

"I don't think … well, no." She felt her face growing hot. Finally she said, "Help me out."

"Sure. Don't worry about it."

"Well, we've always had a good working relationship, Oliver. I don't want to blow that."

"You haven't. It's not a problem."

"Are you sure? I feel like I've caused you all kinds of embarrassment. I mean, I had no idea about you and Tina. I thought—"

"Julie, honestly, do you know how lucky I am to have you? I can't remember how this college ran before you came on board. I'd be devastated if you ever left. You're invaluable."

"Oh God, Oliver," she muttered, and put a hand to her eyes.

"I loved the *Les Miz* night. I wouldn't take it back for anything." He grinned, showing the laugh lines she adored. "Is that a good answer?"

"It's perfect, Oliver. Thank you."

"Want to help me with this letter?"

"Of course."

"It goes to Carol Nixon. Do you know her?"

"I've spoken to her on the phone. She's director of the Miami school."

"That's according to last year's catalog. It's 'TBA' in the new copy. This letter doesn't go to her office, it goes to her home. I've got the address."

Julie gasped. "She was fired?"

"Just. She called me half an hour ago."

"Whatever for?"

"She didn't make January."

"How long has she worked at Burr?"

"Thirty-one years. She was my first 'go to' person when I started here and was learning the ropes. She's a great educator. Problem is, I don't think New York wants educators running the schools."

"They don't want educators?"

"Not as directors. Kind of says something, doesn't it?" At that moment the period bell blatted, and he held up a hand. "Wait a sec. Don't say anything. Just listen."

She did, but there was nothing to hear. The harpsichord piece skittered without pause.

Oliver said, "When this school had its peak enrollment, about eight, ten years ago, you could sit in this office and hear the students thumping up and down the staircase at the end of the hall. It only occurred to me recently that I don't hear that anymore, that I haven't heard it in years. Lily's figures for July and September are starting to look good. Maybe this fall I'll be able to hear students on the stairs again."

"That'd be nice."

"I love this business, Julie. I love watching the students learn, and I love what we're teaching them. I've got another two decades left in me, and I want to spend that time doing what I'm doing, because I think the Burr College is special, and I want to keep it that way."

She said gently, "What about the letter, Oliver?"

"Yes, the letter. Thirty-one years. I have no idea what to say to her."

Yet he articulated a beautiful letter praising Carol Nixon's skill and dedication, blaming without bitterness the times for her misfortune, and his confidence that she was too experienced to remain unemployed for long. He closed reassuring her that he would always be a good reference. The care and generosity he put into the letter tore at Julie's resolve. She closed her pad.

"Oliver?"

"Yes?"

"This is difficult for me, but I'm going to say it anyway. I want you to come out to Manayunk and visit me and my daughter. I want you to get to know us."

He closed his eyes. "Julie …"

"I'm sorry about you and Tina, but that only convinces me I'm right. Kelly and I can do a lot for you. And you know it's what you need."

He was silent.

"Oliver, why don't you take advantage of me?"

He sat up straight in the chair and put his glasses back on. "Julie, what am I going to tell you? I'm sure a smarter man would. The offer is incredible. But it wouldn't be fair to you."

"Fair to me? Oliver, this is my idea."

"You're missing the point. I have this school. I am worried *sick* about this school. It isn't working. The kids coming here aren't getting the education they need and that's my job, to make sure they do. I'm failing them, which means I'm failing Burr, and all the teachers, and all of you, and I can't figure out how to reverse that."

She heard real panic in his voice. Her counter-argument died on her lips.

"If you end up leaving, I'll understand. I certainly don't want you to go. I'm not sure I can function properly without you. But I can't put you in the spot you're in and then expect you to stay."

"You didn't put me here," she said. "I did that one myself."

"There is another reason." He looked at her quietly across the gulf of his office. "You should know that I'm still in love with my wife."

She hid her surprise by biting her lip.

"I have to file the papers, the divorce has to go through. But only because she wants it. If Tina called me tonight and asked to come back, I'd take her in. As long as my feelings are so crossed, I can't start something with you. I can't be so selfish."

"She's divorcing you, Oliver."

"I know. But principles don't derive from happenstance. They come from an honest heart. I don't like this, but it's how it has to be."

"Principles again," she said bitterly. "Oliver, aren't you ever interested in doing what you want? Just simply what *you* want?"

He looked embarrassed. "It's never been a priority."

"Okay." She stood up and gave him a small defeated smile. "Oliver, I'm not going to leave. I'm just going to be the best administrative assistant you've ever had."

"That's what you've been for a year now."

She left his office and relieved Deirdre at the front desk. The admissions rep stared at her but didn't say a word. The lobby was still, and Julie sat alone with her thoughts.

She didn't want to quit this job. In many ways, Burr had been her salvation. After being abandoned by Sam, Julie had struggled for whatever work she could get, hampered by the needs of her toddler and a real lack of job experience. Most jobs—cashier, waitress—paid minimum and offered no benefits. The vulnerability of how she and Kelly were living was frightening. Coming to Burr had given her stable employment, and working for Oliver Dunbar restored her self-worth. She wished she were older, she wished she had met him years ago. She wished, in fact, that God would finally give her a break.

Thinking that last, she quickly crossed herself. Then she opened her steno pad and began to type out Oliver's letter to the fallen Miami director.

30

Though the other department heads suspected what Admissions was doing, it was Ethel who finally attempted a direct probe. One morning she casually knocked on the open door of Deirdre's office. The young rep commanded Trudy's old office, Trudy having moved into Elaine's.

"Hi," said the dean.

"Oh, hi!" Deirdre quickly straightened behind her desk. A graduate two years old now, she was still intimidated by Dean Harris.

"Big come up in the world, hey?" Ethel grinned and sat in one of the client chairs without waiting to be asked.

Deirdre laughed. "Yeah, I thought so too at first, but it's just as crazy here too."

Ethel smiled and folded her hands on her lap, a picture of friendliness, and looked around. The rep's desk was cluttered with blue app forms and files, and the open calendar was heavily marked. "You look busy."

"Oh, it's nutty. I kinda knew it would be tough, the pressure and all, but there's no really knowing it until you're in it."

"Sure. That's very true." Ethel kept glancing about as if admiring the office. She knew Lily would pitch a fit if she learned of this visit, so Ethel wanted to look like she was just making a social call. "And how's Admissions working without a secretary?"

Deirdre smiled. "Kinda ridiculous."

"Oh?"

"Yeah, like now the—" Suddenly the phone rang. "Excuse me." The girl picked up the line. "Sure, I'll take it. Hello, Rashad! Did you get the materials I sent? Well I was looking to book you in at four o'clock on Thursday. I know, but the rest of the week is pretty jammed. Yeah, but—"

As Ethel waited patiently for Deirdre to finish the call, she studied the young rep. What she wanted from this visit was a sense of whether things were going well in Admissions or not. Lily had gotten Oliver to mandate that only Admissions personnel could look at a prospect's file, and Ethel wanted to play by the rules. The dean had strictly forbidden Jean Cavanaugh from peeking at files, and nearly threatened to put her top teacher on probation. But Ethel had developed a bad feeling since the January sit, and she wasn't so sure that playing by the rules was the smart thing to do. Deirdre's cherubic face and easygoing manner had made her one of the most likable students in her class. Ethel's ever-retentive memory recalled that Deirdre's grades were good but her skills so-so; still, she was conscientious and an excellent proofreader—the primary attributes of a good secretary. If something really wrong was going on, the dean reasoned, she should be able to detect it in Deirdre.

The rep hung up and giggled. "Busy, busy, busy."

"You know," the dean said gently, "some of the files you gave me for January are missing high school diplomas or transcripts or even enrollment contracts. Are you aware of that?"

"Shoot." Deirdre frowned but didn't seem too upset. "You're still missing stuff from last September. I'll get it all in as soon as I can, Dean Harris, but I gotta be honest with you, it's not my problem anymore. And I wouldn't vouch for the shape of any files for the upcoming classes either. I mean, I look out for my stuff, but there really isn't time for follow up. The kids either send us everything they're supposed to or they don't. They still get admitted. I don't think Trudy even knows what belongs in a file, though I showed her. And Lily sure doesn't bother."

"Yes. I understand." Ethel hid her concern behind an expression of complacency. "But you like being a rep now, instead of a secretary?"

"Sure," came the cheerful answer. "This is the best job I ever had."

The girl was obviously happy, but Ethel wasn't sure what to base this on. Though it had not been trumpeted loudly at the time, Deirdre's metamorphosis from admissions secretary to admissions rep was a legitimate promotion, with a salary increase and an office of her own. On the bulletin board above her desk, thumbtacked between an organizational calendar and a snapshot of her latest scary biker boyfriend, were several congratulations cards. So why was Deirdre happy? Because she liked the job, or because it was a promotion?

"And how do you feel about the students you're recruiting?" Ethel asked, finally getting down to it. She was trampling etiquette openly now, but feared too much was at stake.

"Oh, these kids." Deirdre groaned and rolled her eyes. "Most of 'em are real sweet, you know, but they're dumber than a goldfish. You should see them sitting in the lobby struggling with the app form, trying to remember what year they graduated from high school, or trying to remember their own ZIP Codes. It's pretty sad."

"Are the admissions scores plummeting?"

"Well, they uh …" Deirdre suddenly dried up. She had sensed, if not actually seen, the light. She smiled and shrugged. Ethel nodded, but behind her friendly expression loud alarms were sounding in her head. Trudy and Deirdre were both grads of the college. Surely they would feel troubled by a drop in quality among applicants for their own alma mater! But Deirdre seemed more amused than disgusted, and Trudy, as far as the dean could tell, did not seem put out in any way. Either things weren't as bad as Ethel suspected, or there was more to it than what she saw here. There was just no way of knowing.

"Well, I guess I'll leave you to it." Ethel stood up.

"Sure. Thanks for stopping in, Dean Harris. It's wicked, isn't it? Me having my own office."

"You've worked hard for it," said Ethel, and she went out.

As the dean walked past Jessica's, Natalie's, and Deirdre's empty cubicles, she wondered if anyone else found it ironic that when this time-honored secretarial college needed to shave expenses it cut first from the secretarial staff. She passed the last Admissions office, occupied by that new boy, Marty Nolan. The door was open and he sat at his desk, scrutinizing his chin with a hand mirror. The sight made Ethel pause. Then he glanced at her, and she moved on. She didn't have this kid's measure yet; she hadn't said more than hello to him since he started working here. Still, she frowned darkly as she made her way down the corridor and up the stairs to her office. She had no reason to mistrust the new rep, but she did, and she heeded gut feelings like this. You didn't raise four boys without developing good antenna for trouble.

Marty was, in fact, sprucing himself for an eleven o'clock appointment, a twenty-five year old African-American woman who was a graduate cum laude from the University of Virginia with a degree in political science. Lily, setting up the interview, warned Marty of all this beforehand. He replaced his bow tie with a straight one, buttoned his jacket to hide his beloved suspenders, and rose to meet her.

"Estelle Tipton?" he asked, gliding like a skater across the lobby with his hand outstretched before him. "I'm Martin Nolan."

"How do you do?" She stood to take his hand. She wore a smartly tailored olive-green blazer and skirt, and towered over him even though she wore flats. Her face was sharp and penetrating, her handshake firm. Despite this show of confidence, she had brought her parents with her, a stocky couple silent with nervousness and seated on the couch with their coats still on.

"Let's everybody come back to my office," Marty said expansively, "and we'll talk about the program."

It didn't take long. Estelle knew exactly what she wanted. She had graduated the previous spring from UVA with every intention of entering Villanova's law school, but then Villanova placed her on a waiting list, effectively checking her plans for at least another year. Restrategizing, she decided that marketable job skills would give her basic security while she pursued her dream. Her SATs were excellent, and Dad was prepared to cough up the $125 app fee and deposit, anything to help his daughter.

"Hey okay!" said Marty. "You're all set for July then. Why don't we take the tour? Get the lowdown of the place, hey?"

"Yes," said her mother. "I definitely want to see the school."

He started the tour in the lobby, showing off the two large portraits of Reginald and Evelyn. "The heads of the Burr dynasty," he said with the subdued reverence of a museum curator. "Reginald Burr started the school in 1907 with his remarkable mother, Evelyn, and then his son Henry ran it, and then his grandson Charles. They changed the whole perception of women in business when the first college was started in Boston ..."

Estelle seemed to like all the pro-female history. Marty played that up.

He took them along the first floor corridor. The parents complimented the rich colonial furnishings so he explained how the home once belonged to a notorious British Tory who was run out of town during the first counter-attack on Philadelphia during the Revolutionary War. "Ben

Franklin stayed here for a while after his own home burned," Marty stated impressively, though he wasn't sure this was true. He thought he heard Oliver Dunbar mention it once. In any case, who could say Franklin *hadn't?*

A table was set up beside the stairway, loaded with cookies, cupcakes, and brownies. Three girls stood behind it, near a sign that read STUDENT COUNCIL BAKE SALE. Marty laughed and rubbed his hands with comic covetousness as he and his charges drew near. "Ms. Tipton, Mr. and Mrs. Tipton, let me introduce you to three exceptionally gifted ladies of the Burr student body. This is Amelia Albretti, our student council president. The woman with the strange green-tipped hair is Heather Feeney, and last but not least is Kristin Rutherford, another cohort of cupcake crime."

The girls snickered. Estelle and her parents smiled politely. Mrs. Tipton said, "Gracious, everything smells yummy, girls."

"Everything's fifty cents apiece," said Amelia.

"Except to Marty," said Kristin. "Everything's a dollar for him."

"Aw, man!" groaned the rep. "You see what I've got to put up with? Do you think I deserve this abuse, Estelle?"

Estelle's smile remained polite.

"It's what you get," said Kristin, "for being one of the few men on the staff here."

"One who loves fudge brownies," said Heather.

"And who we think should buy some more," added Amelia, holding a tray under his nose.

"Ladies, ladies, I indulged enthusiastically when I came in this morning. That was only two hours ago."

"Exactly," said Amelia. "Two whole hours have gone by. Time for a refill."

"And my green hair isn't strange," remarked Heather. She touched it to be sure.

"Don't give him an app deposit unless he buys something," said Amelia.

"Egads!" said Marty. "Well, Estelle, you're seeing first-hand what Burr enterprise is like. As smart a woman as you are, you'll have some tough competition here."

"I'm not worried."

"Well, up to the second floor then."

As they climbed the stairs, Mrs. Tipton said, "You seem to be well-liked here, Martin."

"Ma'am, I always believe it pays to be nice. What I like about working here is these students don't make being nice a chore."

"There seem to be more black students than I expected," the father said, puffing as they reached the second floor landing.

Marty's face relaxed into solemnity. "Sir, I admire educational institutions as much as the next man. But it's a fact that most schools of prestige admit blacks and Hispanics mainly because it wouldn't be politically correct for them not to. In other words, black students are recruited to fill quotas, and are not encouraged to apply once those quotas are answered."

Mr. Tipton nodded with stern agreement.

"But here at Burr," Marty said with a sudden big smile, "I can say with complete honesty that we openly recruit minority students. We feel there is tremendous potential in today's youth, regardless of race or nationality. We have no quotas. We don't believe in them. Any Hispanic or African-American student who meets our admittance criteria is actively encouraged to enroll. You might say we've put the 'action' back into Affirmative Action."

"What is this, Mr. Nolan?" Estelle asked, pointing to a bulletin board covered with photographs and neatly printed index cards.

"That's our Placement board," he said. "We love advertising the success of our grads."

"There are certainly a lot of pictures," said Mrs. Tipton.

"Yes, ma'am, there are." He enjoyed showing off the Placement board. Some of the positions were very good, like the girl who was secretary to Donald Trump, or the executive assistant to Mayor Ed Rendell. Jessie Hershhorn, whose picture hung dead center, was a White House executive assistant. Of course a great many of the placements were older than Admissions cared to mention. Recent grads were not getting the high-profile corporate jobs that previous grads had enjoyed, so some time ago Trudy and Deirdre revised the cards on this board to eliminate the years those alumni graduated. The Tiptons were very impressed.

"Is this a computer lab?" Mrs. Tipton asked, looking through a window in a door.

Marty had to look too. The room was empty, the overhead lights off. The monitors were asleep under their protective polyester covers. "That's right. Burr grads are famous for graduating with typing speeds of a hundred and forty to a hundred and sixty words per minute. It's phenomenal to watch. In fact, *all* Burr students tend to graduate with skill levels that other schools would consider super-human. The training here is that special."

"One hundred and sixty words?" Estelle asked skeptically.

"Absolutely. When you train the Burr way, you're not just a secretary. You're one of the elite."

"We do want the best for Estelle," said Mrs. Tipton.

"We all do," agreed Marty. He pointed to another bulletin board where a full-color poster depicted a beautiful Mexican woman sipping from a straw in a coconut shell. "Estelle, did I mention that Burr students take a class trip each winter to Cancun?"

Down on the first floor, Jean Cavanaugh and Donna Harding each bought a chocolate cupcake from Amelia, and oohed appreciatively as they bit in. "Ladies," Jean said with a pleasantness that shocked them, "you may have missed your calling. You should be running a catering service and making a fortune."

"That's what my mom says," grinned Kristin Rutherford.

"This is exquisite," said Donna. "Of course you're killing my girlish figure."

"And my diet is taking a shellacking as well," acknowledged Jean. She held her cake and napkin close to her chin. "I don't know how I'll maintain class discipline if you ladies keep me plump and jolly."

Any joke by Mrs. Cavanaugh was so startling the girls had to laugh.

"Try to sell the rest of these before next period ends," said Donna. "So I won't weaken again, okay?"

"We'll try," said Amelia.

They watched and waited until the teachers were out of sight.

"Can you believe it?" gasped Amelia. "She's so different outside the classroom. A whole different person altogether!"

"Never mind that," hissed Kristin, for the coast was clear. "Where'd he take you this weekend?"

"Up to New York," said Heather. "We booked a room in a Holiday Inn, and we had breakfast in some big park hotel, and we shopped and finally we rented a limo and toured all of Manhattan like a couple of movie stars."

"God, he must have a lot of money," said Kristin.

"He sure does," said Heather, swelling before their awestruck faces. "He makes thirty-three thousand a year!"

"And you guys are really engaged?"

"Well, like engaged to be engaged. He doesn't think I should have a ring until I finish here, you know? It might be awkward. I dunno. He's probably right."

"God! Wow, it's wild, Heath."

Kristin asked tentatively, "Do you … are you still … you know?"

"Oh yeah, all the time. Every chance we can. Especially at his place. He's got this real cool loft and big fat kitty cat."

Amelia frowned. "Is he really good, though? I mean, he looks kind of short to me. Short legs, and kind of stocky. Maybe he's just not my type."

"Well," said Heather, "there's one part of him that's not short, and believe you me it compensates real nice."

Kristin squealed. They all battled to suppress their laughter, and Heather snitched a brownie.

"God!" Kristin said, "I can't believe it!"

"Sometimes I can't either. Sometimes it feels like a dream. Especially in class, you know, watchin' him teach."

"Yeah," Amelia nodded.

"But it ain't a dream," said Heather, her mouth stuffed with cake. "It's the real thing. The *real* thing."

31

Though the Race Street Meetinghouse went by that name, its entrance was one block south on Cherry, where attendees entered through a gate between the original building, erected in 1856, and the modern Friends Meeting Center built in 1974. Meeting began at 10:30. Oliver always arrived each First Day a half hour early so he could mingle with other Quakers beforehand, including a few academicians who had been classmates of his at Penn. He then entered the meeting room and took his preferred seat on a bench near the northwest corner, half-sheltered under the second-floor balcony that extended along three sides of the room. The Friends sitting around him dressed casually: jeans and T-shirts, though some of the women wore skirts. Oliver's best friend, Dale Thurston, a dean of Humanities at Swarthmore College, always wore suit and tie to meeting, reflective of his earnest childhood upbringing. Oliver tended to wear slacks and a button-down shirt, or a sweater when the weather was cold. His business suit was the rigid uniform of his job; he didn't want to wear it for worship.

A dusty silence settled on the sixty to seventy people sitting in this room which in grander days held four hundred. People sat with heads bent or stared before them. Oliver was also silent. He rarely had trouble feeling God's presence here, although once when he mentioned this to Tina she suggested that perhaps he wasn't feeling God at all but just the sheer history of the building. History and God, she said, tended to feel the same. Around him bodies rustled and small children squirmed. Doors to distant rooms in the meetinghouse thumped shut, and floorboards creaked as inconsiderate latecomers tiptoed in. Traffic grumbled on Race Street, muffled by the heavy windows. There was no choir at meeting, no designated minister, organ, liturgist, or reading of scripture. Quakers communed with God through the purity of their own open minds and hearts. During the course of such communion one might suddenly feel compelled to speak. This was the closest thing to a sermon in a Quaker meeting, and it was a ministration anyone was allowed to do.

It usually took Oliver the first thirty minutes of meeting to shake his mind free of the concerns and stresses of the previous week, enabling him to turn inward toward the light. Quaker worship was, for him, a freeform conversation with God that was thoughtful and candid, replenishing his sanity and giving him orientation to face whatever problems lay ahead. It was a weekly way of catching up with the Lord, like two friends getting to-gether over coffee.

Worship ended at eleven thirty. Over cookies and juice in the social room, Oliver spoke at length with Dale, whose latest book, *Social Impact of Campus Role Models*, had just been published in time to be added to educa-tion catalogs for the next school year. Oliver gave him a hearty congratula-tions, then worked his way to the exit and stepped out onto Cherry Street. It had been a good meeting; quite a few people had spoken, and he felt spiritually centered.

He walked westward on Cherry, which was the way back to
Rittenhouse, but when the red traffic light on Seventeenth Street halted him
his mind shifted gears and he turned north. Not until he crossed the over-
pass for the Vine Street Expressway did he realize what he was doing. At
Spring Garden Street he recognized the campus of Philadelphia Community
College. During the week this intersection bustled with students of end-
lessly varied races passing to class or buying food from rows of sizzling
vendor trucks, but since this was Sunday the curbs and corners were empty.
The blocks north of campus were residential, cramped but reasonably neat,
with the look of student rentals. Oliver cut two blocks west to Nineteenth
Street, just to get clear of the college, and continued north. He reached
Ridge Avenue, which cut a diagonal swath through the otherwise grid-
pattern of the city's streets, and recognized the stone wall bordering the
southeast corner of Girard College. He continued up Nineteenth, walking
block after block, crossing residential streets with names he never heard of:
Berks, Norris, Fontain. The neighborhoods grew shoddy. White faces became scarce. He passed parked cars with NO RADIO, NO MONEY signs
taped to the windows, and spotted swirls of angry graffiti on vans and alley
walls. Trash accumulated on the neglected sidewalks, curbs, and house
stoops. After walking for almost two hours, he reached Cumberland Street
and halted, recognizing the name from a recent drug shooting reported on
the local news. The two-story row houses looked peaceful enough, though
weatherworn and impoverished. Halfway down the block, on the opposite
side of the road, an elderly man helped a child steer his tricycle over uneven
breaks in the pavement, the little boy's face screwed up with effort as his
legs pushed the pedals. Tired and sore of foot, Oliver turned east on
Cumberland, figuring this would take him to Broad Street where he could
either ride the subway or hail a cab. The neighborhood wasn't deserted but
felt that way, as if the cracked bricks and dented cars and boarded up
houses and trash dumpsters and disinterested old men sitting on stoops
proved that nothing mattered, that the whole meaning of living was that
nothing mattered. Weeds turned vacant lots into wilderness, radios twit-
tered softly or pounded like thunder. He passed two young men who stared
at him from under the raised hood of an ancient Rambler station wagon. A
few children could be heard, squealing playfully in hidden backyards. In
fifteen minutes Oliver reached Broad Street, and although it was as tawdry
and filthy as the blocks he just passed through, it was at least populated and

busy, and despite himself he felt relieved. The North Broad Street Station was just one block up. He walked to the subway entrance and caught a ride home.

32

At a quarter past ten David Hurley walked out to the lobby to greet a financial aid applicant who was supposed to come at nine. His irritation at having to interview someone over an hour late dissolved before the appearance of the applicant herself. On the couch sat a middle-aged woman in a dumpy denim coat and stained corduroys. The skin of her face was a purple shell, shiny as if laminated. She held a shapeless brown bag under one arm.

"Mrs. Clarke?"

"Yeah?" Small eyes rolled up as high as David's collar but got no further. Her head and neck would not cooperate, though she smiled easily enough.

David felt goose bumps ripple up his spine. "Won't you come with me, please?"

Mrs. Clarke pushed herself off the couch. She walked with a horrendous stoop, following David through the cubicles at a height no higher than his waist. She kept muttering to herself, and David decided to do this interview with the door open. He showed Mrs. Clarke to a chair and waited until she settled into it before taking his own behind the desk.

"Mrs. Clarke, what program are you interested in?"

"That's right, sir."

"Mrs. Clarke?"

"Well, ain't you a dear?"

David raised his voice as loudly as he dared. "What's the name of your program?"

The woman smiled apologetically.

"You did have an admissions interview, didn't you?"

She nodded at that. "I got my ten bucks."

David had no idea what she was talking about. He stood up cautiously. "Excuse me, won't you? I just need to check something." He walked out to Deirdre's old cubicle, yanked open the file drawer for prospective students, found the file marked PATRICIA CLARKE, and pulled out the blue app form. Mrs. Clarke had been accepted to the July Secretarial Arts Program, recruited through something called "The Mission Strategy." David had never heard of it. A blurry photocopy of a high school diploma from Cheltenham High School dated 1968 was in the folder. The interviewer was Lily Espirito, and in the "Comments" section she had written in her spiky impatient script, *Student needs image improvement but is otherwise an acceptable candidate.* There was no address on the app form, no way for David (or anyone in Admissions, for that matter) to know where Mrs. Clarke lived.

David returned to his office and sat behind his desk. "Mrs. Clarke, you're enrolled in the Secretarial Arts Program that starts in July."

The applicant smiled, humming softly.

"May I ask you something?" David hesitated, not sure this was proper. "Can you tell me why you want this class?"

His concern seemed to cut through her reverie. The woman looked a little worried now, as if afraid she had done something wrong. "I was told it was good to do," she said with slow effort. "They had a sign up. And they give us ten dollars. I'm supposed to get another ten today. Do I get that from you?"

"Who are they?"

"Pardon?"

He said, louder, "Who are 'they'?"

"Heart of God."

Mrs. Clarke shut her eyes, and her gray head hunched low, as if the fluorescent light glowing from the ceiling was a weight pressing down on her. David stared at all the blank spaces on the app form.

"Mrs. Clarke, where do you live?"

"Oh, I don't live nowhere, sir."

"You have no address at all?"

"I ... well, I sleep at the mission whenever I can. Otherwise I got me a grate on Sansom. Wi' Sally. She's guardin' it now while I'm here."

David nodded, his worst suspicions confirmed. "Will you excuse me again, please?"

"You are such a dear. Take your time."

David fled the office.

Lily's door was partially open. David swung it wide and surprised the admissions director who was on the phone. When she saw David's distraught face she raised her brows and said into the receiver, "Bill, can I put you on hold a moment? Thanks." She tapped a button and put the receiver down. "What's up?"

"Lily—" David started too loud and halted. He needed to be careful. He felt at a disadvantage in any altercation with Lily, whose powerhouse energy could make any confrontation risky. "Mrs. Clarke is here."

"Who?"

"Patricia Clarke. You accepted her for July."

"Oh my word, yes! Is she here to see you? Thank Christ, I didn't expect her to show."

"Oh, she showed all right," David said, trembling. "But she's addled. She can barely focus on a word I'm saying to her. How could you have accepted her?"

Lily's brows knotted, her mouth drew tight. "How dare you? That's not your province. You don't pass judgment on applicants, you just get them their funding to come here."

"Lily, for God's sake—"

"We've had this talk before—"

"Lily—"

"—and frankly I'm getting pretty damn sick of it! That woman is a high school graduate." Lily slapped the top of her desk angrily. "We called the Heart of God Mission and asked if we could put up some fliers. We asked if they knew anybody who might benefit from some in-class instruction. The sisters were delighted to have somebody show an interest in their charges. They suggested Mrs. Clarke, who is a very sweet woman and not all that old when you think about it, plus a few others. We're hoping that several of their 'regulars' will come to us."

"But Lily, the woman can't even—"

"And the sisters are not expecting us to pass judgment! How *dare* you, you snot! Do you despise the homeless so much that you think they shouldn't be given a chance? Do you really think yourself so much better than they—"

"No, I don't—"

"As if you've got a lot to be proud of, still living at home with mommy and daddy!"

"*What?*"

"Must be easy to criticize a homeless woman when you've got two people sheltering and feeding you! You should be ashamed of yourself!"

Appalled, David said, "Now wait a minute—"

"I always thought you were too immature for the professional position you hold! Lord *knows* I've been as patient as I know how, but I can see I'm going to have to speak to Oliver about this yet again!"

"Hold on—"

"Now you get that woman her aid! That's your *job,* goddammit! And you will *stop* this high-and-mighty attitude, do you hear me? And I mean *now!*"

David hissed, "I don't answer to you!"

Lily laughed. Her rings and earrings sparkled. "Don't be so sure, sweetie pie. Any trained monkey can do financial aid, but Admissions keeps a school alive. Even Oliver knows that."

David fought hard to control himself. This wasn't true! Financial aid was filled with picky rules and regs. It required proper reporting, fiscal accountability, and fair distribution of limited funds. It involved continuous follow up, in-depth counseling, detective work to find additional resources of scholarships and grants—a whole myriad of duties that few people realized. But he couldn't express any of this to Lily and not sound like a self-justifying jerk.

He asked, "Does Oliver know about this—this mission strategy?"

"He knows the general idea. He hasn't troubled with the details."

"He *likes* it?" David winced, asking this.

"How could he say no to a plan that would help the homeless?"

"But she lives on a frigging *grate!* How am I supposed to complete a financial aid app when I can't put a proper address on it? Banks won't accept it, and neither will Pennsylvania Higher Ed!"

Lily dismissed that with a flip of one hand. "Doesn't she hang out on Tenth and Sansom? I think that's what she said. Just put down Tenth and Sansom. The ZIP is 19107, I think."

"Lily, I can't *do* that—"

"Then use the mission address! For God's sake, stop this noise! Can't you see I have Bill Nostrand waiting? I don't have time for this selfishness! Go do your goddamn job!"

Choking, David backed out. He ducked past the empty cubicles and ran through the lobby to the hallway. Spotting some students standing at the far end of the corridor, he immediately backed up against the wall, hiding behind the grandfather clock. A moment later the period bell sounded its ugly blat. The hallway emptied. David stayed where he was. He was standing near the entrance to the school, and on the wall opposite him was a large grouping of framed memorabilia: notices of praise on White House stationery from Bill Clinton, George Bush, Ronald Reagan, and Jimmy Carter acknowledging the importance of secretaries in America and glorifying the excellence of Burr secretaries specifically. There were also letters from others: Governors Ridge, Casey, and Thornburgh, Philadelphia Mayors Rendell, Goode, Rizzo, and Councilman Thacher Longstreth. A class photograph from 1915 showed students at their desks wearing bonnets and gloves, their skirts puffed out from petticoats. There was a picture of Reginald Burr in uniform shaking hands with somebody named Harry Hopkins regarding the support of Burr graduates in the work force during World War II. And testimonial letters from grateful graduates working in government, on Wall Street, and out in Hollywood.

He felt scalded to the marrow. Lily had spoken out loud his worst fear—that he *should* be embarrassed for still living with his parents and taking shelter at an institution that paid low but otherwise kept him safe, surrounded by women who admired his stance as an artist and otherwise left him to run his one-person shop his own way. If Lily found this reason to hold him in contempt, then quite likely the other women did too—without ever saying it out loud, of course. Trudy, Deirdre, and Julie all liked him, but he knew that in some ways they didn't take him seriously. Out of college and still in the nest. Shit.

But he had studied *art!* Could he help it if the world didn't open its arms for him when he graduated? He was trained to tell the difference between a Monet and a Manet, to critique the regionalist romanticism of Thomas Benton or the brilliant use of light by Edward Hopper, and finally he was groomed to put his own vision on canvas though he hadn't done much painting since leaving school (which particularly bothered his mother). Financial aid was a specialty field. It offered no career paths except to *stay* in financial aid. Did he want to process forms for the rest of his life? And what would he do if he didn't?

David sighed and stepped away from the clock. He thought about Mrs. Clarke waiting in his office and decided he didn't care. He walked back through the lobby to finish the interview.

In her own office, Lily was back on the phone with Bill Nostrand. She held the receiver in one hand and sipped coffee with the other. "So Bill, is there *really* a difference between a regular secretary and a medical secretary? I've got a girl interested in being a medical secretary but we don't teach it. Well, how much of a difference can there be?" She listened, her foot with the diamond ankle bracelet impatiently tapping the floor. "Okay, I know there's special terminology, special forms and such—well, but can't we get around all that? It really makes a difference? Do you think the accreditors *know* the difference? Fuck. Pardon my French, Bill." She issued an exaggerated groan. "Okay. Any chance we can throw in a medical secretary program by July? No, I mean it. If you can set it up, I can bring them in. Hell, the competition does it, so I don't see why not. I know, but this isn't the first time we've lost somebody because they wanted specifically to be a medical secretary. Well if you *can't* do it by July then let me know so I can think of something else. I'm not losing this kid. 'Bye-bye."

She hung up and flipped through her stack of *While You Were Out* messages. She dialed a number. "Yes, I'd like to speak to Jack Brannigan in Public Relations, please. Lily Espirito. He knows me."

While she waited she pinched a Hershey's Kiss from a candy dish on her desk and undid the foil with her teeth. The line in her ear came alive and she swallowed the chocolate fast.

"Jack?"

"Hello, Lily," said a robust male voice.

"How are you doing, Jacky?" Lily put a lot of melody into the question.

"Not bad, snappy lady. What can I do for you? It's been a long time since I heard from you."

"Oh, it hasn't been that long. Say, Jacky, I want you to do me a fave."

"Lay it on me."

"Secretary's Day is a month from now. I think it's April 22nd. I need a big build up for this."

"What do you have in mind?"

"Well I can work up some newspaper and TV coverage for the school, but I want something splashy. I was thinking maybe you could talk to whatever that place is on Market Street, you know what I mean?"

"You're talking faster than you're thinking, love."

"You know, the tall building on Market that flashes lit-up messages on its roof." She snapped her fingers several times. "What's it called?"

"That's the Philadelphia Electric Company."

"Fine! Great! I need to get something up there about Secretary's Day. Something this whole damn city will see."

"Hmmm. Do you want the Burr name in it?"

"Of course." She laughed loudly. "Wouldn't do me much good otherwise."

"Well, that's a problem, Lily. PECO doesn't do advertising, per se. I think they just project city events and public service announcements."

"Well shit." Her face wrinkled. "What's the point then? Do you know that for a fact? Find out for me, will you?"

"Sure. For nobody but you, Lily. I'll see what I can see."

"Okay. If you can, I need something really catchy up there. It has to be secretarial in nature, of course, but it has to kick."

"How about 'My pad or yours.'"

Lily doubled forward, braying so hard her face colored deep red. Trudy Weiser poked an inquiring head through the doorway and the admissions director, still laughing, waved her in. "Oh Jacky, you are the most horrible cornball!"

"Well, it kicks."

"Oh, I love it, but I'm sorry, it won't fly here. This place still thinks it can afford its reputation. I know without asking that it won't fly."

Trudy dropped the latest test answer sheets on the desk. She started to tiptoe out but Lily held up a hand to make her stay. "Work on it, Jacky, for me, okay? Thanks, sweetie. Talk to you soon."

Lily hung up and examined an applicant's test sheet, comparing the kid's responses to an answer chart Trudy had set on top of the stack. "Jesus Christ, Tru, we're not recruiting any rocket scientists, are we?"

Trudy was apologetic. "No, it doesn't look like it."

"How many passed?"

"About twenty this week. These are all the ones that didn't. There's about thirteen there."

Lily read on in amazement. The test was the easiest accepted by ABCAA. The math section, thirty questions to be done in forty-five minutes, offered such challengers as *117 + 432 = x* and *14 x 19.3 = x*. The English comprehension portion offered three essays to read, then asked questions about the texts. One discussed the immorality of animal research, another discussed social awareness in contemporary Hollywood movies, and the third cited straight facts about the galaxy. Students were given forty-five minutes for this section too. The test was supposed to be monitored, but Lily couldn't spare a staff member for the ninety minutes it took, so she tended to group four or five applicants at a time in an empty classroom and just let them go at it. After the first results she quickly scratched the time limit out of the booklets, and applicants could now take as much time as they needed to finish either section. And if the students decided to pool their answers in the unproctored room, who would know? Yet even with these helpful nudges, wrong answers populated the answer sheets in mind-numbing quantities.

"Nothing like measuring the mental prowess of our students to sober a body up," muttered Lily. "Let's see, this one actually took the SAT and scored 610. Jesus, what's it like to go through life like that?"

"Deirdre's got the acceptance letters for the others," Trudy told her. "Do you want her to send reject letters for these?" She pointed to the stack on the desk. Lily had told her staff never to send a reject letter without first consulting her. In the six months since Lily became head of Admissions no reject letter had ever gone in the mail.

"Let me double check your grading, dear, and then we'll know for sure."

"Okay."

"Thanks for these, Tru. Talk to you later."

Alone, Lily studied the tests again. The reading comprehension was a disaster. The galaxy text noted that Mars was often referred to as "The Red Planet." One of the questions that followed simply asked, *"Which planet is known as 'The Red Planet?' Is it a) Earth, b) Mars, c) Jupiter, or d) Mercury."* Lily looked at the applicant's sheet. She had put "d" as her answer. This was worse than sobering, it chilled you to the bone. Lily took a pencil out of her drawer, erased the "d" and made it a "b." She began to go through all the answer sheets in this fashion.

33

It was soon common knowledge among the staff that Oliver Dunbar was missing a lot of work. He did not call in sick, nor did he explain or apologize for his absences on the days when he did come in. He was often remote and distracted, but whatever was troubling him remained his own affair. He did not confide in Dean Harris or Louise Mallory, his two most trusted lieutenants, nor did he give explanation to Julie. The secretary couldn't help thinking his withdrawn behavior was her fault. One morning when he had been absent two days in a row, she sat at the front desk opening the mail with second-nature motions, her worried brain far from monitoring the competent working of her hands. Deirdre trotted in from the cubicles and idly picked up the photograph of Kelly. "I can't get over this, that you're a mom."

"I'll tell you right now, you *never* get over it. I wake up every morning surprised to think I have a kid."

"Yeah." Deirdre put the picture back, then glanced at two prospects sitting on the couch. One was Marty's, the other Trudy's. She sighed. "Well, I got some phone calls to make. You ever have to telemarket, Julie?"

"No."

"I hate it. I know we gotta do it, but it sucks big time."

"Uh-huh."

Deirdre sauntered off. Julie collected her various piles of mail, then walked through the cubicles to the school director's office. She unlocked the door and went in. The empty office seemed freakishly silent without the radio tatting the classical station. The in-basket was starting to pile up. Oliver's chair was pushed in, his window blinds drawn. Julie felt a strange dread standing there. She didn't think he was sick.

There was an open letter on the desk, creased in two places from being in an envelope. The bottom third was folded over, covering the middle third. It was not her place to look at the letter, but the heading was from a lawyer and she couldn't help picking it up. The brief text rebuked Oliver for being delinquent in returning some kind of paperwork. It was about the divorce, she knew. A divorce he wasn't rushing to finalize. She put the letter and his mail on the desk blotter and exited, relocking the door. She heard the tapping of the business manager's calculator and summoned her courage. She looked around the partition. "Louise?"

Louise glanced up. "Yeah?"

"Can I talk to you?"

"About what?"

"Oliver."

Louise looked uncomfortable. "You sure you want to talk to me? I'm not a great confidant."

Julie didn't know what she meant. "It's about him missing so much time."

"Okay." Louise looked relieved. "I just figured he was ill. Isn't there some kind of bug going around?"

"That's not it." Julie stepped into the cubicle and sat on the single client chair. "His wife left him."

"What?"

"Tina and he split up."

Louise sat back as if punched. Her mouth was a round gray hole, like the opening in a birdhouse. "When?"

"Back in January. He told me. He hasn't told anybody else. I know I shouldn't be saying anything but …" She inhaled sharply. "Oh Louise, I'm worried. He hasn't put in a full week in a month. And when he does come in he doesn't say anything to anybody beyond greeting them, and he never has any work for me. He shuts his office door now, when it was always a point of pride for him to keep it open. And I don't know what he does when he's in there. I go in afterward and it looks like nothing's disturbed."

Louise wouldn't meet her eye. "He really told you Tina left?"

"Yes."

"Well … well, I guess we'd better not expect too much from him for a while." She hesitated, then resumed totaling her invoices on the calculator.

"Don't you think we should do something?"

"What did you have in mind?"

"I don't know. That's why I came to you."

"Oh boy." Louise leaned back in her chair. She looked at the secretary for a very long time, then lifted her tea mug and swirled its contents gently. "Anybody ever tell you about Ethel's ex-husband?"

"No."

"I don't think Eth'll mind—she's passed this story along enough times herself. Anyway, a hundred years ago when she was young and stupid, Ethel married this guy Harry. He was a charismatic alcoholic and she thought she could change him. Well, four sons and who knows how many fights later, the S.O.B. remained unchanged."

"Louise, I—"

"Silence. You enter my cubicle, you pay the price. Harry would get in these brutal rages and whack Ethel around. Once he hit her with a baseball bat—"

"Louise—!"

"It was only a whiffle bat. Her kid was two at the time. Still, Eth thinks Harry didn't know the difference. It could have been made of wood."

"Why are you telling me this?" Julie looked pale.

"Because it's one of the great tales of our time. One night Harry came home with a pistol. Got it from a buddy. Walked into the house, Eth said, and swung it around real proud. To prove it was loaded, he fired at the ceiling. The kids upstairs started yelling. Ethel ran up to them, and saw a hole in the mattress of the crib. The bullet passed through both the floor and the crib. A couple inches more and he'd have shot the baby."

"My God!" Julie exclaimed.

"Ethel packed the kids up that same night and drove to her mom's. Only Mom told Eth she'd made her bed and could go lie in it. Eth had a sister willing to take her in, but not the three boys and an infant. And old Harry had managed over the years to alienate all of Eth's friends.

"So she drove to Oliver's house. Now pay attention, because we're going back about eighteen years. Ethel was an accounting teacher at Burr, and had only worked here maybe three months. She had no reason to think Oliver would help. She told him and Tina what happened, and they took the family in. They had a row home in Powelton Village at the time. They sheltered all five of them, and took care of those kids for the two years it took Ethel to get her doctorate. The Ph.D. led to Ethel's promotion to dean, with a significant raise and the extra benefits she badly needed. She's an excellent dean. I know for a fact she's gotten offers from some first-rate colleges over the years. She's turned every one of them down. She'll work for Oliver forever."

"That's an incredible story," Julie said.

"And you'll never hear him tell it. But it gives you an idea what kind of couple he and Tina were back then. They've got deep roots, those two. Don't think you'll be the one to untangle them."

"Why do you think I'd want to?"

Louise just looked at her.

"What?" Julie asked with sudden dread.

"Missy, your feelings aren't as bottled up as you think. Although if it makes you feel better, the general consensus around the water cooler is that Oliver's being an ass."

"Oh my God." Julie felt her skin grow cold.

Louise grinned. "Don't take it hard. People always know more than you think they do. Except Oliver. I'll bet he has no idea, eh?"

"We've talked about it."

"Really? You two had an honest heart-to-heart? Isn't that so him." Louise pulled her payroll ledger from a shelf and flipped through the most recent pages. "Say, he *has* missed a lot of time. Most of the first half of April. I didn't even notice." She glanced at the unhappy secretary. "Maybe you should go back to your desk."

Julie nodded and stood. "Thanks for the time."

Oliver didn't come to work for another two days. When he did return, showing up bright and early as if it were a regular day, he smiled and greeted his surprised secretary, hung his coat in the closet, and opted to walk down the first floor corridor instead of going through the lobby to his office. He climbed the stairs to the second floor just as the bell blatted, and passed among the students on their way to Period One. Caucasian girls, African-American girls, Asian-American, Hispanic-American—he loved the rich mix of the student body even though it made New York nervous. He looked through the windows in the classroom doors, and watched students with headsets writing at various speeds to the dictation of the cassette decks, and others scribbling notes as their teachers lectured. Older second-year students were hunched over terminals in the personal computer labs working on complex assignments, or leaning over someone else's chair to help them. That last he loved the most. Burr students seemed to possess this type of generosity in abundance. It was not uncommon for an entire room to cheer when one student managed without error to reach a new typing speed. Nor was it uncommon for students who finished an assignment early to help their classmates, particularly when it came to learning the different computer software programs where novices sat in terror that a wrong keystroke might wipe away pages of assignment.

In one lecture room ten students sat. Jean Cavanaugh stood indomitably before them, an open text held level with her chin. Her tone was strident but without its usual classroom boom; the students were serious as they listened and read along in their books and raised their hands with questions. Jean was famous throughout the seventeen Burr Colleges for picking out the slowest students and giving them extra instruction. She annually saved numerous flunking students in this fashion. Oliver's heart twanged tenderly to see Keone Robinson sitting there, head down, ankles crossed, her broad forehead puckered with concentration. He trotted briskly down the stairs.

When he clicked the key in his office lock, Louise called out from behind her partition, "Oliver, that isn't you, is it?"

"Hey, Louise. Yes, afraid so."

"God, I thought you'd retired. Come in here."

He stepped through. He was startled to see very few papers on Louise's desk. The business manager wasted no energy asking him about his absence, but handed him a large envelope. "Invoices for you to initial. New York's jerking around some of our best vendors. Get them to cut it out, Oliver. They sure aren't going to listen to me."

"It looks pretty good in here."

"You always get a lot done when the boss isn't in. No offense."

"No, I know how true that is. Say, I saw something that brightened me up."

"And that was?"

"Ten of September's weakest students coming in early to study under Jean."

"She does that with every program."

"I know. It's wonderful. That quiet girl, Keone Robinson, was there."

Louise growled.

"What's wrong?"

"Well, our latest accounts receivable report shows practically nobody from September paying anything beyond what David's gotten them through financial aid. That Keone is one of many on my hit list."

"Well, I don't think her family has much."

"Hell, that's a problem, isn't it? Nutty us, to take in a student who can't pay."

"Do you want to pull her from class?"

"What's the point? I've already talked to her. She's made another promise to pay, and we'll abide by it until next month when she'll just default again. She owes $1,800 now that all her aid is in, and her family doesn't have it. If you don't have the heart to cut her now, at least don't let her come back next fall with an outstanding balance, okay?"

"Put together a list of the worst offenders and I'll talk to them."

"Are you going to put them on payment plans, Oliver?" Every time they had this conversation the business manager asked this.

"Of course," he said, answering as he did every time.

Louise's snort was an unique mix of sarcasm and affection. "Nice to have you back, boss."

Oliver went into his office. Save for the scary height of the in-basket, everything looked unchanged. Flipping hastily through the stack, he saw that most of it was periodicals, *The Chronicle, Financial Aid Transcript*, newsletters from NACUBO, AACRAO, NASFAA, NACAC, PACAC, ABCAA, and The College Board. Also a few policy memos from John Coyne and Bill Nostrand, a survey for *Peterson's Guide to Colleges*, and a faculty assessment report that he had to read and approve before Ethel could barter with Abby DeSalvo in New York for merit raises for Carol Sobolewski and Bob Lawrence. The report was due back on Ethel's desk sooner than he cared to think. Tucked in a corner of his blotter was a stack of pink phone messages as thick as a bar of soap. He riffled through them guiltily.

Opening Louise's envelope yielded the worst stuff. A lot of invoices sent to New York months ago were still unpaid. He shared Louise's anger over this. In the face of all their struggling schools, New York was adopting a policy of only paying those vendors who squawked—a horrid practice on moral grounds, and particularly distressing here where the Philly school enjoyed a good relationship with local businesses. He would have to call Bill about that. The thickest item in the folder was the accounts receivable report. Oliver skipped the mathematical breakdowns and turned to the last page for the wretched punch line. The January class owed \$187,129 in tuition, the Septembers owed \$352,258, and the Julys that had just graduated in March still had an outstanding balance of \$111,043. The small programs were covered entirely by student loans (as they had been designed), so the evening school slate was clean. But to date the Philadelphia college was operating under a bad receivable of \$650,430. He wondered if Bill Nostrand would adjust Lily's goals again.

"Oliver?"

David Hurley stood in the doorway. One hand rested on the doorknob.

"Hey, David," Oliver said. "Come in. What's up?"

The aid director seemed to debate sitting, then did so as if he couldn't avoid it. He looked tired and nervous. "I waited until you came back. I've got some bad news."

"What can I help you with?"

"I'm giving notice."

"Oh." Oliver's smile faded. He sat back in his chair. "Oh, David, what's wrong? How can I help?"

"It's just time, Oliver. I mean, I've been here three years. I have to think of the future. Where I see myself in five years, that old question. You know?"

"Do you have another job?"

"Financial aid at University of the Arts. It's only a counselor position, but it pays more than what I'm getting here."

"You graduated from U-Arts, didn't you?"

"Yes."

"Well, that's great, David. That's a terrific school. Would you go on for your masters?"

"That's part of it, yes."

"In art?"

"Yes."

"I thought you were unhappy with art."

Now David smiled. "Oh, I know art isn't practical, and I'll probably never make a lot of money. But it's the one thing I love, and the one thing I do best. I feel like I'm marking time staying out of it, and I don't want to spend the rest of my life feeling that way."

Oliver laughed. "That's incredibly wise. I'm not happy to see you go, of course, but it sounds like a great opportunity. I've learned to expect this sort of thing when my employees are good."

David smiled at the compliment. "I'm giving a month. I can't give more than that. University of the Arts needs me as soon as possible."

"A month is fair."

David started to get up, then suddenly said, as if he couldn't help it, "It's just gotten so different around here. I'm tired of being pushed around by Admissions. I can't do my job the way it needs to be done."

Oliver said gently, "I could talk to Lily about that."

David's face was politely dull. They both knew Oliver had done that before, many times, without influencing Lily. "It's okay. I thought maybe May 10. That would almost finish out the school year."

"That would be a big help," Oliver nodded. "Incidentally, you can tap me for a hell of a reference. I'll have it done before you leave, so you can take it with you. Do you have a lot of work right now?"

"Stacks."

"Okay." Oliver smiled ruefully to show there were no hard feelings. "You go back to your stacks, and I'll get back to mine. Hey—and congratulations."

The aid director laughed a little. "Thanks."

"Looking forward to it?"

"I wasn't. But now I'm starting to."

"You'll do just fine."

David left. Curious, Oliver reopened the accounts receivable report. Even the most recent class, the January IP, had all the aid credited, student loans, Pell Grants, and supplemental grants. The big outstanding balances were for the portion of tuition the aid hadn't covered. David was terrific at his job. Louise would go through the roof when she heard.

His intercom beeped.

"Yes?"

Julie said, "Mr. Nostrand on Two."

He hit the button. "Bill?"

"Oliver, so you're in, hey? What's been at you, the flu?"

"In a way."

"Half the President's Office is out with it. Feeling better now?"

"Sure."

"You ought to. I just got the numbers for March. You're really sailing, aren't you?"

"Uh, yeah." Oliver started rifling the papers in his in-basket. He hadn't seen the finalized March monthly report.

"The numbers are way up high for July, and even September is pulling together. Dramatic difference from last year, that's for sure. Looks like Espirito's strategy is taking root. Excellent work, Oliver. Keep her at it. Say," Nostrand's voice sounded restrained, an explosion lay behind it. "Know what else is on my mind?"

"No, Bill. What?"

"Nothing!" The line erupted with crazy laughter. "Nothing at all! I saw that report and just felt like calling and praising you! Who'd have thought the day would come, right?"

"Well, you're … you're sure surprising me." Oliver wasn't quite sure how to take this; Bill Nostrand's laughter was the most bizarre sound he ever heard.

"Yeah, well—I've got to get back to work myself. Keep it up. Take your pills and don't have a relapse. 'Bye."

"Talk to you later, Bill."

Oliver hung up slowly. Nostrand had been with Burr for more than two years, and this was the first positive phone call Oliver ever had from him. All because of the numbers? What *were* the numbers? How good could they be? He rummaged through the in-basket in earnest.

"Oliver!"

The shrill yelp made him look up. Louise stood in the doorway. Her hands were liver-spotted fists. "David Hurley just told me he's quitting!"

"Yes."

"We've got to do something! Let's talk to him! Let's *both* talk to him! We can't afford to lose him!"

"Louise, he's been here three years. It's time for him to move on. He said so, and he's right."

"Oliver, that's not why he's leaving and you know it! You know *exactly* what the problem is! Help me with this!"

Oliver's eyes dropped to his desk. His right hand still rested on the in-basket, itching to rummage for the monthly report. He really wanted to see it. Bill Nostrand's laughter was still in his ears. The sound made his heart taut, gave him an exciting sense that something was going right at last and on a profoundly important level. He fought off the lurking possibility that this was a false feeling, that if the numbers were high there had to be a reason, and it might not be one he wanted to know. He didn't want to think about that. He wanted to remember Bill's laughter. He wanted to relish it all the more because good feelings never lasted long, and he wanted to savor this while he could.

But he couldn't ignore Louise. Dimly aware that she wasn't speaking any more, he looked up. He was alone in the office. The business manager was gone.

34

"Let me tell you what I'm looking for," Lily said, upright in the chair across from Clara's desk. Her hands sliced the air. She crossed her legs, and the foot with the diamond ankle bracelet tapped the air. "I need someone personable but with brains. Someone with business savvy. *That's* what I need."

"Well, Lily, we—"

"Someone who will work with my office and not stand on some airhead federal morality and say he's above counting noses."

Clara Peterson said with meek caution, "But we don't have many candidates right now. The second-year September class is graduating in six weeks, and most of those women have already found jobs. I've got some student profiles from the January class, but they won't graduate until September. Besides, it's hard to find someone with financial aid experience. That's unusual, and I don't think the girls in that class have any."

"Oh bosh! I don't care about that! Hell, I don't *want* her to have financial aid experience. Haven't we already learned that lesson?"

Clara raised astonished brows. She tucked her head down, trying to follow the admissions director's rapid words. "But doesn't … doesn't she have to know lots of regulations? Isn't financial aid very regulated?"

"Look, we'll send her to a couple of workshops and she'll do fine. And I happen to know a few financial aid basics myself; every admissions director has to. The *last* thing I want is somebody with preconceived notions of what financial aid is about." Lily slapped the arms of her chair, leaned forward and recrossed her legs. Jewelry flashed from both wrists, that ankle, and a gold neck chain thick enough to tow a trailer. Clara was put off by all the glitter, by Lily's startling rudeness, and by the woman's decidedly too short skirt. The whole attire seemed cheap and dazzling—and poor Clara was dazzled. She wanted to cooperate. Prior to this meeting she had prepared a small selection of candidates she believed would be perfect for the aid director position: girls she knew who were sweet, smart, and pretty in the conservative Burr tradition. A couple were personal favorites of hers, picked simply because she thought it would be lovely to have them work here.

"Lord help me," Lily continued, "David Hurley was a nice guy and everybody loved him, but we lost more applicants through him than for any other reason."

Clara was astonished. "But I thought David was very good at his job."

"He was *terrible!*" Lily recoiled contemptuously. "New York's charging $9,150 beginning July. For the two-year kids David could get federal aid to cover all but about three thousand. Fine enough, except the poorest kids couldn't *afford* the three thou! They just didn't have it!"

A pause.

"Yes?" Clara asked timidly, trying and failing to see how this was David's fault.

Lily thrust both hands in the air. "Well, he would *tell them that!* Goddammit! He'd look those poor devils in the face and actually say, 'You can't afford to come here—why don't you try a community college?' And they'd all have second thoughts and not apply!" The very remembrance was too much for her. She jumped to her feet and paced before Clara's desk, growling.

Clara said, "But that's his job, isn't it? He has to tell them if they can't—"

"*NO!* There's no *goddamn rule* that says he has to tell them about a three thousand dollar gap! You'd be surprised how many kids can get charged nineteen thousand dollars over two years, get aid for about sixteen thou, and never figure the balance has to come from their own pocket. But David *would point it out to them!*"

"Kids don't realize that? I can't believe—"

"A high percentage never do." Lily's laugh was blistering. "Students are only interested in coming to school. Paying the bill is the furthest thing from their minds. You don't mention three thousand dollars, they won't think of it themselves. *That's* the kind of thing the new aid director has to know about!" She stopped before Clara's coffee table and looked at a dish of foil-wrapped candies. "Are those chocolate almonds?"

"Yes."

"Do you mind?"

"Not at all. Please help yourself."

Lily popped one in her mouth and kept four more in her hand. She resumed pacing. "David never understood the ramifications of his job. He was very irresponsible. I can't tell you how many times I wanted to kill him!" Lily's stride widened, her stiletto heels scraped the acrylic carpet.

Clara didn't know what to think. Although she saw Lily in staff meetings, this was her first occasion to deal with her directly. She knew all the stories about the woman's outrageous sales tactics; she knew that some people (mostly faculty) considered the woman a bimbo while others like David and Dean Harris thought her scheming and trashy. Clara herself had never formed an opinion. The great thing about Placement was it kept you away from the regular workings of the school. There was no need to get involved in staff politics. You set up jobs and you matched students to them, and you billed the agencies that took the students, and you made money and helped everybody and everybody was pleased. Clara thrived happily in her little office day after day. Lily was a ferocious blast of energy she was not prepared to deal with.

"A lot of students are too embarrassed to tell you why they want to drop out. They know how much time and effort you've put in on their behalf. They think that saying they don't have money is a dignified way to get off the hook. I want someone who will show them they can pay *no matter what* their circumstances! Keep them from using that as an excuse!" The admissions director popped another candy in her mouth. She returned to her chair but was still restless, still angry. "Tell me what you've got, Clara, and we'll take it from there."

Clara opened her profile book with vague apprehension. "Well, uh … how about—?"

"The person in this position, Christ, should feel the same pain my reps feel when an applicant fails to sit."

"Yes." And Clara tried again. "How about Audrey Martin? She's done very well in algebra. Arthur Cassidy says she's a mental whiz. She'd be a good numbers person. Don't you need that in financial aid?"

Lily's answer was a loud raspberry. Clara looked up, shocked.

"Are you kidding? Haven't you been listening to me? I want someone good with *people,* not fucking numbers! Any joker—pardon my French— joker with a calculator can add and subtract. We need someone who—oh, look do you mind?" A well-tanned arm whipped out for the notebook. Two gold bracelets clicked against Lily's wrist. Hurt and humiliated, Clara gave it to her, then retracted in her chair as if her hands had been smacked.

The admissions director flipped pages impatiently. "Goddamn, don't we have anybody closer to thirty in these classes? Nobody wants their money handled by kids. That's another problem I had with David. In fact, the only thing I ever *did* like about David was at least he was black."

"Would you consider—"

"You don't have any men in the January class? I remember recruiting a nice handful."

"They all withdrew."

"Crap. A lot of parents are more comfortable talking about money with men. Stupid, but that's the way it is." Lily read on. Sometimes she snorted, sometimes she just shook her head. She turned the pages of the book with a fierce *whapping* sound and tore a few, injuries Clara bore in silence though her hands fluttered desperately below her desk. Lily ignored the math, English, and skills measurements of each student and scanned the photocopies of resumes, and also read the quick summaries Clara had made of each student during mock job interviews, something all students did with Placement as graduation approached. Suddenly Lily paused. She read one page a little more intently, flipped to its other side, then reread the first side again. "This isn't bad."

Clara said quickly, "Who is it?"

"Beatrice Genovese. She looks good."

Clara said nothing.

"This is original. She's got a background selling cars. Chryslers. You don't find too many women selling cars, do you?"

"I don't know. I guess not."

"Born and raised in Hazleton. That's a miserable slag city, Hazelton. People from places like that don't crack easily. Yes, I'm intrigued by this one."

"Are you sure, Lily?"

"Well, it's worth an interview, at least. No harm in talking to her. You haven't placed her yet, have you?"

"No." Clara boldly reached for the book. She set it on the desktop and deliberately shut it. "In fact, she's been very difficult to place."

"Difficult? How?"

"Well, she's a little off-putting."

"How?"

"Well, she told one prospective employer that he would have to make an allowance for her to smoke at her desk, even though it was a non-smoking environment. That sort of thing. She's very pushy."

"Oh." Lily did not seem bothered. "How is she with clients?"

"She—well, I don't really know. She used to sell cars, you saw that yourself. But I don't think she did it long."

"She did it for five years."

"Did she? I didn't remember." Clara pouted unhappily. She didn't want to recommend Beatrice, who was aloof and sarcastic. Clara was obligated to place the student somewhere—but certainly not where she herself worked.

"Set me up an interview with her."

"Lily, there's something unpleasant about her. I can't put my finger on it. I can't see her fitting in here at all."

"We'll see."

"Her classmates don't like her."

"What's that got to do with the price of bacon? If I don't like her, I won't hire her. But a woman who used to sell cars," Lily couldn't help chuckling, "even if she wasn't great at it, she's got to have learned *something.* That's a cutthroat business if ever there was one."

"But Lily, there are so many nice students who are much more in keeping with—"

"GOD IN HEAVEN! I don't want NICE! Don't you know anything about business? People don't want *nice* people handling their money! They want somebody tough! Someone who'll make the decisions *for* them! Christ, do I have to tell Oliver you're not cooperating with me?"

"No, of course not! I'll set it up right away! If you really want to talk to her."

"Soon as you can."

"But in any case, she won't be able to start until she graduates. That won't be until September."

"Shit." Lily thought a moment. "All right. We'll get through the summer somehow. The reps can do financial aid. They can fill out loan apps or something. I'll show them how."

The period bell blatted. Lily looked at her watch and rose. Her black eyes twinkled, her gold grape-clustered earrings clicked merrily. She pressed her hands over her hips to smooth her skirt, then reached for Clara's hand and shook it vigorously. "This is great. I feel so much better. Thanks, Clara, for all your help."

"Of course," said the placement director, whose chubby hand would actually hurt for some time from the pumping it received.

35

The September class was deep in its first year exams. A year's worth of study, skill-building, and professional acumen would be measured over two high-pressure, anguish-riddled weeks. The hard tests, the ones to study for, were behind them now: written exams in Accounting, Economics, and English. Students with electives in a foreign language (the College offered Spanish and French) had both oral and written exams. These were all covered the first week. Now came the skills. Over the course of five days students would be measured on typing manuscripts, letters, press releases, and memos. In addition, eight professional letters would be dictated between seventy and ninety words per minute, and students were expected to transcribe and type a minimum of six perfect letters from their transcription.

By Wednesday Keone had already blown her two-letter margin for error. Her first transcribed letter contained nine errors, the second had thirteen. She stood currently looking at a grade of D-minus to F unless she could bring up her points with the remaining four letters. But there was no room to slip.

Carol Sobolewski stood behind her metal desk as the students shuffled in. Normally friendly and supportive, today she was as remote as Jean Cavanaugh. Annual testing was the true baptism of Burr fire. Students who did not have it after a year's training would not be sitting in these chairs again come the fall.

"Everybody take their seats. Get ready. These are all long letters today. Let's get started." When everyone was settled, Carol sat down. She flipped open her teacher's manual to a page marked by a yellow sticker, and held the book in one hand while her other clasped a stopwatch. "I'm going to dictate three letters. The first will be seventy words per minute, the second at eighty, and the third at ninety. You have to do at least the seventy to get a passing grade. At the end of class you'll go to the room next door where I will supervise the typing and transcription. You may pick whichever of the three letters you want to transcribe for today's grade. Ready?"

No one said anything. Pens were poised over steno pads, clutched tightly as if the slightest tremor might cause them to detonate.

Carol raised a small portable microphone. *"Rutherford Company, 134 Clinton Avenue, Union, New Jersey, 17111. Dear Mr. Harcourt—"* The students scribbled swiftly. In their minds they saw each letter in every word the teacher uttered, and the rules embedded from lesson after lesson now had to take those words and crunch them up, spit out the unnecessary, and flick these pens across the little lined steno pages with an athlete's speed and agility.

"... and the paper stock you sent is yellow, when we asked for goldenrod. As you will see clearly in the photocopy of the invoice enclosed, we did not check yellow. We checked goldenrod. Yet when your representative, Mr. Standish, first insisted that we had checked yellow, he produced this invoice to prove us wrong. The invoice clearly shows our selection of goldenrod. Then Mr. Standish tried to tell us there was no difference ...'"

Carol had been doing this for twelve years at Burr, and four years previously for another secretarial school. Her face remained impassive, her voice calm as she paced herself with frequent glances at the stopwatch, but inside she churned with an anxiety that, even after sixteen years of giving final exams, never went away. She yearned for these girls to do well. It was a major temptation to read just a little slower than seventy words, to give them all that moment's special joy of success. But she never cheated. She couldn't forgive herself if she did.

After four minutes Keone's wrist was aching. Her face was a grimace of hard physical labor. She had learned cursive writing in grammar school but never took to it; throughout high school and the two years after she dropped out she simply printed. But phonetic shorthand only worked if the pen never lifted off the paper, and she was trying not only to learn how to do this and do it fast, she was trying to control the unsteadiness of a hand-writing style she hadn't bothered with for more than half of her life. Mrs. Cavanaugh's advice from the private tutorials was lost under pressure like this. Keone simply panicked. The dictated words passed her, moving further ahead than she could write. Keone's marks on the steno pad turned into streaks of indecipherable wire. "If the dictator is moving too quickly," Mrs. Cavanaugh had said, "and you're not in a position to ask him to slow down, then get as much of a sentence as you feel comfortable with and then jump to where the dictator is and go on from there. But leave a gap in your shorthand notes so you'll know there's something missing. You can then go back and piece your notes together afterward." Keone was doing that now, but doing it all over the page. She felt a rising terror that there was no escape from this, that she had clobbered herself once and for all. Her hand shook worse.

"*'... and we will conclude our business with you as of this last order. Our account will be settled, and we will in the future conduct our business elsewhere. Sincerely, Mrs. Faith Bradley, vice-president of operations.'*"

Carol snapped off the stopwatch and looked up. "Pens down. Everybody rest a moment, then we'll try one for eighty words per minute."

Keone had never done a successful eighty-per-minute dictation; her one hope of getting a decent grade lay in transcribing the seventy. Although she tried the next two letters at higher speeds, she quickly trailed behind, gave up, and sat with her head bent down so no one would notice, and let the throbbing ache in her wrist be her sole consolation.

The bell rang. Mrs. Sobolewski collected their steno books, and the class cut through an inside door that connected directly to Computer Lab III. The teacher followed, and did not give the girls a chance to discuss the three letters upon which their academic futures rested. She shut the door and let her voice resonate. "Everybody sit. Do it now!"

Everybody dashed to their chairs. A few mice clicked to clear screen-savers, and to bring up the proper software.

Carol strode across the front of the room, passing back the steno books. "Keep them closed until I tell you," she said needlessly, for by now they all knew the drill. They set their steno pads against the plastic props beside their computers and waited, hands on their laps because Mrs. Sobolewski had a *thing* about hands being anywhere else before a test.

"Pick one of the three letters I just dictated. You have ten minutes to type the letter. You will use semi-block format. Begin!"

Keyboards rattled in loud unison. Keone's too, but only in spurts. She squinted at her handiwork and felt like running from the room. This whole goddamn school, with its impossible exercises and grim-faced teachers urging you to work as hard as you fucking could, and then socking you right in the face with your humiliation. She should simply stand up, knock Sobolewski on her ass and storm off. Keone could see herself doing it, could see it more readily than getting a letter out of the spaghetti in her notebook. She spent minutes groping for words and forgetting grammar, punctuation, and everything else. She couldn't tell where one sentence ended and another began.

"Stop! Hands off your keyboards! Print your papers and pass them forward."

Fuck!

That wasn't ten minutes! Keone was outraged. Around her printers hummed and rolled out paper. Her classmates dutifully passed their letters to the teacher's waiting hand. Keone finally printed her own, and found herself staring at half a letter. That was all she had accomplished. So this was it. All gone. Eight months of hard work for nothing.

Two floors below, Bob Lawrence and Arthur Cassidy walked into the school, returning from lunch. They were about to turn down the hallway when Bob glanced through the glass doors of the lobby and saw a large bouquet of flowers on Julie's desk. "Hey Arthur, dig what Julie's got."

Both teachers entered the lobby. Julie started to speak but Bob clapped his hands. "Well, well! Julie, that's quite a garden there. What is it, your birthday?"

"Not quite," murmured the amused secretary. "But I'm glad you stopped by. These are for you."

"How's that?"

"They were just delivered. The card's in your name."

Julie, who liked Bob even though he was something of an office flirt, was taken aback by the sudden frightened look on the teacher's face. He made no move for the bouquet. Arthur Cassidy stepped close, intrigued. And Deirdre and Trudy, who had been on the lookout for Bob ever since the flowers arrived, now stepped into the lobby with big grins on their faces. Everyone stood around the English teacher, enjoying his embarrassment.

"Well," said Bob after a long pause. He laughed. "Golly. Well, I guess I'll take these back to the lounge."

"What?" exclaimed Julie. "You're not going to open the card here?"

"Oh, come on!" pleaded Trudy. "Come on, Bob! Do it here!"

"Yeah, come on!" nodded Deirdre with a giggle.

Bob pulled the little envelope from the flowers and looked at it. Only his name was printed on it. He didn't know what to do. He couldn't believe Heather had been so stupid. He would kill her.

"You're hesitating, Romeo," said Arthur.

"I really don't know who this could be from."

"That's why there's a card," said Julie. "Hurry up before the phone rings."

He tore open the envelope and looked at the tiny card. In Heather's looping scrawl was the message, *Hi! Hope you're embarrassed! XOXOXOX.* Her name wasn't on it.

"Who's it from?" Deirdre fairly jiggled.

"It doesn't say."

"Oh, it has to say!"

"No, it doesn't," he muttered, too relieved to speak up. He boldly showed the card to Julie.

"Hmmm," she said. "A secret admirer. Any ideas, Bob?"

"No. None."

"God, Bob," said Arthur. "I'm jealous. I never get flowers from any-body."

"That's because you're a priest," said Bob. "Romance to you is reading *The Thorn Birds.*"

"I was a priest," corrected Arthur, who knew his colleague was joking but had to say it anyway.

"I think it's a student," Julie declared with unnerving confidence.

"Sure," said Trudy. "Lots of students really like you, Bob."

"Oh, it can't be," he said hastily. "No."

Julie nodded. "Yeah. Some dreamy youngster who's a sucker for American Lit. Who do you think it could be, Bob?"

"I really haven't the slightest idea."

Arthur said, "I'll bet I know."

They all looked at him.

"Jennifer DeAngelis. I've heard her in the cafeteria sometimes just going on and on about our Bobby."

"Yeah," said Deirdre, to whom Jennifer was a friend. "She does think Bob's pretty cool."

"Guys, this is too much," said Bob. "Julie, you keep the flowers. They look better next to you."

"Bob, I can't take your flowers."

"Trust me, I don't know who sent them. I can't get mushy over flowers when I don't know who gave them to me. You keep them. They'll get some use that way."

"Okay," said Julie with a big smile. "They're beautiful. Thanks."

Arthur said, "Why don't you let me or Carol see the card? Maybe we can recognize the handwriting."

"No. I know this has been a funny episode and everybody's getting a good laugh, but let's not drag it out. I've got a test to give in—" he checked his watch, "five minutes."

He marched far ahead of Arthur down the hall, spurred by anger. Two girls at the drinking fountain smiled at him, but he ignored them. This was Heather's last day of class before summer recess; her last final had been in the morning. He wouldn't see her for most of the summer, since her family rented a shore house in North Wildwood and she wouldn't be able to get back to town. He, of course, had to stay because he worked during the summer. Nevertheless, Heather told him two days ago to come down for her birthday in July, and wouldn't take no for an answer. (She told him while she was straddling him in his apartment, and under the circumstances he couldn't argue.) There was no way to get out of it without risking trouble. So he would finally meet her family. Good Christ. Maybe while she was at the shore some Coppertoned super-hunk would sweep her off her sandy feet and she would forget—

"Bob, are you okay?" It was Arthur, who caught up with him by the stairs.

"Sure. Why?"

"Well, you look a little green. Say, do you really have no idea who sent you the flowers? I love stuff like this."

"No."

A long silence followed, and both men grew self-conscious of looking at each other. They broke into grins, and Arthur punched Bob's shoulder. "You dog. In a way it's more exciting, not knowing. Opens up all kinds of possibilities."

"Yeah, I guess so." And Bob felt good enough now to ask if Arthur really thought Jennifer DeAngelis liked him. He refrained judiciously.

36

On David's last day there was a wine and cheese party in the student lounge in which everyone, including most of the faculty, attended. It was one of the best going-away parties the school ever threw. Jean Cavanaugh said as much over her one glass of Chablis, adding the rhetorical question, "Who doesn't like David?" A few toasts went around, and when it was Lily's turn she echoed the sentiment.

During the afternoon David worked hard to get the financial aid office in order. He felt badly that no replacement had yet been hired, but when he offered to train Deirdre as a backup Lily said in a sweet, motherly tone, "Don't worry, dear, we'll get by." It made him feel very expendable. Gloomily he visited each of the offices in turn, saying good-bye to Clara Peterson, then to Dean Harris, Trudy, Deirdre, and finally he stopped by Louise's cubicle before going in to see Oliver. The business manager was openly bitter about the whole thing.

"Goddammit, you're going to be missed. What a hell this place is turning into!"

"I feel bad about leaving," David confessed.

Louise backed down a little. "Nonsense, this is the best thing in the world for you. But I know what was going on, and it could have been prevented."

"It's just time for me to move on."

"Of course it is. And no one here would ever stop you. But you're not leaving because you want to move on. I *know* why you're leaving. And let me tell you something, buster—you're *damn right!*"

David didn't know what to make of this. He always felt, around Louise, that he was dealing with a superior mind, a woman whose jaded personality was not the result of some harsh past experience but simply because Louise realized that jadedness was the smart way to be. "I guess so," was his best response.

Parting with Oliver was brief, because in the middle of David's goodbye Mr. Nostrand called and he had to take it. David waited obediently, but the more he thought about what Louise said the more he realized that Oliver might have done something to keep his financial aid director, and suddenly David resented that he hadn't. Maybe that wasn't fair, but he felt it anyway, and when the call went on for several minutes he silently waved and withdrew.

It was ten after five and the school officially closed when he finished up. Files were put away, no stray loan applications needed certification, all rosters had been updated. The office looked so neat it was a shame to think he wouldn't be coming back again. Walking out to the lobby, he met Julie taking her coat out of the closet. She smiled and shook his hand.

"Well, David, congrats one more time. We'll miss you."

"Thanks, Julie." He looked around the lobby. The school felt shadowy and hushed with all of the cubicle lights out and the employees gone. He looked back toward the offices and could just barely see the admissions director's closed door. "I guess now that the numbers are increasing she'll be here forever."

"Lily?"

"Yeah."

Julie slung her pocketbook over her shoulder. "You know, David, you might not like her, but she's done you the biggest favor in the world. You're moving on with your life now. You wouldn't be doing that if she hadn't spurred you to it."

"I know. I guess I resent that that's how it happened." He kept looking around. "I feel like there should be something more. I worked here for three years, and put heart and soul into this place."

"It's a chapter in your life," said Julie. "It's a chapter in Burr's life too. I'm sure Burr is grateful. How about you?"

"Yeah, me too." He grinned. "It's tough growing up, isn't it?"

Her sudden laugher surprised him. "God, is it! Good luck, David."

They shook hands again, and then she went out. He stood alone in the lobby, not sure what to do next. From down the hall came the metallic clatter of the cleaning people's equipment. David gathered up his briefcase, the box with the remainder of his farewell party cake, the two Burr College marble bookends that Oliver had presented to him, and went out the door.

37

In the staggered fashion common to schools like Burr, some students in May would finish their studies and graduate, while other programs such as the January start would study straight through, and still others, such as the September two-year students only completing their first year, would break for the summer and resume in the fall. With four major class starts a year—July, September, January, and April—the Burr College technically had four graduations per year as well, but although the students who finished their studies in March, December, and September were given recognition, they were all invited to join the big traditional ceremony in June for which they would be honored with a real cap and gown, a march down the aisle, and issuance of a diploma in a little blue book.

On the day of graduation Ethel walked unannounced into Oliver's office, shut the door, and dropped scowling on a chair. As luck would have it, Oliver was reviewing his copy of the recent April monthly report, which reflected not only the high admissions figures for the upcoming July and September starts, but also increased withdrawal rates among the current classes, particularly January IP and the Evening Accounting and Paralegal programs.

"What are you looking at?" the dean asked.

He told her.

"Well, we tried to hold them," Ethel said. "Frankly, I'm surprised some of these people lasted until now. You know, Lily pulled some fast tricks back in January. You can't satisfy people when you promise something and don't make good on it. She made what we teach here look glamorous and exciting, when being a secretary is really a lot of hard work with very little thanks."

"I suppose."

"And this is how we'll pay for it. I'm sure the withdrawal rates are going to get worse. That won't make us look good when the accreditors come back."

"It doesn't help, certainly." He pushed up his glasses and rubbed his nose. "What can I do for you, Eth?"

"Keone Robinson is in my office."

"Oh hell."

"Exactly."

"What's she getting?"

Ethel folded her arms defensively. "After one year of Burr training, including some wonderful extra help via Jean, Keone is the proud owner of a 1.47 GPA."

Oliver sighed.

"What do you want me to tell her."

He could see that Ethel was prepared to dismiss the student if he said so. He appreciated that she felt compelled to come here and talk to him about it. She certainly didn't have to.

"Well, is there any way we can get around it?"

Ethel shrugged non-committedly. "It's in the catalog, Oliver. You have to complete your first year with at least a 2.0 or you fail out."

"What about academic probation?"

"She's been on probation all spring. I can play around, try to extend it, but what do I base it on? She's not on a medical leave. There's no mitigating personal situation that would justify keeping her on."

"Ethel, you've done this sort of thing before."

"I know. Maybe I'm just uninspired." Ethel looked down at her shoes, saw a run in one stocking. Her gown at tonight's ceremony would cover it.

"You know what irks me, Oliver? I don't feel like flunking this kid. She's tried. Screwed up a lot, but she's worked hard."

"How many other kids are going to fail?"

"Well, there's a good many. More than I care to admit. We just don't get the quality—"

"How many? Got a percentage?"

"I'd say … maybe thirty percent."

"Thirty percent are *failing?*" He was shocked.

She nodded, and studied him with cool brown eyes.

"Well, there's the answer. We can't fail out nearly a third of the class."

"We're going to keep her?"

"We have to."

"Okay." She stood slowly. "She's a lucky kid."

He smiled ruefully. "I was thinking the same thing."

Keone sat by herself in the dean's office. More than any other department head, Ethel maintained her office in a severe state of chaos. Since losing Natalie back in January, the stacks of papers, folders, binders, old textbooks, and periodicals had worsened. It was impossible to navigate any part of the office without stepping over something. Keone sat in the client chair and trembled. She held her academic transcript in her hand, and the reality of her failed grades had knocked the wind out of her. She had already been marched to the business manager's station where that scary Ms. Mallory snarled and hissed about the $1,800 still owed for tuition. Keone had no answer for that, she had assumed financial aid would cover it. "How could you think that," Ms. Mallory bellowed, "when tuition is $9,125, and your total aid was only $7,325?" The numbers were lost on Keone, who only knew she wouldn't be returning next year. She would never pay the loan back, and therefore never get aid to attend another college. She was dead in the water. But even failing out of school was a bureaucratic process, and so she was marched next to the dean's office, scared and ashamed, and now sat in this chair trying to figure how not to care about any of this.

Dean Harris came in. She shut the door and started speaking before she reached her desk. "Ms. Robinson, I've just discussed your case with the school director. We believe there are mitigating circumstances."

Keone looked miserable. Ethel tried again. "What I mean is, both Dr. Dunbar and I have recognized a sizable effort on your part to do well in your classes."

The girl barely nodded, waiting for the blow to come.

"We believe that your work started to improve in January when you began those special sessions with Mrs. Cavanaugh. We also believe that one semester wasn't necessarily enough to really help you catch up to where you ought to be." Ethel did not smile; she never smiled at students until they held their diplomas. "We will allow you to return next fall. You'll be on extended academic probation. That means you'll have the fall semester to bring your grades up to the requisite 2.0 if you wish to continue in the spring and graduate. Do you understand me?"

"I'm comin' back?"

"Yes. Do you understand the circumstances I've just stated?"

"Yeah'm." Dazed, she wasn't even sure she heard the question.

"Keep taking advantage of those special tutoring sessions with Mrs. Cavanaugh. They're obviously helping. And Ms. Robinson—if that still isn't enough, come talk to me. I'll help you too."

The student met the dean's eyes but didn't speak. There seemed no way to set this girl at ease, but still Ethel maintained her cold professional mask. "You've worked like a horse this semester. As hard as I've ever seen any student work. Frankly, I think you deserve to graduate from this school. What do you think?"

"Yeah. I sure want to."

"Well, go home. Have a nice summer. Keep up your skills. *Don't* let the summer take them away from you. You won't stand a chance next fall if you let that happen."

"No, I won't." The realization of her reprieve was beginning to sink in. She stood up, and her thin voice came to life. "Thanks, Dean Harris. Thanks lots!"

Ethel nodded curtly, and watched the girl run from the room. Alone amidst her clutter, she said, "Heaven help us if the accreditors choose her file," then picked up the program for tonight's ceremony and compulsively rechecked it for possible errors.

Strapping on her red bookbag, which had in it only her steno pad and typing book, Keone skipped down the concrete steps of the school and was startled to find her mother standing across Sixth Street. "Mama!" She fairly flew across the road. Doris hugged her girl tight.

"How'd you do, baby?"

"Good, Mama. I'm comin' back next year."

"You pass them tests after all? I thought you said you flunked."

"I musta just made it. They're lettin' me come back." Keone laughed and clung to her mother's ample arm.

Doris could barely breathe. Not since she was a child had Keone looked this happy. She couldn't get over the sight of her daughter emerging from an institution of higher learning. God was creating a miracle here, and Doris was shaken in the face of His handiwork.

They headed for the subway, mother and daughter still holding onto each other.

38

On a July afternoon pressed flat with summer heat, Oliver left the college and headed south. Below the funky college-kid commercialism of South Street the row houses stood in varying degree of love and neglect, for incomes varied in the city's large southern parishes, and poverty revealed itself in patchwork patterns, a couple blocks here, an intersection there, with little open drug selling and a more confident sense of safety. This changed at Fourth and Washington where he stared upward at the twenty-six story apartment towers of the Southwark housing project, dark and mostly abandoned but not quite, as evidenced by swatches of clothes drying on lines hoisted over balconies many floors high. He had walked into Southwark once, and found the stairwells so filled with trash they were insurmountable, and the sight of children playing in the basement amidst the rust of broken pipes and splintered pieces of wood made him tremble worse than any physical fear of standing there. On this day Oliver passed under the shadows of the towers but did not venture in. Below Washington Avenue he wandered in a vague westerly direction, taking side streets no wider than alleys. At Catherine Street near Twelfth he walked through the looming shadows of another miserable set of towers, four of them this time, smaller and stubbier than Southwark but just as bad, dirty and dilapidated and guarded by youngsters who spotted him and ran into the shadows, not to hide but to warn the dealers. This was the Martin Luther King Jr. Plaza, and without venturing inside he could see that so many of the units were dark and dead, with windows broken and only a few with curtains. Crossing Broad Street he worked his way along Wharton to Grays Ferry, a neighborhood rife with racial violence, and over the bridge to Forty-Seventh Street and the Kingsessing neighborhood, where an ongoing rash of murders kept making the news. Here the homes were big, generous townhouses and duplexes standing three stories plus an attic, with bay windows on the second floors and large porches below, grand homes once but now weatherworn and untidy, with trash peppering the lawns and many windows boarded up. Tree roots broke up the sidewalks, and fender-patched cars leaned against the curbs like wounded creatures. Weeds thrust through sidewalks, but also sprouted out of walls and roof shingles. Women in summer frocks sat on the big porches holding babies, and old men in shorts and tank tops sat and exercised by scratching themselves. No one talked while he was in view, but many smoked, and perhaps that was the point, to just sit back, puff, and let the sky pass over. Oliver would nod hello as he walked by, but he was a white man in a business suit; he rarely got a nod back.

This was Oliver's seventeenth walk through the worst neighborhoods of Philadelphia. He had started in the March winter cold and was now traversing in the fresh July heat. Mostly he walked by day but sometimes, like this occasion, time got away from him and darkness advanced with its stirring of nocturnal threats. Previously he had walked Broad Street as far north as Logan, and wandered the blocks at random, passing through dim projects, groups of graffiti-scarred buildings with cardboard covering broken glass in the lobby doors, and trash dumpsters with the green lids torn off. He walked down streets where kids throwing basketballs stopped until he passed, and passed under marquees of former movie houses now proclaiming holy revival meetings. He counted bars and lounges on every third corner. On another day he walked north then turned east on Somerset and circled the begrimed drug neighborhoods under the shadow of Kensington Avenue. He passed through the sprawling Richard Allen project along Poplar Avenue, an odd configuration of three-story buildings facing inward and blocked by walls that made the whole neighborhood look like a giant mouse maze. He saw a lot of drug trafficking there, where the little passageways afforded quick retreat if the lookouts sounded a warning. He walked toward Overbrook, and passed a barefoot man asleep against the stone cemetery wall of the Cathedral of Our Mother of Sorrows. On another day he took the ferry across the Delaware River to Camden, New Jersey's poorest city, and walked squalid residential streets where happy children played around piles of indecipherable rubbish, supervised by parents who watched him with suspicion. He saw row homes flush against cemeteries of toppled headstones, homes with the bricks crumbling to the sidewalks, backyards containing swing sets and broken metal drums and car parts. He felt the massive weight of poverty pressing down on these homes, making the tar roofs sink. He never walked Camden a second time. Back in Philadelphia, he trekked through Yorktown, Olney, and westward to Brewerytown and Strawberry Mansion, ghetto blocks where drug trafficking and violence and battles with aggressive police were as common as trips to the grocery. He walked streets no outsider to the city ever saw, where the porches and railings of row homes when one walked up and touched them (as he did) yielded like sponge, and curb drains collected trash soaked to a primordial pulp. There were large gaps between the row homes where tall grass hid all kinds of small horrors: broken knife blades, syringes, and shell casings. Stores sold fast food behind barred windows, and billboards advertised products he never heard of, cosmetics and shampoos specifically for black skin and hair, and other billboards begged information regarding missing children, and still others showed black arms scarred with multiple injection holes, crack deaths made big and raised high as a warning to all.

There were scores of children playing, for these were neighborhoods despite their reputation, and Big Wheels and strollers and Barbie dolls lay scattered in yards. Occasionally he saw birthday balloons and streamers decorating a backyard, or nicely dressed people walking home from church. He watched a woman in a postal uniform deliver mail door to door with a bored expression worthy of any civil servant, and watched as mothers walked their children to school in the mornings, how cheerfully the adults greeted each other, and how appealing were the children themselves, their young shoulders supporting schoolbags larger than their torsos. The poverty was less visible on these people than it was on their aged-brick surroundings. Yet it was these surroundings shaping the kids who now came to his school. Here, where boredom and a lack of work caused steam to rise, where the night's shadows flooded intimately against windows and thickened in trees, where stripped cars sat orphaned in dead lots, where graffiti in its swirls of illegible anger spattered walls, vans, and storefronts, where the churches locked their doors, where the trolleys squealed, old and gasping and dented from accumulated abuse, where the homeless and homeowner blurred together, and the curbs and park benches seemed unsafe for either, this was the world of so many of his students.

Oliver stood on a corner of Fifty-Sixth Street, his shirt clinging to his ribs. The afternoon was done but the twilight air brought no relief. Lights in some houses flicked on. People began to shuffle off their stoops. Oliver's arches stung from hours of smacking pavement. Six weeks earlier he had walked through this same area and heard gunshots. Now, with the sun gone and the local inhabitants off their porches, the scene was priming for the nighttime enterprise that dominated all. He didn't wish to linger. He walked north to Baltimore Avenue, and while he waited at the corner for a trolley three young men approached and waited as well. They stood aggressively close to him on three sides without seeming to look at him, and he wasn't sure if they were threatening him or just testing him. No one spoke, and when the car pulled up on its squealing tracks, he sat up front and they passed him to sit in the back.

It was a slow ride into Center City, for the trolley stopped at every intersection, and as Oliver waited, staring out his window at the dark night and inky houses, he had a sudden vision of the large storage room in the Burr College basement filled with two decades of graduates' files. Coming above ground at Fifteenth Street, he hailed a cab to take him to Sixth.

Unlocking the Burr College entrance and letting himself into the lobby, he was startled to see an office light shining past the darkened cubicles. Lily Espirito sat at her desk, marking notes on an already well-scribbled computer run. She looked up haggardly. He said, "Lily, it's after eight."

"Tell me about it. That was forty minutes right here, talking that one into coming."

"Will she?"

"Yes. Well, maybe … I don't know. She's insisting that she can't come earlier than next week, so anything can happen."

"Did she sound interested at least?"

"Oh, that wasn't the kid. That was Mom." Lily stood and stretched. She reached high, splaying small fingers over her head. She seemed unnaturally short to Oliver, but then she stepped away from her desk and he saw she was barefoot. "See, they aren't really interested in Burr," she said, snapping off the coffee maker and dumping the used grinds. "They're on a waiting list for Lafayette and Drew."

"Whoa, those are big schools, Lily. We can't expect to compete with them."

"Well, her kid filled out a lead card during a high school assembly. If Mom thinks I'm gonna ignore that she's nuts." She sat down at her desk and pulled sneakers from a tote bag.

"Why don't you take an extra hour tomorrow? Sleep in for a change."

"Oh that's sweet, Oliver, but I'll be in. Can't really afford the luxury right now, and besides I hate to sleep."

"So what are the numbers?" He didn't usually ask this, but she seemed in a good mood.

"Okay, but not great. Well, great maybe, but not what I'm looking for. Dammit, the summer goes so fast. It's the middle of July, can you believe it?"

"Well, I thought the June monthly report looked good."

Lily shook her head. "We've had some recent melts. And hardly any new nibbles. We had a good jump on September, but then it tapered."

"Well, four hundred and seventy students is a hell of a high goal, Lily. New York was unreasonable to set that."

"That's not the point."

"Are we behind?"

Lily looked at him and wrinkled her face.

"Sorry," he said, though he had every right to ask.

"Christ, I don't know if it's the economy or because everybody and their brother is splashing in water off the Jersey shore. By our original forecast we should need fifty-seven kids at this point, and we're short over seventy. Seventy-six, I think it is."

"How much of a problem is that?" He knew the answer, but wanted to hear what she'd say.

"Well, you know me, Oliver. I'm not one to blame other people, but Dee's just not pulling them in like she should. Trudy's been good, especially when school was in session and we had her on the road. And Marty's a goddamn godsend." Sneakers tied, she stood and shouldered her bag.

"Lily, you're doing the best you can. You've worked miracles. Nobody appreciates your efforts more than I."

"Hell, I'm sure *that's* true." She gave him an acid grin. "I've no doubt Dean Harris and those others are pissed by our success."

Oliver reluctantly agreed. Two weeks ago on July 7, and to no small fanfare, Lily's staff had made the July one-year sit. Two hundred and forty-seven students. Some were right at the last second, some had planned to come in September but were coerced into enrolling during the summer instead, but however she had done it, it was done. Oliver made sure everyone, including Louise, congratulated the admissions staff at a wine and cheese bash he threw in the student lounge. The admissions director and her reps were ecstatic, and the phone rang throughout the afternoon as members of the President's Office called with praise. But as historic as the occasion was, everyone knew—and Lily herself made it clear when she offered the toast—that they all still lived in the shadow of the much bigger September goal, almost twice the size of July and only six weeks away. They would still be running ragged. "But a *good* sort of running ragged," she had insisted, bronzed and beaming, and lifted her glass with a giggle.

Lily said, "We aren't going to miss this sit, Oliver."

"I'm sure we won't."

"No, I mean it. I *can't* miss this sit. After all the mouthing off I did to Bill, there's no way."

Oliver said nothing, to suppress a pulse of jealousy that she still felt free to talk to his boss without going through him.

"You know Miami's still in big trouble," she said, starting for the door. "Bill's thinking he might have to go down there and run that shop himself."

"I hadn't heard that," Oliver muttered, and followed her out.

He stopped in his office and rummaged through a file drawer until he found a student demographic report that was, unfortunately, six years old. Lily was waiting in the lobby for him.

"I'll tell you this much," she said as he set the alarm. "Before the staff and I go on that seminar Luis is flying me to Hawaii for at least two weeks."

"Sounds like what the doctor ordered, Lily."

"He doesn't know it yet, but he is."

They walked outside and stopped at the foot of the steps on Sixth Street. "What a warm, beautiful night," she said, looking at the sky. "I didn't get to the shore once this summer."

"It's been a hard season."

She looked at him, as if noticing him for the first time. "What brought you back here at this late hour?"

"I wanted to get this report. I'm thinking of a new program, maybe a variation of the current two-year program. Something that will better meet the needs of all the disadvantaged students we're getting."

"Really? And what will this do?"

"It'll help us to really teach the students. Instead of pushing them through a program they're not qualified for, maybe we can work with them at their level and legitimately teach them how to be good Burr professionals."

She looked genuinely intrigued, which flattered him. "You think you can do this without lowering the academic standard?"

"The standard would stay the same. It's merely revamping the program so the poorer student can achieve the standard."

"Why Oliver, that's wonderful! What a great idea!"

"It just needs to be done, is all."

"Good Lord, Oliver! Wouldn't it be nice if we could actually teach these kids?"

"You'd like that, Lily?"

She gave him a stunning smile. "Are you kidding? To be able to sell a good program and not have to pull all the crap? It's a salesperson's dream. Best of luck. If anybody can make it work, I'm sure you can."

"Good night, Lily."

She shifted her heavy bag to her other shoulder. "Take care."

Oliver felt his ambition steeply kindled, as if the work he was about to engage in was the finest and most important work a man could do. He grinned, watching his admissions director trot up Sixth Street to the garage where she kept her car. She really had the gift. Though his feet still protested, Oliver chose to walk the twelve blocks to Rittenhouse Square. For the first time in ages he looked forward to going home.

39

Bob Lawrence sat in his loft. The only light was a patch of moonlight shining through the north dormer window. The ceiling over his head arched claustrophobically into the apex that was the roof of the building itself. There was no sound but the soft shush of traffic three floors below.

He just sat there.

His computer hummed but offered only a blank screen. His hands were flat on his lap. His blond hair was matted in little bent spikes, dried from two days of saltwater exposure. He stared at the screen. Its darkness behaved no differently from the darkness of the shadows of the room itself. He was staring at an electronic shadow, sitting in a room filled with real ones.

He moved slightly, to lift a glass of ginger ale and take a sip. He felt the carbonated liquid battle the dryness in his throat. The glass left a water ring on the computer table, and when he put the glass down he set it exactly over the ring again.

He had traveled two hours from the Wildwood shore to get back here. After weeks of dodging, of explaining how busy he was during the summer, how inconvenient it was to rent a car, anything he could think of, he had finally visited Heather's family at the shore. At stake was Heather's birthday, and she wouldn't take no for an answer. So the family knew him now. He was happily accepted by them. He was in real trouble.

The trip showed him everything that was wrong. He drove the Atlantic City Expressway and Garden State Parkway with mounting apprehension. His heart began to trip as he passed the last sign for Avalon, and the Wildwoods and Cape May spread before him. Driving on New Jersey Avenue the cross street numbers began to ascend in much too rapid an order: Tenth, Eleventh, Twelfth, Thirteenth, and then Fourteenth, his destination. A fat woman with corn-yellow hair stood in a bleached square yard, watering dead grass.

"Hello," he said gamely.

The woman squinted irritably. Or maybe the sun was just in her eyes. She said nothing and the hose, pointed up in her hand, spit an arc of water.

"Are you Mrs. Feeney?"

"Who are you?"

"I'm Bob Lawrence. I'm a friend of Heather's."

The woman laughed. She turned toward the house, slopping the hose water. "Heather! Your guy's here!"

"Is it all right to park here?" Bob asked.

"Why not?" She resumed swishing the hose around.

Heather dashed out of the house, banging the screen door behind her. As soon as he was out of the car, she grabbed his arm pointedly in front of her mom. "Bob! Bob! This is so great, you coming here for my birthday!" She kissed his face repeatedly.

"How could I miss it?" said Bob, side-glancing at Mrs. Feeney who was looking irritated again.

"Come in!"

She pulled him along. She was in her bathing suit, a red one-piece that compressed her body into a prepubescent boy's although the bottom cut high up her thighs, giving a severe feminine shape to her long legs. Her black hair was tied back with a green band.

Like most shore rental property, the Feeneys' summer house exuded cheapness. The carpet had been pounded bloodless from decades of bare feet, and the sparse furniture included a couch with one arm (designed that way), a Sylvania TV on a wire stand, and several sponge paintings of cresting waves, sailboats, and lighthouses. A portrait of Jesus praying in Gethsemane hung near the front door, but if you stood to the left it changed to a sorrowful figure on a cross.

Heather led him into the kitchen, pushed him on a chair next to a chrome and Formica table, and plopped on his lap. She hooked her feet around his. Her skin was deeply tanned and her hair wet, and in all honesty she did feel nice.

"It's my birthday today."

"I know."

"I'm nineteen."

"Yeah, how about that?"

"I love you."

A large young man filled the doorway. He was barrel-bellied and sported a round lumberjack's beard. "Hey, I'm Patrick. You're Bob, right?"

"Yes."

Heather said, "That's my brother." She kissed Bob's cheek.

The big man thrust out a hand. "Glad to meet you."

"Likewise."

"Thirsty?"

"A little."

"That's a drag ride from the city. Heath, you're supposed to get drinks and stuff for your guests. Don't count on her for hospitality," he said. "In this place you fend for yourself."

"That's not true," said Heather, but she was happy. She let her feet swing and her butt rocked on Bob's lap. He really wished she would get off.

"Want some coffee? We'd have to brew it, but it ain't a prob." Patrick opened the refrigerator, looked bored, and shut it. "Or do you want a beer?"

"Beer's fine."

Patrick opened the refrigerator again. "Heath?"

"Sure."

Patrick seemed to accept his sister on Bob's lap as part of the natural order. He passed out bottles of Coors. This casualness disconcerted Bob. He didn't want to be known by this family, didn't want to get further involved with Heather than he was already. And overcoming every other uncomfortable aspect was the Big Question—where was he sleeping tonight?

A voice from the doorway: "Yo, Dad got any beer left? He's yellin' for some."

The doorway filled with another large young man. As Patrick opened the fridge a third time, this guy studied Bob and smiled. He was wrapped in a towel, naked from the waist up, and his shoulders and chest looked like a prizefighter's. His black hair was long and shaggy, and tapered to an unruly beard that flowed without seam into the hair of his chest. "You must be Bob."

"Yes."

"I'm Frankie. Heath's brother."

"Glad to meet you, Frankie."

"Here you go," said Patrick, tossing a brown bottle at him. Frankie caught it in one hand and sauntered off.

"Heath, why don't you get off a moment?" said Bob.

"Why?"

Patrick said to Heather, "How was the beach this morning?"

"Hot." From the living room the screen door smacked. Heather sat up. "That's Dad."

"Is it?" Bob tried to rise, but she still wouldn't move off his lap. "Heather, come on."

"What?"

"Let me stand up."

"Why?"

Mr. Feeney walked into the kitchen holding a beer. He was tall, but much slimmer than his sons. His face was wide and reddish from the sun, his black hair thick and pasted back behind his ears, his brows and mustache heavy. He saw his daughter on Bob's lap and openly frowned. "How do you do?"

"Mr. Feeney. Nice to meet you." Bob extended his hand past Heather's ear.

"Heather, why don't you stand up and let the man breathe?"

She did quickly.

"My glasses are in the bedroom. Get them for me."

"Yes, Daddy." She left the kitchen.

Feeney took Bob's hand. "So at last we meet."

"Yes, sir. Sorry, but my job goes straight through the summer, and it's the kind of job that involves taking a lot of work home too. I don't get away much."

Feeney smiled. It was a pleasantly crisp, masculine smile, of white teeth and casual authority. "I admire teachers. Hell of a profession. Much harder than it looks, I'm sure. Good to have you on board, son."

Bob's attic grew darker. Through the exposed rafters a creaking noise emitted from the living room below. Mr. Wemmick yowled. The big cat was heavy enough to make the floorboards protest. Bob didn't answer. He sat still, going over this wretched weekend that had been a predetermined nightmare even before he rented the car and set off down the long Jersey highways. He felt bad not answering his cat. Maybe he could rent a movie tonight and sit on the couch with Mr. Wemmick. They used to do that a lot and Wem loved it. They hadn't done it in ages.

This weekend had, in a not-too-funny way, scared him. Heather's older brothers were big men, wide in girth and all muscle. Their thick arms hung out from their sides as if always ready to wrestle. They got a kick out of watching Bob on the pier rides. They thought it hysterical how their little sister could scream and yell and wave both arms going down the coasters while her old man tucked his chin against his chest and shut his eyes as they plummeted. The Feeneys were all hairy, and their summer-drenched tans made Bob with his pale bare skin feel like a fish on ice. The family did not act in a threatening manner, but they were a threat nevertheless. The danger was their easy acceptance of the whole arrangement. They didn't mind Bob's age, they didn't find anything disturbing about a teacher dating a student. For sleep they provided him with a fold-out cot in a spare room, but save for that discretion they enthusiastically kept him and Heather together. Saturday night, after the birthday party, after Mom and Dad had gone to bed and Heather fell asleep on the one-armed couch in the living room, the brothers insisted on taking him to a local bar. There they kept refilling his glass until Bob finally doubled over and vomited on the counter. The establishment kicked them out, but the brothers loved it. It was his initiation; he was one of them now. Sunday evening Bob drove back to Philadelphia in a cold sweat, and never felt so grateful to see the speckled lights of the Philly skyline as he crested the Walt Whitman Bridge.

Out there in the night, the night beyond the closed dormer windows of the loft, a fire siren wailed. This city was always catching fire. He took another sip of ginger ale, diluted now by melted ice, and listened until the siren faded.

He didn't think Heather was interested in fair play. He didn't think she would take rejection gracefully. And the other Feeneys seemed capable of de-limbing him if he did the wrong thing by their sister. It was a delicate situation. But this weekend had proved that it was also untenable. He had let things go far too long. It was finally time to act.

Bob stood up and went down the narrow stairs to the living room, passed Mr. Wemmick who jumped expectantly on the couch, went into the kitchen and opened the doors of his laundry closet. A week's worth of used clothes were piled on the compact dryer. More wilted shirts lay draped on a kitchen chair. On a corner of the kitchen table was a get-to-it-soon pile of mail. He knew there were unpaid bills and possibly even a paycheck hiding in there. A cold saucepan with crusted spaghetti sauce rested on the stove, and other mottled dishes crowded the sink. Dust bunnies rolled like small tumbleweeds before his bare feet, and particles of mysterious snack food dotted the living room carpet. The whole apartment looked like a derelict's hovel.

Bob went to work. He went back upstairs, cleared the bed and made it, then collected all dirty clothes in a laundry basket, took it downstairs and started a load. He washed and scraped the dishes, then set them in the drying rack. He went through the papers on the kitchen table and threw out two-thirds of what was there, junk mail or bills that were already outdated by the reminders lying higher up the pile. He got out his checkbook and paid them all. He wasn't going to fuck around with this stuff anymore.

Both the kitchen and living room needed vacuuming badly, but the hour was too late to turn on a noisy machine. Right after work tomorrow he would give the whole place a good going over. A delicious purity filled his body, a calmness he hadn't experienced in ages. He felt he could put everything behind him, all his mistakes, his dumb decisions, his inability to finish the manuscript that lay like a block of marble beside his Mac. Thirty-six wasn't a bad time of life, not if you didn't waste it. He was through wasting his.

He poured himself a well-earned glass of wine and sat beside his cat on the couch. He flipped channels and recognized *Trading Places* on HBO. He hadn't seen it since college, and left it on. Mr. Wemmick purred against his thigh. Suddenly inspired, Bob went into the kitchen and microwaved some popcorn. He and Mr. Wemmick shared the bowl.

40

During the third week of August, three weeks before the September sit, Lily panicked. She called two staff meetings, one on Monday, the other on Wednesday. Then on Thursday afternoon, right after another phone call from Bill Nostrand, her beehive thrust out the doorway. "EVERYBODY GET IN HERE!"

Other employees watched sympathetically as the admissions staff grabbed their tablets and hustled into the director's office. The door slammed shut like a vault.

"Twenty-two applicants to go!" she screamed. "What the CHRIST is it going to take?"

Deirdre tried, "We're dealing with every lead we get—"

"*Shut up!*" Lily stormed back and forth before them, and each time she passed her desk she smacked the top of it with the flat of her hand. "What do you mean by that?"

"Pardon me?"

"*Shut UP!* Riddle me this, sweetheart—why the fuck are we behind twenty-two commits?"

Marty braved, "Lily, we can only run with what we've got. We've worked every lead—"

"You're full of shit! You aren't salespeople! You don't even know what 'admissions' is! You think it means you admit applicants who come in! Bloody Christ! What it *really* means is you ADvertise and that's your MISSION! As in 'Get out there!' 'Seek and ye shall find!' not to mention the ever-popular *'Get off your ass!'* Look at these GODDAMN FIGURES!"

She snatched up a yellow folder and threw it at Marty. The male rep cringed and covered his face as papers flapped around him. As Lily continued her tirade, he sheepishly put down his hands.

"We've pulled in sixty people from the mission homes, maybe we'll get about twenty out of it, but that's *all!* And they're only head counts, not official commits, because they don't have a dime to give us up front! And the girls from the high schools are still interested in coming, but the little bitches are sending their deposits piecemeal—forty bucks *here*, ten *there*, trying to make the hundred twenty-five bucks! Those papers there—" she jerked her hand at the clutter on the floor, "tell us we need four hundred and seventy-two heads for September! We've interviewed and committed four hundred and fifty, but only three hundred and fifty-two have paid their full deposit! Which means they're not really committed at all! That's ninety-eight students whose promise to us is *verbal!* Well, verbal doesn't count on PAPER, children! It doesn't count with New York, and it doesn't count with ME!"

Of course, the high school girls Lily was talking about were almost entirely from the "C" list: ghetto kids who had no money, and by nature needed to be prodded to do anything. None of the reps dared point this out.

"So you tell me—*what's* it gonna take to get some money in this office?"

"We keep calling—" Trudy began.

"*Hardly!* Hell, you're not calling right now!"

"Well but you made us come in for this meeting—"

"I will NOT accept excuses!" Lily's black eyes leapt from face to face. "You are not only keeping yourselves from a cruise and a big bonus, you are keeping ME from it as well! And you can bet your flaccid asses I'm *not* forgiving anybody who keeps me from my bonus and a cruise! Who here thinks that anything other than UNMITIGATED HELL will result if I miss a bonus and a cruise?" She leaned into their faces, each in turn. Her stiletto heels stabbed the pages of the report, still scattered on the floor, and sheets stuck to both feet. She didn't notice, and no one dared point this out.

"So I'm not going to see any more verbal commits! Is that clear? ANSWER ME!"

"Yes, ma'am!"

"And you've each got forty-eight hours to get those delinquent deposits in! God Almighty, how can you let such a thing go? ANSWER ME!"

"We don't know, ma'am!"

Lily crossed to her coffee maker and poured. The mug shook in her hands. She drank half of it in one shot. "Next thing, I want you bozos on those phones drumming up more business! We've got to get twenty-two new bodies! *I will not start that September class with one empty seat!*" She stepped forward, heard crackling, and looked down at the paper stuck to her shoes. "Shit!" With an agile hop she perched on the front of her desk and reached down. The papers shredded loudly as she tore them from her heels. She wadded the sheets threateningly, and glared at each rep to see if anyone was laughing. The faces before her were stone.

"Now what the Jesus are our road reps doing? That Joyce and, uh, what's her name? I haven't heard from them in a hell of a long time."

The three cowed reps looked at each other. Trudy said with delicate fear, "It's the middle of August."

"So?"

"Well, they get the summer off. High schools are c-c-closed now."

Lily stared incredulously. She slid off the desk and indifferently tugged down her skirt. "Are you telling me my road reps have been off all summer and *nobody told me?*"

"But they—they always get the s-s-summer off. It's understood. High schools are closed—"

"CHRIST!" Specks of saliva flew through the air. "Oh, you are all going to pay for THIS one! I can't be-LIEVE it!"

"They always have it off," Trudy whimpered.

"GODDAMMIT!" Lily's arm blurred toward the ceiling and a wad of rumpled paper smacked noisily off Trudy's head. "You dumb twat! The world doesn't stop with summer vacation! Things still happen! We should have sent them someplace! Maybe we still can! Hey, I know—the Girl Scouts go camping all summer long! We'll have them do tent demonstrations or something! Call around and look into it!"

Poor Trudy said, "I never heard of that."

Lily swiftly bounced another wad of paper off her head. "You never heard of screwing either, I'll bet, when you were a child growing up in your big Villanova home, yet it was happening all around you, in every luxurious house up and down the street! No doubt with all the kinks too, if I know rich people and *Christ I do!*" She bounced a third wad off the girl's head.

Trudy covered her face. "Lily, please stop—"

Deirdre said, "It's awful late in the summer. My sister's already home from camp."

"Then let's set the reps up on the boardwalks at the shore! Christ, let's get them a booth in a mall! WHY AM I THINKING OF EVERYTHING HERE!"

Marty began to laugh. Lily whirled on him. "Is this funny, Mr. Nolan?"

"No, absolutely not!" He looked up fearfully, his jaw struggling. "I'm sorry, I am, I swear. It's just kind of funny, you bouncing that paper off her head. I don't mean any disrespect, honest. I couldn't help it."

"Fine." Lily returned to her desk, grabbed her heavy metal stapler, and flung it at him. It passed Marty's head by inches and struck the wall with a terrible smack before clattering to the floor. Marty's smile went away neatly.

"What's your wife look like, Mr. Nolan?"

"What?"

"Pretty? Tall? Leggy? Nice smile? And your kids, are they walking yet? Learning to talk?"

"Well, I—"

"Because if you can remember what your wife and kids look like, THEN YOU'RE NOT WORKING HARD ENOUGH FOR ME! Now get out of my sight! Get on that goddamn phone and don't leave it until you've got me twenty-two new apps! IS THAT CLEAR?"

"Yes, ma'am!"

"That goes for all of you! I'm going to stay late and work the phones myself, and there isn't ONE REP who'd better go home before me! That's going to be our cheery policy until we have the entire class sat, even if it takes EVERY DAY for the next three WEEKS! Doesn't that sound good?"

"Yes, ma'am!"

"I don't see any smiles! Are you SMILING?"

Everyone smiled.

"And I just might stay until fucking MIDNIGHT! Does that present a problem to anybody?"

"No, ma'am!"

"It's going to be a lot of FUN, isn't it?"

"Yes, ma'am!"

"Get out of here! Bring me results that count for a change! OUT! NOW!"

They grabbed their pads and ran.

Lily stared at the half-open door, her chest heaving. She strode forward and slammed the door shut with the flat of her hand. Then she kicked her desk a few times. She stared at the triangular gash in the wall where the stapler hit.

She was really scared. There were *no more names!* She could make her staff telemarket till doomsday, but what she really needed were fresh leads for them to contact. They had squeezed every possible list out of the computer's database, and called every lead card brought in from newspaper ads. They had phoned alumni to see if they had children or grandchildren interested in attending, and even tapped a few former employees. But it wasn't enough. Why had New York made the September goal so fucking high? Was Bill Nostrand deliberately trying to make her fail? Maybe New York didn't want to pay out the bonuses if a school made goal, was *that* why they made them so unreachable?

She felt the office walls closing in. She put both hands to her cheeks and whispered, "Sweet Jesus, what am I going to do? What am I going to *do?*" No answer whispered back. She looked at the coffee maker, but the brown sludge at the bottom of the carafe made her stomach wrench. She was out of coffee *and* luck.

Her left hand reached for the little crucifix that hung on a gold chain from her throat. Lily was Catholic, but seldom had occasion to be reminded of it. The crucifix was small and made of real gold. She did not generally wear it, but her appointment later this afternoon was with John Duffy and his daughter Shannon, and Lily thought it a nice touch. Her Connemara green dress was conservative yet sexy, covering her properly from neck to knee while fitting snuggly to her body, enough to make clear its ample assets, the perfect dress for a well-brought-up Catholic girl. Mr. Duffy would be charmed. She had already set a figure of St. Patrick on her windowsill, and replaced her diamond wedding ring with a gold Claddagh band. She looked at the clock. One-thirty, and the appointment wasn't until four. She walked briskly out of the office.

"Going on an errand," she announced to Julie as she passed through the lobby. Coming out on Sixth, she turned north and quickly found herself surrounded by tourists clustered about Independence Hall, snapping annoying pictures, eating hot-dogs from street vendors, or climbing into horse-drawn buggies. Business people sat on benches eating lunch in the shade. Lily wended through them all until she reached the front of Congress Hall, then turned west.

Chestnut Street was a drab strip of shoddy outlets and fast food joints, although it still held enticements. At Thirteenth Lord & Taylor beckoned, and once Lily crossed Broad Street the stores grew more upscale: Eddie Baur, Ann Taylor, Burberry, even the Coach Store where she could really use a new pocketbook. She forced herself to scurry by. At Seventeenth Street she was confronted by Liberty Place, Philadelphia's tallest building and easily the city's best shopping mecca, but again she steeled herself. She would not have her mission corrupted by materialism.

Lily turned up Seventeenth. The sun shone hot and bright. She had been walking long enough now to unwind, to enjoy the sound of traffic and scraps of breeze filtering between buildings. She was still a city girl. Low rent shopping venues had filled much of her childhood, flea markets and bazaars where she had haggled enjoyably over prices already marked down, a shrewd customer even as a kid. She remembered such places as a haven from the horrible house on Westmoreland Street in North Philly where she lived with four brothers and two sisters, in total a family of nine, with her father coming home from the machine plant stinking of oil and whipping everybody for no good reason. She would remember to her death the scary plays he made at her when she, the eldest daughter, reached her ninth year and started budding. And how Mama never spoke back to him, ever. It cost Lily nothing to leave that house, and she practiced leaving it years before college finally freed her by haunting the Center City streets, window-shopping without money, hanging out with friends, doing anything to keep from going home. There were a few homeless on Seventeenth and they begged her with silent open hands. Lily passed them contemptuously. She never gave to the poor. No one had ever given to her. And that bolstered her a little, even before she reached the wide Ben Franklin Parkway where the homeless were forbidden. Lily's head was high again, her stride quick and assured. Businessmen turned their heads as she flashed past in the snug green dress that showed her to such advantage. She didn't care. She was grim about her attractiveness. Her looks, like her clothes and education and marriage, had been hard to come by. The businessmen staring after her didn't seem much different from the homeless. Everyone was a beggar for something.

At Seventeenth and Race the Cathedral of SS Peter and Paul rose before her, an austere brown edifice of green domes and enigmatic statues. Lily mounted the steps and pulled open the massive door. She dipped her fingers in holy water, crossed herself, then entered the sanctuary.

Like all Catholics, even shaky ones such as herself, the immensity of a cathedral sanctuary struck Lily with the Big Presence that people kept forgetting about. Far down the central aisle, past a low gate and under a twenty-foot tall tabernacle of marble columns and some kind of dome, a crucified Christ glowed like a distant phantom. Lily walked the center aisle cautiously, her heels delicately tapping the black and white tiles. Marble altars were tucked off to the sides, lit between arches, and the first on the left was for St. Patrick. Lily continued down the center aisle but kept that in mind for afterward. She still had to see the Duffys at four o'clock.

There were only three other supplicants seated in the vast room. Lily reached the first pew and genuflected before a painted statue of Mary. The Virgin looked sweet and serene in a robin's egg blue wrap, her hair covered, dainty hands pressed flat in prayer. Her face was beautiful despite no make-up, her small mouth pale and natural, her eyebrows possibly plucked. Lily grasped her little crucifix, bowed her head, and cleared her mind for humble communication.

"Dear Lord, our Father," she whispered with a childlike hush, "bless my mother and sisters. Bless my brothers. Bless my husband and the home we live in. Forgive me, Lord, for not having gone to confession in … some time. Keep those I know healthy, and protect them from ill harm. Help me too, Lord, to be more worthy of those who live and work with me. And also, Lord, if it be your kind will, please get me twenty-two students for September in the next three weeks. In the name of the Father, the Son, and the Holy Spirit, amen."

41

Traffic buzzed two hundred feet above, headlights whizzing like comets over a span of black. Parked under Interstate 95 in a dirt patch worn grassless from countless lovers' cars over countless years, Keone let Dashiell Lang fuck her. There was no one else in the car. Dashiell had a wide old 1987 Ford, big enough for her small frame to stretch out on the back seat. His voice was a laugh in the dark, but his weight was real. Still, it was good weight. There was no waste on him, nothing that wasn't tight and smooth and tough. She could lie on her back and look up through a side window at the highway traffic streaking past, so very high up. Comets.

A haggard whisper in her ear. "It's good, ain't it?"

"Yeah."

"Say my name, baby."

"Dash," she whispered. "Dash."

She had never liked it. But he was good-looking and Darcy was jealous that he'd come back to Caulfeld and immediately looked Keone up, and he had money. Earlier in the city he took her to a bar where he bought pizza and a lot of beer, then they went to a horror movie, some slasher flick everyone was seeing, and he laughed when she screamed and buried her head in his hard shoulder, and she laughed too. She thought now, with Dash covering her, about the way the movie scared her, the gore and that wild moment when the ax went in one girl's head, they showed it plain as day, and she actually walked around a bit with the thing half in her skull, screeching and clawing the air while her pretty boyfriend backed across the floor on elbows and feet, naked and good-looking like Brad Pitt though it wasn't him. She thought about all the scary parts of the movie, and Dashiell didn't seem to take long at all.

But he wouldn't drive her home afterwards, and insisted they stay in the car. He talked, she listened. He told her about the two girls on his string and the grief they were giving him. He told her about a robbery he took part in one month earlier, a liquor store on Moore Street that socked in over six hundred bucks, cool for one hour's work plus a little planning. He boasted of these things and Keone, growing up with Javaughn, knew he shouldn't be blabbing any of it. She thought he must be real serious about her to do so, and in twenty minutes the reason for his insistence that they stay in the car became clear. He pushed her down on the back seat, and she studied the comets again.

She was almost asleep when he brought her home. The car jostled over the speed bump by the gate to Caulfeld. Through heavy lids she saw the mint green glow of his dashboard, felt the stiff crust of her cotton T-shirt and shorts against her dried skin. Dashiell wasn't whistling or drumming the steering wheel like he usually did, and he could hardly keep his eyes open. He pulled up before her house but didn't shut off the motor.

"Um beat, baby. I see you tomorrow."

"'Kay."

The porch light was on but all the windows dark. She didn't know what time it was but felt it must be close to dawn. She undid the bolts and knob lock and went inside. She flipped on the living room light and heard little scratchy sounds coming from the kitchen. She walked cautiously to the doorway.

"Look what finally come home," Javaughn said. He was flipping the buttons on a Gameboy.

"What you doin'?"

"Got somethin' on my mind. Come in here." He snapped off the toy and set it on the kitchen counter.

Keone stayed in the doorway. Her brother stood with his heavy arms folded. He stared at her for a long time, then pointed to the kitchen table. "When's the last time you used that?"

The computer sat unplugged on the far corner of the table, its keyboard relegated to the floor where it leaned against the wall on one end. At the beginning of the summer she had practiced on it nearly every day, her typing book and papers taking up most of the tabletop. Now it was August, and extended lack of use had pushed the schoolwork aside, and coupons and junk mail were piling on top of the monitor.

"So what?"

They stared at each other. For all his outward anger, Javaughn seemed unsure what to say next. Keone realized suddenly how big her brother had grown. Javaughn's arms and legs were large and stocky, his black boots looked like weapons. Dashiell was a shrimp next to Javaughn.

"Didn't you tell her you had to practice regular over the summer or you'd lose your skills?"

It was true. But she had intended, every night before she went to sleep and every morning upon waking, to put in that practice time. Somehow the summer days slipped past faster than she could keep track, and it had been one of the hottest summers ever. After a while it just got nice to wake up without having to do anything.

"Well, I run outta paper."

"Fuck. I'll get you paper."

Keone rested her head against the doorframe. The lengthy night was eating at her; all she wanted was to go to bed.

"So you'll get me paper," she said coldly. "What are you, my mommy now?"

Javaughn uncrossed his arms and jammed his hands in his pockets. "I ain't tryin' to be your mommy. I'm tryin' to look out for you."

"You?" she scowled. "Who axt you to?"

"Nobody. Just thought I would, that's all."

"Well, I can look after myself. I got—"

"No, I don't think you can. If you was, you wouldn't be traipsin' in here after bein' out all night with Dashiell Lang. You lettin' him fuck you again?"

"That ain't your business, and it ain't true neither!"

"It is true. I already know it's true."

"It still ain't your business." She matched his harsh whisper. She was not going to be lectured by a younger brother. "You're one to talk. What about your doin's?"

"What I do we ain't talkin' about. We ain't from the same mold, and Mama knows it. I made my place here and I'm doin' fine. But you ain't never goin' to. You ain't tough enough. Till this last year I just watched you gettin' eat alive and didn't think nothin' about it 'cause why should I?"

"So?"

He shrugged. He smiled suddenly, and she was startled to see how handsome he was, how adult he looked. "You showed me up."

Keone said nothing.

"You showed Mama too. No one thought you'd stay at that school. But you lasted a whole year, sister. You got somethin' goin' for yourself. You ain't no fuckin' lost cause no more. But you ain't takin' care of yourself either."

"Oh, shut up—"

"You listen to me!" He stepped toward her, and she instinctively shrank back. "I don't want you near Dashiell Lang no more. He's gonna bring you right back where you was. Your whole year is gonna go to shit. You hear me?"

"Dashiell ain't your business—"

"I ain't allowin' it anyway. What you want for keepin' away from him? A new wardrobe? Somethin' businesslike? What a executive would wear? I'll buy that for you. I'll buy whatever you need." His hand jerked out of his pocket and carelessly flashed a wad of bills. "Will that do it? Dashiell—"

"He's better'n you givin' him credit," Keone declared. "He ain't in Caulfeld no more! He got his own place—"

"Dashiell ain't out of here. He keeps comin' back. He's too stupid to leave here for good. And he talks too much. He's gonna get fucked over some day, and you ain't gonna be near when it happens."

Keone looked away angrily. Javaughn said, hard as stone, "You know what I'm talkin' about."

"Why you doin' this?"

"Told you why."

"You ain't been nice like this before."

"Never thought about it. Got my own problems, like everybody else. Just never really noticed you. But now you got somethin' goin' for yourself and it looks like a good thing. That's more'n anybody else got in this family 'cept me. Don't fuck it up. You ain't gonna last in Caulfeld. The wolves, they eat you like a snack."

"I'm tougher'n you think, Javaughn. I won more fights'n I lost."

"Grade school. Look, I ain't askin' you to prove it. I'm askin' you to do what you set out to do, which is get through that school. Isn't that what you want?"

"But Dash's fun," she whined. "I can't just work, I gotta have fun too. He buys me stuff, blouses and things, earrings, he give me these here, see? And he pays for movies—"

"I'll pay for your fuckin' movies. I'll pay for your earrings. Just don't have nothin' to do with him no more, you hear me?"

Keone took three deep breaths, noisy through her dry mouth. She said quietly, "Yeah."

"You know what I'm talkin' about. You don't see him for *nothin'*."

"Awright." But her face pinched. She looked worried.

"What?"

"Well, he ain't gonna like it."

"So he don't like it. The world don't revolve around him."

"But I'm kinda scared of him, Javaughn. He's real strong and he's got connections—"

Her brother snorted contemptuously. "Dashiell ain't got no connections. Trust me on that. He's a fuck-up from day one, and no one smart wants anythin' to do with him."

"He still scares me."

"See, that's why you gotta keep away from him. You don't have nothin' to do with what scares you. You tell him off, or I'll do it for you. You can believe me on this—he ain't gonna do nothin' to you. I'll kill him and he knows it. Which you want? Me to tell him or you?"

"You tell him."

"Okay. And I'll make him think it's my idea, then it won't be you he's mad at."

"He will be anyway."

"That's his lookout. And I'll get you some paper. Tomorrow, first thing."

"Awright."

"Good night, sister."

Keone ascended the stairs in wonder.

42

Muffy McKnight stared at the loan promissory note in front of her. Chris Maloney leaned forward from behind his desk and held out a pen. "I had Mike complete it for you," he said, smiling to show this was yet another service, "but you have to sign."

"I ain't sure I want debt. That's twenty-six hunnerd dollars you're talkin' about."

"Muffy, we went through this before. What you're going to make as a hotel manager nine months from now will more than cover the debt you're signing for."

"Yeah, I know. I just ain't signed somethin' so big before."

"Muffy, you have no reason to be afraid. Don't you know how student loans work? They're federally guaranteed. Do you understand what that means?"

The girl stared at him meekly.

Maloney laughed. "It means that if you don't pay this loan, the government pays it for you. So the bank gets its money anyway. It won't have a reason to chase after you."

"You sure?"

"Yes."

"'Cause I can't have no bank doin' somethin' that would hurt my welfare benefits. That's all I got."

"It won't. You have my complete assurance."

Muffy signed the loan note which was certified for the maximum $2,625. Maloney took the form and told her he'd mail it for her. He never took chances. He never let his prospects mail applications or promissory notes, just as he never told them that although the feds did pay banks for defaulted loans, they then went after the offending students with a vengeance, killing credit, garnishing wages, and retaining refunds from tax returns. Muffy McKnight was nineteen years old and lived in a housing project only a few blocks away. Her sole support was welfare—bad credit and tax refunds didn't mean diddly to her.

"Okay," he said merrily. "You're now enrolled for September. Welcome to the Hotel Institute. You're on the road to a great career."

Muffy laughed and picked up her daughter, who had been playing with her trucks on the floor of the rep's office. Maloney walked them both to the front entrance, which faced the derelict intersection of Fifty-Third and Market Streets.

On his way back through the lobby the pretty receptionist, Jeannine Richie, smiled through huge glasses and looked up from the morning paper. "Call for you on Three. Mrs. Kim."

"Shit. Okay." He fairly dashed to his office. He grabbed the line and without so much as a hello said, "Mrs. Kim, what's the problem?"

"Mr. Maloney," said a shy voice, "I won't be coming in today."

"But Mrs. Kim, you made the appointment. We're going to discuss the restaurant business as a career for you. You know that's a great opportunity."

"I don't … I am sorry. I don't think I am ready for school again at this time."

"Well, Mrs. Kim, frankly you're putting me in an awkward spot. I'm seeing a lot of people today. My whole afternoon is booked. I had to turn two people away because they wanted the two o'clock slot I reserved for you. You're not being unfair to me, ma'am, I'm only here to do what you want. But you did put out two other people."

"I am sorry. I didn't know this."

"Let's just talk about it a moment, okay?" Without pausing for breath or removing the phone from his ear, Maloney held the cord with one hand as he walked around his desk. He dropped on his chair, stretched his back, and crossed his legs.

It took ten minutes, but Mrs. Kim didn't cancel the appointment.

Maloney was only a rep, one of three on the staff, but he had been working at the Hotel Career Institute for a year now and already held highest seniority. He was also raking in more money at twenty-two than he ever would had he pursued his degree in environmental science. He rifled through his phone messages, most of which were two days old. That is, the calls from people already in class who now wanted to talk to him were two days old—his prospective phone message pile was empty. He never failed to return a prospect's call within an hour of receiving it.

It was incredible, the level of stupidity people could reach. To any logical degree, the Hotel Institute didn't exist. There was no real syllabus, no transcripts kept, and no affiliations with area hotels or restaurants. The dean, absent most days, held a degree in geography. Sometimes if a class was unusually small, the school waited the statutory first month, then deposited the federal loan checks while quietly encouraging the disgruntled kids to withdraw. Students were obligated to pay their loan debt whether they completed the program or not, so the school's claim on the proceeds was legitimate. And very few students thought enough about their indebtedness to complain. It meant thousands of dollars profit for HCI with only marginal classroom costs. There was goddamn genius at work here.

And the look of the school should make people wonder, but it didn't. The lobby of the Hotel Institute looked like somebody's basement. The beige carpet was old and worn to sandpaper, the walls a light blue that might have been pretty had the painters bothered to scrape off the old coat. They hadn't, and the subsequent blue paint bubbled and split. There was a picture of Ben Franklin on one wall, Abraham Lincoln on another, and a blown up photograph of the luxurious Ritz-Carlton Hotel over the receptionist's desk. (Ritz-Carlton had no idea it was there.) You'd think all these things would tip off that the school was a sham, but the prospects who walked in never questioned. Of course, if they were willing to pass through the door on the street, which identified THE HOTEL CAREER INSTITUTE via a silver plaque no bigger than a desk name plate, if they were willing to accept the school in a dreadful section of West Philadelphia, with a project (Muffy's) just a block away, and that the school itself was squeezed between a fried chicken takeout and a dollar thrift store, with the Market-Frankford El rattling overhead every twenty minutes—if they were willing to accept all this, then they weren't the type of discriminating applicants who fretted over cracked vinyl furniture or a little bad paint.

Jeannine buzzed. "She still coming in?"

"Natch."

"Damn. You a mean boy, Chris." She laughed and hung up.

Maloney opened his appointment book. He was the only rep who kept one. Generally the people who came to the Hotel Institute didn't make appointments, nor were they good about keeping them when they did. The other reps thought it a waste of time. Not Chris. When he fielded a call he always scheduled an appointment, and then followed up relentlessly to make sure they came. And if they tried to back out, like Mrs. Kim, he let them know they were putting him out. He had thirty-four names scheduled in his personal appointment book for the month of September, and he considered every one of them a fish on a hook. It was one of the reasons why he was the best rep.

He leaned back in his chair, pleased with his handling of Mrs. Kim, and contemplated again the lucky fact that so many stupid people existed. Most of the poor slobs who came in here didn't know *anything*. Most of them, welfare born and bred, couldn't do more than sign their names. He had to fill out everything for them, admissions forms, loan applications, and take what little pocket change they had on them. Even after they started school they didn't question anything. They mutely accepted that half the time their teachers didn't show, or that they had to share books with other students, books which were recycled year after year. They didn't question that the school was unable to place them afterward, that there was no formal placement director even though an office door had PLACEMENT painted on it. Maloney smiled just thinking about it. How could he help smiling?

A businessman named Peter Sherman started the school in the mid-Seventies. He owned it and several other career schools in conjunction with some business friends of his. They had, during the course of two decades, reaped a tremendous fortune from federal student loans and grants and not worrying about placement, enrollment, grades, all the extras of running a school that more or less got in the way of making money from student loans and grants. Sherman's earliest stroke of genius was ferreting out the Academic Commission of Career Schools to accredit his institutions. The ACCS logo was framed in the Hotel Career Institute lobby, though the agency in twenty years never conducted an audit of the Hotel Institute nor expressed any interest to do so in the future. This fine hands-off policy could be attributed to the fact that their sole contact with this New York-based agency was a man named George Denton who lived in Yonkers and evidently worked out of his home. Several times when Sherman called him the guy's wife or little child answered first.

Still there were problems. A federal program review last year put a wedge in the Hotel Institute's future, for their student loan default rate was eighty-nine percent (no doubt the statistic that triggered the review), and the auditors had turned red with anger and most of the staff fired immediately by Sherman out of self-preservation. The final determination was that the Hotel Career Institute owed the federal government over six million dollars in mishandled federal money plus fines. Sherman was inches from an indictment and spent most days on the phone talking to lawyers, some power outfit in Florida that specialized in this sort of thing and must be good, because the feds tried to close the school on the spot and here they were, one year later, throbbing along and still giving out federal loans. Sherman said openly that he counted on the slow wheels of justice when he and his friends first opened their schools. The man had balls.

His phone buzzed and he hit the button. "Yeah?"

"Chris," said Jeannine, "there's a girl out here interested in hotel management. You got time to see her?"

"Sure. What's her name?" He flipped open his appointment book. He had three prospects scheduled this afternoon and one at twelve, but the morning was clear. The majority of students simply walked in off the street. Chris never took lunch out of the building because of this.

"Gloria Rodriguez. She's a walk-in."

The name wasn't in his book. "Sure. Be out in a minute."

He stood before the full-length mirror on his door and checked his burnish-blond hair, straightened his tie, and smoothed the double-breasted jacket. He always looked like someone who managed the front counter of a hotel, the guy who made everybody else behind the counter hop. It impressed most of the zombies who came here.

The girl sat in the lobby. The vinyl on her chair was splitting badly, but she didn't seem to mind. Probably had furniture just like it at home.

"Hello there," he said and flashed his best. "I'm Chris Maloney. Call me Chris."

She smiled. "Hallo. Me llamo Gloria Rodriguez."

"Very pleased to meet you."

She looked about twenty-eight. She *was* cute, but she had pigeonholed herself right off with her blue jeans and white fringed cowboy boots, red satin shirt, and white vest that didn't come with the boots but looked like she might get away with it. Her black hair was tied back in a ponytail, and little curly bangs fell uniformly above her brows. It was hardly the clothes for a career in hotel management, but at the Hotel Institute this wasn't uncommon. Few people dressed up to come here, and many who did misfired this way: dressing up to them meant Saturday night. This woman belonged at the bar of a honkytonk.

"Do you speak English?"

"¿Como esta?" Ms. Rodriguez looked terribly embarrassed. "I speak little," she apologized in a thick accent. She must be right off the boat.

"It's fine, don't worry. Me llamo Chris. Why don't you come back to my office with me?"

"Yes!"

But she didn't move. She sat and smiled. He began to coax with approximate rowing motions of both arms. "Come, come." Behind the desk Jeannine snorted. Well, if Ms. Rodriguez had any deniro he'd ream Jeannine out later. The mutt finally understood and got to her feet. She hefted a large canvas tote bag with JC Penney printed on it.

"This way," he said. "This … this way-o."

The only décor in Chris' office was a poster tacked to the wall. It pictured a seagull flying against the sun, and the script below it read IT TAKES MANY PEBBLES TO MAKE A BEACH. It had been left by one of his predecessors, and Chris didn't know what the hell it meant. "Please have a seat."

"Yes!" She nodded eagerly and sat, clutching the big canvas tote bag.

"Well, let's talk the hotel program, shall we? Now Gloria, if I speak too fast you have to let me know."

"Yes!" She beamed like a child.

"Where do you live?"

"Philly."

"Where about?"

"¿Que?"

He said slowly, "Your *address*. Where do you *live?*"

"Oh! Lycoming Street." She pronounced it very distinctly.

"In Hunting Park?"

"Si. Hawnting Park!"

Chris nodded. A lot of HCI applicants hailed from Hunting Park. It was a North Philly neighborhood with a lethal mix of minorities, and famous for its drug problems. "And you're interested in our hotel program?"

"¡Si! Hotels!"

He picked up a catalog and handed it to her. "Let's see what the program is about."

The catalog was eight typewritten pages photocopied so often the words looked waterlogged. Again, Maloney was saved by the stupidity factor. Kids applying here never questioned the crappy handouts. There was never a need to apologize.

"Hotels are for the rich," he said. "You'll be hobnobbing with society's best. Society?" He looked at her inquiringly.

Gloria nodded. "Yes!"

"We'll train you to handle credit cards, cash registers, show you how to make reservations, handle big conventions and conferences, the whole bit. You'll be qualified to work in the finest hotels, like the Ritz-Carlton, Four Seasons, the Warwick, the Sheraton. Philadelphia is loaded with hotels, and each offers the enterprising student many great career opportunities."

"Yes, I know this! ¡No puedo esperar!"

He laughed at her excitement, then began to describe the program. Gloria would receive her certificate in nine months. As originally accredited years ago (and he did not tell her this), the program required two years to complete, including an affiliation during the second year where the student was supposed to work for experience at a regular city hotel. But since no hotel in Philadelphia would hire any of these birds, that part of the program had been quietly eliminated. Old George Denton in Yonkers didn't seem to mind, as long as his agency got their ten thou a year.

"¡O esto es grandioso!" she squeaked. "I am so exciting. I am so exciting to be here!" She wrung little hands. Maloney laughed appreciatively, for the girl knew she was cute, she wrinkled her nose at him and giggled.

"Terrific. Since that's the case, I'm going to take you to the financial aid office, and our man there will show you how to pay for this."

"Yes! ¡Gracias!"

This was called one-stop shopping. He never let them get away without a trip to the financial aid office. Virtually all applicants qualified for the maximum $2,625 Stafford Loan and $2,340 Pell Grant. Tuition had been scaled to meet this, at $4,965. Students never had to pay a dime. Because the Hotel Career Institute did such high volume business (eighteen class starts a year!), the low tuition was more than compensated.

Maloney took Gloria to another office where a man sat punching numbers into an adding machine. "Gloria, this is our financial aid expert, Mike Powell. Mike will show you how to pay for your program."

"Oh gracias! Hallo, Mike!"

Maloney didn't like Powell, who was twenty-seven, obnoxious, and from New York. His hair was a towering pompadour, his baggy jackets somehow always looked right. Maloney resented how the girls in the office cooed over him, even though he himself had no interest in office girls. Mike, despite a wife who called all the time, sporadically dated the secretaries, and once in a while took out a student. Sherman didn't seem to mind. "Don't get 'em pregnant," was his fatherly advice. Maloney knew before they walked in that Mike would go for Gloria straight off and the bastard did, grinning like a rodent and actually standing up as he was introduced. "Sure," he said. "Have a seat, Gloria. We'll get you squared away."

Maloney propped himself in a corner. He did this with all his applicants. He would not have a sale spoiled by this clown's reckless conceit.

It was a little painstaking, taking Gloria through the forms. There were a lot of questions, but Mike was more than happy to go through them one by one, and the girl sat childishly with her knees and white boots tight together, hugging the tote bag on her lap, gazing with doe-eyed wonder as the aid director completed the form for her. There was no way she'd last nine months at this place without him getting in her pants. Mike used his computer to calculate her eligibility, then brashly announced that she could receive a total of $4,965 in financial aid.

Gloria's eyes fluttered wide. "That is a lot of money! Is it all for me?"

"Well, it's to pay us. But yes, technically it's your money."

"¡Padro Santo! ¡Nunca tuve tanto en mi vida!" She looked at Mike in awe. He smiled roguishly and winked. From his corner, Maloney coughed to get things rolling again.

"What is this?" she asked, pointing to a line on the aid application.

"That's nothing," said Mike. "You're supposed to put your driver's license number there. But we can work around that."

"Oh! I have got that!" She opened the big tote bag and started rummaging.

"It's not a big deal." Mike waved magnanimously. "Don't worry about it."

But with stubborn ignorance Gloria Rodriguez continued to search through her large bag. She set it on the floor before her and leaned forward to dig into it. "No, no, no. I know I have it. It is here somewhere."

"It's not that impor—" Mike's voice died away as he stared down the open V-neck of her red blouse. From the way his eyes enlarged and his body checked, Chris could tell the financial aid officer was impressed by the view.

"It is here, I know it." Gloria practically put her head in the bag. "Ah, ah! Here it is!" She pulled out a black wallet and waved it.

"Good," Mike said, and reached for it. But Gloria kept the wallet, opened it, and happily jotted down the number herself.

"I know I could find it," she said.

"Sure. You'll be a first-rate hotel manager."

Gloria signed the application with Mike's help, then he took it from her and said, "We'll put it in the mail for you. Save you a stamp. Another service we provide here."

Chris asked, "Is that it then?"

"That's it. For now."

Maloney tugged gently on Gloria's arm until she understood that it was time to leave. "Good-bye, Mike," she breathed over her shoulder as she was pulled out of the office.

"Adios," said Mike, who watched the doorway long after she was gone.

Back in his own office, Chris seated her and said, "Now the last thing, Gloria, is a deposit."

"¿Que?"

"De-poz-zit. Ten dollars to hold your seat in class."

She looked confused. "Ten dollar?"

"Yes. It's important, because classes fill up all the time and you don't want to be bumped to a later one."

"No, no, no," she said. "I do not want this, this is for sure." She opened her tote bag and rummaged through again, making the same clattering noises as before.

Chris leaned back in his chair and waited. He gradually became aware that several minutes were passing. Gloria's face as she searched grew perplexed, then whitened with panic. "Oh no!" she exclaimed. "Oh no!"

The front legs of Chris' chair hit the floor. "What's wrong, Gloria?"

"¡Jesus, ayu dame! ¡Mi cartera no esta!"

"Gloria, wait—what? Can you say it in English?" He leaned forward imploringly.

She looked terribly shaken. "Mi cartera—my … my wallet. My wallet is not here!"

"Your wallet?"

"¡Si! ¡Recuerdo haberla puesto aqui antes de irme—!"

"Okay, wait a minute, honey. Just hang on. Maybe you left it in Mike's office when you took all that stuff out."

"¿Que?" She looked at him, scared and obviously not even listening.

He smiled confidently and stood. "Wait here, Gloria. I bet I know where it is."

He went back to the financial aid office and found Mike leafing through *Rolling Stone*. "What's up?" he asked. Chris ignored him, looked at the desk top, then down at the floor near the client chair. A black wallet rested on the carpet. He picked it up.

"The lady dropped something," he said with a grin.

Back in his office, he held up the wallet. "Is this yours?"

"¡O gracias! ¡Mucho gracias!" Gloria giggled and jumped to her feet. With a suddenness that took Chris by surprise, she reached up and kissed his cheek.

"Well," he said. "That's reward enough."

She fished out ten dollars and gave it to him. He didn't bother with a receipt and she didn't know to ask for one. She shouldered her bag and he escorted her out to the lobby, and just to bug the shit out of Mike he took her arm. And Mike saw too, for the aid director had strategically stationed himself at the receptionist's desk, supposedly to chat with Jeannine but really to smile and wave good-bye as Gloria swished past.

"Thank you all so much," she said. "I am so exciting!"

"Yes, you are," said Mike. And then she was gone.

The two men walked back to their offices. Out of Jeannine's earshot, Mike whispered, "Shit, if that's what they're breeding in Hunting Park I may have to move there."

Maloney said angrily, "You copy her phone number off the aid app yet?"

"No, but I know it's there."

"Take it easy."

"Did you see those mams when she leaned over like that? Like a pair of soccer balls hanging in a net."

Chris made it a growl this time. "Take it easy."

"Sure. Don't worry. We just haven't had a piece like that stroll through here in ages."

Maloney left the idiot and entered his office. So far it was an excellent morning. A couple more walk-ins and he'd be finished the September class.

And three *scheduled* appointments this afternoon. Not bad at all. That fucking Mike though. Chris had to speak to Sherman about him. You couldn't run a successful business with such immaturity risking the pitch.

He reached compulsively for his appointment book to check the names of those afternoon interviews. His hand grasped empty air. He looked. It wasn't on the desk. What did it do, fall off? He stood up and walked around the desk. It wasn't on the floor. It wasn't under the desk either. Truly puzzled, he stepped out to the hallway and glanced at Mike's office, but there was no reason for Mike or Jeannine to want his book. And the other two reps, Chuck and Helen, thought appointments books were stupid, and Chuck wasn't even in now, he preferred to stay late and do evening hours. So what ...?

Chris went back to his office and looked around again, but the book wasn't there. A nervous tremor pulled at his stomach. Christ, he'd better find that book and fast. It had all his appointments in it for the next four weeks!

43

On September 10 the Burr College sat four hundred and seventy-eight students. Once again congratulations poured in. Julie's phone wouldn't stop ringing. The Philadelphia school was only one of two Burr Colleges to make the September goal; Atlanta was the other, a tiny school with much smaller enrollment expectations. Up and down the East Coast school directors, admissions directors and deans called to give their blessings, some a little jealously, but none with any malice. The President's Office called several times. Oliver received two elated calls before the morning was out, one from Bill Nostrand, the other from John Coyne. Lily received calls from these men as well, and only Julie at the front desk knew that their calls to Oliver followed the calls to the admissions director.

It was the biggest enrollment for any one sit in Philadelphia history. On Orientation Day there was a shortage of chairs in the student lounge. Many students stood, and some half-sat on the edges of crowded cafeteria tables. They listened, enraptured, as the dean gave her "birth of a diploma" speech. Afterward these new students stormed the stairs and corridors, they jammed and shouted in the locker room, and the staff and faculty looked on, stunned by such a sea of faces. The classrooms, with their colonial smallness, became tangled by the additional desks and chairs. The bookstore didn't have enough texts or supplies, for the cynical President's Office had been caught unawares. Of course Andy Abrams hastily ordered more of everything, but couldn't promise an arrival date. To Louise's growls he merely said, "Hey, congats on the big class!" No one wanted to deal with bad news.

A party started in Lily's office immediately after Orientation. "To the cruise!" she cried and drained her bubbling glass. Perched on the front of her desk, dressed in a purple sequined blouse and tight mini, Lily was all teeth, sparkles and bare legs. "To sunny Caribbean skies and obsequious cabana boys! To moonlit nights and baking sand! Ha! Ha! Ha!" The whole staff was there, crowding the admissions director's office until it felt like a closet. A large case of champagne rested beside the snack table, a gift from Oliver. Lily waved her plastic glass and Marty jumped to refill it.

The mood between reps and department heads was marked. While Lily's staff laughed and chattered like children, Louise Mallory tucked herself in a corner and spoke to no one, and Ethel Harris grudgingly shook hands and smiled stiffly, as if bravely enduring an attack of gas. Louise watched with admiration as the dean managed to drink one glass of champagne and sneak out. Of all the department heads, only Clara Peterson was able to show any real enthusiasm, though it was hard to tell whether her pleasure was over Admissions' triumph or the presence of the champagne. She squeezed her plump body into one of the client chairs, and from this centralized position was able to find plenty of people to keep her glass topped up.

Deirdre poured for Trudy who sat on the love seat. Champagne spilled over the rim of the senior rep's glass and she shifted fast to keep it from hitting her skirt. She giggled, "*When*, Dee!"

"No!" barked Lily. "You take that back! I don't want anybody saying 'when' today!"

"Lily, you're gonna fall off," said Marty. He grabbed her elbow to hold her steady, for the admissions director was rocking wildly, seated on the front edge of her desk.

"I'm fine, sweetie. Your glass is empty. Shame on you! Fill it up! This is one day we *don't* have to telemarket! Ha! Ha!" She leaned far forward and said to Trudy and Deirdre, "Sweethearts, we did it! I told you we would! I've never missed a goal in my life! You are both my daughters and I love you!"

Hidden in her corner, Louise held a glass of champagne and kept her eyes on Lily. The admissions director's face was bright red. Her gold earrings were long vertical bars that tinkled like wind chimes. When someone said something funny she roared with laughter, throwing back her head and lifting her knees so that her feet pedaled the air. She talked faster, drank faster, and laughed harder than anybody, and kept flashing her glass and beckoning the others to drink up. People glanced at Louise's sour face and did not speak to her. The party carried on despite her.

"So who was the hardest?" Lily yelled at her staff. "Who was hardest? Hey? Who caused the most grief?"

"Those sonofabitch homeless people," said Marty.

"That Vicki Kaminsky girl who put me off for months," said Trudy.

Deirdre said, "Or that girl who—"

"I'll tell you the *weirdest* one," said Lily. "That one girl, the one who came all the way in from Ocean City, that Laverne or Lavonia—" She snapped her fingers rapidly.

"Laurel Springer," said Deirdre.

"Right. Laurel Springer. I keep thinking she's black and she's not. Anyway, we got her deposit, signed her up, everything, and then Mom calls." Lily held an invisible phone to her ear. "Mom wants to know—the kid's fine, mind you, she can't wait to start—Mom wants to know what kind of jobs Burr girls get when they graduate. So I tell her about high salaries, big-shot companies, the whole spiel, and she interrupts me. It seems her daughter is very delicate. She can't work a job that might require her to stand for long periods of time. So I tell her how secretaries traditionally sit behind desks. Well, Mom has a problem with that too. She doesn't think her daughter should sit long either."

Clara asked, "Goodness, what's wrong with her?"

"Christ knows! Well, the whole time I'm reassuring Mom I'm thinking that the girl can't work standing and she can't work sitting. All that's left is for her to lie on her back, and I don't think Burr is placing girls in *that* profession, at least not yet, hey? Ha! Ha! Ha!" Her body careened back and forth on the desk, and her purple stilettos nearly gouged Clara in the face.

"Jesus," said Marty. He grabbed Lily's arm with one hand, cupped her knee with the other, and held her steady. "You've got to watch yourself, Lily."

"Darling, we've *all* got to watch ourselves. Ain't nobody gonna do it for us." She grabbed her personal bottle of champagne which was beside her. Although she was now sitting upright, Marty kept his hand on her knee.

Oliver wormed his way into Lily's office, clutching a large envelope. Lily gestured. "Oliver! Right here! Come right here!" Marty hesitated, then relinquished his place by Lily's side for the school director. Lily laughed and slipped her arm around Oliver's waist.

With a fatherly smile he said, "Enjoying yourself?"

"Oh *Lord!* Oliver, it's only taken a year, right?"

"It's certainly taken a lot of hard work. This package just came from New York. It's addressed to you."

"Oh? Thanks! Boy, that was fast." She tore open the large envelope, and found three smaller ones within. She shuffled them like cards, reading each name. Then she grabbed her heavy stapler and rapped the desk until the room quieted.

"Hey guys! Hey! Stop gulping a moment, 'kay? Little announcement here, and then a toast. Fill your glasses." Lily topped her own from the bottle by her side. "We have made goal today—no, please! *Please!*" She grinned and waited for the clapping to stop. "Don't interrupt so much, 'kay? You'll make this short announcement into a long one.

"Like I said, we have made goal with six to spare—" More applause. "—and we have achieved the biggest class in Philadelphia history—" More applause. "—and we have the best fucking Admissions staff in the whole goddamn system!" Wild cheers. "Pardon my French! No other school made goal except Atlanta, and we know how tiny they are so I don't think they even count. At any rate, they'll be sharing the staff improvement seminar with us, but *nobody else is,* and that news rings like the Hallelujah Chorus in my head!" Loud laughter.

Julie appeared in the doorway. She peered in with concern, but didn't try to enter. Oliver saw her, and for the first time felt Lily's arm around him. He disengaged himself gently, and Lily didn't notice. "Okay," the admissions director said, "Oliver has just given me something very sweet. Thank you cards from Bill Nostrand. Just a token acknowledgment of work well done, but still sweet anyway. No—honeys, don't open them here. Take Bill's sentiments home and savor them." So the reps pocketed the envelopes. Trudy's held a check for $800, Dee's for $560, but the big payout was Marty's for $1,650. Lily had arranged a bonus system with Bill Nostrand months ago without bothering to inform Oliver. Commissions to college admissions reps were illegal, and both she and Bill agreed that it just seemed easier to keep the school director out of it.

"Congratulations, you silver-tongued geniuses!" Lily cheered. "You really *are* the best fucking admissions team, and I don't care if you pardon my French or not! Ha! Ha! Ha!"

More cheers. Glasses waved. Furniture arms were pounded.

"So now," she sang, holding her glass high like Liberty's torch, "I would like to make a toast! To our magnificent school director, Dr. Oliver Dunbar!"

"What?" Oliver was startled. "Me?"

"We couldn't have done it without you, Oliver. Your vision of educational quality gave us the fodder we needed to attract all these students to Burr. Your management style fired our inspiration and carried us along this great, difficult road. Every person in this room is indebted to you."

"But Lily," he protested with a sheepish grin, "I never did anything. I pretty much kept out of your way."

She raised her glass to him. "Cheers."

Everyone drank, and Julie took the moment to make her way to Oliver's side. She tiptoed to whisper in his ear, "Bill Nostrand's holding for you."

"Again? Okay, thanks." Oliver put down his glass and started to work his way out of the office.

"See that, Oliver?" the admissions director shouted. "Now that you're a success the big brass won't leave you alone!"

"They didn't leave me alone before." He squeezed out the door and looked back at them all, at the happiest faces he had ever seen on an admissions staff. "Congratulations," he grinned. "You're all terrific."

Julie tried to follow him out, but Trudy trapped her in a hug. The rep's face was pink and hot, her eyes a little crazy. "Jule, we did it!"

Julie smiled and gently pulled free. "Congrats, Tru."

"Gosh, thanks! Here, take a glass!"

"No, I still have to man the front desk."

"One glass, please! You're a part of this too. We all know that."

"How true," caroled Lily from the desk. "This place would die without you, dear!"

Julie accepted a glass and took it with her to the lobby, feeling vaguely depressed.

In his own office with the door shut, Oliver hit the lit button. "Bill?"

"Oliver, it's me again!"

"What can I do for you?"

"Well, you and Atlanta have already done enough, but everybody knows that. Sounds like you're having a little bash there."

"Oh, can you hear it? I've got the door closed."

"I heard when I was speaking to the receptionist. It's fine, they all deserve it. Wish I could say things were as cheerful up here."

"Are we really that bad across the board?"

"It's unbelievable. I don't think I've ever seen such incompetence in my life." Suddenly Bill sounded a lot more familiar.

"I'm sorry to hear it."

"Well, aren't we all? Miami is short thirty percent, Memphis missed by fifteen. New York is hurting bad at forty percent and we don't know why; those numbers stayed high throughout the summer, then suddenly melted. Both Boston and New Haven are down ten percent, as well as Wilmington and New Orleans. Washington's not as bad, just under three percent of goal, but under three is still negative revenue no matter how you slice it." He paused. The silence lengthened. Oliver wondered if Nostrand's own job was on the line. Previous vice-presidents had been fired by Coyne over sits less damaging than this.

"Is there anything I can do, Bill?"

"Hell no. Listen, I didn't phone to cast a pall on your happy day. I want to update you on some items I think you're going to like. Now get this …"

After the toast for Oliver, Louise stirred herself and ducked out of Lily's office. As she passed through the cubicles toward her own, she noticed Ethel Harris sitting in Deirdre's old station. She watched in amazement, for Ethel was doing the unthinkable—rummaging through the drawers of a file cabinet and flipping through Admissions folders.

"Hi. Isn't there a dictum against Education snooping in Admissions?"

Ethel nodded, reading a test score with wide eyes.

"And didn't you tell your teachers this is a no-no?"

"Well, Jean's the only one who does it. Look at this test score, Louise. Thirty-three points out of a potential one hundred. Passing is seventy. Thirty-three isn't even failing. It's failing *cum laude.*"

"Is she accepted? Oh, what am I saying?"

"Certainly she's accepted. And it's illegal. You can't accept a student who fails your admissions test. The test is our accreditation standard. Jean told me about this, and I still kept out of it. I chewed her out for looking, and in my heart I figured she was exaggerating. You know Jean."

"Most of us do. Are these the kids we just sat?"

"Yes. Every one of them was downstairs at Orientation this morning. Did you see them?"

Louise nodded. "Where do you think I've been? The bookstore was hell. Those new kids don't understand the concept of waiting in a line."

"They're the worst-looking kids we've ever had."

"Well, we knew what was going down. How surprised can you be?"

"Maybe. I certainly didn't think it was this bad." There was more pain than anger in the dean's voice. "Look at these essays. I'm not finding a single coherent sentence. And the math scores are appalling. Lily did nothing short of scamming to bring them in."

"A serious charge, that."

"And you know it's true." Ethel slipped the file back in the drawer. "Thirty-three points out of a hundred. We'd better all be damn worried."

"Is that kid ability to benefit?"

"No, that test has to be proctored by an outside party. Looks like Lily's trying to duck that. But this kid is going to take the ATB test before I'm through."

"Telling Oliver?"

"No, I'm telling Abby DeSalvo, executive dean in New York. It doesn't do any good to tell Oliver anything, and you know how I hate to say that."

"Hey, if it's true, it's true." Louise's small shoulders shrugged.

"I'll tell him I'm speaking to Abby, but that's it." Ethel pulled the next file. "Oh look, this one scored fifty-eight out of a hundred. And has a high school GPA of 1.70. We've got a potential valedictorian here."

She dropped the file back and stood up. "I've got to tell Oliver whether he wants to hear it or not. I just don't know if I should do it while everyone is celebrating. I can't afford to have the whole school hating me."

"Why not? The whole school hates me, and it's kind of fun."

As if on cue, a burst of laughter erupted from the open door of Lily's office. Over a fresh round of hand-clapping they could hear the roller-coaster cackle of the admissions director. Ethel hunched angrily, and her nostrils flared.

"Lots of happiness in there," remarked Louise.

"God, I hate this." Ethel looked at Oliver's closed door. "Want to come in with me?"

"Sure."

They knocked on Oliver's door, but no one answered. "I know he's in," said Ethel. "I saw him when I was standing in Deirdre's cubicle."

"He probably can't hear you over this."

Ethel pounded again. Lily's party drowned out everything. Finally the dean simply turned the knob. Oliver sat at his desk, on the phone. He saw them and pointed to seats.

"Yes, Bill. Okay. I hope it all works out for everybody. And thanks again. I know they'll be thrilled. Good-bye." He hung up, and looked at the two women who remained standing. "What's up?"

"You gave a speech at Orientation today," said Ethel. "You saw the new crowd. You tell *me* what's up."

"Okay, I know. Frankly, they were a shock to me too."

"Well, that's what you get, Oliver, for not monitoring your Admissions Office."

The old tiredness crept back in his face. "Ethel, it's not that simple. I *never* monitor the Admissions Office. I don't monitor yours either. When you hire a professional for a job, you have to give them their space."

"We're not talking *space!* We're talking street people. We're talking some mean-looking girls sitting in that new class."

"And we'll teach them," Oliver said with firm conviction. "It's going to be hard, maybe harder than it's ever been, but we'll do all we can for them. I don't believe Lily's done anything wrong by accepting them. I'm sure they weren't what she wanted either. She hasn't committed any crimes worse than what the rest of us have."

"What do you mean by that?"

"All those September kids who will return next Monday to start their second year, that we put on academic probation when we both knew they should have been dismissed. That wasn't Lily's doing, that was you and me."

"But we had to."

"So what?"

Ethel's hostility lost its edge. "Well, at least we did it to try to help them."

"No, we were thinking about ourselves, mainly. We couldn't afford to lose so many from the class."

Ethel felt her anger brought up short. She didn't want to be thwarted by Dunbarian candor. "Dammit, what I faced this morning was the worst class in the history of this school. July and September are always our best sits, the best kids, the quality!"

"Yes, I know."

"Then what the hell were those people doing in that lounge today? *Don't* tell me they all passed the admissions exam. *Don't* tell me Lily isn't doing something wrong. A few in the back looked like the window light was blinding them, like they're not used to sunlight. They kept putting their hands over their eyes."

"Don't be ridiculous, Eth."

"Screw you, Oliver! Did you see the faces on the few *good* students? They looked scared to death to be sitting next to those others."

He steadfastly met her eye. "We'll take care of it. Incidentally, I just had a wonderful conversation with Bill Nostrand."

"Did you really? How marvelous!" The dean looked ready to spit on him.

"He's thrilled to death by this sit."

"Great. Do you think I give a damn about impressing a weasel like Bill Nostrand?"

"And he said you can now rehire yourself a secretary."

Silence.

Ethel's mouth hung open in mid-word. Oliver watched her with a sly smile.

She muttered, "Well, that's nice, of course. But I don't want a secretary at the expense of these students. They've been duped into coming. We've become exactly the type of institution we've scoffed at all these years. We're another Stanley School, for God's sake. One of the infamous dregs of post-secondary education. Who'd have thought you, of all people, would let that happen?"

"He also said that because we made both the July and September goals, you can now put in a capital request for the new computer equipment and he'll approve it."

Another, much deeper silence. Ethel held her breath. Off to one side, Louise smirked at her.

The dean asked, "He really said that?"

"Just now. That's what this phone call was about. Said you should advertise in the paper right away for a secretary, and write up what you want for the classrooms. I'm to take it to New York when I go to the November budget meeting. Keep it reasonable, he said, and he'll approve it."

"Shit," said Ethel.

"It's a real lesson in how the world operates, isn't it? Have a seat, both of you."

Ethel took a chair. Oliver put his hands behind his head and watched her with a bemused smile. Only Louise remained standing.

"Anything for the long-suffering business manager?" she asked.

"Louise, I'm not even sure Bill knows what the business managers do. But as long as he was in a generous mood I took a plunge for you. I didn't ask about the walls; I really didn't think that would go over. But I tried for something else that I know you've always wanted."

"Not the bookstore manager?" gasped Louise.

"Bill said yes. Go ahead, put an ad in the paper. We can now afford it."

Another burst of applause resounded from beyond the wall. Both women stared at Oliver in disbelief.

"Ladies," he said, and spread his hands wide, "welcome to prosperity."

On the Corner of Cambria

44

AMELIA ALBRETTI THUMBTACKED a poster to the bulletin board near the second floor staircase. It was eight-thirty on the first day back for the September two-year students, and she wasn't wasting any time. The poster afforded a cutout magazine photograph of wild ponies running through a green meadow, and the block-letter caption underneath declared DON'T CHANGE HORSES! *Vote Amelia Albretti for Student Council President!* The poster bore Julie Fitzgerald's initials, which authorized the student's right to hang it up. Jennifer DeAngelis stood nearby, passing out blue fliers as girls swarmed past.

"Re-elect Amelia," she shouted happily. "Go with Albretti, she's done it already! Go with Albretti, she's done it already!"

The second floor corridor clamored with dense traffic. New and old students eyed each other with mild suspicion. The staggered program starts throughout the year tended to isolate each class, and the returning September students viewed the new Julys as interlopers on their own familiar turf. The Julys, already on the premises for two months, viewed the returning Septembers much the same way.

"God," said Amelia. "Look at this place. When did the hallways get so packed?"

Jennifer looked dour. "Can't say I like the new class. There are a lot more—" she leaned close and whispered, *"black* students here, did you notice?"

Amelia nodded absently, watching the crowd for familiar faces. They went to the third floor to hang more posters. Amelia was running this campaign with the same aggressiveness that showed in her schoolwork, where she was one of the tops in her class. She tacked another poster on a bulletin board so that it overlapped by two inches a sign for yearbook volunteers.

"Hey guys! Amelia! Hello!"

"Karen!" they both cried. Karen Louden ran up and kissed them both. Karen's face was thinner, and her short blond hair had bleached white over the summer. She popped gum with quick motions of her long jaw.

"God, Kare," gasped Jennifer. "Look at your tan! You're beautiful! Did you even go inside this summer?"

"Not if I could help it. Avalon was great. You both look wonderful. Hey, have you seen some of these new girls?" Karen crossed her eyes. "I mean, I can't believe they let some of them in the school."

"We were talking about that." Amelia glanced down the hall, and pitched her voice low. "In fact, look at that one."

A washed-out redhead none of them knew appeared at the top of the stairs and trudged past, heading toward the bookstore. She was sleepy-eyed, with a willowy body that moved in a gloomy haze all its own, perhaps explained by the unhealthy bulk pushing under the hiked belt of her dress.

"Jesus," Amelia said, then quickly crossed herself.

"I guess she's learning for two," whispered Karen.

Jennifer giggled nervously. "How old do you think she is?"

"Old enough for somebody," Amelia said with deep disapproval. And because her mother was an obstetrician, she said importantly, "It's not set good either. It'll never get through her hips."

In the bookstore, Louise Mallory was on a rampage. She hated first days more than any other part of her job. There were locker assignments to give, new books and supplies to sell and distribute, and she didn't even try to hide her irritation. With no secretaries available to assist her, she shanghaied Deirdre Smith to help in the bookstore at the end of the third floor corridor. To make matters worse, the Septembers were returning simultaneously with the start of yet another Evening Accounting class plus a new Paralegal class. Boxes of books for all three programs lay piled in the hallway outside the store. Louise stood at the half-open Dutch door and squinted at Frances Page, a returning September student who was next in line. "What?"

"I came for—for ..." Most students withered before the business manager's glower, and Frances was no exception.

"For *what?*"

"I—my books."

"Why didn't you say so? You're holding up the line."

"I'm sorry. I only—"

Louise leaned past her and bellowed, "EVERYBODY FORM A SINGLE LINE! I'M NOT WAITING ON A MOB!" She grabbed an armload of books, tablets, and a ream of fake letterhead, and balanced it on the half-door. "That's two hundred and forty-two dollars."

"What is? I already paid for these."

"You did not."

"Back last year I did."

"That was for last year's books." Louise's magnified eyes slitted ominously. Every year she had this argument with the returning students. "The two hundred forty-two is for these books here." She whacked the pile with the flat of her hand.

"How come I wasn't told about this?"

"You *were* told about it. You got a notice last spring before you left on break, and another notice was sent to you in the mail."

"Well, I never got it."

"Well, I don't care. You can't have these books until you pay for them."

"But I don't have any money," said Frances, going into the standard student whine. "My parents are paying for everything."

"Then go tell your parents you need two hundred and forty-two dollars so you can get your books for the second year."

"You mean I can't get these books today? What about my classes?"

Louise lowered the books behind the door, in case Frances tried to grab them. "Think of this as yet another enriching academic experience. We'll call it Reality-101."

"Shit!"

Frances stormed off furiously. Louise watched her go with genuine satisfaction.

Deirdre called out, "D'ya know where the Third Edition Calculus books are stashed? This set doesn't have one." She was making sets of supplies and books to help the purchasing move faster. "We're also getting low on steno pads."

"Look in that box behind the overhead projector." Louise faced two girls who stood side by side at the Dutch door. "What do you want?"

"We need books," said one.

"Yeah," said the other.

Louise didn't recognize either of them. "What program are you? Accounting or Paralegal?"

Both girls' hair stood up in vertical coils, and one's was dyed orange. Enormous gold loops swung from earlobes stretched by the weight, and a small ring protruded from a crusted puncture hole in the tongue of the girl with orange hair. "We're paralegals," she announced happily.

The phone rang and Deirdre answered it. "Louise, Julie's on the extension."

"So what?"

"Emma Jones is at the front desk. Says her locker won't open."

"Well, I can't fix it now."

"I told her that. But Julie says the student wants to talk to you anyway. She doesn't know where to put her books."

"Christ!" The business manager banged open the Dutch door. "Man the fort, Dee. I have to grab the crowbar out of my desk." She cleaved an angry path through the crowd of students.

Deirdre got the books for the two paralegals. From her vantage at the Dutch door she saw that the line of waiting students stretched the length of the corridor. She hoped they would all be patient with her.

The next student stepped to the door. She was slight of build, with a narrow head embedded in a distinctive cloud of puffy dark gray hair. She wore a white button-down shirt and simple blue skirt, about as plain an out-fit as a student could get away with and still meet the dress code. She said, "Hey there."

"Hi," said Deirdre.

"Looks crazy back here."

"It *is* crazy." The admissions rep rolled her eyes. "Who are you?"

"Stephanie Homan. I live on Naudain Street. You live in the city too?"

"No, I meant—what program are you?"

"Second year Executive Secretarial Arts. What's wrong with your eye?"

"My uh … my eye?"

"Yeah. Somebody hit you?"

"No." Yet Deirdre's hand flicked up, covering her right eye. This gray-haired kid was sharp. Deirdre had thought her make up hid the bruise.

"I know a couple guys'd be more than willing to straighten out who-ever did that."

"No thanks." Deirdre laughed uneasily. She stepped back to collect the books for this student, and felt depressed and anxious, depressed because of her situation with Denny, who *had* hit her the other night in his apartment, and anxious because this student seemed kind of creepy. Deirdre brought the books to the Dutch door. "That's two hundred and forty-two dollars."

"Okay." The student reached into an enormous vinyl pocketbook, but instead of pulling out a purse or checkbook she removed a small red object and flipped the top end of it with her thumb. Deirdre assumed it was a cigarette lighter, then realized it was a Pez dispenser with the grinning head of Bill Clinton. "Want one?"

"Huh? No thanks. God, I haven't had Pez since I was a kid."

"I've got about three hundred of these. Greatest pop icon of the Twentieth Century."

Deirdre tapped the books. "Two hundred and forty-two."

"Sure." The student reached into her pocketbook again. "Say, does Ms. Mallory really keep a crowbar in her desk?"

"Yeah. And a small hand-ax too, which she swears is only there in case of fire." Deirdre looked past her at the line, which seemed longer than ever.

The student handed over the check. "Lemme know if you want something done about that eye. Nice meeting you."

"Uh-huh."

The impact of the new class hit Donna Harding first by its size. Average classes ran to twenty students. The small rooms in the two-hundred-year-old mansion couldn't accommodate more. Now she was faced suddenly with a classroom of thirty to thirty-five students. Everybody had to bunch up, and their chairs with pallets attached kept tangling together. The second thing to strike Donna was, of course, the students themselves. She had never confronted so many poorly dressed students in one class. Many wore jeans and T-shirts, totally against the dress code. And so many were black. Not that she was prejudiced, of course, but ... but it was still a shock. The sullen faces turned toward her were bleak with ignorance, and one or two rocked in their chairs as if such motion was necessary for their circulation. Donna stood by the front desk feeling like a nervous beginner, and she had been teaching for over nine years.

"Okay, this is Professional Development. In this class we'll be talking about your professional image and behavior. Office etiquette, proper clothing style, make up, all of it. You need to develop a positive work ethic that will carry you through the worst pressures and indignations that a boss can throw at you. And they'll throw you some doozies too. For example, how many of you would be willing to work late to finish an important pending project?"

Most hands went up. A few raised theirs after seeing how many of their classmates did.

"Good. Because businesses will expect it. It doesn't matter if office hours are nine to five. Even the kindest boss knows that the work comes first."

Faces stared at her. Donna let her voice ring with a cheer she did not feel. "Now, what would you do if the boss expected more of you than what was on your job description? For example," and she pointed to a student on the first row, "what would you do if your boss expected you to complete a statistical report that *he* should do, but he just drops the assignment in your work basket because you've been around long enough and he knows he can dump it on you. What would you do?"

The student glared at Donna, resentful at having been singled out. She wore a cheap denim dress, and her fingers were covered with Band-Aids. "I'd tell the fucker to stick it up his ass."

Donna stared at the student in horror. The rest of the class howled joyfully. "Well," she said, and wet her lips, "although I'm sure we'd all feel like using those same words, that's not the proper response you should give."

"I don't care," said the student. "That's just what I'd tell him."

"Well, that won't work in an office. You never show anger before a boss. You take it on the chin, then maybe go into the bathroom and kick the wall or something. Then you come back out all smiling and professional again as if nothing—"

An unrelated burst of laughter issued from the back of the classroom.

"Can we have a little more decorum, please?" Donna said, craning her neck to be heard. She couldn't see anything, there were so many students shoved together.

"More what?" someone asked incredulously.

"Please be quiet," said Donna. "Everybody, open *Office Procedures* to Chapter One."

The class did with an incredible amount of bumps, thuds, and low mutterings. Donna's voice trembled with growing indignation as she started to read out loud. *"In an office environment the administrative assistant plays a key role in the daily management of his or her department. Client contact, organization and efficiency, are critical in the functioning of any office. Bosses and supervisors of both small and large companies rely on specialized support employees to maintain calendars, take minutes at meetings, present the company to clients with polish and courtesy—"'*

"Yeah, right," someone muttered, and the class laughed.

"No talking," said Donna. "This is important, people. It doesn't matter what skills you learn over the course of this program if you don't possess a professional attitude. No office will hire you without a proper presentation of yourself both in appearance and in behavior—"

"Unless you got big tits," said a voice, and the class roared.

"All right!" said Donna sharply. "That's enough. That's exactly what I'm talking about. In this classroom we don't use language like that. Okay? I like to have fun too, but not in an irresponsible manner." She winced and raised her voice high. "And can we *please* have it quiet in the back of the room?"

The first day back was an interminable one for Bob Lawrence. He conducted his classes in a state of wracking suspense. He didn't want to run into Heather; he wasn't sure he had built up the nerve to break with her today. And heightening the suspense was the slim chance that he might not have to face her, for the schedule called for him to teach her section of the returning Septembers on Tuesdays and Thursdays, and this was Monday. Unless he and Heather crossed paths in the hall there stood a good chance of his not seeing her. Of course, this was just one day's grace, and he would still have to call her tonight. But another innocuous phone call was safe to the point of tenderness compared to a personal confrontation.

He almost made it. When the bell sounded the end of his last class he dashed to the lounge, grabbed his briefcase, and ran down the hall. He waved a fast good night to Julie through the glass lobby doors and jogged outside. Old and new students were gathered in idle clumps along the sidewalk, but no Heather. God had let the dice roll his way. Thank you, thank you!

Bob started south on Sixth Street, heading for home. There she was, waiting for him by the first intersection. He cursed through a big smile and walked up to her.

"Hi, sweetie!"

"Heather, you shouldn't be doing this."

"Well, hello to you too."

They waited side by side for the light to change. "You know what I mean," he said. "We're in full view of everybody coming out of school. This is risky."

She laughed, and he thought with real fear that she might kiss him. He hadn't seen her since that shore visit in July and Heather had added to her tan. Her face looked golden, her eye shadow much less intense. Her black hair was noticeably longer, and she had stopped dying the tips green. She looked good.

"Bob, I already decided I was gonna do a little shopping on South Street. So we're just coincidentally walking in the same direction."

"All right. That's okay, I guess." The light changed, and they started across. "But don't do this again, you hear me? This is a one-time thing."

"Oh, I thought the summer would never end," she said gaily. "I can't believe how little I saw of you."

"Well, I had to teach through, you know."

"I know. But it was agony. Wasn't it for you? Didn't the summer just drag forever?"

"I got down for your birthday."

"Well, you *had* to visit me then. I wouldn't of forgiven you otherwise."

Her short gray dress flaunted shapely legs that kept pace easily with his nervous gait. Her face was flushed with careless joy, her long hair bouncing. Turning west on Lombard Street, they were far enough from the college for Heather to take his arm. Bob didn't know how to object, and felt an unwilling desire not to. There was status to having this beautiful creature on his arm. Philadelphia, eat your heart out.

"I can't believe I'll be able to see you every day again."

"Yeah."

"Oh, I want to do something special! Something *real* special! Don't you?"

"Well, Heath, it's your first day back. Aren't you a little tired?"

"Not one bit. I was thinking about this last night. We can go to your place, and I can make us dinner. That'd be great, huh? What do you have in the fridge?"

"No hamburger," he said. It was her specialty.

"Well, I'll come up with something. Or I'll run over to the Super Fresh. We can make a real evening of it. I can even stay over."

"Oh Christ. Heath, what will your parents think when you don't come home—"

"I'll call them. They won't care. They trust us."

And they did. He still couldn't get over it.

"Gee, Heather, I don't think so. Let's just—"

"Bob, why not?" She stared at him, and her grip on his arm tightened.

"Why not? Well, because … because …"

Because there were rules to this game. Because you didn't sleep with someone you planned to break with. It wasn't right, and they got pissed at you when they found out.

"Bob?"

"Well, I'm not really prepared, and the apartment's a mess."

"Oh, I don't care about that." She tugged his sleeve until he bent his head. She whispered in his ear, "Bob, can I ask you a real personal question?"

"Well, sure." Her pulling his face down directed his eye line to the lovely inward curve of her waist. His arm ached to slip around her.

"Bob …" She couldn't go on, and he was startled to see her blushing very deeply.

"What, honey?"

"I just …"

Heather's embarrassment was sincere enough to be cute, and he smiled. "What?"

"I wanted to know if …" She giggled and clung to his arm, buried her face in it.

He chuckled. "Honey, what's on your mind? You can tell me."

"Well, I was thinking about this last night too. I really want to do something *special*."

"Well, we can think of something. Maybe we should eat out." That would be better than taking her home. He might stay in control of this situation if they remained outside the apartment. He doubted he could if they went there.

"I guess we could." But her face fell. "I sort of had something else in mind."

"What's that?"

"Have you ever made love from behind?"

The question confused him. "Sure. Of course. We've done it that way ourselves any number of times."

"No, I mean … made love from behind. I mean … in a girl's behind."

Bob stopped walking.

Heather giggled nervously. She tried to measure the shock to his brain, and there was plenty of shock there.

"Heather, God—"

"Are you angry?"

"What? No, but uh …" He laughed weakly. "You've, uh, really started my heart pounding."

"Then have you?"

"No, I haven't. That is, if you're talking about … I mean … if you're talking about—" Good Christ, he couldn't say it. Not and look at that young face. A dignity which he normally took for granted slipped away, and he was suddenly a blundering schoolboy. "No, I never have."

Heather gripped his arm. "You gotta admit it'd be real special. Something to remember."

"Well, yeah, it would be that." He felt nerves snapping loose in his head, pinging against his skull. Dare he? With this kid?

"Please?"

Please. Good God. "Well, I just … I'm not sure it's even … well, doesn't it hurt? I've been told that—"

"Not if you're careful."

Ah!—some experience behind that answer. Heather's glowing face filled his vision, but he knew what the rest of her looked like. He had taken her from behind any number of times in the conventional way, and on those occasions Heather was just a beautiful functional object, shoulder blades flexing, spine arching, pear-shaped buttocks undulating against his groin. Just a wonderful fleshy surface with only a tousle of black hair and not a face to answer to. It was on the occasions when they made love this way that he truly felt he was getting all he needed from this whole sorry relationship.

Heather kissed his hand softly, then pressed it against her cheek. "Please, Bob. Let's."

"Heather, I … I just … well—"

Okay, so maybe tonight wasn't the best night to break up after all.

45

Beatrice Genovese started her job as financial aid director in the last week of September. Oliver greeted her initially, then passed her on to Lily who showed the new employee her office. Beatrice found herself staring at a desk full of financial aid applications, loan promissory notes, Student Aid Reports, and 1040 tax returns. The backlog dated to June, for after David Hurley quit no one bothered to do more than dump the financial aid mail on the desk. Still, Beatrice was undaunted. She didn't know anything about financial aid, so there was no way for her to measure how critical any of this was. Had she spoken to Louise she might have gotten a hint, for the business manager was going crazy trying to deal with students who hadn't paid a dime in months because their applications for federal aid had never been processed. Beatrice looked at the mountain of forms and shook her head in ignorant bliss.

Lana Kaufmann, the executive for financial aid, came down from New York and spent three days training her. She introduced Beatrice to the forms, taught her the complex methodology used to calculate eligibility, and showed her how to document the applicants' financial data in accordance with federal guidelines. She showed Beatrice what to look for on tax returns, how to submit Pell Grant batches, and walked her through the certification of loan applications. Beatrice found herself boggled over theories defining student dependency and independency, base-year income and current year income, how to extract custodial parent income from a tax return when the student's parents were divorced, and how to police untaxed income, assets, social security, child support payments, and AFDC. She finished the three days convinced she had bitten off more than she cared to chew. After Lana Kaufmann left she stormed into Lily's office.

"You must be crazy," she exclaimed. "This is the stupidest job I ever had in my life!"

"Really, dear?" The admissions director, darkly tanned from two weeks in the Hawaiian sun, gave her a pleasant but knowing smile. She motioned her to sit. "Beatrice, honey, I haven't met a financial aid director yet who didn't go on about how complicated her job was. As if the rest of us just sit on our butts reading *Cosmo.*"

"I don't care. I've pushed enough paper in my life to choke an elephant. I don't understand any of this regulatory crap and I don't want to learn."

"Well, that sounds normal to me. Dear, have you heard of something called 'professional judgment?'"

"Like in what way?"

"As an actual concept—something in financial aid that's legally called 'professional judgment.'"

"No. Well, I guess Lana mentioned it, but I don't know what it is."

"Let's talk a moment. Would you like some coffee?"

Lily hummed to herself as she fixed two mugs. She gave one to Beatrice, then returned to her desk and immediately took a sip from her own. "Did you know that in 1986 Congress mandated a power to financial aid directors called 'professional judgment?' Essentially, it gives you authority to change any aspect of a student's file so long as you feel the change is warranted. You have to document why you're making the change, but in principle you can do anything: increase the cost of attendance which would increase the student's financial need, decide not to include the parents' income, even change the federal formula which calculates eligibility. Just as long as it's documented. Did you know this?"

Beatrice studied the admissions director cautiously. "So what exactly does this mean?"

"Why, it means," Lily nearly rose out of her chair with joy, "that you have carte blanche manipulation of the entire financial aid laws and regulations!"

"You're saying I can do anything I want?"

"Yes! Just as long as the student gives you proof. But here's the great thing. In order for the concept of professional judgment to work, the determination of what is or isn't appropriate documentation has to be left to the aid director. Ha! Ha! Do you understand? You can get statements from the students, something in their handwriting with their signatures on it, and if in *your* professional judgment the statement is convincing, no auditor can legally argue against it!"

"You're kidding," Beatrice said. "That can't be what they mean. It's too damn easy."

"It's in the regs." Lily shrugged happily. "We used professional judgment at my old schools all the time, and I'm here to tell you it really helped a lot of kids get money when originally they weren't eligible."

"So how come Hurley wasn't doing this?"

Lily's good humor dimmed. She put her mug down with a thunk. "David had a lot of high-minded prejudices. Since I never agreed with them, I can't defend him. In your job, Beatrice, you can be a bureaucratic snob and tie up the process, or you can use the regs as leniently as possible to help the most kids get aid. David loved rules and process and didn't care about the kids. I want the rules to *help* our students, not hinder them."

"Well, sure. That makes sense." Beatrice chuckled and shook her head. "This is nuts. But what the hell, I'll take another look at that stuff."

Thanks to professional judgment, most of Beatrice's backlog swiftly melted away. One student was ineligible for aid because her parents earned over $130,000. Beatrice told her to write a note that said, "My parents don't give me nothing," and Beatrice used that to justify excluding the parental income from the eligibility formula. An older applicant showed a $50,000 business profit on her tax return and wrote a note to Beatrice stating that she didn't know how that amount got on the form, that her accountant must have erred in completing the return. Beatrice therefore calculated her aid eligibility without including any business profit. The new financial aid director decided when tax returns did not need to be collected ("My parents can't find theirs, they don't think they filed.") and even used professional judgment to dispense with the bother of doing an eligibility calculation at all. ("This student told me she has no income," she wrote in the student's file herself. "Therefore she should get everything.") Beatrice found herself saving lots of time and not documenting half the crap her predecessor had pursued so diligently. Hurley, she decided, must have been a dope.

The only drawback was her colleagues. Beatrice miscalculated for two days, making wisecracks about the students, the Admissions tactics, and the idealistic Burr image of working women as spelled out in the catalog, before she realized that the rest of the staff actually cared about the school. They could get real touchy about it too, like the time the fat placement director, Clara, knowing Beatrice was new, pointed to the portraits of Reginald and Evelyn and ticked off the proud history, and Beatrice, just meaning to be funny, interrupted to say, "My Mom's mom used to wear that same dippy hat." She pointed at Evelyn. "Like walking around with a doily on her head." She was surprised to see Clara bristle. Another time she was walking through the cafeteria with Oliver Dunbar when they passed leggy Bonnie Beecher, and Beatrice whistled and said that *that* one would make a fine "sex-retary." With a hand on her elbow, Oliver steered her into the faculty lounge and firmly admonished her. Hell, no one could take a joke.

One Friday, about three weeks in, Beatrice returned to her office with a package of Skittles from the vending machine and found Marty Nolan rifling through the tall stack of files on her desk. She flared with outrage. "What do you think you're doing?"

Marty straightened. "Looking for one of my kids. She's on the phone. Says she hasn't heard anything yet about her financial aid."

"Well, I'll find it. What's her name?"

"Ruby Johnson."

"Ruby? What is she, black?"

"Yeah."

"Well, then they must have been color-blind when they named her." Beatrice chuckled, but didn't get a laugh from the rep. Fine. She had determined early on that Deirdre and Trudy were ditzes and Marty a jerk.

"You even know where the file is?" he asked.

"Move," she snapped, and pushed him aside. She dug the file out of her sagging in-basket. "Yeah, her app got here a couple days ago."

"What's she getting for aid?"

"I haven't calculated it yet."

"Can you do it right now?"

"*Right now?* What, you expect me to just drop everything and do this chick because she's one of yours? Take a message and I'll call her back."

"Call her back when?"

Beatrice snarled, "This afternoon, okay? You can see the file's on my desk. I'm *getting* to it."

She felt a lot better after he left. Ruby's file lay before her, but Beatrice didn't feel like working on it; catching the black rep going through her files had pissed her off too much. She drained her coffee and wandered out to the lobby. "Hi," she said to Julie.

Julie looked up from her computer. "Hello, Beatrice."

The financial aid director scanned the empty lobby. "Kinda slow."

"Fridays usually are. It'll pick up as we get closer to January."

"Yeah. Lily warned me."

Beatrice moved closer to the desk. Of all the people working here, she thought she might get along best with the director's secretary. She figured she and Julie were about the same age, herself being thirty-two. Julie seemed pretty cool, and less inclined to take herself so seriously like the others. "So where do you live?"

"Manayunk," Julie answered.

"Yeah? I'm just on the other side of Fairmont Park. Got an apartment in a big old house in West Mount Airy. I moved there when I dropped out of Temple in '86."

"That sounds nice." Julie tried to go back to her letter but Beatrice spoke again.

"Yeah, I've had lots of jobs now, just drifting. Then a friend tipped me to this place, so I decided to learn some office skills. I sure wasn't getting anywhere where I was. Not that this place is anything to—" She caught herself. God, it was hard keeping back the wisecracks.

"Well," Julie said pleasantly, "it was probably a good decision."

"Jury's out, we'll see." Beatrice grinned. She looked at the framed photograph on the desk. "This is your little girl, right?"

"Yes. Her name's Kelly."

"She's a cutie. Looks like her mommy."

"Thanks. She's gonna be eight in October. Smart as a whip."

"Yeah, looks it. Now you had her before Oliver, right? I mean, the kid isn't his, is it?"

Julie jolted upright. She looked at Beatrice, aghast.

"It's okay," Beatrice said easily. "Trudy and Dee clued me to that my first day here."

The secretary turned back to her computer in fury.

"Come on, hon, that's nothing. You should've seen the creeps chasing me around the minivans at Chrysler. Though at least they were my age and some a little younger. Can't really say that about Oliver, can you? Though of course it's your life."

Julie said coldly, "You don't really want a good working relationship, do you?"

"Hey, I've been around the block. I know how guys are. Especially in middle management. Nothing creepier than middle management, let me tell you."

"There's nothing going on between Dr. Dunbar and me."

"If you say so." Beatrice shrugged. "Probably for the best, anyway. I mean, these academic types might be well-read and all, but I doubt they've got the zip later in the evening when it really counts. And you're too good-looking a chick to settle for that."

"Get the hell out of here," Julie said. "Go bug Lily."

"Lily's got an interview right now."

"Well, go away anyway."

"Sure, if that's how you want it." Beatrice backed off. "But this is pretty ironic after your talk about good working relationships."

The financial aid director returned to her office and spent the next twenty minutes perusing a *National Enquirer* pilfered from the student lounge. Marty passed her open door and peered in. "You calculate that student yet?"

"No. Give me a break."

"You do it now or I'm telling Lily. If Lily suspects you're blowing off a prospect, you'll get your ass kicked faster than you can say shit."

"I don't know," said Beatrice with affected boredom. "I can say 'shit' awful fast."

"You want to cross swords with Lily?"

Beatrice's boredom faded. She was new, but not so much that she didn't know which way the wind blew.

"Do it now," said Marty firmly. "And call that kid back. Then tell me how it went. That's how we do things here."

"Fuck you," said Beatrice.

He shook his head smugly. "You're not fucking anybody but yourself, babe." He walked away.

Beatrice glowered across her desk. She closed the paper and tossed it aside. "Bastard nigger," she said, and opened Ruby Johnson's file.

Marty walked back to his office and grabbed a computer list of fresh phone numbers. "Goddamn bitch," he muttered, and shut the door.

46

He stood on Germantown Avenue near the corner of Cambria Street, watching drug dealers hard at work on Indiana, one block north. It was after ten at night, yet no windows were lit in the row houses facing any of these streets. Oliver stood by an iron fence bordering the western edge of Fairhill Cemetery, his presence hidden in the shadows cast by the branches of a large tree planted on the cemetery side of the fence. The September night was warm and inviting, and the drug activity along Indiana was aggressive. Familiar as he was now with the common signs of urban poverty, the vacant buildings, the decaying houses, the grassy gaps where homes once stood, the junked cars, the storefronts and vans plastered with graffiti, the ever-present garbage, and the boredom of the youth, the fear in the old, and the defeatism felt by all, he was still shocked each time he saw drug dealers operating out in the open, transacting business with the bored faces of cashiers at a supermarket. They swarmed fearlessly around any car that slowed.

Oliver's measure of the world was shaped by a childhood in a white middle-class town with good schools and a community code of honor that canceled out the worst temptations of adolescence: thievery and vandalism, and where any eddy of drug abuse was small and covert. His parents' upbringing plus years of First Day School taught him that the world was filled with people in need, and that God wanted these people helped. He had done food drives and clothing drives as a boy scout. He had given blankets to the homeless, and brought toys to children in shelters. He had studied poverty at college and watched the evening news. Nothing had prepared him for this. Arriving here a little before seven, with the sun already setting to the south so that its blood light reflected off second-story windows and trolley wires, the residents already tucked inside, all shades pulled, he had circled a few blocks, spotting the things he always did: syringes in flowerpots and bottles broken on the curbs, lots with grass higher than a child's waist, old cars and plastic toys crammed in wood-fenced yards, and perhaps saddest of all, the derelict factory like a dead heart—which in fact it was— locked and deteriorating, vines spilling over its meshed fences, the parking lot a prairie of weeds and duff, pocked with broken wooden pallets and engine parts.

Despite the hour, and the fact that he had been walking all afternoon, Oliver felt alive. He finally saw the problem the way it needed to be seen. It wasn't that the wrong type of student was applying to Burr. Rather, Burr was ill-suited to help these students. The implications were huge. For nearly a century the one thing about Burr that *hadn't* equivocated was the education. That standard was still high. There was integrity in such strictness; it was not something the school could afford to lose. But these kids couldn't hack it.

The trick then, would be to make Burr's education more accessible. Some approaches were basic. Since most economically disadvantaged students learned at a slower rate, the curriculum would have to adjust its pace to accommodate them. He didn't know yet to what extent; he would need Ethel to help with that. But if the two-year program started in July instead of September and continued through the following summer, it would increase the classroom time from eighteen months to twenty-four. That in itself wouldn't be hard to do. The difficult part, as he saw it, would be giving these students the extra time *without additional charge*. That alone would make it a tough sell to New York. Still, he believed it could work. Up front it would cost the school more to put these kids through, but it would pay off because they would stay the course. They would get their education without being pushed along a high-speed conveyor belt, they would acquire their skills and polish, they would learn the language arts and math and science that made a Burr education rich, and upon graduation Clara could place them in good jobs with confidence. Employers would like them, and there was Burr's reputation made whole. And admissions could accept students like Keone Robinson without shame.

He only hoped Ethel, in the clear light of day, wouldn't punch too many holes in the idea.

Cars rolled off Germantown Avenue, and legs and sneakers flicked before their rocking headlights. He watched as adults and children of varied ages executed transactions so fluidly he couldn't tell who was buying and who was selling. There was some rustling in the trees of the cemetery to his back, and he knew small drug-related desecrations were taking place in there. It was the drug culture that made him feel the most out of touch. The idea of needles, injecting, snorting, burning, and the filth, the unending sickness and waste, completely spooked him. All addictions scared him. Substance abuse, gambling, sexual dependency, alcoholism, all stripped people of everything that was precious. Stripped them of freedom, thought, spirituality. Stripped them of the God he loved so much. He looked at the small homes facing all this and tried to fathom the lives huddled within. There were hints of an effort to lead normal lives: porches or backyards with plastic basketball hoops set at a small child's height, princess play-houses, deck furniture even when there was no deck, bicycles, flowers. Some homes had wreaths of welcome on the doors. He did not believe his new program would patronize these kids. They were coming to Burr to get out of here. He would see to it that they did.

"Buddy, you lost?"

Oliver turned. Two teenage boys were walking up Germantown Avenue from the south, strolling alongside the cemetery fence. One was grossly fat with a soft jaw and bald head, the other short but lean with a pencil mustache. Oliver's heart picked up tempo. This was it. The law of averages.

"No," he said quietly.

"Got a light?"

"I don't smoke. Sorry."

"How 'bout a coupla bucks? My buddy here, he and I ain't eaten good in days."

"Forever," the fat one nodded.

He stood between them and the drug activity one block north, with the cemetery fence at his back. Their stance was casual, but their eyes gleamed with predatory confidence. He didn't know what to do.

"Just a coupla bucks. You gonna tell me you standin' here empty-handed?"

They thought he was a customer. He was standing in a gray business suit half a block from the action, the very picture of a novice druggie, shy and indecisive. He was so scared his lungs hurt.

"Where's your car?" the fat one asked. He tilted his head back, and studied Oliver down the barrel-bridge of his nose.

"I don't have a car."

"You don't got much."

The thin one said, "You a cop?"

"No."

"Sure you ain't a cop?"

"No."

"Then what the fuck then?"

He had only himself to blame. He pulled his hands from his pants pockets and let them hang, letting the boys know the next move was theirs. He would not fight back.

They seemed to understand this, and perhaps it was what saved him. One took his elbow, and without resistance he was led across Germantown Avenue to a weedy alley between two houses. Behind the houses only a shaft of streetlight filtered through, and the second-story windows of these houses, since they didn't face the street, offered some dim wattage. The thin boy pinned Oliver's arms tightly behind him while the fat one with the soft face pounded him. It was all done in silence. The punches were random, though most hit Oliver's chest, and he only gasped once when the fat boy socked him in the stomach. The lean boy let go of him and it was easy to drop to the ground, a grass surface so far away and yet rising up in a second to catch his body and hold it still. They rifled through his clothes, took his wallet, watch, and tried unsuccessfully to pull off his wedding ring. Their feet squeaked on the grass as they scampered away. Loose change jingled against some rubble, the one clear sound he heard.

He didn't quite make it into unconsciousness. His hip lay against a rock or brick, and the discomfort was enough to let him know he was still breathing. His first real shaft of pain came when he lifted his head. He grimaced, and for a moment felt it might be better to just lie here until morning. Except it was someone's property and he really ought to move. He raised himself to his hands and knees, got a sense that everything still worked, and with an effort pushed himself up on his feet. His tie was twisted over his shoulder. He straightened it and pressed it smooth, then worked his way out of the alley, keeping one hand on the wall of someone's house to stay erect.

The boys were nowhere to be seen. Activity continued uninterrupted to the north. Oliver walked gingerly down Germantown Avenue, away from Indiana, and spotted a pay phone by the corner of St. John's Church.

He had to cross the wide Avenue to get to it, and imagined the whole time that the phone couldn't possibly work. Yet a dial tone buzzed in his ear as soon as he lifted the receiver, and with a swift prayer of thanks he pressed for the operator.

"Bell Telephone."

He tried to speak and choked.

"Hello? This is Bell Telephone."

He gave the operator a number that came instinctively to his lips, one he had memorized from so many occasions when he needed to call outside office hours to ask a favor.

"There will be a momentary pause while the other party is contacted."

He glanced nervously up the Avenue while he waited, but no one was coming for him. He could still hear cars and a few voices, but the cemetery now blocked most of the view.

"Oliver?"

Her voice, dreamlike in its familiarity. How selfish of him to summon it to this land of cold shadows and brutal avarice. How could he ask her to do what he needed?

"Julie, this is Oliver."

"Yes, Oliver?"

"Thanks for accepting the charges. I'm sorry to disturb you at home. I … I haven't got any money on me or I would have …"

"Oliver, what's wrong? Where are you?"

"I don't know. Wait." He squinted at a green street sign. "Cambria."

"Where?"

"Cambria Street. It's North Philadelphia."

"Where exactly, Oliver?"

"I don't, uh … don't … Germantown Avenue. The southwest corner of Fairhill Cemetery. Lucretia Mott's buried there."

"Is that a safe neighborhood?"

"No, as a matter of fact, it's not. That's why I was wondering if … if you would mind coming to get me."

"All right. I'm on my way. Just stay where you are. Can you do that?"

"Sure. I don't real … really have much choice."

"Oliver, is everything all right? No, never mind—I'm on my way. Just wait for me."

The click in his ear released all the pain held back in his chest. His ribs expanded from a fire inside. He almost slid against the pole supporting the phone. He opened his eyes and made out the church steps just a few yards away. They looked inviting, but a metal fence blocked their access. Oliver slid against the phone pole. He felt the descent but never remembered reaching the pavement.

47

He awoke with sore lungs and diaphragm. A large white landscape filled his vision, interrupted a moment later by a hand reaching to touch his forehead. Julie Fitzgerald, dressed for work, bent into his vision and smiled self-consciously. The white landscape lost its mystery, turned into a ceiling.

"I'm sorry. You were so still, I had to be sure."

She had parked on the wrong side of Germantown Avenue. From his slumped position he watched as she ran across the road, barelegged in shorts and sweatshirt and sandals, pale and courageous in the face of the derelict homes, the unlit alleys, the graffiti, the trash, the darkened cemetery, the pitiless activity just one block north, everything Action News taught about danger in the ghettos. The best secretary he ever had.

"I'm going in now. I have to. Listen, it's almost seven. Kelly's been told to make your breakfast whenever you get up, but if you want something better than cereal you may have to fix it yourself. You're not going to work today."

"Okay."

"Kelly doesn't have school. It's an in-service day for her teachers. I was going to drop her off at my parents, but I'm letting her stay here with you. I told her she's your adult-sitter. You are to take the day and rest. Don't do anything."

"All right."

"When I get home tonight we'll talk about what to do."

What to do. She had begged to take him to the hospital and he refused. She in turn would not drop him off at his apartment. He sat huddled in the passenger seat, hugging his chest for the whole trip out to Manayunk.

"Have a nice day," he said.

"You too." Their eyes met. It was the moment when husbands and wives kissed each other before splitting up to face the day. Julie straightened and shouldered her pocketbook. "I left some money on the kitchen counter, just in case. And I'll call later to see how you're doing."

His eyes were shut before she was out of the room.

Oliver slept fitfully. When he finally awoke for good he stared at a neon-green starburst on a blue night table. It was a clock, but he didn't have his glasses. He sat up on a narrow single bed and straightened his cramped legs. Morning light filtered through a pink window curtain.

His glasses were beside the clock, his pants and work shirt draped on a wooden rocking chair. A white bunny sat in the rocker. Now that he could read the clock it startled him, shining at 10:40. He stood up in his underwear to reach for his pants, and only then realized that Julie must have undressed him last night. How was he ever going to work with her again?

Barefoot, he stepped out to the living room. He could see a television glowing with cartoon figures but the sound was off and the couch before the set was empty. It made him suspect that he was dreaming. A smell of over-cooked coffee led him through an archway to a small kitchenette, and there he found Julie's daughter seated at a table, her back to him. Her hair was almost pure white, and her feet dangled off the floor. Her left hand curled tightly around a crayon, her wrist and elbow resting on a coloring book.

Confronted foremost with the fact that she was deaf, he tried to think of a polite way to get her attention. Figuring a tap on the shoulder might startle her, he walked around the table where she could see him. He smiled.

Kelly looked at him but did not smile back. Oliver felt like what he was, a gigantic stupid stranger. He found a mug and poured black coffee, then pointed at another chair with an inquiring look.

Kelly nodded.

Oliver sat at the table and watched the girl color. It was a picture of two children on a seesaw. The girl sitting on the upraised arm wore a buttoned coat, her hair flying, her mouth open in a happy shout. The boy's unbuttoned coat revealed green pants—well, green after Kelly finished with them—and he was laughing too. Her coloring of the figures was even and meticulous.

"Why does he have a red nose?" Oliver asked.

Kelly frowned. She held her right hand with palm up, and with the index finger of her left hand made a slashing motion against it.

He tried to remember if she could read lips. "Why is his nose—" Oliver pointed to his own and over-pronounced, "re-hed?"

Kelly grinned. She pointed to the boy's open coat, then touched her nose with index finger and thumb, gently stroking the ball of her nose.

"He has a cold?"

She nodded, and Oliver laughed. Kelly executed a whirlwind of hand motions. He shook his head helplessly. She got up, opened a drawer near the sink, and returned with a pad of paper and a pencil. With the same coiled precision that had guided the crayon she printed, *Do you want some breakfast?*

Oliver took the pencil. *You don't have to make it for me. I can make my own.*

She took the pencil. *But I know where it is. Do you like Froot Loops?*

He watched while she got the cereal, a bowl and spoon, and even a carton of orange juice, which she poured unsteadily but successfully into a plastic mug. Utilizing a few amateur mime moves, he got her to bring a second spoon and share the cereal with him. In return she offered the coloring book, and so they colored, keeping the pad between them so they could jot to each other.

Thank you for this great breakfast, he wrote.

You're welcome. I got to stay home from school today.

Do you like school?

Yes. But a break is nice.

How do you say "thank you?"

She put the tips of her fingers to her chin, then drew her hand downward. *This is how you say "you're welcome."* And she did a little salute near her forehead.

He wrote, *I'm going to have to learn a better way to talk to you. You're too smart for me to do this by writing.*

Kelly laughed, and her feet swung below her chair.

After an hour Oliver excused himself and wandered into the living room. He turned off the TV and stepped carefully around a pile of laundry that must have been balanced on the couch arm but subsequently fell to the floor. Poor Julie hadn't anticipated company. A picture on a wooden hutch showed a curly-haired man in uniform, another showed a fat woman scowling on the concrete steps of an apartment doorway, holding the hands of two little children on either side, everyone dressed for church. The tallest child looked the most like Julie. With her wispy blond hair and inquisitive squint at the camera, she could have been the girl coloring in the kitchen.

It made him uncomfortable. Julie worked for him, and he was seeing her clothes strewn about, her family pictures, her deaf child, her sparse hand-me-down furniture. The evidence of a young mother struggling on very little income socked him everywhere he looked. Julie never let any of this show at the office. He wasn't supposed to know. Yet he couldn't leave, he had promised to stay. In which case he needed something to do.

In a wide closet off the kitchen he found a compact washer, dryer, and a jug of soap tucked under more dirty laundry. He walked through the apartment gathering clothes from a hamper in the bathroom and another in Julie's room, plus the pile on the living room floor. He started a load in the small washer, then went to work on the dishes. Kelly came to help. He washed, she dried. It still hurt some to breathe, and Kelly made a motion of cupping one hand and dangling something over it with the other. He nodded yes without the faintest idea what she was asking. He walked into the living room and rested on the couch, and a few minutes later Kelly appeared with a brimming cup of tea. Deeply touched, he thanked her by drawing two fingers away from his chin. She took the TV remote and turned on some cartoons. The set showed dialogue printed in black boxes at the bottom of the screen. Oliver found himself trying to read and listen simultaneously. He was surprised at how deep Kelly's voice was when she laughed at the slapstick. None of her articulations were actual words, and he tried to imagine her voice with the discipline of language.

At noon the phone rang. He picked it up in the kitchen. "Hey," Julie said. "How's it going?"

"Pretty good. Your daughter's a charmer. She made breakfast and insisted on helping me clean up. Though she was happy to let me do the vacuuming."

"Oliver, are you cleaning my house? I'll kill you."

"I'm not doing a lot, don't panic. It's giving me something to do. I'm having trouble closing my eyes. I keep seeing the boys who hit me."

"Okay," she said.

"We're also having a Sign Language lesson. She points to things and shows me what the signs are."

"Well, good. What have you learned?"

"Curtain. Ceiling—or maybe it's roof. Window. Chair. Table. Crayon. I've also—and bear with me, I'm quite proud of this—managed to resurrect some extremely old Boy Scout knowledge. I had to learn the Deaf Alphabet for a merit badge when I was nine or ten, and I've recalled maybe twenty out of twenty-six letters."

"That's fine. That's really good."

"How's the fort?"

"Quiet. Everybody's interviewing, all the students just started Fourth Period."

"Doesn't sound like they miss me."

"Right now you're better off where you are."

"I'm inclined to agree with you. Oh, you're going to have to let me go, the commercial's over."

"Oh? What are you and la princessa watching?"

"*Anamaniacs*. Does that sound right? Oh, you know she made tea for me without asking. Your girl is a wonder."

"Glad you think so. But Oliver, don't let her watch cartoons all day. That's the one favor I'm asking you."

"Got it."

"Take care."

Out the living room window he saw a spectacular view of Manayunk. Julie's apartment sat high up the hill, and the town dropped like a staircase toward the Schuylkill River, revealing the shopping district, the gentrified warehouses, and the expansive slopes of Belmont on the other side. Once again he felt like he was dreaming.

Kelly switched to Bugs Bunny cartoons that were not closed-captioned. She seemed no less attentive, although she didn't laugh. Oliver wrote, *Your mother doesn't want you watching TV all day.*

What do you want to do? she responded.

What is there to do?

We could go to a park.

Do you know where one is?

Yes.

Ok. Let me check the laundry.

He started a second load, then off they went. The park Kelly led him to was only a few blocks away. Oliver wasn't sure what they would do when they got here, and he was dismayed to realize they had forgotten the writing tablet. He needn't have worried. Kelly had her own entertainment planned. The child could climb anything. Oliver clapped and gave her thumbs-up as she shimmied up poles and dangled upside-down at him from hanging rings. She crawled through tubes and zipped down the slide. They both shared the swings. Oliver bought hot-dogs, sodas, and fries from a vendor, and they managed to communicate nicely without the tablet. (When he asked if she wanted a hot-dog, Oliver fanned himself as if perspiring greatly, then pointed to someone walking a terrier. Kelly thought it very funny, but also understood him and nodded.)

Back at the house, the second load was ready for the dryer. That started, they took the rest of Julie's money and walked to the store. They bought a bouquet of summer flowers, chicken and pasta and a bottle of red wine, and came home filled with culinary ambition. He cooked the food while Kelly focused with great intent on arranging the flowers in a glass vase on the kitchen table. She tugged his sleeve and whipped her hands in a blur. Oliver shook his head. She got the tablet and wrote, *Are you and Mommy sweethearts?*

Oliver signed no, which she had taught him earlier in the morning, and Kelly seemed a little confused, if not disappointed.

They played Mousetrap on the living room floor, and he let her fit all the pieces that were her personal favorites. They were just about done when the front door opened.

"Goodness," said Julie, "what smells so good?"

"Just your standard chicken and pasta," said Oliver.

"It's not standard if I don't have to fix it." Julie stepped into the kitchen and saw the table crowded with place settings, candles, and a completely impractical centerpiece of flowers. "Oh my God, I don't believe this! Oliver, this is beautiful!"

"Don't credit me. Kelly had final say over everything."

She saw the wine on the counter. "It's too much. You shouldn't have done this."

"You didn't have to come get me last night. I'm sorry I had to use your money. I'll get to the bank tomorrow and pay you back."

"Don't be silly."

He shook his head. "It's not a 'thank you' if I don't."

Kelly cranked the trap, and the red cage rattled down over his mouse. "Way to go," he said to Julie. "You distracted me."

Julie changed to house shirt and jeans while he finished up the dinner. It had been a full day, she reported over dinner. A good number of applicants showed for their appointments. The highlight, in Julie's eyes, was when Lily took the parents of a prospect out for an expensive two-hour lunch while their daughter took the Admissions test, and they came back thoroughly convinced that Burr was *the* place for their child to get her education. At this tale of blatant salesmanship, Oliver merely shook his head.

Kelly waved, for Julie wasn't signing any of this. Julie explained that it was just shop talk, but Kelly wanted to be included anyway. So Julie and Oliver talked about his leisurely day with Kelly, and Julie's hands interpreted both sides of the conversation.

At six-thirty they sat in the living room and watched the news. Because it was live, the closed-captioning was tardy and sloppy. Kelly grew bored and went to her room with *If I Ran the Zoo*. Julie followed to tuck her in. When she returned, she said, "What time is it?"

"Almost seven-thirty," said Oliver. "I've really overstayed my welcome. Julie, I can't begin to thank you for what you did for me. Both last night, and today."

"Oliver, you're not going back to the city tonight."

"I can't infringe on you two days in a row."

"I don't want you to do that either."

"What then?"

"Sit with me a moment."

They both sat on the couch. With a quick jerk of the remote Julie shut off the TV. Her hazel eyes fixed on him. "I want you to stay here. This couch folds out."

Oliver grimaced. "Julie, you're not thinking right. I can't stay here. You've got a little girl."

"I'm well aware that I have a daughter, Oliver. I never have a thought that doesn't include her. I was at my desk all day running this through. If you try to live by yourself in that place on Rittenhouse you'll never get better."

He knew the truth of that.

"This is one friend helping another. That's all."

"Is it, though? Forgive me, but are you sure?" Oliver smiled lamely. "I mean, even I'm not sure."

"Fair enough. This might get complicated, which also means we won't thrash it out tonight. Right now I'm mostly interested in what's best for you. We need to talk. Over a period of days or however long it takes. But do this for us both, please."

"What would Kelly say?"

"She's already hoping you'll stay."

Oliver felt a terrible pressure on his heart, felt it struggle to beat through its own oily weight. "It's still not a good idea, Julie."

She looked at the blank TV with an irritated sigh. "Then do what you think is best. I can't hold you here. But I truly believe this is what you need. I care about you. I love you. I'm not going to be shy saying that to you."

"Well," he said, overwhelmed.

"You don't have to stay here. I admit, that's a big jump, and I spoke too soon. But I want to see you. I want you to think seriously about building a life with me and Kelly. You're a kind man, Oliver. Kelly and I need kindness. God, Kelly needs it."

"Listen," he said, "there are just problems everywhere. You work for me. I've got what—fourteen years on you?"

"Don't give me that crap," she said sharply. "You're the best man I ever met, Oliver. Am I really supposed to ignore that just because you didn't have the sense to be born in 1962?"

"Was that what I did wrong? I knew it was something."

This made them both smile. Julie took his hand, and was heartened to feel him squeeze hers back. Gently she asked, "Do you still think about Tina?"

"Yes."

He said it simply, but it was a confession, and in the single soft-spoken word she felt the depth of his unhappiness, all his guilt, and realized he could have made this moment easy for himself by saying no, except he was incapable of lying to her. She felt bad for getting annoyed with him.

"How about this?" she said. "Why don't you take me to dinner Saturday night?"

"This coming Saturday?"

"Sure. Or do you already have something hot and heavy going?"

"No, I don't."

"Then say yes."

"Yes."

She was startled. "Really? Are you sure, Oliver? I don't want to push you."

He smiled. "No, not much."

"I'm serious. You've taught me some things this past year, you know. Patience, for one thing. And a whole new way of caring about people."

"Saturday sounds great." He stood and slipped on his suit jacket. She walked him to the door. They stood so close that it was ridiculous not to kiss. It was sweet, short but gentle, and they both blushed a little as their faces pulled away.

"Well, now you have to take me out," Julie said.

"I think I do." He opened the door and stepped outside. "Dress smart for Saturday. I'm going to take you some place nice."

48

In late September the push for January kicked into high gear. Bill Nostrand called every other day to check numbers, and Lily's office laid out a scheme to cover high schools and the most remote of local public events.

Success had sharpened the reps. The respectful manner advocated by the Elaine Margolis era was dismissed for a more persuasive approach. One day a prospect named Sonja Flores handed her app form to Trudy in the lobby, then mentioned that she wanted to come the following July, not January.

"What was that?" Trudy stared hard at the applicant. "When you called, Sonja, you said you wanted to come in January."

"Yes, I know." The girl looked about nervously. She had dressed carefully for this interview, and her desire to be accepted by the college was palpable. "But I forgot that my family's going to California in March. That's why I have to come in July."

"Well, I'm sorry but you can't."

From her desk, Julie looked up in surprise. Sonja's eyes fluttered in confusion. "But don't you have a class that starts in July?"

"Yes, but you can't attend that."

"Why not?" It wasn't asked indignantly, just out of disappointment.

"Because you applied now. Students who apply now have to come in January. That's institutional policy."

"But what if I wait and apply in the spring?"

"Can't. You already applied now." And to prove it, Trudy held up the pink receipt made out for Sonja's one hundred and twenty-five dollars.

"But I've never been to California. My family's planned this for a year."

"I appreciate that, Sonja, but you didn't tell me about it when we set up today's interview. There's nothing I can do about it now."

"But that means I can't attend." And the girl looked crushed.

"Well, you can decide that if you want. I feel badly about it though, because you already paid the app fee and deposit."

"You mean I don't get that back?"

"No, I'm sorry."

"But I only gave it to you ten minutes ago!"

"I know. But don't you see, Sonja? I gave your check to the business manager, and I'm sure she has it logged into the system. Once it's in the system we can't delete it."

"But that's my money!"

"Look, what am I supposed to do?" Trudy finally let a little annoyance show. "I accepted your check in good faith to hold your seat in the January class. Now you want to back out. Is that my fault? Do you really think you should get mad at me because you changed your mind?"

"But—"

"Seriously, Sonja, do you think you're being fair to me? Do you?"

In the end Sonja decided she had better attend in January after all, and was grateful when Trudy volunteered to break the news to her parents.

On another occasion Deirdre had an applicant sitting in the lobby. Irene Perkins was interested in Accounting, but after watching the video she thought she might do better in the Information Processing Program. Deirdre, elated to have a prospect change her mind for a more expensive program, praised Irene's intelligence and ran to get a catalog and an app form. At that moment Marty strolled into the lobby holding a Coke.

"Hello."

"Hi."

"Are you being helped?"

"Yes. Ms. Smith is getting me some stuff about a program."

"Really?" Marty stepped closer, all smiles. "And what program is that?"

"Information Processing."

"Ah. January. Well, good for you. That's our best program. What's your name?"

"Irene."

"Well, you know, Irene, I have that same information in my office. No reason for you to wait here. Why don't you come back with me?"

"All right." The girl stood and returned his smile. "Thank you." She followed him out of the room.

Julie sat at her desk, appalled. She turned sideways and concentrated on her typing. A moment later Deirdre returned, clutching a catalog and app form. "Hey, where'd she go?"

Julie tried to keep typing.

"Jule, where'd she go?"

"Well, uh …" Having no choice, the secretary faced front. "She went back with Marty."

It took a moment to register. Deirdre's eyes dilated and her small mouth popped open. "What!"

Julie nodded wordlessly.

"That rotten creep! I'll break his neck! That's *my* prospect!" The junior rep raced out of the lobby.

By the middle of October the drop in morale could be felt throughout the school. Teachers complained so incessantly that it was no longer enjoyable to eat lunch in the faculty lounge. From the front desk Julie saw the dissolute faces of staff and faculty as they trudged in each morning, and noted how few greetings were exchanged between them.

On the second Monday in October Lily held a B.A.M.—Big Admissions Meeting—for which the TV and VCR were wheeled in from the lobby. Marty, Deirdre, and Trudy sat with notebooks on their laps. Lily dispensed coffee, then sat at her desk and aimed the remote control. "Three good ones, people. Check 'em out!"

The first commercial was a thirty second spot. A handsome dark-haired male model in a pinstripe suit sat behind a desk in a posh office talking on the phone. He hung up, looked at the camera, and smiled with Fortune 500 dash.

"Hi. I'm the executive director of a top publishing house for several fashion magazines. I need a secretary. Wouldn't you like to work for *me?* If you're a graduate of the Burr College of Business, you're exactly what I'm looking for. In this high-powered, exciting business, I wouldn't hire any other kind of administrative assistant." His smile grew rakish, and his brows lifted knowingly. "I hope to be talking to *you* soon."

It was an instant hit. Trudy and Deirdre giggled happily, and Lily said proudly, "Gets the point across, doesn't it?"

After a black leader the next one came on. To a bouncy music track a harassed businessman and his ditzy middle-aged secretary went at it. She cut off his phone calls, spilled coffee on his lap, couldn't find anything in her files, put *him* on hold, and deleted several major accounts from her hard drive. The bald and portly boss wrung his hands. "I should have gotten a Burr secretary!" *Flash cut!* A stylish, beautiful woman in her twenties sat before a spotless computer terminal and effortlessly handled calls, typed massive reports, and greeted clients in a mere twelve seconds of air time. Her handsome dark-haired boss (the same model from the previous commercial) appeared and acknowledged his appreciation of her abilities by bringing her a cup of coffee. The voice on the soundtrack crisply extolled Burr secretaries and gave the phone number to call.

"His getting her the coffee was my idea," Lily said. "Wait folks—this one's my favorite."

A beautiful professional woman strolled between desks in an open office area. Two good-looking male employees admired her from the water cooler. "Hey," said one, "that's some secretary. When'd she come on board, Tom?"

"Jackie's been here two months now, Bill. Was hired as secretary to the vice-president of advertising. She's just finished the Oakland account."

"No way!" exclaimed Bill. "They wouldn't give a secretary an account that big."

"Oh, she's not a secretary any more. She's corporate administrative assistant to the president."

"But she just started here two months ago!"

"She's a Burr graduate. What can I tell you?"

"A Burr graduate?"

"Sure. They're the best. They're more than just secretaries, they're the elite. Jackie's proved herself so quickly that the boss wants her on the Portland account."

"Wow," said the other. They watched the woman stroll out the door. "Wait a minute," Bill suddenly cried. "Portland's *my* account!"

The woman walked into the boss' office without knocking and set a folder on his desk. The boss picked it up and said, "Jackie, this is brilliant. The Portland account is definitely yours."

"Thank you. I owe it all to my Burr College training."

"Yes. We never hire from any other business college."

She walked out, and passed Bill at his desk without noticing him. The camera stayed on Bill, who was speaking into his phone with one hand cupping the receiver. His eyes darted about to make sure no one was listening. "When's your next class? So soon? That's great. I'll definitely be there. I realize now that I need to be trained the Burr way!"

Lily shut off the TV to great applause. "Okay," she said. "I've got these airing on the local stations in a format called block-booking. It's the least expensive way to get time. These ads will play at different hours over an eight-week period. Prime time, which is really what we want, but also during the day for housewives to see, and in the wee hours of the morning, just because in this kind of package we have no choice."

"So we'll be mixed in with the two a.m. psychic phone commercials and the miracle hair-growth ads," commented Marty.

"Big deal. We're not so different. Those ads cater to people unhappy with their lives and so do we. Why else do people bother with education? Ladies, Marty—this is what I've wanted for a long time. It's taken a bit of coaxing to get New York to agree because these ads, especially that last one, cost a lot. But mind you, we have some clout now. As you know, we are the top selling admissions office in the Burr system. Of course, now we have to *stay* the top selling office, so the pressure on us will be greater than ever."

"What's the January goal?" asked Trudy.

"One hundred and twenty students."

"One hundred and twenty students in three months?"

"Plus two Evening Accounting classes of twenty-five each. It's going to take a lot of hard work, ladies and Marty, but we're going to be rolling in some heavy dough when it's done. We're on a magnificent rebound here, and we can finally make the most of it. Ha! Ha!"

"What about Paralegal?" asked Marty. "Aren't we sitting one of those too?"

"Paralegal is on hold right now due to that student who's suing us."

"Who's that?" exclaimed Deirdre.

"I forget her name. Some sour-grapes kid with a pole up her butt. Don't look so worried, dears, stuff like this happens. There's no pleasing everybody. This girl says no law agency will hire her because her background's so limited, and we must have known that but admitted her anyway." Lily took a deep swallow of coffee. "Less ambitious students always think their college is responsible for getting them jobs, and they get ticked off at us when they don't find work."

"What do you think'll happen?"

"Nothing to us, that's for sure. That program was accredited and she met the admittance criteria. Let her take us to court. She'll come away with some good law experience after John Coyne's attorneys get through with her. Any other news? No? All right. Get your new computer lists and start working leads for January. The ads start running on TV tonight, so I expect to see plenty of appointments in the book by the end of the week. Now *scoot!*"

The reps hopped up and ran for the door. Lily called out, "Marty, wait a sec!"

He turned around and grinned. "What can I do for you, Lily?"

"Close the door."

Lily turned in her chair and plucked a truffle from a plate on the windowsill behind her. "You never told me about your trip this morning."

"Oh, well sure. I had an appointment at the Diamond Career Training School."

"How were they? What were they like?"

"Pretty piss poor. No catalog to give me, and they've got kids doubling up on computers because they don't have enough in each classroom. Really bad."

"Now wait." Lily pursed her brows. "Where the hell are they located?"

"Up around Tioga. The area's a dump. The school's got iron bars on all the first floor windows."

Lily snorted. "Wonderful. Honey, tell me why we shouldn't be worried about this place."

"Oh, it's absolutely not in our league at all."

"But they're competitive with the 'C' schools."

"Sure, but—"

"See, that's what Oliver and New York don't understand! Those are the high schools we have to tap into to make goal, now that the wealthy white girl population isn't coming to us. We lost that market a decade ago."

"It's true. You're right, Lily. You're right."

"Sometimes I think you and I are the only ones who understand that. So did they want to take you?"

"Ha! That was never an issue. They were begging to get me enrolled."

"Good, good. What a riot."

They both laughed, and Marty dropped on the love seat and crossed his long legs. He gave Lily his most dashing smile. Now that he had proven himself with the July-September sits, his boss was relying on him more and more, and all kinds of possibilities kept twisting in his head—and not all of them were professional. Lily Espirito was the best-looking woman he had ever seen. He didn't know the details of her marriage, but it was obvious from all the hours she spent working here plus the fact that both girl reps said the guy was old that she wasn't getting it like she should. Lately she was flashing looks at him during staff meetings that were like little private messages—as if Trudy and Deirdre weren't even in the room. And hell, she *never* took the girl reps out for a drink, whereas several times recently she had treated Marty at a local pub. He loved going to bars with Lily. He loved the fire a few drinks put in her cheeks and black eyes. He loved watching her miniskirted ass perched on a barstool. They didn't come sexier than Lily.

As if to confirm her own thoughts along this line, Lily stood and stepped casually around her desk. The admissions director wore a tight-fitting minidress of deep plum, with a pattern of silver paisley that clung like ivy to the rich curves of her body. She gave him a wide delicious smile.

"Listen, honey, I may have to give you some of the North Philly schools. I hope you don't mind."

"Of course not, Lily. Not at all."

"Yeah. Little Tru's doing great in the 'burbs, but she's not connecting like we need in the poorer urban schools. Since you're ..."

"Black." He laughed.

"Babe, because you can relate, or at least they *figure* at those schools you can relate, you might do better than Tru. Which isn't meant to be a reflection on her."

"Of course not." But it was. A rep who lost a school only did so because she wasn't bringing in the leads. Trudy would have a conniption when she heard. Tough titty.

"Her fashion shows outside of town are a big hit," Lily added, as if feeling a need to defend her senior rep, "but in North Philly we need someone with a little more … charisma."

"You got it."

They were silent a moment. Marty could tell she was debating whether to join him on the love seat. She asked, "What's on for the afternoon?"

"Well, I have an interesting appointment at four. A divorced mom and her daughter. It's really the daughter's appointment but I figured I'd try for both."

"Of course. You're good with the divorcees, aren't you, love?" Lily reached out and caressed Marty's cheek. "I guess all of us older girls better watch out for you." She smiled with a high arch of her brows, then walked back to her desk with an arresting swing of her plum-colored hips.

Marty returned to his office and closed the door. He grabbed a fistful of phone messages and began returning calls with unbridled vigor.

49

The fight started in Carol Sobolewski's Business Comp class because Rose Becker arrived late. Few crimes struck a deeper nerve with Carol, and before the student reached her chair the teacher broke her lecture to say, "Ms. Becker, I am going to record you as late for this class, and it will be a permanent mark on your transcript."

Rose was twenty years old, squat and heavy. A lifetime of poor posture had given her shoulders a permanent slope, thrusting her head forward like a surly bull. She glowered at the white middle-aged woman at the head of the classroom. "You ain't puttin' me on no report."

"Yes I am." Carol flipped open her attendance book. "This is not the first time you've been late."

"So what?"

"So what? Ms. Becker, do you understand the importance of punctuality in an office job? This is the eleventh time in six weeks that you've been late. It's an appalling record. Absences and latenesses are logged on a student's transcript, but your excesses deserve a report to the school director, and that's exactly what I'm going to do."

"No you ain't."

"You wish to explain to me why I shouldn't?"

"'Cause you ain't."

The rest of the class sat rigidly in their chairs. They smelled the danger. So did Carol, but she didn't dare back down. She raised her voice with practiced authority. "Sit down this instant, Ms. Becker."

The student's protruding head swung back and forth like a wrecking ball. "You ain't tellin' me what to do."

"Yes I am," declared Carol, "as long as you're a student in this class!"

"Oh fuck this." Rose wedged thick fingers between her computer and the desk it rested on. She flipped upward, and both monitor and CPU somersaulted to the floor. The students on either side leapt out of their chairs.

"Ms. Becker!" Carol shrieked. "You did that deliberately!"

"No shit!" The student laughed and lumbered forward. "Let's see what else I can do."

Carol's heart beat wildly but she stood firm. Her glare was designed to intimidate, but Rose's eyes were dangerously cool and impervious.

"Get out of my classroom right now!" Carol ordered.

"Then you comin' with me."

Traci Cunningham and Tory Polumbo jumped up from the front row. Their chairs clattered backward. They lunged at Rose and grabbed her arms.

"No!" shrieked Carol.

Rose Becker roared. She yanked backward, pulling both girls, then twisted her thick body and spun Tory and Traci around with her. Tory stumbled into Danielle Lazzaro's desk but kept her hold. Danielle jumped up as her computer hit the hardwood floor with a horrendous crash, missing Tory's toes by inches.

"Motherfuck … mother—" panted Rose, struggling.

"Girls! *Stop!* I can handle this!" Carol waded in. Books thudded. Students screamed. Someone knocked the trashcan over. Arms locked on all sides. Backs bent, legs strained. "Watch out for her teeth!" someone shouted.

"Stop!" the teacher yelled. "Stop! Stop!"

More students lunged and grabbed hold. Desks scraped and heels slipped. The classroom door opened and Bob Lawrence peered in. "What the heck's happening? We can hear all this next door."

"Mr. Lawrence!" Danielle screamed. "Help!"

"What?"

"They're killing each other! Help! Please!"

Bob looked in amazement at the locked mass of people at the front of the room. With only the slightest hesitation he rushed in. "Hey, come on! What is this! Come on now!"

A sudden lurch pushed everybody against the blackboard. Carol's spine cracked painfully against the marker ledge. Someone's elbow jabbed the wind from her and she gasped, clinging desperately to Traci Cunningham's arm. Bob yelled, trying to pry everybody apart, "Come on, this isn't—"

"Let go! Oww!"

"Shit! Fucker—"

"Get *off* me—"

"Mr. Lawrence! Pull them apart! Mr. Lawrence—!"

Bob tried. Several other students joined in, and everyone pulled at everybody.

"Girls, please!" Carol gasped. "Someone's going to get—"

"Look out!"

The tangled mass shoved against the teacher's metal desk and pushed it scraping across the floor. Carol's arms were wedged between Dorothee Jackson's shoulder and Rose Becker's elbow. She couldn't get her hands free and tugged in panic. Amidst the shouting and shoving, a big hand gripped the back of her collar, and she felt herself pulled around to face the large woman at the center of the melee. Rose Becker's eyes burned inches from hers, and her lower lip stretched in an ugly grin.

Donna Harding looked through the door. "It sounds like a riot in here—oh my God!"

Carol gasped and shoved without effect against the weight of everybody. Rose Becker's big hand squeezed tighter on the back of her neck. Suddenly, incredibly, Carol felt her feet lift off the floor. She screamed.

"Everybody off!" yelled Bob from the other side. "Come on now! I'm serious!"

Carol wiggled one hand free and beat sloppily at the big student.

"Fuckin' ain't got long to live!" hissed Rose.

Another lurch, and everyone fell apart. Carol's feet hit the floor and her right thigh whacked against the edge of her desk. Rose Becker shook Traci off and stood clear. Everyone panted hard, watching Rose. The big woman kept turning, fists up, waiting to see who would jump her next.

"Enough!" yelled Bob. "Come on, let's not get crazy here!"

"Yes!" said Carol. She straightened with dignity and said, "Girls, go back to your seats. Ms. Becker, leave this room at once!"

"Shit." The student hitched her fat shoulders and the other girls quickly stepped back. Rose lumbered to the door. She turned and shouted, "I ain't leavin' 'cause of you! I ain't stayin' here anyway! You bitches can all fuckin' die!" She elbowed a stunned Donna Harding out of the way and disappeared.

Carol put a hand behind her neck and felt swellings underneath her fingers. She tried to control the trembling in her legs. All eyes were upon her, and that was enough to restore her composure. "Thank you, everybody," she said with a smile. "I'm sorry about this. We won't let her back in, I assure you."

"Are you all right, Ms. Sobolewski?" asked Tory.

"Yes, Ms. Polumbo. Well, why don't we all take ten minutes and just ... walk around the block or something, if you want to? Then we'll come back and continue the lesson. Mr. Lawrence, thank you so much. Maybe you could help me set the computers up again."

Donna Harding said, "I'll get Dr. Dunbar," and disappeared out the doorway she had never fully entered.

The class filed out with breathless whispers. A few girls started to straighten the room but Carol shooed them out. "Ten minutes," she said softly. "Just come back in ten minutes. Thank you, girls."

When the last student left, she sank onto the nearest seat and rubbed her thigh, wincing.

"Are you okay?" Bob carefully lifted a monitor off the floor.

"Yes. Thanks, Bob."

"So what was that? A withdrawal or a dismissal?"

"I'm going to buy flowers for every girl in this class," said Carol. "And then I'm writing one hell of a report to Ethel!"

Donna Harding buzzed Julie and told her what happened. Louise was standing by the photocopier in the center of the cubicles when the school director dashed out of his office, passing her without a word. Louise was copying checks from the few students still paying out of their own pocket. She returned to her office, wrote up a deposit slip, and paper-clipped the five checks to it. She looked at the stack of outstanding tuition bills sitting on her desk. The pile was higher than she had ever seen it. Louise sat at her desk in one of her blackest moods.

After a while Oliver returned. He passed hastily into his office, but a moment later stepped out and looked at her.

"What the hell's happening?" asked the business manager.

"There was a fight in Carol's classroom."

"Oh God. Is everything okay?"

"Well, no one's hurt. Two computers are busted. I just had Julie call New York. I want to talk to Larry Soames. I need to know what our responsibility is."

Louise nodded. Larry Soames was Burr's legal consultant as well as John Coyne's personal attorney.

"Who started it?" she asked.

"Rose Becker. I don't even know her."

Louise laughed harshly. "I do. Suddenly this doesn't surprise me."

"Talk to you later." Oliver pushed up his glasses and vanished back into his office.

Louise finished auditing the tuition accounts. She was just starting on her regular mail when somebody rapped the edge of her partition. She looked up irritably. A student stood there, dressed in a small brown wool sweater and charcoal skirt. The girl's hair was entirely gray and puffed out from her head like a dramatic spongy cloud.

"What do you want?" Louise asked.

"I have an appointment with you."

"You do?"

"Stephanie Homan. I'm in the two-year Executive Secretarial Arts. I want to interview for the bookstore manager job."

Louise shook her head. "That position isn't open to students. That's why we didn't post it on campus. We put the ad in *The Philadelphia Inquirer.*"

"Well, I read *The Philadelphia Inquirer.* Why can't a student do the job? It's part-time, right? I can make sure it doesn't conflict with my classes."

"Now look," Louise said, pissed that a student would dare argue with her, "I don't want a student in that job. It involves too much responsibility."

"But I'm having trouble keeping up with my tuition. Having this job will help me pay my bill. Don't you want to help a student pay her bill?"

"I just told you—"

"Yeah, I know what you just told me." Stephanie stepped into the cubicle and crossed her skinny arms. "Ms. Mallory, I am not a baby. I used to keep the cash box for a veterinary office in Bryn Mawr. I'm extremely responsible, and I'll do a great job for you. Why are you being such a hard-ass?"

Louise leaned back in her chair. "First off, 'hard-ass' is not an expression the bookstore manager is expected to use."

"Okay. Why're you being such a jerk then?"

Louise's eyes closed to viper slits. "How long did you work at that veterinary place?"

"Two years. And they didn't lose one goddamn cent."

"You in your first or second year here?"

"Second."

Louise growled and rifled through some papers. She extracted a one-page job description and passed it over. "Here's the deal. It's ten hours a week and pays a quarter above minimum. It's not hard work, but the hours listed have to be covered without exception. There's not much flexibility I can give you, because the store has to stay open during lunch hours, between classes, and sometimes in the early morning and late afternoon so the students can have access."

"Yeah, so I figured." Stephanie scanned the nine points of the job description. "Ms. Mallory, this is nothing. If I were brain-dead I could do this job. The cash register and the inventory need to be handled with accuracy, but that's still just adding and subtracting, big deal."

"Might need to work on your attitude," remarked Louise.

"My attitude's fine," the student answered smoothly. "I just don't see what the issues are. I'm bright, I'm honest, and I can use a calculator. What more are you expecting, considering that pay scale?"

Despite herself, Louise grinned. "Not much, that's for sure."

"What about these 'other duties as assigned?'" asked Stephanie. "Is that there 'cause all job descriptions have that, or do you really have something in mind?"

"As a matter of fact, Admissions would like someone to help load lead cards into the computer and run reports. It's easy, mindless work. Deirdre Smith will show you. She's an admissions rep now, but she used to be the secretary, and she still has to load lead cards on top of her new duties. Rather a pain for her."

Stephanie's blue eyes lit. "Deirdre Smith? Really?"

"You know her?"

"I know who she is. She's a honey."

"Well, she's been doing all the work for a while now, so I'm trying to help her out." Louise looked at the student. "What?"

Stephanie was smiling to herself, gazing at her lap. "I won't mind that. She had a black eye right around when classes started, didn't she?"

The business manager did not answer.

"She tried covering it up but I saw it. She shouldn't take that shit from anybody."

"Bookstore managers don't say 'shit' either," said Louise, but it was almost a whisper. She watched the student as if waiting for a trap to spring.

"I think it's time Deirdre developed a new outlook on life." Stephanie nodded slowly. She glanced up at the business manager. "Are you okay, Ms. Mallory?"

Louise said, "You're hired."

"I am? Really?"

"Yeah. Show me your class schedule. Let's come up with something workable."

"What about your other candidates?"

"What about them? They'll get jobs somewhere. Not our problem. What are your classes like?"

Stephanie began fishing in her red Burr bookbag. "This is great, Ms. Mallory. Thanks a lot."

"You're welcome. I'll be expecting great things from you."

50

For the faculty, the Rose Becker incident confirmed the worst. Ethel Harris sensed that conversations were stopping when she entered the faculty lounge, and more than one teacher was spotted after hours in the personal computer labs. Resumes being updated, the dean figured. She didn't mention it to Oliver. Until something happened, she preferred to keep it her problem.

Perhaps it was ironic that Jean Cavanaugh was the first champion of the new class. It happened after she gave her first quiz and over forty percent failed. She was teaching business math this semester, and it was not difficult material. Matrix multiplication was a basic principle of algebra. Grading the papers in her kitchen that night, she kept complaining to her husband Frank, who was trying to watch a baseball game. "I don't know if these kids are stupid or lazy," she told him.

"Could be either," he said. He was a Philadelphia cop, and familiar with the economically depressed areas where many of Jean's new students lived.

"So what am I supposed to do? I've got one student right now—" Jean kept marking papers as she talked. "Tessie Whales. She seems interested, but rarely raises her hand. And when she does she's usually wrong. I finally looked at her notebook one day and she has misstatements all over in it. I couldn't understand why. Know what her problem was?"

"Hmm."

"She can't see. I write notes on the blackboard and she doesn't see them. So I put her up near the front of the room and now she's doing all right. Not great, but okay."

"Well good," said Frank.

"It's *not* good. How am I supposed to help these kids if they won't tell me when something's wrong?"

"Hon," said Frank gently, and kept saying "hon" until finally she stopped railing and heard him.

"Yes?"

"I don't think you understand these kids."

"Well, I guess you're right," Jean said resentfully. "If a kid can't see the board and doesn't tell me, I guess I *don't* understand that."

"These aren't kids you're used to. They aren't going to come out and tell you what's wrong with them. They've got pride."

"Pride?" exclaimed Jean. "What's proud about not seeing the board?"

"The pride is not admitting a weakness. Don't you see? These kids live in a world where weakness is exploited. They aren't going to tell you what's wrong with them."

Jean looked at her stack of heavily marked quizzes.

"At the same time," Frank went on, "I'll bet they resent you for not spotting the weakness and being compassionate about it, like teachers are supposed to be. You've got a tough group of kids, dear. I wish you weren't teaching them."

"I wish I knew what to do," said Jean.

The next day she passed the papers back with the hardest face she had ever presented to a class. "The quiz yesterday was a disaster. I cannot believe that so many of you did this poorly except by choice. Who actually studied for this?"

Most of the class raised their hands.

"That's a lot more who studied than passed," Jean remarked, letting her disbelief show. "Can anybody account for that?"

Silence. Then one girl raised her hand.

"Ms. Forsythe, yes?"

The kid said, "I never got this in school."

"You never got this in your high school? This is standard business algebra!"

"No, I never."

Jean scanned the others. "How about the rest of you?"

No one said anything, though a few scared faces nodded.

"Well, dammit, then you should have! Problem One." Jean turned to the board and started to write it out. The eyes of the class pressed against her shoulders. The click of the chalk grew louder. Her mind echoed the words "You should have," and Jean began to feel ashamed. Why had she said that? Was it really these kids' fault? She finished the problem and turned around.

"All right. We'll take it from the top. We'll go down the whole page together. If you didn't get this in high school, you're getting it now. After today you won't have an excuse."

It was all the incentive she needed. Jean went after the new students with the full force of her crusader's spirit. She didn't care about the heavy minority make-up of the class, or that the students came from poverty backgrounds. The crime-riddled neighborhoods they lived in only made her worry about their well-being. What she hated was their weak educational upbringing, and so she worked her classes to the hilt. She threw pop quizzes, pushed slower students with extra-credit assignments to boost their study habits, and extended her office hours. This same attitude carried to her after-school sessions. Her original six students from the previous September class soon swelled with additional students until she found herself meeting almost nightly with twenty-six students, more than a normal-sized class. They met every day, and sometimes stayed as late as eight o'clock. It was hard on both Jean and her husband. Frank's police knowledge of Philadelphia made him uneasy about the types of kids his wife was staying late at the school with. But Jean would not be smothered by Frank. She had students who needed her more than ever.

Nothing put a student in Jean's good graces better than a display of earnest hard work, and as the weeks progressed she recognized that the new class was not so bad. The girls of even the most questionable academic backgrounds were still spirited enough to try. They slung their red Burr bookbags over their shoulders with happy pride, and when a fellow student got a good grade or did well on a skills test they applauded as selflessly as the affluent Burr students of years and decades past. They had hearts and souls like any other student; they worked hard and concentrated, and began slowly to achieve a modicum of success.

Keone was back for these special sessions, digging in her heels and expecting to hate every minute of it. But a funny thing happened. The after-school time with Mrs. Cavanaugh was still tough, but not as bad as before the summer. She couldn't believe the teacher was letting up on the pressure, but somehow it felt that way.

Actually Jean was *not* taking it easy on the students. The reason Keone thought so was because the special sessions were making a difference. Despite herself, Keone was developing a grudging respect for Mrs. Cavanaugh. She understood now that the teacher was less upset with her than with her high school and parents. And now that Keone felt herself learning, actually grasping what was going on in the classroom, now that she had someone who actually believed her capable of achieving something, she reflected on her home life with deep bitterness. By helping her, Mrs. Cavanaugh was showing how no one had ever helped her. Even Doris had never expected much from Keone. And the teachers at Southwest High School had marked a passing grade on every paper she submitted.

The after-school sessions covered whatever Mrs. Cavanaugh decided the students needed to know. On most nights the teacher split the students up and gave typing assignments to some while others struggled through poetry or performed math problems. Keone found that she liked some of the poetry. And the math wasn't difficult, really. There was always a logic to it, even if the problems were complex and initially despairing.

English was tougher. Mrs. Cavanaugh made them write two essays a week, a terrible burden on top of their regular homework, and always returned the papers not with a grade but with copious notes crammed in the margins. When Lula Gomez, a July student, complained that the work was too hard to not receive a grade, Mrs. Cavanaugh told her to leave. Jean declared that everybody came to these special sessions to learn, not to get grades. Lula was shocked. She stayed, and no one complained again. The teacher also attacked them personally.

"It's not 'axt,' Ms. Robinson. The word is 'ask.' Let me hear that 'esskay' sound."

"Ask."

"Well good. If you can say it here, why can't you say it in normal conversation?"

There was a girl from Keone's class who joined the after-school sessions. Shaney'ah Bacon had also gone to Southwest High, but she and Keone never really met until Mrs. Cavanaugh sat them together in the library to research the history of Rohm & Haas, a Philadelphia-based chemical company. It turned out that Shaney'ah lived with a grandmother in Tasker Homes, another South Philadelphia housing project not far from Caulfeld, and both students remembered seeing each other in the high school cafeteria. They talked for most of the hour instead of doing the assignment.

"We could get together more often," Shaney'ah suggested, "and try to learn this stuff. This extra work is killin' me."

"You said it," said Keone. "Let's do it. Yeah."

So they tackled the workload together, and it didn't take long for a solid friendship to form. Shaney'ah was as eager to get out of Tasker as Keone was Caulfeld. It was the best friendship Keone was to make at the Burr College, and the feelings of loss and alienation that plagued her so much the first year did not trouble her again.

November deepened, crisp and gray. Jackets became coats. A cold front whipped through the city. Wind cut faces and hands, then warmed slightly by a diffuse noon sun, only to cut again by the end of the day. It was already dark when the students finished school each afternoon.

Late one night the phone rang. Keone woke, but since there was no phone in her room she didn't move. She heard a chair scrape the kitchen floor downstairs. The phone never rang a second time. Dad often woke up during the night and wandered the house, but he would never answer the phone. It had to be Javaughn.

She sensed the call was bad. It had been picked up on the first ring, like it was expected. Keone got out of bed and tiptoed in her floppy pajamas to the door. The hallway was dark, which meant the kitchen must be dark too, for an indirect glow from downstairs could always be seen in the hall when the kitchen light was on, and there was no light at all.

Why was Javaughn sitting in the kitchen with no lights, not making a sound?

The chair scraped again. She heard steps pad the kitchen tiles, then brush lightly on the living room carpet. Still no lights though. He was down there in the dark. Keone tiptoed to the landing and rested a hand on the stairway banister. "Javaughn?"

"Keone? That you?"

She stepped lightly down the stairs. Her eyes were adjusted enough to see the living room through the silver-beaded haze of moonlight shining through the large front window. Javaughn was fully dressed, even to his boots.

"Who was that?" she asked.

"Friend of mine. Why're you up?"

"Phone rang. Why you got the lights out?"

"Don't turn 'em on."

"I ain't. But how can anybody see?"

"Come here."

Javaughn walked back into the kitchen. Keone followed, groping carefully.

"I got a problem," he muttered. "But it's serious."

The kitchen window shade was pulled, and she wasn't sure where he was. The roar of highway traffic just a few feet beyond made the window rattle gently, a sound the whole household was used to. "Like what?"

"I had something fall through. I ain't sure how it happened, but I got my ideas. It's put me in some shit. I'm gettin' out tonight."

"Where?"

"Just out. I won't be back for a long time."

"Javaughn, what happened?"

"Nothin'," he said with a hint of anger, so she asked no more. She sensed movement in the dark, and suddenly felt him close to her. "You look scared," he said. "Don't be. After I'm gone you won't have no trouble. This'll blow over, I juss don't know how long."

"Someone tryin' to kill you?"

"No." But his voice went angry again.

"You sure?"

"Why do bitches always think the worst? Yeah, I'm *sure*."

So someone was. The knowledge registered easily, for there had been other times during their lives together when Keone thought her brother as good as dead. Yet it hurt a little this time, and the hurt scattered her thoughts. She wasn't used to worrying about Javaughn.

"I can't hang 'round long. Gotta get some stuff together and go. Touch's comin' in a car for me. I don't wanna take mine. Listen to me, sister, I got somethin' for you." He rustled his clothes. "It's somethin' I promised you." He pulled a fat envelope from a pocket and held it out.

Keone reached for it quickly. "What you givin' me?"

"Money. It ain't like what I wanted, but it's all I can spare. Was gonna surprise you with it on your birthday, but it don't look like I'll be here for that now."

Her birthday was four months away. Javaughn's shit must be real serious. This awareness wrestled with her excitement as she tried to pry the envelope open. She couldn't see well, but it certainly felt thick.

"Don't open it now. I don't got time and I need you."

"For what?"

"Come in the other room."

Keone followed him back to the living room. Javaughn led her to the front window. "Stay here and watch for me. I'm goin' upstairs to get some things. Touch'll come in a red Pontiac. He's gonna pull up to the curb with the engine runnin' and wink the headlights. You tell me if you see him. Anybody comes and don't wink the headlights, you let me know that too."

Touch was Javaughn's partner. She was really scared now, for herself as well as him. "You want me to yell upstairs?"

"No. Don't wake Mama. I can't get in no argument with her." He thought a moment. "Well, only if the lights don't blink, okay?"

"How long you gonna be?"

"Just a few minutes. Now stand there and watch."

Keone stood by the window as he padded upstairs. She faced the street and kept herself to the right edge of the window even though the living room lights were off. Virginia Street was one block long with two apartment buildings on either side. The street dead-ended in a left turn just past her family's building. A single streetlight out of view up the block cast a sidewise yellow sheen, enough for Keone to discern the whitewashed buildings across the street, a few leafless trees, and the restless movement of the Tarrants' Dobermans in their large cage.

Javaughn stayed upstairs a long time. Just as she was about to go see what he was doing, the tree shadows bobbed. A car pulled into view and idled by the curb. Keone crouched below the windowsill and squinted, trying to see if it was red. The headlights shut off, and a second later flared back on.

"That's him," Javaughn whispered.

Keone jumped and he laughed.

"Listen now, you don't tell 'em nothin'. After a few days they'll catch on and stop worryin'. I'll come back when I can, or maybe I'll get a message to you or something. That present," he tapped the envelope, "is just a down payment. Good luck, sister." He moved quickly to the door. "If I can get to your graduation, I will. No promises though." He opened the door a crack, then slipped out and shut it behind him. Watching from the window, she saw him dart to the car, and somebody flung open a door for him. Javaughn jumped inside, the car crawled forward, picked up speed, and rolled out of view, taking the left turn. Keone heard it go around the block and head for the east gate.

Back in her room with the door locked, she tore open the envelope and counted fifty one hundred dollar bills. She counted the money over and over, and rubbed the bills between her fingers. She thought of all the things she could buy with it. She thought how generous Javaughn was, and hoped he'd be all right. Then she realized, with a spasm of fear, that Dad would take it away from her if he found it. Keone sealed the envelope as best she could, and spent the rest of the night figuring the best place to hide it.

51

Ethel sat at her desk admiring her new secretary. Dawn Hitchcock was thirty-four years old, and a graduate of the previous July Secretarial Arts class which had finished last March.

"Your day starts at nine. You'll have to rotate lunches at the front desk with Julie Fitzgerald, who is both the receptionist and the school director's secretary, and Deirdre Smith who works in Admissions."

The door opened and Arthur Cassidy strode in holding a sheaf of papers. "Excuse me, Eth. These are my attendance sheets for last week."

"Fine. Arthur, do you remember Dawn Hitchcock?"

"I do indeed. Welcome aboard." They shook hands.

"Where was I?" asked Ethel.

"The front desk," Dawn said.

"Oh yeah. It's up to you, Julie, and Deirdre to make sure the front desk is always covered."

"I met Julie. She seems very nice."

"She's the best," said Ethel with emphasis. "You won't get any sniping or gossiping from Julie." She looked at Arthur. "Dawn had a bad experience at her last job."

"Really?"

Dawn looked self-conscious. "Well, it was just a crazy situation. I was working for this group of CPAs in Wilmington—"

"Don't call it a crazy situation," growled Ethel. "That makes too light of it."

"Bellman Accounts," Dawn continued. "I loved the work, but there were these three male CPAs on the floor, one of whom I reported to, and soon after I started they began dropping weird racial comments."

"Like what?" asked Arthur.

Dawn grimaced. Ethel quickly said, "It doesn't matter."

Dawn nodded. "It wasn't until they started doing it that I realized I was the only African-American woman working on the floor. Anyway, I told one of them politely that his comments were offensive, and I asked him not to say such things to me again. He apologized. But then he told my supervisor, and I got chewed out."

"Your supervisor was one of the three?" asked Arthur.

"Yes. He said I was not to make trouble for Mr. Craig, that anything he said was surely harmless, and it was time I stopped acting persecuted."

"Persecuted?" Arthur echoed with a rise in his voice.

"It got me so upset I couldn't sleep or eat. All I wanted to do was quit but I didn't think I could, I hadn't even worked there a month yet. So I called Mrs. Peterson, just for advice, and she said, 'I have a perfect position for you if you're willing to work in Center City.' And she set me up with Dean Harris."

"Call me Ethel," said Ethel. "You've moved up now."

"You should sue them," said Arthur.

"I am. I have an appointment with a lawyer Thursday afternoon." Dawn looked at Ethel. "Is that okay with you?"

"Absolutely. I hope you smack 'em hard. They were stupid to treat you that way." The dean turned to Arthur with a big smile worth savoring. "Dawn's a graduate from NYU's film school. How about that? When's the last time I had a college grad for a secretary?"

"How long have you been without one now?"

"Ten months. Natalie left last January." She looked at Dawn. "What else do I need to tell you about the job?"

"We were still discussing the front desk," said Dawn. "Ethel, would you like me to go downstairs and refill your coffee?"

"God bless you. We'll both go. I'll give you the guided tour."

"Don't be too nice to the dean," Arthur cautioned. "Ethel, what will you do if this one likes it here and actually sticks around?"

"Give her my job," Ethel said with a warm smile.

At noon, and to everyone's wonder, the dean was still smiling. Dawn Hitchcock reviewed the stacks of files, folders, memos, and grade sheets piled in both Ethel's office and the cubicle that used to be Natalie's, and pitched right in. She worked steadily, regrouping, filing, purging, organizing, and after three hours made more positive impact on the dean's office than Natalie had in a year.

Julie looked up in amazement when Ethel came into the lobby at midday and pulled her coat from the closet. "Are you actually going out to lunch, Dean Harris?"

"Yeah. And I might just make that a habit from now on." Ethel hummed as she went out the school entrance.

Julie buzzed Lily to let her know her twelve o'clock appointment had arrived. A teenage girl sat on the couch with a short elderly woman. A moment later Lily emerged breezily from the cubicles.

"Hello! Hello! Nancy, isn't it? For the Information Processing Program? My, I'm happy to see you! And who's this? Your grandmother?"

"Yes," the elderly woman nodded. "I'm Mrs. Collins."

Nancy said, "Mom and Dad work, so Gram brought me."

"That's wonderful. That's family values at work, hey? Well Nancy, I need you to fill out this little blue form, but why don't you both come back to my office? Mrs. Collins, may I ask where you are employed?"

The grandmother laughed. "Oh, I'm retired. I haven't worked in decades."

"Really? How about your husband?"

"Mr. Collins passed away fourteen years ago."

"Oh dear. Gracious, I'm sorry. If there is anything I can do, please let me know. Now, does this mean you have no income?"

Mrs. Collins took the prying good-naturedly. "I'm sixty-nine years old. I have a pension, and social se—"

"Oh, but of course you do!" Lily laughed and took the woman's arm. "Still, in this day and age, I'm not sure it's wise to put all our eggs in government baskets, hey? After all, federal funding may come and go, but secretarial positions will *always* be out there …" They disappeared through the cubicles, Nancy trailing behind.

The bell blatted, and a moment later Julie heard the corridor thunder as students changed classes. Bob Lawrence walked into the lobby holding a folder. "Hi, Julie, how's it going?"

"Well enough, Bob. How about you?"

"Rocking and rolling." He strolled through the cubicles, and rounded the partition wall of the dean's secretary station just as Dawn was snapping shut her purse and getting up from her desk. "Oh, hi," he said, caught off guard.

"Mr. Lawrence, hello. I'm Dawn Hitchcock."

"Yeah, I remember. So you're starting today?" He smiled warmly. "Welcome to the zoo. Now you get to see how the sausages are made." He held out a folder. "Speaking of which, can I give you these before you go off to wherever you're going? They're my mid-term grades."

Dawn took the folder and checked the pages within it. "Weren't these due at the beginning of November instead of the end?"

Bob frowned, impressed. "Pretty knowledgeable for your first day."

"Not even that. It's barely afternoon. Ethel has already given me a list of the teachers who are behind on their grades. It's not a long list, Mr. Lawrence."

"Ethel needs to loosen up and enjoy life."

"As I'm sure you do." The secretary grinned.

Little nerves tingled. Bob had perfect radar for even the mildest office flirtation. Ethel's new secretary already appealed to him simply by meeting the rote standards of good clothes and a fetching figure. Standing close, he was now taken by the contours of her oval face, her large brown eyes, and black hair set in tiny pristine waves behind her ears. He remembered her as one of the older students back when she attended, and now he wondered by how much. "Where are you heading?"

"Downstairs for lunch."

"You're eating in the faculty lounge? You can't do that, it's your first day. Killigan's is just up the block. They've got the best roast beef sandwiches in the city."

"I'm a veggie."

"Are you really? Wish I was. Well, they also have an excellent quiche. And the service is fast, so you can do it in an hour. What say you?"

"Sounds good to me." She picked up her purse. "Let me get my coat."

At the deli he ordered the quiche as well, even though Dawn said she would not be offended if he chose to eat a smelly, disgusting, blood-red, bacteria-riddled sandwich.

"You're broad-minded. I like that." But Bob didn't change his order.

"Ethel told me you're writing a novel."

"Oh God, I wish she wouldn't keep telling people. It's embarrassing."

"Why? I think it's great. You should be proud of yourself."

"I'll be proud if it ever gets published. Until then I'm not a writer, just a wannabe."

"No, don't think like that," she said quickly. "I never got in the film industry, but I made a couple of films when I was in college and I still consider myself a filmmaker."

"You made films in college?"

Dawn smiled impishly. "Cinema was my major. I'm only a secretary because I couldn't crack the industry."

Bob's interest in her sharpened. "What kind of movies?"

"Oh nothing deep and cerebral. My stuff was more the bittersweet Joan Micklin Silver variety."

"*Chilly Scenes of Winter.*"

"Well, well. Very good."

"And your last name is Hitchcock?"

She put up a hand. "Don't start. I got four years of that at NYU."

"Okay," he said with a laugh. "I won't say a word. But you'd think a name like that would open doors."

"Well, I thought it looked good on a resume. But the movie industry is too close-knit. I needed money and contacts and didn't have either. Oliver's wife is Christina Dunbar, isn't she? That's what Trudy told me."

"Yeah."

"That's something. You ever talk to her?"

Bob shrugged dismissively. "Not really, though I've met her. She doesn't come around much."

The food arrived. Bob felt both relaxed and stimulated, a very good sign. He and Dawn discussed their favorite books, restaurants, and films. He soon learned that she lived in town, shared an apartment with a sister, and was three years his junior. The lunch went too quickly. As they split the check he asked, "Would you be free for dinner some night?"

Dawn didn't look too surprised. "Is this something you do with all the secretaries on their first day?"

"Look, I get teased a lot because I'm single and there are so few guys working at the school. But God's honest truth, this is not something I normally do. I'm just enjoying this too much, and I want it to continue."

"Well, I'm enjoying it too." Dawn smiled, and he thought how lovely it would be to wake up to that face in the morning.

"Should I get Ethel's permission?"

"You are so silly. Bob, I don't think I should be dating co-workers my first week on the job. I've got enough to worry about right now."

"Is that a no?"

"It's a 'give it time,'" she said. "You seem like a nice guy. Just let me get acclimated, okay?"

"Of course."

Returning to Burr, he almost followed Dawn through the lobby instead of going down the hall to his classroom. He was tempted to see if Louise Mallory was away from her cubicle so he might grab a peek at Dawn's personnel file. It was embarrassing to think like that, but he also recognized the high school crush in the impulse and laughed at himself. He went to class.

Had Bob looked, he would have found the business manager's cubicle empty. Louise sat in Oliver's office with the door closed, perusing the latest draft of the Achievement Program, a seventeen page white paper with a three-page syllabus and course description. Oliver sipped tea nervously as he watched her read it. This was an important moment, for no one took more pleasure from being cruelly honest than Louise.

She didn't take long, even though she skimmed the syllabus a second time. "It's good, Oliver. You've been an ambitious boy."

"Me and Ethel."

"How long have you been working on this?"

"Most of October, and all of November."

And tough work it had been. The problem with attacking a curriculum like Burr's was that its structure of learning had not been tampered with since the early Twentieth Century. The recognition that women were as intelligent and competent as men was already fundamental when Reginald and Evelyn designed the curriculum in 1907; the psychology of eighteen-year-old women, and older women with ambition but no practical experience in business, had been scrutinized and mapped into the programs, and lessons and academic pressure increased to a preconceived pace as skills and experience advanced via classroom exercises. This was not to say that Burr education had never undergone revision; in fact, the colleges prided themselves on their ability to adapt with the times. Programs had evolved as women advanced in management during World War II, and other changes took into account the gradual erosion of small businesses where many early Burr grads worked in the days when large corporations still wouldn't take them seriously as managers. And of course now Burr was racing to keep pace with the new technological innovations, personal computers, cell phones, e-mail, and the ever-expanding Internet. Burr education was elastic this way.

Oliver and Ethel were trying something different. They weren't changing the curriculum because of the times, but because of their students. They did not touch established program content, but did go after the structure. This was a serious acknowledgment that their student demographic had shifted. As fewer wealthy middle-class women considered secretarial careers, the door swung open for those who had limited career options at best: poor, and poorly educated women. With this in mind, the dean and school director took the two-year program and extended it six more months. They chose the extra time to attack the basics: reading, writing, and math. But they went further. They got personal. Ethel incorporated lifestyle classes to teach the students basic professional comportment, hitting negatives hitherto taken for granted such as gum-chewing, foul language, and talking back to the boss. A personal finance class was added to teach students how to handle money, including their precious student loans. The extra class time was quickly filled with lessons and lectures. Then Oliver and Ethel rethought the progression of all these classes. The workload was kept tight and relentless, a traditional signature of Burr education, but the gradation of pressure was slowed enough to keep the weaker students from despairing. The end result was a six-semester version of the four-semester (or two-year) Executive Secretarial Arts Program. Oliver christened it the Burr College Achievement Program, a cryptic name he hoped would distinguish it from the existing programs without sounding condescending.

"We did our homework," he told Louise. "We interviewed the principals and counselors of the 'C' schools, we examined the transcripts of the recent July and September girls to see what academic level we were really dealing with. It took us most of October to scheme it out. I think it does the job. No one will think of this as the 'dumb students' program."

"Well," said Louise, "if we're ever going to help these kids, this is the way to do it. Of course it's going to cost."

"I know. Here, look at this." He dug around for another folder on his desk. "I've got some estimates cooked up by an accountant I know who has no experience with education, I'm sorry to say. But I think it's accurate. We figure we should sit two classes of fifty each the first year. That's high for a new program, but we thought a sudden big start would be attractive to John Coyne."

"We don't have the classroom space."

"There's the Dungeon. That's a fine big room." Oliver was referring to a large room in the basement just off the cafeteria, currently home to all student academic files dating back twenty-two years.

"We've talked about that before. We'd have no place for our records."

"We'll scan them on disks. There are places that do that now."

"God, Oliver, you're talking massive electronic storage on top of a full room renovation. We'll need overhead fluorescent lighting, new desks—how about computers?"

"That'll be tight," he admitted. "Obviously we need more, but I think we'd have to get through the first year with what we've got before I spring that on John. I want to contact Microsoft and Dell and IBM for possible grant funding."

"You know, some business supply stores have older equipment they might donate."

Oliver nodded. "We've a lot to look into."

"I see you're talking about hiring six teachers."

"Well, we want a double session."

"Swell. That's at least two hundred and eighty thou right there. Couldn't Ethel stretch with at least one in-house faculty member?"

Oliver shook his head. "They're stretched too much as it is. Besides, our people aren't right for this. We'll be teaching girls who've never had positive role-models, whose parents might be drunks or drug addicts or just simply never around. Ethel doesn't think our teachers are equipped to teach a student body like that, and she's right. They're good teachers, but they're bound to see this as a comedown, and I'm sure they'll unconsciously communicate that to the class. We need good teachers already experienced with kids like this. Ethel will look into that further after we get New York's go-ahead."

"Hmmm. New York." Louise laid the folder flat on her lap. "Oliver, how enthusiastic is John Coyne going to be about this?"

"We don't know. But since New York's most obvious way of attacking the program will be the cost, we need to be as prepared as possible. That's why I want you to vet this. Try to come up with a total expense figure so I know what I'm up against. Everything you can think of, from the cost of renovating the Dungeon to the number of pens these girls will need. We have to prove that the volume of students we get will more than pay for the program."

"That wasn't what I was talking about. I didn't mean New York would object to the money."

"Oh." His face clouded. "Yes, I know what you're getting at."

"This whole Achievement Program thingy is an open invitation for ghetto kids to come to Burr. How are you going to get the President's Office to feel pleased about that?"

"I don't know," Oliver admitted. "I've been to meetings where Bill has stressed—without actually coming out and saying so—that minority students aren't really what the Burr Colleges are about. Said he doesn't consider minority enrollment a bad thing, but …"

"There's always that 'but,'" said Louise.

"Yes."

"And here you are with this plan."

"I know. This program could knock our overall yearly enrollment of minority students close to fifty percent. And as long as we're being candid I should say I don't know what effect it will have on the white population. I like to think it'll have no effect, but I don't want to be naïve."

"Gets awfully sensitive, doesn't it?"

"Yeah. Well, maybe John won't mind. He takes lots of trips to the schools and boasts that they keep him in touch. If he's really been looking, he must see the changing demographic. Maybe he's learned something."

"Maybe he has," said Louise.

"I mean, it's possible."

"Sure."

They looked at each other, then suddenly, simultaneously, they laughed. Louise's guffaw sounded like a gear in need of oil, and Oliver's shoulders shook so hard he had to push his chair away from the desk to make sure he didn't knock anything over.

"God, that felt great." The business manager wiped a tear from her eye. "I'll get this back to you before the end of the week, okay?" She stood, holding the folder.

"Thanks, Louise."

He worked the remainder of the afternoon on his overdue November monthly report. At five o'clock Julie buzzed him. "Oliver, I'm closing up."

"Okay. Have a good evening."

"How late are you staying?"

"Not late. Not past six, I promise. I'll call you tonight."

"That'd be nice. Be safe walking home." She hung up.

They were seeing each other more and more, for dinners, for weekend jaunts with Kelly, and for each other's company. They had yet to spend a night together, but the bond between them stayed sweet, and perhaps grew stronger without this last intimacy. He even met her parents over Thanksgiving when Julie drove him and Kelly up to Roxborough. Jerry and Lisa Fitzgerald were a quiet, serious couple living in a modest apartment above a hardware store on Ridge Avenue. Their faces couldn't hide their concern over the fourteen-year age difference between their daughter and her new boyfriend, but softened once they saw how respectfully Oliver treated Julie, and were won over entirely by his tireless attention to Kelly.

Julie's voice from the phone stayed in his head, and Oliver didn't get much work done on the report. At six-fifteen he put it aside and stretched. He took his coat from the lobby closet, feeling deep in his bones that it was Manayunk and not Rittenhouse where he should be heading. How easy it would be to catch the No. 9 and ride out to Manayunk, ascend the hill, knock on Julie's door, surprise her, and take her in his arms. The more he thought about it, the more it became the only thing to do.

He set the security alarm and snapped off the lights. The phone rang and he almost ignored it, but the light on Julie's phone indicated the call was on his office line. Professional integrity kicked in, and he picked up the receiver. "Burr College of Business."

"Oliver? Are you answering your own phone now?"

The voice couldn't have caused a deeper mental wrench. Oliver's head dizzied, and he suffered an irrational split-second of guilt. "Tina—hello."

"Have they cut your staff *that* badly, hon?"

"Huh? Oh, no. Just—it's just everybody else has gone home."

"Except you, of course. I figured I could reach you there. How are you?"

"Fine. Hey, your film got some good write-ups. I read all the reviews, you know. Everybody seems to think you were great."

"Did you see it?"

He hadn't; the Sidney Wallace courtroom film had come out in September and disappeared from theaters in less than three weeks. To cover himself, he asked, "Any Oscar talk?"

"Oh good Lord no! Not until next February at best, but who could even *dare* think … well, you know I can't say anything that might jinx things."

"I know."

"But other than that everything's good. I'm getting quite a few scripts and so is Dennis. Don't worry, I'm not going to talk about him."

"Thank you."

"But things are bopping, and in a very good way. How about yourself? That nuclear woman of yours still bringing them in?"

"Lily. She sure is. The place is packed."

"That's nice to hear. I mean that. I was pretty worried about you."

"How do you mean?"

"Well, you never returned the lawyer's phone calls or letters, and recently I talked to Dale Thurston—"

"Oh did you?"

"Yes. He wasn't seeing you at meeting, and thought you might be falling into a serious depression. If you're really all right, tell me again."

"Tina, I'm fine."

"Good. Are you going to—oh wait. Oliver, can I put you on hold a moment?"

"Sure."

The line clicked in his ear. Oliver adjusted his glasses and looked out the dark windows at Washington Square. His heart pounded through his overcoat. Another click and she was back. "Sorry, hon. Now let me bring up the nasty issue."

"Sorry about the divorce dragging."

"You're telling me. Oliver, this is taking too long. Up to now I haven't felt much pressure, but there are things happening that sort of dictate I get my freedom. It's been nearly a year."

"I know."

"Will you do me and my checkbook a favor and start cooperating? I could have these extra expenses charged to you, but so far I haven't. I mean, I *do* feel somewhat guilty about the whole thing. But I need your co-operation to get this finished."

"I'll go through whatever I've got as soon as I get home."

"That would be great. You can't imagine how aggravating this has been."

"Well, I probably can. I have no excuse."

"Fine, then. I'll let you be. Take care. Glad your school is doing well."

"Tina, good luck next February."

She laughed and hung up.

Oliver stood in the darkened lobby. The wall with the two big portraits blanked to whiteness and on its surface, like a movie screen, he saw old Penn campus days and late-night café discussions over pressing subjects like *The Pentagon Papers,* Watergate, and the China embargo, *Catch*-22 and *A Clockwork Orange,* and old chestnuts like *Ulysses* and *Tropic of Cancer.* Arguing with Dale Thurston and others over social issues and picking apart art in all directions. Pointy-heads they all were, enjoying an elite campus attitude that accepted brains and culture as true status symbols. One tipsy night Oliver stood on a bar chair and trumpeted his plans for an educational reform that would transform America, and Tina, the only undergraduate in the group and sort of odd-man-out, looked up at him with a light of pride in her eyes that would stand the test of time; he could still see clearly her gray cotton blouse and tight jeans, the tall glass of beer in her hand, and the crazy disco lights swirling behind her.

Oliver stood in the lobby of his empty school, lost in the days when he had made Tina proud.

52

It was as Javaughn said. Doris was upset but not surprised. She called the neighbors, who knew nothing. When more than a week passed she called again, and still no one could tell her anything. So she waited for word to come to her. She went to her grocery job each morning, came home and made dinner for the family, and tried not to think about it. She told Bella,

Darcy's mom, that she hoped Javaughn would show by Christmas. Doris' boss had found her a nice live tree, and she, Keone, and Corey planned to decorate it, and Doris had two gifts wrapped for her eldest son.

On the second Wednesday in December, during the first week of the fall semester finals, Keone got an A on her exam in Arthur Cassidy's Advanced Accounting class. It was her first A at Burr, and she showed the grade to Lisa Wallace and Shaney'ah Bacon as they all descended the stairs to reach their lockers.

"Great job," said Lisa. "Congrats."

"Best I done so far," said Keone.

"Is it? Great."

The white girl wasn't as excited as Keone hoped, but Shaney'ah was properly impressed. Both girls knew Keone was on probation. This A in Keone's hand, an A from Burr, was a true certificate of glory. She couldn't wait to show it to her mother.

Shaney'ah, Lisa, and Keone opened their lockers. Lisa said, "Keone, you look so pretty today."

"Yeah," said Shaney'ah. "I was just gonna say. Not that you don't look good other times," she hastily qualified. "But I mean, today you look *real* good."

"Thanks." Keone beamed happily. She had waited all day for someone to say something. With three hundred dollars of Javaughn's money, she had bought a red satin dress, red shoes, and new gold earrings, and at the last second got her hair done, a 'do that piled her hair thickly over her forehead while trimming close to the sides of her head, a style she had seen in *Glamour*. Nothing had prompted the make-over except she had the money, it was almost Christmas, and she just felt like doing something fun for herself. Getting these compliments from her classmates made all the effort worthwhile.

"You think this looks okay?" she asked, indicating the bright dress. "I got it 'cause I love red, but it's not real office-like."

"It don't look bad," said Shaney'ah. "It's kinda loud, but it's sharp."

"I know what you mean," said Lisa. "You get away with it, but you'd never see, say, Mrs. Harding wear that bright red."

"I'm not good at buyin' clothes," Keone confessed. "Not work stuff, anyway. I look at magazines and I go in stores, but it's so different when it's right there in front of me. I never know what I'm doin.'"

"You just need confidence," said Lisa.

Shaney'ah asked, "Got any spending money on you?"

"Yeah."

"What you got?"

"It's uh … at home."

"You want to spend some of it on clothes?"

Keone was confused by the question. "Well, sure."

"Right. You come with me this Saturday and we'll go to The Gallery. I'll dress you up."

"Okay."

Shaney'ah looked at Lisa. "You wanna come?"

"Oh, I don't know. Maybe next time. But you gals have fun."

Keone said, "I gotta buy dinner."

"You're on!"

Keone banged shut her locker and they all stepped outside. Lisa went her own way, and Keone and Shaney'ah strolled bustling Walnut Street for eight blocks to the Broad Street subway. They passed business people, diners formally dressed for the theater, and shoppers overloaded with Christmas tote bags. The two project girls squeezed through, red bookbags weighting their shoulders, and went below the street to catch the southbound train.

Keone emerged by herself twenty-five minutes later. She passed some boys hanging before a donut shop on Broad Street, and cut across four lanes of traffic to the west side. The lights of Veteran's Stadium flared into the night sky. She walked down a residential street occupied by a lot of Mafia families, and the neat clean-swept yards and pretty bay windows were decorated with religious icons and Christmas figures. It reminded her of the Burr College's upcoming holiday party. Her Pollyanna was Ruth Conant, and she knew Ruth didn't like her, yet she was afraid not to buy her something. Keone turned down Haggard Street and passed through the open gate of Caulfeld. She crossed the playground in the dark and walked down Virginia Street. She unlocked the bolts of 183 and pushed the heavy door open.

Her father looked up from the couch. "Where you been?"

"At school." She stood half through the door.

"Okay."

Warren Robinson sat in the center of the couch with his large arms stretched across its back on either side. He was a big man, six-foot three with a build like Javaughn's, though at thirty-seven his gut was soft and paunchy from alcohol and long stretches of unemployment. His red flannel shirt was open to reveal a T-shirt gray from a need of changing. A beer bottle stood on the floor by his feet but it was still capped. He grimaced as if in some kind of pain.

"Don't bother Mama," he said. "She's upset about Javaughn."

Keone stepped quietly to the kitchen doorway. Doris sat at the table with her hands over her face. Corey stood with his back pressed against the sink counter, looking at his mother with big frightened eyes.

"Mama?"

Doris looked up. Her face was washed with tears. "Honey, you ain't heard nuthin' 'bout Javaughn, have you? Nuthin' among your friends?"

"No, Mama. I wish I did."

Doris covered her face again. Keone picked up Corey, whose snuffling was now choked by a liquid run of snot down his nose, and carried him out to the living room.

"What you doin'?" her father asked. He hadn't changed his position on the couch.

"Takin' Corey to my room. Lettin' Mama be."

He nodded. "That's good. You do that."

The bottle of beer was still capped. Keone knew that he tried not to drink when Doris was upset; for all the times he hit her, he was still Dad and still here, which was more than most Caulfeld families could say. Darcy had called four guys dad since childhood, and never knew her real father at all. Keone carried Corey up to her room and laid him on her bed. She wiped his nose, and kept cooing at him until his shakes stopped. She bounced him on the bed to make him giggle.

Downstairs the kitchen phone rang. It was picked up with a hasty clatter, and Keone sat still so she could listen. "Hello? Oh Bella, yeah. You hear somethin'? No—I just don't know. He never left me nuthin'."

Keone got the Etch A Sketch from Corey's room and let him play with it on her bed. She pulled the night's homework from her bookbag and sorted through it to see what needed to get done first. When she went shopping on Saturday with Shaney'ah she would buy one dress. Just one, and it would be a practical dress. A business suit, because she needed one. The rest of Javaughn's money she would save. As soon as she graduated she would get an apartment or something, and that would be the best use for the money. She had to get out of here.

53

Two days before Christmas Lori Clayton sat at a card table in the kitchen of her one-bedroom apartment in Riverside and scanned the help-wanted ads in the paper. The metal folding chair she sat on was the only other furniture in the room. This minimalism carried to the rest of the apartment where a futon served as a bed in the bedroom, and a small portable TV rested on a coffee table in the living room. A miniature stuffed reindeer stood on the windowsill, her sole Christmas decoration. Lori was forty-five and heart-broken from recent events, and though she had bought the paper on Sunday it wasn't until Monday that she finally made herself look at it. At the top of the employment section was an ad two columns wide that shouted the very question at the heart of her problem:

DO YOU WANT A JOB?
The Career Office of the
BURR COLLEGE OF BUSINESS
Is looking for you!
Martin T. Nolan, *Job Representative*

She stared at the ad for a while, then finally gave Mom a call. Mom had gone to the Burr College after graduating high school in 1948. So had Lori's sister, Jeannie, in the Seventies. Lori was the daughter who married straight out of high school. Lori the dope.

Mom was encouraging, so she called the school. By noon she was showered and dressed and driving into the city. She was impressed that Mr. Nolan would see her right away. Walking down Sixth Street she spotted the quaint brick building and liked it immediately. It wasn't what she expected a snobby business school to look like. Stepping inside, the old-fashioned furniture, the Nineteenth Century boats framed over the reception desk, and the tall potted plants made her feel less ashamed of her situation. The woman behind the desk was young and blond, and Lori had low tolerance for young blondes these days, but at least she was pleasant.

"Hello, may I help you?"

"Yes, I'm here to see Mr. Nolan about a job."

"A job?"

"Yes. He made an appointment for me. Told me to come in this afternoon."

The receptionist looked at a heavily marked calendar page. "And your name?"

"Lori Clayton."

"Well, yes, you're here. Are you sure it's about a job?"

"Yes." Lori wondered why the receptionist looked confused. Maybe she was new.

"I'll buzz him," the blonde said. "Please have a seat."

Martin Nolan was a very nice black man with a charming smile and firm handshake. He insisted that she call him by his first name, then took her back to his office and offered her a seat and a glass of iced tea.

"Tell me your situation, Lori," he said soothingly, "and take your time. I know some of it already from our talk on the phone, and I respect what you're going through."

"Martin, I'm in real trouble. This is very difficult for me."

"Of course."

"I appreciate your seeing me. I do truly."

"I haven't done anything yet, Lori. Take your time."

"Okay." She took a deep breath. "I'm going to turn forty-six in two months. Three weeks ago I—" She stopped. Martin waited patiently. "I left my husband. I did it two Sundays ago. I had to leave choir practice early 'cause of a headache, and I found Tony with Edie Hagel in a clinch on the living room couch. Edie's divorced. She lives six houses up. I don't know her well, but you can hear her kid all the time, he screeches at the top of his lungs."

Lori burst into tears. In a flash Martin was beside her, a box of tissues in hand. She grabbed a clump. "Oh God, I'm sorry."

"You're fine, you're fine. Don't even think about it."

"I kept that house running for twenty-seven *years!* I stayed home while he pursued his business degree and then his frigging masters! I watched our kids crawl and walk and grow up. I went to the little league games and the PTA meetings. I counted every goddamn dollar as if it were blood from my own veins, saving for band uniforms and school trips and—oh God!"

Martin passed more tissue. "What did he do when you caught him?"

"I can hardly remember. I know Edie just said 'Excuse me' and got her coat and walked out. Oh—I know what he did. He said he wasn't happy. Married twenty-seven years and not happy! I moved out that same night. I got this little crappy place on High Street. I took the deposit money from the account Tony and I share. I thought that would signal him I was serious, and he'd better fix things fast to get me back."

"Yes, of course."

"So he called a couple times to see how I was getting along. After the second week he stopped calling. I started driving by the house. I couldn't help it. I saw Edie's car in the driveway and that did it, I couldn't take it anymore."

"Lori, I'm very sorry."

She stared morosely at her glass. "I guess he drew his own conclusion from the lesson I was trying to teach him."

"Lori—"

"How can a man do that? Edie's thirty-five, I *think*. She's not *that* young. How can a man leave his wife so completely after twenty-seven years? Our kids aren't around. One's in college and the other has a job in Chicago. I have to go back to the house and get things, but I don't even know how to do that. What if she's *there?* But I have to, 'cause I don't have anything."

"Do you have a job, Lori?"

"Well, kind of. That's why I'm here."

"I think we should talk about that, don't you?"

"Yes." She blew her nose. "It's so exhausting to call the phone company, the electric company, the water company. Everything's so complicated. My sister is giving me some furniture. I should have it by the weekend."

"What about your job, Lori?"

"It isn't much. Just thirteen thousand a year as receptionist for a dental clinic."

"Okay," said Martin. "Obviously that's not enough."

"I know, I know." She dabbed her eyes.

"Do you have a resume?"

"Yes. It's got some typos on it which I can fix. I had to write it out this morning. I'm sure it needs work."

"Well, let's look at it, okay?"

She pulled it from her pocketbook and unfolded it. She knew already that it didn't look like much. Her dental receptionist job was listed at the top, but the remainder of her experience—a shoe clerk, a ceramics teacher—dated more than twenty years ago. As Martin read it, the silence began to eat at her, and she grabbed more tissue.

Finally he put down the paper. "Lori, what we need to do is put you where you don't have to count on anyone else for your security." He tapped the paper. "This isn't bad, and we can definitely work with you. But your job experience isn't strong enough. The receptionist job is good, but the rest of your work experience doesn't project a lot of marketable skills."

"Well, but I do have some computer training. I mean, I'm using a computer now. They have them at the clinic. And I'm a very good typist."

"Certainly. But I have to be blunt because it's the only way I can help you. This part-time receptionist job is not going to be taken seriously by employers. Not if you want a *good* job. Would you like another glass of iced tea?"

"Please."

He hopped up to serve her.

"Right then. I'm thinking about your resume and I've got an idea. Something that can really punch up your resume and do what we want. Interested?"

"Oh yes. Certainly."

He plucked a brochure from a plastic stand on his desk. "Take a look at this. It's our Information Processing Program. It's the best program we run, and a new class starts first week in January. It goes to next September, and when you get out you'll have all the qualifications necessary to be a top executive secretary."

Lori's heart sank. "Next September?"

"Lori, you know you're good, and I know it too. But on paper you're not qualified. Right now I can't get you any job better than the low-paying one you already have. But if you take this class you'll be set. We're talking a big salary instead of an adequate one. We're talking real financial security as opposed to just getting by."

She stared helplessly at the brochure. "I just don't know. September seems so far away. When does it start? And what does it cost?"

"It starts January 5. Now look, I have to be honest. The January class is pretty full and they don't allow us to overbook. I'm going to have to pull some strings to get you in. But that's okay—" He held up a hand to block her protest. "I respect the situation you're in. I realize you can't afford to wait. Let me go talk to the director of admissions right now. I'll probably have to fight her about this, but you really need to get in this class."

"Oh, but I don't want you to get in trouble—"

"Don't even think about it. This is too important. You wait right here."

Marty walked out of his office, saw that Lily's door was closed, and passed through the cubicles. He walked the first floor corridor to the men's room, entered and stepped into a stall. (The Burr College, female for so long, had no urinals in any of the bathrooms.) Marty peed leisurely, then washed his hands while enjoying his reflection in the mirror. God*damn* but he was good! When he had proposed this job service idea at staff meeting, Lily had been enchanted and the two girl reps jealous. As well they should be. Nice girls, Trudy and Dee, but they didn't have the edge. Marty sure did. He was without a doubt the best rep, pulling in the biggest numbers and therefore the biggest bonuses. Trudy and Dee tried, and sometimes it was touching to watch them, but face it, it wasn't their fault. To be a salesman—a *real* salesman—you needed that cannon between your legs. There was power there beyond simply pleasing the ladies. Here it was the middle of December and the January goal nearly made, and Marty was responsible for more than half the commits. The Rep with the Pep. He combed his hair, straightened his bowtie, and strolled back up the corridor to the lobby. Walking into his office, he squeezed Lori's shoulder as he passed her chair.

"Good news," he said. "You're in."

54

Early Christmas morning Oliver rode the bus out to Manayunk. The door to Julie's apartment was answered by a flushed, agitated Kelly in yellow Belle pajamas. He signed, *What's your problem?*

Santa was here!

Evidence of that good-hearted philanthropist lay under the tree, more gifts than Kelly had seen in seven previous Christmases. With no experience at buying for kids, Oliver had overdone the Kringle department. His major gift to both child and mother was a computer, and it was the biggest box under the tree; but he was unable to let it go at that. Kelly opened Barbies, books, earrings, Stratego, Clue, pictures for her room, Disney videos, and an alarm clock that flashed brightly when it went off. Julie, sweet in a blue bathrobe although exhausted around the eyes, laid out fruit and muffins, and kept the coffee coming. Oliver's gifts to her included a set of emerald earrings, two novels she had wanted to read for years, and tickets to *Rent* on Broadway. Julie gave him a black-belted Burberry overcoat and refused to say what she paid for it. They sat together on the couch and watched the child tear through her treasures.

By nine-thirty they were dressed and climbing into Julie's car to go to meeting. Oliver drove. As they wended their way through the scant holiday traffic, he said, "I hope this isn't too boring for Kelly."

"Why do you think it will be?" Julie signed for both of them, since his hands were on the wheel.

"Well, it's such a simple ritual. There's no preacher or choir. You just sit and worship. Lots of kids get antsy."

"So you're saying Kelly might find it boring because nobody speaks and there's no music?"

It sunk in and he looked over. Kelly was laughing from the back seat. "Okay," Oliver said. "I'll get used to this someday."

They parked near Race Street. *Who is that?* Kelly signed as they passed a statue of Mary Dyer. Oliver showed her the caption on the pedestal. Kelly signed, and Julie interpreted. "Do people really get executed for saying what they believe?"

"Yes," Oliver answered.

"Do they still do that?"

"In some places."

"Do they do that here in America?"

Oliver hesitated, then nodded. "Some places," he said again.

The lobby was jammed with holiday worshippers waiting for the meeting room's double doors to open. "It's not usually this crowded," Oliver said. "A lot of these people don't come during regular Sundays."

"Sort of like us."

"Exactly. But that's going to change."

"I think it should too." Julie held her daughter's hand tightly.

"Hey, Oliver!"

Dale Thurston waved and tried to cut through a family blocking his way. He was a large individual, with thick jowls and a heavy moustache. Oliver whispered in Julie's ear, "Remember me talking about an old school chum? Brace up, you're about to meet him."

"Oliver, glad to see you!" Dale shook his hand with barely a glance at Julie.

"Merry Christmas, Dale."

"Yeah, merry Christmas. Forgive my stunned face. How long has it been since you were at meeting?"

"Almost a year," Oliver admitted.

"And you haven't kept in touch or anything. I was worried about you."

"Yeah, I heard that. Say Dale, this is Julie Fitzgerald and her daughter Kelly. You have to wave to Kelly, she's deaf."

"Oh?" He examined afresh the young woman and her child. "How do you do?"

"Fine, thanks," Julie said with a smile.

Dale looked from one to the other, sensing a need for explanation. Oliver smiled and offered none. Dale turned to Julie. "Are you a Quaker?"

"No. Oliver's the Quaker. I'm just a 'friend.'"

Oliver groaned, and Dale rolled his eyes. Julie said, "Sorry. I've been waiting all morning to say that."

"God, Oliver, she's funny. Julie, I like you already. What are you doing after meeting? Did you eat yet?"

Oliver said, "We're having dinner at my mother's."

"Then you'll have to explain yourselves now. Let's move over this way." He steered them out of the crowd to a corner beside a rack of brochures, half of which explained what it was like to be a Quaker. "So all right. You look like a couple. What's happening here?"

"We're lovers," Julie said.

This startled both men. Dale looked at Oliver, who said simply, "I do love her."

"Well, I'm flabbergasted. Julie, where did you meet this flake?"

"I work for him at Burr."

"She's my administrative assistant," Oliver explained.

"Holy cow! Now you *are* pulling my leg." Dale leaned back and squinted suspiciously. "Since when do you date employees? I thought you had some private rule about that sort of thing."

"Live and learn," Oliver said.

"What would Tina say if she knew?"

"I really couldn't care."

Dale looked stricken. "God, Julie, that was tactless. Forgive me."

"It's quite all right."

"No it's not. I'm being stupid and rude. Though in fairness," he gave Oliver a reproving glare, "this guy did surprise me. Julie, don't let me be a jerk. It's a real pleasure meeting you." He bent down to smile at the child. "And you're Kelly?"

"She's Kelly," Julie signed.

Dale straightened up. His eyes were reddening. His large face grew soft and he smiled. He shook Oliver's hand, then Julie's. "Good for you *both*. I've been worried about you—" he stabbed Oliver with a finger, "ever since Tina bought that place in New York. I always felt that was the beginning of the end."

"Thank you, Dale."

He turned to Julie. "Now if you can just pry him away from that dinky school of his."

"Now now," said Oliver. "Be nice on Christmas Day."

The doors opened, and the crowd began to jam through. "God bless you," Dale said with a wave. "Have a good meeting." He worked his way hastily through the doors to get his usual seat.

Keeping a tight hold on Kelly's hand as the crowd shuffled forward, Julie said, "He's nicer than I was expecting."

"He's very nice," said Oliver. "Comes off a little self-important at times, but name me one person in education who doesn't?"

"Why does he disapprove of Burr?"

"He just thinks it's beneath me. It's an opinion shared by every classmate I had at Penn. He's dean of Humanities at Swarthmore, and he gets published a lot. He's definitely following the right track." He took her hand as their turn came to squeeze with the crowd through the doors.

Any worry Oliver had about Kelly proved unwarranted. Julie had managed to get them both to church a few times over the years, so Kelly had a basic idea of worship, although Quaker meeting offered none of the visual trappings of a Catholic mass, and certainly no bulletin to help keep track of things. But she did not appear bored, and Oliver was touched each time the child bowed her head to pray. Julie spent a lot of the hour praying as well. Oliver sat in his own quiet world, his concentration divided over his frank enjoyment of Dale's reaction to Julie and Kelly, and his own recognition of how appealing these two were. The three of them must look awfully good to Dale, whose wife Myra and four intellectual kids had no patience for meeting, which was why Dale always attended alone. Julie signed to Kelly whenever someone stood and spoke, and because it was Christmas quite a few people did.

Coming out of meeting into the sunlight of Cherry Street, Julie said to Oliver, "That was something. I've never experienced anything quite like that."

"It can take some getting used to."

"Take me again, will you?"

"Of course."

Christmas dinner at Barbara Dunbar's home in Abington was pleasant and fun. Oliver's mother was tall and spry at seventy, with her son's cleft chin and straight nose. Oliver's brother Earl brought his family down from Allentown, and his children, Elliott and Pam, sprawled on the floor with Kelly and her new Clue game, and although neither child knew any Sign Language they all managed just fine.

It was a warm, friendly way to spend Christmas. Barbara had prepared a traditional turkey dinner, and the snug home with its beige wallpaper and wood decorations of blue geese, ducks, and sunflowers felt like something out of a storybook. When they held hands around the dinner table to say grace, Julie felt she was part of a genuine family circle, and that the prayer offered by Barbara was received by something real.

It was eight o'clock when they returned to Manayunk. Oliver carried Kelly asleep into the house. She stirred when he laid her on her bed, and fussily pushed him out the door so she could change. Oliver returned to the living room to find Julie taking wine glasses from the hutch.

"Light the tree," she said. "I'll make sure Kelly's tucked in. The rest of the evening is ours."

He plugged in the tree and dimmed the room lights, then stared out the dark window at the decorated homes sloping downhill toward the black Schuylkill River. Beyond it, traffic moved in gold dots along the West River Drive. The sight made him feel isolated and safe.

The floorboards creaked behind him and he turned. Julie approached, barelegged in her blue bathrobe, holding two glasses of Shiraz. The tree lights winked off her lenses. "Quite a view, isn't it?"

"You got changed."

"Do you mind? I've been wearing that Christmas dress all day."

"Of course not."

She joined him by the window and passed him a glass. "The tree looks nice, Oliver. Merry Christmas."

He clinked her glass. "A couple weeks ago I got a call from Tina."

"Oh?" Julie stood very still.

"She wanted the divorce papers signed. As soon as I got back to Rittenhouse I rummaged through every envelope on my desk. Anything with her lawyer's mark on it I opened, signed, and put in the mail. I didn't read any of it. I have no idea what I've agreed to, and I'm sure my lawyer will be pissed. But it's done and on its way."

"Oliver!"

"You were right at meeting today. You can hold against me my time of indecision, but I needed to know within myself that I wasn't setting you up for a fall. I love you."

Julie took a long sip of wine, then raised her hands and shrugged. "Well," she breathed. "Well, good God! Merry Christmas!"

They kissed awkwardly, still holding their glasses. Julie set them both down on the coffee table, and then they embraced, standing before all of Manayunk. Julie lifted her arms around his neck and the bathrobe slipped open. Oliver found himself holding her naked body. "Julie, what—"

"Shush."

She kissed him slowly and sweetly. Oliver spoke in a voice that wasn't his, his breath plucking a vocal cord so deep it had never been used. "This is too real for me."

"I know what you mean," she whispered. "It's larger than life. That's how it's supposed to feel." Her face was so close he could trace every line of her lashes. They kissed again, and in a sudden surge of joy he grabbed her around the waist and lifted her off the floor. Julie made a fumbled grab for his shoulders, and broke into choked laughter. "Oliver, good God! Wait! Stop that!"

"Say, you're kind of light."

"In a pig's eye. Put me down."

He did, and they smiled and kissed again, gentler.

"Come on, sweetheart, before my daughter decides she wants a glass of water."

Sweetheart. The word tilted his gravity as he followed her into her room. As the night passed in pleasures and shadows and small talk, he realized as he never had before how much a haven was a lover's bed. Covered by un-familiar sheets and cocooned in the tender reception of this young woman, he felt the stubborn mantle of his collected failings break and his heart lift in wonder, as if in the chemistry of Julie's breath and the beat of her heart, her voice in his ear, the exquisite intimacy of her body, and the soul-union of their close eye contact, he could feel a miraculous, long-awaited yet never expected, gift of absolution.

55

At six p.m. it started to snow. Within half an hour the streets were lightly dusted. By eight o'clock car hoods and rooftops were crowned by an inch of flawless white.

Doris stood before the large living room window admiring the flakes as they drifted down. Corey was sucking on a SpongeBob Sippy cup and getting fidgety. She laid him on a blanket on the credenza next to the TV so she could change him while watching *Who's the Boss?* on TBS. From the kitchen came the steady keyboard rattle of her daughter's computer. She couldn't believe how fast Keone was typing now, sixty words a minute her daughter said, like a real office worker. Doris never stopped praising God's gift in the rattle of that computer, in her daughter's staying in school, in the A's and B's she was coming home with, in the goodness of one particular teacher Keone kept talking about, whom she wanted Doris someday to meet. Doris looked down at her baby son, the only son she had left, and realized as she hadn't before how personable little Corey was. Yeah, he got into trouble, he tried to eat everything he could get his hands on, he tested his Mama's nerves until she wanted to smack him. But look at that face! Those chubby cheeks, the big round eyes, the little black brows that raised so happily at the sight of anybody, even Doris who *had* smacked him once too often. Yes, he was a funny boy. She would have to start thinking about him too.

Glass broke, and something thudded the wall over her head. It made her jump.

"What was that?" she asked, though she knew. Everyone in Caulfeld knew. Corey started to cough, and she saw strange white specks of dust dotting his face.

Glass broke a second time, sending small shards into the room. Doris screamed and looked about for the light switch. It was on the far side of the room. She threw her large body over Corey, pulling them both to the floor. The boy whimpered and pawed at his eyes.

"Mama!" Keone cried from the kitchen. "What is it—"

"Stay out!" Doris shrieked. "Stay out!"

More pops sounded from the street, shattering the left half of the big window. Keone dropped to the floor by the kitchen doorway and lay there, eyes and mouth tight shut. The wall above Doris thudded like a drum. And then the TV exploded in a wicked electric blue flash.

"Stay down!" Doris yelled.

More glass broke. The wall over the couch cracked, spitting plaster, nails, and hardened gobs of glue. The room grew cold. Ozone from the TV tainted the air. "It's all right!" Doris yelled at Corey. She huddled over him like a tent. "It's all right! It's all right!" But the child shrieked from the pain in his eyes and his mother's shouting in his ear.

Warren's legs appeared at the top of the stairs, visible below the living room ceiling. He crouched, putting his head into view. "Everybody stay down!" he shouted. "Where are you?" He squinted through the gray plaster smoke. "Are you here? Call out, godddammit!"

"Help me!" Doris yelled. "I got Corey!"

"Are they still shootin'? I can't hear nuthin'!"

"Where's Keone?"

"I dunno."

"Keone!"

On the floor by the kitchen, she was too scared to answer.

More pops. The wall thumped and a lamp jiggled and fell to the floor, close to Doris' head.

"Lord! Oh Lord! Lord—"

"Who the fuck are they? Why can't—*ow!*" Warren fell onto the steps in a sitting position and gripped his knee. Blood seeped swiftly through his pajama pants, leaking between his fingers. Moaning, he fell sideways against the banister railing and it cracked, nearly pushing out. Plaster chips fell about his shoulders.

Corey kept howling. Doris gasped over him, her breath cold puffs against the toddler's face. "Keone!" she yelled. "Where you at?"

"Here, Mama!"

"Where—?"

"Here!" Keone crawled forward on hands and knees until she was beside the stairs. She blinked up at her father's grimacing face, visible between the bars of the banister, directly above her. She sat up cautiously and craned her neck to look out the window across the room.

Doris started to get up.

"No, Mama!" shouted Keone. "Mama, don't move! They still out there!"

More pops whistled through. Doris screamed and fell back. The credenza splintered, the wall cracked. Doris' beloved picture of Javaughn and Keone, taken as youngsters, dropped off its hook and smashed. Bullets hit the afghan covering the couch, stirring tiny tornados of dust. A bullet hit Warren in the shoulder, knocking him against the stairway wall to his right. "Fuck," he breathed. Rocking in pain, he moaned and fell to his left, toppling against the banister a second time. There was a loud crack of wood, and suddenly he had no equilibrium. He realized weirdly that although he was flush against the banister he was still falling. His body pushed through the banister, pushed it out with his big shoulders and fat gut, and he plummeted several feet to the living room floor. He lolled half upside-down atop debris, posts of wood—

Doris shrieked. Out the window an engine gunned. She got to her knees as bright headlights swung the length of the living room, filtered through glittering snowflakes. She crawled frantically across couch cushions and chinks of glass to get near the stairs.

"Get off her! Get off her! Get off her!"

Warren was crying. Blood trickled up his neck from the shoulder wound. Doris stretched sideways on the floor and kicked him viciously until finally he rolled off the broken section of banister. He raised his head, saw his wife pulling at the mess, pulling at an arm—

He shuddered, shut his eyes and dropped his head to the rug.

Doris dragged Keone free and turned her over. Her daughter's face was pouring blood. Doris wiped wildly with her skirt.

"Get an ambulance!" she screamed at her husband. "Move! Lord! Dear Lord!"

She pressed her hand against Keone's small face but there was no reaction.

"Do somethin'!" she yelled. She kicked her husband in the side. "Call for help! Oh Lord have mercy! Lord have mercy!" She pressed her face against her daughter's cheek. She arched her broad back over Keone to shield her from further attack. Her strength dissipated from fright and tears, and her voice dropped to an exhausted whisper, but she continued her prayer without pause: "Lord have mercy ... Lord have mercy ..."

Feds

56

ON JANUARY 5 four new classes sat in the student lounge for Orientation. There were forty students in the two Accounting classes and eighteen in a fledgling Conference Planning program. But the big news was the January Information Processing class with one hundred and twenty-seven students, seven over goal.

The Philadelphia admissions department was beginning to take success for granted. There was another champagne party in Lily's office, and behind her closed door fat bonus checks were passed to the reps. Trudy got $970, Deirdre $475, and Marty a staggering $2,400. Lily had a giant mock check drawn on a piece of cardboard and presented it to him with comic cere-mony, remarking that she had never seen a larger bonus check paid to any rep for a single sit. Marty grinned and strutted and tugged his bow tie. Trudy and Deirdre sat in silence on Lily's love seat, and didn't even try to smile when Marty shook their hands.

Philly, Washington, Atlanta, and New Orleans were the only schools to make goal. Bill Nostrand wasn't happy. He assessed the situation even as Orientation began, and called Lily with some news. He didn't call Oliver, but left it to the admissions director to pass the word. Lily stewed on it for most of an hour, letting her champagne grow flat, then finally went to see the director.

"They're reinstating April," she said without fanfare, interrupting a conversation between Oliver and Ethel Harris.

"What?" he said.

"Bill just got off the line with me. Only four schools made January. Bill needs a way to compensate for the loss in revenue, so he's making us reinstate the April Secretarial Arts class."

"Oh shit," said Ethel.

Lily ruefully laughed. "How's that for a kicker, Oliver? We're now *sup-porting* the Burr system. Big schools like Boston and New York can't cut it, so little Philly is needed to carry the load."

Oliver said anxiously, "Does Bill remember that we've never made the April goal? And that the students who come are so weak academically that—"

"He said he's sure we can do it. He expects miracles from us now. Funny position to be in, hey?"

"Can we do it?"

"Oh, of *course!*" Lily laughed and flipped her hands. "It's actually quite flattering. I'll let you know how it goes." And with a pert twirl of her little pleated miniskirt, she flashed out the door.

"Jesus, Mary, and Ralph." Ethel slumped in her chair. "Not another lousy April class! Can't you call Nostrand and talk him out of it?"

Oliver looked grim. "I can try, but I doubt it'll do any good. If the schools as a whole are doing badly, Bill's job will be on the line. If he thinks running an April class will save his neck, he's not going to listen to me."

"I feel like we're right back where we started."

"It's not that bad."

"No—it's probably worse." Ethel stood and took a deep breath. "It's time for my speech to the new class."

Ethel went to the Orientation in the student lounge and proclaimed the merits of birthing a diploma. Then she walked up two flights to her office, shut the door, took off her blazer, and sat at her desk. In front of her was a blue folder containing the finalized Achievement Program proposal. Twenty-one pages, including Oliver's cover letter and Louise's cost sheet. It didn't look like much to help the dull-eyed kids she had just faced. She opened the folder, read it from beginning to end, and wished she had more confidence in it. She walked back downstairs to Oliver's office and rapped on the doorframe. "Okay, this is it. Anything to add, once and for all?"

Oliver looked at the blue folder and smiled. "No. I called Bill on Friday and told him about it. He was a lot more excited than I expected him to be."

"Fine." Ethel walked out to the lobby. "Julie, I need you to FedEx this. It goes to Bill Nostrand. And handle it reverently."

The secretary looked unusually haggard. She took the report, and Ethel went back upstairs.

Sitting in the lobby, up front and vulnerable, Julie had dealt all morning with the new students' questions regarding room locations, class schedule errors, bill disputes, locker troubles, and lateness slips. The phone rang nonstop, and students still plied their questions even as she tried to talk to the caller. She lost her lunch hour dealing with all this, and by midafternoon felt nauseous with fatigue. She wrapped the binder in a FedEx envelope. Except for the dean, no one else knew how hard Oliver had worked on this, the program that would save the school. No one had seen him hunched for hours at the kitchen table, checking stats in manuals, cutting here, pasting there, the phone calls to Ethel, to colleagues, to social workers, even lawyers. At the same time Julie had never seen Oliver so vitalized. This was his life's work, making education possible. He would never be thanked for his efforts. A student receiving a diploma was the only reward he would get.

She buzzed him at five to tell him she was leaving. "Okay," he said. "I'll get home as quick as I can."

"I'll have dinner for you, no matter what hour. You be careful on the road."

"Thanks, Jule. See you tonight."

This was as familiar as they got at the office. No one at Burr knew about them. Oliver's lease had finally terminated on the Rittenhouse apartment, and his pertinent belongings were now crammed in the small apartment in Manayunk. It was agreed that by next fall Julie would get a job somewhere else, and Oliver was even encouraging her to try for admission to some of the local colleges. Julie loved him for this, for she hated never having gotten her degree.

Oliver worked until six on an ABCAA midyear survey, then put it aside and stretched. He got his coat from the lobby and double-checked that he had the car keys. Normally he and Julie bussed into town; it was cheaper. But tonight he needed wheels. He retrieved Julie's battle-scarred Olds from a garage on Seventh, and drove westward on Walnut.

Days were short, the sky black. Oliver crossed the Schuylkill River and turned west on the Expressway. From there the Lincoln Drive shuttled him through a dense woods that was part of Fairmount Park. He took Gypsy Lane and pumped hard to get the car up the steep hill. He drove along School House Lane, then turned onto the driveway for the Pennsylvania School for the Deaf. Just inside the foyer two women sat at a table with notebooks and a tin cash box. Stacks of books lay at their feet.

"Hi. I'm here to register."

"Basic or Advanced?"

"Basic."

"That's sixty dollars," the woman said, "and $24.95 for your text."

Oliver made out the check and received a spiral-bound book. He entered the room she pointed to. It was a children's classroom and the wooden chairs were too small for Oliver and a handful of other adults. He took a metal folding chair from a wall. Other students entered, adults and quite a few children. Over the next twelve weeks he would learn that many of the young ones knew a lot of Sign already from having deaf brothers and sisters, and some had parents sitting in the Advanced class right next door.

A woman dressed in jeans and a La Salle sweatshirt entered, went to the blackboard, and wrote MARIE RENSICK in block letters. She smiled at the class, pointed to the name, then pointed to herself. Then she pointed to each letter in the name and executed its hand symbol. Oliver was mesmerized. It hadn't occurred to him that his teacher might be deaf.

Marie swiftly led the class through the hand alphabet, then quizzed them each in turn on numbers. Oliver made it to twenty, but several classmates including most of the children counted higher. Marie herself whipped through both letters and numbers with incredible dexterity, and even the most experienced of the hearing people could not keep pace with her. They opened their books, and she taught them basic grammar and forty vocabulary words, mostly nouns for parts of the body plus various emotions like love, hate, sad, happy, tired, and also a few verbs. Then Marie paired them, and watched as they labored through the simplest conversations with each other using the book as a guide. ("Are you mad?" "No, I am happy.") Then she went person by person, and executed the same introductory exchange, again taking it from the book.

Hello, she signed to Oliver. *My name is Marie.*

Hello, my name is Oliver.

How are you, Oliver?

I am fine, Marie. How are you?

Fine. Thank you.

Oliver felt something close to enchantment as he sat in this room. It was more than talking in Sign, more than the strange experience of having information imparted from teacher to class in nearly two hours of ethereal silence. It was sweet nostalgia, the throb of something fresh and forward-driven that hadn't fluttered through his heart and mind in ages.

He was learning again.

57

James DePriest guest-conducted the Philadelphia Orchestra for Shostakovich's Eleventh Symphony. It was, for Bob, one of the most richly stirring works ever written. "Long, slow, brooding," he gushed to Dawn as they sat in a coffeehouse after the performance. "Taking all the time in the world to build those crescendos. The marches, the attacks, the longing, the triumph. I swear, there's not an emotion known to man that's not recorded in that symphony."

"Except maybe discovering a bargain at Bloomies." Dawn laughed guiltily. "I'm only kidding, Bob. It was beautiful."

"I've been waiting all my life to hear it performed live. Now I can die happy."

"Well, pay this check first."

It was midnight when he walked her to her apartment near Fitler Square. "You free this weekend?" he asked. "I mean, the *whole* weekend."

"I can be."

"Let's do something. Let's rent a car and go to the shore."

"The shore? This time of year—"

"This time of year is terrific. The beach is deserted. We can walk for hours and relax."

"How about this?" Dawn said. "We rent that same car and go to my parents' house in the Poconos. That'll be deserted also, and it has a big fireplace. You can even bring Mr. Wemmick if you think he'd like it."

"He might. He's pretty docile on car trips. You didn't tell me your parents own a home in the mountains."

"You never asked. Dad develops computer software. He's not a suffering artist like you and me."

Bob slipped his arm around her waist as they walked. "You, me, a fireplace, and a cabin in the chilly mountains? It's positively profound."

She kissed him. "I'll get all the food supplies, but you have to stock the wine."

"Deal."

The big miracle that she didn't mind his paltry teaching salary was still holding. Dawn had been to his apartment several times now, had seen it all so to speak, and was still going out with him. She thought Mr. Wemmick was a wonderfully big teddy bear cat, and was impressed by the fat stack of manuscript on the computer table. Bob had also been to her apartment and met her sister Connie, who was just as nice as Dawn. She was a legal secretary studying to be an actress. Many nights after work they would all three hook up for a drink, and sometimes Connie brought a guy with her and sometimes not. But they got along splendidly.

Bob and Dawn held each other by her doorstep for a long while before she reluctantly pulled free and undid the three locks and went inside. Walking home, Bob hummed the symphony afresh, and his timpani impression made other late-night city pedestrians switch to the opposite sidewalk.

The next morning he awoke with the music still in his head. He continued to hum it as he walked up Lombard to work. Heather Feeney stood at the door of the school, letting her classmates pass. She gave him a mean look. Bob nodded casually. "Good morning, Ms. Feeney."

"I gotta talk to you."

Several students stood chatting by the steps. Dropping his voice, Bob asked, "Is this a good time?"

"I don't give a shit."

Alert, alert. "All right, come with me." He entered the school ahead of her and passed down the first floor corridor. He found an empty lecture room and walked in. Heather followed, pouting. Bob shut the door and strode hastily to the teacher's desk at the front of the room. "Heather, what's up?"

"I want to go someplace this weekend."

"This weekend?" He kept calm. "Don't you have studying to do?"

"I'm sick of studying. We haven't done anything special in ages."

"We went to dinner on Monday."

"That's all we've been *doing* is dinner. I can do that with my friends. I want something romantic."

Christ.

"Let's do something fun. We haven't done anything fun in ages."

"I see." He stood beside the teacher's desk with his hands behind his back. He hoped this professorial pose would fool anyone who might chance to peek through the window in the classroom door. "I can't see you this weekend. I've already got plans."

"What kind of plans?"

"Just plans, Heather."

"What are they?"

"Come on, Heather. Why do you need to know?"

"Well, why can't you tell me?"

A familiar knot of exasperation formed in his stomach. "It's not that I can't tell you. I'm entitled to my privacy. I shouldn't have to explain everything I do."

"We could stay in a hotel," she said. "Get one with a big king-size bed. Wouldn't that be great?" She gave him an ardent look.

The poor kid. If she only knew what a sexual neuter she had become to him.

"Look, I can't afford a hotel, and I'm not taking you anywhere this weekend. That's final. Now go to your class." Even as he said this he watched her face change from bratty vexation to livid outrage.

"What are you doing this weekend?" she demanded.

"Look, I'm not telling you."

"Bastard! You're probably—"

"All right! You win! I shouldn't have to tell you, but I will. I'm taking the weekend and staying at my brother's. His wife's away. They're having some marital problems, and he wants to talk to me. Just brother to brother with no one else around. Understand?"

"Yeah."

"All right. That's why I can't see you this weekend, and why I can't take you where I'm going. It's a personal thing for Phil."

"Oh Bob." The girl's face relaxed, though it still looked a little flushed. "Why didn't you tell me?"

"Because I shouldn't have to."

"Baby, let me come over tonight."

"Tonight?"

"Please, honey. We haven't seen each other in ages."

"What about your studying?"

"I've studied enough. I'm sick of studying."

"But still—"

"Please, Bob. I miss you."

He was silent.

"I love you."

What could he do? He had no good reason not to invite her over. She knew he didn't have a social life, she knew too much about him. He couldn't think. As if one inspired lie was the best his brain could manage. And at least he had saved the weekend. "All right."

"Really, Bob? Great. I love you *so much!*"

"All right, Dawn. Just go to class. We're both late."

"I know what I'm gonna do. You go straight home. I saw this dress in a store window on Chestnut Street—it's to kill for. You are gonna *die* when you see me." She suddenly looked puzzled. "What did you just call me?"

He was wondering himself. Running back his last words, he realized exactly what he had called her, and shook his head fast in ignorance.

"What did you say?"

"I don't know. I, uh …"

"Did you just call me darling?"

He hesitated. "Yeah, I did."

"Oh, Bob! That's so nice!" She rushed forward and embraced him. "You haven't called me that in a long time. Honey, kiss me."

A window in the door. "Not here. Can't right here."

"Come on. *Please.*" She pulled his face down and kissed him hard, holding the back of his head.

"Heath—" he managed. "Anybody can—can look in here!"

Heather broke off and stepped away. She gave him a wicked carnal grin. "Rest up, Mr. Lawrence. I'm gonna eat you alive tonight."

She swept out the door. Bob stood alone in the classroom in turmoil, as guilty as if he were committing adultery.

58

It didn't take Bill Nostrand long to get back to Oliver. One week after Ethel shipped the Achievement Program proposal to New York, Julie buzzed

Oliver to say the vice-president was on the line. Oliver hesitated before picking up. He wasn't sure a quick response from Bill was a good omen.

"Philly, good morning!"

"Good morning, Bill."

"Is it raining there? Pouring like the devil up here."

"We got some, but I think it's already stopped."

"Well, the streets here are soaking. Listen, I want to talk to you about that Achievement plan of yours. I had to read it while I was traveling. Had to kick-start all those schools that fell below January. You can't believe how screwed up so many of them were."

"Really?" Oliver was a little disconcerted. Why was Bill complaining to him? Bill never talked like this to a school director.

"Miami—well, Miami, you know how bad that's been. I think they're turning around now, but we had to put that school under martial law. I was calling the Marriott home. Didn't even see my family on weekends."

"Sorry to hear it, Bill."

"It was madness. Well, about your plan."

Bill paused, and in that silence Oliver felt it all. He couldn't shake the tension out of his back, he couldn't just sit and take it. He already knew the answer—and he also knew why.

"It was a tough call, Oliver. We're not going with it, but I want to give you our reasons. In a way, you already saw it yourself. You explained in the letter the price tag for mounting a program like this. Twenty-four months, six consecutive semesters, six extra teachers, the room renovation—"

"Bill—"

"It's not practical. Hell, it's very humane. I think in many ways you've hit the nail on the head. It's too damn costly to educate people, and that's the trouble—"

"Bill, did you show it to Abby DeSalvo? To anybody in Education? What did they think about it?"

"Oh, everybody thought it was academically sound. We weren't surprised by that. We know how good you are at that sort of thing. You and Ethel. That's why we admire you—"

"Bill, can I come up and talk to you and John about it? What did John say?"

"And your insights about the changing demographics are acute. Nothing anybody wants to hear, but it's honest—"

"John. What did John say about it?"

A pause.

"Oliver, candid truth?"

"Of course, Bill."

"He hated it."

Oliver quailed. "What did he say? Did he think it was too expensive?"

"Of course he did. But that wasn't the real problem. He felt it encouraged a type of student we don't really want to see come to Burr."

"You mean the minority students?"

Bill said *"No!"* with swift defensiveness. "He meant the *poor* students! Poor students wreak havoc with a school's reputation, you know that. And this thing of yours encourages them to come. It *accommodates* them. John couldn't imagine where the hell your head was at."

So there it was.

"Bill, it doesn't accommodate them, it *trains* them. The current programs don't take into account—"

"Oliver, it's a no-go. And I'm sorry. It's obvious you and Ethel put a lot of work into it. But it's not feasible, and it's not strategic."

"Strategic?"

"Now your show of initiative is terrific. At least you guys are trying to do something, which is more than I can say about the rest of the system. Most of the schools act like they're scared to talk to me. In fact, while I was in Miami we had …"

Oliver set the receiver on the desk. Bill's voice rasped against the blotter. Oliver leaned back in his chair and stared at the ceiling. It was papered, not painted, and he could see some rippling in the corners. In twenty-three years he had never had the ceiling redone. The paper over his head had been here as long as himself.

He finished with Bill and walked out to the lobby. Julie was handling a barrage of calls, and he stood in a corner, admiring the skill of it. When he was able to catch her eye he nodded, then returned to his office. She followed a moment later and took a seat, her steno pad ready.

"I feel like putting my fist through a window," he said, "and I'm hoping you can talk me out of it."

"Was he calling about the Achievement Program?"

"Yes. It's been axed."

Julie gasped. "No! Did he say why?"

"Money. And prejudice. I've got to break the news to Ethel."

"I'm sorry, Oliver."

"Yeah, it's too bad. I think it would have saved us." There was no rancor in Oliver's voice. He merely sounded tired.

"Do you want to talk about it?"

"That's nice of you, Jule, but there isn't much to say. The whole thing was chancy. Ethel, Louise, and I always knew we were asking more from New York than we were likely to get."

"What can I do?"

"Just keep me company for a moment."

So she sat with him, holding her steno pad and watching him draw therapy from the silence of the room. The radio was off, and the little pendulum of the ABCAA clock clicked with each swing. Children could be heard in Washington Square, laughing as they fed who knows what to the pigeons.

"You know what bothers me most?" Oliver said at last, pushing up his glasses. "Doing this through Bill. I'm sure John saw my report, but I have no idea if he felt the care we put into it. The stats and estimates by themselves are pretty cold. He could easily have dismissed it out of hand."

"Is there any way you could find out?"

"Not without talking directly to him. Bill wouldn't like it."

"Is that so important?"

Oliver smiled ruefully. "Only on a practical level. I report to him."

"Fine. Except what if you can't do your best work because of him?"

He looked at her.

Julie's face had an earnest glow. She leaned forward eagerly. "What if you took a train up to New York? Talked to John and found out what he really thinks."

Oliver laughed. "Gee, I don't know."

"Ethel tells me you use to do things like that. Whenever New York made decisions you disapproved of."

"That was a good many years ago."

"So what's different now?"

He shrugged lamely.

"Then answer this. What are you going to replace the Achievement Program with?"

"What do you mean?"

"Do you have a back-up plan? Is there anything that can take its place? Or are we just back at the beginning, facing the same problems?"

"I sure don't have any other ideas."

"Then it sounds like you'd better make a stand for this one."

Oliver gave her a bemused, appraising look. "There's some steel in you, did you know that?"

Julie grinned. "I'm second-generation Irish. You should see me in a bar fight."

"How fast can you get me a cab?"

"Twenty minutes."

"Call one, will you? Looks like I'm taking a trip."

After she left he put on his suit jacket. He searched through his file drawers for a spare copy of the Achievement Program and grew anxious when he couldn't find one. Possibly he had sent Bill his only copy. Coming out to the lobby, he grabbed his coat from the closet and took a red Burr umbrella from a stand. Julie was handling a call with the phone receiver tucked between her chin and shoulder, and passed him a copy of the proposal without interrupting her conversation with the caller. Oliver tucked it in his briefcase, mouthed "thank you," and went out.

It was a dismal train ride to New York. Rain rapped the windows and darkened the landscape to a midday twilight. Oliver sat perspiring in his overcoat, trying to keep the speeches rehearsing in his head from maundering into frantic pleading.

Wind tugged the umbrella as he walked up the Avenue of the Americas; he had to hold it with both hands while gripping the briefcase, and this left his pant legs wet from the knees down when he entered the lobby of the building on Fifty-fourth Street. He rode the elevator to the forty-third floor and startled Eloise, Bill's secretary.

"Dr. Dunbar? Forgive me, I wasn't aware that you were coming today." She automatically reached for the intercom.

"Don't bother him," Oliver said. "I'm not here for Bill. I need to see John."

"President Coyne?"

"Yes. I know the way."

He walked down the hall to another small reception area where Coyne's personal secretary was dictating into a microphone. Pages of an official report lay before her. "Hi, Carlene."

She looked just as surprised as Eloise. "Dr. Dunbar, hello. Is John expecting you?"

"No, but it's okay." Oliver strode past her desk.

"Dr. Dunbar, excuse me—I'm not sure—"

Coyne's door was open. The president of the Burr Colleges sat behind his large desk at the end of the long paneled office. He looked up from his correspondence and squinted. "Who is that?"

"Oliver Dunbar. Sorry to barge in, John, but there's something important we need to talk about."

"Good Christ! What are you doing here?"

Oliver strode the length of the office. "I want to talk to you about the Achievement Program."

"The what? Did Carlene let you in? You don't just walk in—"

Bill Nostrand burst through the doorway. His face was scarlet. "Son of a bitch, Oliver! What the hell are you doing here?"

"John." Oliver stood before the president's desk. "The Achievement Program. Talk to me about it. Just a few minutes of your time."

"The what?" said John Coyne.

"Oh Christ," said Bill.

Oliver faltered. "The Achievement Program, John. What did you think of it?"

"Oliver," said the president, "are you out of your goddamn Ivy League mind? What the hell are you talking about?"

*

It proved a long, difficult day for Julie. She couldn't keep her mind on anything but what might be happening in New York. As if to deliberately gall her, other staff members kept buzzing her, wanting to connect with Oliver, and she had to bluff with a lame, "He isn't in today. He's off-campus on business." Of course everyone wanted more details, and she had none to give. At one point Ethel actually came downstairs and stood before her. "What's he doing?" she demanded. "I need him to review the fall probation appeals. We're past deadline already. Jean and Carol and everybody want to know if they should keep admitting these kids to class. Oliver has to make a decision."

"Ethel, he's on a business trip. That's all I can tell you."

But the dean was too experienced with the art of evasion. She scrutinized the hapless secretary. "He hasn't gone AWOL again, has he?"

"No, I'm sure."

"Well, is he sick or something?"

"Ethel, he's on a business trip. That's all I know."

"No it isn't," said the dean. "Have him call me when he checks in. Jesus, Mary and Ralph, I hate the way nobody tells anybody anything in this place." She went out the door grumbling.

At four o'clock Julie turned on the promotional videotape for one of Lily's prospects. She was just returning to her desk when Oliver charged through the door. "Julie, greetings!"

"Good God, Oliver! What happened?"

"Tell you in a moment. Where's Ethel? Get her down here. And Louise and Lily too. Oh, excuse me," he added, stopping short before the prospect on the couch.

"Goldie Jenkins is here to see Mrs. Espirito."

"I see." Oliver smiled at the young woman. "Good afternoon. So glad to have you here. Julie, get the others at least."

"I'm calling now."

Oliver paced the lobby while Julie buzzed Lily, sent the prospect back, then summoned Ethel and Louise. As the two women walked into the lobby Oliver pumped their hands. "Congratulate us. The Achievement Program is on!"

"Oh Oliver!" cheered Julie.

"Was it off?" asked the dean. "What's going on, Oliver?"

"I talked to John Coyne, and he's thrilled with it. He absolutely wants to see it happen."

Louise asked, "This is where you've been all day?"

"Yes." Oliver looked ready to perform handsprings on the couch. "Bill called this morning to say John hated it, but in truth John never saw it. Bill stopped it from reaching his desk. So I appealed to John's sense of social justice. I don't know how well you know John, but he has always envied Reginald Burr for having an opportunity to seize a good cause and make an impact. He loved how Reginald started these women's colleges at a time when women were treated like second-class citizens. So I said what Reginald did for women in 1907 we now have a chance to do for today's underprivileged. And he bought into it. The more we talked, the more excited he got."

"Oliver," said Ethel, "you're amazing."

Hearing loud voices in the lobby, Deirdre and Trudy came out. They stood by the cubicles and marveled to see the school director prancing about so excitedly.

"So the Achievement Program is on! Ethel, you can start work on getting faculty for it. Louise, we'll have to work out the space. John won't do the renovation in the Dungeon, not this first year. That's the one thing he asked me to concede this time around. Let it work a year, he said, and then we'll put money into tearing up the downstairs."

"Good job, Oliver," said Louise. Ethel applauded, and everyone else followed suit.

"Bravo," yelled Julie.

He looked at her. In two long strides he was behind her desk. He seized her by the shoulders, lifted her to her feet, and kissed her. Gasps exploded around them. He faced them, keeping his arm about her. "Does anybody need an explanation?"

"Hell no," said Ethel. "You do whatever it takes to keep the staff happy."

Julie beamed. "He's doing that."

"Oh my God, Julie!" exclaimed Trudy.

"I'd still rather have a raise," said Louise.

59

In the fourth week of January Ethel sent a letter of dismissal to Keone Robinson.

The dean's policy was to send a warning letter to a student after three days unexplained absence from class. If there was no response after ten days, the letter of dismissal was sent. Ethel waited fifteen days for Keone, but when no word came from the student she finally did her duty.

Two more days passed. Then one afternoon Dawn buzzed her from downstairs. "Ethel, there's a man and woman here to see you. They don't have an appointment, but they're Keone Robinson's parents. They just walked in."

"I'll see them. Is Oliver around?"

"Can you hold a moment? I'll check." Ethel waited, all kinds of thoughts running through her mind. Dawn was back in a second. "Oliver's at lunch."

"Then Louise. Find her, will you, and tell her who it is. And you can show the Robinsons up."

There was only one client chair in the cluttered office, for Ethel rarely talked to parents. She moved a heavy stack of files off it to a small computer table. The door opened and Dawn appeared. She said to the hall, "This way please."

Mr. and Mrs. Robinson stepped in. The mother was short and stocky in a black wool coat. The husband was a big man, puffy-faced, with dark brows and moist eyes that kept blinking. He moved slowly, and gripped both a ski cap and a cane in his right hand. His open coat revealed his left arm in a sling. For all his size, he seemed strangely quiet, and throughout the visit deferred to his wife.

"You the dean?" Mrs. Robinson asked. "Excuse me. Are you Dean Harris?"

"Yes. Come in."

Mrs. Robinson took the client chair. Her husband stood behind her. The woman wasted no time getting to the point. "Mrs. Harris, would it be possible for Keone to come back to school?"

Ethel raised her brows and pursed her lips. As a courtesy, she pretended to consider it. "Mrs. Robinson, she's been absent over three weeks now."

"Yeah, I know."

"A student is withdrawn from the college once an unexcused absence extends past ten days. I gave Keone a break waiting as long as I did. She never came to me for help, or to say there was a problem. She simply disappeared off the planet."

"Yeah."

"I hope you can appreciate that. Here at Burr we train students to be professionals. We can't give a Burr degree to a student who stops coming to school without an explanation. We can't have students believing they can do that in the work force."

"Yeah, okay. What if she got in a accident?"

Ethel paused, again only as a courtesy. "That could prove mitigating, certainly. But Keone never contacted us. At the very least we should have received a phone call."

"Mrs. Harris—" The mother put her head down. When she looked up, tears shone on her dark cheeks. "Please let her come back to class. She wants to finish."

This was the side of education they didn't teach you at college, even at the doctoral level. Crying students, crying parents. They came to school with a dream, and you had to play both dictator and therapist when they didn't make it.

"I'm sorry," said Ethel.

"Mrs. Harris, you don't understand. She was in a real bad accident. My older boy, his name's Javaughn. He deals crack. I don't know where exactly, not where we live. But that's what he does."

"Doris," rumbled her husband, "you don't gotta tell her that."

"I *am* tellin' her that!" snapped his wife, glaring at him with a fury that impressed Ethel. "I'm tellin' her whatever I got to to get Keone back here! We don't got room for pride, not you and me!" She faced Ethel. "Mrs. Harris, please believe what happened. Juss around Thanksgiving Javaughn got in trouble. He lit out. Didn't say good-bye, didn't say where he was goin'. Juss told Keone he was in trouble and had to leave. He's never come back."

"Go on."

"So right after Christmas someone shot at our house. They shot through our livin' room window. Keone got a bad gash acrost her face. She was bleedin' real awful. We rushed her to the hospital. Warren here got shot in the leg, and he had to crawl to get the phone. I was tryin' to protect the baby."

Ethel listened in horror. She knew Keone was a project girl, and she knew very well what that meant. This woman sitting before her had been shot at in her own home. The dean held her breath, for she also had experience with guns.

"She's good now, but she knows you won't let her back. I says, go check it out anyway, you come so far. She says no. I think she's scared of you a bit, Mrs. Harris."

The door opened and Louise entered. She closed it behind her and stood there, a gray embellishment hardly noticed by the others.

"Dean Harris," said Ethel. "Call me Dean Harris or Dr. Harris."

"Yeah, ma'am. So that's why we're here 'stead of her. She'll come see you if you want, but she hates that her face got banged up."

The mother's face was mortared with a terrible pain. Behind her the father shifted his weight and grimaced.

"Mr. and Mrs. Robinson," said Ethel, "don't let me put you in a begging position. If all this really happened, Keone can certainly come back to school. If she's well enough she can rejoin her class and finish out this semester. If not, we'll put her in the next one and she can graduate then. Whatever it takes."

"Oh lord! Thank you, Dean Harris! Thank you so much! Lord bless you!"

"Have her come see me before she goes to class. She needs to talk to me."

"I will, ma'am. I'll tell her that soon's we get home."

"What about her bill?"

The question chopped the air with the bluntness of a guillotine. Everyone faced Louise. Ethel made a quick slit-throat motion that the business manager saw but didn't understand.

"I'm glad the dean is allowing Keone to return, but she hasn't paid us a dime in a year-and-a-half beyond what she's received in financial aid. I've had her down to my office any number of times. She keeps promising to pay, but then we never get a cent."

"Louise," said Ethel, "you don't understand the situation."

"Well, how much does she owe?" asked Mrs. Robinson.

Louise brandished a green bill. "Three thousand one hundred and forty-eight dollars and thirty-two cents."

Dead silence from the Robinsons.

"Louise, for God's sake," said Ethel.

"Eighteen hundred of this is a carryover from last year. You have to understand—even if the dean lets her back, she'll never graduate if this doesn't get paid."

"Lord," whispered Mrs. Robinson, staring at the bill. She looked at her husband.

Louise smiled grimly. "She never talked to you about this, did she?"

"No. We'd of done something if she had, I swear it. Lord, Warren, what we gonna do 'bout this?"

"I have to tell you," Louise went on, "I've had it up to here with promises from your daughter. She hasn't kept any. And at this late date I can't accept fresh promises from her parents. I need to know *right now* if you intend to pay this bill."

"Ma'am," said Mrs. Robinson. "Sorry, I don't know your name. I just … well, we got to pay it. It just gotta get paid."

"Of course," said Louise. "How?"

"I dunno." The woman looked shattered by this new problem. "Ma'am, we didn't know 'bout this, and we got to give it thought. But we'll pay it. We'll work on it right away."

"Look, a promise isn't good enough," Louise said. "If your daughter comes back to class you can all go on a payment plan for the remaining four months of her program. But that'll come to …" She looked around for a calculator, saw none handy, and concentrated. Ethel pulled one from a drawer but Louise waved it away as a distraction. "Eight hundred and fifty-four dollars and fifty-eight cents. Payable the first of the month and starting in February. And since this is January 26 you'll need to make the first payment in five days." She watched as the parents struggled with this.

The mother said, "We need eight hundred and fifty-four dollars in five days?"

"And fifty-eight cents."

Mrs. Robinson stood up. She put a hand on her husband's shoulder. "We'll get it." She didn't look at Louise, she looked only at the dean. "Thank you again. For Keone, thank you."

Both department heads watched as the couple moved slowly out the door. Louise shut it after them, and grinned at Ethel. "Oliver's turning you into a Quaker."

"Somebody shot up their home. Keone was taken to a hospital."

"What?"

"This is no joking matter," said Ethel. "I'm ashamed of myself for not fully understanding what we're dealing with when we get students like Keone. I think it's a bigger miracle than we realized that she's gotten through three semesters. We should let her play out even if they don't come up with the money."

"We're not a charity," Louise said, but with no real venom. "They did seem sincere, didn't they? The mother at least. Little hard to read Dad."

"Except to know he's got more sauce in him than blood. I have an eye for that."

"Well, letting her back is admirable of you. I didn't expect it. You made me the heavy, you know."

"You like being the heavy."

There was a knock on the door. Ethel sighed. "Lord, who is it now? Come in!"

The door opened and Mr. Robinson peered in. He winced a little, and his fingers clutched the cane. "Excuse me, Mrs. Harris?"

"Yes, Mr. Robinson?"

"I need to talk to this woman here."

"Ms. Mallory," said Ethel. "Certainly."

"What can I do for you?" asked Louise.

He shuffled a little, trying to find a comfortable position for his weight. "My wife's downstairs. Ms. Mallory, I got to axt you something. If we don't get that money in five days, are you gonna throw Keone out?"

"Mr. Robinson, this is a business. What do you think should happen?"

"Ms. Mallory, I got to axt you not to do that. We ain't … we ain't gonna have no eight hundred fifty-four dollars in five days."

Louise's face was stone. "Well then."

"But that's just this month," the man said hastily. "What if I got you double by March? That'd be like a thousand seven hundred, wouldn't it? How about I get you that much by then?"

"Mr. Robinson, if you can't get eight hundred and fifty-four dollars now, why would you have twice that by March?"

"'Cause I can work and have it by then."

"You're not working now, are you?"

"No. Please don't kick her out. I … Ma'am, she's my wife's only girl." To both women's embarrassment, he started to cry. He leaned forward on the cane. "I'll pay that bill if you just promise to keep her in class. Doris' been countin' on it so much." He looked at them miserably. "I dunno if we'll ever see our boy again. Keone, she's all Doris' got. Doris'n me, she's all we got."

"All right," said Louise. "One thousand seven hundred and nine dollars and sixteen cents by March 1. A deal, Mr. Robinson?"

"Yeah."

"And she's out of here March 2 if you don't come through."

"Yeah. Right. That's fair. Thank you, ma'am." He turned carefully and walked out, holding the cane, not using it. He was still crying.

"Hell," said Louise. She glowered at the dean.

"Don't look so pained," said Ethel. "It's called a good deed."

*

Warren Robinson stayed sober for two days, then called social services. Ms. Hooper was long gone but the new guy, Jim Peters, gladly came out to the house to talk. Afterward, Peters called around, and finally told Warren he might find something through Primoni's on Twelfth and Dickinson. He found Warren a decent tie, wished him luck with a smile that might or might not be genuine, and saw him off to the subway station. Warren didn't bring the cane, and didn't wear the sling. He forced his right leg to bend naturally as he walked.

The receptionist was a middle-aged South Philly woman with a large yellow perm and at least fifteen bracelets on each wrist. She gave him an application and ushered him to a back office. A big man with a florid face mottled with acne scars stood and shook his hand. "You Robinson?"

"Yeah, sir."

"I'm Alex Jameson. Glad to meet you. Have a seat."

Warren sat, easing his leg without changing the look on his face.

"Peters talk to you about this?"

"He just said you needed men."

"Well, for what I'm talking about we need men of a somewhat imposing nature. Which certainly you are. You drink?"

"No."

"Looks like you do."

"I ain't drinkin'."

"'Kay, I don't really care. That won't stop you from getting hired. But once you're on you can't touch the stuff. Is that clear?"

"I ain't touchin' it now."

"Fine. Here's the deal. We didn't inform Peters fully. That wasn't in our best interest."

"What am I doin'?"

"I got a company in Chester. They cut lumber. The workers went on strike a month ago and the latest settlement just broke down. The company's trying to hire replacements and the union's getting ugly. So now they're looking for scabs. That's you and nine other guys. The work's easy enough. Just do whatever the supervisors tell you. But you gotta cross a tough picket line coming and going. That's why it pays so nice. Eighteen fifty-five an hour. Any of this a problem for you?"

"No."

"You ain't scared of things like that?"

"No."

Jameson leaned forward. His eyes didn't leave Warren's face. "You want to tell me why you wouldn't be?"

"I need money."

"What for?"

"Is that your business?"

"I'm making it my business. You don't like it, scram."

Warren swallowed. There was no reason to hide the truth. "I'm tryin' to pay my daughter's school."

"Oh yeah?"

"They gonna kick her out if I don't get it paid. I can't let that happen."

Jameson looked doubtful, then shrugged. He pulled a form from a file drawer. "Why not? It's a better reason than most. You gotta be out there tomorrow morning by seven. Lemme give you the particulars."

60

On Valentine's Day Stephanie Homan was in the bookstore by eight a.m. putting together supply packets for yet another new Evening Accounting class. The phone buzzed.

"Bookstore."

"Steph? It's Deirdre."

"Hi, girl. Good morning to you."

"Morning." The high voice of the admissions rep hesitated, and Stephanie gripped the phone in quiet, quick suspense. "Steph, you shouldn't have left the flowers."

"Hey, I know. But I saw 'em in the shop window and couldn't resist. Then once I had them, who was I gonna give 'em to?"

"I understand. I mean sure. But …" A longer, and therefore more worrisome pause. "I *told* you I'm not … you know … I mean I'm not gay. I mean, I've given it thought like you asked. I *really* thought about it. But it's not me. I mean, it's not *for* me."

"And I knew that when I left the flowers on your desk," Stephanie responded breezily. "But I bought 'em on impulse, and once done it was done. And it's stupid to buy flowers for yourself. So if you're gonna give flowers, they gotta go to someone you admire. I admire you, that's all."

"That's—that's nice. Thanks. But this is exactly what I was talking about—"

"And admiration is something one friend feels for another. In fact, you can't have friendship without it."

"I realize that. I guess I do. But considering it's today, and after you and I talked—"

"I remember the talk, and what did I tell you? I said I'd be happy to just be a friend, right?"

"Yeah—"

"And that's all I've been, right?"

"Well, yeah—"

"We've loaded lead cards together, we've had some terrific gossipy girl talks. We've even gone to a couple of movies. We're supposed to go again this weekend. Am I embarrassing you?"

"No. It's been fun, actually. I told you that."

"Well, that's good." Stephanie hooked the phone to her shoulder so she could resume making the supply packets. "Look girl, I meant the flowers to be nice, but if they bother you, chuck 'em. I won't be offended."

"Oh God no, I don't want to do that!" Deirdre giggled nervously. "No, Steph, they're too nice. Actually, they're the nicest flowers anybody's ever given me. Everybody here's asking who the guy is. But … well, considering it's Valentine's Day, I just had to be clear with you."

"Totally understand. In fact, I was expecting your call. Sorry to put you in a quandary."

"Thanks, Steph."

"Talk to you later."

Stephanie hung up, and whistled a little as she worked on the packets. At age twenty-five she had already trekked most of the United States, published several chapbooks of poetry, survived a total of three failed marriages between her two biological parents, plus one failed marriage of her own. She rented a house on Naudain Street just below Bainbridge, and made ends meet teaching piano and violin when she wasn't working this bookstore gig or going to class. It was a hectic life but it was all hers, and she thrived on the nonstop pace. At the same time, she could appreciate when progress was best served in slow, steady steps. Sometimes patience could make the payoff all the sweeter.

At ten to nine she tallied her early morning sales and took the register receipt and cash downstairs to Louise. The business manager was hunched over a form, making low angry noises. Her pen dug hard as she completed blank lines.

"Hi, Louise."

"Steph."

"Wha'cha doing?"

"Filling out an inventory questionnaire Andy Abrams sent me, because that's exactly how I want to spend my time. What have you got?"

"The morning's receipts." She passed them over. "I also have an idea about the clocks."

"Oh yeah?"

"At least an idea that's better than trashing them."

"Let's hear it." Louise gave the student her full attention. Last year New York had shipped cartons of plastic clocks with the Burr logo to each of the schools. They ran on quartz batteries that were supposed to last five years, and were shaped like computer terminals with the time shown on the "screens." New York wanted the dinky things sold for eight dollars. It was a ludicrous price, and since then perhaps five of the two hundred and fifty sent to the Philly school had actually been purchased. Now, to help clear space for the extra supplies necessary for Oliver's new Achievement Program, New York was permitting the school to dump the lot. Louise asked, "What do you want to do?"

"Let's sell 'em for a buck."

"Just a buck?"

"Sure. They're not bad clocks. The students like them, they just don't want to spend eight dollars. But make the price a buck and I'll bet the whole batch goes. That's two hundred and fifty dollars. New York doesn't even have to know about it. We can take the money and throw an office party."

Louise laughed. "Yeah, we could. All right, whip up a sign and do it. Good job."

Stephanie left for the bookstore. Passing Dawn Hitchcock's cubicle she noticed a large vase of red roses mixed with baby's breath on the secretary's desk. She stopped and whistled. "Hey, not bad. What'd they cost you?"

"Oh funny," said Dawn. "They're beautiful, aren't they?"

"Yeah."

It was an impressive bouquet. The roses billowed from the vase, taking up half of Dawn's desk, and the open blooms were the size of coffee mugs.

"I'm totally blown away," Dawn said. "I really didn't expect anything so nice."

"You're real lucky."

"I know it." Dawn grinned and blushed.

Stephanie walked through the cubicles. Passing Deirdre's office door, she stole a peek at the rep, who was busy on the phone and didn't notice her. The vase of flowers, twelve yellow roses (yellow for friendship, of course), stood high on the windowsill catching the morning light. Dee's moving them off her desk was kind of a demotion, but at least she hadn't thrown them away. And better still, there were no more pictures of those hairy bastards tacked to her bulletin board. Crossing through the lobby, Stephanie saw yet another big bouquet of flowers on Julie Fitzgerald's desk. What a great day!

Her first class wasn't until 9:50, so Stephanie bounded up the stairs to reopen the bookstore. A small queue of students was waiting for her.

"Hello, Dorothee, what can I get you?"

"A ream of letterhead," said the student.

"Coming right up." One of the nice things about this gig was getting to know all the students and not just the ones in your class. It made her feel a part of the school. "Here you go. That's $7.45. Who's next? Mona, what can I get you?"

"Just need a pen, Steph. My last one finally went."

"Good enough. That's a $1.95. Amelia," she said to the president of student council.

"Hey, Steph."

"That's a nice brooch."

Amelia laughed. "Thanks. Vinnie gave it to me."

"Valentine's Day?"

"Oh you bet!"

"What can I get you?"

"A steno pad."

"Coming up. Here. $3.49. Thanks. Hello, Heather."

"Hi, Steph."

"Those are beautiful roses."

"Thanks." The student laughed and hugged her bouquet, huge red roses wrapped in colored paper and highlighted with baby's breath.

"What can I get you?"

"I need a steno pad too."

"Coming right up."

61

Sedately tapping the stairs with her four-and-a-half-inch red stiletto high heels, Trudy Weiser descended from the second floor where she had just set up an applicant to take the admissions test in the library. Nick Persichetti was that rarity—a male applicant interested in a secretarial career—and she had put him at a corner table with the test booklet and some scratch paper, then placed her own proctoring materials one table over. Trudy hoped the boy would pass the test or, barring that, be smart enough to peek at the answer sheet planted practically under his nose.

As the senior rep passed through the cubicles to Lily's office she slowed, hearing the admissions director's strident voice. She approached the door cautiously.

"Bill! Bill!—come on now, you have to be reasonable! No, that's not the case! Because it's *not!* I know, but you have to look at the whole—

what?" Lily looked at the rep peeping in the doorway. "Bill, Bill—*BILL*, wait, will you? Just a sec." She lowered the phone. "Urgent?"

"No," said Trudy.

"Okay. And close that, will you?"

Trudy stepped back and shut the door. Although it muffled Lily's voice she could still hear her half of the conversation.

"Now look, Bill, I know as well as you what the numbers are. You are not going to accuse *me*, of all people, of being neglectful! Well, I thought the TV ads would bring in more too. Okay, but they did bring in *some*. Bill, that's not fair. Now listen—what? Hey, I don't need this kind of pressure! It's not productive, Bill! Don't you know how important staff morale is? You really shouldn't be talking to me this way—"

Trudy bristled for Lily's sake. They were all amazed at how quickly the spring was passing. April 4, with its looming sit of sixty students, was getting closer all the time, and the numbers did not look good. The staff had done all the right things, gone to high schools, attended college nights and career fairs at local malls, and Trudy herself was back on the road doing fashion shows. And they were all telemarketing night after night until each rep believed a phone receiver attached to the ear was a design of nature. Despite all of it, the numbers for April remained low. It was a lesson in Admissions that successful reps never quite learned: namely, that success did not breed success, achieved goals were yesterday's headlines, recruitment was never-ending, and there was never a time when even a phenomenally successful rep could afford to relax.

Lily shouted through the door. "Okay, come on in!"

Trudy entered to see the admissions director standing by the window staring out, arms akimbo, her shoulders stiff with resentment. Her right foot tapped the carpet rapidly. Trudy said with some hesitance, "Lily, can I get you anything?"

"Yes, you can get me thirty-two fucking prospects!" Lily spun about and jerked an arm toward the phone. "That son of a bitch's got the shortest memory I've ever known! I've never *seen* such ingratitude! He does nothing but point out that we're still short thirty-two students for April. It's March 6. The sit is April 4. That's four weeks! It's one prospect a day! Why doesn't he think we can reach that?"

"I don't know, Lily."

"Should be a piece of cake for us. Fuck. Pardon my French." She took a deep breath and smiled. "Tru, hon, I'm not mad at you. Goddamn Bill Nostrand is seeing bad numbers throughout the system and he's in a panic. But we're doing okay—not spectacular, but what do you want for a dopey late-spring sit? I know we'll make goal. He knows too, but he's being bitchy. I can't stand it when people take their frustrations out on others. Want some coffee?"

"Sure. Thanks."

Lily poured and they sat down. "You're doing that wop boy from St. Paul's Parish."

"Yes. He's in the library right now taking the test. He wanted evening steno, but I convinced him to take the full-time April class instead."

Lily smiled at the senior rep's low-cut cherry blouse and ass-tight miniskirt. "Well done. Get the app fee and deposit?"

"I insisted on the app fee before I toured him. The deposit he's hanging onto until he passes the test. He's nervous about taking it but I'm not, so I let it go. He really wants to be a secretary."

"What's his problem?" Lily snorted, and both women laughed. The admissions director sipped coffee, her good humor restored. "Listen, Tru. Give me half an hour, then buzz the others and let's hold a staff meeting. There's no reason why we can't get thirty-two students in four weeks, but the sooner we do it, the quicker Mr. Bullysnot will get off our backs. Shoot, we should each be averaging fifteen commits a week *minimum*. We could have the whole goddamn thirty-two in *two* weeks if the leads would just pick up."

Trudy stood. "Did you hear about the purse snatcher?"

Lily frowned. "The what?"

"There's a purse snatcher in the neighborhood. I read about it on a poster by the lobby door. Someone's been running up to girls in Washington Square, pushing them over, and grabbing their purses. There've been like three incidents in the past two weeks."

"I didn't know about this." Lily looked alarmed. "It wasn't in the paper, was it? Shit—we have enough trouble trying to convince the Jersey girls that Philly isn't dangerous. You say you saw a poster?"

"Yeah. It details the whole thing, and tells the girls to be careful and not let any strangers approach."

"And this thing is hanging *right by the lobby?*"

"Uh-huh. Julie said Oliver's real upset about it."

"So am I! Imagine putting something like that right where the prospects can see! Why can't the teachers simply make an announcement in the classrooms?"

"I can always take it down when no one's looking."

Lily sighed. "No, let me talk to Oliver first. One more yip to have with him. Go tell the others. Half an hour."

Trudy left.

Lily sat and brooded. This damn April sit was killing them. Lily knew (as did Ethel Harris and the faculty) that the best students in any academic year came in July. Those kids proved their initiative up front by the very act of sacrificing fun in the sun for education. And the September students were usually okay, because September was at least a traditional time to go to school and attracted normal kids. January classes began to show the quality drop. Many students beginning a program in January had already attended one school in the fall and failed out. Or they had wanted to start in the fall but never got their act together. Still, January wasn't a *weird* time to start school, and the students who began in that month were not necessarily bad, just not choice.

By April, however, a school was asking for trouble. April kids were so disorganized they couldn't get their act together in time for either September *or* January. Lily's staff had learned this quickly. Nearly every April prospect needed complete hand-holding. Interviews that should have taken thirty minutes stretched over an hour as reps helped students fill out app forms, financial aid forms, and explained and re-explained the course descriptions in the catalog.

Lily opened the pencil drawer of her desk for a Hershey bar and found it empty. The vending machines were downstairs in the student lounge. Lily sighed and got up. As she walked down the hall to the staircase the bell blatted and classes changed. Students converged around her, bumping shoulders and laughing among themselves. Lily passed these blurred bodies, former prospects obviously, but she couldn't put a name to a single face.

At two o'clock the cafeteria was slowing down. Four or five students sat at separate tables, munching and studying. The vending machine was out of Hershey's almond, so she bought a Snickers. Turning away, her eyes lit upon one black girl who was not studying although a textbook lay open before her. The kid was sitting alone, staring straight ahead. She sat profile to Lily, but the admissions director could see there was something wrong with her. Curious, she walked over.

"Excuse me, hon, but are you okay?"

The student's voice was barely audible. "Yeah'm."

"Are you sure? Look at me."

The girl lifted her head, and Lily stifled a gasp. The kid's right cheek was swollen and purple, the skin mottled where leftover stitch marks crossed the bone. A pink scar sliced her right brow in half. Her chin was also crooked, with purple discoloring on the right side although there were no stitch marks. "Sweetie, what happened to you?"

"I was in a accident."

"Looks like a bad one."

The student said nothing.

"I'm sorry."

The kid's shoulders flinched indifferently. With a knowledgeable eye Lily saw that whatever cretin stitched the jaw had done a sloppy half-ass job. She turned away and unwrapped her candy, but when she reached the foot of the stairs she stopped and looked back. Two girls at one table were chatting happily. The student with the damaged face was staring at nothing again. She looked totally defeated. Lily bit into the Snickers and walked back.

"Dear, can I sit a minute?"

"Awright." The student looked apathetically at her book.

"Want a piece of this?"

"No thanks."

"Looks like it hurts to chew."

No response to that.

"Look at me a sec, will you, please?"

The student did so without expression. Hers was a tiny face, and even without the damage her features were crunched naturally in a mean pinch. Some challenge, the admissions director thought, and was immediately stimulated. She chewed briskly.

"Did a doctor tell you if that scar there, where the stitches were, would be permanent?"

The girl didn't answer but looked pained. Lily smiled. "May I?" She reached so gently, and the smile was so cheerful, that the student didn't even flinch. Lily placed gentle fingers on the girl's chin and examined her, turning the marred face left and right. To herself she wondered if it was a father or a boyfriend who had damaged her. She didn't believe it was an accident. She had had enough "accidents" herself when she was a kid. "The bruises are nasty," she remarked. "Let's see. Your face is a nice rich brown. And you're lucky, it's even in tone all the way around. What color do you use?"

"Ma'am?"

"You don't use much make up, I can see. But you must use some. Every girl uses *some*. Let me think." Lily's eyes passed over the narrow face, took in the hairline, the high forehead, the small squarish ears. She grinned, opened her purse, and took out a small pad and pen. "Do you have a yellow base? You need that. Mix it with your foundation. It'll take the purple right out of those bruises." Lily's eyes flicked around the student's pointed jaw line, assessing the color. "Yellow, absolutely, for both the chin and the cheek. You know who's got a nice yellow base? Dear old Mary Kay. You must know *some*body selling Mary Kay. And for the foundation itself, with your pigments, I would suggest … Origins. I love their line." She wrote down the name. "Now the scar. Hmm." Lily puzzled in silence for some time. "Okay, hon, this is going to be tough. The line starts up near the left temple and curls down to your jaw." It was truly a wicked scar. A crack like the Mississippi River running down the left side of the kid's head. "Honey, that's gonna be permanent. You're gonna have a line, unfair as it seems. We can't hide it, but what we *can* do is—are you interested?"

The girl nodded.

"What we *can* do is make the rest of you look so terrific no one is ever going to notice. What do you use on your eyes?"

The kid started, "Well—"

"I would try driftwood for a wash. Do you use that?"

"I ain't—"

"It's perfect for an almond skin like yours. And then raisin on the crease of your lids. Do you know what the eyes are, honey? They're the gems of your face. Everyone looks at the eyes first, because ninety percent of a woman's beauty is shining right there." Lily took her pen and held it vertically alongside the girl's nose. Then she held it diagonally from the bottom of the nose to the outer corner of the eye. She nodded approval and put the pen down. "You should use a charcoal liner. Do you?"

The student watched Lily, fascinated. The admissions director kept jotting down notes and brand names on the pad. "Origins makes a rouge that is just perfect for dark skin. Ever notice how red can sit on a black woman's face as if it's just floating there? Origins blends flawlessly. Allows the red to look like it's coming from within, which is what it's all about, of course. And try coral for your lips. With a driftwood wash, there's nothing more sensual than coral lips on a black woman. You use an oil-free base?"

The student nodded.

"Honey, you are going to look so cute. Do you ever smile?"

The very question made the student break into one.

Lily leaned back and grinned. "There you are, sweetheart, you're beautiful! Take this list." She tore off the page and turned it upside down so the student could read it. "You get this stuff and try it. Get that lipstick for your mouth, get that foundation and shadow, get the yellow. Honey, there won't be a man on the planet who'll see that little line you got there—trust me. Now come see me when you're set, hey? I'm gonna want to look at you. You know where my office is?"

"Up front?"

"That's right. I'm Lily. You come see me if you have any questions. I can tell you *everything*." She stood up.

"Thanks, ma'am."

"You lost the smile. Where's the smile?"

The kid grinned self-consciously.

"Gorgeous! You come see me."

Lily finished the rest of her candy bar as she trotted up the stairs. She returned to her office and rifled through a small accumulation of phone messages. Six were complaints. She smacked her intercom buzzer. "Beatrice? Lily. Can I see you for a minute?"

"Sure."

Lily drummed the desktop rapidly with all five digits of her left hand. Beneath the desk, her foot tapped the carpet.

Beatrice stuck her head through the doorway. "Hi."

"Come in."

"Is there a problem?"

"Looks like it."

Beatrice sat and stretched, putting both hands behind her head. "So what's the deal?"

Lily let the casual pose stoke her anger. At least the financial aid director was wearing dresses now. When Beatrice started last September she wore slacks and sandals to work, and one day even wore jeans. Lily chewed her out before all the department heads at staff meeting, and Beatrice showed for work thereafter in proper business attire. She never used make up, not even lipstick, and when she wore knee-high skirts little black hairs poked through her pantyhose, but Lily tolerated these infractions since the alternative was to search for a new aid director and she couldn't afford the hassle.

"I have six phone messages here," said Lily, "from parents whose daughters are set for April. They haven't heard about their aid yet. Now I know that at least two of these girls applied last week, and I thought they had submitted their forms to you."

Beatrice took the phone slips and read the names. "Yeah, I think they did."

"Well, why haven't they heard from you?"

"They will, Lily. I've got a backlog right now."

"And why do you have a backlog?"

"Lily, Christ, you brought in a ton of people last January for both day and evening classes. I've been playing catch-up ever since."

"And you think that's good?"

The aid director shrugged. "It's what it is. I can't help it."

"Well, you'd *better.*" Lily smacked her hand on the desk with such violence that Beatrice sat up straight. "Financial aid is critical in this business, and speed is of the essence! Do you hear me?"

"Sure." Beatrice slouched again, resentful at reacting so strongly to Lily's loud hand smack.

"Paying for college is the big concern of these kids. They need to know *immediately* that they can afford to come. I won't have you screwing up my sits, understand?"

"Sure."

"So what are you going to do about it?"

"Well," Beatrice looked at the slips again. "I guess I'll do these right away and send them out."

"No! You will *call* them with the results. *Then* you'll send out the aid notices. And not just for those two, but for anybody else who's still sitting on your desk. I want everybody who's applied here up to yesterday to get a package in the mail today."

"Up to yesterday?" Beatrice laughed out loud. "Are you nuts? Nobody can work that fast."

"*Everybody* here works that fast. Go back to your office and get started. I'll be over in five minutes and we'll go through your in-basket together."

"You're gonna what?"

"You heard me." Lily's eyes gleamed with faint malice. "Beatrice, I'm going to light one hell of a fire under you. You won't like it, and maybe you'll quit. That's up to you. But I'll tell you this—*if* you stick it out you'll get those fringe benefits we talked about, hey?"

Beatrice kept her mouth shut.

"You know I'm not bullshitting you. We've talked about some nice stuff for you. But you sure as hell won't get a cent with your current work performance. Got it?"

"Yeah."

"Say yeah again."

"Yeah, Lily, I get it." Beatrice stood up, looking annoyed. "Let me get started. But you don't have to come over. I'd rather organize it myself."

"No, I'm coming. We'll look at what you're doing and determine how to handle the work flow. Don't take it as an insult. You're still fairly new at this game. I know we can work out some good shortcuts that'll benefit all of us."

"Lily, you don't have to—"

"I'm coming."

Beatrice walked out in a quiet fury. She didn't like people telling her what to do, and she sure as hell didn't want to be monitored. But Lily held all the cards, and some of them—extra vacation time, bonuses—were pretty attractive.

She entered her office and dropped behind the desk. She looked at the in-basket, which was fairly high and had been since January. The April prospects were submitting stuff piecemeal—a tax return here, a financial aid application there—and the work pile never went down. She figured she could work around the clock for days and still not catch up.

In the midst of this perplexity, wondering what she should fix first before Lily stuck her nose in here, the intercom buzzed. Beatrice hit the button. "Hello?"

"Beatrice, there's a call for you on Line One," said Julie.

"Okay." She punched the white flashing light. "Financial Aid."

"Yes, I'd like to speak to the financial aid director, please."

"Speaking."

The voice on the other end was pleasantly masculine. "May I have your name, please?"

"Beatrice Genovese."

"And you're the director of financial aid?"

"You got it." This didn't sound like a parent. Beatrice couldn't understand what was going on.

"Ms. Genovese, my name is Richard Parkinson, and I'm with the Program Review Unit of the Department of Education."

"Uh-huh. Sure, what can I do for you?"

"Well, I'd like to schedule a program review of your office. Say some time near the end of this month."

"A program review." Beatrice stated the phrase, even though she meant it as an inquiry.

"Yes. Can you name a time that would be convenient?"

"Well," Beatrice picked up her vinyl calendar book and flipped through the March and April pages. Most days were blank but that didn't mean anything. She wasn't particularly good at keeping her calendar up to date. Appointments were always showing up in the lobby and surprising her. "I'm not too sure what my schedule is. You may want to talk to the school director."

"All right. That's Oliver Dunbar, isn't it?"

"Yeah. Hold on a moment, I'll see if he's in."

"Thank you."

Beatrice punched hold, then hit the intercom button for Oliver's office. Maybe after Oliver talked to this guy he would tell her what the heck was a program review.

62

Heather passed one hundred words per minute without error in Carol Sobolewski's Fifth Period shorthand transcription class, and it was too good a victory not to share. Clutching a thick biography of Bill Gates, her office Procedures II book, and a steno pad, she skipped down the stairs to the second floor where Bob's drama-lit class for the first-year September students was just finishing. The Gates book was for a report in Bob's class, and though she was annoyed that he assigned her something so thick, she realized all the other biographies on the list looked just as bad. This fourth and final semester was really getting tough.

She reached the second floor landing and wormed through a bottle-neck of jabbering July students. Bob stood by his classroom doorway, talking to Nicole Richardson. Heather's bright feeling evaporated on the instant. She stood in the middle of the hall, hugging her books and ignoring the students trying to pass around her.

"The thing about Williams you have to watch out for is his sentimentality," Bob was saying. "It's a weakness all southern writers possess."

"But I think the ending of *Glass Menagerie* is so sad," said Nicole, wide-eyed and standing close. "Don't you think so?"

"Sure it is. And it's to your credit as a sensitive person that you feel the sadness. But you have to remember that *Menagerie* was Williams' first major play. He wanted it to be tragic, even if such an ending didn't make sense. After all, how likely is it that the gentleman caller would develop a compassion for Laura, court her and even kiss her, then blurt out that he's going to marry somebody else—all in the space of one forty-minute act?"

"God," said Nicole. "I would never have thought of that. You really know how to read these plays, Mr. Lawrence."

The bitch!

"You have to be careful with *Streetcar* too," Bob lectured happily. "Poor Blanche doesn't stand a chance because Williams is too enamored with Kowalski. Williams was a homosexual, you know, and couldn't resisting loading the dice in favor of his primitive Adonis. When—"

"Hi," Heather cut in.

He turned and smiled. "Heather. Ms. Feeney. Hello."

"Hi, Nicole."

The other girl studied Heather coolly, then turned back to Bob with a fresh airy smile. "You were saying, Mr. Lawrence?"

But Bob was studying Heather. He sighed and said to Nicole, "It's not important. You better get to your next class."

"Okay. Thanks for giving me the time." Nicole's tart smile in front of Heather lasted two seconds longer than it should. She hefted her bookbag and jogged up the stairs.

"The Red Tavern!" Heather snapped. "Right at five o'clock! You hear me?"

"Yes. What—"

"Just be there! We got to talk!" She spun on her heel and ran up the stairs.

When Heather's last class finished at four, she grabbed her homework and bookbag and stormed out of the school. The Red Tavern was eight blocks west on Broad Street where it could draw the upscale City Hall and Philadelphia Orchestra crowd. It was too expensive for most students, and Bob considered it safe because of this. Heather entered the pub and took a seat at the bar, knowing she had an hour to kill before Bob would be able to join her. As five o'clock approached the pub began to fill with clean-shaven, well-tailored yuppies. Sitting alone in her short-skirted lavender business suit, Heather received plenty of appreciative looks, but the first time she tried to order a drink she got carded, with the apprehensive manager requesting that she please wait by the door until her older companion arrived. Heather was able to soothe the poor man by flashing bright eyes and laughing at his apologetic jokes about the stupid law, and was able to get away with keeping her seat and sipping Cokes.

Bob showed shortly after five, saw her, and requested a table in the dining room. As soon as they were seated she said, "I want a daiquiri. Order me one."

A waiter approached and Bob did. "And I'll have scotch and soda," he added. The waiter jotted down both orders without so much as a glance at Heather. She watched him go with mean satisfaction.

"All right, Heather. What's the problem?"

"You really don't know, do you?"

"Not until you tell me."

She nodded dramatically to let him know she was seeing through him. "So now you're what, making moves on Nicole Richardson?"

Bob was nonplussed. "What are you talking about?"

"Right! You mean that wasn't what you were doing, when you thought I was up on the third floor?"

"Oh hell. Dammit, Heather." He looked angry, not guilty. "When you saw Nicole and me we were talking shop. We were discussing … hell, I don't even remember."

"I don't care what you were talking about. What I object to is her standing close and chummy with her tits practically in your face, and you lettin' her—"

"Oh get real. That's crazy."

"It's *not* crazy!" she shrilled. "Don't tell me it's crazy!"

"Hey, hey! Keep calm, honey, okay?"

The drinks arrived. Bob waited until they were alone again. "It was between classes, Heath. People get bunched together in that narrow hall. Maybe we just looked like we were close together. Neither of us realized it, I can assure you."

"I don't think so."

"Stop it, Heather. I couldn't even tell you what Nicole was wearing to-day. I don't think about her at all."

"White blouse and red skirt, kinda short. Red shoes, white stockings."

"Sounds like a candy cane."

"She's got fat legs."

"She does?"

"Thunder thighs. She looks stupid in miniskirts."

Bob tried to remember. Nicole's legs weren't *that* fat. Actually her calves had a curvy sensuality that thinner girls like Heather missed out on. He contemplated this a little too long, and when he looked at Heather she was clearly mistaking his musings for reverie.

"You son of a bitch! You *have* noticed! I can see it in your eyes!"

"Oh for God's sake, Heather. She's a student in my class!"

Her eyebrows raised. "So?"

Really. He tried again. "I have no interest in Nicole Richardson."

"You didn't look it when you two were in the hall."

"Oh Christ," he snapped. "I'm tired of this! Your damn jealousy and your stupid arguments!"

"You sayin' I'm stupid?"

"You don't even want to see reason! That's the really unforgivable part, that you aren't interested in even *trying* to be fair." Bob's heart sparked. He was showing more anger toward her than ever before, and it felt wonderful. "Don't you know anything about guys? They *look* at women! It's a natural thing, like breathing. It doesn't mean they want to have sex with them."

"Oh really?"

"Yes! Christ, it's just a … a … I don't know, just a thing all men do. I wasn't flirting with her."

"You are a bastard," she said, and chomped the strawberry on her glass.

"I am not." He indulged his own drink. The scotch burned the back of his throat, the very gasoline he needed. "Maybe you should grow up more, and get an understanding of what people are like."

"Oh yeah, take *that* attitude. I don't need to grow up to see what a shit you are. I think you're ashamed of us."

"I'm not ashamed."

"You really piss me off. I feel so good about us, I get so excited. I want to tell everybody, the feeling gets so big."

He said too quickly, "You haven't, have you?"

"Shit! That really worries you, doesn't it? What a fucking coward."

Bob shut his eyes. In a swirl of hastily swallowed scotch he made his decision. He didn't care about the consequences. He had always known it would end, but the delicacy of waiting for the right moment wasn't worth all this grief.

"Okay, you win. You're disgusted with me, and I can't deal with your insecurities. Let's break up."

"Insecurities!"

"Sure. You're jealous too many god-awful times, Heather. I'm sick of it. Let's break up and go our separate ways."

She sat straight. "What?"

"You heard me. I think it'd be best for both of us."

"Oh no!" Heather wasn't angry any more. Flushed from alcohol on an empty stomach, she said loudly, "I don't want to break up, honey! Please don't say that!"

"I don't see any other way. I can't stand this childish behavior of yours, and that's exactly what it is—childish!"

"Okay. I guess it is. You're right. I'm sorry, Bob."

He downed more scotch, felt it bolster him. "Heather, sorry isn't enough. We've had these talks too many times. It takes me forever to convince you when your behavior is bad, then when you finally promise to act better nothing happens. You don't change. Tomorrow you'll catch me talking to, say Bonnie Beecher, and you'll throw the same damn tantrum all over again."

"I won't, Bob! I promise!"

"I just don't believe you anymore." Dear God, sunlight after all! Why hadn't he done this sooner? Why, when this was over he *could* talk to Bonnie Beecher. Or Nicole Richardson. He'd be free again. But the main thing, the real blast, was that he could stop seeing Dawn Hitchcock in secret. Nothing had frustrated or depressed him more than trying to date Dawn around Heather's schedule.

Heather sat very still with one hand on her glass. She looked devastated. "I can't believe this."

Bob's elation ebbed. He really didn't want to hurt her. "I'm sorry, Heath."

"Bob, *please!*" She grabbed his hand with frightened urgency. "Can't we try again? I know I acted bad today. You gotta let me make it up to you!"

He knew what that meant, and immediately didn't want to stand firm. Whenever they argued and she realized he was truly angry with her, she would get this same frightened look, and would afterward submit willingly to whatever method of lovemaking he desired. It was an intensely powerful lure.

"Heather, I'm sorry," he said with real effort. "It wouldn't be right. We have to be fair to each other."

"Then you don't want to marry me?"

"Honey, we aren't suited for each other. Why marry someone you don't understand, or who doesn't understand you? You'd be asking for misery if you did that. We both would." He picked up the check. "Let me just settle this and we'll go, okay?"

He didn't wait for an answer. Bob walked to the bar and broke a twenty. Waiting for change, he leaned against the counter and exhaled slowly. He had to stop doing this shit with the students. Even without

Dawn in the picture it was getting tougher and tougher. Or perhaps he was finally just outgrowing it. Bob collected his change and returned to the dining room, half-wondering if Heather would still be there.

She was, and pouted as he stood there figuring the tip. "I'm telling Dean Harris."

Bob's scalp tingled. "Why do that?"

"Because you're a jerk. I feel used, I really do."

"Heather, that's not true. How can you say—"

"And I don't think you ever intended to marry me. That's why we never got a ring, right?"

"I told you why you shouldn't have a ring. Remember you agreed—"

"Fuck you." Her fingers gripped her pocketbook. "You big jerk, I can't stand it!"

Bob sat down fast and lowered his voice. "Hey come on. There's no reason to tell the dean except to get me in trouble. You're an adult, Heather, you can behave better than that."

"I don't care. I hate you, Bob."

"Heather, don't tell the dean. I'll—"

"That's really got you scared, doesn't it? I got you there, don't I?"

So he sat back defiantly. His voice sharpened. "All right, go ahead. Tell her. You know I don't care about my job. I'll find some kind of work."

"Good. Then if nothing else it'll get you out of the school! I won't have to look at your ugly face!"

She meant it. She was going to do it.

Bob tried to conceal his nervousness. Even if he *didn't* care about his job (and he did—or at least he feared unemployment), he realized with a dreadful pang that Dawn would find out. How could she not? She was Ethel's secretary. And when she learned she would think … she would think … *Jesus!*

"Heather, what would be the point? You don't want to hurt me."

"It's me who's hurt!" she declared with a vehemence that brought out all her youth. "And I have to hurt you back. Go fuck yourself."

"Heather, please—don't tell the dean."

"I am. First thing in the morning." She started to get up.

He slapped his hand over hers, making her stay in her seat. "All right, what do you want?"

"What do you mean?"

"For not telling her. What do you want that will keep you quiet until you've grown up about this?"

She studied him silently. Her face broke into a smile of wonder at the possibilities.

"Tell me," he said again, but his forcefulness slipped before that smile.

Heather nodded. "Sure, okay. First off, I want to keep seeing you. I want you to take me out to dinners and movies so we can talk this out."

"All right, I expected that."

"And I want an A on my Bill Gates book."

"Your what? Oh come on, Heather. You can't blackmail me over a grade."

"Then I'm telling the dean!" she shouted.

"All right, keep your voice down!" People were glancing at them. He hissed in a low tone, "Heather, that's crazy. I can't do that."

"Then don't, and see what happens."

Good God! His worst scenario, imagined with every student he slept with, finally come to life! His heart pounded hard enough to hurt.

"Heather, how can you expect to iron things out between us if you're blackmailing me?"

"I gotta get something out of this. You're causing me a lot of pain. There's no way I'm reading that stupid book when you're my teacher. I want an A."

"All right. But do me a favor, okay, and make a reasonably intelligent effort. So I can justify the A."

"You can take care of that," she said. "I don't care if you write the report."

"Heather!"

"What?" The challenge was clear.

He took a deep breath and let it out slowly, to calm himself and keep from lunging across the table at her. "Okay. You get an A on the paper."

"And we keep seeing each other. Not for sex unless I feel like it, but for dinners and movies and things. Whenever I want to."

"Okay. But think about this, all right? You know you're not going to get us back together by doing this. This is the worst thing you can do."

"Are you agreeing?"

"Yes."

"All right." Heather drained her glass. "I want another daiquiri. Buy me one."

"Go buy your own," he snapped.

"Buy me one or I'm tellin' the dean."

"Oh come on! You just used that threat for the other stuff! You can't use it again!"

"Why not?"

They stared at each other. Waiters hopped briskly around them. In one corner a three-piece combo executed a few preparatory licks and twangs.

Bob asked, "What flavor?"

"Strawberry."

63

On Tuesday Marty interviewed a young woman for the April program, then walked her out to the lobby where her boyfriend waited. He watched them go out together and speculated on something that normally would not have crossed his mind: he wondered what would become of her. She had failed the admissions test with as low a score as he'd ever seen—twenty-eight out of a hundred. When he discussed the curriculum she seemed to think him funny, and would laugh one moment and look on the verge of tears the next. Like she wasn't in control of herself. Like she was ... well, *on* something. Who could know?

He accepted her anyway, of course.

Marty was no sooner back in his office when the phone buzzed. Lily's voice rapped in his ear. "How'd it go?"

"She signed up."

"For April?"

"Yes."

"Did you get the deposit?"

"I tried for the deposit. She didn't have a cent on her. But at least she signed up."

"Fucking hell, Marty! I've told you a *thousand times* that a verbal agreement means nothing! What's it going to take for you idiots to understand that—!"

"Lily—"

"I can't do everything around here, you know! Don't you realize where our numbers *stand?*"

"Lily, did you hear me? She didn't have a cent. I tried, but she had nothing. Not even a checkbook. Just train fare."

"Ask me if I care! Did you set up this appointment?"

"Yes, but—"

"Then you could have told her to *bring* a checkbook, couldn't you?"

"Lily, that might have put her off—"

"*Couldn't* you?"

"Yes," he conceded, and stifled his annoyance.

"You could have reassured her if she suspected something. You know how to do it. Face it, you fucked up."

"All right, Lily. I guess I did. It won't happen again."

"It better not, Marty. The numbers are too serious. April orientation is getting closer all the time, and we're still twenty short! I am not going to miss this goal, do you hear me? So get on the goddamn ball!"

Click!

Marty banged his own phone down. Christ, was it his fault the April numbers were coming so slowly? Was it his fault those expensive TV ads didn't pay off like Lily promised New York? She shouldn't be busting his balls like this. He could leave, and *then* where would she be? Stuck with those two namby-pamby bitches. He was the best rep she had and she knew it. She should be more deferential to him. Fucking *grateful.*

Marty buzzed Deirdre's office, and when the rep answered he asked, "Say Dee, is there a new lead list for today?"

"Yeah. It hasn't been run off the computer yet, but I saw it on the spool queue."

"Well, can you print it for me? I need some fresh phone numbers fast."

"Steph's working there. She knows how to do it."

"All right. Thanks." Marty went out to the cubicles. At Deirdre's old station he found the student sitting at the computer terminal loading lead cards. Her spongy gray hair was pressed into bizarre funnels on each side of her head, thanks to a radio headset, and she bobbed to an invisible beat. "Excuse me," he said. Getting no response, he raised his voice. "Hey!"

She turned and stared vacuously. She didn't remove the headset.

"I need you to run something for me."

She nodded without a word. He could hear tinny rock music coming out of her hair.

"Are you listening to me? I need you to run a report."

"Sure. Okay."

But she didn't do anything, just sat there watching him. Marty felt his blood rising. "Look, kid, take that off and run what I want."

"Well, what *do* you want?"

"I need a lead run. Make it from March 5 to the present. That'll give me almost two weeks' worth."

"Okay."

"Did you hear me?"

"Sure." She looked at him like he was demented, then turned and punched the keys. Marty returned to his office in a foul mood and shut the door. He dropped behind his desk and rubbed his forehead. Why the fuck was some kid loading lead cards, running reports, doing mail-merges, and the like? Why wasn't Deirdre doing it? She'd done it before, and she sure was better doing data input than trying to recruit. With each sit, she always had the lowest enrolls. He would have to discuss it with Lily.

A knock on the door. He raised his head and adjusted his bow tie. "Come in."

The student strolled in with a very small computer run. He despaired at the thinness of it.

"Thanks. Just give it to me here."

"Okay." Stephanie plopped it on the desk and walked out.

Marty grabbed the list. It consisted mainly of phone numbers pulled from inquiry calls. Part of the April problem was that at this late time of year the reps had to rely solely on phone contacts and walk-ins to generate business.

Running his eye down the list, some of the names seemed strange. Like people he had talked to a long time ago. Why would that be? Marty double-checked the upper left corner of the first page and his heart stopped. The report was from March of *last* year! The names were inquiries for the previous July class! Blood rushed so fast to Marty's head that his vision clouded. He was out the door in a flash.

"Goddammit!" He whisked the report before Stephanie's wide eyes. "Get that damn thing off your head right now!"

She complied. "What's wrong with you?"

"You couldn't take that thing off to listen to me, and now you've run the wrong report! This is last year's inquiries! A fat fucking lot of good it's gonna do me!"

"All right, I'm sorry." She shrugged. "I'll fix it right away and get you another."

"You better! This is worthless, you stupid bitch! I don't care if you are a student!" He slammed the pages into the wastebasket.

Stephanie's little body straightened and she crossed her arms. Her small face pinched in a tough grimace. "You watch what you call me, mister."

"I'm not apologizing to you!" screeched Marty. "Do your job and you won't get called names!"

"It's probably not good strategy to yell at somebody you're asking a favor of."

"I'll get you fired!"

"I'd like to see you try."

Even in his anger he realized she probably had him there. Students were little gods around here. "Just run the report."

"Run it yourself."

"Look you," he shouted. "You're paid to do a job. *This* is your job. Now run that damn report."

Stephanie stood and stretched. "Gosh, I think I'll go get a soda." She started to walk past him.

"Hey!" He took hold of her arm.

"Oh, you don't want to do that," she remarked. He let go immediately, and she sauntered off.

Marty stared at the computer terminal in baffled fury. He had absolutely no idea how to run the report. He let fly a vitriolic stream of profanity and headed back to his office. Passing Trudy's open door he looked in and saw her seated at her desk, chatting on the phone with a large computer printout of names and phone numbers spread across her desk. Marty lingered in the doorway until she finished the call.

"Hi there," he said with his best grin.

Trudy leaned back in her chair. "What do you want?"

"You mind if I make a copy of that report?"

"Yeah, I do."

He was caught off guard. "You *do* mind?"

"Sure. This is my report. Go get your own."

"I just tried. That little—that kid Louise hired won't run it for me."

"I know." She smiled. "I heard you out there."

Marty was baffled beyond belief. "What the hell kind of attitude is this? Give me that report. I'll bring it right back."

"Uh-uh."

"Christ! You want me to go tell Lily that you're—"

"Oh Marty, shut up."

"This is totally unprofessional!"

"Golly."

"Look, this isn't fair! You give me at least a page off that report or I'm going to Lily! You hear me?"

"All right, all right." Trudy stood up. She picked up the computer run and approached him.

"Good," said Marty. He squared his shoulders. "I don't want to see this kind of attitude again. We're supposed to be a team, you know?"

"Yeah," said Trudy. "Ain't it the truth." Still holding the report, she shut her office door on him.

Marty's "GOD DAMN YOU, YOU LOUSY FUCKING BITCH!" could be heard all the way out to the lobby.

64

Richard Parkinson and Kristina McClure of the Department of Education arrived at the Burr College at 9:30, Monday, March 31, thirty minutes late. Parkinson was a tall robust man with jet black hair and brows. McClure was pale and petite. Both wore glasses and carried briefcases, and McClure also clutched a spiral-bound notebook. Parkinson identified himself to Julie with a genial, "How do you do?"

"Hello," she smiled. "I'll get Dr. Dunbar right away." After buzzing Oliver she said, "Let me take your coats. Would you like some coffee?"

"Thank you. That would be nice."

The whole school had been on the lookout for these two since eight o'clock. As prearranged, Julie buzzed Dawn who came forward to cover the desk. "Please have a seat," Julie said to the auditors, then went for the coffee. Parkinson and McClure sat on the couch and simultaneously crossed their legs.

Dawn said, "Did you have a good ride in?"

"We came last night," said Parkinson. "We're staying at the Sheraton."

"Oh, that's nice."

"But it was a pleasant train ride up," McClure offered, and smiled.

"Do you both live in Washington?"

Parkinson nodded. McClure said, "Yes."

Dawn smiled pleasantly but asked nothing more. She was nervous and didn't want it to show. Program reviewers came from either the federal or state level to review schools for compliance with the ever-growing myriad of financial aid regulations and laws. Like the IRS, they were conceived as a positive force designed to maintain quality control, yet were considered The Enemy by those whose doors they knocked upon. Program reviewers could fine schools, make them pay back financial aid incorrectly given to students as far back as three years and, in cases of profound abuse, petition that a school's eligibility to participate in the Title IV federal aid programs be severed. That last would cut even a small college from tens of millions of dollars annually, and would almost surely cause it to fold. Dawn tried to look busy by pretending to proof the half-finished letter in the computer, which was silly because it was Julie's letter, and she had no clue to its contents.

Oliver came through the cubicles with Beatrice close behind. Oliver had donned his suit jacket which usually hung forgotten on his office door, but it was the aid director that Dawn stared at. She had never seen Beatrice look so nice. Beatrice wore a dark wool business suit, short blazer and silk blouse with an out-of-fashion ruffled collar. She stood beside Oliver in the lobby, the perfect picture of a business professional, flawed only by the chubby face that seemed to sorely miss its chewing gum.

"Hello," said Oliver. "I'm Dr. Dunbar. This is our director of financial aid, Beatrice Genovese."

"Yes," said Parkinson. "We talked on the phone."

The auditors stood up and everyone shook hands. Oliver said, "I'm glad you both made it safe and sound. We're at your disposal. Shall we go to my office? Dawn, would you buzz Ethel and Lily and ask them to join us?"

The auditors retrieved their briefcases and followed Oliver and Beatrice through the cubicles. Dawn called the others, then sat alone in the lobby. Julie returned shortly, pushing a silver coffee set on a rolling cart, a set that was not school property but a loan from Clara Peterson.

"I see you don't mind doing the coffee thing," Dawn joked good-naturedly.

"They're the Department of Education," said Julie. "I'll cook 'em a turkey dinner if they ask. Back in a minute."

She navigated the coffee set through the cubicles, but because Oliver's office was full of people she had to keep the cart outside. Every chair was taken save one, reserved for Lily, and small talk went around while they waited for her. McClure unzipped her briefcase. Julie made sure everyone was properly served, then stepped out. Parkinson finally decided to go ahead.

"Well, what I'd like to do is give you the list of files we want pulled, then really all we need is a quiet place to work. It's not our intention to bother any of you unless specific questions come up as we go along."

"How many names have you got for us?" asked Oliver.

"Forty-five." McClure pulled a computer printout from her case and handed it to Beatrice, who was seated beside her on the couch. "They're a random selection of aid recipients we have on record from this institution. We pulled fifteen each from the last two years, plus fifteen from the current year."

There was a knock on the doorframe. "Lily," said Oliver. "Please come in. Everybody, this is our admissions director, Lily Espirito."

"Hello, hello! Hope I haven't missed anything fun!" She strode into the room with a jolly laugh. Everyone stood, and the handshaking started anew. Lily's bronze and gold hair was swept up in a regal beehive, her minidress a dazzling sheaf of rose-gold sequins that reflected every light in the room. She singled out Parkinson immediately and crinkled her eyes at him. "I understand you're here to give us lots of trouble. Ha! Ha! Shame on you!"

"Oh no, we're not here for that," Parkinson said, suddenly shy. The woman standing before him was brazenly beautiful, her body shimmering with light, her legs bare to the thigh, her eyes fixed on him with utter joy.

"Of course you're not! You guys are the best! Actually, I've always had a *thing* for accountants. Nothing sparks a girl's interest more than a man who does math for a living, hey?" She winked at McClure.

"Beatrice," said Oliver, "Why don't you go collect the files they need?"

"Sure." Beatrice grabbed the computer list and left.

Everyone sat again, and Lily took the empty chair across from Parkinson. She faced him directly and crossed her naked legs. The foot of the upper-crossed leg tapped the air gently, making the ankle bracelet wink. Parkinson couldn't stop glancing at her, and every time he did she smiled.

"We'll need copies of each student's academic transcript," said McClure. "Unless there are copies in the financial aid files."

"I keep them separate," said Ethel.

"And a copy of each student's account."

Oliver said, "That's our business manager. I'll let her know."

"And all admitting documentation, plus the college catalog, to be sure that all policies have been followed."

"Oh! Oh!" Lily chirped. "That's my area! You have any questions at all, just come see me."

"And we'll need a copy of your Title IV Program Participation Agreement and certification of a drug-free workplace."

"I have those," said Oliver. "How long do you think this will take?"

McClure looked at her colleague. She was only the assistant and couldn't answer that. Everyone looked at Parkinson, and after a long pause he said, "What?"

Oliver repeated, "Do you have any idea how long this will take?"

"Well we'd, uh, like to finish by Wednesday, though we're allowing a full week. Let's say through to the end of Wednesday."

"That's fine. Will we get an exit interview? I'd like to hear what you have to say before you go."

"Oh yes. That's mandatory. We'll meet with you before we leave."

"Good. We're going to put you up in our library. It's on the second floor, and it's nice and quiet. We've put a sign up so students will know they can't use it until after five."

"Thank you."

"Meanwhile it'll probably take Beatrice a little time to collect the files. Perhaps you'd both like to tour the school with Lily while you wait?"

Lily bounced to her feet. "Oh yes! Come with me, everybody. This'll be fun. I love showing off this place."

The two auditors followed her out. Oliver looked at Ethel. "What do you think?"

"I guess they're all right."

"You don't look happy."

"I just resent the way they barge right in and disrupt everything while they snoop around."

"It's their job, Eth. I don't like it either, but they're necessary."

The dean sighed and stood. "I'll get Dawn after those transcripts. Oh, Kurt was asking about you, did I tell you? He graduates from Temple this year."

"Oh my gosh. How is that possible?"

"He's a man now. I think that's the first time I've said that out loud." Ethel chuckled and shook her head. "Anyway, he wondered if you would come to graduation. Usually they just give tickets to immediate family, but his daddy won't be attending."

"You tell Kurt I'd be honored."

Beatrice collared Deirdre Smith and they went downstairs. Past the faculty lounge was a black door with a glass knob and a hole for a skeleton key. Beatrice produced such a key, given her by Louise, and clicked the lock. The door opened on a large room filled with deep shadows and only the barest gray light. A pull-chain dangled from the ceiling. Beatrice gave it a tug, and an overhead bulb lit. The gloom was not much alleviated.

"Shit," she grumbled. "If I get anything on this suit Oliver's paying for the cleaning."

"Who's on the list?" Deirdre peered timidly past her.

They stepped down two wooden steps to a concrete floor. The Dungeon was fairly large, forty by sixty feet, with metal tiers in the middle holding carton after carton of files, with still more cartons stacked on tiers running along all four walls. Financial aid files had to be kept for three years, but academic files were permanent. Files in this room dated back twenty-two years to the first Philadelphia Burr class of 1973. Deirdre was familiar with this room from her days as admission secretary, but it always gave her the creeps, and she was much heartened when Beatrice spotted another chain and forged ahead. A second ceiling bulb flared on. Deirdre asked, "Financial aid files are in the back, right?"

"Yeah."

"Figures."

The back wall yielded some natural light through a window set high up the wall and level with the Sixth Street sidewalk outside. The legs of passerby strobed the window light.

"Are the names in alpha order at least?" asked Deirdre.

"On this list, yeah. But they're not alphabetical in these boxes."

"They aren't?"

"No. Hurley had them all packed away by programs and classes. This list doesn't say what class they're in. We're just gonna have to dig 'em out."

"Dammit," pouted Deirdre. "I don't have time for this."

"Who does? Look, Oliver said you were supposed to help me. Let's just do it, okay? The first is Abbott, Jane."

Together they pulled a large carton off a shelf, then squatted in the gloom to root through the manila folders crammed within.

In the lobby directly over their heads stood Lily and the two auditors. Lily pointed smartly at the two portraits. "Now these, of course, are the founders of the famous Burr Colleges. Reginald Burr and his mother—"

"Evelyn," McClure interrupted brightly. Lily stared at her. The auditor smiled apologetically. "I'm sorry. I just did an audit of your Washington school."

"Oh, you did?"

"I was very impressed by it. The students appeared very enthused."

"Yes, that's a wonderful school. I should think auditing a school that good must be a lot of fun."

"Well," McClure laughed, "auditing is never what I'd call fun. But it was a nice school."

"See that," said Lily. "And I would think auditing schools would be exciting. I mean, it's such a special job that you both do."

Parkinson and McClure grinned at each other.

"Oh, I know," Lily acknowledged with a flip of her hands. She began leading them down the first floor hall. "Auditing, accounting—I realize they don't sound glamorous. But when you think about jobs, you realize they *all* have a certain amount of drudgery to them, don't they? In the end it's really what your drudgery *accomplishes* that counts, and that's where you two are to be admired. This is a lecture room. We can't go in right now, there's a class in session. Let's trot up these stairs, hey?

"What I mean is, your job is a vital part of the whole educational process. It's very noble, the work you do. You could be crunching numbers for some fat-cat firm that exists solely for the people on top to get rich, but instead you're working to preserve the quality of America's colleges. It's wonderful! And I'm sure you don't get any thanks. The students you're protecting don't even know you *exist*. I think you guys are heroes." She laughed self-consciously and put a fist to her mouth, blushing before Parkinson as if afraid he would think her silly.

"Oh no," he said hastily. "Actually for those of us on the road, that's the only way to think—"

"Oh yes, you must travel a lot. Isn't that an exciting part of the job?"

"Well, sometimes—"

"This is our Placement board. Lots of graduates, as you can see. Working some terrific jobs with big salaries."

McClure said, "Your catalog reports a ninety-seven percent placement rate."

"We're very much in awe of Clara Peterson. No one loves the students more."

"We'll be talking to her," said Parkinson.

McClure said, "About the travel, Rich has done a lot. I'm just starting."

"You will though," Parkinson said. "This business is eighty percent travel. A good bit of flying too—"

"Flying as well!" exclaimed Lily. "My goodness, surely you don't audit the whole *country!*" She gazed at Parkinson with childlike wonder.

"Oh no," he laughed. "Usually the regional offices handle local territory. Personally I've—"

"Gracious, I don't know how you do it! Now this is a transcription room. Believe it or not, we still teach shorthand. Fewer employers are asking for it, yet everyone loves seeing it on a resume. Over here is Computer Lab II. It holds up to twenty-five students at a time, though sometimes the students will double up. Not that they have to, mind you, but some like extra time on the equipment and the doubling is their own initiative. We're hoping someday to enlarge all three computer labs but right now our space is limited. Old historic landmarks have such tiny rooms! Ha! Ha!"

"It's very nice. Tell me, does the college—"

"Well, this is the library." Lily unlocked the door with a sprightly flourish. "It's small but neat. I just love this room. I find it so relaxing."

"It's very pleasant," said McClure.

"Yes." Lily turned to Parkinson and laughed. "Oh darn it! They didn't do what they were supposed to do!"

"Oh? What's that?"

"They left the lights working. I told Maintenance last night that auditors from the Department of Education were going to review files in this room, and we wanted as little illumination as possible. Ha! Ha! Ha!"

Parkinson laughed loudly. "Why, sure. And keep the room freezing and the air vents clogged. Of course!"

"Ha! Ha! Ha! Ha! Ha!"

McClure sat down and unzipped her briefcase. "We should be ready as soon as they bring the files up."

"Of course. I'll get after them. Oh, I remember what I wanted to ask." Lily spun about and smiled eagerly. The light from the library windows flashed off her sequined dress like a bundle of match flames. "Oliver and I were wondering if it was okay for us to take you both to lunch?"

Parkinson smiled immediately, but glanced at McClure. "If it's separate checks," she cautioned with a sudden lack of humor.

"Separate checks," he told Lily. "But otherwise fine."

"Terrific! And at least we'll have each other's company! I really can't wait to hear more about the wonderful work you both do! I'll leave you at it then. See you soon!" She sparkled out of the room.

McClure pulled out her guide sheets with a shake of her head. "There's a character. She looks like a human disco ball."

"But she's nice," said Parkinson. He sat down and opened his brief-case, and found himself staring wide-eyed at his papers with spots before his eyes.

Downstairs, Oliver called New York to tell Bill Nostrand that the auditors had arrived. As he hung up, Louise appeared in his doorway and held up a letter.

"Barney Kaplan sent this. He won't renew our food contract as of April 1—which of course is tomorrow—because New York hasn't paid him since January."

"Oh dammit," said Oliver.

"I've called Andy Abrams about this before. He's just not listening to me."

"I know you have. You've done your job. Want me to talk to Andy?"

"No, I want you to scream at Andy."

"Okay. And I'll bring Bill into it, if I have to."

"Thanks." Louise's mouth twisted cynically, and her eyes flicked upward at the ceiling, indicating the library one floor above their heads. "How are *they?*"

"Okay, I think. Even Ethel thought so, and she hates any kind of government interference."

There was a knock on the doorframe. Beatrice stood there, rumpled, with a dust ball clinging to the side of her head. She looked hot and angry. "We're missing two files."

"Christ," breathed Louise.

Oliver said calmly, "We can't be. Who are they?"

"June Schoedsack and Merrie Carson. They're from a year ago. We've looked everywhere. Dee's still down there."

Oliver glanced at Louise. "Let's go."

They followed Beatrice down to the Dungeon. Deirdre was on her knees in a corner designated for Placement files, and cartons were open all around her. Her hair was askew and, like Beatrice, she was tired and hostile. "I found one. It was over in those Admissions files. The other one's just gone. I don't know where it is."

"Which one's missing?" asked Oliver.

"June Schoedsack. Merrie Carson I found."

"She wasn't in her corresponding Admissions file?"

"I just said she wasn't."

"Okay," said Oliver gently. "Why don't you take a break? Sit in the cafeteria and get your breath back. Louise and I will take a shot at it."

"Fine with me." Deirdre moaned as she got off her knees. Walking past them she said, "But I really think it's lost."

"It better not be," said Louise.

"All right now," said Oliver. "Beatrice, how about you go through the Admissions files anyway, just to be sure? Louise, let's you and I dig in."

They went at it for an hour. The missing file was not among the Financial Aid, Admissions, or Placement files. Louise cursed openly, and Beatrice began to take long rest breaks. Deirdre never returned. Oliver alone maintained a cheery countenance. "This always happens," he kept saying. "We've never had an audit where at least one file didn't prove difficult to find. Beatrice, are you sure you looked among all the file drawers in your office?"

"Yes," snapped the aid director. "It was the first place I looked when we didn't find them down here. I *told* you that."

"Well, why don't you check again, just to be sure?"

"Look, I can't keep searching the same places over and over!"

"But we have to," Oliver said with an imperturbable patience that grated on Louise as well as Beatrice. "Until we find it, that's what we're going to do."

"Goddamn ..." The rest was lost as Beatrice stomped out of the room.

Oliver said quietly to Louise, "I don't think it's down here."

"So what do we tell them?"

"It's got to be around. We'll tell them we're having a little difficulty finding it but are still looking. I don't think that'll cause too much trouble. It must happen a lot."

Now dusty themselves, Oliver and Louise emerged from the Dungeon and shut the door. Climbing up the stairs he said, "There was something we were discussing just before this happened."

"Food. As in getting some in the cafeteria again before tomorrow."

"Right. I'll call Andy right away. If he blows me off I'll talk to Bill."

"Okay. And I'll make sure Beatrice is really looking in her office again."

But when they reached the top of the stairs Beatrice walked toward them with a manila folder in one hand. "Here it is. I got it."

"That's the Schoedsack girl?"

"Yeah."

Louise asked, "Where was it?"

"In one of the file drawers in my office. I must have missed it the first time." Her chubby face offered no apology.

"Well fine," Oliver said. "Take it to the auditors right away." As Beatrice tromped up the stairs he rubbed his smudged forehead and smiled at Louise. "Crisis averted."

"That kid worries me," Louise said with a scowl. "Why didn't she find that file the first time she looked? Lord, what I wouldn't give to have David Hurley back, if just for this week."

Oliver said, "I'll make that call."

65

Bob's phone rang at eleven-thirty p.m. Deep in a rum-and-coke slumber, the noise could not have jarred him harder if the bell had been inside his head. Late-night phone calls meant a wrong number, but once it had been a hospital calling about a fall Dad took back home in Baltimore, and ever since Bob made the effort to answer. He pulled the receiver to his ear. "What?"

"Bob?" A man's voice.

"Uh-huh."

"Yo man, did I wake you? Didn't know you went to bed so early."

The voice was familiar but Bob was too fogged to think straight. He grimaced at his clock. "It's eleven-thirty."

"Is that late for you?"

"Who is this?"

"It's Patrick, man."

"Patrick?" Bob struggled to sit up. "What are you doing? What's up?"

"Well hell, Bob, I'm feelin' awkward about this. You're a good guy, and don't think I don't know it. And this isn't even my business, I guess, except I care too much about Heath. In fact, she came to me. I just want you to know that, so you don't think I'm buttin' in."

Bob put a hand to his eyes. "What's up?"

"Well, uh, she's not too happy with some of the things you said the other night. I don't know if you're aware of that."

"She's not happy?"

"Well, Bob, you called her a—" His voice dropped. "You called her a bitch, guy. I know sometimes she can be a real good one, but still—you don't got to tell her to her face, do you?"

"Patrick, do you know what we were arguing about?" Bob snapped on the light. From the foot of the bed, Mr. Wemmick issued a groggy meow.

"Something about a gift you got her. Look, Bob, I know this isn't my—"

"No, it *wasn't* about a gift I got her. It was about a gift she *wanted*." Bob spoke sharply, reckless from sleep. This was really something, calling him at home and at this hour. What was wrong with these people? "It just happened to be an emerald ring that cost seventeen hundred dollars, thank you very much. I'm a teacher, Patrick. I don't have money like that to burn."

"Bob, I know that kind of makes sense, but you got to see it from the girl's point of view. Women set a store on that stuff, especially from the guy they're gonna marry. Considering that circumstance alone, you probably shouldn't of said no."

The tone was amiable, yet it filled Bob with dread. He didn't like Patrick's voice penetrating these walls. Heather's younger brother was always cheerful, always drinking, always wanting to arm wrestle and lift things, just to compete. He and the other brother, Frank, were amazingly strong. It seemed to Bob, whenever he got trapped into visiting the Feeneys' house in Norristown, that the brothers spent a lot of conversation describing the altercations they got into on buses, at football games, whatever. Just recently Patrick had it out with a gas attendant who tried to cheat him out of three dollars. "You should have seen his eyes," Frank laughed, telling the tale, "when he had that gas nozzle shoved in his mouth. We got gas for free that night."

Holding the phone, feeling an unpleasant pulsing on the left side of his forehead, Bob said, "Patrick, that's crazy. I don't have the money."

"Well, Bob, I guess it really goes deeper than that."

"Deeper?"

"Yeah. You see ... well, she thinks you're taking her for granted. She doesn't feel the love from you she used to. Shit, you know I hate to be the one tellin' you this. It ought to be her."

"Oh for—"

"It ain't true, hey? I mean, that's what I told her."

"No, Patrick. It's not true." Gas nozzle. Seen his eyes. "Look, can I talk to you a minute? Maybe you can help me reason with her. Heather doesn't listen when I try to talk to her."

"Shit. That's what she keeps sayin' about you. I don't want to get caught in the middle—"

"And you shouldn't. I respect that, Patrick. But I need somebody to understand what's going on, and I'd like to—"

"What's going on?" Patrick was silent a moment, and Bob's skin prickled nervously. "What do you mean, what's going on? *Is* something going on?"

"Nothing's going on. I just—"

"Look, Sis stayed over your place last weekend. We're both grown men, I can figure what you guys were doing. You goddamn better *not* have something else going on."

"Patrick, that's not the case, I swear. But I need Heather to understand—"

"She means everything to this family, you know. She's Dad's only daughter."

"Of course. I know. But—"

"Oh hell, listen to me." Suddenly Patrick laughed. Bob had seen this before. Patrick could switch emotions with the speed of a hand clap. "Christ, I know how you feel about Heath, right?"

"Sure."

"Can't deny she's an armful, Bob, but she's my sis. And she's still a teen, you know, she's pretty sheltered and innocent."

"Of course."

"So why don't you guys make up? Give her a call and ask her out. Buy her the bauble if that's what she wants. I can tell you this—" and he dropped his voice in gleeful conspiracy, "if she sports that ring and Dad finds out she got it from you, that would really cement you once and for all with the family. Dad already likes you tremendously."

"Ah."

"So will you give her a call?"

"Patrick, that's not the issue. I tried to talk to her about it, but she wouldn't listen. She's the one who cut off communication—"

"Hey, hey, I know what you're talkin' about, man. My own girl, she flies at me all the time. I never know why. But I know it's always me who's got to make up. Come on, you're helluva lot smarter'n me. You can do it with style. Give her a call."

"Patrick, in all fairness, you or Heather can't expect me to blow seventeen hundred on a ring. It isn't even like it's Christmas or a birthday or something—"

"Well, but isn't that's what makes it so great? Come on, make the call."

"Patrick, I'm not going to do it. It's a ridiculous request."

Another silence. "Bob, man to man, okay?"

"Okay."

"You ain't stringin' her along, are you?"

"No absolutely not." Bob's loft felt very cold.

"Okay. 'Cause you should know—the way you sounded just now—if you talked to her like that I can see why she's upset. You gotta watch that, Bob. Heath's pretty delicate."

"All right. I'll call her. Tomorrow. Fact, I'll talk to her when I see her in class."

"Oh, I didn't think you guys could say much during school." Patrick was his jovial self again. "Just straighten it up over the phone, she'll like that."

"Okay."

"Great. Fantastic. Listen, you get back to sleep. Sorry to disturb you. She should of called you herself, Bob, I know that. I feel like such a prick doin' it for her. But she's still young. She'll learn, you know. Take it easy, man."

"Good night, Patrick."

Bob hung up and snapped off the light. He put his cheek to the pillow, and his one unburied eye stared at an amoeboid flickering of shadow off the ceiling from a streetlight filtering through a maple tree out the window. Mr. Wemmick started to wash himself, and Bob heard each pristine lick, and felt the bed by his ankles jounce from the cat's rhythmic activity.

66

The federal program review continued with little interruption. Business went on, students were interviewed, financial aid was packaged, classes were taught, and for most of the next two days it was easy to forget that federal auditors were even on the premises. New York kept calling, particularly Lana Kaufmann who, as the executive director of financial aid, had her own job riding on the result. But even she wasn't that worried. Federal program reviews weren't common, but schools were audited annually by hired firms, and the Philly school had never once suffered a fine or citation. This did much to assuage a President's Office already beleaguered by other problems.

The first hint of trouble came at the end of Tuesday when Kristina McClure told Beatrice that they wouldn't be finished by Wednesday after all, but expected to stay through the rest of the week. This triggered an impromptu meeting in the school director's office between Beatrice, Oliver, and Louise. The latter made sure the door was shut.

Oliver said, "Look, it doesn't have to be bad news."

Louise glared at Beatrice. "Have they mentioned any problems to you?"

"No."

"Have you been checking on them? Just seeing how things are going once in a while?"

"Sure." Beatrice was angry and defensive, as if the auditors' extended stay was her fault. "Sometimes they've got questions about something or other, but when I don't know the answer I come to you."

Oliver asked, "Like what kind of questions?"

Louise said, "Mostly they want to know why someone's aid was calculated in a certain way. But David's notes are so complete I can figure it out."

"Were they satisfied with your answers?"

"Yes. I just wish they would look at the notes themselves. Then Beatrice wouldn't have to bother me."

"Hey, I can't help it if I'm new," said Beatrice.

"You're not *that* new!" snapped Louise.

"All right," said Oliver. "So we're able to answer their questions satisfactorily. Maybe the audit itself is just taking longer than they expected. That can certainly happen."

"Or maybe they're just saving the big guns to fire at us when they're ready to leave," said Louise. "Every question they've asked is about David's files. But there were a lot on that list of theirs that go back to this past July and September. Beatrice was new then. There *have* to be some mistakes. Law of averages if nothing else."

"Hey, stop making it my fault—"

"All right," Oliver said again. "Look, we can't expect the auditors *not* to find something. Probably their own bosses in Washington would think them suspect if they didn't. Like cops with traffic ticket quotas."

Beatrice said, "I swear, more often than not when I stop by the library the two of 'em are just jawing at each other. And not about the files either. They're talking about different schools they've visited, and vacations with their kids, and stuff like that. I think they're just taking their time finishing."

"It could be." Oliver nodded encouragingly. "We've had auditors like that before."

Louise shook her head angrily. "Oliver, they finished with the financial aid files at noon today. Parkinson told me so right before they went to lunch. Do you know what they were looking at this afternoon? The admissions and education files for those same forty-five students. Are you gonna tell me there's nothing wrong with *those* files? The *Admissions* files?"

"We'll find out in the morning. If there really is a problem they'll let us know."

The next day, Wednesday, at nine a.m., Kristina McClure caught Beatrice in the lobby as the aid director walked in and presented her with a list requesting thirty additional files. Beatrice gave the list to Oliver, who studied it resignedly then handed it back. "Okay. Get whoever you need to help you and go collect them." Beatrice left, and he walked out to Louise's cubicle.

The business manager sat behind her desk with the latest invoices stacked in a perfect square before her. She said, "They want to look at more, don't they?"

"How'd you know?"

"I thought as much when I saw that woman sitting in the lobby waiting for Beatrice. We're in trouble."

"Not necessarily. They might simply be doing a spontaneous check. I wouldn't be surprised if something like that wasn't procedural with the feds."

"I wouldn't be either, but that's not what they're doing. Yesterday you said they'd tell us if there was a problem. I think they just did."

He went into his office and tried to concentrate on work. At ten o'clock Julie walked in with a small bundle of mail. "There's a letter from your lawyer."

"Is there? Stick around, this could be it. In fact, why don't you shut that?"

Julie closed the door. Oliver opened the letter and read. He nodded briskly and put it down.

"Better take care, Ms. Fitzgerald."

She smiled. "Are you a free agent?"

"As free as your dinner. Call your mom and see if she wouldn't mind entertaining the Princess a little longer tonight."

"That sounds special, Dr. Dunbar. I will." She hesitated. "Oliver—seriously, how does it feel for you?"

He took a moment to answer, leaning back in his chair. "Tina and I almost made twenty-two years. There's no recouping that. But it's turned out best for everybody, hasn't it? I know I'm not complaining."

"Good. Thank you." The secretary smiled and went out, leaving the door open.

Oliver reread the divorce notice, then folded it up and stuck it in his jacket pocket. He opened the middle drawer of his desk and removed a small photograph in a gold frame. The picture showed Julie and Kelly, both smiling, clad in ski outfits on a snowy slope. He had taken it during a February vacation in the Adirondacks. Oliver propped the picture on his desk beside the gold clock.

One wall over, Lily was close to panic. Orientation for the April class was Friday. This was Wednesday. She had seven empty seats and two days left and *no appointments scheduled in the book!* She felt as if she'd been worrying about this goddamn sit for years. She had excoriated her reps too many times already—still, what else was there to do? Seven bodies had to spring from *some*where! Pouring coffee with a shaky hand, she returned to her desk and buzzed Deirdre to go round everybody up.

Her doorway darkened. "Hello, Lily," Ethel said.

"Why—hello." Lily was surprised, for the dean never came to see her. Weeks sometimes passed without their paths crossing. "Is there something I can do for you?"

"Did you admit a student named Renee Hawkins to the April program?"

Lily's chin became a shield. "Have you been looking through our files? You're not allowed to—"

"Yes I was. Go ahead and report me."

That silenced the admissions director. The dean, like herself, held no fear of a reprimand from Oliver. Lily said primly, "Well, I don't believe I have to talk to you about her."

"Lily, Carol Sobolewski just quit."

"Pardon me? Oh—Carol? Goodness, why?"

"She's burned out. She can't deal with the effort of trying to teach the kids you're bringing in."

"And you think that's an admirable attitude?"

"No, I don't. But I can't blame her. I know what she's feeling."

"Ethel, do you have any idea how busy we are? Why, just this day I—"

"God damn it, Lily! You're letting in a student with a criminal record. Renee Hawkins was here with a probation officer."

"Was she?"

"You should know. You interviewed her. It's your notes scribbled all over the file. What did you do? Strike a deal?"

"I don't know why you're so negative," said Lily. "As a matter of fact, her lawyer cut a deal with Judge Auburn. Do you know him?"

Ethel shook her head.

"Auburn is in his late sixties, a very sweet man. He admires the Burr Colleges, always has. Loves our secretaries. He saw that Renee's high school record was not particularly bad, and he decided that as a condition of her probation she has to attend our college."

"What did she do?" Ethel demanded.

"It was a street thing." Lily flipped her hands. "Something with a gang."

"What did she *do?*"

"I really don't know." She saw Ethel's angry skepticism and repeated irritably, "I *don't* know. But I trust Judge Auburn. I'm sure the girl will profit from being with us."

"Jesus, Mary, and Ralph. So now we're accepting street hoods, is that it?"

"Dean Harris, I never realized you were so biased."

"Shut up," said Ethel. "I just lost one of the best teachers I have, and I lost her because she knows she can't do justice to the students you're bringing here, and she knows this administration allowed it to happen."

"We're just doing our job," said Lily.

"*Don't* talk down to me, bitch! I'm not the trusting soul Oliver is."

Ethel took a step forward and Lily leaped to her feet. Their stances were the same: heads thrust forward, shoulders hunched, eyes glaring, feet spaced apart, arms and hands at the ready.

"What are we doing, Lily?" Ethel asked.

"You tell me."

"Are we taking this outside?"

"If you want."

They crouched lower, eying each other for an opening. Ethel had a flash image of the two of them scratching and kicking on the floor of Lily's office while the Department of Education reviewed files in the library over their heads. She started laughing, and straightened up. She turned to Lily's coffee maker, took one of the client mugs, and poured herself a cup. Lily remained crouched, watching her carefully.

"Well, Lily, we almost did it." Ethel mixed in cream, then looked toward the door. The three reps stood there, holding notebooks for Lily's meeting. They watched the dean and admissions director with visible fear.

"Don't panic, guys," Ethel said. "No catfight today. We'll try again tomorrow." She passed through them, going out the door.

The reps stepped timidly into the office. "Lily," Marty asked, "are you okay?"

"Of course," said the admissions director. She dropped in her chair, sipped coffee, and smacked the desktop with the flat of her hand. "What have you got?"

Ethel went upstairs to her office. A stack of spring mid-term grades sat in her in-basket. She was reviewing the first few when Dawn entered with some more.

"Strong start," remarked the dean.

"Good."

"Actually, some of the weaker girls are surprising me. Shaney'ah Bacon is getting B's for the first time on her papers. Keone Robinson has two A's and a B, and in English comp II she got a B-plus. This is amazing."

"I see those kids staying here most nights."

"That's what it is." Ethel nodded proudly. "Jean's special classes. All these kids are doing time with her."

Dawn left to return to her cubicle downstairs. Ethel alternately read through grade reports and a *First For Women* to keep herself awake. There was a knock on the door and she glanced up.

Bob Lawrence stood there. "Got a minute, Ethel?"

"Yes, Bob. Come in."

"I can come back later if this isn't a convenient time."

"No, by all means." Ethel leaned back and stretched. "Have a seat. What can I do for you?"

He shut the door with a strange reticence. "Well, I just wanted to know if, uh, I could discuss something with you."

"Of course."

"Can I sit?"

"Help yourself. I just said you could."

"Right." Bob sat in the chair cautiously, as if it might collapse under him. Ethel waited.

"Bob?"

"Thanks."

"For what?"

"For letting me sit."

"Sure." She stared at him, not sure whether to smile or call a doctor. She had never seen him like this.

"Ethel, I've got a friend with a ... problem." He laughed and quickly raised his hands. "Okay—okay, now I need you to know that this really *is* a friend. I mean, this isn't that old thing where you say it's a friend but it's really you, you know?" His eyes focused on the little figure of the Blessed Mary on the desk. "I mean, this is kind of a serious matter, I don't want you suspecting there's a problem here that involves, say, me—or you—or anybody here, who works here, I mean. Okay?"

"All right, Bob."

"The thing is, I'm not really sure it's all that serious either. I mean, I called it a serious matter but that would really depend on how you look at it. You're a dean, someone higher up, so maybe it would seem more serious to you than it really is. Everything's relative to perspective, don't you think? But this friend of mine, he got himself in kind of a jam. He works for a different school—you don't mind if I don't tell you which one?"

Ethel shook her head.

"I just—well, I know you know a lot of people at other schools, and it *is* possible that—well, you know. Anyway, if it's not that big a deal then there really isn't anything he should be nervous about, right?" His hands drummed the arms of the chair.

"Bob, may I speak candidly?"

"Oh sure, Ethel. I wish you would."

"I don't know what you're talking about."

His eyes darted to her face. They hovered there, then passed on to the filing cabinet behind her. "Yeah, right. I know." He laughed loudly. "Of course you don't. But he's been pretty good up to now, more considerate than he really ever needed to be, so there isn't any reason for him to get slapped, at least that's how I look at it. And what kind of offense is it, anyway? It's not one at all—from, from some points of view. I think there really isn't a problem."

"Bob, what is the problem?"

"A good question, that. I'll try to clarify. He—my friend, this is—" He looked at her cautiously.

"Yes, Bob."

"'Cause I can't help suspecting that I sound like I'm trying to put something over." He grinned, started to get up, then leaned back in the chair. Then he leaned forward, both hands on the armrests. "You know, it really is a friend. I can't help it if that kind of thing's become a cliché."

"Bob, you're—"

"What bothers me is she's so unfair. That's the part I can't deal with. If she rationalized what was going on, she'd be … well, kind of … out of it, I think. That makes sense."

"I thought he was a he."

"What?"

"Your friend. Isn't he a he?"

"Yes."

"Then who's the 'she'?"

Bob stared at her. "She who?"

Ethel couldn't help it. She started to laugh. "That's what I'm asking *you!*"

Bob's left cheek twitched. "But I don't know her. Remember, he's a friend of mine. This is his problem with her, not mine."

"I realize that. But you're talking—"

"Ethel, don't you think people can slip into a bad situation not because they're bad people or even stupid, in fact they might be pretty smart, it's just that they maybe expect more from another individual than they actually get, and the next thing you know—" He paused and took such a deep breath it nearly lifted him out of the chair, "it's a quagmire. You're stuck. I mean, how hard-nosed can you, the dean, get over something like that? It could happen to anybody. Even you or me."

Ethel folded her arms across her chest and watched him as if he were a circus performer.

"You do realize he's just a friend?"

"*Yes*, Bob."

He laughed. "All right, I *know* I'm asking that too much. Now I'm probably arousing suspicions *because* of that."

"Bob, I'm having a difficult time figuring what my half of this conversation is supposed to be."

"Yes, exactly. A good point. So how can you pass any kind of judgment, in all fairness? That's *my* question. Am I right? I mean, it's not like he'll ever do it again. He's definitely recognized that it's time to quit. As long as you know that, then there can't be that much anger you'd vent toward him. I mean, anybody can make a mistake, that's just mortality. What's important is when the person who makes the error recognizes it and learns a lesson. That's the proof of the pudding, you know. That's what separates animals from civilized people. Yes, that's absolutely right." He laughed again, much more cheerfully now, and stood up. "Hey Ethel, thanks a lot."

"Glad I could be of help, Bob."

"Look, I know this is confusing for you. But you've been more help than you know. It's very appreciated."

"Of course."

He inhaled deeply, then laughed and went to the door. "Want me to leave this open?"

"Would you, Bob. Thanks."

He waved and went out. Ethel returned to the grade reports in front of her. She was as familiar with these forms as she was with the utility bills she paid at home, but now she stared at them incomprehensibly, as if they were cuneiform inscriptions.

67

Louise forced to silence a growl in her throat, squeezing it flat with sheer esophageal muscle. "Amber, you have a balance of $2,868. It has to be cleared or you can't use Placement next month or graduate in June."

"But I don't understand why that is," the kid said. "I was told my financial aid covered it all."

"Amber, your financial aid *never* covered it all. This was reflected on the award notice you signed last September."

"I never signed nothin' like that."

Louise whipped from her desk a blessed photocopy of the award notice. Amber's signature adorned the bottom. She flashed it in the kid's face.

"Well, I don't care what that says. Mr. Hurley told me financial aid would cover my bill. He told me so."

"Mr. Hurley never told you anything of the kind. Nobody gets enough financial aid to pay the entire bill."

"Well, I ain't lyin'."

"I'm not saying you're lying," Louise said, lying. "I'm saying that it doesn't make sense for Mr. Hurley to tell you financial aid would cover everything when he knew that *nobody* ever gets enough aid to cover everything."

"Well, that's what he told me." The girl was less stubborn than simply pragmatic. "And he ain't here anymore, is he?"

"I don't care what you think he said." Louise tapped the balance on the computer screen with a chipped fingernail. "You owe the money and you have to pay it."

"Well, I ain't got twenty-eight hundred whatever."

"Twenty-eight hundred sixty-eight. Then you can't use Placement or graduate in June."

"Aw, come on!" whined Amber. "You tellin' me I come through all this and now I can't graduate? That's unfair!"

So Louise loosened her throat muscles, allowed some of the growl to emerge. "*What's* unfair? Paying your bill? Everyone else is paying theirs—" another lie, "so why do you think you don't have to?"

"Well I guess you should of done something about this sooner. There's no way I ain't graduatin' after two years of this shit."

Louise grinned. "Wanna bet?"

"Look, I don't see why I got such a balance anyway. I made some payments."

"Yes you did." Louise tapped the screen again. "In October you gave us forty dollars, and in February you gave us twenty. It's now the beginning of April and we haven't seen a dime from you since."

"Well, how is that? How is that twenty-eight hundred and sixty-eight?"

"Because that's how God designed math. Tuition this year was $9,950. You were eligible for $7,022 in aid. Mr. Hurley got you that, then you paid sixty dollars yourself. This is what's left."

The student looked from the damning computer screen to Louise's savage grin and crumpled. She had learned from her parents, all living with four brothers and sisters in a cramped apartment in Kensington, that defiance before authority usually worked best. But Ms. Mallory was old and mean, and Amber was lost.

"Well, I gotta graduate, Ms. Mallory. I gotta get out of where I am!"

Louise heard the panic and savored it. With a leisurely pass of the hand she opened a drawer and extracted a form with many blank lines and a certification at the bottom.

"Amber, if you agree to cooperate we can let you use Placement and graduate. You have to sign this contract, and you have to stick to it. It's a post-graduation payment plan. If you ever breach it you'll be sent to a collection agency, and you'll lose all the privileges of a Burr grad. You understand?" Louise said this with a straight face, but it was a pretty weak threat. Post-grad privileges meant lifetime use of Placement plus a quarterly alumni magazine that was lucky if the President's Office got out two issues a year.

"I'll do what I got to."

"That's the spirit. We'll fill in the amounts now. It's dated the first of every month. What I need from you is an idea of how much you can pay per month."

"After I graduate?"

"Well, you have two more months of school. You can still pay something now."

"But I ain't got nothin' now! Or my parents neither!"

The cords in Louise's throat flexed, ready for another growl. "Okay, after you graduate then. How much do you *think* you can pay?"

"Well, I don't know."

"How about a hundred dollars? That would nearly cover your bill in two years."

Amber's eyes goggled like Ping-Pong balls. "A hundred dollars! Who the fuck's got that?"

"Watch your language," hissed Louise.

"But I don't got no hundred dollars!"

"Not now, but you'll be using Placement. You'll be earning a salary."

"I still don't think I'm gonna have a hundred dollars! That's so much, Ms. Mallory!"

The two huffed at each other. Louise had a problem here. Oliver needed everyone with an outstanding balance put on a payment plan before New York complained, and Louise had quite a few, all the poorest students and, naturally, the least cooperative. Oliver couldn't afford to cut them from class, and he needed an answer when all the bad debt came due. So she had to wring a payment plan out of Amber Williams one way or another.

"If not a hundred, what can you pay?"

"Well, I don't know."

"How about eighty dollars?"

"Shit, that's just as bad. I can't pay no eighty dollars. I ain't that good at this stuff, Ms. Peterson told me so. She don't think I can get a good job at first, not until I get some real experience."

"Fifty," Louise said, flat and disgusted. Who was fooling whom? This little grifter would graduate two months from now and they'd never see a dime no matter what she signed. "Let's be done with this. Give me an amount."

"I could pay maybe ..." Amber's eyes rolled. "... maybe twenty a month. But that's it, I swear."

Louise spluttered, "Twenty? Twenty *dollars!* Five bucks a *week?*" She resisted throwing her cup of black tea in the student's face.

Amber said indignantly, "I got a family and brothers and a sister and we ain't got much. I can't be payin' this school. I got other things to worry about."

"Fuck!" said Louise right in the girl's face. But she surrendered, and began to pen the amount on each blank line on the contract. She ended up going to five pages. At twenty dollars a month starting in September, Amber's account would be paid off in twelve years. Louise, who was sixty-five, figured she'd be dead or in a nursing home by then.

"So long, Amber," she said, after the student signed the form. "Enjoy yourself."

"Thanks, Ms. Mallory." The girl grabbed her book bag and skipped merrily out of the cubicle. Nothing fazed these kids. Oliver saw it as a strength, but it only made Louise want to throttle them.

She was still nursing the bad feelings from this exchange when Beatrice walked in. "One of the files isn't downstairs."

"What are you talking about?"

"Tamara Garling's file is missing. It's one of the one's the auditors want from this stupid new list of theirs."

"So?"

"I can't find it."

"Why the hell not?"

"I don't know. It just disappeared. It's really the Admissions file that's at fault. The kid withdrew last September. I think it got packed downstairs."

"Then look downstairs."

"I did that. I've been looking for an hour."

The business manager turned wrathful eyes upon her. If Beatrice possessed any intuition at all, she might have fled for her life. Not so blessed, she blew out her cheeks and said, "Is it really so bad to be missing a file? I mean, it's just *one*, right?"

"Beatrice," said Louise, "find that file or I will flay you alive. I will haunt your dreams! Now get the hell out of my office!"

"Hey, what's the matter with you?"

"*OUT!*" Louise scanned her desktop for a weapon, but there wasn't anything on her desk that she wanted broken.

Now Marty stuck his head past the partition. "Louise, I got an app fee check for you."

"What? Fine, give it here."

"But what about this missing file?" asked Beatrice. "I've looked everywhere!"

"You try the crack in your butt?" asked Louise. "That's large enough."

"Hey!" Beatrice was outraged.

"Look," snarled the business manager. "Take him and find that file. Now both of you get out of here!"

"I can't go looking for a file," said Marty. "I've got a prospect sitting on the couch out there."

"Want to be too crippled to tour her?" asked Louise.

"No, but—" Marty made eye contact and couldn't go on.

"You're elected," said Beatrice, who would never take a no from Marty. She pulled him physically by the arm through the cubicles. "Now look, the auditors are being a pain in the ass. The student's name is Tamara Garling. Lily says she was one of yours. She started last July but then dropped out. Dee thinks she got filed in the Dungeon, but I can't find her."

"So what am I supposed to do?"

"You're coming downstairs to help me look."

"I've got a prospect!"

"Oliver said everybody has to help."

Marty shook his arm free. "I don't answer to Oliver. Lily isn't gonna want me downstairs when I have all this work to do."

"I spoke to Lily. She says we gotta look good for these auditors above all else. Now move your ass. I don't want to do this anymore than you do."

"God damn it!" He stomped after her. As they passed through the lobby he glanced at a young woman sitting on the couch wearing worn jeans and a flower print blouse. She smiled and started to rise.

"Caroline, wait," Marty said quickly. "I have to help with something. I'll be right back. Have you seen the video tape yet? Julie, could you run that for her?"

"Sure, Marty."

"I'll be right back."

He grumbled all the way down the corridor. "This isn't what I get paid for."

"So what?" said Beatrice. "I *do* get paid for this. I think that's worse."

They passed Trudy coming up the stairs as they went down. She was still chewing the last morsel of her lunch. "Hi, Tru," Marty said automatically. She made a disgusted face and passed him without a word. For a split second he thought about asking her to prep his prospect with an application, then thought better of it.

Stephanie Homan was in the cafeteria eating lunch by herself. She looked up, and when Marty obligingly waved to her she stuck out a tongue coated with some half-chewed horror.

Beatrice said, "Popular with everybody, aren't you?"

"Shut up and come on." He was beginning to feel nervous about leaving his prospect unprotected in the lobby. "Let's get this over with."

They reached the Dungeon door and Beatrice turned the skeleton key in the lock. With the ease of recent practice she strolled ahead, yanking on the lights. Marty followed impatiently. He couldn't believe he was down here. Beatrice stopped by the back wall where student files in cardboard boxes were crumpling from the weight of other file boxes stacked on top.

"All right," he said. "Where would it be?"

"How should I know? It's an Admissions folder."

"And they're over here?" Marty had never been in the Dungeon before.

"Yeah. But I can't find any box marked with last year's kids who withdrew." Beatrice shook her head in annoyance. "I wish those goddamn auditors would just go away."

"Well, I haven't the slightest idea where that file is."

"Lily said you worked on it."

"Yeah, but not after the class started. You should ask the dean."

A voice called in. "Hello? Beatrice?"

It was a man's voice. Both looked over. Arthur Cassidy leaned through the gloomy doorway. Beatrice called out, "Yeah?"

"Someone upstairs just called. There's a student in your office needs a loan check signed."

"Which one?"

"I don't know." The teacher looked apologetic. "They called the faculty lounge and asked for you."

"Yeah, they'd have to. There's no phone in here. All right. Thanks, Arthur." To Marty she said with visible contempt, "You start looking. I'll be right back."

"I can't look long. I've got somebody waiting upstairs."

Beatrice shrugged indifferently and left.

Marty looked at the long file boxes stacked against the wall. He didn't know where to begin, and wondered how he was going to do this and not get dust all over himself. Was Louise out of her mind letting Beatrice drag him down here? Once a kid was in class they became an education problem. Dawn Hitchcock should be down here, messing up her clothes looking for this stuff and not him. He studied the highest boxes, which towered over his head, and knew with animal intuition that if he touched one they would all cascade down. He reached up, having no choice, but set himself to run the minute they teetered in his direction.

A sudden bang made him jump. He spun about, but nothing had fallen off the shelves. He walked about, checking the metal tiers, but nothing seemed disturbed. Then he saw the shut door, and his heart jolted.

"Hey!"

He ran and tried the knob. It wouldn't turn. He pushed at the door but it wouldn't budge.

"Hey!"

No sound on the other side. He tried the knob again.

"Open up! This isn't funny!"

He pounded on the door, and even as he did so he remembered Stephanie Homan sitting in the cafeteria. The memory gave him a cold feeling. He called out again, trying hard not to sound panicky. "Hey, open up! Come on now! I'm stuck in here! Somebody open the door!"

He looked around, but saw only cardboard boxes and bare light bulbs. At the far end of the room a hint of the outside world flickered as shadowy legs passed the small window that was level with the sidewalk on Sixth Street.

"I know this is you, Stephanie! Now open this door! Enough is enough!"

Marty stepped back and looked at the door. He turned and walked the length of the large room, then turned and walked back. If he didn't do anything, she'd get bored and finally open the door. He sat on a heavy carton and waited.

Ten minutes later he was still sitting there.

"All right! This isn't funny anymore!"

He ran to the back wall and tiptoed to look out the window. He watched feet pass on the other side of the iron grating, level with his nose. He could open the glass panel and call out but ... but the very *idea* was humiliating—his head at sidewalk level begging passerby to go get help.

Marty looked at the door again. Maybe that brat had unlocked it, silently so he wouldn't know. The idea filled him with hope. That would be part of the prank, to make him pound on an unlocked door. He had done as much to his sisters when they were kids living in a cheap complex in North Jersey and playing in the laundry room. Very gently, because she would still be listening on the other side, Marty grasped the doorknob and turned it ever so slowly. Nothing happened. The door was still locked.

"God damn it! Somebody open this door!"

He pounded furiously. As a joke, it was going far too long. Where the hell was Beatrice? Wasn't anybody in the cafeteria? Or in the teacher's lounge? He tried to remember who he had seen right before he and Beatrice walked in here, and that led to a truly scary thought.

"Trudy! Trudy, don't you dare take my prospect! Trudy! I'm warning you! don't you dare!"

He pounded frantically on the door with both fists.

68

On Friday the new April class sat in the student lounge listening to the dean's opening remarks. There were fifty-eight women of varying ages, and the looks they gave Ethel ranged from eager attention to icy stupor. Still it was a large class, enormous by April standards, another Espirito miracle. The goal had been sixty. No one was going to criticize Lily for two empty seats. New York was ecstatic. On the phone with Oliver, Bill Nostrand confessed that he never expected Lily to come close to the goal, and his adulation for Philadelphia's crackerjack admissions team rang in the school director's ear.

Only one staff member was upset by the barely missed goal, and that was the admissions director herself. As the new class gathered downstairs for Orientation, Lily closeted herself in her office and ransacked her records, searching for two more prospects.

There was only one appointment in the book for the day. Though that was frustrating, this single entry was still a heaven-sent miracle. Selma Levy had planned to attend the April class starting at the Boston Burr College when suddenly her husband accepted a job in Philadelphia. Because of the relocation, she hastily made plans to attend the Philly school instead. Selma and Moshe Levy arrived at 10 a.m. even as Orientation began. One quick call and Boston faxed her application, test scores, and a copy of her high school diploma, and Deirdre reviewed it speedily while Trudy took Selma through the motions of a tour.

"We'll get you all caught up," Trudy said, leading the way along the first floor corridor. "And maybe still have time for you to attend part of Orientation."

"I'm sorry we're late with all this," said Selma. "Moshe's job offer was so unexpected. He applied for it months ago and never heard. And then all of a sudden—boom!"

"No prob. We're glad to have you with us. What kind of work is he in?"

"Resort management. Well, that's what he's aiming for. His new job is assistant to the supervisor of the dining facility at the Penn Valley Country Club. It's not great pay and mostly evening hours, but there's real promise of moving up. We think the dining supervisor is going to retire in a few years."

"My parents are members of that club. It's huge." Trudy was genuinely impressed. "How long have you been married?"

"Eight years. Straight out of high school for me. Moshe was in his junior year at B.U."

"Wow. Here's hoping that other guy retires real soon."

Selma laughed. "We've got our fingers crossed."

In his office, Oliver finished his call with Bill Nostrand and walked next door to share it with Lily. He found the admissions director at her desk tearing through a computer list, striking out names with a furor and throwing page after page in the general direction of her wastebasket. "Lily, I just spoke to—"

"Oliver, I need a phone number! We've called all these too many times!"

"Lily, Bill Nostrand just said—"

"What's *he* want?" She looked up sharply.

"He didn't want anything. He received the preliminary numbers from Deirdre and all he wanted—"

"What?"

"Just … well, nothing. It was all praise. He said it's fine that you're short two students, he'll still consider the goal a success. I've never heard Bill sound like this. Even back in September—"

"We'll only be short one. Trudy's touring somebody who was planning to go to Boston. Her husband just got a job here, so they moved."

"Really?"

"Yeah. Hubby's out in the lobby. Thank God he got that job. I believe in those things. Miracles, that is." She resumed scanning the computer run. "We can't stop shy of one, Oliver. I told New York this goal wouldn't be a problem. I talked Bill into shelling out for those goddamn commercials that were supposed to bring in so many kids and didn't. We can't come up short, not after July, September and January. Think the other schools aren't watching us? Think Terry Kruger, Gayle Schwartz, Don Hogan, and all the other admissions directors wouldn't love to see us fail?"

"Oh Lily, I hardly think—"

"Shit!" She tossed the ragged computer sheets aside. "There aren't any appointments in the book until next week. I need a lead *now!*"

Deirdre trotted in. "Here's the fax of Selma's test score." She held it out.

"Did she pass?" Lily asked.

"Yes. Boston said as much before they sent—"

"Then why do I need to see it?"

"Well, but—"

"Put it in her file. I'm working here."

Deirdre backed out. Oliver felt bad. "Lily she was just—"

"CHRIST, Oliver! Why are you here? Do you need something?"

"I just wanted to tell you that Bill—"

"All right! So Bill's happy! Hot diggity! I'm *not!* I've got to dig up another student! There just isn't anyplace left to look! I can't squeeze blood from a f—oh Christ! Oh goddamn it! Where the hell is my head at?" She jumped to her feet, passed Oliver in two strides, and peered out her office door at the cubicles and lobby. She shut the door and glanced down at herself, frowning at her satin V-neck blouse and short blue business skirt. She passed him again, returning to her desk where she grabbed her pocketbook and fished out a set of keys. She passed him a third time, undid the padlock to her closet, swung the doors wide, and scanned the multitude of tops, skirts, and costumes hanging there.

"Lily, what are you doing?"

"Mmmf!" She fluttered a hand to silence him. After some contemplation she selected a hot pink knit blouse and laid it carefully on the back of the love seat. Then she pulled out a matching pink miniskirt with a pleated hem, clipped to a hanger. It didn't look much bigger than a washcloth.

"Lily, what are you doing?"

"Oh for God's sake, Oliver. I'm taking a little initiative. They're married, and they're young. He only has a B.A. and his new job is mostly evening hours. I know the Penn Valley Club and they pay the understaff shit."

She laid the skirt on the back of the love seat, then swiftly grasped the neck of her blouse and whipped the garment up over her head. Her breasts in a cocoa-brown brassiere joggled above trim stomach muscles. Startled and appalled, Oliver spun about and stared at the wall. With one quick jerk Lily undid the zipper behind her lower back and let her business skirt drop to the floor. She stood for a moment in the center of her office, wearing nothing but bra and panties, then strode back to the closet and grabbed a pair of gold stilettos. She pulled the knit blouse over her head with a grunt, tugged the tiny miniskirt up her thighs with brute callisthenic force, and stepped into the shoes. Her height shot up five inches. Turning to check herself in the full-length mirror on the closet door, she spotted Oliver in its reflection, standing with his back to her.

"Oh goodness!" she said with a giggle. "You can turn around now. Did I embarrass you?"

"Frankly, yes."

"Sorry, Oliver. I forgot you were there." She squared her shoulders and assessed the vivid pink outfit. The tight blouse not only flaunted her full breasts but forced four inches of cleavage to bulge up from the neckline. The miniskirt fit snugly over her buttocks before dropping a few inches, enough for the pleated hem to swing playfully when she moved her hips. Lily tested this very effect, and smiled approvingly.

"Lily! Wait a minute—I can't condone this!"

"Who's asking you to?"

"No—don't you see, Lily? You shouldn't lower yourself—"

"Oh for *God's sake,* Oliver! What's your problem?" She strode to her desk and started rummaging in a drawer. "Want to tell me this is demeaning? That it makes me a sex object, a *thing,* something not to be taken seriously? Is that it, boss?"

Oliver was baffled by her anger. It was exactly what he wanted to say.

"Shit, Oliver, do you want to know what's *really* demeaning? Try stupidity! Well, I'm *not* stupid, but you know who probably is? The grown man sitting in your lobby who is about to base a decision on how to spend several thousand of his hard-earned dollars on the shape of my ass. *He's* the one you should be talking to." She lifted a Star of David brooch from the drawer and swiftly pinned it above her left breast.

"Lily, wait! You can't lower yourself to this sort of—"

"Oh will you STOP!" She spun on her heels and glared at him. "You sensitive intellectuals drive me crazy! All talk of feminine equality and sexual freedom, hey? Except when a woman actually *uses* her sexuality you scream bloody murder and go on the attack! Oliver, what do I care if that guy stares at my face or my boobs as long as he makes the decision I need him to make? It doesn't cost me anything, and it gets me a sale. And you can pretend to be offended by that attitude all you want, but we both know what you really are is scared by it."

"Scared?"

"Yes! Because you know it's going to work! Because your gender is just dumb enough to let it work! Now get out of my way. I have a client to see." Lily opened the door and strode out. He could hear her stiletto heels thocking the carpet.

After a moment he followed. He passed through the cubicles but stopped short of entering the lobby. Lily stood before Mr. Levy, all smiles and perky hand gestures. Her laughter rang across the room.

"Why yes, I've always heard that about Boston, how *clean* it is. Not like this city at all! I wonder why that is."

"Boston," Levy said importantly, "is Philadelphia done right."

"Do you really think so?"

"Absolutely. First, it's got the better history. Both cities claim to be the birthplace of America, but Boston has all the action. Night rides to warn of British troops, colonists dressing as Indians and dumping tea, it's got the first black American getting killed. Philadelphia's got the politics: the First and Second Continental Congress, the writing of the Constitution and the Declaration of Independence. Those are important, but hardly a lure when you're on vacation with the kids."

"Gracious! I never thought of it that way!"

He laughed easily. Levy had thin straight hair that emphasized pink ears. He sat on the couch holding the school's latest copy of *Money,* clearly happy to have some company while he waited for his wife.

"Oh dear," Lily exclaimed. "This coffee table is such a mess! Will you pardon me while I do a little housecleaning?"

"Not at all."

And there it was. Lily bent forward and restacked the magazines and yearbooks, going at it methodically with her eyes cast down. Levy stared in wonder at the protuberant cleavage bobbing gently before his eyes. When Lily reached the end of the table she turned sideways with a little flick of her pleated skirt, and even from where he stood Oliver could see Levy's eyes circle the admissions director's buttocks and skate up and down her legs.

"Are you a well-traveled man, Mr. Levy? I ask, you see, because you seem to know both Philadelphia and Boston quite well."

"Well, I went to school in Boston, but I'm actually from this area. Bryn Mawr."

"My goodness! I had no idea. I live in Radnor, we're practically *neighbors.*" Lily finished with the table and straightened, clasping her hands behind her back and squaring her shoulders. "You know, your wife's orientation is going to take a while. Would you like to come back to my office? I can offer you a cup of coffee and, in fact—" she grinned puckishly, "if you wouldn't mind indulging me, there's a brochure for a program I'd like to show you. It's the same one your wife is discussing with Ms. Weiser right now."

He laughed, seeing through her. "Once a saleswoman, always a saleswoman, eh?"

Lily colored and crinkled her nose. She rocked her hips slightly, enough to make the pleats swing. "Well, I just feel you should know what Selma is getting herself into."

Mr. Levy grinned and stood up. "Sure. No harm in discussing it."

They were going to have to pass him. Oliver started walking so they wouldn't realize he was spying. "Hello Dr. Dunbar," Lily chirped as she trotted by. Levy followed with a feeble nod in Oliver's direction, his eyes fixed on the back of his hostess. Lily led him into her office, then laughed and shut the door. Oliver was sure he heard the bolt lock.

He wandered out to the lobby, feeling like he'd been whacked on the side of the head. Julie sat at her desk, looking equally dazed. He asked, "Are you okay?"

"What? Sure. I'm just recovering from the show out here."

"I saw it. Am I only now becoming aware of how my Admissions Department works? I feel like I've been out of touch with everything." He stared at the secretary for such a long time that Julie finally smiled.

"Yes, Dr. Dunbar?"

"You look very pretty."

"Thank you."

"Extremely pretty. Too pretty to have to work."

"I absolutely agree."

He frowned suddenly, puzzled. "What time is it?"

Without looking she said, "Eleven forty-five."

"Aren't I supposed to be doing something?"

"You mean beside speaking at Orientation?"

He looked at her blankly.

"Orientation," she repeated distinctly. "You speak right after the dean."

"Oh my gosh." He looked at his watch. "When was I supposed to talk? Eleven-thirty?"

She smiled. "Or whenever you get there."

"Damn it!" He dashed out of the lobby.

Julie opened mail for the next fifteen minutes. Deirdre strolled into the lobby to see if she had any phone messages. "Nothing, huh?"

"Phones have been quiet today," Julie agreed.

Deirdre sighed and looked around the empty lobby. "We need one more to make April. Lily's going bonkers trying to track a lead. Wish I could be the one to bring it in."

"She's working on a possibility right now."

"She is? She told me she didn't have a lead. Well, leave it to Lily. Talk to you later."

The rep wandered off. The Fourth Period bell blatted, and a moment later Stephanie passed through to go work for Louise. Julie's intercom buzzed.

"Front desk."

"Julie," said a high melodic voice, "is Trudy finished the tour?"

"Uh, well they haven't come back yet, Lily. In fact, they may have gone down to Orientation. I haven't seen them."

"Okay. Listen, I'm discussing things with Mr. Levy. Tell Trudy she should take Mrs. Levy some place nice for lunch. Tell them to take their time. You got that?" The admissions director tittered suddenly, but not at Julie—Julie could tell.

"Sure."

"Good." Lily hung up.

Julie sat still with the receiver in her ear. An obscene phone call could not have chilled her more.

Trudy and Selma Levy did return shortly, and Julie gave them the message. Trudy was happy enough and Selma, without the slightest suspicion, seemed impressed that the school was courting her with such style. They went off together to freshen up.

A few minutes later Kristina McClure walked in, carrying her briefcase. "Hello, Julie."

"Mrs. McClure."

"We're finished now. Rich'll be down in a minute. We've left the files up there, but we locked the library door."

"That's fine, thank you." Julie was dying to ask them how the audit went, but it wasn't her place.

"Is Dr. Dunbar available?"

"He's at Orientation right now. We have a new April class starting on Monday. He shouldn't be long. He usually makes a short speech and that's it."

"Would he be able to see us afterward?"

"I'm sure."

"Then I'll just wait here. Oh Rich," she said as Parkinson walked in, carrying his briefcase in one hand and a notebook in the other. "Dr. Dunbar should be able to see us shortly."

"Fine." He came forward and held out his hand. "It was nice meeting you, Julie. Guess we better shake hands now. I know I'll forget when it comes time to leave."

"He will too," said Kristina.

"We're hoping Oliver and Beatrice can see us now," Parkinson said amiably. "We might be able to catch the early shuttle back to Washington."

"He should be right back."

"Thank you. We'll wait."

Both auditors sat on the couch. A clatter of voices and feet grew louder, and Julie knew Orientation was finished. A moment later Oliver entered, flushed and happy.

"Hey Jule, they don't look like such a bad lot. I think Ethel's being over-judgmental. Any messages?"

"No. Oliver, the auditors are here."

He turned to the couch. "Oh, hi. Are you finished? What do we do next?"

"We'd like," said Parkinson, "to have the exit interview now, if you wouldn't mind. Kristina and I have a chance to catch a two o'clock train."

"Of course. Julie, would you see if Beatrice is free? And Mrs. Levy, did she sign on?" To the auditors he explained, "We have a transfer from the Boston school coming in today."

"Trudy took her to lunch," Julie said, cool and casual. "They left about thirty minutes ago."

"Where's Lily?"

"In her office with Mr. Levy."

The answer took a moment to register. Oliver looked hastily at his watch. "How long have they been in there?"

"A fine long time."

Kristina asked, "Is anything wrong?"

"Nothing." He looked around the lobby. "Nothing. Julie, call Beatrice and have her come in. Thanks."

He led the auditors through the cubicles, and tried not to look at Lily's closed door. In the safety of his own office he said, "Have a seat, please," and dropped behind his desk.

A moment later Beatrice walked in, clad in the same dark wool suit she had been wearing all week. Parkinson flipped open his notebook and cleared his throat. In her own notebook, McClure scratched notes.

"Dr. Dunbar, Ms. Genovese, I want to touch on this quickly, but don't let me make you feel rushed. Any questions you have, please feel free to ask."

"Good," said Oliver. "We're all set."

"Okay. Well," and he sighed deeply through the word, "we reviewed forty-five files initially and then an additional thirty. There were quite a few findings on a number of counts, mostly in the admissions records." Beatrice smiled. On the word "admissions" Oliver lost it; before his eyes was not Parkinson's serious face but the closed door of Lily's office. He saw her cocoa brown brassiere and bare flat stomach, her dark penetrating eyes, her wide smile at Levy in the lobby. His ears bypassed the auditor's voice and strained toward the adjoining office wall. He couldn't hear anything, but he might—he just might.

"From the original forty-five, eleven admissions files are missing proof of high school graduation. Five do not have enrollment agreements. Two have enrollment agreements for students under twenty-one but do not have the necessary parents' signatures. Nine don't even have the students' signatures." He paused a moment to let the gravity of that sink in. "Upon reviewing the additional thirty, we found that within that group nineteen students were missing proof of high school graduation, and sixteen enrollment agreements were missing. Eleven students have high school transcripts instead of diplomas, which is all right, but the transcripts only include the first half of their senior year and are not acceptable as proof of graduation." Parkinson coughed into his hand. He gave Beatrice a severe look. "Now this next is particularly bad. There are twenty-seven files which show a receipt slip for either twenty-five dollars or the hundred dollar deposit, yet no credit of such appears on the student's account, and the students were then billed full tuition without having the deposit subtracted. There was also ..."

Something important was happening here, but Oliver couldn't focus. He kept thinking he heard noises on the other side of the wall, unexplained thumpings, or maybe the movement of furniture.

"Regarding the financial aid files, there are numerous omissions and discrepancies. Out of the total seventy-five files reviewed, fourteen students are missing proof that a need analysis formula was even done. There's no electronic record, no hardcopy Student Aid Report, nothing to show that their eligibility for aid was ever calculated. Yet they got maximum federal loans and even some supplemental grants. Also, there were nine students who withdrew within the first month of school, requiring the school to process a tuition charge reduction. Although records show this was done, no *financial aid* refund calculation is in evidence, and it appears that these students still received their full year's aid even though they all attended less than two weeks. Also, there are twelve students who went on a leave of absence one full year ago, and are still in that status even though all evidence shows they never returned. The regulations firmly state that for financial aid purposes no leave may extend longer than one hundred and twenty days. These students are clearly not here, yet your financial aid office processed them with a full year's aid. They were never charged by the college and no funds were ever posted to their accounts, yet loan checks were issued that have never been returned or otherwise accounted for. Not only that—" Parkinson's eyes widened; his own astonishment was putting a swell to his modulated accountant's voice, "but it appears that one or two had financial aid processed for them again *this* year, even though attendance records show they still hadn't returned."

Oliver's stomach was really cramping. He fixed upon the Renoir print hanging on the wall between his office and Lily's as if it might clue him to what was happening on the other side. Rattle maybe, or fall off its hook.

"This next is also extremely serious," said Parkinson, flipping to a new page. "From May of last year to the present there have been no entrance or exit interviews conducted for any of your student loan borrowers. Federal Regulation 682.604 and Section 483 of the Higher Education Act state that all schools must conduct entrance interviews before disbursing student loan checks. This is intended to protect students from being talked into taking unnecessary loan debt and to ensure that they understand all rights and responsibilities regarding such indebtedness. The exit interview reaffirms this …"

Wonderful work, that Renoir. Little dabs that were nothing by themselves, simple blotches on a stretched canvas. Dabs that from a distance became flowers and vines entwined in a fence. Incredible.

"After finding all that," Parkinson said tersely, "I guess it wasn't surprising to find this. Over forty percent of all reviewed files show tremendous overawards. We're talking thousands of dollars given to students beyond their calculated need, with no documentation in the files to explain why." He was angry now. Reading this summation was affecting him. "The Omnibus Budget Reconciliation Act of 1989 and Regulation 674.14 clearly forbid overawards of federal Stafford loans and campus-based aid. All this money will have to be returned. My God, it's like no one even bothered to check the info on the applications against the tax returns even when this material *was* collected …"

Were students like dabs? If you put them all together and viewed them from afar, from a helicopter maybe, what would they look like? Would there be a structure? Would they look like a college? Was he getting weird here?

A briefcase snapped shut, and he looked up.

Parkinson set the case on the floor. The creases in his big face curved like pond ripples, deep and damaging.

"I don't think it's going to end here, Dr. Dunbar. More than likely there will be further reviews, additional files checked. You'll get the full report in about three months' time, and you'll have at least thirty days to respond to any regulations cited as being in violation, as well as explain the restitution and corrective measures you plan to employ. In the meantime, we have a list to give Beatrice of the students and the omissions and discrepancies that we noted. You may try to clear up as many of these as possible between now and when you receive our report and plan to make your response."

Oliver said vaguely, "What damage are we talking about, Mr. Parkinson?"

"Well, no damage yet, Dr. Dunbar. But there are enough violations in the files to warrant additional review. The issuing of overawards and the missing loan disbursements are both highly criminal. There will be liability, but I can't tell you how much at this time. And potentially the school could be suspended from further participation in the Title IV financial aid programs. Of course, if the Department makes such a decision, you will have forty-five days to appeal."

"Appeal?"

"Yeah. If we make a move to fine you, or if additional reviews show justification to suspend you from Title IV, you can appeal. A court hearing will be set, and your lawyer will present briefs justifying what your college did. If the judge decides against you, another appeal can be sent directly to the Secretary of Education. His decision, however, is final. It would probably be best, Dr. Dunbar, to get in touch with counsel as soon as you receive our report."

Funny how the bad news had separated them, made them all business people again, using formal names.

Oliver forced himself to stir. He looked at Beatrice, who sat on the couch, bored, her arms folded. He said to Parkinson, "Listen, how bad is it? Is it *really* going to reach a point where lawyers are necessary?"

"I'm fairly sure it will." Parkinson's manner offered no solace.

"Well … what exactly are we talking about? I mean, assuming the worst, okay? What's the worst scenario that could happen?"

"Well, you'd be responsible for returning all financial aid funds that were incorrectly collected. That would come to a sizable amount, probably hundreds of thousands of dollars. There would also be fines levied for mishandling the financial aid funds, and they would also come to a substantial amount. Technically we can fine up to $25,000 per violation, but of course that's a worst-case scenario."

"How could this have happened?" Oliver whispered it.

Parkinson sighed. His face relaxed, grew friendly again. "Look, Dr. Dunbar, I can see this has taken you by surprise. Most schools with violations this big know they're in trouble before I even step through the door. When I talk to them the guilt and fear is all over their faces. I've seen good schools that run their shops like a textbook, and others run so incompetently the owners should be burned at the stake. And I've seen schools like yours."

"Like mine?"

"Yeah. You're not a bad school, Dr. Dunbar. But you've allowed your staff to treat the regulations very lightly. I won't say they did it deliberately, I won't go that far. But ignorance is still a form of contempt. There's a lot of contempt for the regs in what we looked at. From a legal viewpoint it doesn't matter how good your curriculum is. All that matters is these files were mishandled."

"I see."

"All right." Parkinson looked at McClure and they stood up. "Listen," he began, "what you should probably do—"

The door banged open. Lily stood in the doorframe, grinning wickedly. Her face was flushed, and strands of bronze hair dangled loose from her beehive and played about her neck. Her pink blouse was askew, the neckline stretched well beyond its design and slipping down one upper arm, baring her shoulder. She swaggered past the startled auditors, slapped the flat of her hand on Oliver's desk, and when she withdrew it a pink receipt remained.

"One hundred and twenty-five dollars," she gurgled with victory. "That's April, Oliver. Call Bill Nostrand and tell him to FedEx the champagne!"

"Lily?" Oliver stared at her. The admissions director's mouth was puffy and bruised. She was panting hard.

"Sorry for sniping at you back there, Oliver. I was just stressing a bit, you know. Nothing a good Christmas bonus wouldn't cure. Do we get Christmas bonuses?"

Oliver had to think. "I, uh, don't really know. We haven't had Christmas bonuses in about, what?" He looked at Beatrice who, only in the job seven months, had no idea.

"Well, you might call New York and get that tradition kick-started." Lily grabbed the neckline of her blouse and tugged it back over her shoulder. "I didn't count on a lot of this when I signed up with this damn school." She blew out her cheeks, met his eye, and giggled. She sashayed out the door.

A locker room dampness lingered in the air. Oliver realized that Kristina McClure was staring at him. Parkinson's head was turned toward the door, but Oliver registered shock there as well. He coughed foolishly. "Well now—let me show you to the door."

Parkinson turned. "Thank you," he said with a smile as weak as Oliver's. "You'll be hearing from us."

The Class of 1997

69

TWO WEEKS INTO the new April class, Jean sprang her first essay. Dealing with the basics of economic methodology, the students were expected to produce five pages. She didn't insist on footnotes or a bibliography this early in the game, but she did want some evidence of library research. She gave them a week to do it. On Friday she collected the papers, read and marked them at home over the weekend, and returned them the following Monday. Several students did well, but that didn't stop Jean from filling the margins of their reports with comments. When the period ended, the students shuffled out, depressed and silent. One visibly irate girl lingered until the room was clear, then approached Jean. "I gotta talk to you."

"Ms. Hawkins, what can I do for you?" Jean pulled open her desk drawer and fished out her purse. After marking Renee's paper last night, she had anticipated a confrontation. It was never hard to predict which students would take their bad grades as a personal attack.

"I got a F on this paper." The student flashed the report angrily.

"Yes, I know."

"Well, I don't think I deserve a F."

Jean looked at the wall clock. "Ms. Hawkins, you know when my office hours are. You can make an appointment through Ms. Hitchcock if you want to discuss this with me."

"No, you talk to me now!" The student stretched her lower lip, revealing gray teeth.

"I will talk to you during my office hours," Jean said with firm authority.

Their eyes locked.

Most of the large April class was obedient and interested in learning, but all classes had a blemish and in this one it was Renee. There was already a rumor circulating the faculty lounge that Renee was extorting money from girls in the lavatory by threatening physical violence. If it was true, no one had yet to come forward with a complaint. Nice reputation for only two weeks. Looking at the student, Jean didn't doubt it. Renee's blunt-boned face was a history book of schoolyard fights and serious trouble, with a pencil-thin scar across her forehead and another running down the right side of her nose. She lived in Strawberry Mansion, a city neighborhood rife with drugs and gang violence that was a far cry from any neighborhood her teacher had ever lived. Still, Jean knew that students who wanted to do well in class could not afford to use their unhappy home life as an excuse to fail.

"Look what you done." The student pointed all over the page. "Look at these marks. This is all punctuation stuff. That ain't what the paper's about."

"The punctuation and the spelling, Ms. Hawkins, are not why you got an F. Your paper is badly organized and incorrect in much of its data. *That's* what the grade is about."

"Then how come there's all marks and corrections and stuff in the margins about periods and words?"

Jean looked at the clock again. It was her lunch hour. Even she had her limit, and right now she didn't want to deal with Renee Hawkins. "If I see incorrect grammar or punctuation in a report, I always note it. That's how you learn."

"But you don't teach that. We get that stuff from Mr. Lawrence."

"That doesn't stop me and it shouldn't. And this is grammar you ought to know by now. Look at this." She took the paper from the student and did some pointing of her own. "Starting sentences with 'and' and 'but.' That's bad in professional writing and you should know that. Look at all these passive verbs. I circled them for you because I want you to start thinking of expressing yourself actively. And look here—you're missing whole words in this sentence. Do you ever read back anything you've written? This is your paper, Ms. Hawkins. You should make it the best you can write."

"That's not what you teach," the student insisted.

"And I didn't grade you for that. Do you want to talk content? Let's see exactly why you got that F. Here, right at the top. Look how this paragraph starts. *'Economic theory, distilled from cumulative data, reflects the interface of human and institutional behavior with materiel and divergent services.'* Do you talk like that, Ms. Hawkins?"

"What you mean?"

"When you write a paper in your own words, it should come out the way you talk. You copied this straight from the encyclopedia. You think I couldn't tell? That's why you got an F."

"You sayin' I cheated?"

"Well, plagiarized is a more grown up word."

"I didn't plagiarize! No way!"

"Really?"

"Yeah!"

Jean handed the paper back. "Okay, then I'll tell you what. We'll go down to the library, you and I, and review the encyclopedia together."

"Fine!" The student breathed fast.

"But this is the deal. If I'm wrong and you didn't copy this, I'll not only give you the A, I'll apologize to you in front of the whole class. But if it *is* copied, then you'll face suspension and probable dismissal from the school."

"*What?*"

"Plagiarism is a serious offense, Ms. Hawkins. Check your student handbook. It's punishable with dismissal. You see, I gave you a break. I didn't report you when I read this paper, and I should have. But I don't like dismissing students, even ones like you who lie about it when they get caught. However, I will *not* give you the break if you make me flip through encyclopedias during my lunch hour to prove that you're lying."

Renee stretched her lips again as she weighed her options. Jean faced her with the bold determination for which she was famous. The student stepped back, wadded the report, and threw it to the floor. She grabbed her books and threw them with a loud crash against the wall, then started for the door.

"Ms. Hawkins!"

She kept going.

"Ms. Hawkins! You *stop!*"

The student did. She looked back, livid.

Jean had one hand on her hip. "You pick up those books right now!"

Renee wavered.

"NOW, Ms. Hawkins! I'm not playing games here!"

The student returned and picked up the books. She slapped them together in her hands loudly.

"And this report too. Pick it up!"

The girl wavered. Rarely had Jean confronted a student who so clearly wanted to knock her on her ass. But she held her ground, let her own cold fury show, and the student finally walked back to the front of the room and picked up the crumpled report.

"Don't ever behave like that again," said Jean. "I wouldn't tolerate it from a four-year-old. Now go to your next class."

"You bitch!" Renee ran from the room.

Jean took a couple of deep breaths. She hefted her text book and attendance folder, shut off the lights, and stepped into the hall, carefully checking to be sure Renee wasn't lurking about. She noticed Ethel Harris by the bookstore.

Standing behind the half-door, Stephanie Homan was holding up a sign for the dean's inspection. Written in exotic calligraphy, it declared, A SHIRT TO WEAR WITH PRIDE AS YOU TAKE THAT CORPORATE RIDE.

"Well, the design is wonderful," said Ethel. "I may reserve judgment on the poetry."

"I've written better," Stephanie conceded. "But I was mainly interested in catching the eye."

"It does that all right." The dean leaned over the half-door so she could look around. "You certainly have this place organized to the hilt. Wouldn't want to stay on full time after you graduate, would you?"

"I thought about it, 'cause I love this place. But Ms. Mallory figures I can make tons more on the outside."

"Ms. Mallory is correct, I'm sorry to say."

"I'm planning to hit Dad for a job in his company. He's got to find a good spot for me though, 'cause I'm not taking just anything. He owes me."

"Does he?"

"Big time."

Ethel's smile grew uncertain. "Does he know this?"

"Oh sure. He married Mom then busted up our family. Then he remarried and busted up that family too. He owes everybody." Stephanie related all this quite cheerfully. "Anyway, he goes on these guilt binges and that's the time to hit him up. We all know how to do it."

"I see why you and Ms. Mallory work so well together."

"Yeah. I really like her style."

Jean Cavanaugh drew near. "Am I hearing correctly? Somebody likes Louise Mallory's style? Hi, Ethel."

"Hi, Jean."

Jean moved to the door. "Ms. Homan, can you spare me a steno pad? I've run out."

"Sure. But I can't just give it to you, you have to pay for it." This because Louise kept complaining that teachers wanted free steno pads and pens, as if those supplies didn't cost the school a penny.

"Of course." Jean handed Stephanie four dollars. Stephanie went to the cash register to make change. Jean added, "It's definitely an improvement having you back here instead of Miss Sourpuss."

Ethel glanced down the hall. Fourth Period had begun and the corridor was empty. "Jean, I have to ask you something."

"Sure."

"We have a list of the students who were cited during the federal program review. Beatrice and Deirdre are trying to clean up this stuff now, after the fact, transcripts and loan applications and whatnot, before we actually get the final report."

"Okay."

"I need to ask how Keone Robinson is doing." And again Ethel glanced down the empty hall.

"She's fine," said Jean. "She'll do well on her finals. She'll never be valedictorian, and I doubt we'll be able to place her somewhere grand, but she'll make it. She'll be a lot better off than when she came here, that's for sure. What's the problem?"

Stephanie gave Jean her change, and the two teachers walked away from the bookstore. Ethel didn't speak again until they were clear of the classrooms and going down the stairs. "Keone's was one of the files cited. There was no proof of high school graduation. No diploma or transcript was ever collected by Admissions. So Deirdre called the girl down and guess what?"

"I can guess."

"She never graduated from Southwest. We called the school and they confirmed it. They said she dropped out after her sophomore year."

They reached the second floor. Ethel opened her office and they went inside. Jean asked, "So what do we do?"

"Oliver looked like a sick fish when I told him. He thinks we should cut her. She lied to us, and now we're in a vulnerable position with the

Department of Education. On the other hand, she's been in the program for almost two years. She's supposed to graduate in six weeks."

"But if you let her graduate it won't be fair to the others."

"Yeah, that's how I thought at first." Ethel sat behind her desk and pushed a stack of papers out of the way. "Now I'm not so sure. A prerequisite isn't supposed to make or break a student from graduating. It's meant to establish a level of preparation before a student attends a program to make sure she can handle the work. Keone was grossly unprepared for the two-year program, but you said yourself she's doing okay."

"With a lot of concessions over the past two years."

"But never to her grades. I've been looking at her work. She's currently holding a 2.3 GPA. She's *earned* that, we haven't carried her. And if she came to us without the proper requirements beforehand, that only emphasizes what she's accomplished here."

"I agree entirely. But is it fair? She did lie."

"I think it's better than fair. She lied, but a few months later we started ATB and legally accepted students who never finished high school. If she'd come half a year later this wouldn't even be an issue. And if she had been up front with us, we never would have accepted her. I checked with Louise, and slowly but surely her bill's getting paid. The kid's really all right."

"She has worked hard," Jean agreed. "If you're asking how I feel, I'd hate to see her not graduate."

"Good. That's what I'm going to tell Oliver. I know he'll go for it."

"What does this do to the audit?"

Ethel shook her head. "It means we get cited, and if they want to fine us then we have to eat it. But nobody is going to face that girl two months before her program finishes and tell her she can't graduate."

Someone out in the hall shouted. Ethel and Jean looked at each other, then went to the door. "Now what?" muttered the dean.

Donna Harding was running down the stairs from the third floor. "Ethel—oh Jean! Come upstairs, both of you."

"What's going on?"

"You have to see! Hurry!"

A crowd of students stood in front of the ladies' room on the third floor. Arthur Cassidy was trying to usher them back. "Go on, ladies," he was saying. "It's nothing. Go back to class."

"What is it, Mr. Cassidy?" asked Kristin Rutherford.

"Nothing. Do what I say now. Go back to your classes."

With the appearance of the dean, the students had no choice but to disperse.

Donna said, "I saw it first, but I don't think any of the students have yet."

"Excuse us, Arthur," said Ethel. The three female teachers squeezed into the lavatory. The room was small, with two sinks and two stalls. They stared silently at a message scrawled in red lipstick across the mirror which spanned both sinks:

> Cavanaugh is a fat fucking Whoor!

The handwriting wavered with apparent haste and anger. The period of the exclamation point was a coiled swirl.

"W-h-o-o-r?" spelled Jean with a lift of her brows.

"Who would write something like that?" asked Donna.

"Any ideas, Jean?" asked Ethel.

Jean looked at the handwriting and shook her head. "Probably Renee Hawkins. I just had a spat with her."

"Renee," groaned Donna. "She's a devil, that one."

"What about?" asked Ethel, all business. She had no tolerance for this sort of thing. Everyone knew she would personally hang the student responsible.

"A paper grade. She got an F and didn't like it. But it was an F paper, so that was that."

"Jean," said Donna, "you really need to watch it with some of these kids. Renee's the kind who would slit the tires of your car if you talked back to her."

"I ride the train," said Jean calmly.

"Still," said Ethel, "there's something to it, Jean. I think someone like Renee should be handled with caution. She's a kind of student we're not used to."

"She's a devil," Donna repeated.

"Oh right," said Jean. "Ladies, we can't afford to be afraid of these kids. They need our help more than ever." She stood next to the mirror and pointed to the word *whoor*. "See what we're up against?"

70

April 23 was Secretaries' Day. Though actually a rep, Deirdre still found a card from Lily on her desk that morning, even though the admissions director was not on campus. Lily had prepared for this day well in advance, and got herself booked as a guest on *Hello Philadelphia!*, a local talk show. At ten a.m. the entire staff invaded the student lounge, which boasted the only TV with a cable hook-up, and the three reps yelled and clapped when Lily was introduced.

"Why, the whole perception of secretaries has changed!" Lily chattered to the hostess, her hands flipping in all directions. "Computer technology has modernized the secretarial profession and made it highly specialized. At the same time, the old adage that it's the secretary who makes an office run still holds true. A tremendous power is wielded by secretaries and administrative assistants throughout this great country. At the Burr College we prepare students to handle this responsibility by utilizing the most advanced equipment of the Twenty-First Century ..."

It was a brilliant performance. Lily tripped off salary figures and employment statistics, she joked and fluttered and showed an excellent talent for knowing which camera was on her at a given moment. The other two guests, a thirty-year career secretary and a female marketing consultant who started as a secretary and now ran her own company, hardly got a word in.

The show finished at eleven, but Lily's day was not done. She taxied back to the school in time to greet two local networks that arrived at noon to do feature stories on Burr for the evening news. The small two-man crews took shots of Oliver at his desk, and photographed students walking the halls and sitting in classrooms taking dictation, but mostly it was Lily who again took center stage.

"Coffee?" she laughed at the camera. "Goodness, I would *pity* the boss who tried to ask his secretary to fetch him coffee in this day and age! He'd be likely to get it dashed in his face! Ha! Ha! Ha! Good heavens, secretaries aren't servants any longer, they're vital cogs in the work force! Businesses everywhere respect them for the power they command—"

After the news crews left Oliver collected Ethel and Louise, for the three of them were taking Julie to lunch. Normally Ethel would have taken Dawn, but Oliver had asked her the week before to join him with Julie, who had so often been the glue of sanity holding the front office together. To compensate, Ethel bought a bouquet for her own secretary.

With Deirdre covering the front desk, the four of them went to Elena's on Spruce Street. Julie was more than a little surprised, for Elena's was famous for both its dining excellence and exorbitant prices. As her boss steered her under the entrance canopy, the secretary said, "Oliver, you don't have to do this for me."

"What an unarguable truth," he declared, and led her inside anyway. A middle-aged maître d' with a Mediterranean complexion and just the right amount of comb over led them to a table set with glittering china and silver.

"This is, of course, in honor of the day," said Oliver as everyone squinted at menus in the darkened light. "Julie graduated from the July Advanced Program two years ago. She's been with us that long. She's done an excellent job, I think everybody's unanimous on that—"

"Hear, hear," said Ethel.

"Amen," said Louise.

"And so it's nice to take Secretaries' Day, designed by greeting card companies to generate some off-season business, and turn it into a sincere occasion. Julie, I thank you for everything you've done for us."

"We all do," said Ethel.

Julie smiled sheepishly. "This is getting thick."

"Sure it is," said Oliver. "That's part of the fun. Everybody, order whatever you want. Lobster, filet mignon, it's all on Burr."

"Really?" said Ethel. "Burr's paying for this?"

"Bill said okay when I told him I wanted to do it. I think he'll say yes to anything Philly wants right now."

"Well, then I'm looking at the wrong section," said Louise, who had been limiting herself to the appetizers—already expensive enough.

Julie said to Ethel, "You should be taking Dawn to lunch, shouldn't you?"

"This is Oliver's thing," the dean said. "He asked me to come. I'm taking Dawn to lunch tomorrow."

They ordered, and talked shop as they waited for the food to come. Ethel mentioned Carol Sobolewski's recent hiring at a community college in Wilmington, Delaware.

"She ought to do fine there," said Louise, "but she lives in South Philadelphia. That's a wretched commute."

"Maybe I shouldn't be saying this," said Julie, "but sometimes when I'm eating lunch in the faculty lounge I hear similar talk from Arthur and Donna."

"All the teachers are making those noises," said Ethel. "We might wind up with a whole new complement by next year."

"You don't really think so, do you?" asked Oliver.

"No, not in my heart of hearts. But I know morale is down. Arthur still has kind things to say about the kids, but Donna has a blind spot. So did Carol, if it comes to that. They can't get their own preconceived notions about these kids out of their heads before they face them in a classroom."

"That's a serious issue. Can you talk to them about it?"

"It's not something you can talk about," said Ethel. "Not and expect to make a difference. But I'm looking very carefully at the teachers I hire for the Achievement Program. I want instructors who already have a lot of experience working with disadvantaged urban kids. Carol, Arthur, and Donna are nice people, but we changed the rules when they weren't looking. Jean, of course, is still a godsend. She pushes those kids along, no matter where they come from. She complains to me about it, she always has, she always will, but the best grades these kids get come from her class."

"And she doesn't curve," Oliver added. "We should do something for her. Maybe present her with something at graduation in June."

"That'd be nice, Oliver. Did you know it's her tenth anniversary with us?"

"I didn't. Give it thought." He put down his fork. "Meanwhile, if you women will indulge me, I have something for our guest of honor." He withdrew a small wrapped box from his jacket pocket. "Secretaries' Day is more than half over, and I have yet to present a token of appreciation to my own secretary."

"Oliver," Julie said with growing nervousness, for the box was small and square, and looked very much like what it might be. "What did you do?"

"All things considered, I couldn't think of a better day to give you this." He set the box before her.

She looked as if it might bite her. "What is it?"

"I don't remember."

She unwrapped the box and opened it. Satisfactory gasps circled the table as other diners in the restaurant turned their heads to see.

"Oh," she said helplessly. "Oh my *God!*"

"Ethel, Louise, you're my witnesses this day." He took Julie's hand, and smiled because she was too dumbstruck to grip back. "You asked me once why I never did what I wanted, and I remember telling you it was never a priority. I can't say that anymore, for what I want now is too important. I want you to quit Burr and go to college. I want you to find out what you really want to do, and get the education to do it. And when Kelly is old enough I want her to do the same. I want to watch Kelly grow up, and I want to grow old with you." He raised her hand to his lips and kissed it.

Julie shook visibly. "I … can't speak."

"Will you marry me? I can't promise a lot of excitement, but it could be nice."

Julie started to laugh. She grasped the diamond ring and tried to put it on, but couldn't hold her hand still.

Oliver said, "This isn't the reaction I was hoping for."

She got the ring on and looked at him. "Yes, I will. You know I will."

They leaned close and kissed. Cutlery rattled. Ethel and Louise grabbed their water glasses. The tables around them applauded, which made Oliver and Julie break into embarrassed laughter. One woman cried, "See, *that's* how it's done!" and elbowed her male companion until he applauded too.

Walking back to the school, Oliver and Julie tarried on Spruce Street, savoring the momentousness of the hour, and the two department heads easily left them behind. The bright April sun glinted off the clean brick row homes and cast speckled dots of light on the large leafy trees. Washington Square was occupied by children chasing dogs, college kids lying on the grass reading, and retirees throwing seeds for squirrels. The central fountain spouted its vertical plume. Coming out on the east side, they could see the three-story brick building on the other side of Sixth Street. Julie took his hand.

"As long as you're making plans for us, I should tell you what I want to study when I go to college."

"All right."

"I want to teach."

He looked at her with surprise and pleasure. "Do you?"

"I think teaching is the noblest job there is. I didn't know how much until I came to Burr. Even when I was a student, I knew I was experiencing something special. My classmates felt it too. And after I started working here, I got to witness that specialness each day, plus come to realize all the hard work that goes on behind the scenes to make it happen. It's a little school, but it's a great one."

"I love you," he said.

"Thank goodness, because the feeling is mutual. I can't believe how easy it is to love you."

They crossed the street and entered the building, still holding hands.

71

Marty stood before Lily's desk, helpless. The admissions director's black eyes were incendiary coals, and her square chin looked ready to explode.

"What the CHRIST is the matter with you? Three accepts this week? Three goddamn Julys *only?* Are you bored working here, Mr. Nolan?"

"Lily, it's—"

"Don't you DARE interrupt me! These kids were all young, female, with marginal high school GPAs and coming from miserable neighborhoods. They were *tailor-made* for you! And yet you only got three deposits! How do you account for that?"

"Listen, Lily, you need to understand—"

"You're interrupting again!" The admissions director banged her desk with a fist, startling a pigeon outside her window and making her coffee mug hop in the air. "You're just fucking up right and left anymore, aren't you?"

"Lily, it's been a bad time, I know. But I have—"

"Bad time? BAD time? You idiot! There's no such thing as a GOOD time in admissions! Don't you dare talk to me about bad times! Bad times are what sales reps RISE ABOVE!"

Marty shut up. His hands were tight fists at his sides. He couldn't give his real reason for the low numbers, and just had to take this.

"You still want to work here, Mr. Nolan? 'Cause unless your damn numbers start to pick up and real fast, I'm not sure we want you."

"You firing me?"

"Baby, if you don't start producing I'm gonna *fry* you."

Marty bit his lip. How could he tell her that he was being sabotaged? How to say it and not look like a desperate loser grasping at straws?

But that was what was happening! That goddamn student worker of Louise's was blowing all his leads. She wouldn't run his reports for him, even though she was more than happy to run them for Trudy and Deirdre, and she kept spilling coffee and whatever on the reports he managed to get out of the computer on his own. He hadn't really known what he was up against until a week ago when these same prospects Lily was ranting about started canceling their appointments. He couldn't understand why until he looked at some envelopes stuffed for a mailing and found his home phone number penned on the back of his business cards with the message *Do you believe in love at first sight? Having met you, I know I do. Call me, darling, and let's get together—Marty*. He had stared at the cards in disbelief, then tore through all the envelopes and found the same inscription in every one.

He knew it was Stephanie. When he confronted her in Deirdre's old cubicle she denied it, but she also laughed her head off. He would have killed her, but she was a student. *That* was the problem—she was a goddamn untouchable student! He couldn't do *anything* to her! He couldn't get rid of her, he couldn't take revenge! And he couldn't get her to stop!

Now how to explain all this to Lily and not sound like a fool?

"Okay, bozo." Lily jerked a gilt fingernail at the door. "You're on probation. *¿Comprende?* You used to be good, Marty, but I'm not interested in history." She took a file from her in-basket and began to read.

"Lily, there's some real problems right now. I have to—"

"PROBLEMS! Get out of my office! I'll give you *problems!* You get your percentage of Julys up or you won't have to worry about any more *problems!* We are not losing this sit, do you understand? And if we DO, I will explain it to Bill Nostrand by shipping your head to New York on a STAKE! Now scram!"

Marty stumbled backward out her door.

He returned to his office in a sweat. Once and for all he had to get his resume together. He couldn't stay here any longer. That damn student! If it had been one of the reps doing this to him he would have found a way to deal with it, but students were little goddamn saints. You couldn't look cross-eyed at them without getting in trouble. And that cold-blooded bitch with the weird gray hair knew it too.

He flipped open his calendar and saw he had an appointment in just a few minutes. Jesus, he'd almost forgot! Marty ran out through the lobby and down the hall to the men's room to spruce up. He splashed a little water on his face, squared his shoulders, and looked in the mirror. His reflection was a tonic in itself. He did look good with his broad shoulders and hatchet profile. He tightened his bow tie. *Voila!* Attired to be admired. He felt up to the challenge once more.

He walked back up the hallway with a bounce to his step. He slowed, however, hearing a familiar voice in the lobby. Anger whipped through his veins with corpuscular friction.

"He's a nice guy, but you just gotta watch him. Don't let him talk you into anything you don't want. I mean, he's real slick."

"He is?" said a thin nervous voice. His applicant.

Marty entered the lobby. Stephanie was sitting on the couch next to a brown-haired girl in a polka-dot blue dress. Stephanie looked up, wide-eyed, at his angry face. "Marty, hi. How are you?"

Through clenched teeth he said, "Please get out of here. Go back to where you belong."

"Marty, you were gonna call me last night and you didn't."

"*What?*"

"I waited by the phone all evening. I canceled a date with friends. And you didn't call." Stephanie's lower lip trembled.

"What are you talking about?" He stared at her, stupefied.

"Baby, please don't shout at me."

"Stop it! Just get out of here!" He looked at the bewildered applicant. "Jeannie, isn't it?"

"Ruth," she said, and looked afraid of him.

"Ruth, I'm Marty Nolan. Please come back to my office and I'll explain what this—this person is doing. Please."

"Marty, why won't you talk to me?" Stephanie whined.

"Shut up! Will you stop it? Enough's enough!"

Stephanie looked at the applicant. "Careful. He's a goddamn heartbreaker."

"Aren't you a student?" asked Ruth.

"Yes." Stephanie looked painfully at Marty. "And he's still a heartbreaker." She ran out of view through the cubicles.

Marty sighed and offered a hand to help the prospect up from the couch. "Shall we go back to my office and discuss the program, Ruth?"

She didn't take his hand, but stood on her own. She collected her purse and jacket. "I don't think so. I'm sorry. Good-bye."

"Ruth, wait! You don't understand. Something very crazy is happening. You've got to—"

The prospect went through the double glass doors. Marty skipped after her.

"She's doing this on purpose. Look, I know it sounds foolish. What about the school? You want to learn about the Advanced Secretarial Program, don't you?"

From her desk, Julie heard the outer door shut. She busied herself typing as Marty slowly walked back into the lobby. In a terrible low voice he said, "Where's Louise?"

"In her office, I would imagine."

She kept her eyes on her keyboard. She felt him standing there, breathing heavily. Then he darted back through the cubicles. Julie pressed her hands to her face, shaking with laughter.

Louise's cubicle was empty. Disoriented for a moment, Marty spun about and saw the business manager standing in Deirdre Smith's old station, talking to his nemesis, who sat primly before the computer terminal. Marty banged on the partition edge. "I gotta talk to you!" he said to Louise.

"Good God," responded the business manager. "What's your problem?"

"My problem? I'll tell you what my problem is! That b—her there, your assistant, is killing my prospects!"

"Steph's doing what?"

The little student blinked meekly at the rep.

"Don't play innocent! I can't believe she pulls this crap and doesn't tell you!"

"What do you think she did?" asked Louise.

"She just told an applicant not to trust me! She's trying to make me look like I'm a sleaze … sleazy—I don't know what!"

"You *are* sleazy," said Stephanie. She started to input data from a card.

"Shut up, you—you—God! Look!" he implored Louise. "She's a student. I can't do anything to her. I tried reasoning with her, she doesn't want to reason. I apologized, she's not interested. But she's … she's …"

Louise said coldly, "What did you do that required an apology?"

"He was fresh with me," Stephanie said.

"I WAS NOT!" Marty screeched. "Leave me alone! Okay? Stop fucking with my leads! You're gonna cost me my job!"

"Good!"

Marty raised a fist. Louise immediately stepped forward. "Get out of here," she said, slitting her eyes.

"You keep out of this!" Marty yelled. "I can't stand this anymore! One time I yelled at her—just once! And she won't let it go!" To Stephanie he roared, *"Get off my case! Once and FOR ALL!"*

"Stop being a dickwad and maybe I will."

"I AM NOT A DICKWAD!" Marty yelled so loudly Louise started to laugh. From the other side of the cubicle, they heard Dawn Hitchcock chuckle as well.

"Marty, enough," the business manager said with a smirk. "Go back to your office and leave my student worker alone." She walked out of the cubicle.

"I swear," hissed Marty, and waved a fist in Stephanie's face, "if you were a man I'd sock you right in the balls!"

"Oh yeah?" said Stephanie. "You mean like this?"

72

"Jasmine," Jean said briskly, "you get computer time tonight. I want to see you doing assignments eighty-seven and ninety-six in the workbook. I'll go to the PC lab to check on you in forty-five minutes. Maris, you need more transcription time. Go practice with the eighty-words-per-minute tapes, and use the ones in Steno Room II. You're already too familiar with the tapes in Steno Room III. Shaney'ah, you stay here. I'm going to dictate an eighty-word-per-minute to you. I want you to concentrate now. You've got to get your speed up or you'll never make it."

Final testing had only one more week to go. The last day was May 28, Friday, and graduation itself was June 2, the following Wednesday. For students not doing as well as they should there was very little time to spare.

"Lucy, I think you better stay here for that transcription too. Keone, you still haven't finished your multimedia report, have you?"

"No, ma'am."

"When's it due?"

"Ms. Harding wants it Monday."

"And this is Friday night. I guess your priorities are worked out for you, am I right?"

"Yes, ma'am."

"Go downstairs. You'll find the library's already unlocked."

It was five o'clock and they planned to work deep into the evening. It was understood among everyone now that on Friday nights they would stay until nine. At seven-thirty Jean, working from the third floor lecture room adjacent to Computer Lab III, sent runners down to the first two floors to announce a pizza break. Jean thought this a good morale boost, and Oliver was more than agreeable about footing the bill. "Half an hour," she said as they all crowded into the lecture room. "Don't stuff yourselves, ladies, or you'll fall asleep at your keyboards. Do that on a job and see how long you last."

A few students laughed. With the non-stop intensity of these sessions, and the lateness of the hour night after night, a lessening of the old Cavanaugh tyranny had to come. The forced extra time had in some ways made them intimate with each other. They were united by a common cause of self-improvement, and to the teacher's great pleasure genuine progress was showing. As she sat with the kids and munched pizza she was one of them, calling them by their first names, and laughing as they chatted about family and boyfriends and future jobs. She wished she could do these special sessions with all her troubled students. She wished there wasn't such a price to pay in terms of time and exhaustion to do this, and that husbands would understand. And most of all, she wished her colleagues would do it too.

"There are jobs out there for you," she told them, reaching for another slice with pepperoni. "Think of all the work you've done these past two years. Heavens, think of the *money* you and your parents have invested. You don't want to be receptionists only or data input clerks. You want to be administrative assistants. You want to take responsibility and prove worthy of upward movement in an organization.

"Now let's be honest. Associate degrees don't take you far in business. Business is too specialized. Even bachelor's degrees don't carry people as far as they used to. The trend in business is to hire people with masters and multiple degrees, and the requirements are becoming extreme. Look at the qualifications listed in job ads and you'll see what I mean."

"Then what do we get by being here, ma'am?" asked somebody.

"You get your foot in the door," said Jean, "and the skills to keep you there. Understand what your Burr education is doing for you, ladies. The trick isn't getting a job. A person who gets a job only proves they're good in a job interview. *Holding* the job after you've gotten it, *that's* what counts. Burr has helped you achieve a level of competency that will give you the security to keep the job."

"Do you think we should continue our education past Burr?" asked Dorothee Jackson.

"Absolutely. Most of you will be good enough to get jobs in large companies that pay for further education. That's your ticket. Get yourselves in a good company, work hard, use your new skills, and take advantage of anything the company has to offer. And if it doesn't have what you want, work and look until you find one that does. You're qualified. You all will be."

Jasmine said, "We just gotta get through final testing."

Jean laughed. "You will. Okay. It's eight o'clock. We'll put in one more hour. Everybody ready?"

"I'm stuffed," said Melissa Parker from the January class.

"Then there's a lesson," said Jean. "When you're in the work force, never eat a heavy lunch or you'll fall asleep at your desk in the afternoon. These are subtle but important things to remember, ladies. Now back to work."

At that moment there was a knock. Everyone looked up. A fat man with greasy black hair slicked to his head, and wearing a gray uniform vaguely like a gas attendant's, stood in the doorway.

"Clyde," said Jean. "We're still working in here."

"Yes, ma'am," he said, and smiled at the students in such a friendly fashion that his impression of some slimy figure from the lower depths was instantly dispelled. "But we've done every other room. This one's the last."

"But we really don't want to stop now. It's getting so late. Why don't you just skip this room tonight?"

"Well, I tell you, Mrs. Cavanaugh, I'd be more than happy to do that. But Miss Mallory, she'll notice on Monday and give my boys hell. She always notices."

"I'll take responsibility, Clyde."

"I don't think that'll help me." He chuckled good-naturedly. His whole staff of six cleaning people thought Louise Mallory tough but eccentric.

"Just the same," said Jean, "if she squawks I'll take full blame. We simply can't stop now."

"Okay. Can you lock up? We'll be heading right out from here."

"I have a front door key."

"Okay." Clyde smiled at everyone one last time and did a cocky little salute with his lacquered hand. "Good night, ladies. Happy learning." He went out the door.

"Goodness," said Jean. "It's pretty bad, isn't it, when you're staying later than the cleaning people. Well, we can all sleep in tomorrow. Ninety words, now. Everybody get out your steno pads. Let's pass it this time, and go home feeling super about ourselves. Ready?"

The two letters took another forty minutes, what with correcting each student's notes afterward. Everyone felt good but extremely weary, including the teacher. Jean collected the papers and bid the students good night.

The teacher sat still and listened as the last footstep echoed down the stairs. She inhaled until her lungs prickled within her chest, then released the air and wearily stretched. This was the moment, with black night out the windows and the classroom empty, that Jean let her mortality surface. She rubbed her eyes and tried to work up the energy necessary to start her commute home to Narberth. These were brutally long days, self-inflicted though they might be. She didn't regret it, she didn't believe she was trying to do too much. She just wished, in a lull like this, that there was an easier way.

She stood up and looped her pocketbook over her shoulder. She collected the six fat textbooks she used to help her cover the many subjects taught during these sessions, and went to the door. The hallway was dark, with only a light in a copper sconce at the end where the staircase began. She started for it.

"Ms. Cavanaugh?"

The shy voice was so unexpected Jean jumped. She looked at the hallway behind her. There was nothing to see but shadows. The classroom doors were shut, the windows in their doors dark. The bookstore at the far end was shut, and its Dutch door had no window.

"Hello?" she called. "Who's still up here?"

After a pause the voice said, "It's me, ma'am." It was a student's voice. "I'm havin' some trouble. Can you help me?"

"Ms. Robinson?" Jean hugged her books a little tighter. She could now see that the lab door was open part way, but the lights inside were off.

The voice said, "Yeah ma'am. I need help movin' this thing. Can you help me?"

"Of course," said Jean. "What is it you're trying to do?" She walked toward the open door. When the girl didn't answer she asked again, "Ms. Robinson, what's the matter? Are you hurt?"

She stepped through the door and started to shift her books to free a hand to get the light. The room was unusually dark, for the shades had been pulled down all the way instead of half-mast as Louise Mallory preferred. Had they been like that when her students used this room just a short time ago?

"Ms. Robinson?" she said, worried now. "What's wrong? Keone, where are you?"

Something hard struck the side of her head. Jean tripped sideways with a yelp and fell against the wall. It happened so fast she still hugged her books. She was startled by presences in the dark with her, then she was hit across the face. She gasped and dropped the books. Her arms were grabbed on either side and pulled outward. Jean heard a squeak of footsteps behind her and the classroom door banged shut. *Sneakers!* She felt swift motion before her face and cringed. A fist cracked against her eyes and blinded her. Her knees buckled; she hung limply, supported by the strong grips on her arms.

She was pulled to the front of the room. She saw someone off to the side, standing by the windows, holding a soda. Jean couldn't focus. Her head swirled in a racing pain that made thinking impossible. They pushed her down on her knees. Something shoved at her face. Tough hands forced her arms behind her, pulled her hands close together. Cold metal touched her wrists and clicked. A hand grabbed her hair and yanked her head back. The pain triggered a conscious terror and Jean screamed. She tried to rise. Voices circled over her and hands pushed hard at her shoulders to keep her down, other hands grabbed her arms, and still others grabbed her legs. *Oh God! Oh God! How many were there? What were they going to do?*

"Help!" she screamed. "Help me! Help—"

She was struck across the face again.

"Come on," hissed a distant voice. "Hurry up before something happens!"

It was a female voice!

Was anybody still in the building? "Help me plee—!" A bulky wad was shoved in her mouth, choking off her cry. It tasted like wool. Large hands pressed a smelly tape over her lips and wound the tape in tight hasty loops around her head. She saw hands, jeans, the floor, some furniture. She was too terrified to look higher. *God please! Let someone hear this! Let someone still be in the building!* Her stuffed mouth muted her screams back at her, little pig squeals that made someone standing behind her titter.

"Come on!" said the voice again with childish urgency.

"Shut up!" hissed a male voice behind Jean.

God please help! Help! HELP!

Whoever had the tape was now wrapping it around her torso, binding her arms to her back. One part of her brain tried to think but she was too scared, nothing came to her aid. She was a police officer's wife, but she couldn't tell them this now, she couldn't scare them with it. Jean blinked and saw a gun barrel close to her face. Her blood went cold. She whimpered like a puppy and reared back on her knees.

"You're taking too long," whined the voice.

"We're doin' okay," huffed a boy. He sounded young, like a teenager. "Now shut up!"

Hands pressed on her shoulders, shoving her face down on the floor. Someone quickly undid the zipper on the back of her skirt, and Jean squealed with real animal panic as she felt the loosened garment being tugged eagerly down her legs. Cheers and wolf-whistles filled her ears.

"Nice big ass," a boy said.

"Chubby girl," another agreed, and giggled.

"Come on," the girl's voice snapped.

Everything happened faster than her shocked wits could absorb. They lifted her to her feet and dragged her to the instructor's desk. Two boys forced Jean to bend over the desk while others pulled the teacher's legs wide apart and lashed her ankles to the desk's front supports. Jean screamed. She screamed for God. She screamed for Clyde, praying his crew was still in the building. She couldn't get her voice past the thick gag. She felt hands tearing at her pantyhose, ripping the nylon clear of her buttocks. Her heart pounded the desktop. She tried to count how many boys were in the room. And the girl—*where was she?* Jean turned her head and saw her standing by the windows, holding her can of soda and *watching*.

And Jean realized who she was.

She went crazy. With a grunt of outrage she lurched upward, writhing furiously in the boys' hands. Someone smacked the side of her head with a metal pistol butt and she dropped flat on the desk. She burst into a muffled wail.

"Shit, don't knock her out," the girl exclaimed. "She's gotta know what's happening."

"She will," said a boy. "We got all night."

All around her was chaos as chairs and desks were knocked over and kicked about and even thrown against the walls, and computer units toppled to the floor and smashed. The male laughter never ceased. Jean shrieked when the first boy fucked her, his body ruthless atop her buttocks and pinned arms, his hands holding her tightly by both shoulders. Her tied legs strained helplessly against the desk. There was no fighting him off, no way for her to fight *any* of them off, and through the brutal crush of her pain and terror Jean willed herself to shut down, closing her heart, her mind, her nerves, numbing every part of herself to protect the remnants of her sanity. But the one thing she could not shut out was her awareness of a student standing by the windows, watching all that was happening.

And sipping a soda.

73

Oliver got the call a little past 2 a.m. Julie, knowing the phone was on his side of the bed, determinedly lay still. His voice was groggy as he asked the caller's name, then he sat up and said no more. Years of raising a deaf child taught Julie how to read silences, and she raised her head to look at him.

Oliver held the receiver with both hands. "How bad is she?" He listened for a very long time. "All right. I'll be there as quickly as I can." He cradled the phone and put a hand over his mouth.

"Oliver, what's wrong?"

"God help us." He swung his legs to the floor. "Jean Cavanaugh was attacked at the school. She's at Walter Welles in Emergency. Watch your eyes." He snapped on the bedside lamp. "I've got to get over there right away. I don't know if you want to come or not. You can." He turned and looked at her. Julie was sitting up, hugging the sheet. "Jule?"

"Oliver—she was attacked?"

"Yeah." He grabbed his jeans from the foot of the bed. "Somebody broke into the school. She was late teaching her class. Where's my belt?"

"I don't know. Was she—how badly did they hurt her?"

"I said she was in Emergency. Do you want to come? Frankly, I could use you."

"What about Kelly?"

"Oh, right. Listen, I'll be back …" He thought about it, then shrugged. He pulled a shirt from a drawer and looked around the room as he pulled it on.

"Were they thieves, Oliver? What exactly happened?"

"I don't know. That was the police on the phone. They're at the school. I'm going there, then I'm heading for the hospital. They didn't tell me much."

"Is she okay? How bad is she?"

"Jule, I really don't know. God damn it, where's my belt?" He dropped on all fours and looked under the bed. He stood, thrust his bare feet into loafers, then leaned over to kiss her. "I'll call you as soon as I can."

Oliver drove into Center City with no awareness of the route he took. Traffic lights, the zigzag curves of the Kelly Drive, his hands did it all by rote. The call he'd gotten was every school director's nightmare. He kept thinking about Jean, her passion, her caring, and couldn't put it together. A red light halted him, and in the isolation of the car with the windows rolled up he gripped the wheel and screamed a little, short sharp barks, loud enough to deafen his ears. He reached Washington Square and slowed as he turned onto Sixth Street. Four police cars were parked in front of the school. Two officers stood on the steps. So it was real after all. He pulled over and got out.

"I'm Oliver Dunbar. I was called down here by Lieutenant Stephens."

"Okay. Please wait here." One officer nodded to the other, who disappeared. Oliver heard him running up the staircase. Police in his school.

A moment later a middle-aged man in a white shirt and necktie appeared and shook Oliver's hand. "Dr. Dunbar? Charlie Stephens. Come with me. Sorry to have to wake you."

A ridiculous comment, and Oliver answered it ridiculously. "Quite all right."

The walk up the staircase felt longer than the drive into the city. All the lights were on, but shadows from the copper sconces spun shadows around them as they climbed the stairs to the third floor.

"Frank Cavanaugh called us," said Stephens. "Got worried as the hour grew late and she didn't come home. We sent a car over, found the broken window, and investigated. She was half-conscious on the third floor. Lieutenant Cavanaugh's wife—Jesus! There isn't a cop in this town who'll rest till these animals are caught."

Oliver just walked beside him.

"They came in through a basement window," Stephens explained. "Your kitchen."

"Yes. We've had thieves break in that way before."

"You'll have to look the place over and see if anything's taken. Doesn't look like a robbery though. In fact it's kinda weird. They busted in downstairs, and they broke open one of your vending machines, but that's about it. We haven't been able to set a time yet, but it must have been late. Mrs. Cavanaugh was the only one in the building. Did she stay late often?"

"Uh … well, yeah. Pretty often. She used to give extra lessons to students who needed help." Used to. Oliver chastised himself. Jean wasn't dead.

"How late did she stay, normally?"

"I don't know. My dean could probably tell you. But no later than eight or nine, I imagine."

"Anybody else here after hours, normally?"

"We have a maintenance crew, but they're out by eight every night."

"How long have they worked for you?"

"Years. Well, the head man at least. His name is Clyde Zaccaro. I trust him completely."

"Okay, that helps," said Stephens. "They might have known the cleaning people left at eight. Until we talk to Mrs. Cavanaugh we can only guess." He gestured the door as they approached. "She was assaulted in here. I don't think they expected her to be in the school. They probably got in this room, and she heard them banging around and went to check it out. She surprised them, but they were certainly prepared. They handcuffed her and gagged her with duct tape."

"Don't tell me this."

"She was beaten and sexually assaulted. Looks like the attack went on for some time, judging from the condition of the room. See for yourself."

Stephens stood by the computer lab door to let him pass. Oliver hung back, and looked entreatingly at the police lieutenant. Stephens went in first.

The room was a wreck. Computer monitors, components and keyboards lay smashed on the floor. The chalkless blackboard was scrawled with angry lines and epithets. The instructor's desk had been pushed askew, facing more the windows than the students' chairs, with dark scrape marks on the tile floor from the desk's legs. A terrible coldness washed over Oliver.

"Is that …?"

"Yeah. She was still tied to the desk when we found her."

It couldn't be true. He was living a horror movie.

"You've got some other rooms busted a bit," said Stephens. "None as bad as this one, though. The ambulance took Mrs. Cavanaugh to—" he looked at the officer by the door. "You know where they took her?"

The officer shook his head.

"Walter Welles," said Oliver. "You told me that over the phone."

"Yeah. Listen, doc, what I need you to do is think who might have some kind of vendetta against this place."

"A vendetta?" Oliver looked at him uncomprehendingly.

"You know—a grudge. Somebody went to a bit of trouble to damage your school."

"I can't think of anyone."

"Anybody get fired recently? Or some kid maybe get expelled? We think actually that the perps were young."

"You do?" Though he avoided looking at it, Oliver could sense the desk's presence. He had trouble following the lieutenant's words.

"Anybody?"

"Well, there are always disgruntled students, sure. But I can't … can't imagine anyone who could hate us this much."

"Well, give it thought. How about this? Anybody report any incidents like students talking back, or maybe …"

It was two hours before they let him go. He walked the four blocks to Walter Welles Hospital and wandered aimlessly through the corridors for twenty minutes, confused by the signs to Emergency. When at last he got there, a tired woman at the counter heard his story and pointed to a row of seats along the wall. All were empty save for a thickset African-American woman reading a magazine. It took him a moment to recognize Ethel.

"Sit down," she said simply.

"How long have you been here?"

"Since about three. Frank called me right away."

Oliver sat. "How is she?"

"She was conscious for a bit but then they sedated her. Frank's the only one they'll let in. She's in a lot of shock, a lot of pain. Do you know what happened?"

"I've been with the police all this time. They think it was vandals."

Ethel closed the magazine and dropped it on a stack beside her chair. "Jean's tough."

"Is Frank with her now?"

"He's in the cafeteria. They finally got him to leave her bed about fifteen minutes ago. She's completely out. They're monitoring her closely."

Oliver started to get up. "Where's the cafeteria?"

"Oliver, he doesn't want to see you."

"Well, just for a moment. It's only to tell him—"

"No. He *said* he doesn't want to see you."

"Oh."

"My guess is Jean's gonna feel the same way."

"Okay." Oliver sat down and said no more.

Hours passed and nothing happened. No one came to talk to them, and they had little to say to each other. Several times Oliver stood and walked the floor. Once he returned and said to Ethel, "The sky outside is pinking."

Ethel nodded without looking up from her magazine. Oliver sat again.

Julie showed up a little after nine, and found them both asleep in their chairs. Ethel's magazine was face down across her lap. Julie sat beside Oliver, and though she was as quiet as possible the dean stirred and opened her eyes.

"Julie, hello."

"Good morning, Ethel. How is she doing?"

Ethel rubbed her eyes. "I don't know. How long have I been out of it?" She looked at Oliver, then at her watch. "Two hours. Let's see what I can find out."

She went to the counter and talked to a nurse. In a moment she was back. "Status quo. But she's doing okay. It's just going to take a lot of time." She glanced at Oliver's slumped form. "I guess somebody should call Louise. The cops are probably all over the school, and she'll want to know about it."

"I can't believe it happened," said Julie.

"None of us can. This sort of thing isn't supposed to happen. Say, let's you and me go get breakfast. The cafeteria's not bad."

"Well …"

"He'll be safe. No one will steal him."

Within twenty-four hours the Philadelphia police, ravenous to avenge one of their own, caught their first suspect. An easy confession led to four other offenders plus Renee Hawkins. Frank Cavanaugh relayed this to Ethel Sunday night, and she telephoned Oliver. The local news programs followed up, and that evening Oliver and Julie watched shots of the hospital as they listened to the story of a policeman's wife, a teacher at a "business college in Center City" who was raped in her classroom by companions of a failing student. Stephens was interviewed on two stations, but out of deference to the Cavanaughs none mentioned Burr by name.

The student body, returning to class on Monday, had its suspicions confirmed when Ethel Harris substituted for all of Mrs. Cavanaugh's classes. Whispers and speculations fired up and down the halls. Where it happened was obvious (the police had closed off Computer Lab III), and there was intense guessing as to which student might have done it. More than one guessed Renee Hawkins, whose name had not been released.

Classes that day were chaos. No one wanted to teach, and no one wanted to learn. Arthur Cassidy was approached by Amelia Albretti's student council and asked to hold a school assembly, and he passed the request on to Oliver. One was scheduled for three o'clock that afternoon.

The student cafeteria was packed. Oliver and Ethel led the discussion, and listened as the students expressed feelings of admiration for Jean Cavanaugh they never knew they had. Everyone was appalled and sickened, and quite a few tears flowed. In a wonderful show of communion everyone held hands, the poor and well-to-do students, the black, white, and brown students, and sang a heartfelt song from some current pop artist while the dean and school director watched, not knowing the words. A hat was passed for a gift, and not one student failed to put something in, even if it was just a few coins. Many decided to write Jean get well letters, prompting the only joke as Ethel remarked that anybody who did so had better get the grammar right. Oliver went back to his office and dictated his own letter to the Cavanaughs, in which he described the emotional outpouring of the assembly for Jean's well-being.

None of which did any good. A week later Ethel got a typewritten letter from Jean, the signature so crunched she almost doubted the veracity of it, tendering resignation. Ethel wasn't surprised. She phoned the Cavanaughs and spoke with Frank, but was unable to make them change the decision. She gave the letter to Oliver, then asked Louise to run an ad for a new business teacher.

*

Among the faculty, Bob Lawrence took Jean's tragedy hardest. While his fellow teachers sat in the lounge and discussed the incident in hushed tones, Bob couldn't even choke out an opinion. He didn't know anyone who had been a victim of violent crime, and every time he thought about Jean he felt sick to his stomach. It was all he could do to stay on his feet and teach his classes.

On May 26, the last day of finals, Heather Feeney entered the student lounge with Jennifer DeAngelis. Both were excited at having achieved one hundred and ten words per minute in their transcription final. They passed through to the locker room and Bob Lawrence watched from the doorway, his hands clasped behind his back.

"Ms. Feeney?"

Both students turned. "Bob?" she said, surprised. "Hi."

"Hi." He nodded to Jennifer. "Hi there."

"Hi, Mr. Lawrence," said Jennifer with wide eyes.

"Ms. Feeney, I need to talk to you about a pressing matter. I'm sorry to trouble you. I know this is your lunch hour."

"That's okay." Heather didn't know what to think. She couldn't believe Bob was talking about getting together right in front of Jennifer! Didn't he know what a tattle-tale Jennifer was?

"I'll be in the faculty lounge. Come in as soon as you can." He withdrew from the doorway.

A moment later Heather entered the faculty lounge. Bob was the only one there, seated at a table with one hand hooked to his belt. His legs were crossed, and his face was granite. "Heather, we're done."

"What do you mean?"

"I mean we're through. This relationship. We are no longer two hearts beating as one."

"You want to break up?"

"We *are* breaking up. Right now. As of this minute." He reached for his briefcase and stood up.

Heather immediately attacked. "No way! I'll go tell the dean!"

"I guess you will."

"You think I won't?"

"I'd like to think you won't but I guess you will. I can't expect better of you."

"Oh yeah? What do you mean, better of me? You're the bastard in this!"

"Well, maybe I am. But not after today."

"I *am* telling the dean."

"Then go ahead."

Heather stared at him uneasily. She couldn't tell if he really thought she'd do it, or if he hoped she was bluffing. His face refused to give her anything, and this infuriated and panicked her.

"What about all we've gone through? Doesn't that mean anything?"

"I wouldn't bring that up. What we've gone through is more of an argument for splitting up than staying together."

"No, Bob, please! What about—"

"I don't want to talk about this. I certainly don't want to listen to any more threats. I told you not to blackmail me. I told you it wouldn't work. We're done."

She saw it. His face revealed that much. He didn't care at all. He looked so blank, so calm, so unfeeling—

"You fucker!" she cried. She stepped forward and slapped his face, slapped him even before she realized that this was what they did in the movies. She looked around, but no one was there to see.

Bob took the blow with a grimace, but held his ground. He stepped around her. "I wish you the best, Heather. Good luck with the rest of your finals."

She shouted, "My brothers are gonna get you when they hear about this!"

"Your brothers have better things to do than come after me." Although he wasn't really sure. Heather's brothers were the scariest element in this decision.

"They're gonna kill you." And she leered saying it.

"Good-bye, Heather." Bob walked out the door.

At the first floor landing he broke into a sprint that lasted the length of the corridor. He dashed through the lobby and weaved through the cubicles. Dawn was at her desk, going over a long list.

"Hi," he gasped. "What are you doing?"

"Well, hi. Not much. Checking the cap and gown orders. What'd you just do, run the Marathon?"

"No." He thought he heard Heather's voice in the lobby and looked nervously past the cubicles. No one but Julie sat out there. "Listen, Dawn, I need to tell you something. I know I've been acting a little evasive and strange lately."

"Yes you have," she conceded, but with warm affection. "Is this the stress of a creative writer?"

"What? No—uh, not exactly. Look, I need to take you to dinner tonight."

"Tonight? I can't."

"Please!"

"No, I really can't. Connie has a show at the Walnut Street Theatre, and I promised to take some videos."

"Call her and say you can't come."

Now she looked surprised. "Bob, are you all right?"

"Yeah. Well, I've been better. But it's imperative that I see you tonight. Maybe you can get off early."

"Early? Graduation is next week. I can't get off early." She looked at his pallid face. "What's happened?"

"I can't tell you here. Tonight. I'll buy you dinner someplace. Any place. Screw the cost. Then we can talk."

His fervor was too weird. Dawn laughed. "You're such a nut. Okay, I'll give Connie a call."

"Meet you right after work?"

"*Yes,* Bob."

"That's great. Thanks!"

But he didn't leave the desk. After a moment she looked up from her list. "Bob?"

"Listen ... I have to ask you a favor."

"Sure."

"Um ... if between now and tonight ... if something happens, something that's kind of bad ..." He was breathing hard again.

"Bad?"

"I mean, like if you hear something ... hear *some*thing, and it involves me, say, will you do me a favor?"

"What?"

"Wait till tonight and hear my side of it?"

"Sure, but …" Dawn was so puzzled she laughed. "What do you mean? Come on, Bob, you can't stop here. Now you have to tell me."

"No, I can't. Tonight I'll tell you all of it—okay?"

"You're scared of something," she said in slow wonder.

"Only of you. I swear, if you'll just listen to me tonight I'll never be evasive again."

"Okay, Bob."

He left her desk, shaking. He couldn't meet Julie's eye in the lobby. He passed Arthur Cassidy in the corridor without a word and ducked into the men's room. He leaned against the tile wall and gasped for air.

Dawn sat at her desk, bewildered. Then gradually she smiled. She and Bob had discussed some wonderful plans recently. She couldn't help suspecting what surprise he would spring over dinner, and began to imagine how she could most romantically answer him. Her intercom buzzed and she picked up.

"Dawn," said Ethel. "I'm taking lunch with the boss. I'll be back in time for the one o'clock PC Lab exam."

"Okay. I'm finished with the cap and gown list. Everyone's name is on it."

"Good. Now all they have to do is pass. How about Amelia's plaque?"

"The engraver said it would be ready this afternoon."

"Great. See you."

"Oh—Ethel? Can I ask a favor?"

"Sure."

"I know this is a crazy time, but do you think I could cut out at four this afternoon?"

"At four? I don't see why not. Is anything wrong?"

"I don't think so." Dawn felt sweet joy pluck upward inside her. "You really don't mind?"

"Why would I mind? I know you're on top of things. Go ahead."

"Thanks, Ethel."

Dawn hung up just as a student stepped around the partition and approached the desk. "Hi. Can I see the dean?"

"Right now?" Dawn asked.

"Is that possible? It's kinda urgent."

"Let's see. She's just about to take lunch." Dawn held the receiver to her ear and buzzed. "Dean Harris, I have a student who would like to see you. Would that be possible? I know you're almost out the door, but she says it's urgent. Ms. Feeney. Okay, one moment."

Dawn lowered the receiver and smiled at Heather. "May I tell the dean what this is in reference to?"

74

In a small basement office of Walter Welles Hospital, Keone Robinson prepared to take a typing test unlike any she had taken before. The woman who proctored it loaded the printer with a paper that had special green margins dictating the shape of a semi-block letter. It would show if the document was formatted incorrectly.

"Are you ready, Keone?" asked Mrs. Lee.

"Yes."

"Get set. I'm timing you … *now.*"

Keone was doing well in her typing finals, holding at the moment a level of sixty-two words per minute with two errors, just enough to qualify for a C. But she had already blown one job interview by messing up the typing test. Clara Peterson had sent her to the city's PBS station for a job in the membership department, but although the personnel people were nice, the new surroundings and the fact that she was being tested by strangers stiffened her hands so badly that she finished the typing exercise with twenty-three errors and was promptly screened out.

She was determined not to be so nervous this time. When Mrs. Lee said, "Now," Keone didn't start typing right away. She let the first few seconds tick by while she took a long cool breath. Then she started typing slowly. Gradually she let her speed pick up. It worked. Stiffness didn't come to her fingers, and she felt more relaxed than at PBS. Energy flowed through her hands. She forgot about the green margin paper, she even forgot about Mrs. Lee. As luck would have it, the letter had many small words and her fingers flicked comfortably over the keys. She wasn't nervous at all when the five minutes were up. Mrs. Lee pulled the paper from the printer and sat at her desk to check it. She looked up with a smile.

"Keone, this is very good."

"What did I get?"

"Seventy-nine with one mistake. That's just fine."

Seventy-nine! Keone couldn't believe it.

She was ushered to a different office where another woman looked up from a desk that was cluttered with papers and coffee rings. She stood and held out her hand. "I'm Mrs. Ballantine, director of human resources. And you're Keone, right?"

"Yes, ma'am."

"Please be seated. Sorry about the mess. We're a little short-staffed right now."

Keone sat and put her briefcase on the floor. The briefcase was Mrs. Peterson's, and the placement director had suggested that if anyone asked why it bore the initials "C.P." Keone was to joke it off by saying she was a Conscientious Professional.

"Keone, tell me about your school. I've always heard good things about Burr. What exactly did they teach you?"

"Well, it's a two-year program. I get a associate's degree when I graduate."

"When is that?"

"This Wednesday."

"Really? Are you excited?"

"Yeah, ma'am." Too late, she remembered she was supposed to say "yes."

"So they teach you typing and filing and such?"

"Yes, ma'am. And dictation too. They taught us Business English, office procedures, economics—" The names of these classes tripped off Keone's tongue enthusiastically, although the courses themselves had plagued her for two years. They were all listed on the resume Mrs. Harding had helped her compose.

"It sounds very good. Have you enjoyed going there?"

"I think it's the best school in the world."

"Very nice. Well, let me tell you what we're about."

A short while later Clara Peterson left her office and trotted excitedly up to the lobby. "Hello, Julie."

"Hi, Clara. Anything I can do for you?"

"No, I'm just waiting for a student to come back from an interview. The appointment was at twelve and it's just a couple blocks over."

"Who's this?"

"Keone Robinson. We sent her to Walter Welles. They have a situation there that I think is perfect for her. Cleric in their Social Services office. A lot of work with not-for-profit agencies that are associated with the hospital. Planned Parenthood, child care, shelters, that sort of thing. They coordinate fund drives and such. It pays twenty-two, but the hospital benefits are incredible. Major medical, dental, and they also cover seventy percent tuition to employees who want to continue their education."

"God," said Julie. "That's what I need."

"They'll pay one hundred percent if the classes are related to the medical profession. Keone's thinking about becoming a nurse, did you know that?"

"No, I didn't."

"I hope she—oh, here she is!"

Keone shuffled into the lobby, perspiration beading her face, her new interview suit wilted from the hot spring sun. The borrowed briefcase hung from stretched fingers.

"Keone," said Clara, "listen to me. Mrs. Ballantine called."

"She did?"

"Yes. They're very pleased with you, and they want you to start work there beginning a week from Wednesday. You've got the job!"

"Really?"

"I just got off the line with her. The job's yours if you want it."

"Sure. Thanks, Ms. Peterson."

The placement director came forward and they embraced. Julie stood and extended a hand over the desk. The news sank into Keone very slowly. She had a job. A desk job. In a hospital. She had done it.

"Now listen." Clara put a motherly arm around the student's shoulders. "Remember what we talked about. You work there and get your experience, but don't forget the other thing."

"I won't."

"Good. Because Walter Welles encourages its employees to educate themselves. They'll help you work out an evening school schedule and then you go for your G.E.D., like we talked."

"Yeah, ma'am. Yes."

"Don't slack on that last."

"No, I don't want to."

"Okay. Congratulations. Come back to my office and tell me all about the interview. Mrs. Ballantine was quite taken with you."

"Uh, Ms. Peterson, I will. But I got to do something with Ms. Mallory first."

"Okay." Clara couldn't resist giving Keone one last squeeze. She retreated down the hall, humming to herself. Keone stood before Julie's desk.

"Good work," said Julie.

"Thanks." It was still sinking in that she had a job. A job in a hospital. "I need to ask Ms. Mallory something. Can I see her?"

"I think she's in. Let's find out."

A moment later Keone passed through the cubicles to the business manager's station. Louise looked up from a fistful of last minute tuition checks for the graduating class. There was nothing like withholding a diploma days before graduation to get the delinquent bucks in. "Hello, Keone, how'd it go?"

"I got the job."

"Good for you. Do you want to pay the rest of your balance?"

"Yeah, ma'am."

Without looking at the computer screen, Louise said, "It's $147.39."

"I know." Keone opened her purse and pulled out eight twenties. Louise opened the petty cash for change.

"Ms. Mallory?"

"What?"

"I, uh …"

"What?"

Keone tugged a rumpled envelope from her purse. "I was wonderin' if you could give me Ms. Cavanaugh's address? I want to mail her this letter I wrote."

"Sorry, but I can't give out addresses. That's confidential information. But if you want I can forward it for you."

"Would you, ma'am?"

"Of course. I know she'll appreciate it."

Keone handed it over.

"Some two years, huh?" said Louise.

Keone wasn't sure what she meant. "Yeah, ma'am."

She came out of the business manager's office feeling incredibly liberated and thinking about the job. Twenty-two thousand a year was more money than her parents *ever* made! And if Shaney'ah Bacon got the job at United Way for twenty thousand like Ms. Peterson hinted, then they could get an apartment right here in the city and be roommates. Suddenly walking wasn't good enough, and Keone skipped through the lobby and down the hall to her next exam.

She passed Bob Lawrence who crossed through the lobby with just a quick glance at Julie. He went through the cubicles. Dawn's desk was empty—as it had been all day. He already feared the worst. Last Friday she had stood him up. He had waited in vain in front of the school after work, then finally ran from office to office without finding her. At last he went home and called her, only to get the answering machine. He called again every half hour until four a.m. without anyone picking up, then called repeatedly throughout the weekend. He went several times to her apartment, but neither she nor her sister ever answered the buzzer. Had she gone out of town? Or was it something worse?

Bob turned away from the cubicles in deep despair. He walked through the lobby and out to the hall with his eyes on the floor. What was he going to do? He had to find Dawn and talk to her. She had to give him a chance to set the record—

He bumped into somebody and drew back. "Sorry," he muttered without looking up, and started to pass.

"Hello, Mr. Bob," rumbled Dean Harris.

Bob raised his eyes. Ethel's face filled his universe, her deep-set eyes dark and forbidding. He felt a critical need to disappear.

"Come up to my office, Mr. Bob. We need to chat."

"Sure, Ethel. What about?"

"Oh, let's wait till the door is shut, shall we?"

So he trudged after her, a prisoner with his warden. Down the hall, up the stairs, and into her office. He sat quietly in the client chair as she reeled off a blistering tirade. She called him names, she spoke about faculty ethics, the trust of parents, the gullibility of students, and finally she told him he was fired.

"And I mean today. Take whatever crap is yours and get out of here."

"Ethel," Bob said, "is this really necessary? I mean, I guess the thing with Heather is bad—"

"It's a little more than *bad,* Bob. I want you gone in fifteen minutes. After that, if I so much as catch a glimpse of you, I will have you arrested. I'll have you blackballed. Swear to God, I'll make sure you never get a job at a school again."

"Ethel, look," he said with a halting need to defend himself, "I know you don't approve of this sort of thing, and I realize the school has a no-fraternization policy. But it's not against the law. Age of consent in Pennsylvania is sixteen. So you can't talk about having me arrested."

"No?" she said, letting the single syllable swoop high in the air. "According to Ms. Feeney you and she became intimate two Decembers ago, over a Christmas dinner in your apartment where you served her alcohol. Not only that, but alcohol was served pretty much every time you two got together. That's called furnishing alcohol to a minor, Bob. I looked it up for you. A thousand dollar fine and a year incarceration."

Bob went silent.

"If you're still in this building fifteen minutes from now I'm making a phone call. Is that understood?"

"Yeah, okay." He rose slowly, for this was beginning to feel like a dream. "Look, Ethel, I don't know if this means anything to you, but ... well, I want you to know I'm sorry."

"Get out of my office."

Bob went down the stairs and passed through the lobby one last time to check Dawn's work station. She wasn't there. She had managed to avoid him completely.

There wasn't much to leave with; he never had his own office. He walked down Pine Street with two textbooks and his briefcase, and wondered about references, wondered about his monthly bills. When he unlocked his door, Mr. Wemmick mewed from the living room and ran to greet him. He picked up the enormous cat and sat on the couch cradling him. Then he went into the kitchen, tried Dawn's number again, and again got the answering machine. He came back to the couch and held the cat close.

"Want to go live with Granddad in Baltimore?" he whispered. "Because it doesn't look like *this* dad'll be able to support you for a while."

Which really meant they would both wind up in Baltimore. Thirty-eight and living off Dad again. He buried his face in the cat's flabby tummy, felt the warmth and fur, and cried. Mr. Wemmick was bewildered but allowed it. Bob was family.

75

One hour before Commencement began, in the giant sanctuary of St. Peter's church, Ethel Harris doggedly rehearsed the graduates. Although the graduating class was mainly comprised of September students, the ceremony was open to any July or January student who had graduated the previous March and September. All in all, Ethel intended to hand out over two hundred diplomas tonight.

"Let's go, people," she commanded from the lectern. "We haven't got much time. Now listen while I play the music. There's a fanfare first, then the processional. You don't start marching until the first beat of the processional. Listen up." She pushed a button on her son's CD player and Jeremiah Clarke's *Trumpet Voluntary* resounded the length of the room. "Starting with your left foot, you march like this: one and, two and—one and, two and. Keep your head up, don't look at your feet. Keep in time with the music."

"Looks kinda dorky," said Karen Louden.

"Shh," Oliver said gently, standing near. He and Trudy were directing the excited, talkative students into straight lines at the back of the sanctuary.

Ethel snapped off the music. "Everybody hear that? I'm going to play it again, but let's try the march. Watch me. Remember, start with the left foot or you'll be off step the whole way—"

Julie entered through a door behind the pulpit, spotted Oliver, and came up to him. "They're here."

"Okay."

He walked with her down a hall to the Fellowship Room, a large space used by the church for social functions. Tonight long tables were set up at one end, which would later hold coffee and refreshments. The near end was crowded with excited girls trying to get into their gowns, with Deirdre and Dawn helping as best they could, armed with safety pins and hairpins. The room was a cacophony of happy chatter. Bill Nostrand and John Coyne stood by the double doors that led to the room, peeking in and clearly enjoying the action. Oliver shook hands with both.

"How are you, John?"

"Fine. Looks like you've got a nice turnout."

"Ethel Harris puts on a good show."

"Wonderful." The president of the Burr Colleges was making his annual trek to all of the schools, attending each graduation. The Philadelphia school was his eighth stop, and Coyne, who was now seventy-two, looked white and fragile. But his manner was animated and cheery, and he watched the girls sorting through their robes with a pride that matched Oliver's own.

To Nostrand Oliver asked, "How are you, Bill?"

"Me? Tired." But Bill smiled saying this. If the boss was feeling good, then the world was good. "We finally got a smart director for Miami. Jim Miller. He's taken the place by storm."

"Fired a lot of people." John nodded curtly.

"Yeah. The staff hates him, but the numbers are finally starting to pull up."

"I have something for you," Oliver said. He opened his briefcase and fished out a large brown envelope with *Department of Education* printed in the upper left corner. It was the audit report from the Department of Program Review. The addressee was William Nostrand, but Eloise Mahwat in New York was forwarding both men's mail to each of the schools as they traveled. Oliver gave the envelope to Bill with a sense that the remainder of his career rested within it.

The students who had been rehearsing in the sanctuary now thundered down the hall to the Fellowship Room. Trudy stopped them by the double doors, then yelled into the big room, "Okay, Group C, it's your turn. Come with me to the sanctuary for rehearsal. You others get your gowns fast. We gotta move now."

At eight p.m. the congregational pews of St. Peter's Church were packed. A hired brass quartet began the *Voluntary*. Parents and family members stood solemnly as the black-gowned students marched double-file down the central aisle, most of them keeping in step. Standing within the audience, Doris Robinson clutched her husband's arm. "There she is. Ain't that her?" For it was difficult to identify any of the grads under their mortarboard hats in the subdued church lighting.

"Yeah," said Warren in mild confusion.

As they reached the front of the sanctuary the double line of grads split left and right, moving toward marked-off pews on either side. Already seated on the first row were faculty and staff. Oliver and Ethel had chairs on the dais itself, near the lectern, and also on the dais sat Bill Nostrand and John Coyne. All wore robes reflective of their educational status save the president, who wore a business suit. Camera bulbs flashed from families in the pews and even from a few press photographers, for Lily had done her part and corralled a small representation of the local media.

The last of the grads paraded in and stood facing the dais. The conductor-less quartet played for another twenty seconds before realizing everyone was in place. The trumpeter waved a hand, and the big church silenced.

Oliver leaned both hands on the lectern. His robe was purple with puffy bell-shaped sleeves, his hat not a mortarboard but a round tam topped by a pompom. It was his own robe, bought when he received his doctorate in education at the University of Pennsylvania. "Good evening, everyone, and welcome to the Twentieth Commencement of the Burr College of Business. Students, Moms, Dads, give yourselves a major pat on the back. You did it. You *all* did."

It was a remark calculated to pull a cheer from the five rows of solemn grads, and it worked. They yelled and whooped.

"Well done!" Oliver smiled. "You're not only graduating with superior job skills, but you all have tremendous lung power."

This encouraged a second loud cheer.

"The invocation will be given by Father Martino."

A gray-haired priest took the lectern and made everyone bow their heads. Seated on the first pew in a robe with a hood bearing the colors of Montclair State, Marty was very conscious of being sandwiched on either side by Trudy and Deirdre. He didn't like it; he and the two female reps were no longer speaking to each other. And when the first row of students filed into the pew behind him his one assured nemesis sat directly behind him. He didn't realize it until the prayer ended and her little scratchy voice intoned "Amen" over his shoulder. Marty still felt a residual soreness in his groin whenever their paths crossed, and with barely suppressed fear he turned around. Sure enough, Stephanie sat behind him. She winked.

Father Martino blessed the class, offered his own congratulations, then returned to his chair. Oliver assumed the lectern.

"Ladies, this is a wonderful moment. For some of you it's been a long road to get here. For others the time just zipped by. Some of you had the support of family as evidenced by all the people seated behind you, and some of you managed it on your own. Some of you are looking forward to the working world, some are still a little intimidated by it, and a lot of you already have jobs."

A lone voice shouted, "All right!" drawing laughter from the grads.

"Ladies, I've been conducting graduation ceremonies for twenty years now, and I've come to know something about these rituals that I want you to recognize. Your parents supported you, but this is not their night. Your faculty helped bring you along, but this is not their night. This is *your* night. You worked too hard to share the limelight with anybody. You are among the best people on the planet, and I'll tell you why."

Oliver paused, and the great thing about churches was they were designed for pauses; he felt everybody digesting the last few words. "You knew you needed an education and you went and got one. Sooner or later everybody—a hobo, a millionaire, a scientist, a politician—has a moment when they discover they are dissatisfied with their life and realize a need to improve themselves. It's a fierce and sometimes frantic feeling. But statistically very few actually take the plunge and do it. This is why you are special. This is why we are proud of you. You not only did well in school, you *chose to go*."

Stephanie leaned forward. "Psst, Marty, I can't see. Would you mind scrunching down a bit?"

He tried to ignore her.

"Marty?"

"Don't belittle this accomplishment. You've avoided complacency, you've kept your life from existing in a rut. It takes tremendous energy to study, and great character to sacrifice a social life to become a better individual. You have achieved for yourselves a wondrous turning point in your lives—"

"Come on, Marty. Move your fucking head."

Deirdre snickered. The male rep glared at her but kept his mouth shut. This brat behind him was capable of anything. The only thing to do was sit still and take whatever shit she threw at him until this was over. Thank Jesus she was graduating tonight!

"So be proud of yourselves. You are genuine quality. Heck," Oliver added with a grin, "you not only have brains, ambition, and the skills essential to build a successful career, but you also look terrific in what has got to be one of the least-fashionable hats designed by humankind."

The entire congregation laughed, and a few grads whooped.

"God bless you all, happy dreams, and happier lives."

Applause and more cheers. Doris Robinson watched the back of her daughter's head, just a few rows ahead of her, with tears in her eyes. She gripped her husband's arm.

"I am now going to introduce the president of the Burr Colleges. John Coyne has presided over the Burr Colleges since 1972, having taken the reins from Charles Burr, grandson of the founder of the first college in Boston. President Coyne is traveling to all the campuses with a special message for the graduates. Please join me in welcoming President Coyne."

Applause thundered through the sanctuary. John stood and took the lectern with radiant pleasure. The microphone rang slightly when he spoke.

"Ladies, gentlemen, graduating class, Dr. Dunbar, staff and faculty of the Burr College, I have a funny confession to make. I *never* received a college degree." He grinned, hoping for a chuckle, but the audience wasn't sure and remained silent. "You see, I went from high school directly into the Navy, and studied finance while I was at sea. I took to finance, and did well. But I missed the college experience, and I've always regretted it. It's a piece of life I'll never know.

"I was both a friend and colleague of Charles Burr, and worked with him for many years. When I was elected to the presidency of the Burr Colleges, I had full understanding of the importance of a Burr education. Taking the presidency was a chance for me to support the very thing I had missed out on in my youth. As I look out over all of you, I am filled …"

"What are those colors dripping down your back, hey?" Stephanie whispered to Marty.

"Just shut up," he said.

"But what do those colors mean? Come on, Marty, what do they mean? What do those colors *mean?*"

"Shit!" He turned partially. "They're for my degree. Don't you know anything?"

"You got a degree, Marty? Gosh. You got a B.S.? Is that what you got? I can picture you getting a degree in B.S."

"Oh ha! ha!" he said and faced front. He felt a flick on the back of his mortarboard, and the hat dropped forward onto his lap. He turned around fast. "What is wrong with you?"

Stephanie said, "Something's hanging from your nose, eww!"

"For once and for all, *shut up!*" The rep faced front, put his hat back on, and rubbed his nose.

"It's disgusting," said Stephanie.

"… for these days there is a wealth of technology at the disposal of any true careerist. More than ever good education and training are essential. I don't know where I would be myself today, if it weren't for Carlene Nichols, a Burr graduate and my own personal secretary. She keeps my schedule, balances my books, runs my errands …"

Doris Robinson kept losing track of Keone among the rows of mortarboards. But she was there somewhere, and Doris squeezed Warren's arm. He had already tuned out the man speaking up front, but he did squeeze Doris back.

"You are all earmarked for success. You are Burr College graduates. The world is yours. You have my fullest respect, and I bid you good luck and God bless you."

A flashbulb went off from the press, and John belatedly smiled. He sat amidst applause.

Ethel Harris stood and took the lectern. Her black robe reflected doctoral status with colors shown as stripes on her sleeves. "Each year the Burr College presents a Student Achievement Award. It so happens that this year's recipient is also our valedictorian, which makes her accomplishments all the more noteworthy. She has been visibly active throughout the college. As president of student council both years of her Burr career, she has organized more bake sales, clothing drives …"

Keone finally spotted her parents. She had asked Ms. Hitchcock for three tickets, but it didn't look like Darcy had come. That was disappointing, although Keone hadn't seen much of Darcy over the past two years anyway. She looked over at Shaney'ah, who was sitting nearer the front. Shaney'ah had gotten the United Way job, and kept looking back at Keone and grinning. No one from her family was here tonight.

Amelia Albretti nearly tripped running up the dais steps. She thanked Dean Harris and took the plaque, then stepped up to the lectern and pulled out a sheet of paper.

"Members of the graduating class, parents, families, faculty, administration, it is with great honor that I speak before you tonight. It is so hard to believe that two years have gone by already, and here we are today, graduates of the Burr College of Business. Tonight, my classmates, we are all successes. But what *is* success? What does it really *mean?* Webster's defines 'success' as …"

"How're your numbers for July, Marty?"

"None of your business."

"Can't be doin' too well. You got gray hairs all over you. Lord, look at them!"

Amelia finished to a spattering of applause and skipped back to her pew. Oliver resumed the lectern.

"We are about to issue diplomas. I want all parents to know that picture-taking during this part of the ceremony is unabashedly encouraged."

Ethel rose and stood beside a table of neatly stacked blue books. Oliver leaned into the microphone. "In recognition of successful achievement in all the requirements thereof, the degree of Associate in Applied Science in Secretarial and Liberal Arts is bestowed upon the following individuals:

"Eve Abrocelli … Amelia Albretti … Tamika Angel … Shaney'ah Bacon … Michaela Beal …"

It was happening. Keone grew nervous as the alphabet worked its way toward her. All she had to do was walk up those steps, go to the table, and let the dean hand her one of those blue books. She didn't have to say or do anything, but she was afraid she'd screw up anyway. She watched Shaney'ah get her book, and couldn't stop grinning.

"Ellen Harper … Jolene Hollister …"

"Wait a minute," said Marty, looking over his shoulder. "What are you doing here? Your last name is Homan. The H's are on the other side."

"Huh," said Stephanie. "I guess I got mis-shuffled."

"No, I don't think so." Marty glared at Trudy and Deirdre, who were both struggling to look interested in the ceremony.

More students filed up to the podium. Oliver kept intoning names while Ethel passed out blue books. Keone Robinson's row began to shift to the aisle, then one by one the students went up to the dais. It struck her that at this point nothing *could* go wrong. She was going to graduate.

"Keone Robinson," Oliver said.

She walked up to him. Oliver squeezed her hand and paused in his roll call to watch her move to Ethel. He couldn't hear what the dean told her, but Ethel grinned and Keone laughed. Oliver watched her run off the dais, then found his place on the list again. "Kristin Rutherford …"

Stephanie's row began to move. She stood and leaned forward to kiss Deirdre on the mouth. Deirdre responded by putting one hand on the back of Stephanie's neck, letting the kiss linger. "See ya in a few," Stephanie said, then side-shifted toward the aisle with the other students in her row.

Marty's eyes popped. "What the hell was that?"

Trudy and Deirdre applauded, watching Stephanie's row work its way to the dais. Stephanie's gray hair was pushed out in all directions by the mortarboard pinned to her head.

"Did you two just do what I think you did?" Marty looked completely flabbergasted.

Instead of answering, Trudy turned to the junior rep and spoke as if he wasn't sitting between them. "So Dee, tell me. Which one was your favorite?"

"Mine? Gee, I don't know."

"I think I'll always treasure the time she pretended to be the financial aid director, and called all those kids to offer them a fifty-dollar Marginal Intelligence Grant. You had a lot of cancellations after that one, didn't you, Marty?"

"What?" he gasped. "She did *what?*"

"Oh yeah," Deirdre laughed. "Although I don't think anything beats the love notes on the business cards. That was just brilliant."

Marty glared at Deirdre. "How'd you know about those business cards?"

"What?"

"I never told you."

"Oh." The junior rep suddenly looked flustered. "I guess Steph told me."

"That's right," said Trudy.

Marty looked hard at them both. "You ganged up on me!"

"Oh, Marty, of course not. Don't be crazy."

"Bullshit!"

Nearby heads turned their way. Dean Harris glared severely from the dais. Marty lowered his voice and growled at Trudy. "I'm gonna kill you if you don't come clean. What's been going on here?"

"Oh all right. I guess it won't hurt to tell you. See, Dee and I couldn't do this stuff to you. You'd have gotten us fired. But Stephanie was a student. You couldn't touch her."

"I know!"

"All we did," said Deirdre, "was offer her a slight percentage."

"What?"

"We gave her ten percent commission on whatever portion of our recruitment exceeds yours," explained Trudy with a chuckle. "She did pretty well too."

"That's what we're here for," said Deirdre, "to help students get through school. Aren't you proud?"

"You BITCH!" Marty lunged at her. Deirdre screamed and covered her face. Trudy threw her arms around Marty from behind and tried to pull him back.

"Help!" she cried.

From the dais Oliver looked over. Students standing by the diploma table turned in surprise. Stephanie immediately pointed. "Look out! He's gone nuts!"

"Get off her you jerk!" Trudy grabbed the colored hood of Marty's robe and pulled. The cord caught around his throat, snapping his head back and gagging him.

Oliver was off the dais in two bounds. Ethel ran down the steps. As Marty twisted in his seat to fight off Trudy the school director grabbed his shoulders and pulled him to his feet.

"What the hell's going on?" Oliver yelled. "Stop it! Stop—"

Marty jammed an elbow into his ribs. Oliver coughed and stumbled backward. Trudy gave Marty a shove, but he grabbed her gown as he fell, and they both rolled into the church aisle. People in the surrounding pews jumped up, some to get out of the way, others to see better.

Ethel grabbed Trudy from behind and pulled her arms back. "Enough!" she thundered. "Now get back to your—"

Marty took quick advantage of Ethel's pinning Trudy's arms, and landed a solid punch in the senior rep's face. "You little shit!" Trudy sputtered. She whipped up a leg, sporting a vicious pointed heel, and gouged him in the stomach. Marty doubled backward with a howl.

Stephanie ran back and forth across the dais. "He's crazy! He's a madman! Get a straitjacket!"

Fumbling in the aisle, Oliver and Ethel managed at last to separate the two reps. "Trudy! Marty! Stop it! Stop it right now!" Oliver stumbled backward, holding Marty by the arms.

"Dr. Dunbar! Hey!" a voice shouted. Oliver looked over and a flashbulb went off in his face. Marty took advantage of his sudden blindness to shake free.

He ran up the aisle toward the back of the church. People shifted in their pews to give him a wide berth.

"Don't let him get away!" yelled Stephanie.

The high-pitched voice pierced his rage. Marty spun about. His hands were fists, his black gown torn along the collar. He stared the length of the large room, past the commotion in the aisles, past the sea of mortarboards in the front rows, past the musicians huddled behind their stands. In a red haze he saw one person clearly, a gray-haired monster jumping up and down on the dais and pointing at him. With a venomous roar he charged down the aisle. Oliver tried to block him but Marty shoved the director back against a pew. Oliver stumbled against Ethel who fell on top of Trudy.

Marty was halfway up the steps when his arm was grabbed by Bill Nostrand. Arthur Cassidy rose from the faculty pew and tackled the rep from behind. Marty and Arthur hit the floor with an ugly thump. The force of the landing was enough to make Marty stop struggling.

It didn't take long to restore order, but it was impossible to get the congregation to calm down. Arthur and Louise shipped Marty out the door, and Trudy readily agreed to wait in the chapel adjacent to the sanctuary. Oliver returned to the lectern, but his purple robe was torn at the shoulder, the flat tam missing, and he was bleeding at the mouth.

"Are we all okay?" he spoke into the mike. "Ladies and gentlemen, is anybody hurt?"

The students, staff, and congregation examined themselves and each other, and no one seemed damaged. Ethel returned to the diploma table. After a long pause, Oliver resumed reading names, but looked foolish and hypocritical. The dean handed Stephanie her blue book, but when the student tried to take it the dean held on.

"So you're in with the W's, huh?" she remarked severely.

"A screw up with the names," said Stephanie. "It was fate."

"I see," said the dean. She let go of the book. "It's all fate, isn't it? Every bit."

76

"The worst! The absolute worst! You can't even put into words the … the absolute *stupidity* of what went on!"

Well, that's one word, Oliver thought.

"John ripped my ear off for two hours at the hotel. What the Christ! What the … the—*CHRIST!*"

Oliver nodded contritely. *The Philadelphia Daily News* was spread across his desk with FIGHT BREAKS OUT AT BUSINESS COLLEGE GRADUATION leaping off the front page. And oh, that picture! Oliver puffy and bewildered, holding a snarling Marty Nolan and squinting into the camera as if about to sneeze. Other pictures: Bill scolding Stephanie on the dais with his hand on her shoulder, Trudy with a bloody nose being led out by Donna Harding. PUNCH AND CIRCUMSTANCE was the clever sub-heading. What great wit was working at *The Daily News!*

"You think it stops there?" Bill slapped a thin vela-bound report on Oliver's desk. "Top of everything else, I had to read *that* last night too!"

"What is it?" asked Oliver.

"Your dismissal, you stupid bastard!"

Oliver looked at the binder. It was the program review report from the Department of Education. His stomach knotted further. "How bad is it?"

"Who knows? There are forty-seven individual citations in that report! At least $252,000 allegedly mishandled via financial aid overawards alone. That's not counting whatever they feel like fining us for documentation infractions. Just how far up your ass *was* your head these past two years?"

Oliver stared wordlessly at the report.

"Yeah!" Bill nodded maniacally. "Two hundred and fifty-two thousand dollars! Think about it! Let it sink in! You think we've got a quarter million bucks on hand to bail out this school? You're dead, buddy! This is it!"

"Well, but we can appeal this, can't we?"

"Sure, and we will. You see the intro letter? 'Possible litigation.' I'm telling you right now, they're just being polite putting in the word 'possible.' Make no mistake, the feds are gonna want us to cough up a lot of money or they'll close us. We won't let them kill us without a fight, but it damn well won't be *your* fight. You're out of here!"

"I understand that part." Oliver's eye moved from the report to the *Daily News* front page, as if the two documents were somehow working in collusion.

"Lawyers' fees, appeals, additional audits. And the *fines!* All on top of that quarter mil! And did you know they can publish these findings? I've seen this happen to other schools. Wait till the word gets out. You'll have Pennsylvania Higher Ed coming in to do their own audit, and then New Jersey Higher Ed—"

"Okay," Oliver said. "Sorry, Bill. It shouldn't have happened."

"You're fired, Oliver. I want you out of here now. Cleanout whatever personal stuff is yours and go. I'm taking an eleven-twenty back to New York. When I get there I will immediately call this school. Julie better tell me you're gone. I am *not* having another conversation with John while you're still on campus."

"I understand." Oliver reached automatically for the report.

"Don't touch that!" Bill snapped it up. "Two hundred and fifty-two thousand dollars! I can't believe it!" He clicked open his briefcase and dropped the report inside. He looked around for his coat.

"It's on the sofa," said Oliver.

Bill retrieved it. "Where's the bathroom in this place?"

"At the end of the hall."

"Show me, will you?"

Oliver led him out to the lobby and through the glass doors. Once Bill was gone, he walked to Julie's desk and gave her a wan smile.

"It sounded terrible in there," she said nervously. "What happened?"

"What we thought."

"Oliver, I'm so sorry."

"Well, it hasn't sunk in yet. Better call the department heads to my office. And come yourself."

"All right." She picked up the phone with a trembling hand. Oliver returned to his office.

Louise was the first to arrive. "Staff meeting a day early, hey? Never a good sign." But even her acerbic wit was subdued. Nostrand's tirade had carried through all the cubicles. Lily, Clara, Beatrice, and Ethel arrived, and took their seats with few words.

Oliver leaned back in his chair, putting both hands behind his head. "Bill and I just had a discussion. It seems our graduation ceremony last night didn't measure up to John Coyne's standard for Burr decorum. Because of this, and certain fiscal issues that have come to light, my service to the Burr College is no longer considered necessary."

"They fired you?" said Ethel.

Oliver nodded.

"Oh my!" declared Clara.

"The sons of bitches!" snapped Louise.

"Now hold on—" Oliver began.

"No, *you* hold on!" said the business manager. She slammed her yellow notepad to the floor. "They can't do this! You made this place! You don't—"

"We have to protest this—"

"They're out of their goddamn minds—"

Oliver held up a hand. "No, no please. Actually Bill's right. I've let the place down. I really have."

"I'm quitting," said Louise.

"Me too!" said Clara. "The very idea!"

"No," Oliver said swiftly. "Please, don't start thinking that way. I don't want anybody doing anything rash. Listen to me a moment."

"Oliver," said Ethel, "what do you think will happen to this school with you gone?"

"She's right!" exclaimed Louise. "Without you this place is nothing!"

Oliver stood and came around the desk. From the corner Julie stopped taking minutes. She simply watched him. "I appreciate what everybody is saying. And I'm flattered, because I respect every one of you. We've fought through many a hard time together. But things do come to an end. People move on, and change doesn't have to be bad. Bill's reasons are valid. You need to understand that."

He looked at them all. Ethel met his eye, but Louise glowered hostilely at her lap, and Clara silently bit her lower lip. Perched on the couch, Lily's black eyes studied him. She leaned down and rubbed one ankle thoughtfully.

"I do not want any of you to quit. This is a good college, and you shouldn't abandon it just because I screwed up. It isn't right, and will only cost you and the school."

"Tough!" grunted Louise. "You think I'm going to work for some clown Bill Nostrand hires?"

"Jesus, Mary, and Ralph, she's *right!*" exclaimed Ethel. "Oliver, I'm not staying. Louise and I are both vested. I've got my connections."

"I wish you wouldn't do this."

"It doesn't matter what you wish," said the dean. "Like it or not, you've been the soul of this college."

"I positively agree," said Clara.

"And what about the students?" Oliver asked.

That silenced them.

"We've got a large student body still counting on you. You can't in good conscience make a hasty decision." Oliver returned to his desk. "I guess Louise was right—this is a staff meeting held a day early. I have to be out of here within the hour, so I can't make any formal good-byes. We'll all have to get together soon, and then I'll do it properly. Thanks."

Julie lingered after the others left. "What can I do?"

"See if you can find me a couple of boxes, okay?"

He sat by himself, deeply moved by the protests from the staff. This was starting to hurt. He began noting what was his in this office, what wasn't, and what might be his but he wasn't sure. The correspondence in his in-basket was nine inches high. He brooded, looking at the pile. There were some important papers there—a student job placement questionnaire for the Pennsylvania Department of Education, and the preliminary self-study for Burr's ABCAA reaccreditation, which was due in five weeks. He also thought about the Achievement Program. With himself out of the way, Bill would probably convince John to kill it. Ethel wouldn't have the clout to stop him. Nor would her superior in New York, Abby DeSalvo. On the other hand, John did like the program. Maybe it would be spared.

Julie returned with two large cartons and set them by the desk. "Oliver, I can't stay. I've got to cover the front."

"It's okay, Jule. I can deal with this. Thanks for getting the boxes."

She walked around the desk and did what she never did at the office, put her arms around him and kissed him. "I'm sorry."

The bookshelf held volumes on education that he hadn't perused in years. Going through them was oddly nostalgic. Paulo Freire's *Pedagogy of the Oppressed*, Charles Silberman's *Crisis in the Classroom*, Raymond Callahan's *Education and the Cult of Efficiency*, Kenneth Feldman and Theodore Newcomb's exhaustive *Impact of College on Students*. Plus a thin book called *Enhancing Faculty Careers* which he suspected was Ethel's. He took a snowflake water ball of the Boston skyline that was given to him when he attended a Burr directors' meeting in 1979, two potted ferns on his windowsill, the gold-plated ABCAA clock, and the radio. From the desk he retrieved a silver Tiffany letter opener Tina gave him many Christmases ago, and which, because his secretary always opened the mail, had never been used. The calculator, blotter, and stapler were all school property. He took the first three inches of paper from his in-basket and stuffed it into a drawer in his desk. He opened a panel in the credenza behind his chair and stuffed in the rest. There was a foot-high stack of education files on the credenza, problem cases Ethel needed him to review: students failing academically, students going on leaves of absence or outright withdrawing. Oliver carried the stack untouched to Dawn Hitchcock's cubicle. Back in his office, he flipped through another small stack of forms and files which represented work in progress: surveys by AICUP and the College Board, journals, the May monthly report, budget worksheets, new TIAA-CREF options, letters from parents (both complimentary and critical) that needed to be answered—and shoved all of it into the credenza as well. He locked the credenza and then the desk, then pulled those two keys off his ring. He looked around, impressed. With the paperwork out of sight, the office appeared quite organized.

He didn't know where to put the keys, and decided to hand them to Julie on the way out. He put on his suit jacket and placed the first carton atop the second. He hefted both, snapped off the light with his elbow, and went out.

Lily's door was open a crack and he heard voices within. Oliver stopped at the sound of Bill Nostrand's tenor. So the vice-president hadn't left yet. Lily was laughing.

"Oh Bill, so much of it is just the proper attitude, you know that! You've seen this place wallow on the bottom as well as triumph at the top. I can make any place pay off, as long as I get the support from your office."

"I know that, Lily. I'll take it under consideration."

"You could do a lot worse, you know."

"Believe me, I do. We'll be talking."

The bell for Second Period blatted, and the sounds of students traversing the outer hall grew louder. It got Oliver moving again, and he took his cartons out to the lobby. "Can you have these shipped home?"

Julie said, "Just put them in the closet."

"I'll see you tonight."

"Be careful, Oliver."

The daylight stupefied him when he first stepped outside. He crossed Washington Square, stopping briefly to admire some children splashing in the central fountain, then headed up to Walnut Street to catch the bus. At the northwest corner of the park he suddenly realized that he still had the desk and credenza keys. At Eighth and Walnut he dropped them in a wastebasket.

There were plenty of empty seats on the No. 9. Oliver rode up Walnut, crossed the Schuylkill River, and watched Manayunk and Roxborough spread into view on the right. He was commuting home in morning light, and it felt like hooky.

The message light was blinking on the phone when he entered the apartment. He started a pot of coffee and hit the playback button, expecting Julie. Instead it was Dale Thurston.

"Oliver? Are you there? Give me a call, friend. Here's my direct line."

Oliver let the message play out without writing anything down. The coffee was hot, but after the first few sips he felt drowsy. He fell asleep on the couch, still in his suit.

When the kitchen phone rang he had to crawl up from a dark pit to reach it. "Hello?"

"It's me," Julie said.

"Hi."

"Are you okay? That's the first question."

"Sure, I guess. I've been asleep this whole time. How is it there?"

"Kind of spooky. Your leaving has rocked the boat. Lots of office doors closed with who knows what conversations going on. I think everybody's scared."

Oliver frowned. He was starting to feel the loss again. "I guess it'll sort out."

"I wish I could be there with you."

"That'd be nice. Though it's probably good to have one of us employed right now."

"You take it easy. It's already afternoon, I'll be home before you know it. I love you."

"Thanks, Jule. Love you too."

He put on the TV and made a sandwich. The coffee in the pot was cold, and he poured it down the sink. The phone rang again.

"Hello?"

"Oliver, it's Dale."

"Dale, hey."

"You all right?"

"Sure. What's up?"

"You're asking me that?" The voice in his ear chuckled. "With your puss in the paper this morning?"

"I've taken better."

"Maybe, but I don't know when I've read a juicier story. Listen, you don't have to answer this if you don't want to, but are you in trouble now?"

"Well, you called me at home and I answered."

"So they let you go?"

"First thing this morning."

"Hell." Dale went respectfully silent for a moment. "Hell, Oliver. I'm sorry."

"I don't think they had much choice."

"I just called your office, but all Julie said was that you were out. Hey, talk to me. What's going to happen to you now?"

"I can't say. I haven't given it much thought."

"Would you object if I start looking around for you?"

"You mean like a job?"

"Of course, nit. I don't know what's out there, but I'll make some calls. You've got good friends in good places, Oliver. It's time you started taking advantage of that."

He couldn't deny it. At the same time he felt a strange reluctance taking help from Dale. After all the years fighting off his colleagues' jokes about Burr, junior colleges, associate degrees and career school education, to take his assistance now felt like they were being vindicated.

"Seriously, man, that story's gonna travel. Every college in the Tri-State Area saw it today, and you can bet there'll be something about it in next week's *Chronicle*."

"You know my experience is exclusively junior college."

"Oliver, you're immensely qualified. You've seen things the rest of us only read about. All you have to do is talk and any intelligent search committee will grab you. Send me a vitae by the weekend, will you? I'll get the word out."

Oliver felt genuinely humbled. "You're a good friend, Dale."

"Coming to meeting on Sunday?"

"All of us."

"See you then."

Oliver hung up. He snapped off the TV and went into the bedroom, thinking of all the things at Burr that needed to be done.

When a hand shook his shoulder he started. Julie smiled down at him.

"Hi, I hated to wake you, but dinner's almost ready. Do you think you could eat something?"

"Dinner? How long have I slept?"

"I can't say. But it's six-thirty now."

"Gosh." He put a hand to his eyes. "Okay, let me get oriented and I'll be right in."

Over dinner he told her about Dale's phone call. "They're a good crowd," he said, "the people I went to graduate school with. Of course they're all in elite colleges with highly selective admissions practices. It would be a completely new environment for me, even as a teacher. I'd have to learn how to be an academic stuffed shirt."

"They won't want a stuffed shirt," Julie said. "Dale is helping you because he knows you're the real thing, and that's what any good college wants. Certainly it will be different, but I know you can adapt."

"Sort of an old dog learning new tricks?"

"Such an old dog too."

Kelly waved for a translation. They stopped talking while her mother explained everything to her.

That night in bed he put his arm around Julie and she snuggled close. He pressed his cheek against her forehead. A breeze moved the window curtain, a dog barked somewhere up the block. Oliver held Julie as one holds a tremendous gift. He loved the smoothness of her skin, the feel of her bones, the thump of her heart, all the fundamentals that made her both real and larger than life. Their arms squeezed tighter about each other. Gently and caringly they coupled. Weight, muscle aches, loss of his school, the undefined cloud of unemployment drifted into darkness beyond the bedposts. Had he a life before her? He figured he must have, but if so then its sole purpose was to temper him for the existence he shared now, in this room, with a child sleeping down the hall and two hazel eyes shining at him with more love than a man could earn in a lifetime. So much heart and blood, this woman. This colleague, friend, this intrinsic part of himself who, for the sake of principle, almost got away.

The End